Phantom at the Feast

Also by Tony White

NOVELS

The Fountain in the Forest
Shackleton's Man Goes South
Foxy-T
Charlieunclenorfolktango
Satan! Satan! Satan!
Road Rage!

NOVELLAS

A Place Free of Judgement (with Blast Theory)
Missorts Volume II
Dicky Star and the Garden Rule

NON-FICTION

Another Fool in the Balkans

SHORT STORY ANTHOLOGIES

Croatian Nights (co-editors Matt Thorne, Borivoj Radaković)
Brit-pulp! (editor)

TONY WHITE

Phantom at the Feast

NO EXIT PRESS

First published in the UK in 2026 by No Exit Press,
an imprint of Bedford Square Publishers Ltd,
London, UK

noexit.co.uk
@noexitpress

© Tony White, 2026

A Maxim Jakubowski book

ISBN
978-1-83501-579-7 (Paperback)
978-1-83501-580-3 (eBook)

2 4 6 8 10 9 7 5 3 1

Typeset in 10.75 on 13.4pt Garamond MT Pro
by Avocet Typeset, Bideford, Devon, EX39 2BP
Printed and bound in Great Britain by
CPI Group (UK) Ltd, Croydon CR0 4YY

The manufacturer's authorised representative in the EU for
product safety is Easy Access System Europe, Mustamäe tee 50,
10621 Tallinn, Estonia
gpsr.requests@easproject.com

For absent friends, with love and gratitude

Author's Note

Words **emboldened** in the text of this novel are the solutions to successive *Guardian* 'Quick Crosswords' that appeared in that newspaper through sixty days in 1985 from 3 April to 1 June, and which – day by day, chapter by chapter – play a key role in the story.

1 June 1985 saw the infamous Battle of the Beanfield near Stonehenge, England, when Wiltshire Police brutally ambushed the so-called 'Peace Convoy' to prevent them from setting up that year's Stonehenge Free Festival. It remains one of the largest civilian mass-arrests in British history outside of the Second World War.

The chapter headings – Abeille (Bee), Laitue (Lettuce), Mélèze (Larch), Ciguë (Hemlock), Râteau (Rake), etc. – mark a conversion of those days in 1985 into the French Republican Calendar, a secular and non-hierarchical system adopted briefly after the French Revolution, in which each week had ten days (rather than seven) and each day was dedicated to an item of everyday rural life.

While the story told in these pages ranges freely backwards and forwards in time, if the sixty days leading up to the Battle of the Beanfield are seen through the lens of the Republican Calendar, they become six revolutionary weeks – but revolutionary how? In order to investigate that question I needed a detective…

CONTENTS

PART ONE

PART ONE

1: Morille (Morel)

Wasn't it always the way with holidays?

Just as you're starting to **relax**, to shake yourself **free** of work, and – in Rex and Susan's case – take some long-awaited time out with **each** other, Sod's Law says that something, or more likely someone, is going to come along and spoil it.

And in Rex's line of work, that someone would often be dead.

Detective Sergeant Rex King of the Homicide and Serious Crime Command at Holborn Police Station in the new Central North London BCU was used to that, even if Susan wasn't.

It had been a crazy few months at Holborn. Some of the upheavals had been long **foreseen**, and even planned for – financial cutbacks, mergers of the former London Borough Operational Command Units, and the dreaded Safety in Custody inspection – but anticipation didn't lighten the load.

Compared to all of that, the discovery of a deceased of known identity in Russell Square felt more like business as usual.

Even if the victim was the key witness in a longstanding Critical Incident investigation – two years and counting – known as Operation Kayak.

Even if a couple of his fingers appeared to have been severed in the preceding day or so, and someone had jammed an ornamental brass **horseshoe** into his mouth. It almost felt as if everything was getting back to normal.

The real **breakthrough** – the one they were supposed to be celebrating right now – had been meeting Susan Hollander in the middle of all this. She'd been visiting London to look after her niece, who was spending a week in Great Ormond Street Hospital for Children.

Susan was a godsend, and Rex knew he'd lucked out when he met her – on Derby Day, no less. They'd both taken a bit of a punt, and now here they were. Things had got serious quite quickly. Not that it had been completely straightforward. Susan lived in York, so they were forever juggling distance as well as the respective demands of work.

When the subject of their going away for a short but much-needed break had come up, Rex had said he didn't care where they went.

'You choose,' he'd said, and meant it.

They could go wherever she wanted. And as long as they were together, Rex didn't care if it was a week at a four-star **Red Sea** resort or a long weekend in **Rosyth**.

Well, maybe not. Although, yes, Rex was speaking from experience. He had been to Rosyth, albeit just for a stopover, and in another life.

Susan had laughed: 'Ooh, you **globe trotter**, you.' But Rex was pretty sure she felt the same way, and in the end they'd put Sharm El Sheikh on hold and instead taken up Rex's old friend Terry Hobbs's standing invitation to check out his new bolthole in Dungeness. Tel had offered to show them around and then make himself scarce, so they could have the place to themselves for a few days.

'Whenever you want, Rex,' Terry had said. 'I'd be delighted.'

And here they were.

It was barely an hour since he and Susan had arrived and they'd already had as much of a wander as they could with what little luggage they'd brought, then stopped for a snack from the seafood stall, which they'd eaten with wooden forks looking out at the sea: smoked salmon with a squeeze of lemon juice for Susan, and a polystyrene carton full of vinegary whelks for Rex.

'Do I know you?' said Susan.

'Poor man's octopus, if you ask me,' said Rex, holding up a gnarly-looking whelk on his wooden fork before chewing it with great relish. 'But you like conch?'

'That's different.'

'Yeah, ten times bigger – must be like chewing an old sock.'

'You wouldn't say that,' said Susan, 'if you tried my grandmother's curry conch. There's no comparison.'

'I'm waiting for the invitation,' said Rex. He'd saved the last scrap for a patient **rook** that had been sitting on a fence post this whole time, watching them closely. And quite frankly he didn't blame it. From where he was sitting, Susan looked even more stunning than she had when they'd first met. A tall, slim Black woman with a short black bob, she had ditched her usual blouse and skirt in favour of white Levi's jeans, gold wedges and a slim-fit, pale-blue, tie-dyed Tennessee **Titans** T-shirt that her sister Jane had picked up for her on a stopover en route to the Caribbean the previous summer.

Rex and Susan had both seen pictures of Dungeness in the colour supplements, or on television, but neither of them had actually been before. And, so far, they liked what they saw. The nuclear power station was so big that for a few minutes they hadn't even registered its presence. Instead they'd been entranced by the picturesque fishermen's huts that seemed to have been strewn randomly across the shingle. Not so much **town planning**, perhaps, as divvying up access to the water.

Rex reached into his pocket for Terry Hobbs's postcard so that he could check the house number, which turned out to be just a few minutes' walk along the shore.

Terry answered the door of the white-stuccoed detached house in a well-used boiler suit and paint-spattered trainers. He was a bit taller than Rex, and stockier. What little hair he had left was closely cropped. He smelled of chemicals and thinners, linseed oil and white spirit.

'Terence!' said Rex.

'Ah!' he said, showing them in. 'Great. I was just finishing off. Susan, we meet at last. I'd better not shake your hand; don't want to get paint on you. Come through! Rex, put the kettle on while I go and clean up. I'll be with you in a sec.'

The tour started out in the garden, which stretched beyond a couple of raised flower beds made of old railway sleepers.

'I inherited these from the previous owner,' said Terry. 'But it gets pretty windy.' He pointed at some stunted shrubs that dominated the beds. 'Lavatera seem to like it. And there were loads of poppies last year.'

Just as they were going back inside, they heard a train whistle, and with a sudden rush and a burst of steam a small locomotive flashed past on the other side of the fence at the bottom of the garden, hauling several empty passenger coaches.

'Romney, Hythe and Dymchurch,' said Terry. 'Miniature railway. You'll get used to it!'

'How often does that happen, Tel?' asked Rex.

'A couple of times an hour when it's open. Weekends all year round, and a couple of weekdays too through the summer. It's closed today – that must be a maintenance run. The timetable's in the kitchen if you fancy. I think they leave Dungeness around twenty past the hour.'

As he showed them around, Terry explained that this wasn't your average 1940s detached house, even though that was clearly what it had been designed to closely **resemble**. In fact it wasn't really a house at all. It was a PLUTO, which had nothing to do with Walt Disney but a little to do with the underworld, since it stood for 'Pipe Line Under The Ocean'. There were a number of them scattered along this part of the Kent coast: military infrastructure from D-Day, 6 June 1944, when Allied troops had landed on the Normandy beaches and begun the long battle to free mainland Europe from Nazi occupation. The PLUTOs were designed to look like houses, but this was a relatively crude camouflage, and in fact they were, or had been, fortified pipeline terminals carrying oil and petrol to the invading troops on the Normandy coast.

'Wait until you see this!' he said, showing them upstairs; first their bedroom, and then his. What looked at first glance like a solid-concrete dressing table under the front window in the master bedroom was in fact the original mounting for a first-floor machine gun emplacement that had overlooked a wide stretch of the beach.

Terry opened a window and pointed out along the coast to where a large industrial structure of some kind was laid on the beach. It looked like spaceship wreckage in a science fiction film. 'You can just about see,' he said. 'Look, that's a bit of the old Mulberry harbour from D-Day right there. I'm not sure whether it's a section that didn't get used or something that was brought back.'

'I love how you've taken everything right back to the original features and materials,' said Susan, admiring the woodwork as they walked back downstairs, which Terry had stripped back to bare wood and then treated – with linseed oil, it turned out – to give a natural finish. 'Instead of ripping it all out.'

'Yeah, and the concrete too,' said Rex, running his hand along the polished surface of a thick concrete balustrade that surrounded what looked like cellar steps in the centre of the kitchen, leading down to a walk-in-cupboard-sized wine cellar.

'That's where the pipe went,' said Terry, proudly. 'It's bomb-proof. Like the dressing table. First thing I did when I bought the place was excavate that. Someone had filled it with hard core. It took bloody ages.'

He pulled down a local history book and showed them pictures of other PLUTOs – not just detached houses like this one, but some Art Deco-style bungalows too. After the war, the gaps between these houses had gradually been filled. And where you might have expected **obsolescence** and dereliction, the PLUTOs themselves had mostly been renovated and converted for full domestic use. They were now broadly indistinguishable from the post-war development that stretched uninterrupted along the coast to the east as far as Dover.

Terry opened the kitchen cupboards in turn. 'Everything's in the usual place. Use whatever you want. Goes without saying. Here' – he picked a glass jar from one cupboard and took off the lid, offered it to them in turn – 'smell that.'

It was a deep, woody, mushroom smell.

'Wow,' said Rex. 'What's that?'

'Dried morels. Wild mushrooms. Good, eh? They're last year's crop. Friend of mine picks them. Knows what he's doing.'

'Well, I think you've done a brilliant job, Terry,' said Susan. 'The whole place is **utterly** charming.'

'Thank you,' said Terry. Then, as Susan went back into the living room, he nudged Rex and nodded in her direction. 'She seems really nice,' he said, then, sotto voce, 'Everything okay?'

'All quiet on the Western Front.'

Whistlestop tour concluded, Terry went into the cellar and reappeared with a couple of bottles of wine. 'Are you two hungry? I was going to **reheat** some *melanzane*—'

That was when Rex's phone rang.

'Oh, typical – excuse me.' He turned it over to see who it was, gave an apologetic shrug, then took the call.

'Alright, Chief? This had better be good. I'm at the seaside with Susan.'

It was Lollo. Detective Chief Inspector Jethro Lawrence, Rex's line manager, superior officer, and mentor for most of his time in the Met.

'I need you here pronto, Kingsy,' he said. 'Tonight if you can. Dicky Sharp's turned up dead, and with Webbo out of action—'

'Fuck!'

'Poor sod. But there was always a chance. He'd have known it was a risk.'

Perhaps Rex was more shocked than he realised. Certainly, he should have known better than to start thinking out loud, but he supposed that, yes, if they left now and put a fair **clip** on, got the timings right, they could be on the high-speed link to St Pancras within the hour, and back at the station by—

Susan was looking at him, incredulous. Shaking her head.

'Just a moment, sir,' he said, pressing the 'mute' button and looking at Susan.

'It's because you just live around the corner,' she said. 'He thinks he can say the word and you'll be there. We've only just got here. What use are you going to be at midnight? Wouldn't it be better to get up early and be at your desk first thing? Then at least we can enjoy tonight.'

Terry looked on approvingly. 'Makes sense, Rex.'

She was right, and Rex agreed.

Going back to the call, he stood his ground and Lollo grudgingly conceded. Then he brought Rex up to speed. The gist? Fatal road traffic accident, but Sharp's hands had been tied with a **three-foot** length of copper wire, and he'd lost a couple of fingers. 'Looked like someone had been at 'em with a **hack-saw** – that's what Sue Stanza reckoned, anyway. Ragged wounds. Messy. First responders found a brass horseshoe in his gob.'

'Nice,' said Rex. 'Hang on…' They'd already heard from Sue Stanza, the Forensic Medical Examiner? 'Fuck Me's reported back already?'

'No, but me and Sue were just there. It's only up the road. She's fast but not that fast. Full report in a day or two, she reckoned.'

Sue Stanza would as ever be true to her word. When her report did come in, the headlines would include the strong adhesive gum residue on Sharp's face and jaw, and a close-textured pressure pattern that appeared post-mortem – the gaffer tape that had been removed by first responders. An ornamental horseshoe-shaped horse brass complete with black leather martingale was found in his mouth, and was the likely cause of a number of broken teeth. The bone abrasion on the missing fingers was indeed consistent with a 24-TPI hack-saw blade. More surprising were the contents of his nasal cavity. His upper respiratory tract contained a large amount of lint: the kind of fluff that you might find in the filter of a tumble dryer. Might he, Sue Stanza would ask, have been held in a garment factory, or a sweat shop of some kind? Somewhere that dried fabrics on an industrial scale? They were isolating the fibres right now, she would say, and running analysis to more precisely identify the type of fabrics and processes involved.

'When did all this happen?' Rex asked Lollo.

'Couple of hours ago. **Taxi rank** on Russell Square.'

'Russell Square? Are you joking? What the fuck was he doing in Russell Square?'

'Beats me. Coming round to yours?'

'Don't even joke about it,' said Rex. 'But DS Webster's team's on tasking, not mine. Couldn't one of them handle it while he's off? Binder Singh's doing great work, and he's been looking for more responsibility...'

'What? In at the deep end? No: Singh's got enough on his plate already. I need a senior body on this, and you're the best man for the job, Kingsy,' said Lollo. He paused for a beat or two, then said, 'I'll give Webbo bloody "stress-related", the fucking idiot.'

'No disrespect, sir,' said Rex, when the Chief was done, 'but there's no taxi rank on Russell Square.'

'Aye, there is,' said Lollo. 'North-west corner – always bloody lined up there, they are. Current status: closed until further notice.'

'It's not a rank, though, sir,' said Rex firmly. 'They don't do pick-ups. The green hut's a cabmen's shelter. It's like a cafe, but just for black cab drivers. Somewhere to get a **bacon** sarnie and a cuppa – you know this, right?'

'Alright, Mastermind. First thing tomorrow, alright.'

And that was how Rex and Susan's holiday was cut short, and why Rex would shortly swap the weird stony landscape of what was – technically, at least – Britain's only desert for the architectural and **arboreal** splendour of Russell Square, London, WC1.

2: Hêtre (Beech)

'**Yes sir**,' said Rex, with no hint of sarcasm.

Lollo owed him, that was for sure, and Rex would find some way in which his superior could make **amends**. He usually did.

But for tonight, Lollo and the late Dicky Sharp could wait their turn.

Since the weather was unseasonably good, Terry had suggested they **decamp** outside to eat. He could start the barbecue while it was still light.

Rex had jumped at the idea. Anything to keep his mind off work for a few more hours.

Terry had been down here a lot recently. Work had been slack so he'd figured doing the place up might be a better use of his time. One of the first things he'd done had been to knock together a barbecue – nothing fancy, just a few bricks – on the shingle over by the rusting boat winch that had come with the house. For tonight's dinner he'd bought half a dozen local marsh-grown lamb chops.

'How lovely,' said Susan.

'Let's do them on the **griddle** and have the aubergine cold on the side.'

'Sounds good to me,' said Rex. 'What can I carry?'

As they trod noisily over the stones, laden with barbecue supplies and some folding camping chairs, Rex found himself humming an old Congo **Ashanti** Roy record from back in the day: 'Breaking Down the Pressure'. Chance'd be a fine thing.

'Do you actually own this beach?' Susan asked.

'Kind of,' said Terry. 'But the whole of the Ness is shingle, so it's hard to tell where the beach actually stops or starts.'

He explained that the freehold of some of these shoreline houses in Dungeness covered plots that stretched all the way to the high-tide line. Not just the PLUTOs, but sites currently or formerly occupied by fishermen's huts like the ones further round the point. The winches were here so that you could pull your boat right up the beach. As he said this, they all noticed that a large seabird was perched majestically on a nearby post. It held its beak in the air and its wings outstretched like some mythical creature from medieval heraldry.

'Look at that. I want to call it a **guillemot**,' said Rex, racking his brain, 'but I know that's wrong.'

'Cormorant,' said Terry. 'There's thousands of them here. Literally thousands. They feed in the warm water by the power station. It's quite a sight: two thousand cormorants coming in to land at the same time. Beats your David Attenboroughs.'

'Wow,' said Rex. 'I'd like to see that.' Then he remembered that they were going home first thing. 'I see the odd one down by the Embankment.'

'Twitchers' paradise, this place. Look, see that white bird on the shoreline?'

'It's an **egret**,' said Susan. 'We have them in **Tobago**.'

'Do you still have family there, Susan?' Terry asked, dumping the gear next to the barbie and starting to unpack what he needed. He hung an LED lamp on an iron fence post, then gave the firebox a quick sweep.

'Yes,' said Susan. 'Grandparents on my mother's side, and a few cousins in Trini.'

'Nice.'

'Have you been?' Susan asked him.

'No, but I'd love to. Always wanted to go to the carnival. Do you get out there much?'

'It's been a while. Jane and Alaric, my sister and her husband, took Ashley over in the summer holidays, once she was feeling a bit stronger. Ashley's my niece. The one who was in Great Ormond Street last year – Rex told you?'

'He did – that's how you two met, right?'

Susan retold the story: Sid's cafe on a busy Saturday morning, it was Derby Day, they'd had to share a table.

While he was sorting the barbecue, Terry put the radio on low.

'I've never quite got into **opera**,' said Susan. 'I'm sure it's my loss.'

Rex was a convert. 'It was the World Cup for me,' he said. 'Italia '90. Couldn't have cared less before that, but "Nessun Dorma" still brings a tear to my eye.'

'If you fancied, I could get you two some tickets,' said Terry while he got the fire going.

'Are you sure?' said Susan, before remembering that their host made a living painting theatrical scenery. 'That'd be lovely. How did you get into it?'

'When I left art school I started getting scene-painting gigs through a friend of a friend, and I'd always go and see whatever show the cloths were for. But I'd been listening to classical music since I was a kid. We had to make a radio in O-level physics. Soldering a coil – you know. Oscillators. **Modulated** frequencies. I could probably still draw you the diagram: demodulator here, amplifier whatever. Power source over there—'

'**Dry cell**,' said Rex.

'Exactly. Anyway, we had to tune it in to something, and the strongest signal I found was Radio 3. Took it home like that – I was very proud of it – and never got around to changing it. Fair to say that I probably enjoyed being a bit of a contrarian, going against the **grain**. All my friends were into punk, of course, and so was I. Loved The Clash, The Jam, Pistols, The Damned.'

'You know I was more of a Stranglers fan, Tel,' said Rex.

'"No More Heroes" – *love* it,' said Terence. 'Classical music used to be all about the conductors. They were your way in: household names. **André Previn** was an international superstar. Men like **Malcolm Sargent** or **Thomas Beecham** were long dead by then, but that was what you got on the radio: their recordings. I suppose the contemporary equivalent would be someone like **Simon Rattle**.'

'Any women conductors?' asked Susan.

'Marin Alsop is pretty great. First woman to conduct the Last Night of the Proms. But it took until 2013, if you can believe that.'

'Yeah,' said Susan. 'I can believe it.'

'Rattle is a good bloke, supposedly,' Terry went on. 'I'm sure I've told Rex this before, but a busker mate of mine, an old Covent Garden face named John McKeon, an artist, he showed at the old Acme Gallery as was on Shelton Street once upon a time. Anyway, virtuoso violinist, he used to busk down at the Elephant. He was playing

Johann Sebastian Bach's *Partita No. 2*, if you please, spectacularly difficult – google it, Rex – and Simon Rattle happened to pass by. This would have been, I don't know, late eighties? It stopped Rattle in his tracks, apparently. He stayed for the whole thing – maybe half an hour? – applauded, then shook John's hand and gave him fifty quid. And I tell you, fifty quid was a *lot* of money back then.'

'So what's this on the radio now?' Susan asked.

'Mozart. One of his piano concertos.'

'I've got the box set of these at home,' said Rex. 'I always used to think it was a bit **elitist**, the old classical music, but Terence put me straight. Didn't you, Tel.'

As he fanned the flames with a bit of old plywood kept handy for the purpose, Terry laughed, then said that actually what he liked about music was that it really was simply there for the taking, that anyone who had even the crappiest old transistor radio had full access. In that sense at least it was the opposite of elitist. But more than that, for him the whole of classical music was also like a kind of **elegy**, not only to the people who made it – the composers and the musicians, and all the people who had ever listened to it – but also for earlier stages in human history and thought. Music was a way for the past to speak to us now, and all of it absolutely **gratis**, just by listening...

'That's a nice way to think about it,' said Susan.

'I'm just an old softie,' said Terry. 'Can you pass me those beech chips, please?'

'Doesn't it make you nervous?' Susan asked, glancing at the nuclear power station as she handed him the bag. 'Being right next to that thing?'

'Not really. If it did go up, I don't think we'd know too much about it.'

'You'd be alright,' said Rex. 'The PLUTO houses would probably be all that was left standing.'

They weren't the only ones who were enjoying the mild evening. Later, when it was dark, and Rex and Susan were snuggled together with a blanket around their shoulders, they watched a red point of light flickering across the vast concrete face of the nuclear power station. They'd both forgotten all about it for a few hours, but now it seemed to loom noisily on the horizon, only a mile or so away.

'Look,' said Rex, 'someone's got a **laser** pointer!'

The next morning they got up early. There was just time for quick showers and a slug of coffee before the minicab arrived from Lydd to take them to Ashford, where they jumped on the first train they could. But last night's loved-up vibes were long gone. Susan was so cross that she didn't even have it out with him, preferring to look out of the window in silence for most of the journey. Rex tried to persuade her to stay in London, but she said that she'd been looking forward to their little break and didn't fancy rattling around his flat on her own if he was going to be busy covering for Webster. Not much of a consolation prize, was it? Besides, she had an open return, so she might as well use it.

'Sorry,' he said for the umpteenth time as they crossed Pancras Road to King's Cross, so she could get the train back to York.

'Stop saying sorry,' said Susan, 'when you're not. I understand. It was fun while it lasted. Just a bit disappointing not to have had more time. Terry's lovely. It felt like meeting your family. It's good to know you've got someone like that looking out for you.'

She didn't know the half of it.

'Yeah,' said Rex. 'Tel's a lovely bloke.'

Rex knew Susan well enough by now to pick up that she was closing down on him. 'Maybe we should have gone abroad after all,' he said. 'Out of Lollo's reach.'

'Don't, Rex. Don't just say that. It's too late now. I think you secretly like it, the way he relies on you. Good old Mr Indispensable, always eager to please. You must do. Ring me later, maybe.'

She said it like it was the last thing she wanted him to do. And with a peck on the cheek, Susan was off, through the turnstiles, and she didn't look back.

Not once.

Damn.

Rex had royally fucked up, and he knew it. Susan was one of the best things to have happened to him in years. They hadn't known each other long, and he hadn't felt like this about anyone for ages, but now he knew that he'd been taking her for granted.

As he waited at the lights to cross Euston Road for Judd Street, all of their plans for a long weekend in Dungeness seemed an age ago: snuggling up around the fire, having Susan all to himself for a few days, going exploring, lunches at the seafood stall, walks on the beach and a pint or two in The Pilot. But right now, as he cut down Judd Street, Rex realised that it might not be so easy to get that intimacy back. 'Fun while it lasted,' she'd said. Did she mean their brief night away, or the relationship itself? He wasn't quite sure.

Rex felt the beginnings of a cold wash of shame.

But there wasn't time to feel sorry for himself because he had things to do and needed to focus. He'd drop in to the flat, dump his bag and freshen up before walking around the corner to the station. Catch Lollo before the meeting, then go and take a look at the scene.

◆ ◆ ◆

Arriving back home on Old Gloucester Street, Rex let himself in to the front door of Falcon, then jogged up the stairs, two at a time as usual, door keys in hand.

He saw the trainers first, as he neared the top of the stairs.

A young woman of secondary school age was sitting on his **doormat**. A child, in other words, and, right now, a child in a vulnerable situation. She was wearing skinny, faded black jeans and red Converse sneakers, with a Nirvana 'smiley' T-shirt under a grey hoodie, and she was reading a book. Whatever it was, it had a lurid cover. She had pale skin, and had tucked her straight, shoulder-length, mousy-brown hair behind one ear. On the ground next to her was a somewhat incongruous *Star Wars* rucksack.

As station lead – for his sins – on SD (Safe Detention and Handling of Persons), Rex had done some specialist training in engagement with young people over and above the standard police training modules, so he was more up to speed than most on safety and welfare protocols, National Referral, but he also knew that needs and vulnerabilities were not always visible.

All of this was second nature to Rex now, so he kept his distance and remained calm and open.

Hearing his steps on the landing, she looked up and caught his eye.

What did she see?

A man of average height and in not bad shape (not out of breath, anyway), wearing khaki Dockers, navy-blue deck shoes and a black Harrington jacket over his red Fred Perry. Slightly tanned, five foot ten with a forty-four chest and shortish dark hair, with a soft brown leather Samsonite overnight bag slung over one shoulder. He was almost certainly not her idea of a policeman, which was a good start in terms of keeping things on a level footing, but also a challenge.

'Hello,' said Rex, flashing his warrant card in his calmest, most non-confrontational manner. 'It's okay. I'm a policeman, but I'm not at work right now. What are you reading? Any good?'

She held it up so Rex could see the cover: *Boudicca: Queen of the Iceni*. 'Yeah, it's alright. I just bought it up the road.'

'Oh right – there's some good shops,' he said. 'Been here long?'

'About half an hour.'

'Are you waiting for someone?'

Silence; but of the inner-city kind.

A pause big enough to rent out on Airbnb.

He could hear traffic on nearby Theobalds Road and Southampton Row, and the automated verbal warning of a lorry reversing. Closer by, but unseen, a blackbird clucked out its distress call against the backdrop of more distant and undifferentiated birdsong in the Queen Square treetops.

Finally, she spoke. 'Are you Rex?'

He wasn't expecting that. 'Who wants to know?' he said.

'I'm Jennifer.'

He looked at her blankly, then felt the strap of his bag slipping, so shrugged it back onto his shoulder. This obviously wasn't ringing any bells.

'Jennifer, your daughter?'

3: Abeille (Bee)

As soon as Jennifer had said it, all thoughts of work, of Susan, and of Lollo – not to mention the investigation and the team meeting he was supposed to be attending – fell away.

'Of course, Jennifer! How lovely to see you.' He could hear himself saying something about how great it was to finally meet, that he'd heard so much about her, and hadn't she grown, and so sorry he hadn't recognised her, but the photos on her dad's desk must have been from primary school…

He was aware that he was babbling, but he meant every word. His brain was going a mile a minute, and for a second he felt like Wile E. Coyote in the *Road Runner* cartoons, propelled into the void by his own momentum before realising that the ground beneath his feet had disappeared.

Rex didn't let on, but even as he was experiencing it, he knew that this was one of those moments when everything changed. Not mere historical change of the 'Where were you when Thatcher resigned?' variety, or the collapse of the Berlin Wall. This was change of a greater order of magnitude. Like suddenly and irrevocably crossing your own private Rubicon, whether you wanted to or not. When everything that had gone before suddenly seemed too simple, and too good to have been true, or to have lasted, and you were abruptly shoved – for better or worse – into a different dimension, with its own new multiplying factors of complexity and risk, and maybe eventually some pleasures too, once you'd adjusted, if you were lucky.

We'd all been there.

Everyone had their own: some good – the marriage proposal, the new job, the pregnancy test; and some bad – the diagnosis, the divorce papers, the 4 a.m. phone call.

The police officer on the doorstep.

The script: 'I'm afraid I've got some bad news.'

Or, 'I'm sorry, but there's been an accident.'

Or, 'Can we come inside for a minute, please?'

This was different; the wrong way around.

Because nowadays Rex was the policeman. This was his own doorstep, and for once it wasn't him breaking the news.

It was his daughter, Jennifer.

The words were simple enough.

And it was true. She was his daughter. But he had never, ever expected to hear her or anyone else say it. Much less expected to ever meet this – what? – fifteen-year-old who had for the past thirty minutes been sitting on his doormat reading a book about Boudicca.

He liked her style and her chutzpah, but he was glad he'd come back home when he had.

Once he got over the initial surprise, all he could think of to say were questions. How did you get here? Shouldn't you be at school? Does your mum know you're here? Or your dad? (God forbid.) But he held back because he knew that what was probably needed was for him to say nothing and let Jennifer do the talking. What he needed to do was encourage her to fill the gaps.

She'd come and sought him out, after all.

There must be a reason why she was sitting here.

And he knew that all of his smaller questions were just a way of avoiding asking the big one: how the fuck had she found out? He wasn't about to ask, though. Not until he'd spoken to Helen and got a bit of background. No point blundering in before that.

Surely Helen wouldn't have told her.

So, Webster?

If so, what on earth had he been thinking?

Christ! They'd done pretty well to keep it from Webster all these years. But a part of Rex would have loved to have been there when he'd found out; to have been a fly on the wall. Because he knew that DS Eddie Webster would practically have had a heart attack at the idea that Jennifer was Rex's daughter and not his.

But supposing Webster had found out, he definitely shouldn't have told Jennifer. Because to all intents and purposes Webster *was* her father, and not Rex.

So, what exactly was going on here? There was no way he was going to call Webbo, but he'd better let Helen know.

And, in the meantime, what was he going to do with Jennifer all day?

He wished that Susan were with him. She'd know how to break the ice, what with having a teenage niece and everything. He thought of giving her a bell too, to ask her advice, but then thought better of it. 'What? Because I'm a woman?' – he could almost hear her saying it. 'She's your daughter. You deal with it!'

Of course, this wasn't the only reason he didn't phone Susan, but he doubted she'd pick up, and it would be far too much information for a voicemail.

'Hang on a sec,' said Rex, playing for time. 'I'd better let them know at work that I won't be there for a bit...' Although it wasn't Lollo he was texting.

Hi H, Jennifer is here? She's safe. Found her on the doorstep.

What's going on? I can take her to work or whatev until you can get here. BTW she knows. R

Lollo would have to wait.

A bumblebee flew past them on the landing. Perhaps it had been awakened by the warm temperatures, these welcome few days of sun. For a second or two Rex wondered if he should point it out – 'Oh, look. A bee!' – but then he remembered that she was fifteen, not five. Keep it simple, he thought to himself.

'Right!' he said at last, in what he hoped would seem a moderately cheerful and practical tone of voice. 'Have you eaten?'

Well, what else was he going to say? After all, everyone's got to eat. Sid's would be a safe bet: home turf and neutral ground all in one. And it was a good way to kill an hour or so.

'No. Not really.'

That settled it.

'Okay. Let me drop my bag, then we'll go to Sid's around the corner – best greasy spoon in London.'

Jennifer looked at him blankly.

'You know, just a traditional egg-and-bacon type of builders' caff? But a good one. I go there all the time. They know me. Maybe you can phone your mum when we get there? Then you might have to come into work with me and read for a bit.'

He unlocked the mortice lock and then the Yale, unzipped his Samsonite and took out the newspaper, then swung the bag through the open doorway onto the hall carpet, pulled the front door to and double-locked it.

'Bring your bag,' he said, then turned and walked towards the stairs. 'Sid's is just near work. I'll show you.'

'K,' said Jennifer.

Something about her manner reminded him of Helen. Hair colour too, perhaps. Other than that, maybe not so much.

'You look a bit like your mum,' he lied.

'I'm hardly gonna look like my dad, am I?'

Don't rise to the bait, Rex thought, but he also recognised that she was giving him an in. 'How's she taking it?'

'...' She batted the question away with a derisive roll of the eyes and a shrug that nearly knocked him over.

Bloody hell.

It wasn't her own mum, not Helen, that Jennifer took after.

It was Rex's mum, Geraldine.

Jennifer's grandmother.

Rex's mum who'd been dead these past thirty years.

4: Laitue (Lettuce)

Now – an hour or so, one 'Mega Breakfast' for him and a fish finger sandwich for her, two mugs of tea, a flat white and a Diet Coke later – Rex and Jen, as she preferred to be known, were sitting in the sun on a bench in Coram's Fields. When Jen had gone to the loo before leaving the cafe, he'd quickly phoned Rebecca Fernie, Lollo's PA.

'Fend him off for me, Becky. I'm on my way, but something urgent has come up – a family emergency.'

'I'll try,' she said.

'What's the mood?' said Rex.

'Crisis mode. You can imagine. They've convened a Gold Support for ten o'clock Monday that he'll want you at.'

Coram's Fields. Rex had attended once or twice professionally, but never had the excuse to visit as a punter. He'd been about to launch into a little local history spiel: 'accompanied children only', the Foundling Hospital, Handel and all that. But then he'd wondered if the subject matter might be a little insensitive in the circumstances. They could pick up a leaflet on the way out. The crossword was safer ground, and kind of fun. So that's what they were doing: the Quick one. Rex was letting Jen fill in the solutions. They'd started the other way around, but he'd had to stop himself from filling in half the answers on autopilot without even waiting for her to have a go.

'Four across,' she said, '"Concerning".' She paused, 'Um, then it says "arch-ache"? In brackets? Five letters, second letter "N", ending with "T".'

'Hmm. Let's have a look.'

She showed him.

'Oh yeah. "Archaic". That means it's an old word. Archaic – like in "archaeology". You'll never get that one. Shall I tell you?'

She shrugged.

'It's **anent**. A-N-E-N-T.'

'A-N—?'

'E-N-T.'

'You're just making it up now,' she said, filling in the squares.

'No, I swear that's right,' said Rex, holding his hands up. 'Sometimes they say "Scots". It's an old Scottish word.'

'How's anyone supposed to know that?'

Rex shrugged. 'It's the kind of thing you pick up if you do enough crosswords. It's just one of those words that crops up a lot, I suppose. Useful in Scrabble, though. Next!'

On the short walk to Sid's, Rex had successfully maintained the tone of cheerful practicality that he'd established on the landing outside his flat. It was slightly friendlier than his usual 24-7 performance, the public-facing neutral professionalism that his job entailed, but not a million miles away. They'd chatted about school: weren't she and Rachel both at— Oh, what's it called?

'The Beal, yeah.'

'That's right,' said Rex. 'Your dad told me. He's very proud of you, you know.'

Her favourite subjects were English, French, Spanish, history and biology, and she'd put those down as her A-level choices.

'Favourite teachers?' he'd asked.

She'd narrowed her eyes and glared at him.

'What do you want to do when you grow up?' had elicited a similar response.

Then he'd asked if she came into town much.

'Course,' she'd said, all blasé, although along with the school trips to the zoo and the museums, or to see some Shakespeare at the **National**, it had just been the usual sights: the London Eye, South Ken, Christmas shopping, concerts at Wembley and the O2. And of course most weekends she and her schoolfriends would come in on the tube to go shopping or to Camden Market, and to one or two of the Sunday-lunchtime gigs at Underworld.

'Good,' he'd said. 'You know your way around.' But still, when they'd got to the corner with Theobalds Road, he'd stopped for a second. 'It's a great place to live,' he'd said, then pointed out that

Holborn tube was just down there, the British Museum over there, Tottenham Court Road that way, Camden Town in walking distance. 'Everything's on the doorstep.'

'What's that?' she'd asked, pointing at some arrangements of fabrics and **drapery** and ranks of dazzling floodlights that shone out of some upstairs windows of the old Central School of Art and Design building opposite.

'Filming something, probably,' Rex had said. 'Or more likely a photo shoot. Used to be The Central – an art school – but the building's empty now. They use it for things like that all the time. There's a part of the Met that just deals with filming requests, you know? If a feature film needs to be shot in a particular street or something.'

'Cool,' she'd said. 'Do you meet them, though?'

'Who?'

'Film stars.'

'Not me, personally, no. I don't work on that unit. It's not particularly glamorous – more like dealing with producers and location managers, checking the paperwork's in order.'

'Oh.'

Rex could tell that not only had he succeeded in not impressing Jennifer; he was now boring her too.

'I've bumped into one or two celebs, though,' he'd said, quickly trying to claw back some credibility. 'Jude Law, the actor? I once literally turned a corner and bumped into him running the other way. Had to grab hold of each other so we didn't both fall over. He saw the funny side.'

Turning onto Lamb's Conduit Street, she'd recognised the station – they'd used to come to the children's Christmas parties when they were younger, but it had been a while. He'd pointed out the broken blind on the sixth floor – 'That's where me and your dad work' – and assured her that, no, there wasn't always a line of tents along the pavement outside.

And now here they were, sat doing the crossword in Coram's Fields. How surreal was that?

'**Produce**,' said Rex, pointing at the paper over Jen's shoulder. 'Look, twelve across: "Yield or make", seven letters. The fifth letter's "U", the last letter's "E"? The answer's "produce", as in' – he paused for a second – "'If you look under twenty-one you will be asked to produce ID.'"

Jennifer merely snorted as she filled in the blanks.

She was reasonably chipper, considering.

But how was Rex doing?

He was doing fine. Making sure to mention Jennifer's mum and dad every now and then. Keeping things low-key. Not over-investing, for now.

It was the police training kicking in. Always the training: stay in control, steer things gently, watch and wait, don't get too involved. Which might seem a bit cold to your average civilian, but what else was he going to do? Was this the point in their story where they were meant to bond? To go on a shopping spree? Buy her a new pair of Doc Martens and a K-pop T-shirt? Where he'd suddenly realise what he'd been missing? As if he'd just left the **cave** and was seeing the brightly **coloured** world outside for the first time? Making **landfall** on some vast Terra Incognita of parenthood? Bewilderingly unfamiliar **scenery** in all directions as far as the eye could see?

Well, yes, maybe so.

Except this was something that he'd known was there all along.

Just he'd thought he could ignore it. They could ignore it. Which was all very well until it turned up on your doorstep to **smite** you one.

It?

She.

This girl who at particular moments looked like Rex's mother, and who was now sitting on the bench next to him in Coram's Fields, reading out the crossword clues.

Bloody hell.

His daughter.

'Why didn't you and Mum—' Jen had asked at one point when they were walking from Sid's to Coram's Fields.

'What? Make a go of it?' said Rex.

Jen nodded.

'That's a good question. We loved each other,' said Rex truthfully, 'but maybe I didn't treat her very well. Let work get in the way.'

'Oh.'

'And then she fell in love with your dad.'

Rex and Helen's break-up, her running off with Eddie Webster – Rex's colleague since Hendon days, the by then Detective Constable Edward Webster – was ancient history. But it had been a bit messier and more protracted certainly than Webster had realised at the time.

Back then, Rex had been alright with it: when Helen had told him she was pregnant, that the child was definitely Rex's but she was going to let Eddie think it was his. It was for the best, she'd thought. And Rex had agreed, been relieved even – You're well out of it, son, he'd thought – and then they'd both forgotten about it and got on with their lives. Well, Rex had, anyway. But clearly it hadn't been only their decision to make.

Rex felt a wave of affection for his former girlfriend. He had to think for a second to remember why he hadn't fought harder for Helen, and tried to get her back once they knew she was pregnant. Couldn't they have made a go of it? Couldn't they have had a couple more kids, instead of letting Webster – fucking Ed Webster of all people – bring up his daughter?

Well, he knew the answer to that.

Helen and Eddie had wanted it more than he had. They'd been totally loved up by then, and it – Helen – had actually been the making of Webster, Rex was convinced of it.

Meanwhile, no amount of couples therapy or **self-help** books could have saved Rex and Hel's relationship. He recognised that now, just as he'd known it then. But for all that it was true, the rational response felt like **cold comfort** now that he was faced with exactly what he'd been missing all these years. The whole business suddenly felt like a **gross** mistake. It was as if he'd given his daughter away as part of a **transaction** the price of which he'd never understood, and probably never thought he'd have to pay.

How could he have thought it would be a good idea not to be part of his own daughter's life? That this would somehow be for the best?

All of a sudden, it didn't really feel like that.

How could they have simply assumed that Jennifer would never find out?

And what might his life have been like these past fifteen years if he'd been able to share it?

The ups and downs of a life in policing seemed like **chicken feed** in comparison.

What if it had been him and Helen standing around the **crib**, and changing their first nappy?

'An endless stream of shit,' a beaming Webster had announced when he'd come back to the station after the then standard few days' paternity leave. 'Unstoppable.' He and Hel hadn't known what to do, he'd said, until a nurse had told them they'd better get used to it, and to clean it up and be quick about it. Then she'd taken **pity** on them, apparently, and told them that if they lifted baby's legs up like that, they were effectively pumping out the poo every time. 'It's like pulling a pint,' Webbo had announced, miming the action, to general hilarity among the younger officers, 'but a pint of shit!'

It could have been Rex taking his turns at feeding, burping, changing, and then – if all else failed – feeding, burping and changing all over again. Then later, it might have been Rex taking his turn to pace around the flat at all hours of the night with a crying baby on his shoulder so that Hel could get some sleep. Rex with little epaulettes of baby vomit. Rex getting up early to assemble the *Millennium Falcon* or the Playmobil pirate ship for Jennifer to **play** with on Christmas mornings. Rex going to the parent-and-toddler group when the two-two-two shift pattern allowed it – two earlies, two lates, two nights – or down to swimming classes at the Oasis. Rex who'd **heave** the sleeping child onto his shoulder, and tuck her up in bed. Rex who'd wheel her in a pushchair down to Maison Bertaux for a treat, to the Phoenix Garden, the Wallace Collection, or around the British Museum. Rex watching children's telly: 'All aboard the *SkylArk*!' What was that from? *Roobarb and Custard*? Something like that. *Noah and Nelly*. That was it. He'd used to watch it at his gran's.

But could he really see himself and Hel ordering groceries, and unpacking the bags from the Ocado **delivery van**?

Steady on.

Things had turned out the way they had for a reason, after all.

It was easier said than done, but it wasn't worth thinking about what might have been. If only this or that.

There was enough to do here and now.

For a start, Rex was unclear exactly how things were going to play out over the next five minutes, let alone the rest of the day-week-month. Perhaps Jennifer was getting bored of the crossword.

'What do you want to do?' he asked. 'Feed the rabbits? We could go and buy some lettuce and come back.'

Jennifer was staring at him, her expression a mixture of scorn and incredulity.

'They've got animals,' he continued. 'A little farm: rabbits, goats—'

'Feed the *rabbits*? Mate! I'm fifteen.'

That was when his phone rang.

Saved by the bell.

He didn't recognise the number.

'Hang on. Got to take this,' said Rex. Then, lifting the phone to his ear: 'King.'

It was Helen, calling from a work phone.

'Oh – hi, Hel,' he said, looking pointedly at Jennifer. 'Yes, we're fine. Jen's fine – I'll put her on in a minute. Where are you?'

5: Mélèze (Larch)

'Seriously?' Amelia stopped in her tracks. 'The Clash played a free gig in the beer garden of your local pub? The Clash?'

'Yeah!' said Spike. 'It was a bit surreal.'

'You're telling me!'

'Woah!' said Deedee. 'You saw The Clash?'

They still had a couple of hours' drive ahead of them, but they'd taken a detour to show Deedee Loch Lomond, and this had seemed as good a place as any to stop for a break. Spike had parked in a lay-by down below and they'd yomped up into the trees, to pee and stretch their legs.

The tall, straight larches towered above their heads, and all around them was the white noise of the running, splashing water that rushed unseen down every hill, in every channel and every crevice from crag to valley floor, from highest boulder to lowest bog. It might even have been idyllic if the air wasn't full of tiny midgies: clouds of them blustering against your face and neck, going in your eyes and up your nose, all over your lips and in your mouth. Lone mosquitoes seemed almost reserved by comparison. These bastards bit you anywhere, and en masse – eyelids, ear-holes, mouth – leaving a rash of tiny and infuriatingly itchy spots.

'Smoke,' said Spike, swatting the air uselessly. 'Quick. It's the only thing they don't like.'

They didn't have a name for their Chapter yet, but the three of them had got together after Amelia put ads up in Housmans and in the Friends Meeting House. She'd read the Isaiah Movement Handbook and wanted to start her own Chapter, make the Peace Pledge and get involved in the anti-Trident nuclear missile protests. She'd roped in Spike. They'd been hanging out a bit already so he hadn't needed much persuading.

He'd first met Amelia at the Nuclear Train protests in Hackney at the turn of the century – vigils against the secret and untimetabled trainloads of nuclear waste that had used to rumble through Hackney Central at four in the morning. At the time, she'd worn boiler suits and Breton shirts, walking boots, and had kind of punky short hair. They'd got chatting when a bunch of them had gone for a drink in the Samuel Pepys afterwards. Her face was familiar too. Maybe from meetings at Friends House? Thought so! They'd had a bit of a fling, nothing too serious. But things had cranked up a notch around the time of the anti-Iraq War march back in the spring. Both freely admitted that they didn't think marching achieved anything – and they'd been proved correct when war had been declared only one month later – but each of them had also felt that the need to demonstrate had never been greater. Diana and Amelia were both Quakers. Spike was more agnostic, but admired the Quakers' ideas about faith being a journey, not an arrival. Now, after some back and forth, they were heading to the Isaiah Movement training camp and a week of direct action.

They'd arranged to meet up in Edinburgh. Deedee – short for Diana – had come over from Holland via a peace camp in France and a stopover at Amelia's place in London. She was ten years older than Amelia, small and wiry, and dressed a bit hippyish. She usually wore her frizz of greying hair in a purple headwrap. They'd got the coach up to Scotland and spent a couple of days staying with a friend of Amelia's sister who had a sprawling flat in Saxe Coburg Street in the New Town, and mooching around the city: seeing the sights, swimming in Glenogle baths, walking up to the Botanics. Spike had joined them later on.

'Don't you love his dreadlocks?' Amelia had said to Deedee. 'Are you going to grow them really long?'

Spike had had things to do down south. He'd been on the lookout for some new wheels to convert, and long-short his mate Tree had spotted a half-decent ex-Royal Mail fleet 1995 Leyland DAF 400 van among the write-offs and non-runners that were stacked up to sell for parts on the edge of the British Car Auctions site at Blackbushe, Surrey, a few days before. Half-decent in that it had the longer body and larger capacity than the 200, plus two months of MOT and a country fleet number, so had probably done more motorway miles than town, meaning less likely that the gearbox and suspension would be completely fucked.

Spike had paid a tiny bit over the odds, was how he told it, but sod it, he needed this. They'd got it back to Tree's place and given it a quick service. He'd ripped all the plastic panelling out of the cab, with its damp, yellow foam lining, and then Tree had welded some chunky hooks onto the inside of the frame, one up behind the driver's seat and another above the back nearside door, so Spike could hang a hammock diagonally across the interior. Hey presto: no need for a bed or a sleeping platform. He was also planning to ply-line and insulate all round, and put in a couple of windows and a wood-burner; maybe a simple folding table. But those would have to wait. And actually he quite liked the fact that, without windows, it still looked like a regular work van – less conspicuous. These were lessons learned the hard way, in the Beanfield. He'd been lucky to get away, riding pillion on the back of some girl's Honda 125. She'd happened to be making her own escape and taken pity on him. But that was then and this was now. And Spike had loaded up the DAF: box of rice cakes, a crate of moody carrots that Teazel on the market would have chucked otherwise, a kilo tub of peanut butter, half a sack of spuds, Primus stove, teabags, some old bed sheets and a selection of household gloss paints in various colours, plus assorted brushes, white spirits, et cetera, in case any banners needing doing, tents and sleeping bags, inflatable dinghy, a roll of carpet, pliers, superglue, liquid cement, hack-saw blades, hammers, chisels, and two sets of heavy-duty bolt-cutters. Then he'd slung his tools in and headed north, slept in a supermarket car park off the A1 somewhere round Morpeth way: 'Finally got to test out that hammock,' he said.

'And how was it?' asked Amelia.

'Like a dream. Best night's sleep I've had in years,' he said with a grin.

They'd needed an early start to come via the National Park. Spike had picked them up on the corner of Henderson Row at 5.30 a.m., and they weren't due at Dani's place until later that afternoon. Spike and Deedee hadn't met Daniella yet, but Amelia had met her a couple of times before, when she'd stayed at Faslane Peace Camp. Dani was a legend in the movement, and every few months for the past couple of years she'd been hosting training camps on her land, which overlooked the loch.

They'd been on the road for a few hours now, trading life stories. He'd finished telling the two women about his new van, and as they yomped up the hill they'd moved onto the altogether more serious topic of how they'd got into all this: anti-nuclear activism, direct action. It was Spike's turn, and he was telling them about the day The Clash turned up at his local and played a free gig.

'When was this?'

'Oh, seventeen, eighteen years ago. Just after the Miners' Strike, so it must be summer of eighty-five. In the Royal Park pub in Leeds. D'you know it?'

Amelia shook her head.

'Is this where you are from, Leeds?' asked Deedee. 'How is it like?'

'No, I'm from Essex, but I went to university in Leeds,' said Spike, shielding with both hands the light that Amelia offered, then blowing out a long puff of cigarette smoke. 'Economics. Dropped out midway through the second year, but stayed on for a bit. How about you two?'

'Chemistry, of all things,' said Amelia, lighting her own roll-up. 'At Bristol. Thought I could be a scientist, but I got into computers instead, thankfully.'

Deedee looked up. She'd been rummaging in a rucksack that was almost as big as she was, first taking out a paperback, neatly folded jumpers and T-shirts and a pair of lightweight khaki trousers before triumphantly pulling out a stout cardboard tube – the kind that might contain rolled-up paper. Or a certificate. 'I graduated *cum laude* in media studies and human geography at UvA,' she said.

'Cum louder?' said Spike with a snigger. 'As the actress said to the bishop.'

Deedee ignored him. A breeze was rustling the higher branches far above them, and sunlight dappled the forest floor. Spike rested back on one elbow and took a drag from his cigarette, enjoying the warmth of the sun on his skin, the break from driving, and the momentary reprieve from the midges.

'Look,' she said as she removed a plastic lid from one end of the tube and tipped it up over her open palm. What emerged, root-first, was a small conifer sapling – no more than ten inches high – its root-bundle wrapped in clingfilm.

'Wow,' said Amelia.

'It is my gift to you,' said Deedee, looking around at the tall straight trees that surrounded them in every direction. 'It is also a larch, like these ones? I take it from the forest near my home as a symbol of our friendship, which is about creating things, not destroying them.'

Amelia's eyes sparkled. 'From Holland? Oh, that's so sweet of you, Dee!'

'Shall we plant it?' said Spike, getting to his feet. 'As a revolutionary act?' He had already taken a pocketknife from his coat and was looking for a likely spot, to give it the best chance of doing well. Perhaps a sunny spot that was equidistant from the larger tree trunks that surrounded them. Once he'd found it, he stooped and – smoking cigarette dangling from his mouth – began scratching through the surface litter and soil with the largest blade, clearing it away with his other hand.

'Yes, I would like that very much,' said Deedee.

'What do you think, Dee?' asked Spike. 'This okay? Give it a bit of space, it should be alright!'

She nodded enthusiastically, and carefully passed the sapling to him.

As he unwrapped the root-ball, Spike thought for a second and said, 'Let's all visualise this sapling growing into a mighty tree.'

Job done, Spike tamped the earth down around the slender stem, then wiped the knife on his trousers and pocketed it, before ceremonially pouring a little water onto the freshly disturbed soil.

Amelia picked up the loose conversational thread: 'So that's what got you into all this? Seeing The Clash in your local pub?'

'Ha, yeah, kind of,' said Spike, dusting the dirt off his hands. 'Well, you know. Indirectly.'

Spike and a couple of his housemates had been out clubbing the night before, and it had turned into a bit of a late one. Rising the next afternoon and all decidedly the worse for wear, someone had suggested a hair of the dog, so they'd staggered down the hill to the Royal Park, got a round in and sat down in the lounge bar. One of Spike's friends had looked over at a group of blokes dressed in black with guitar cases who were standing near the bar, then did a double-take.

'I swear that guy with the orange hair is Joe Strummer,' she'd said.

The others had looked over blankly.

'No, seriously. I love The Clash. I'd recognise him anywhere.'

At about that moment Strummer and co had picked up their guitars and their pints and trooped out into the back garden, and with a growing sense of excitement Spike and his mates had followed suit. By the time they got outside, the band were tuning up. It was Joe Strummer and Paul Simonon, plus a couple of guitarists and a drummer that none of them had recognised.

They'd already done a couple of gigs in Nottingham, supposedly, then landed in Leeds on the Monday. The Royal Park was one of several gigs that they'd play in the city over the next two or three days. Spike's eyes lit up as he set the scene. 'There were only about twenty of us in this little pub garden,' he said. 'Watching The Clash – incredible!'

'What songs did they play?' asked Deedee.

'The funny thing is I can't remember exactly,' said Spike. 'They definitely played "Straight to Hell" – oh, it was so great – plus some newer songs and a couple of cover versions. I'm pretty sure there's a bootleg of one of the other gigs, though.

'Anyway,' he went on, 'I'd never written anything before – or since, really – but the next day I went down to the *Leeds Other Paper* office, and offered to review the gig.'

'What's that?' asked Amelia.

'*Leeds Other Paper*,' said Spike. 'It was a radical weekly newspaper and listings magazine. Kind of anti-racist, anti-nuclear, anti-sexist, pro-trade unions. Run by a co-operative; really kind of lo-fi. A bit like *SchNEWS* down in Brighton, if you ever saw that?'

'Did they run your review?'

'No!' said Spike. 'They said they already had it covered, but they were always looking for people to help out if I wanted to get involved. So I did: selling ads, making tea, sweeping up, whatever needed doing. But I also started actually going to the things we were covering, a couple of CND demos in Leeds city centre, then spent some time up at the Peace Camp at Menwith Hill, the American air base on the Yorkshire Moors, you know, the "golf balls"? Stop the City demos, that kind of thing. And *that's* how I got started in all this.'

'All because of The Clash!' said Deedee, laughing. 'Thank you, Joe Strummer.'

'Yeah, and rest in peace,' said Spike.

'What?' Deedee looked aghast. She was genuinely shocked.

'Oh man, I'm really sorry,' said Spike. 'It's so sad. He died just before Christmas. Didn't you hear?'

6: Ciguë (Hemlock)

'Yes, of course it is very beautiful,' said Deedee. 'But it also depends what is your **criteria**? You cannot, for example, **regard** this landscape as natural any more. Hey, you should **quit**, you know that?'

Amelia was lighting a last rollie. Her nerves were beginning to show. The magnitude of what they were planning to do. Give up smoking now? Not likely. She remembered the last time she'd tried: the whole **fractious** round of headaches, nicotine patches and displacement eating. Deedee was right, of course, but this was simply not the time.

It might have been summer, but it was **not so hot**, now that the sun had disappeared behind the brow of the hill above them. Having planted her larch sapling, and finished the cheese **scones** that Amelia had baked the night before, Deedee was sitting cross-legged on the ground putting everything neatly back into her rucksack: T-shirts, jumper, wetsuit, washbag, a large Afro-style **comb**.

Spike picked up her book and had a flick through. It was the Penguin Classics edition of *The **Hunchback** of Notre-Dame* by **Victor Hugo**. Deedee had bought it from a second-hand bookstall near the Grassmarket in Edinburgh. The painting on the cover was not of **Quasimodo**, but an atmospheric image of stonemasons building— What was it? Yes, the arches of a bridge over the Seine. It must be. While the familiar outline of the great Gothic cathedral brooded darkly above them. Before he could look to see who the painting was by, Deedee put out her hand to take it back. She placed the book on top of everything else, then tightened the drawstring over it and fastened the flap.

'Well, of course,' she said, getting to her feet and hoiking the rucksack up onto her back, 'the mountains are not man-made, but their appearance and the landscape itself is, completely. Forests

don't really grow in straight lines, you know. We studied this at
UvA.'

She told her friends how in prehistory most of what was now
Scotland would have been covered in the ancient Caledonian Forest,
a mix of dense woodland, savannah, heath and bog, populated
by wolves, bears and lynx, but how centuries of deforestation and
farming, the industrialisation of hunting and shooting, would slowly
denude the landscape, an effect compounded by the forced removal
of many tens of thousands of people in the successive phases of
the Highland Clearances, and more recently by the management of
vast estates for game shooting and by industrial forestry practices.
Larch plantations like the one they were standing in right now hadn't
been a feature of the Scottish landscape at all. The trees had only
been introduced 250 years ago, but larch had proven a particularly
resilient timber for shipbuilding, as well as being suitable for paper
production, and even – in the twentieth century – for old-fashioned
wooden telegraph poles.

'Typical of mankind,' said Amelia, shaking her head, 'to find Eden
and' – she paused, looking for the right word – '**debase** it.'

They all felt the same way. With **Icarus**-like levels of hubris,
man was now capable of committing nuclear **genocide**, or, worse,
destroying all life on earth. Didn't they know where this would
end? Where was the resistance? There'd been some progress. Recent
proceedings at the International Court of Justice had proved beyond
legal doubt that any nuclear missile launch was in and of itself a war
crime, since it was impossible not to target civilians in a nuclear strike
or its aftermath. That's what this trip and the entire Isaiah Movement
was about, after all. The name came from the Old Testament of the
Bible, Isaiah Chapter 2 Verse 4:

And he shall judge among the nations, and shall rebuke many
people: and they shall beat their swords into plowshares, and
their spears into pruninghooks: nation shall not lift up sword
against nation, neither shall they learn war any more.

Anti-nuclear protests were no longer limited to vigils and
petitions, handing out leaflets on the high street or attending peace
camps, but now included testing the law. And it seemed as if the law

– according to the ICJ, at least – was finally saying that protest could extend to active disarmament. That the prevention of a war crime was justification enough.

Spike stood up and dusted himself off. The rest stop, this **dreamy** interlude, was over. There was important work to do. It was time to **scramble** back down the slope and drive to Dani's place, to meet the other Chapters from all over the country who'd be converging on Gare Loch over the next few days. He gestured to the others and they formed a circle, linking hands for a couple of minutes of silent prayer, each communing with their own understanding of God: Deedee with her head bowed, and swaying – almost dancing – on the spot, and Amelia standing straight with eyes closed, while Spike gazed up at the sky through the gaps in the canopy far above.

After a short while, Amelia lightly squeezed her friends' hands and wordlessly nodded, as if both to reinforce their bond and to draw their respective prayers to a close. The gesture was returned by all. 'Amen,' they said.

As they neared the road, Amelia stopped, ankle-deep in vegetation on the damp and shaded edge of the plantation, and pointed out something they'd missed in their rush to get up the hill and empty their bladders: a thick covering of the distinctive glossy, arrow-shaped, purple-speckled leaves and standing flowers sometimes known as Lords and Ladies. She pulled a tatty, green-cloth-bound *Observer's Book of British Wild Flowers* from her pocket, and read the entry aloud: 'Cuckoo-pint...'

She pronounced 'pint' to rhyme with 'mint'.

What it didn't say, she added, was that ***Arum** maculatum* was supposedly exceedingly unpleasant to the taste, as well as mildly irritating to the skin and mucous membranes, so best avoided, though hardly the most poisonous plant in the British woodland.

Spike jumped down onto the road, unlocked the van and flung the door back with a flourish. Climbing in, he reached across to flip the lock on the passenger side, and slid that open too. 'All **aboard** the *SkylArk*!'

7: Radis (Radish)

For one **awful** moment, with half a dozen machine guns trained on them and the bandit alarm sirens going off all over the base, Amelia wondered if they'd simply be shot, and their bodies dumped in the water. Perhaps they'd been guilty of plain old **self-deception**, thinking that they'd be allowed to get away with it. Not that they were running away or resisting. They weren't even pretending that they hadn't done it. Quite the reverse: they'd hung around waiting to be arrested. Their particular brand of radical resistance might have involved confronting evil systems, but they did so in a manner that prioritised accountability, openness and the safety of all involved.

Later, Amelia would tell Spike that during their arrest she'd suddenly thought of Angela **Lansbury**, that **mainstay** of the daytime TV schedules, with her trademark **wink**. But you didn't need to be Jessica Fletcher to figure out that a crime had been committed here, nor whodunnit. They'd even left a **note** inside explaining their actions, before coming up on top of the barge to eat a picnic breakfast comprising the last of the food they'd brought from Edinburgh – oatcakes, radishes and some farmhouse cheddar from Mellis's – while they waited for someone, anyone, to notice they were here and arrest them. It went through her mind that in the past what they had just done might have been called 'treason', and that people had been sent to the **gallows** for less, although to her mind, here and now, with the human race and the earth itself facing the greatest threat it had ever known, she had faith – they all did – that the greater **sin** was to do nothing.

Over at the main gate the ceilidh was already in full swing and would be for most of the day – they could hear the bagpipes and fiddles from here. Some of their Isaiah Movement comrades would by now be locked on to each other in a human chain, while other

Peace Pledgers, and a few Labour and SNP MPs who'd buzzed in for the day, would be singing and dancing, chanting out their slogans and giving soundbites to the local and national press. The original plan had been that, having broken into the base under cover of nightfall, Amelia, Deedee and Spike would take advantage of the distraction caused by the blockade at the main gate to slip into the water and swim around to the submarine and explosives-handling jetties, where Her Majesty's Ships *Vanguard* and *Victorious*, two of the UK's four SSBNs – nuclear-powered ballistic missile submarines – currently wallowed in berths 10 and 11.

Only two days before, from the banks of Gare Loch, they'd watched HMS *Vengeance* gliding serenely away through the water on its way to the Gulf and Iraq. They hadn't gone looking for it; they'd been out for a walk because Dani had enlisted Spike and Amelia's help to forage for scurvy grass. She'd pointed out the glossy heart-shaped leaves that grew along the side of the track leading to the beach, and picked a couple for them to taste. She was going to make a good and peppery scurvy-grass-and-nettle pesto for the communal supper. Then they'd heard its engines and all turned to watch it sail past. Amelia had seen the subs before, of course, but Spike had been shocked by the sheer size of the vessel. There'd been a crew of sailors – submariners, he supposed – crawling over its broad back. They were dwarfed by the sub. It was a **monster**. And what was with the pantomime names? *Vengeance*? *Disgrace*, more like. This was ugliness and violence redefined and made manifest. Enough to **mar** any **vista**, to besmirch and defile any field of vision through which it passed. No wonder they hid them underwater. These machines were shameful.

After a convivial and good-spirited communal dinner, they'd piled into Dani's Land Rover and driven down to the Shore Road by Kilcreggan to watch the sun setting over the luminous waters and the low hills beyond, where – Dani had pointed them out – the Clyde meets Loch Long and the Holy Loch and becomes the sea, with Dunoon and the Isle of Bute beyond. Amelia had some pictures left on the disposable camera she'd bought in Edinburgh, so she took a few photos of the sunset and the beautiful golden light. Spike had suggested a few minutes of t'ai chi to make the most of it, and led them through some simple breathing and stance-based exercises, and the eight brocades. Then they'd taken turns to photograph each other. When they were driving back to Dani's, Amelia had given the camera to Spike and asked if he could keep it in the van for now. It was a slightly self-conscious gesture that at once seemed rather silly and melodramatic, but the reasoning was serious and Spike had received it with due solemnity, promising Amelia that he would look after it for her.

Later, after comparing notes with comrades from the more experienced Chapters, Spike had got kitted up and been out on a recce under cover of darkness. He'd found a weak spot where the fence was shielded from the casual glance by a gorse thicket, and where there was reasonable cover close by on the other side. When he'd appeared back at the camp several hours later, mission accomplished, he looked like he'd been dragged through a hedge backwards. He'd made a hole, or more accurately a flap, in the fence and camouflaged it with brambles. You wouldn't see it if you didn't know it was there.

Then, before dawn this morning, he'd lifted the mesh so that they could go through. He'd already gone through once, twice, and spread pieces of carpet over the razor wire. Then he'd helped the others. They'd estimated that they would only have a minute or so to both get through the hole and reach 'base camp': a **lean-to** bin shelter on the blind side of a catering block, from which a service road would take them deeper into the base. Safely inside, adrenaline had taken over and the women had scrambled off the broad dirt road that followed the line of the perimeter fence and ducked behind the line of wheelie bins. Spike wasn't coming in. His job was to be a 'decoy', to loiter by the fence until he could be caught by one of the regular perimeter foot patrols, with wire-cutters in hand, apparently in the act of breaching the fence. Sure enough, from their hiding place the women had heard the crackle of walkie-talkies, and if they'd dared to look they'd have seen Spike being unceremoniously rugby-tackled to the ground by two soldiers.

The women hadn't moved, and hardly dared to breathe for half an hour or more. Spike's subterfuge had clearly worked. Otherwise the bandit alarms would have gone off. According to Dani, that was the routine when any intruder was suspected. Spike must have convinced them that he was acting alone, that the hole in the fence was preparation for an action planned for later that day. Confident the coast was clear, they'd zig-zagged from the shadow of one service building to the next, finding safety exactly as planned in the trees behind a line of decommissioned Nissen huts that were awaiting demolition.

Deedee had been worried about Spike.

'He'll be alright,' Amelia had said. 'He's survived this long. Got **nine lives**, that one.'

At first light, they'd broken cover, expecting simply to dash to the water and chance a brief swim, perhaps chip a few anechoic tiles off the flank of one of the subs if they got that far, but there'd been no one around. Never mind the five hundred extra police outside; the quarters on the base – functional blocks which reminded Amelia of the sprawling halls of residence at a regional university – seemed largely empty. Perhaps they should take this opportunity to be more ambitious.

In training they'd talked about the possibility of targeting one of the floating labs, a 'comms barge' so-called, that was usually moored in berths 1 or 2, and which was able to be towed out into the loch during testing. More than Amelia or Deedee, Spike had felt keenly that the time for symbolic protest – songs, marches, swims – or delaying tactics like blockades and lock-ons had passed, that the ICJ's advisory opinion offered them both a possible defence and freer rein to aim for maximum disarmament. He was right, and it had caught the mood in the camp. Now was the time to put the boot in and do some actual damage.

Bizarrely – or perhaps not – there was a well-maintained flower bed in front of one of the Nissen huts, a tiered display backed up by tall and waving arms of **hollyhock** and golden rod. Admittedly the hollyhocks were a little bent and ragged-leaved, their deep pink or yellow flowers slightly frayed and torn, but that was no surprise given the prevailing winds and the weather out here on the west coast. The middle of the bed was filled out with finely red- and white-flowered salvia, foxgloves and some cistus that had gone to seed, while in front of these half a dozen lavenders in full bloom were planted alternately with silver-leaved senecio. The soil between the plants was bare from regular weeding. The **neat** grass verges almost made Amelia laugh out loud in relief. The fact that this gardener, whoever they might be, had gone to such lengths to create something of beauty amidst these great engines of destruction gave her hope.

The comms barge didn't actually look like a boat, more like a Portakabin on a pontoon, a two-storey building floating on stilts. On board, monitoring staff, engineers and analysts would gather to collate and test the data on every aspect of each sub in real time, checking their invisibility to radar, monitoring and testing the reactors, the telemetry, the personnel, crunching the numbers, examining, modelling, predicting, tweaking; then starting over.

They'd known exactly where to find the barge; Daniella and some of the older hands had pointed it out, and it was quite close as the crow flies, although it had taken a while to reach on foot. Both women had been well aware that just to be here on the base had already involved committing a whole string of serious criminal offences, and at every turn they'd expected the alarms to go off, or to bump into a patrol, but it had seemed there really was nobody around.

No one to stop them as they approached the barge.

No one to prevent them walking up the gangplank onto the gantry, and testing each window and door. Was this place even alarmed? Where were the movement sensors? The cameras? Amelia had started to feel invisible, untouchable, as if they were being protected – but she'd also known that this was an illusion that could be shattered at any second. Of course, they hadn't been able to get in the main door – it was locked and they didn't know the keycode. But it hadn't taken long for Deedee to find an unlocked lower-level window on the **larboard** side.

They'd squeezed in and looked around, unsure what they'd find, but fully expecting at least to startle a nightwatchman or two. They'd wondered if at best they might have a few short minutes to unplug a couple of computers before then. But the barge had been deserted.

Inside, it had looked like any office anywhere: desks, computers, filing cabinets and meeting rooms. No nautical accoutrements to speak of. Next to the kitchen there'd been a noticeboard with photos of the **trainees** on an outward-bound day, and on the wall in the wardroom was a photo of the Queen. In the kitchen itself, postcards had been Blu-tacked to the cupboard doors: Durdle Door, the **Norman** great hall of **Oakham** Castle, the **Nairobi** skyline at sunset.

Brazen as anything, Deedee had put the kettle on, and found some Earl Grey teabags.

It had been totally surreal, sitting there and drinking tea. But when it had become clear that no one was coming after them, they'd decided quite rationally that, rather than **ransack** the place or smash a few things, they could afford to be more methodical.

This was a once in a lifetime opportunity.

The **moment of truth**.

No one would ever be allowed to get in here so easily again.

To miss this chance would be **tragic**.

The realisation had dawned that they could simply clear the place out, throw everything in the water. All the windows on one side of the barge were shielded from wider view by the jetty.

Amelia had walked over to one of the workstations and gathered up all the lever-arch files, then – as if not quite believing it herself – she'd walked to the window and thrown them out. A second or two later they'd heard a series of light splashes. Deedee had followed suit with a printer, then a PC, then another and another. They'd gone from desk to desk, unplugging each unit, then pushed them through the window one by one. They'd opened filing cabinets, grabbed sheaves of paper and flung them out of the window hand over fist. They'd watched rolls of blueprints, chart after chart, **flop** into the water.

Anything that wasn't screwed down had gone out of that window, and most things weren't screwed down.

All in all, it had only taken them an hour or so.

It had been like a workout. Deedee had hardly broken a sweat, but by the end Amelia had felt particularly **unfit**, more than a little out of breath. Deedee had been right: it was definitely time to quit smoking.

They'd stopped to survey their handiwork: a room full of empty desks and orphaned power leads. As the magnitude of what they'd done sank in, Amelia and Deedee had both burst into tears. They'd embraced and said their own silent prayers of thanks for the great privilege they'd been granted.

Down below, shoals of papers floated on the oily surface of the water, lapping against the jetty and spreading out with the current. Everything else, everything that really mattered – the tech, the kit, the PCs and the servers, and along with them all the data and the computer models – was at the bottom of the loch.

Job done, they'd taken out their pre-typed statements and left them on one of the desks, then made more tea and taken it up on deck.

It was a beautiful, fresh morning. Not hazy like the day before. The mountains looked impossibly detailed in the clear air. It was still early, but the base was waking up around them.

After ten minutes or so a young soldier appeared at the top of the ladder and said, in a slightly **nasal** voice, 'What the hell are you doing here?'

He was more shocked than they were.

'You'd better arrest us,' said Amelia, then held out her little Tupperware box: 'Would you like an oatcake?'

That was when the bandit alarms went off.

More soldiers appeared, this time with guns.

The women recited their statements from memory.

They both knew that this was the beginning of what would no doubt be a long and testing journey, but as they were being led away they drew strength from their faith and from the knowledge that it was they who were on the right side of history, not Tony Blair and George W. Bush, and that this was a journey that many brave men and women had made before them.

8: Ruche (Beehive)

It was fair to say that the minute he walked in late to the team meeting Rex knew he'd **incurred** the wrath of Detective Chief Inspector Jethro Lawrence. You didn't have to be Ernő **Rubik** to work out that Lollo was not in the best of moods. The atmosphere was sombre. Two years' worth of investigation was at stake, with a budget to match, but far from moving forward to arrests, Operation **Kayak** now seemed in danger of sinking.

'Operation Kayak' indeed. The oppo names given to big investigations and policy initiatives were intended to be neutral, meaningless in relation to the subject of whatever operation. Words were chosen at random from alphabetical and sometimes themed databases: antelope, bullfinch, cedar, **dik-dik,** through nightjar, **oak-leaf,** poplar, queen bee, et cetera – so 'kayak' must have been the first and best available 'K'.

'Sorry, boss. I—' said Rex, closing the door behind him. He knew better than to even try explaining the kind of morning he'd had: Jennifer turning up on his doorstep, the sudden imposition of fatherhood, and whatever all this meant in terms of DS Eddie Webster. Jennifer, who at that moment was reading *Boudicca* and drinking a cup of vending machine hot chocolate in the station canteen. Jennifer, who was expecting him back in half an hour.

He could never broach such a sensitive subject in this company: that Webster's daughter was actually his. He and Webster would never hear the last of it.

Rex had worked with DCI Jethro Lawrence for years now. Yet how much did he really know about Lollo's personal life? That he was born in a pit village near Barnsley, a Holgate Grammar School boy who cut his teeth in the South Yorkshire Police before transferring down south, as he still called it. That he was partial to a bit of Gilbert and Sullivan and a **Jura** single malt, ideally at the same time. And that his favourite films were *Zulu* and *In Which We Serve*.

All those pith helmets and polo necks, **musketry** and stiff upper lips told you a lot about Lollo.

Rex and Susan had watched *In Which We Serve* a while back when it popped up on the BBC iPlayer after they'd binged a few episodes of *Parks and Recreation*. The classic Second World War film made a refreshing change from all those endearingly quirky personalities in **Pawnee**, Indiana. It was stirring stuff alright. But Rex couldn't quite see it – did Lollo fancy himself as a bit of a Captain **Kinross**? That was a laugh. More Alex Ferguson than Noël Coward, Lollo was pathologically incapable of keeping his cool. There were plenty of people in this job whose bark was worse than their bite – there was more barking than **Crufts** in this place sometimes – but Lollo was not one of those. With him it wasn't mere **bravado** or trying to win a pissing contest. Lollo really meant it.

Everything was a fight to the death.

He had a short fuse at the best of times, but even more so now, following a fraught few months for the station that had included a 'root and branch' Safety in Custody inspection *and* a hastily implemented London-wide shake-up of local policing structures that had squeezed the city's thirty-two Borough Operational Command Units into twelve larger Basic Command Units or BCUs.

The SiC inspection had been carried out by an eight-strong team comprising representatives of Her Majesty's Inspectorate of Prisons and the recently rechristened HMI of Constabulary and Fire & Rescue Services – HMICFRS for short – and one Care Quality Commission inspector. For two weeks in June these drones had crawled all over Holborn and Kentish Town Police Stations with their clipboards and their detailed questionnaires, taking an audit of management and reporting structures, and examining everything: treatment and conditions, Risk Assessment, Use of Force incidents ('UFOs'), custody records and cleaning. They'd looked at individual rights, grounds for arrest, and translator and interpreter services. They'd also explored healthcare provision, Forensic Medical

Examiner response times and liaison with mental health service providers.

They'd given questionnaires not only to detainees on both sites, but also to a sample of prisoners in HMPs Pentonville and Wormwood Scrubs who'd passed through Camden custody suites within the previous few months. As part of the liaison team, Rex had had these questionnaires coming out of his ears: *What is your ethnic origin? What if any would you classify as your religious group? Are you a foreign national? Yes No.*

One thing Rex had learned over the years was that the very fact of being inspected made you feel like you'd done something wrong, even if you hadn't.

But especially if you had.

Thankfully it had all gone off okay, or so it had seemed. But the delivery of the resulting SiC report had then necessarily been held up by the rollout of the new structure and the amalgamation of the former Camden BOCU and its arch-rival Islington into a new Central North Basic Command Unit.

Enquiry Desk Officer Eric Jinks had been incredulous. 'Oi, Rex,' he'd said. 'Did you know Islington call overtime "fat", not "gobble"? And they call Socks "Soccos". Bloody weirdos.'

It had been a matter of personal pride to Lollo that Camden be seen to 'win' the merger. Victory had been cemented by the appointment of Holborn DCS Tabitha Churchill to a newly created post of Chief Superintendent of the merged BCU. But any celebrations were long-forgotten.

'Oh, deary me, alas and **alack**!' the Detective Chief Inspector bellowed sarcastically now, as Rex took his seat. 'Before you say owt, Kingsy, you can fucking shut it and all. Spare me the fucking sob story. I don't want to fucking know. I'm getting it in the neck from **Evelyn** Gummer and the bloody Comms team, and my inbox is now **chock-a-block** with arseholes wanting answers on Operation Kayak. And I've got nowt to give 'em except a room full of useless twats.'

'What's happened, sir?' said Rex. 'Aside from the obvious.'

'Oh, nothing much!' said Lollo. 'Just that this morning's CPS evidential advisory meeting was cancelled. They've chucked the whole fucking lot back. Said we were over-fucking-reliant on our star witness – anyroad, we need to think again. It's put a right fucking **kink** in my week, I can tell yer.'

Rex knew better than to interrupt. Lollo was just getting into his stride.

Rex could well believe that Evelyn Gummer was breathing down Lollo's neck, Detective Chief Inspector or not. Operation Kayak was big and it needed careful management. Gummer was the Met's overall Head of External Relations. Rex had met her several times, not least when the shit had hit the fan with **Trevor** Tennyson, a protester who'd died in police custody on Rex's watch a few years earlier, when things had got a bit **kinetic** during processing. Once the dust had settled on the Tennyson acquittals – or died down temporarily at least – Rex had told Lollo that he'd heard one of the journalists in court refer to Gummer as a '**king-maker**'.

'Not fucking much!' Lollo roared. 'She could **ordain** you **Kabaka** of Buganda if she bloody wanted.'

'The what?'

'Buganda! You know, "Good King Freddie"? Assassination by vodka, remember?' said Lollo. 'Like that scene in *Get Carter*. Michael Caine. Nefarious deeds in Rotherhithe. None of your fucking Georgi Markov bollocks, or your Novichoks, if you can just use vodka, eh?'

Rex still hadn't a clue.

'Oh, I forget you're just a kid,' Lollo said. 'Ask Binder Singh. He'll know his fucking Ugandan history.'

It was true that Evelyn Gummer had got the Met out of more scrapes than Rex could remember. And just because she was on familiar and friendly terms with every hack and **subeditor** from **Hackney** to Heathrow, from the *Ilford Recorder* to the editor of *Newsnight*, didn't mean she wouldn't cheerfully throw any of them under a bus if they didn't do what she wanted.

'And that's the last fucking thing I need,' said Lollo. 'I can't fucking believe it. First off, Webbo goes AWOL, then' – he pointed at Rex – 'Jack fucking **Kerouac** here picks today to go fucking walkies. I needed you here first fucking thing, Kingsy. I assured Evelyn that you were a safer bet than **Arkle**. Fucking CPS – we should have been delivering all the Kayak warrants next week. So unless sommat gives, we've gone from Blue fucking **Danube** to Shit Creek overnight. And now you waltz in after lunch like we've got all the time in world. But

I'll tell you sommat for nowt, sunshine' – Lollo homed in on Rex – 'if we don't get on top of this one PD-fucking-Q, then that's two years' investigation down the fucking pan, and you know what, Detective Sergeant? I'll fucking blame you for it. Fuck this up and by the time I've finished with you you'll be lucky if you can get a job as a lollipop lady.'

9: Gainier (Judas tree)

All things considered, it seemed that **Dicky** Sharp might finally have done something useful.

With Lollo's bollocking still ringing in his ears, and Jennifer happy to read in the canteen for a bit longer, Detective Sergeant Rex King quickly brought himself up to speed with the investigation. Or the headlines at least, because there was a **limit** to how long he wanted to leave Jennifer alone.

My daughter, he'd been thinking to himself. Turning the words around in his head. Getting used to the idea.

It was maybe just as well that Webbo wasn't around right now, but thankfully he'd been running a relatively tight ship before his sudden leave of absence. On this quick read-through the files seemed to be in order – the ones King had access to, at least – plus the Operation Kayak synopsis and the evidential advisory briefing doc that the CPS had just thrown back in their faces.

To say that Dicky Sharp had been known to the police was something of an understatement. He might have come from Metro-**Goldwyn-Mayer** central casting. A six-foot **vegan odd-ball** in his early sixties from the **fag-end** of **Ilford**, Sharp was well-built, with a trademark bald head resulting from his daily appointment with an electric **shaver**. Distinguishing features? Facial scarring and a continually weeping left eye. He'd lost part of the upper **eyelid** in an **unfortunate** work-related incident involving a **hot iron**. Reports mentioned him constantly dabbing his cheek with a large paisley handkerchief, or throwing his head back to sluice the socket through with an eye-bath that he always carried for the purpose. A **flawed** dandy who always dressed in black, they said. He affected the appearance of the kind of old-school East End villain who'd be angling for a **cameo** in a Kray Twins movie. The kind of bloke who, if served with a **law-suit**, would have asked if it came with a **Nehru** collar. To his early criminal ambition there'd been neither let nor **trammel**, but in real life there'd been obstacles at every turn. He had dreamed – for example – of retiring to his once-favoured holiday spot of **Antigua**, which was understandable, but crime did not turn out to be quite the **milch** cow he might have hoped it would. Perhaps he wasn't **really** cut out for it after all, much as he looked the part. You wouldn't want him to **darken** your door, unless he worked for you as a bouncer. But even then, maybe not. Because if he'd garnered a reputation, it was for fucking things up. Handed the ball, so to speak, he would probably **fumble** it. In truth, he was a bit of a loner. None of the real villains trusted him, and with good reason, as it turned out. For the last few years he'd been living with his mother in the family home near Fullwell Cross, dreams falling by the **wayside** as he slowly ticked off the successive stages of incipient diabetic **renal** failure.

It was sad, Rex would reflect later, when he scrolled through the photos from the scene and the autopsy. So sad that Dicky Sharp, his crushed skull cleanly **partitioned** by the pathologist's electrical saw, could not even **outlive** his dear old mum.

10: Romaine (Cos)

'"**Vaunt** in their youthful sap"...' thought Rex. There was a brief **lull** in the conversation and he'd drifted off in his own thoughts for a second, remembering O-level Shakespeare. How did it go? Something about 'men as plants increase'?

That was it: 'When I consider every thing that grows...' Sonnet 15. In English lessons at school he'd found it **inane**. He and his mates, completely missing the point, had used to **snigger** at the word 'sap'. They were more interested in chewing up bits of paper torn from the backs of their exercise books so they could flick a damp **pellet** at the teacher. No surprise there: mortality is purely theoretical at that age.

Unless or until it comes knocking on your front door.

But there was nothing like being confronted with your own offspring to remind you that your own 'youthful sap' was itself fast becoming a memory, even if you finally – well, *duh*! – understood that the 'brave state' referred to might be as much to do with the physiology of male arousal as with psychology or youthful courage.

Russell Square – the garden – was as busy as ever. Above their heads the leaves on the great old plane trees were starting to come out, and the beds amid the ornamental box hedges and shrubs were full of spring flowers, tulips and daffodils. Behind them, a line of police vehicles was parked out the back of SOAS. Every bench was occupied with couples and colleagues, solo newspaper readers, packed-lunchers, phone-fiddlers and vapers. A dog snapped at the water from a fountain that was embedded into the pavement in the centre of the square. Rex made a mental note to let Emma in SNT know about the group of skate punks smoking weed in the quietest corner. Maybe one of the PCSOs could have a quiet word and move them on. Nothing too heavy-handed, but this was a family amenity after all, and that smelled like some strong shit.

Russell Square was more a thoroughfare than a destination, with a main drag that crossed the square diagonally from south-west corner to north-east corner. A continuous stream of people – office workers, students, museum-goers – heading for the tube or towards King's Cross. Men in shirtsleeves – it didn't take much: one sniff of sun – walked in twos and threes; wheelie cases and headphones. A young woman in a light mac and pedal-pusher jeans caught Rex's eye, and drank from an orange Styrofoam soup container as she walked. Another dressed all in black chatted animatedly to an unseen phone, and tucked her long black hair behind her ear. A boy in school uniform stood next to a litter bin picking the lettuce leaves out of his burger and dropping them in. As one, the pigeons took to the air and wheeled over to where a man on a mobility scooter was chucking bread – whole rolls and pieces of loaf – from a carrier bag on his lap over the railings into the fenced-off area around the statue of the Duke of Bedford. An ambulance sped up Southampton Row with its lights flashing and quick stabs of siren. On the other side of the square a busker was playing **flamenco** guitar.

Helen had stopped crying and blew her nose. She'd whizzed in on the tube at the end of lessons to pick up Jennifer, and suggested this as a meeting place, which suited Rex for obvious reasons. Lollo could spare him for half an hour. Rex had managed to get through the afternoon without mentioning Jennifer to the Detective Chief Inspector. He'd figured it would only complicate things; for himself as much as for Webster. He didn't want to give Lollo the ammunition. The way Lollo worked, you'd get it back tenfold.

Jennifer was queueing to get some hot chocolates from the little coffee van on the eastern end of the square, which at least bought Rex and Helen enough time for a quick debrief. Normally he'd have suggested the cabmen's shelter, which – unlike most such establishments – served the general public, though the inside was reserved for licensed black cab drivers. But of course it was closed.

'She's a great kid,' said Rex. 'I took her to Sid's.'

'Course you did,' said Helen. 'How is he?'

'Oh, he's retired. It's not Sid's any more. They've got a new sign and everything.'

The irony of it all, Helen told him – **without tears** this time – was that the DNA tests had been Eddie's idea.

'Typical Ed,' said Rex. 'What was he thinking?'

'Trying to please the girls, I suppose,' said Hel. 'Keep them interested in family life. They're growing up, after all.' She paused. 'Or maybe it was to keep himself interested in family life.'

It turned out that, when Jennifer's class had finished their mock GCSEs in Year 10, they'd been given a family history assignment for the last few weeks of term. They'd each had to keep some sort of **journal**, an investigation of their family tree. How they wanted to approach that had been up to them: some combination of photos, oral history, art or creative writing. Jennifer had really got into it, and Rachel had joined in a bit too: going to the library, looking at census data online, interviewing family members, the lot.

'What could I do?' said Helen, shrugging. 'I dreaded where it might end up, but I had to go along with it and just hope they'd get bored.'

But they hadn't got bored. Because the next thing was that Eddie and the girls had had the bright idea of surprising Helen with some posh family tree type thing that they'd had done professionally – calligraphy, **gold leaf**, the works – and framed for her birthday.

November the twenty-third, thought Rex. He hadn't forgotten.

'When I opened it my heart sank,' said Helen. 'I can't tell you. I had to pretend I loved it, but I felt terrible, knowing it was a lie. I even had to hang it on the sitting room wall.'

It got worse.

'Eddie told us it was a dummy kit for training,' she said. 'A refresher course for work. That you all had to practise taking DNA samples. And I believed him. Well, I had a lot on my mind with work. That must have been the new year, because we'd had the people in to clear the Himalayan **balsam** in the back garden.

'Yeah,' she went on, 'Eddie had all the kits, you know, the little plastic stirrer type thing, "Open wide!" then he'd **daub** your saliva into the little test tube. Well, you'd know all about it. I honestly didn't think anything of it. Stupid cow. I could kick myself!'

'Come on,' said Rex. 'It's not your fault.'

Helen sighed, and Rex knew why.

'But it is,' she said. 'You know it is.'

'That's not what I meant,' said Rex, but she was right.

Well, half right.

It was both of their faults. But what could you do?

When Rex and Helen had split up, there'd been things to sort out. Nothing too complicated, just simple stuff like feelings. And one thing had led to another. Once or twice. Several times. But in truth everyone had just been doing their best in a difficult situation.

It's not like Rex and Hel were the first people on earth to have had break-up sex.

Rex became aware of a large crowd milling around them, and gathering beside their bench. A booming voice behind them: 'Like Bloomsbury Square, Bedford Square and much of Regent Street and Regent's Park, Russell Square was designed by James Burton at the beginning of the nineteenth century. The garden itself was laid out by the great British landscape architect Humphry **Repton**, and was restored to his original layouts in 2002. So what you see now—'

'Fuck sake!' said Rex. He rolled his eyes at Helen and waited for the guide to **expound** on whatever was coming next: the great plane trees with their swollen, vase-shaped trunks, the fountains that had replaced Repton's original gardeners' hut, T. S. Eliot at number 24, blah-di-blah – he'd heard it all before. In fact, Rex had learned a lot from the tour guides over the years. Historical trivia that he'd mentally filed away. That Russell Square had once been the northernmost edge of the city. That when it was being built there'd been no interruption to the view across the fields to the hills of Hampstead and Highgate. That a wave of less high-spec property developments nearby – coupled with the building of the New Road and developments in Somers Town that spoiled the view – had depressed the prices almost immediately.

Rex and Helen had used to come here quite often. And even now Rex would often stroll up to the square if he needed a bit of headspace, if not exactly peace and quiet. This was tour guide country, after all: the Blue Badge brigade. But hopefully this one'd piss off in a sec and continue the guided walk elsewhere. 'Walk' being the operative word, after all.

Helen ignored them and carried on. She wasn't bothered by the crowd, and they weren't interested in her little drama. The DNA results, when they'd come in, had posed a bit of a **riddle** for everyone else, she told him. But she'd known what they meant immediately.

'You must have been angry?' said Rex. He could well imagine. He'd seen Helen angry.

'Everyone was,' said Helen. 'Well, upset at least. But I was incandescent. At being tricked, at the fact that he'd given away our data – listen to me with my teacher hat on! – and, even worse, our girls' data, without even discussing it? Words fail me, Rex. And that's not even taking into account the obvious. Course I didn't want that to come out. He's been a good dad. A great dad.'

'So presumably Ed now knows about us,' said Rex. 'I mean, he'll have done the maths?'

'Yes, and he asked me straight. I didn't have to spell it out for him.'

'Poor bloke,' said Rex.

'He's so great with the girls…'

'Must have been a shock.'

'Yes,' said Helen. 'But it's not just that. I know it sounds heartless, but you shouldn't poke around if you might not like what you'll find.'

It had been simmering and had blown the family apart these past couple of weeks, she said, smiling and waving at Jennifer, who was now walking back across the square towards them with three takeaway cups in a cardboard holder. The **glue** that held them all together as a family was coming unstuck. She and Jen'd had yet another blazing row this morning, which had ended with Jennifer running out of the door screaming at Helen to '**Get off my back**!' or words to that effect. They'd assumed she'd gone to school, until Helen had picked up Rex's message during morning playtime.

'Eddie's taken it really badly. But you know him. He doesn't like change. He'd rather just **stand pat**.'

'Just glad I was around,' said Rex. He didn't need to explain.

'Yeah, me too. This must have been the last thing you expected. How are you taking it?'

Good question.

'She looks like my mum, you know,' he said. 'More in her movements than her face, if that makes sense. It took me aback.'

Helen put a sympathetic hand on his closest shoulder and squeezed it briefly: 'Poor you. I bet it did.'

It had turned out that her and Eddie and Rachel's profiles had loads in common: a combination of Germany, Scandinavia and Central Asia, and a bit of Genghis Khan.

Peasant stock, basically.

'What would my mum have said,' said Helen, laughing in spite of herself.

It made Rex think of haystacks and pitchforks, quaint folk customs like morris dancing and **well-dressing**. But yeah, centuries of grinding poverty, disease and servitude would not have gone down well at the golf club.

'She'd probably have put on her posh voice,' said Rex. 'I was sorry to hear about your mum, by the way. Ed told me. I liked her a lot, as you know.'

'She was fond of you too. I'm glad she's not around to see this. Well, not really, but you know what I mean.'

Jennifer's profile had been wildly different from the rest of the family. It was all over the shop: North Africa and the Iberian Peninsula, Native American, the Middle East. She could have been descended from the **wandering Jew**, there was that much of a mixture: DNA from every-bloody-where. The **logic** was inevitable. You didn't need to go too far out on a **limb** to see. And the kit specifically tested the paternal line, so there was no getting around it.

Part of Rex was intrigued. He wanted to see the test now, and do his own. He wanted to tell Susan. He knew that both of his maternal great-grandparents had moved to rural Devon from Galway at the start of the twentieth century, found work in domestic service and on the railways. And hadn't Galway been a trading post for centuries, between Spain and Portugal and the Americas? That must be it.

It would probably **appal** the Little Englander mob, but Rex felt a genuine sense of pride in the diversity of his own genes. Out there in the world, all that movement over the centuries, generation after generation, to arrive right here, at this point, now. It was mind-boggling.

'Well, me and Jen have had a good day, considering,' he said. 'Actually, it was fun: we did the crossword. But no pressure, eh? We're all friends, aren't we, so let's just keep in touch. Play it by ear.'

'Okay.'

'Jen's a credit to both of you, Hel. You know that, don't you.'

And here she was.

'Hey,' said Rex.

'Took ages. I got you sprinkles and marshmallows? What even *are* marshmallows anyway?' Jennifer reached down awkwardly with one hand to gently jostle first Helen's hot chocolate out of its recess in the cardboard tray, then Rex's, before sitting down beside her mum.

None of them said anything for a bit.

It had been quite a day.

There was almost too much to take in; so they didn't even try.

If you saw them sitting there – drinking hot chocolates and laughing as they watched a Jack Russell noisily trying to retrieve its ball from the fountain's jets, Rex pointing something out with his rolled-up newspaper, Jen raising her eyes to heaven at something Helen said, then putting on her headphones – you could be forgiven for thinking they were just a regular family on a day out.

11: Marronnier (Horse chestnut)

As Rex walked Helen and Jen across the square to point them at the tube, he couldn't help thinking about Dicky Sharp. Kayak wasn't one of Rex's – not until now, at least – but he'd seen Webster and the team tearing their hair out over the past couple of years. It was not an **overstatement** to say that almost in spite of himself Dicky Sharp, the self-styled hard man – in reality a mere bit-player – had come to their **aid** when they'd most needed it. And by coming forward of his own accord, Sharp had unwittingly saved an investigation that he hadn't known existed, but which had otherwise been **teetering** on the rim of the toilet pan. Talk about the **underdog** bites back. He'd helped them **even** up the evidential **trade gap**, as it were. Meaning that until they'd lucked on Sharpy they'd been buying in much more than they could sell, evidence-wise. The sums just hadn't been working.

Lollo was by nature a **sceptic**, but that had come from years of successfully pitching to the CPS and by extension to the jury: 'Come on, don't keep me in **suspense**,' he'd always say. 'Cut to the fucking chase. Have we got enough to convince the **floating voter**? Because if not we've got to fucking double down and find it.' And invariably he was right.

He had a reputation for it. He'd been part of a regular hit factory in South Yorkshire.

And that'd be your **cue** to get the team together for a scrum-down and try to think of another angle, to **vary** the approach until you could come up with a more coherent **plan**. 'What are you waiting for,' Lollo would say, 'a fucking invitation? Okay, here's one. I **invite** you to do some real bloody police work for a change. Everyone's in-fucking-vited. *Répondez, s'il vous* fucking *plaît!*'

From what Rex had already seen of Kayak, there were obvious

similarities with Operation **Lavengro**, a major investigation he'd had the misfortune to be involved in down in **Aldershot** back in the early noughties. Up and down the M3 – they'd been based at Barnes Common in South-West London but mainly working out of some Portakabins on the edge of the former Cambridge Military Hospital site in Aldershot. Home of the British Army? That's what they used to call it. You could keep it. Talk about privates on **parade**. By the end of it, Rex joked that he wouldn't mind if he never saw another squaddie's dick as long as he lived.

Stuck down there, you had to do something of an evening, but they'd quickly learned that the nightspots of Aldershot were best avoided. Like a post-traumatic stress disorder research project set to a jazz funk beat. Insomnia and hypervigilance were assets in nightclubs like Owls or The Palace. Acute stress reactions kicking off left, right and centre, predictable as a middle-eight. It was safer to stay in. One time, Donal dropped Rex back off in London with a boxful of reggae 12-inch singles that he'd picked up in a charity shop on the high street on one of their afternoons off. They'd been gathering dust in Rex's flat ever since, and there were some he'd never got around to listening to at all until Susan persuaded him to buy a new hi-fi. They'd popped round the corner to Richer Sounds on Bloomsbury Way one morning and got a cab back with the various separates, spent a couple of hours wiring it all up: the turntable, CD player, amplifier and speakers. Then they'd sat on the floor like a couple of teenagers, playing one record after another.

'You're a dark horse, you are,' said Susan, lifting the stylus on a 12-inch single of Slim Smith's 'You're My Everything' on the Lord Koos record label so that they could listen to it again. 'These are brilliant.'

Lavengro had taken a couple of years to unpick too. Locals didn't have a clue. That's why they'd had to bring in the big boys, sneaky-beaky style: softly, softly, **catchee monkey**. Rex shuddered to think of it. Endlessly fast-forwarding through the slightly out-of-**focus** surveillance footage or audio tapes until you were **giddy** with it, looking and listening for the obvious but simply not seeing or hearing anything. Sifting it again, but through a finer and finer **mesh**, until you knew what you were looking for. Then – if you were lucky – you realised it had been there all along. A few hours of that every day and it fried your brain; you'd have to nip out for a fag break just to look at some trees and clouds for half an hour. One time they'd stopped at Fleet Services on the drive back to London and he'd thrown up in the car park like a cadet at a crime scene.

They'd been a funny old bunch in Barnes. The cream of the crop, they used to say, drawn from all over. Based in a modern, brick-built police station on the corner of Mill Hill and Station Roads – long gone now. To all intents and purposes it was a fully staffed and functioning police station, except for the fact that it wasn't 'public-facing', as they used to say, and operated outside the regular chain of command. The normal police station was half a mile away, on the river. Barnes Common was lower-profile and housed Flying Squad mostly, plus Special Demonstration Squad, and child abuse investigations. Conveniently out of the way and anonymous-looking, it could have been the country-town HQ of a regional insurance company. And that Donal especially had been a right joker. He was ex-RUC from the leafier suburbs of Belfast and a grand old laugh.

'Oi, Rex,' he'd say. 'Why aren't there any aspirins in Aldershot?'[1] or, 'What's the only type of biscuit that can fly?'[2]

Or, 'Oi, Rex. What's long and hard and full of semen?'

'Eh?'

'No, go on. What's long and hard and—?'

'I don't fucking know. A submarine?'

'No – David **Seaman** in a suit of armour! Big bloke, that David Seaman.'

'Oh, *fuck* off, Donal!'

Never mind Russell Square, those lucky bastards had Barnes Common on the doorstep – a few square miles of heath and ancient woodland: weeping willow, birch, horse chestnut, sweet chestnut. It was a perk of the job. Like being out in the country. For a while Rex had taken to wandering on the common at dawn. To stretch his legs and try to forget what he'd been looking at. He'd got quite into it too. Once, he saw a badger, and woodpeckers were two a penny. He even saw a kingfisher – well, a flash of metallic blue – where Beverley Brook flows under Station Road. Until one morning he'd wandered a bit too far down the brambly byways over Gipsy Lane

---

1 'Because the Paras ate 'em all.'

2 'Just a wee plane one.'

and bumped into an elderly **nudist**, out saluting the sun. Rex had stuck to the cricket pitches after that, or just gone and sat by the pond.

When the Lavengro convictions had all come in, the team had gone out to celebrate. They'd been **to hell and back** – a.k.a. Aldershot – so they figured they'd earned it. Rex had suggested the new Pizza Express opposite the old police garage, but the local boys had overruled him, said ASK was quieter. They were right. But no wonder. You had to laugh, though. The only other people in the place were a certain Mancunian rock star and his **retinue**. They must have been recording along the road at Olympic Studios. Well, that dated it. But the funny thing was that he'd had them all sitting in what was then the non-smoking section of the restaurant. Not very rock 'n' roll. The band had been up and down like yo-yos, nipping out to smoke every five minutes, while he just sat there scowling.

Rex realised that he'd been making too many assumptions. Until he'd spoken to Helen, he'd just assumed Webster was off sick because of the pressures of Kayak.

As they approached the crossing, heading towards the back of the Brunswick Centre and that little row of shops, Rex said, 'Thanks for coming in, H. I appreciate it.'

Helen glanced at Jen, who still had her headphones on and was now bopping her head gently to the music. 'I appreciate what you said just then,' said Helen quietly, 'about "no pressure". It's just that, well, I wouldn't get too used to it.' She paused. 'I know you, Rex,' she said. 'So don't go getting all wistful about what might have been, or thinking you'll suddenly become this great hands-on dad. Even if you feel it, that might not be what she needs right now. Kids are like that. They make you feel things. But it's not about you, it's about them and what they need. So don't flatter yourself, okay? I don't even know if, now that she's seen you, that might be the last of it. Satisfied her curiosity. But—'

Helen paused again, and Rex wondered if she was going to cry.

'Go on,' he said.

Helen steeled herself. 'No, it's just that, if she did say she wanted to see you again, would that be alright?'

'Yeah, of course,' said Rex. 'I'd love that.' Well, what else was he going to say. He thought for a second, then added: 'Sorry, I meant to ask. All of this business with the girls, with Jen. Is that why Ed's been off work?'

Helen stopped dead and looked at him, stunned: 'What do you mean, "off work"? Since when?'

12: Roquette (Rocket)

With Helen and Jennifer safely on the tube home, Rex ducked down through Queen Square and along to The Lamb for a restorative pint on his way back to the station. He'd never have admitted this, let alone volunteered it, but meeting Jennifer and now seeing Helen had shaken him up a bit. This had been the first time he'd seen Helen in years. She'd stopped coming to the station Christmas parties or pub quizzes long ago. Understandably so, with two kids to bring up and a demanding job as a teacher.

'I know you, Rex,' she'd said, 'so don't flatter yourself.'

And she was right.

It was maybe no wonder he felt the need to take a twenty-minute time-out to begin to process it.

When he and Jen had got to Russell Square to wait for her, he'd seen his ex a mile off, even before Jen had. He'd recognised something about her, whether it was her gait or her posture, the shape of her face or the way light fell onto it. Or was it how she held her head? He couldn't be sure, but whatever the reason that was unmistakably Helen.

'Here she is now,' he'd said confidently.

'Where?' Jen had said. 'Are you joking?'

'No, there,' he'd said, pointing. 'Look. Just crossing over now.'

'You can see *that* far? I don't believe you.'

He'd been surprised to find that he still felt so at ease in Helen's company, sitting and chatting in the square with her and Jen like that. He couldn't help wondering if she was thinking something similar now herself, as mother and daughter rattled home on the tube.

Outside Great Ormond Street was yet another tour guide, gesticulating towards one of the hospital's side entrances and talking in a priestly monotone: 'In a house on this site in 1914—'

Like Buckingham Palace, the Houses of Parliament and Big Ben, South Ken, Oxford Street and the Tower of London, Bloomsbury attracted its fair share of the capital city's tourist traffic, with something like sixteen thousand people a day coming into the area to visit the British Museum alone. Just as in policing, with the number of 'boots on the ground' needed per head of population, or with public library provision per capita, or schools capacity or children's health services, there was probably a rule of thumb, a calculation you could do on the back of an envelope, to work out how many tour guides would be needed to service whatever quantity of tourists. But what was it with all the tour guides today? It was hardly the height of the tourist season, yet he'd had to dodge half a dozen of them in the last five minutes. Were they like fruit trees, blossoming early because they were confused by the unseasonal warmth? A few days' sunshine before Easter and suddenly they were everywhere. Like animals coming out of hibernation prematurely. Holding aloft their furled brollies. Like this one who was speaking into a headset as he turned left out of Great Ormond Street and led his line of headphone-wearing tourists up towards Coram's Fields.

Just here in the immediate vicinity you might find a 'Blue Plaque Tour of Bloomsbury', or 'Radical Social History', a Charles Dickens tour, Karl Marx in London, Swedenborg's London, Virginia Woolf's London, the Bloomsbury Group, Literary Bloomsbury, the squares and gardens of Bloomsbury, Great Ormond Street Hospital: past, present and future, the Bloomsbury Group in general, radical women, London's public libraries, bomb sites of the First and Second World Wars, the IRA in London, detective novelists, suffragette women, Georgian neoclassical domestic architecture from the Adelphi to Red Lion Square. If there was the interest, there'd be a guide to cater for it. Some were charlatans, chancers, but most were salt of the earth; pavement scholars. Some actual scholars too.

All that patter. Rex imagined the din if they were all going at the same time, shepherding their little flocks. All those personal routes and bowdlerised histories overlaid on the map.

As he approached the pub, there was one tour guide standing in the centre of a small crowd outside Ciao Bella. He had a fluorescent-green fake-fur fox-tail dangling above his head from a repurposed car aerial that stuck out the top of his rucksack. He was pointing at the restaurant and telling them that this – what is now Ciao Bella – was the actual site of William Lambe's fountain. The very spot where, having dammed a tributary of the River Fleet in order to divert some of the water into his cistern, and to supply fresh water to Snow Hill in the City of London by means of his conduit, after which the street was named, William Lambe had built a public fountain – not a fountain of the ornamental kind, but perhaps some kind of continually flowing spigot – *and* he'd also supplied one hundred buckets to local women so that they could come and get free water. When the original building was demolished, a stone sign marking the site of the fountain had been preserved and set into the wall just around the corner of Long Yard. And look, said the tour guide, waving around an A4 piece of paper on which was printed a reproduction of a detail of Robins's leases map of 1752, and pointing to the several convivial conversations that were going on at the tables on the pavement outside the restaurant and then back to the map, on which the sign of Lambe's fountain was clearly marked right in front of what is now Ciao Bella. The fountain may have gone, he was saying – and he was speaking now as much to the smiling patrons of the Italian restaurant as to his audience – but *to this day* its precise location remains a popular gathering place and watering hole.

Rex waited for a lull in the presentation, then leaned in and excused himself – 'That was fascinating' – and asked the tour guide if he had a business card. Maybe this would be something that he and Jen could do on some future visit. If, that is, she wanted to see him again. He realised that he was hoping that she would. He wondered if she liked Italian food, then thought better of it. *Everyone* likes Italian food.

Helen did, after all. Or she'd used to, at least.

The times they'd eaten here.

Rex looked in the window, scanning for the familiar faces of the patron and his family. And, finding them, he waved. Didn't want to be rude.

In some ways it felt to Rex as if he and Helen had just picked up where they'd left off. As if no time at all had passed. But Rex wasn't entirely stupid – although he'd be the first to admit that he occasionally had his moments. He knew that a couple of decades would show up on anyone's face, that unmistakable thickening of the features, but who could really say how people changed inside. Rex had no idea at all about what Helen had been through in the intervening years – her mother dying, for one thing, and they'd been very close – or how she might have changed as a person. And for all her slightly piss-takey 'Have you been working out?', Rex could tell that she'd been a bit shocked by how much he'd aged.

There was no point going over the circumstances of the break-up again. He'd replayed it in his mind often enough, and he'd always blamed Webster, the opportunistic prick. But maybe it had been just as much Rex's fault.

As if shift working wasn't bad enough, he'd been away a lot. That would have been the early days of his secondment or thereabouts, and it had kept him away much more than either he or Helen had expected. At the time he'd told himself that Lollo had obviously seen something promising in his performance. That he'd had the makings of a decent policeman, a good officer. But having made the sacrifices required, the promotions hadn't exactly come thick and fast. Now he wondered if Helen had been right, and he'd been simply too eager to please. Was it just that he'd been the only one willing to sacrifice his family life for fuck-all, and still say thank you into the bargain?

There was Helen, at the time, doing her PGCE at Westminster Polytechnic and getting her first teaching jobs, working pretty hard herself. Making the flat in Falcon nice with her vintage wallpaper, a retro neon-lit cocktail bar and a handmade mattress from Alphabeds down on The Cut, olive oil soap from Habitat, and fresh parmesan and big bunches of Italian parsley from Camisa's on Old Compton Street. She'd been good at finding the best china and kitchenware in the Heal's sales, and had had an eye – on her daily walks – for the quality furniture that used to get thrown out around Fitzrovia, 'free to a good home' for any takers.

Whatever Lollo's motivation, in those days Rex was always being put forward for new professional development opportunities over and above the standard training programmes. Which was how for a couple of years either side of the millennium he'd come to spend so much time over at Barnes Common, how he'd been seconded to Operation Lavengro down in Aldershot, or doing Police Liaison in the early days of ESCU – the London-wide Economic and Specialist Crime Unit – with the Childline operators in their necessarily secret offices, which were then on the top floor of the former Royal Mail sorting office, now the Islington Square 'luxury housing' development, behind the Almeida Theatre on Upper Street. One time he'd bumped into the Childline founder and broadcaster Esther Rantzen on the stairs, and been surprised at how tiny she was.

'Pint of Guinness, please,' Rex said now to the young man behind the bar. While he waited, he looked around for an empty seat. The clientele was mostly the quick-drink-after-work crowd, it looked like. Always a reliable indicator of a good boozer.

But if it had been Rex's own mistakes that had cost him his relationship with Helen, just as much as Webster seeing an opportunity and grabbing it, was Rex in danger of simply repeating those mistakes now, with Susan? Was he putting work first, just because he felt flattered to be asked?

That reminded him: he needed to phone Susan. Not least because he was dying to tell her about Jen. She hadn't called back yet, so she was obviously still pissed off with him. But it wasn't the first and it probably wouldn't be the last time they'd argue about work and priorities. It came up every month or so, fuelled by what Susan described as Rex's general lack of availability.

When things were going well, which a lot of the time they had been, he and Susan tended to phone or text each other a few times a day. It was just something they did: trading little tokens of affection; even just a single 'X'. But lately it seemed they'd been playing voicemail tag. And there'd been nothing yet today of all days: no texts, no missed calls, no voicemail.

Rex handed over a tenner while his Guinness settled in the glass, then pocketed the change. When the pint came, he took a ritual tentative sip, then made his way to a table and took a seat on the banquette. He put both pint and newspaper down and took the pen from his inside pocket. Might as well finish the crossword. Flattening the paper, it was strange to see some of the squares of the crossword grid filled out in Jen's neat hand. They hadn't quite finished it earlier, because Rex had held back. He hadn't wanted to go into 'Competitive Dad' mode, so there were a few easy ones left unsolved, or rather that he hadn't filled in yet: '23 across: Salad science – Stephenson's? (6)'. Too easy. But it confirmed that '5 down: Pile stamps (anag.) (10)' also ended in 'T'. Well, of course. He started to fill it in: P-A-L-I-M-P-S-E-S...

He'd finished the last few clues before he finished his pint. Figured he'd try Susan once more before he went back to work. It rang a couple of times then went to voicemail.

'Hi, it's me,' he said. 'How are you doing? I've got some news, but I'll save it for when we speak. Call me, okay? Love you.'

13: Pigeon (Pigeon)

Seeing the charges against Amelia and Deedee laid out in the arcane language of the Scottish legal system had come as a bit of a shock.

> That on 22 August 2003 on board the vessel *Newt*, then moored in the waters of Gare Loch, Argyll, you Amelia Alison Johnson and you Diana Andries did wilfully and maliciously damage said vessel.

It was all 'indicted at the instance of The Right Honourable The Lord Boyd of Duncansby' this and 'By Authority of Her Majesty's Advocate' that.

Later, Amelia would say that the whole thing reminded her of the suffragist writer Evelyn Sharp, a personal favourite of hers, who described encounters with provincial Church and Law as being like shaking hands with the Middle Ages, or words to that effect. But right now, wrapped up in all the archaic pomp and jargon was plenty of contemporary language that they all recognised: the charges. Not just 'malicious damage', but also 'theft' and 'endangering the **crew**'.

There had been three days of court proceedings, which, until they were suddenly and loudly interrupted, had been going exactly to plan. Deedee had been represented by a sympathetic advocate who'd successfully defended previous Isaiah Movement defendants, but Amelia was defending herself.

In her letter, Amelia had told Spike that she couldn't exactly remember smashing the contents of the electrical equipment cupboard and damaging the cables it contained, but she did recall putting superglue in all the locks. The only computer monitor that she had actually smashed was the one that she hadn't been able to throw out of the window. They had all been amused to learn that the comms barge even had a name: HM survey ship *Newt*. According to the charges, the damage the women had done to the ship's radio and range-finding equipment had posed a danger to the *Newt*'s crew. They had also wilfully and maliciously damaged acoustic equipment and an amplifier, books, a briefcase, a case and contents, chairs, computer equipment, documents, electrical and office equipment, electronic components, fax machines, office furniture, recording equipment, records, telephones, tools and a wall clock. Several tens of thousands of pounds' worth of high-spec military kit, in fact, that by depositing it in the waters of the loch they had rendered waterlogged, useless and inoperable.

Thoughtfully, Her Majesty's Advocate had also laid out an alternative charge of theft. Presumably this was so that, if the wilful and malicious damage charge couldn't be made to stick, they still had endangerment of crew, or a serious burglary charge in reserve.

As they filed back into the courtroom after the short recess, with order now restored, Amelia was clearly distraught, and no wonder. She had just completed her introduction and been about to move to the witness stand to give her evidence when it had all kicked off.

The two of them looked well, if exhausted. Three months in the women's wing at HMP Greenock had clearly taken a physical toll on them both. But their morale was good, considering. They hadn't been cellmates, but Amelia and Deedee had maintained contact during permitted acts of worship and in recreational activities.

In the one letter she'd managed to write to Spike during her remand, Amelia had also told him that she was quite enjoying working in the prison's bicycle repair shop a couple of days a week – she called it 'Re-cyc-a-bike' – and that Deedee had managed, of course, to get a horticulture job. She also wrote that they had decided to change the name of their Chapter from Larch to **Andromeda** because the constellation symbolised a woman in chains, and hoped he was okay with that. In his letter back, he said he was honoured that she would even ask, that he was in awe of what she and Deedee had done, and that he hoped he would continue to justify his place as a kindred spirit alongside them.

During the trial, eloquent expert witnesses from the UK, Europe and beyond had been called and questioned on matters of international law, nuclear weapons and the history of non-violent protest. They'd outlined and expounded the ethos of the Isaiah Movement, and explained that the movement's core principles of safety, openness and accountability were things they all took very seriously. That these applied to everyone. This was why drink and drugs were banned from the movement, and why it was vital that everybody from the biggest, hairiest MOD police officer to the maintenance staff, to the presiding Sheriff, to the Lord Advocate – the poshest of the posh, a real **blue blood** type – was to continue to be treated with the utmost respect and civility. The movement was designed to **heal** differences, they said, not to exacerbate them. A trial like this, with the whole world watching, was an opportunity to underline this and to put it on record. Every trial was an opportunity to **implement** the movement's ethos, and to express their argument by every means at their disposal, which also meant respecting the representatives of the legal system whose diligence and good faith were also being counted upon.

But now all of that had been put in **peril**.

Years of planning and research put at risk by a group of hotheads acting entirely outside the spirit of the movement.

Before the unexpected recess, as Amelia was being led back to the prisoners' holding area, she had caught Spike's eye and a silent message had passed between them: a single, stunned and exasperated look that expressed love and solidarity, but also – accompanied as it was by an almost imperceptible shrug and shake of the head – 'What the fuck was that?'

None of them had seen it coming. It was exactly the kind of thing that could undo all of the good work that had gone before. Had that been the objective? If not, then who exactly were these people? Spike looked down at his feet. There was still confetti on the floor.

An hour earlier, as they'd waited outside in order to be allowed into the public gallery to watch the day's proceedings, Spike had picked up where they'd left off the night before, trading war stories – protests they'd been on and lived to tell the **tale** – with Plum, who had just arrived to join the vigil along with some other members of **Free Wheel**, a Chapter from down south; Kent or thereabouts, he said.

'Well, it's not for me to say, but the more the merrier,' said Spike. 'Hey, but I'm sure we know each other, right? Everyone calls me Spike.'

Plum took a drag from his rollie and narrowed his eyes. 'Yeah, I thought I recognised you, man. Where do I know you from?' He spoke with a soft Northern Irish accent, and stroked his chin as if regarding Spike critically. 'London?'

'Yeah, maybe,' said Spike, thinking of likely raves or protest sites. 'Whirl-Y-Gig? Claremont Road?'

'Fuuuuuuck!' said Plum. 'Of course. That's mental, mate.'

They embraced like veterans, like the survivors of some great battle.

With its abundance of towers, turrets and crenelations, and a central, oversized clocktower, Greenock Sheriff Court looked like some sort of hyper-real fairy-tale Scottish castle. A large group of protesters had gathered in the west central Lowland town, from Chapters all over the country, and the plan had been to **cram** as many people as possible into the courtroom every day, while those that couldn't get into the trial itself would maintain a **polite** vigil behind some crowd-management barriers on the pavement outside.

'I was bound over last week,' said Spike, 'so now I'm not allowed to go within thirty miles of Faslane. We maybe could have fought it, but you've got to choose your battles. These two are more important. I'm just a grunt. Have you ever been to Menwith?'

'Aye, no,' said Plum. 'Got to admire them, though, keeping that up for so long!'

'To the max,' said Spike. 'But listen, once you get away from the base, the skies are so clear up there. It's beautiful. We did the peace march one time, a few years ago now. A bunch of us stayed over, and it was during the **Leonid** meteor shower, November time. Fuck me, there were so many shooting stars. One every few minutes – all coming from the same part of the sky. Unbelievable. It felt like the sky was blessing us.'

A more radical group of Menwith Hill marchers, of which Spike had been a part, had taken compost and a few dozen oak saplings, plus pickaxes, bolt-cutters, the works; a whole fucking garden centre's worth of gear. The plan had been to break in and get onto the base so they could plant trees along the runway, on the actual airstrip. But someone must have tipped the MOD police off because they had been waiting for them mob-handed. There was no way they were going to be allowed to break in, let alone get near the **strip** itself. He told Plum how they'd put their heads together and instead decided to yomp further out onto the moor, where they'd planted the saplings as a living CND symbol, one hundred feet across.

'Visible from the air?'

'Exactly,' said Spike, remembering how they'd marked out the circle, compass-stylee, with Spike standing in the centre holding a length of nylon rope, slowly turning on the spot as the two people at the other end traced out the perimeter of a circle, one of them walking and trying to hold the rope taut while the other sprayed an 'X' every few steps with fluorescent-yellow line paint. Ditto for the vertical, which pointed north, and the downward-pointing outstretched 'arms'.

Plum nodded. 'I like that even more,' he said. 'There's a lesson in that, eh? That could be there for centuries. It's got to be better than just inconveniencing them for a day or so. And they'll see it every time they come in to land. Every. Fuckin'. Time!' He thought for a second or two. 'That's brilliant. Is it still there, d'you know? I'd fuckin' love to see that.'

Spike shrugged. 'Pretty brutal up there in winter, so who knows.'

'You *from* London, then? What's your story?' Plum asked.

'No,' said Spike. 'Originally a place called **Dedham**.'

'A Suffolk man,' said Plum.

'No, that's Denham. Everyone says that. Dedham's in Essex, near Colchester.'

Plum was a wiry guy maybe in his late thirties or early forties, with an ingrained field tan and a **sleek**, grown-out green mohawk plastered back on his head, dark roots showing through nearer the scalp. He wore army surplus boiler suits – as long as they fitted, he wasn't fussy – and a battered leather biker jacket with holes in the lapels where the odd **stud** had fallen out. On the back of his right hand was a tattoo, a thick black outline of an **isosceles** triangle.

'What's that mean?' Spike asked.

'That my right hand will always be eighteen,' said Plum with a shrug.

Plum's usual gig was taking an anti-nuclear and pacifist bookstall from festival to festival during the summer. A couple of trestle tables and boxes of books and pamphlets: everything from old paperbacks of Bart de Ligt's *The Conquest of Violence* and selected writings of

Gandhi to more recent titles on feminism and non-violence, on nuclear disarmament or the Chernobyl disaster. He told Spike that he got a bit of stick in some circles for 'cashing in' or 'exploiting the movement', but he just laughed. 'I fuckin' put them straight. "Me, a **profiteer**?" I tell them. "You think there's any money in this shit?"'

Spike laughed too.

'I'm just trying to keep the information out there in the public domain,' said Plum. 'Taking it to where young people actually are. How do you think we're gonna **foster** the next generation, get them active, unless we do that? Look.' He gestured at the other Free Wheelers who were ahead of him in the queue to get into the courtroom. 'How d'you think this lot got involved, eh? You've got to be prepared to put in the hours and educate people. Talk to them. Like the old socialist slogan: Educate, agitate, organise.'

Plum's strategy evidently worked. He told Spike and the others how the young people who came to his stall often considered themselves politically conscious, but once you started to talk to them it was all conspiracy theories about contrails and **germ** warfare or whatever: pure stoner talk.

'You've got to remember,' he said, 'they've been fed a diet of pure shite since they cut their **milk teeth**. All they know is whatever daily **ration** of bullshit they've been spoon-fed from the TV. It's all fuckin' *He-Man* or the *Animaniacs*. *Big* fucking *Brother*. Their idea of a controversy is whether it was *Stop the **Pigeon*** or *Catch the Pigeon*.'

'And it was neither, right?' said Spike with a chuckle.

'Fuck sake!' said Plum. 'You know what I mean? You've got to shake them up and show them the real conspiracies – blow their fuckin' minds. Look, the nuclear weapons **stockpile** is a relic of another age, an obsolete geopolitics. If bin Laden is really hiding out in Afghanistan, what good are nuclear weapons? What are you going to do? Obliterate **Kabul**? It would be genocide.'

In court, the formalities over, a shuffling of feet and a **rustle** of papers meant that it was Amelia's turn to speak.

Spike had a vague idea of what to expect. In her letter from prison, Amelia hadn't gone into too many details, for obvious reasons, but she'd told Spike that she planned to begin her defence by telling the story of her own introduction to CND, her Quaker faith and a lifetime of anti-nuclear protest, so when she began talking Spike wasn't surprised to hear the same story that she'd told him and Deedee up at Loch Lomond those few months ago. How her awareness of the Campaign for Nuclear Disarmament had begun with her accidental purchase, aged about eleven, of the grey Penguin paperback of John Hersey's *Hiroshima* from the bookstall at the 3rd Farnham Scouts' jumble sale. *New Yorker* journalist Hersey's book-length article, with its personal eyewitness insights into the obscenely destructive force of nuclear weapons, had affected her deeply, and a couple of years later the knowledge had prompted her to attend a private screening of the then still banned anti-nuclear film *The War Game* at Farnham Maltings. Then she'd seen Monsignor Bruce Kent speaking on the Pyramid Stage at Glastonbury, when the festival was still primarily a CND fundraiser.

She had also told Spike that she would try to weave together defences in common law and international law, as well as statutory and moral defences, all of which would demonstrate not only the unlawful nature of the Trident nuclear missile programme but also her corresponding right to actively disarm it, in order to prevent the far greater crime.

They'd known from previous Isaiah Movement trials that giving evidence would take most of the day, and because she was representing herself she would need to be in complete command not just of all of the relevant information but also of the overall argument she wanted to communicate, which had to be carefully constructed – it would need to be the speech of her life.

Spike had heard her speak in meetings at Friends House and at Housmans before they'd actually met, so he knew that Amelia was an eloquent orator, but she wouldn't be able to rely on a barrister for support. Not only was it essential that she not bore the jury, but her speech would need to leave them sympathetic to the cause, and even empowered by it. She needed to give the jury both the tools *and* the motivation to acquit herself and Deedee, and to do so whatever the Sheriff's recommendation might be. Moreover, she'd of course had to do all of this preparation within the literal constraints of imprisonment, so had asked Spike and other colleagues in the movement to collate the many pieces of supporting material that would be needed, in order that these could be duplicated for circulation in court. It was painstaking work, but Spike had been only glad that he could help. He knew that every word had been carefully weighed.

Amelia's voice had been trembling at first, and Spike knew that she felt the responsibility keenly. She was speaking not just for herself, nor the movement in general, but on behalf of humanity itself. She quickly got into her stride, however, and when she said, 'I will now present my evidence from the witness stand' and picked up the large pile of papers from the table in front of her, Spike knew that something special was going to happen. Though he hadn't been prepared for exactly what that would turn out to be. Out of the corner of his eye he saw Plum **pucker** up and kiss **Eden**, the young woman sitting next to him. But then, as one and before Spike could question the inappropriateness of what he'd seen, Plum and the rest of the Free Wheel Chapter – the whole **tier** of seats to Spike's left – suddenly stood up, threw confetti and red paint and shouted: 'Free the Gare Loch Two!' Eden quickly took her top off. She was wearing nothing underneath, and with a few twists and turns, having handed an end each to the people on either side, she quickly unfurled the fabric to reveal that she had in fact been wearing a long banner made of parachute silk, upon which those same words were painted.

'Free the Gare Loch Two!' they shouted. 'Free the Gare Loch Two!'

Spike couldn't believe what he was seeing. How could they?

Disrespect to the court was one thing, he supposed, but how could anyone think it was a good idea to disrespect the people you were meant to be there to support? He was only relieved that press photographers were not allowed into the courtroom, otherwise that was your headline right there, the kind of coverage you could do without: 'Gare Loch pair freed!'

He saw Amelia staring at them with an expression of utter shock and incredulity. The timing literally could not have been worse, unless some sort of psychic attack had been the actual objective here. Amelia began to crumple, but somehow managed to stay upright for long enough to put the huge pile of papers safely back down on the table in front of her without dropping them, before slumping back down in the chair.

'Free the Gare Loch Two!' the Free Wheelers shouted as the constables rushed in and began to drag the protesters out of the courtroom, one of them using his jacket to cover up the young woman's nakedness. 'Free the Gare Loch Two!'

Amelia was holding her head in her hands and crying. Spike knew what she was thinking: who the fuck were these people? How could they do this to her? And how on earth would she be able to recover her composure sufficiently to start again and satisfactorily do the job she needed to do? Worse: how could she restore the court and the jury's faith not just in her but also in the entire movement, after such a crass, ill-timed and destructive gesture from within their own ranks?

14: Lilas (Lilac)

Strolling back down Lamb's Conduit Street to the station, Rex felt superficially better for the Guinness, though still perplexed that Webster was giving Helen the **run-around**. All these tour guides had reminded him of that old story of Webster's. How did it go? He'd have to tell Terry **Hobbs** next time he saw him. He liked a good story, did Terence. He'd appreciate that. Of course, Webster would tell it better if he were around, but he wasn't, was he. Some great yarn about a rookie constable, from the days when they'd still been pretty green themselves. This would have been back when Rex and Webster were still mates.

They'd had a right old laugh about it at the time, if Rex remembered rightly. It hadn't even been a big investigation. Not that it hadn't been a serious crime. A rough sleeper stabbed in broad daylight up by St Pancras Old Church had sadly died on the way to UCH. There'd been nobody around and door-to-doors had yielded precisely nothing, so they'd put a couple of Inquiry Boards up, one on each side of Pancras Road – yellow 'Serious Incident' signs – appealing for witnesses.

In the event, a couple of postmen had come forward. They'd have been knocking off earlies at what was then the NW1 mail centre on St Pancras Way – and that closed in what, '94, '95? So this was before that. Both of the witnesses had mentioned seeing a tour guide in the vicinity. Which was not surprising because it's a historic spot, St Pancras Old Church. You've got a Saxon church built over a Roman temple, Thomas Hardy, the coming of the railways: the works.

This had seemed like a lead, anyway, and let's say maybe someone in the team meeting had suggested that if they could interview this tour guide it might at least **enable** them to eliminate him from their enquiries. Problem was they didn't know which one it was. So one of the rookie PCs had been tasked with pulling together a list of all the tour guides operating in the borough – broad brush, just the most active ones – and off the bat this young constable had assumed that they were all licensed, so he'd gone to the Guild of Registered Tour Guides, as they were called at the time – the Blue Badge people. But when he'd come back all pleased with himself with a photocopy of a typed list of guild members, instead of the big pat on the back he'd been expecting, job well done et cetera, he'd just got a massive bollocking because of course tour guides don't have to be licensed at all. Any fool can set up as a guide. And he'd been sent back to do a better job.

But what was Webster playing at? Approaching the station, Rex saw a youngish – mid-thirties? – and smartly dressed man and woman – well, smart-casual – standing on the pavement looking at a familiar and ubiquitous device that was positioned on the wall near ground level: a small yellow square upon which was an embossed and black-painted letter 'H'. They were standing close, her arm linked in his. She pointed with her other hand.

'The top number is the diameter of the water main,' she said. 'Eighty mil. And the bottom number tells you how far away, usually in the direction the plate is facing, so two metres in this case. They're for firemen to connect their hoses.'

'Wow,' said the man, looking at the **hydrant** plate and then at a rectangular iron cover set into the pavement near where they were standing. 'I suppose I'd always wondered.'

'I'm actually really chuffed you didn't know that!' the woman said, dragging him in the direction of the nearest pub, a few doors down on Theobalds Road. 'Look! They have foosball.'

Quite frankly Rex would rather be playing table football. He had better things to think about than the daily whereabouts and motivations of his long-time colleague, but being so resoundingly cuckolded would have to hurt!

Rex was secretly glad. He was enjoying the sixteen-year payback; talk about a slow burn.

But he knew that such a bombshell would not sit well with a man like Ed Webster. It'd be enough to **numb** the most jovial and thick-skinned of men, and see them retreat and lick their wounds for a bit to try to avoid the inevitable **scorn** of their colleagues. In a job like this, that's the kind of thing you'd be reminded about every day of your working life. Everyone would be singing that Kid Creole and the Coconuts song under their breath, every time Webbo walked into any room, forever.

It was lucky for Webster that he'd managed to have at least one daughter of his own. He'd never get called a 'Jaffa', and be accused of shooting blanks. But if he knew that she knew that he knew – Jesus! It was like that old Kursaal Flyers song – what did Webster have to gain from neglecting to tell Helen that he hadn't been coming into work the past few days?

Rex jogged up the steps and into reception.

Jinksy usually had his ear to the ground. He'd know.

The EDO was on front desk for the late shift, and when Rex walked in, Eric Jinks was using a biro to stir a glass of cloudy water, and there was a box of **soluble aspirin** on the desk. He had a broad white dressing strapped across the bridge of his nose and what looked like the beginnings of two black eyes.

'Fuck sake, Jinks,' said Rex. 'What happened to you? Plastic surgery?'

'Very funny,' said Jinks with a decidedly **nasal** twang. 'You know you're the first person to say that?'

Rex didn't rise to the bait.

'Nah, walked into a fucking plate-glass door, didn't I.'

'Broken?'

'Luckily not,' said Jinks. 'I hear you're filling in for Eddie Webster, then?'

Rex raised his eyes to heaven. '**Hurrah**. Yes. Thank you, Webbo,' he **apostrophised**. 'Thank you very fucking much!'

Jinksy chuckled, then downed the aspirin in one.

'Did he say anything to you?' asked Rex.

'Eddie?'

'Yeah.'

'About being ill? No, but to be honest he never **looks** that great, does he.' Jinksy puffed out his cheeks to reinforce the point, and lifted his arms to nurse an imaginary belly. He was right. Webster was more **Eamonn** Holmes than Sherlock: no fine-chiselled **Basil Rathbone** figure he. 'Looked like he'd seen a ghost last time I saw him, though.'

'When was that?'

'Few days ago?'

'And?'

'Well, white as a **sheet,** like I say,' said Jinksy. 'I didn't ask.'

As white as Pik **Botha**'s bathroom, thought Rex. He had a sudden brief flashback of the living room in his childhood family home in Spenser Avenue, Exeter. He could almost smell it: sun-warmth on the net curtains. Seagulls at the beach. He remembered that time watching the Exmouth Lifeboat being scrambled, then coming back half an hour later towing a small yacht. They'd deposited the rescued sailors **on shore** and it had been somebody his dad knew from work, some guy called Mervyn who'd been out sailing with his family when they'd got into trouble. It had all happened so quickly. At home, they often listened to that Elkie Brooks song his mum liked, 'Lilac Wine', or **chamber** music on Radio 3. His dad's dark-green-ribboned Plymouth Argyle **rosette** that always stood on top of the carriage clock on the mantelpiece, a souvenir of their 1975 promotion to Football League Division Two. To be a Pilgrim was an intent that Rex's dad did **indeed** first **avow**, when he'd been alive – loudly and often. It had been the least of Rex's worries at the time, but it was too bad that his parents had died before his father could see them get to the semi-final of the FA Cup. They did 'with giants fight', after all. Catching the light in the glass cabinet would be his mum's small **ormolu** pieces, an ornate ring box and a vase that was shaped to look like a miniature oil lamp, with its faux-chimney made from opaque bright-blue glass. And propped up in the centre of the sofa, the doll-sized, furry, green **Atlanta** Braves mascot that another friend of his dad's had brought them back from a work trip to the US. This 'bleacher creature' – product of some Deep South **sweat shop** – was meant to be the Braves' official **opossum** mascot, but it just looked like a generic Muppet. Rex remembered the three of them laughing at something his father had said: that something was as white as the then long-time South African Foreign Minister's bathroom. Rex couldn't recall what they'd been talking about, or why the apartheid minister's name had been invoked. But he did know that they'd all found it funny, and remembered his mum saying, 'Oh, Charles, don't!'

But that old story about the rookie constable looking for a tour guide...

Somehow he'd got lost in the task, whether through inexperience or stupidity or both. It turned out he'd spent days traipsing round the West End and the City tracking down the unlicensed guides. He was stealing bundles of flyers from the tables in the foyers of 2-, 3- and 4-star hotels, going to the pubs that the guides drank in, being pointed in this or that direction, tapping into networks of Ripperologists in Aldgate gambling clubs and having whispered conversations on Millbank with greasy-trousered ticket touts for fly-by-night sightseeing bus companies. Days had turned into weeks, supposedly, but novice that he was, he hadn't said anything or asked for help. And probably no one had thought twice about some rookie's absence from whichever team meeting. Meanwhile he was still out there, with no plan, digging himself a deeper and deeper hole, frightened of not bringing back enough intelligence, so not turning up to briefings, and eventually going off sick with the stress of it. And even then he'd carried on working on the project in his own time, writing it all up; by hand, probably. This being the early nineties, not many people had personal computers.

Webster was definitely better at telling the story. How did it go? Something like, by the time this young constable crept back into the station, by the time he'd emerged back off sick leave and dropped this massive 'report' on whoever's desk it was – well, it could have been Lollo in his Detective Sergeant days, he was terrifying even then – this great list of all the unregistered tour guides, in truth a filthy, dog-eared pile of handwritten papers, all anecdotes and crossings-out; by that time, supposedly, the investigation had already been wrapped up. Done and dusted long since. Turned out it was another rough sleeper had done it. Motivation: robbery. Got caught trying to sell some piece of crap down King's Cross and someone had recognised it. Something like that.

The rookie constable had left the force shortly thereafter, if Rex recalled correctly.

There was probably a lesson or two in there somewhere, about shouting if you were getting out of your depth.

Or maybe it was just the way that DS Eddie Webster used to tell it.

Webbo had been a right old laugh in the Sports and **Social** back in the day.

15: Anémone (Anemone)

It was obvious to Rex that Operation Kayak was not going to be a week on the Costa del **Sol**, or a leisurely **amble** in the park, even if he was joining the investigation at this late stage. But luckily he would not be unsupported in his task, for, just as at the end of every rainbow there is a **crock of gold**, so underlying any investigation that fell within the definition of a Critical Incident was a Gold Strategy. And with its complexity, its family liaison and community-impacts considerations, its need for expert advice and multi-agency working, and potentially its media requirements, Operation Kayak was clearly a Critical Incident. And for every Gold Strategy there was a Gold Support Group, a GSG, to ensure good practice, for monitoring and successful delivery. The functions, membership and content of the Gold Support Group would of course vary according to the nature of the major crime under investigation, but could include specialist advisers and partner organisations, staff associations and lay advisers, all working towards a remit that might include everything from simple knowledge-sharing to a discussion of which sentencing **tariff** the investigation might be seeking. If it was a really big investigation, there would be someone from the CPS at the GSG meeting **too**. Not to mention the comms angle. There was no point setting sail with your major investigation all shipshape only to immediately encounter a PR **iceberg**. You needed to stay afloat, not sink before you'd started. Which was where the Met's press and comms genius Evelyn Gummer came in, to embed the media strategies from the beginning, and to give the press what they thought they wanted. Gummer was the best in the business. She could be barking orders at you through a loud **hailer** and you'd think you'd thought of the ideas yourself.

Rex had already made a diary note of Monday's Gold Support

Group meeting after Becky's tip-off, so he wasn't surprised when Lollo brought it up. What was surprising was Lollo's joviality. He was clearly in more conciliatory mood, if not exactly waving a **flag of truce**.

'Alright, lad,' he said. 'Sorry about having a go earlier. I needed a scapegoat, and you walked in.'

'That's alright, sir,' said Rex, **pragmatic** enough not to have taken it personally.

'SiC report lands this time next week,' said Lollo. 'What d'you reckon?'

Rex shrugged. He could do without the reminder.

'Weren't that fucking bad, though, were it, Kingsy?'

'Speak for yourself. Not exactly my idea of fun.'

'Tennyson weren't your fault, you know,' said the Detective Chief Inspector. 'You do know that, don't you?'

Well, Lollo had put his finger on it there. The DCI didn't know the half of it, but Rex wasn't about to argue with him. Even if pressed he still wouldn't say it, but Rex was fully expecting the SiC inspectors to go to town on Trevor Tennyson. An 'Adverse Incident' like a death in custody was enough to skew the whole report, even if the officers involved had eventually been acquitted. It had been Rex who'd told them to call an ambulance, immediately realising the seriousness of the situation, but as station lead on Safe Detention and Handling he would still be right in the firing line.

He'd been turning it over in his mind, unable to stop himself from thinking how Trevor Tennyson might have responded to the SiC detainee questionnaires if he were still alive:

Were you told about the Police and Criminal Evidence (PACE) codes of practice (the 'rule book')? Yes ☐ *No* ☑ *I don't know what this is / I don't remember* ☐

Did you feel safe there? Yes ☐ *No* ☑

Did another detainee or a member of staff victimise (insult or assault) you there? Yes ☑ *No* ☐

Were you handcuffed or restrained whilst in the police custody suite? Yes ☑ *No* ☐

Were you injured in police custody, in a way that you feel was not your fault? Yes ☑ *No* ☐

When you were in police custody, were you on any medication? Yes ☑ *No* ☐

When you were in police custody, did someone explain your entitlements to see a healthcare professional if you needed to? Yes ☐ No ✔ *Don't know* ☐

Please rate the quality of your healthcare whilst in police custody: I was not seen by healthcare ☐ *Very Good* ☐ *Good* ☐ *Neither* ☐ *Bad* ☐ *Very Bad* ✔

'You've got to see them just like any other **regulator**' – Lollo was still talking – 'in any public sector, really. If this were a school or a **college** it'd be Ofsted, right? They're not an enemy. We all want the same thing, see. We offer them some low-hanging fruit, they make a few recommendations, identify where a bit of training might be needed, and we say thank you very much we're going to take those recommendations on board. Then we tell them how we're going to go about learning the lessons. And everyone's happy.' He leaned in and lowered his voice: 'Listen, don't quote me on this, but I'll lay you evens that Kentish Town'll come off worse.'

Aha, thought Rex. So that was it. Lollo had had a tip-off.

'What have you heard, sir?'

'I've heard nowt, but call it an 'unch,' Lollo continued, sotto voce. 'All over the place up there, they are. And Tabitha's not going to let any shit stick to us while they're around.'

Well, maybe Lollo was correct in that respect, Rex reflected. Tabitha Churchill could do no wrong right now, it seemed. As well as being in overall command of the new Central North BCU since the merger, she was also BCU Rep – and chair of several influential committees – on the National Police Chiefs' Council.

'Listen,' Lollo went on. 'Speaking of which, Gold Support Group's at ten a.m. Monday. I want you there, but I'm sending you in with a **listening** brief, alright? You've only just picked up the reins, so they'll know you can't be expected to be on top of it. No one'll put you on the spot. Just follow your instincts.'

'Sir,' said Rex.

'Tabitha will be chairing. Not sure who SMT'll be sending because Jane Milligan's about to drop. The new Police Federation rep, what's his name—'

'Simon,' said Rex.

'Simon Rose, that's him. Evelyn, of course. Child protection team leaders from Camden, Newham and Redbridge social services. Oh, and Clifford Heath'll be there as specialist adviser. He's an old South

Yorkshire mate of mine. Now a Detective Inspector in Thames Valley, so he's been through something similar on Bullfinch, and he knows how to win it and how not to. You must have seen him about over the years: handsome Black bloke, about my age – terrible **rug**.'

Rex laughed. In that case he had seen Cliff Heath around once or twice, but Lollo was being **unfair**. It *was* an awful syrup, but was there any other kind?

'Obviously you won't be in a position as SIO to give the status update. I'll do that based on my last one-to-one with Webbo. Just feel your way, Kingsy, old son. Listen and learn.'

'No problem,' said Rex. He could hold his own in a meeting. He'd been to enough of them over the years.

'Course, you won't have read Dicky Sharp's statements yet. I've asked Becky to send you an invite to the group, but she might not action that until first thing.'

'Right you are,' said Rex.

'Just to give you fair warning, Kingsy, my angle is going to be "Let's pretend Dicky Sharp never existed." Take his evidence out of the picture completely and see what's left.'

'That'll surprise them, sir.'

'Maybe so,' said Lollo. 'But if that's the steer from the CPS, I'll take it.'

'One more thing, sir,' said Rex.

'Aye, go on, then,' said Lollo.

'Any chance of a quick one-to-one in the next twenty-four hours, sir? Personal matter.'

'Sunday?' said Lollo. 'Drop Becky an email to remind me.'

'Shouldn't take five minutes.'

'What did I just say?'

'To email Becky, sir.'

'Fuck off and do it then!'

'Yes, sir.'

'Oh, Kingsy?'

'Sir?'

'Lion or **hippo**?'

Back at the flat later on, and cutting the top off his **boiled egg**, Rex had to laugh. Lollo had clearly been in a good mood, and if the

Detective Chief Inspector had heard a whisper about the outcome of the SiC, then that boded well for the whole **outfit**.

'Lion or hippo?' Lollo had said again. 'Who d'you fancy in a fight?'

'Have you just discovered Facebook or something, sir?'

'Lion or hippo?'

Rex had just stared at him.

'Living as we do in an **age of reason**,' Lollo had said, 'I'm simply asking you to engage the old grey matter: Lion or fucking hippo?'

'Lion, I suppose.'

Lollo had shaken his head. 'No fucking way. Hippo every time. Seen how big they are? Size of them fucking teeth. They're fast and all, and them little legs are surprisingly springy.' He pronounced it with a hard G. 'They can turn on a sixpence. Imagine that: four and a half fucking ton of muscle and them bloody jaws coming at yer.'

'Lions've got to be faster though, sir. And they've got the killer instinct. Two lions, for sure. Hippo wouldn't stand a chance.'

'One on one, Kingsy. You don't **anger** a fucking hippopotamus. That's one beast whose **ire** you do not want to draw. The only way a lion's coming out on top is if there were a decent-sized tree in the vicinity he could climb up sharpish.'

'Or if the hippo had a handicap,' Rex had said, playing along. 'One hoof tied behind its back. Or maybe it's anaemic.'

'Whoever heard of an 'ippo with *anaemia*? All that fucking water-weed they eat?'

You had to laugh.

'Thanks, sir,' Rex had said.

'Aye, go on, then. Fuck off.'

Rex had taken the lift for once, but immediately wished that he hadn't. It reminded him why he always took the stairs. It wasn't just about keeping fit. The lift reeked. All those smokers up and down the building popping out for a **breath of air** every few minutes – 'I'm just going to **freshen** up!' or whatever the latest euphemism was – smoking two or three in quick succession to make the journey worthwhile, then getting straight back into the lift and bringing all that second-hand smoke back in with them. The whole place smelled like a pub ashtray, as people had once been fond of saying. Next time: stairs, he thought.

By the time Rex turned in and set his alarm, there was still nothing from Susan, no sign of the usual little late-night goodnight text. He'd texted a couple of times, and left one voicemail, so he wasn't about to leave another. She'd call in her own good time, and besides, he didn't want to look desperate.

Rex was planning to spend most of the weekend catching up before Monday's Gold Support Group meeting. While he waited for Becky to send through the invite, he'd be going through Webster's files with a fine-tooth comb, to see if the Detective Sergeant had missed anything obvious.

Sometimes that was all it took: a fresh pair of eyes. As SIO – especially on a long investigation – there was a risk you'd get so involved you couldn't see the wood for the trees. Which was where Rex was at an advantage, parachuting into a well-established investigation. Meeting up with Helen earlier, the whole business with Jennifer, might have thrown him a bit, that was for sure, but Rex was starting to feel like his old self again. Fuck Helen, and fuck Susan.

Now he remembered precisely why it was that Lollo always entrusted him with the difficult projects.

Why Lollo put him forward for things.

Why Lollo pushed him.

And why it paid Rex to keep Lollo close.

It wasn't because he was gullible, or always available, or a people-pleaser.

It was because he was good at his fucking job.

And you know what? He enjoyed it too.

So, Rex was going to do precisely that. He'd have a bit more of a dig around and follow his instincts, like Lollo said.

And he'd find something alright.

It'd take a while, but Rex would find something that stood out as bright as a flash of yellow **gorse** on a Scottish hillside.

16: Pensée (Pansy)

They celebrated the verdict in Deedee's brother's room at the B&B. It was a tiny room with lacy net curtains, an embroidered sampler reading 'Ars longa, vita brevis', and a framed poster for the film *Titanic* on the wall. On the way back from the Sheriff Court they'd dropped into the baker's and bought a **cream bun** each, and a small **iced chocolate cake**. Deedee had wanted to buy some fruit loaf, but asked for **sweetbread** by mistake.

'I don't think that means what you think,' Spike had said good-naturedly. He'd bought Amelia a little 'get out of jail' present: nothing fancy, just a brick of Savon de Marseille olive oil soap.

'Thanks, babe!' she'd said, holding the rough green cube to her nose to savour its fresh clean bouquet. 'You remembered.'

They'd also bought paper cups from the newsagent, so they could toast their freedom with some **ouzo** brought over by Deedee's brother, who worked at the Dutch Embassy in Athens. All washed down with cups of **instant coffee** made with the tiny electric kettle in Tomas's room.

'Well, it was your evidence that did it, Amelia,' said Spike, raising a paper cup. 'The judge said so: "In light of submissions made yesterday on the part of the accused." That's you.'

'She was quite a woman,' said Amelia. 'Sheriff Sarah Disraeli. I liked her.'

'Any relation, d'you think?' said Spike.

'Probably. Who knows? I bet she gets asked that all the time.'

Spike was right. Amelia had successfully argued a common law defence of coercion or necessity for their actions, as well as a statutory defence, and a defence in international law.

Based on these arguments – for which she had praised the defendants – Sheriff Disraeli had directed the jury to return verdicts of not guilty on all charges. Though she did add the necessary caveat that the same defence might not work a second time.

Disraeli had also made the express point that she was well aware that the defendants had had as little warning as she had of the disruptive protest that had taken place the previous morning, saying 'It is clear that you had no part in the disruption, and it was not representative of your movement nor of the exemplary manner in which you have conducted your defence.'

'Free Wheel?' said Amelia. 'Give me a break.'

'Plum, his name is,' said Spike. 'From Belfast originally. I've definitely met him before. Seen him around in London: M11 protests and that. They weren't at Dani's in August, but he said they'd been up for the 2001 blockade, when Galloway and Sheridan were arrested. He seemed sound enough when we were chatting the other night. He runs an anti-nuclear bookstall these days, takes it to all the festivals, apparently.'

'Oh, he hangs out at pop festivals – I wonder why,' said Amelia, pointedly. 'D'you think all of his friends are beautiful and **aloof** young hippy women half his age? I nearly died when she got her tits out. What do they think this is, the sixties?'

They sat in silence for a moment.

'Were they actually trying to fuck it up, d'you think?' said Spike. 'To set us back? That would be a good way to do it, if you wanted to. A different judge might have assumed we were all in it together.'

'What do you mean?'

'I don't know…' Spike measured his words carefully. 'You hear about…'

They all knew what he was thinking: agent provocateurs, undercover cops.

Amelia was **defiant**: 'Well, fuck them!'

Deedee and her brother had been speaking softly to each other in Dutch, but turned to join in. 'Yes!' said Deedee, laughing, then: 'Who are we fucking?'

'I think she means the… commotion? in the courtroom?' said her brother in English.

'Oh, him!'

'**Lovable** rogues,' said Amelia, 'are the worst. In my experience.'

'Here's to Sarah Disraeli,' said Spike, topping up the ouzo in their paper cups. 'Who'd have thought she'd be one of the good guys!'

'*Proost*,' said Deedee, and they all said it back: '*Proost!*'

Once the trial had finished, they'd had to hang around the Sheriff Court for half an hour or so. Then, outside, arm in arm with Amelia, Deedee had read out one of their two prepared statements. The other, written to be read out by Deedee's barrister in the event of a conviction, would not now be needed. And then they had spoken to the press. Deedee's English was not quite up to an in-depth interview, but Amelia actually didn't mind doing it. She was happy to talk to the papers, local radio, anyone, and saw press and publicity work as a necessary element of what they were doing. 'I think of it as a **tithe**,' she'd said to Spike once. 'Like in the Bible? Genesis, chapter twenty-eight, verses twenty to twenty-two? "Of all that you give me I will give you a tenth." If I can give ten per cent of my time to helping spread the word, whether that's updating our website, photocopying, giving out leaflets, speaking to a journalist, then that's a good thing.'

'What are you two going to do now?' asked Spike.

'I will go to Athens,' said Deedee, 'and be an aunty for a week or so. It is still warm there!'

'I'm going to go and see my dad and his wife in Gloucestershire, and do nothing but read and sleep for a week,' said Amelia.

'Oh nice,' said Spike. 'Whereabouts?'

'Chipping **Campden**,' said Amelia. 'Do you know it?'

Spike shook his head. 'I only know Stroud, and the Forest of Dean. It's lovely round there. If anyone needs a lift, I'm driving down to London in the morning. Getting back to **urban** life. A man can have too many mountains!'

'Yes please,' said Amelia. 'That would be great. Can we go via Edinburgh, maybe stay over, so I can pick up a few things?'

'Your friend in the New Town? Yeah, of course. I love Edinburgh.'

'You know what I've been fantasising about in prison?' said Amelia with a **grin**.

Spike looked up.

'Stop it, you,' said Amelia. 'I mean food-wise. I've had real cravings for kiwi fruit. Just to have a **fridge** full of fresh veg again! We've been eating **tinned fruit salad** for three months – except once I managed to **cadge** some raw carrots from the kitchen before they boiled them to death. I need some **vitamins**, spinach, anything!'

Amelia hadn't said anything to the others, but she was also worried about the press interviews she'd done back at the court. She hoped that at least the *Herald* reporter who'd come down to Greenock would play it with a straight bat. Assuming she herself hadn't let everyone down by saying something stupid, Amelia was hopeful that the *Herald*'s piece might be more than the usual **hackwork** demolition job. At least they'd sent a woman, which made a change: a rather wry and sensitive-seeming American from the women's pages, who'd actually done her research and asked one or two decent questions. So that was a good start.

The reporter had laughed when Amelia had said she was glad they hadn't sent a man.

For a start, a man might have been more readily distracted.

Luckily it wasn't quite so easy to **bedazzle** a seasoned female journalist by painting CND symbols onto a young woman's naked breasts.

17: Myrtille (Blueberry)

Sitting at DS Eddie Webster's desk in the relative quiet of the sixth floor on a Saturday morning, Rex tried to ignore the archive boxes filled with hard drives and the associated paperwork that were stacked up behind Webster's laptop docking station and on a trolley next to the desk. The quiet suited him. He wanted to be able to **leaf** through Webster's notes and the various reports in peace, get up to speed before Monday's meeting.

He'd brought his own coffee in with him, in a University of York-branded reusable cup that Susan had given him. He'd found one of her blueberry yogurts in the fridge too, which was still in date, and he'd eaten that while he waited for the stovetop espresso pot to do its business. His phone had rattled in his pocket as he walked along Great Ormond Street, but it wasn't Susan. To be fair, it was a bit early. It was a text from Becky Fernie, who was evidently up and at 'em even earlier than Rex. She had teenagers too. Rex could remember when they were born. She was probably just getting ahead before the Saturday-morning onslaught of ferrying the boys to and from football, and had texted through the password to the Kayak folder on the shared drive: **Shanklin**_1985. In brackets she'd added 'capital S Shanklin underscore 1985 all one word. Call if any probs.'

That was a date to conjure with. Rex wondered who had been admin lead when Operation Kayak was being set up, and what if any connection they might have had to the Isle of Wight. Maybe a childhood holiday, or perhaps someone had been born there, or – in family legend – conceived. Maybe it had simply been the next UK place name on a list.

Rex's family had had a couple of holidays on the Island in successive years when he was maybe six or seven. Never mind '85, this would have been in the mid-seventies. They'd have driven up to Southampton in the Rover and got the car ferry: suitcases in the boot, box of groceries on the back seat, listening to Radio 1 because it was the first day of the holiday. The summer jingles: 'It's a great good morning!'

He didn't remember too much about the holidays themselves. A poky caravan on a small site near the beach. The only-very-slightly-larger caravans at the top of the slope, which had picture windows facing the sea, had seemed posh. Walking to the farm shop with his father to get the milk in the mornings, and the breakfast **bowl** of Weetabix, the taste of tinned new potatoes and of tea made with diluted evaporated milk when the fresh ran out; making sand castles and finding some fossils on the beach. He was pretty sure they'd have been to Shanklin. He had a slightly vague memory of a souvenir tea tray that featured an image of those famous thatched cottages.

Rex was experienced enough to know that he should enjoy even these scant memories while he could, because after a few log-ins they would **wither** like an old **turnip**. The name of that picturesque tourist destination would instead become an unthinking muscle memory, no more than a practised sequence of finger movements on a keyboard, both the prelude and the inevitable daily 'open sesame' to – and forever associated with – its own particular world of systematic violence and coercion, a pile-up of stories to be pieced together, dramas with their own overlapping casts of characters and associations, individuals whose faces he had not yet come to recognise or give nicknames to but would end up knowing better than his own family. Operation Kayak, a major investigation into a criminal network that right now was hiding in plain sight and operating with impunity, or so they thought. Material that – Rex was well aware – he would never be able to unsee. It was just how it went, the luck of the draw that it had been Webster and not him who'd been on tasking duty the week it had first blown up. But now it had landed in Rex's lap in any case.

Operation Kayak had started with a concerned mother from out Romford way coming in to the front desk rambling distractedly about her sixteen-year-old daughter who'd gone missing for the umpteenth time on, as it turned out, a vodka-soaked day trip to Camden Lock with some schoolfriends. When the girl hadn't come home on time, rather than waiting around, her mother had driven into town and looked for her, and somehow wound up at Holborn Police Station rather than Kentish Town. Luckily the woman had been possessed of sufficient fortitude to not take the habitual, generic and institutionally sexist response of the jovially dismissive EDO for an answer.

'Tough as **whip-cord**,' was how Webster had put it, shaking his head in admiration. 'Mum in a million, thank fucking Christ!'

They'd found the girl relatively quickly – she was in University College Hospital having her stomach pumped. And usually that would have been that, but for the rather circuitous route she'd taken from Chalk Farm Road to UCH, which turned out to have involved her panicking friends bundling her into a minicab with a fiver for the fare, which in turn had led to several missing hours, a significantly more complex toxicology report than first expected, and an immediate referral to the rape unit. Even then, there'd been no indication of how that single missing persons enquiry would subsequently **snowball** into the major oppo that Kayak had become.

Not unlike Lavengro, with its comings and goings in cab offices and barracks, army admin blocks. There had been weeks spent intelligence-gathering, identifying the key locations and players. Then poring over everything, weighing up your options, looking for a sweet spot, the best place to put your kit.

In the case of Lavengro, that had meant recognising that the various individuals were all converging on a dingy, **pine**-panelled sitting room out the back of some closed-down former **bucket shop** travel agent's near the old Wellington Centre, and creating some street theatre to ensure the building was empty for an hour or two. It had been similar with Operation Kayak – a 'gas leak' in the building next door to necessitate an immediate evacuation that lasted long enough to put the cameras in. Back then it had been mainly audio for indoor surveillance jobs. In those days, cameras were too big and cumbersome to hide in some wainscoting or a skirting board. But then as now it was just a matter of watching and waiting, and hauling it all in. Everything leading up to the moment when you'd make your own appearance on the tape, the moment when you'd burst in: the **raid**. Even then you'd have to avoid looking where you knew any devices had been hidden, much as you'd want to admire the engineers' handiwork: a unit that would have been operating unseen for however long it might have been – a month, a year. Two years, in the case of Lavengro. By the end of it he'd spent that much time in Barnes that he was on more than nodding acquaintance with half a dozen dog walkers and shop workers – all the Barnes early birds. Conversations with some of them had been easier than with Helen, who was justly feeling somewhat neglected back at home.

Working away for sustained periods like that, **oftentimes** with little **prospect** operationally of anything that you might call 'success', was more or less guaranteed to drain the love out of your real-life relationships. You could tie yourself in a **knot** just trying to keep track of where and who you were meant to be at any given moment. At the time it hadn't seemed significant, but looking back he could see that he and Helen hadn't stood a chance: their relationship had been a **disaster** waiting to happen. No wonder she'd run off with Eddie Webster. A simpler life had beckoned, with a partner who might actually be there – well, most nights at least.

It had had its moments, though. The lads were a good laugh. One time, towards the end of Lavengro, they'd been working through the night to pull it all together and most of the lads had been taking a nap up in the Sports and Social. Donal had popped out to stretch his legs, but he'd come running back in a few minutes later, laughing his head off. 'Call the police!' he'd said. 'Someone's nicked Barnes Pond!'

Well, everyone had needed a fag break anyway, so they'd all jogged and huffed down Station Road to Barnes Green like schoolboys, lighting up and hawking phlegm into the gutter. And, sure enough, the pond was gone. It had drained overnight, exposing some iron gratings and brickwork structures as well as the inevitable junk: mobile phones, scooters, traffic cones and a couple of Tesco trolleys, as well as some freshwater mussel shells the size of a man's foot. All left high and dry in a large wallow of thick, black mud that now contained less water than your average **bird bath**.

It was early in the day – not long after eight – but there'd been a gang of hi-vis-wearing surveyors already at work. One pair with theodolite and levelling rod gridding the area off and marking the positions of the newly exposed features, while others were out on the mud in their waders, poking at it with long poles. When they came off, Donal had gone over and asked one of them what was going on and he'd said something about how, once upon a time, a lot of Barnes was oyster beds, something about drainage and subsidence and Beverley Brook, and an old pipeline feeding this pond from the

Leg o' Mutton up Lonsdale Road – no, not a pub that Donal had inexplicably missed, but a reservoir – and how there was rumoured to be a plug hidden in this mud somewhere, like a giant-sized bath plug, the only problem being that no one could quite remember exactly where that was, or where the water went from there. But they'd find it, no doubt. 'Can't be that difficult, can it,' he'd said. 'Not exactly searching for the source of the **Nile** here, are we, eh?'

Community jollies over, everyone had got a bit bored, so the lads had wandered back to the station, punched in the code at the front door and – too awake now to go back to sleep – gone back to whatever horrors they'd stepped away from an hour or so before.

You had to be good at compartmentalising in this game. Maybe too good. Because by the end of it you'd have seen the clips – the final selection of evidence – so many times that you didn't even really see the violence anymore, but just knew the filename of the best version of each one, the running order and where it fitted in the case about to be presented.

All of which might have been why, despite his best intentions at this early hour, Rex was still avoiding logging in with 'capital S Shanklin underscore 1985 all one word', or at least putting it off for a while. Working up to it.

Technology had moved on even since the Lavengro days. What was that thing the tech boys loved to talk about? Moore's Law: how processing power doubled every two years in relation to size or whatever it was. You didn't want to grill them too closely about it or they'd start ranting about CPUs and infinite numbers of transistors. And that was angels-on-the-head-of-a-pin territory. But roughly speaking, yes, they'd concede there was a general trend towards miniaturisation. It wasn't rocket science, or theology. If you wanted proof, you only had to look at the old mothballed edit suites they'd had at Holborn. A couple of rooms packed from floor to ceiling with rack systems and big CRT monitors, edit suites daisy-chaining obsolete analogue VTRs that had only been got rid of in the 2002 refurb, but had sat there gathering dust until then. Roy had been the video technician in those days. Rest in peace. He was a big guy. Even in uniform he looked like a farmer. He was the kind of bloke who in days gone by might have been a blacksmith. He had an eye for how things ran, and a way with wires. Give him half an hour and a screwdriver and he'd get anything working again. Christ, he could smoke too. It had been a different age. The sheer size of those U-matic video cassettes, boxes of them, the waste of materials. You used to need a van to hide a camera in, and whole libraries of tapes for just a single operation. And on top of that there were the routines and protocols, the paperwork and infrastructure that size created: packing the boxes of numbered tapes off to storage in the warehouse up by the canal in Islington, yet all told still only a fraction of the capacity or processing power of your average mobile phone today. A perk of the job back then was to have to drive the archive boxes up there and get 'stuck in traffic, Sarge'. Rex remembered being on one such delivery and looking out of the window to see a couple of fishermen skinning up on the towpath below, their roach poles stretched out over the still water; watching and waiting.

It was the same difference, really.

How many warehouses' worth of video footage would be equivalent to, contained on, just these couple of dozen hard drives that were stacked up on DS Eddie Webster's desk right now? Two weeks a pop, times that by a couple of years, and it would be a fair few.

It was before Rex's time, but he knew that Tabitha Churchill had come into the Met as a graduate of the Computer Science Tripos at Cambridge. An **avid** proponent of the applications of emerging technology in policing, Churchill was still celebrated in certain geeky police engineering and 'policy wonk' circles for taking a leading role – early in her career, so probably mid-eighties? – in the formation of TARC – the Technology and Research Committee, later simply the IT Committee. That would have taken some doing for anyone, let alone a woman, in those sexist 'There, there, love' days. It was well known now, how she'd always **champion** the new and try to keep the Met at the **vanguard** of policing. And she'd been correct. IT was now ubiquitous. It wasn't just an 'add-on' after all. It wasn't simply a single database on one un-networked PC in each station any longer, with documents printing out onto green-striped concertina paper with perforated edges, but an integral part of every committee and every aspect of police working whether internal or public-facing, from Terrorism to Traffic.

These days you didn't need a **degree** in order to point and click, but there was a limit to the amount of information that a single viewer could reliably process. In the **new society** this would probably be a job for artificial intelligence and facial recognition software. The thinking was that such **ends** would justify the means, and Churchill herself had been joint lead on the facial recognition pilots that had been running in the Met for several years now. But in the meantime it was still wholly dependent upon a human touch. Meaning there was no alternative but for officers to watch every second of every recording.

Postponing the inevitable log-in, and just for starters, Rex began flicking through the pages of the lined pad next to Webster's phone. This was partly a wilful distraction, but he was also thinking that it might be useful to see the unprocessed thoughts, the telephone notes and the random raw materials, the list of assets with dates and time codes, key words and crossings-out, rather than the raw video, or even the end product: the ring-binder volumes of statements and reports and screen grabs. It was the phone notes that caught his eye, because they all followed a similar protocol: date, time, number, initials and a few words, all accompanied by heavy doodles, usually of three-dimensional figures – a cube, a pyramid, a sphere – drawn and overdrawn. It would be simple enough to cross-reference these calls against Webster's detailed log. Who – other than Dicky Sharp – had he been talking to the most? Rex was looking for anything that might give him a shortcut or a way in. If he was going to follow his instincts, like Lollo had said, then he needed some kind of search criteria. An appetiser, if you could call it that, something to sharpen the senses. As starters went, Webster's desk pad was hardly a plate of **petit fours**, but if Rex knew one thing, it was that people were generally **honest** when they doodled.

18: Greffoir (Graft knife)

Rex watched Cliff Heath sprinkle some red *copra idli* – dried coconut chutney powder – onto the shard of popadom he held in his left hand. Heath then took a teaspoonful of mint yogurt, which he proceeded to drag along the toasted wafer's bubbled and bumpy surface, where it absorbed some of the red colouring of the coconut powder. It was like watching an artist at work. Heath regarded for a moment the way that the red colouring leached into the yogurt, then carefully bit it off and ate it.

'You've got to feed the **inner man**, Rex!' he said, before repeating the process. 'You tried this? Amazing!'

'Don't you have curry houses in Oxford, Cliff?'

'We've got some good ones, but nothing like this. Me and Jethro used to come here in the eighties. **Once** you've had the best, eh.'

Thanks to DI Cliff Heath, the Gold Support Group meeting had been more useful than it had at first seemed. They'd convened in the tenth-floor conference room as per usual, and when Rex had arrived people were queueing to pour themselves coffees from the **gallon** or two that Building Services had provided in the usual pump-action beverage dispensers. Before the cuts, a morning meeting at such a senior level might have warranted pastries. Now, such things were down to the individual, but someone had evidently dug into their pocket on the way in and bought a packet of supermarket-own-brand chocolate digestives.

The blinds were drawn, and one of them was rattling in the breeze from an open window. Rex caught the eye of Jane Milligan from Senior Management Team, very much *not* yet on maternity leave, as she lowered herself carefully into one of the chairs nearest the door.

'Just in case,' she said with a wink.

'When's it due?' Rex asked.

She looked at her watch.

Funny.

'No,' she said, 'only kidding. Got three weeks yet.'

There was no sign of Lollo – he'd probably arrive with Tabitha Churchill after their pre-meet – but that was Simon Rose, the Police Federation rep, chatting with Evelyn Gummer. They were sharing a joke about the piss-up after the National Custody Awards, from the sound of it.

Tommy Bee, one of the FLOs – Family Liaison Officers – present, was telling FLO Coordinator Winston Edwards about his new **Tanglewood** acoustic bass. Before joining the police, Tommy had been a bandsman in the Household Cavalry, a trumpeter, and he still gigged occasionally when shifts allowed it. He was in a three-piece folk band, a proper one. **Opus Peacock**, they were called. They'd performed at the Christmas party a couple of years back, and they were pretty good. Did a few folk standards: 'John Henry', and 'Follow the Drinking Gourd', plus a couple of crossover numbers like 'La Bamba' and 'Anarchy in the UK' – for the oldsters – and some Flanders and Swann track about the **Beeching** cuts. That had got a few **hoots** of laughter; anything to do with cuts. It had to be said that having a musician in the ranks made a change from your usual **staid** copper. Rex had heard tell that Opus Peacock had once auditioned for *Britain's Got Talent* but hadn't made it through to the actual televised heats.

Tommy was one of five FLOs on Operation Kayak, each of them with an allocation of up to a dozen 'families' – the term covered anything from an individual to a huge extended family grouping, you could never tell. Tommy and Winston were already working with their full allocation; the other three were being briefed, and liaising with the relevant local authority child protection teams ready to work with a further thirty or so victims once the warrants had been delivered. It was a stressful job, keeping track of all those conversations, keeping every scrap of paper, typing it all up, telling victims and their families what they needed to know, yet withholding plenty that they might have wanted to hear. You had to stick to your guns, **step** carefully, or they'd **drag** you into one family **saga** after another, never mind one-to-one relationships that could easily cross the line.

The role led to all kinds of emotional fallout, both during and after the event.

Not something Rex had ever really fancied.

It was a job that you really had to want to do, but hats off to them, because he knew from colleagues who had chosen or been steered into that particular career path that it was all too easy to get too attached, especially at stressful times in their own lives.

It was difficult to remember sometimes that the FLOs' primary function was still investigative and not pastoral, however considerate and carefully planned your 'exit strategy' might need to be; and however fine-tuned your emotional **literacy** or empathic your scripts and behaviours.

Winston had once confided to Rex – strictly on the need-to-know, line-of-duty basis – that Tommy was 'in recovery'. Aside from the alcoholism which was now, hopefully, under control – whisky on the breath in morning meetings now a thing of the past – Tommy's problem was that he could be too empathetic. He tended to over-identify with the victims of crime. This was just, Winston had said, by way of letting Rex know, confidentially, that Tommy occasionally needed to go *to meetings*, at any number of nearby venues depending on the day and time. Well, meetings were part of everybody's job. But *meetings*? 'Where's the nearest *meeting*?' someone might say. Or, 'I've got to find *a meeting*.' And Rex had known exactly what kind of meeting Winston meant.

It was no wonder Tommy Bee liked to wind down after work with a bit of a sing-song – and good luck to the bloke.

Rex had recognised Detective Inspector Clifford Heath immediately. He'd definitely seen him around once or twice, and Lollo wasn't wrong about the syrup either. It *was* terrible: too dark – almost blue-black – and it stuck out at the back like wigs always do. It was also weirdly shiny, as if made of some strange acrylic material. And yet presumably he thought it looked good.

Cliff and Lollo went way back, apparently. Far enough that the Detective Chief Inspector was allowed to crack the other joke that everyone else in the world had to make a continual effort to avoid: '**Heathcliff!**' he exclaimed as he shut the door behind him. 'It's me! Cathy!'

'Jethro!' said Cliff. 'Looking good.'

Once everyone was seated, Chief Superintendent Tabitha Churchill and Frances, her PA – Frankie for short – had come in right on cue. 'For God's sake, will someone open those bloody blinds,' she said immediately. 'Bugger protocol, let's have a bit of light in here.'

Rex did the honours, coaxing the blinds up while Frankie got herself set up, laptop at the ready to do the minutes, then poured herself and her boss a glass of water each from one of the jugs on the table.

'Right, then,' said Churchill, before **briefly** going through the formalities, cantering through and agreeing the minutes of the last meeting and confirming that there was no change to the terms of reference. 'Apologies from Ed Webster, I gather,' she continued. 'Sorry to hear that, and I understand Jethro's going to give the Investigation Update – that right? – and DS Rex King, who I think most of you know, is here observing in DS Webster's absence. Welcome, Rex.

'But looking at the agenda,' she went on, 'I'd suggest that we roll the Investigation Update and Critical Issues into one – can you make a note, Frances? – since that's all within Jethro's purview.'

And once everyone had reported back on their various respective actions from the previous meeting, that was precisely what happened. Lollo reconfirmed the bad news, and drew their attention to the summary report that CPS evidential advisory had thrown back. It was in the file of papers that everyone had been given, each in its own transparent plastic **sheath**. He told colleagues that Rex had been brought in to cover DS Webster's position as SIO for the time being, and that the team would now be proceeding on the basis that Dicky Sharp had never existed, seeing if, in the first instance, that might help them to make a broader case. He'd welcome any feedback or suggestions.

Heath stepped in first with a bit of a pep talk, urging them to look again at the evidence and how it was framed. 'It's all in here,' he said, slapping a hand down on the pile of papers. 'Not to be a pedant, but it's "when", not "if". The **goal-post** has not shifted one iota – just the way you get there. So stick to your guns. Fifty-odd victims might sound like a lot, but, believe me, it's not. That means you've caught this gang early. You can still nip it in the bud if you don't fuck it up.'

Winston Edwards agreed with Heath's assessment. 'If we went back to the families now,' he said, 'and told them we couldn't proceed, after everything they've been through, I promise you they'd go ballistic. They'd think it was a **smoke-screen,** that we were covering something up. We'd lose their trust just like that.'

'Thinking aloud here if I may, Tabitha,' said Cliff Heath, 'and I don't want to teach anybody's grandmother to suck eggs, but what I'd suggest, *sans* Dicky Sharp, is a bit more focus.'

Lollo caught Rex's eye. He pointed at the paper on the table in front of him, and mimed the action of writing. The meaning was clear: we're not waiting for the minutes on this one. Rex picked up the pencil and started taking notes.

'Number one,' said Heath, 'keep that warrant delivery date on a heavy pencil, so everything's in place and you don't have to start from scratch lining up arrest teams, FLOs and custody capacity all over again. Number two: task your top officer to go back through and find the "best bits" for each individual: one incident that's got (a) a watertight facial ID, (b) the clearest depiction of one or more offences, (c) where the victim's known to us and (d) has given a statement, and (e) where it can be tied in to Dicky Sharp's diary or one of his statements. DNA would be an obvious bonus. Line up your second tier where the victim's identified but not yet statemented, and so on. Tick, tick, tick – shouldn't take the team too long to filter those out. Get that back to CPS this week and suggest in light of their feedback that we arrest and charge each individual based on just those tier-one offences in the first instance. They all present enough risk that you can press for remand, to give you time to process the second tier and put the other charges together. Have Winston's team ready to move in the minute the warrants have been delivered. You'll keep all the other however-many offences it is in reserve for now, ideally to add them to the charges. Or tell CPS that you're thinking of asking for the other – what? few thousand? – offences simply to be taken into consideration. That'll wind them up.'

Heath got a laugh, but he was right.

Lollo wrote something down on the sheet of paper in front of him and held it up so that Rex could see it: 'Put Binder Singh on that.'

Rex nodded.

Then Lollo wrote something else and held it up again: 'NOW!'

'Clifford,' said Churchill, looking at where Frankie had written a note on her print-out of the agenda. 'You wanted to add something, I believe. On a related matter.'

'Yes. Thank you, Tabitha. One other piece of advice,' said Heath. 'And I'll give you this for free. And this applies to all of you, no exceptions. One thing we learned in Oxfordshire, and we learned it the hard way, because no one sat us down and said what I'm about to say to you – but you've got to have a means of relaxing. Because if you don't, it can mess you up, working on a case like this, let me tell you. Because it can get in your head, an investigation of this nature. People have breakdowns over less, believe me. And where you are now, we've been there – with bells on. Now, me, I'm lucky, I have transcendental meditation...' Heath paused to allow a slight titter to go around the room at the idea of big old Clifford Heath and his syrup in the lotus position going 'Om'.

'Listen,' he said, 'it works for me. Find what works for you.' Heath looked slowly around the room, making eye contact with everyone at the table. 'And I want it added to the agenda for the next GS, okay? Some of you think I'm joking, but I'm not. Under a heading: "Team well-being" or something.' He looked at Frankie: 'That make sense?'

Frankie nodded.

While Cliff Heath was talking, Rex had got busy with his phone; first off, a quick email to brief Binder Singh – 'Urgent: A1 Kayak' in the subject line. Knowing Singh, he'd have dropped whatever he was doing and started immediately.

Tabitha Churchill moved on down the agenda. First came the families update, which took half an hour on its own, then community and partner agencies, resources update, a quick overview of media strategy from Evelyn Gummer, and a round-up of any takeaways from the Ethical Group.

Lollo passed a note to Rex, then turned and nodded to Churchill. He was expected at St James's Park; the car was waiting.

Rex looked discreetly at the note, then pocketed it.

Can't take it any more LOL

Sly old bugger.

Rex's phone beeped. It was a text from Singh: 'Message understood. On it, Skip.'

And eventually, thankfully, since there were no AOBs, the Gold Support Group meeting drew to a close. That was it and all about it, as Rex's mother had used to say.

'I've got an urgent appointment with Ravi Shankar,' Cliff Heath had announced over the scraping of chairs. 'Curry and a debrief. Who's in?'

Rex was the only taker. 'Let's stroll,' he suggested, steering Heath away from the lift.

It was sunny outside. Bright, but a bit fresher than it had been.

'Thanks for that,' said Rex. 'Cutting to the chase like that. I've put our best DC on the data-crunching already: Binder Singh. He knows the material. He reckons he'll have it done in a day or so, tops.'

'No problem,' said Heath, stepping around an old filing cabinet, a scuffed and grubby white-painted MDF plinth and a sagging **esparto** laundry basket that someone had left on the pavement for collection. 'I always felt that they were over-reliant on that one witness. But looking at our experiences with Operation Bullfinch, I can tell you a sole witness is always an accident waiting to happen. Too good to be true. And here? Relying on some charismatic villain who's had a crisis of conscience? For goodness' sake. Geezers like Dicky Sharp don't have consciences. More like the old grafts were no longer working, and he was trying to cash in what he knew before being put out of his misery. To be honest, Rex, I'm surprised that Jethro let DS Webster get away with that. From where I'm sitting, Webster seemed a bit lost, like a rabbit in the headlights, reluctant to move on from intelligence-gathering mode and make the leap; too much information and not enough strategy. I can't see what was holding him back. Any idea?'

Rex shook his head.

'It's understandable,' Heath continued, 'to be a bit daunted by the sheer scale of the operation. But you've got them all bang to rights many times over, no question. I think, if anything, Sharp was a distraction, to be honest.'

'Never look a gift horse in the mouth, I suppose they thought,' said Rex. 'Put him on the stand and that'd be it: job done. I can see the attraction.'

'Well, if someone gave you the keys to a rusty **Allegro**,' said Cliff, stretching the metaphor, 'would you take it? No. You wouldn't need to look under the **hood** to know it was a dog.'

The waiter at the Ravi Shankar Bhel Poori showed them to a table and brought them menus.

'Been here before?' asked Cliff.

'Yeah. Love it,' said Rex. 'I live just down the way, so we used to come all the time.'

'I've been coming here must be thirty years,' said Cliff. 'This is London to me. You can keep your Fortnum's. I always used to get the same: number thirty-five, number thirty-nine with lemon rice and roti, and chutney on the side, but I think—' Cliff explored the menu. 'No, look, they've changed the numbers,' he said. 'Bhindi bhaji's number thirty-eight. What about you?'

'I'm going for the buffet lunch, Cliff. Bit of everything. You can't say fairer than that.'

'Delicious. But you're a braver man than me.'

'How so?'

'I never know when to stop. They'd have to kick me out at closing time, prise my fingers off the potato pooris. At least this way' – he leaned back and patted his stomach – 'I can *try* and control the old intake.'

The waiter came for their order.

'Buffet for me, thanks,' said Rex, nodding in the general direction of the serving dishes that were laden with all manner of bhajis, koftas, vegetable specials, sauces. When Rex said a bit of everything, he meant it.

'I'll have popadoms to start, bhindi bhaji, daal, lemon rice, roti,' said Cliff, pointing at each invisible dish as if it were in front of him, 'with chutneys on the side. And a salted lassi. Please. I'll order pudding later.' He turned to Rex. 'Barfi here is amazing.'

'Yes, salted lassi for me, too,' said Rex. 'Barfi? Never had that. I usually go for the jalebi. What's it like?'

'Like a spicy **fudge**,' said Heath. As the waiter turned away, he leaned over conspiratorially: 'Hey, you know what they used to say about Jethro back in the day?'

'No?'

'A real hard nut,' said Heath. 'You can imagine. And chippy with it. It got him into trouble more than once.'

'I'm all ears, Cliff,' said Rex. He was going to enjoy this.

Once Cliff's food arrived, and Rex had returned from the buffet, the two of them observed an almost silent half-hour ritual of epicureanism and thanksgiving, punctuated only by the occasional grunt as one of them would shake his head in appreciation and point silently at something on his plate, but Rex was also working, pondering the delights of the Gold Support Group meeting; turning it all over. He might have had a lot on his mind, but he could still follow his instincts.

Then he remembered something.

Before he went back for thirds, Rex said, 'Thanks, Cliff, actually that's really helpful.'

'Delighted to hear it,' said Heath, wiping the daal from his plate with the last piece of roti. 'Not sure what I've done, but happy I could help.'

19: Rose (Rose)

It was only a ten- or fifteen-minute walk back to the station, but Rex decided to take the scenic route, ducking down by the Bartlett School and the Bloomsbury Theatre. The tea hut in Gordon Square was open because of the warm weather, and one of the little tables was free so Rex stopped for a quick coffee. He had plenty to think about – not least now that he had a way in to Webster's notes – but he was still chuckling about everything Cliff Heath had told him.

Lollo had been right: old Heathy was a good bloke – and a quite a raconteur. They were well-practised anecdotes, of course, honed at countless dinners and dos over the years. But some of the scrapes that he and Lollo had got into in the South Yorkshire force in the 1980s didn't bear thinking about. Talk about hair-raising. You wouldn't get away with crap like that now. They'd been lucky, Cliff reckoned, to have had an Inspector who could see some potential and saved their bacon on one or two occasions; smoothed the waters. Not so different, Rex supposed, from what Lollo had done for him and Webster.

'I didn't realise you and Lollo went back that far,' said Rex. 'You haven't got the—'

'Accent?' said Heath. 'No, well, I was born in Luton. Didn't go to Sheffield until I was ten. My mum was a nurse. We moved when she got a staff nurse job at the Royal Hallamshire.'

Heath had been regaling Rex with stories about the two of them going down to Aldershot on a recce during the Miners' Strike.

'Home of the British Army,' as everyone always said.

Everyone but Rex.

If anyone mentioned Aldershot to him, he'd just shake his head and say, 'You don't want to know.'

Cliff Heath was more garrulous on the subject – at least the parts that weren't covered by the Official Secrets Act. 'Paras were still there in those days,' he said. 'Don't know about when you were there. Gone now, I gather.'

'Well, they were just clearing out,' said Rex. 'And I certainly helped one or two on their way.'

'One thing I do know, there was a lot of hanging about on that job,' said Heath. 'More for paperwork than anything else. It was just simple inter-agency work – procurement, you know, but hush-hush, of course – but everything took ten times as long to do in 1985. You could be waiting days for something to be typed, or for one single form to be countersigned and travel back through the internal mail. On top of that we were liaising with the Surrey and Hampshire forces, and those lads were all hoovering up as much overtime as they could get. It was like a holiday for them. They were staying in the same barracks as us, and halls of residence or whatever. So you'd hear them getting up for reveille at two or three in the morning, laughing and joking, then breakfast in the NAAFI and piling in coaches to go up the M1 on Police Support work. Jethro and me'd be left to hold the fort. We used to kill time playing football with all-comers on the old Polo Fields on the Farnborough Road, and the Paras'd be doing training jumps at eight hundred feet from an old barrage balloon. Rather them than me. I say football, just passing and heading. Jethro had a preference for the oval ball, of course.'

'Pimpled ball these days,' said Rex.

'Oh, I don't doubt it, but in those days he was a rugby man and he had the physique to go with it. Heavyset chap, he was, and couldn't dance for toffee. Not light on his feet like me. He clattered me once and broke a rib, and we were only having a kickabout. But I got off lightly. Luckily for us the chief mechanic in Camberley was already on a disciplinary and subject of an internal investigation or Jethro would have been out.'

How did Cliff's Camberley story go? One of the lads in the police garage, the chief mechanic – arrogant as they come – had started taking the mick, trying to get a rise out of the Yorkshire boys: calling Lawrence a northern get, mouthing off about him being a traitor to Yorkshiremen, and was he happy that Surrey and Hampshire lads were getting overtime to kick shit out of his people and fuck their women, and why wasn't he up there defending 'em, and what was he, a scab?'

'Fuck's sake,' Rex said. 'What did Lollo do?'

'Excuse my French, but he kicked seven shades of shit out of the bloke without breaking a sweat. You can imagine. In those days it'd be like being punched by a brick wall. They'd probably have thrown the book at Jethro if the mechanic hadn't already been under investigation. As it was, it was him that got arrested, for theft on the job – some long-running scam involving recommissioned tyres and forged certificates or something, God knows – convicted too, or so I heard. Jethro just got a ticking off, jammy bastard, largely thanks to old Tommy Orwell, our Inspector, may he rest in peace.'

'Sorry to hear it,' said Rex.

'Thanks. It's a few years ago now. But he'd left the force long since – turfed out for taking money from the tabloids for Hillsborough tittle-tattle. And just as well, if you ask me. No disrespect. He was a nice enough chap, Tommy, but a bit old-fashioned. He wouldn't have been able to hack it in today's force, if he were still alive. Couldn't keep his hands to himself. One or two chickens would have come home to roost, if you get my drift.'

'Say no more,' said Rex.

'Look, we both got these done in Aldershot.' Heath was rolling up his sleeve. 'The tattooist was a chap called Jeff Jaguar. He had a place out the back of the amusement arcade on the high street, if you know it.'

On Heath's tricep there was a thickly lined tattoo, bluish with age: not quite a skull and crossbones, but a skull in a miner's helmet over a crossed pickaxe and shovel, above a scrolling banner on which was written the legend 'The A-Team'.

'What's that, then?' said Rex.

'Most blokes had "A.S.P.O.M.",' said Heath. 'They'd say it stood for "Anti Strike Police, Operation Miner", if anyone asked. Or they'd say the "A.S.P." bit stands for "Avon and Somerset Police", but it really stands for "Arthur Scargill Paid Our Mortgage". But we called ourselves "The A-Team", so that's what we put. Jethro's got the same, only up here.' Heath patted his left shoulder. 'And with a white rose of Yorkshire on top. Ask him, he'd show you.'

'I will,' said Rex.

'For goodness' sake,' said Heath, shaking his head. 'You don't call Jethro Lawrence a scab if you know what's good for you. Talk about a red rag to a bull. Especially after what happened to his father.'

20: Chêne (Oak)

'See **yonder** door,' said Lollo firmly. 'I want you to turn around and go back out through it right this fucking second, Detective Sergeant. And then I want you to go straight home to your wife and family, and I want you to fucking well stay there until I call for you, son. Understood?'

DS Eddie Webster made to speak, but Lollo cut him off: 'Shut it, Webster. Don't fucking **tempt** me. Go!'

Not usually a **violent** man, the beaten Webster turned and limped away. A minute or so later a door slammed somewhere in the building, but otherwise the sixth floor was quiet once again. At five o'clock on a Tuesday morning, it was early enough that the cleaners weren't here yet. It was still dark outside, and apart from the lights in DCI Jethro Lawrence's office, and Rex's laptop screen, only one or two desk lamps were on.

Rex and Lollo just stood there for a second or two until – excitement now over – Rex bent to pick up the swivel chair and set it back on its wheels.

'What the fuck were that?' said Lollo, shaking his head. But before Rex could answer, he added, 'And don't tell me you don't know, Kingsy. I wasn't born fucking yesterday.'

Rex hadn't yet had a chance to tell Lollo about the whole business with Jennifer and Helen, but given that Detective Sergeant Edward Webster had just stormed into the office effing and jeffing and taken a swing at him in front of the Detective Chief Inspector, Rex realised he was going to have to fill him in. Thank Christ the rest of the team weren't here, or neither of them would ever hear the last of it.

'Long-short,' said Rex, 'it's all gone a bit **topsy-turvy**. He just found out that Jennifer – his oldest – isn't his.'

'You're fucking kidding me,' said Lollo. 'And you knew this.'

'Only just found out myself,' said Rex, bending the truth slightly. 'Who's the—'

'...'

'Oh, don't tell me. You? What is it with you two, eh?'

'It was a long time ago, sir.'

'For fuck's sake, Kingsy. Why didn't you fucking say? You know better than that. If I know about sommat, I can manage it. But not if I'm blindsided and it blows up in our faces I can't.'

'Yes, I know, sir. Sorry, sir.'

'One stupid twat on the team I can handle. But two?'

Lollo was seething, so Rex said nothing for a minute or so.

Then: 'To be fair, I did book a one-to-one,' he said, setting Lollo straight on that at least.

'Oh aye, you did that.'

'Can we keep it between us for a bit, though?' said Rex. 'Till things calm down.'

'And that'll be when?'

It was a rhetorical question.

He had a point.

Prior to his going off sick, and before this latest outburst, Detective Sergeant Edward Webster might have flattered himself that, as Senior Investigating Officer, he was indispensable to Serious Crime in general and Operation Kayak in particular, but after this exhibition DS Rex King was wondering – and not for the first time – whether Webster hadn't always been a bit of a liability. Right now, he was about as useful as a Hallowe'en **pumpkin** on November the first. And after what had just happened, if Rex decided to take it further and make this a disciplinary issue, you could probably argue that Webster was **unfit** to have a leadership role at all.

On the other hand, maybe it was the strain of the job. It was a lot of responsibility, after all. And perhaps, on top of everything else, Webster was simply worried that Operation Kayak might **turn turtle** on his watch.

It had already been a long day and a longer night. Rex had been looking forward to getting finished here and going round the corner for a quick couple of hours' kip at home. What was it that Heath had said in the Gold Support meeting? Something about how the goal-posts hadn't shifted one **iota**, it was just how they'd get there that had changed; which had got an enthusiastic '**Hear, hear**' from Winston Edwards.

Both men were right, of course, and Cliff Heath was a diamond.

There were always those in the police who thought it took a **pike** to catch a **trout**, but Rex favoured the gentler, more patient and methodical approach advocated by Heath.

It was abundantly clear that if they couldn't now build the case around Dicky Sharp – knowledge drawn from his unique vantage point of two years' **gainful** on night security at the **Lido** Cars minicab office in Romford – then they'd have to spread the load a bit, and do it with documentation and paperwork.

Not impossible, just more of a slog, and ultimately harder to convey the story persuasively to a jury.

He could understand why Webster would have gone for what looked like the easy win.

But to Rex, Cliff Heath's suggestion seemed a welcome **outbreak** of common sense. And since Heath had held a senior position in the notorious Operation Bullfinch, and taken that all the way to multiple high-profile convictions, you had to respect that his opinion was hard won.

But it was something else Heath had said that had nagged slightly at Rex, and so as soon as he'd got back to the office, almost before he'd sat down, Rex had begun leafing back through Webster's desk log until he found the pages he wanted: manual notes made for each hard drive, of the time-signatures of the various assets, cross-referenced with serial numbers, locations and other relevant data needed to complete a DEF11, the Digital Evidence Form that accompanied each hard drive in the evidence store. He took scans of the several pages of notes on his phone, and sent them to the nearest printer. He was glad they'd had a good lunch because, even if he just checked through a random sample, Rex could see that he'd likely be here a while. He plugged his laptop in to the docking station and – capital S Shanklin underscore 1985 all one word – logged in to the closed drive, then clicked his way through to the folder marked 'Surveillance Video'. He opened the first folder, then found the corresponding hard drive, bagged up with its DEF11, from the archive boxes on Webster's desk, and began to compare them line for line, ticking the numbers off on his own copy.

This whole business with Jen was a facer, and – perhaps obviously – it was making Rex think more about his own parents, both long dead. Right now, opening up video files in Windows Media Player, he couldn't help thinking how mystified his mum would be by the contemporary world of smartphones and computers. Just getting a record player had been a major event in their household, and she'd struggled with the simplest VCR. He remembered once hearing a loud burst of white **noise** from the living room of their red-brick semi on Spenser Avenue and finding her sitting in front of the telly in tears of exasperation, the screen full of static. All she'd been trying to do was watch a video. His more mechanically minded father would always come to the rescue if he was at home.

'Charles,' she would say, with her slight West Country **burr**, 'are you busy?'

'Coming, love.'

Rex's father would appear from the garage, and slowly wash his hands with green gunk from the pot of Swarfega that he kept under the sink. Then he'd come and find her and say, 'What is it, Gerry, my love?'

Rex remembered the signed photo of the dapper British racing driver Mike Hawthorn that had been hung with pride in their kitchen. Hawthorn was the Lewis Hamilton of his day. In the photo, Hawthorn was posing with another champion, Juan Manuel **Fangio**, on the podium of the 1957 German Grand Prix at the Nürburgring, the year before Hawthorn became World Champion. In the young King's mind, the racing driver had become inextricably linked with the coincidentally named Hawthorn Avenue around the corner from their home on the Burnthouse Lane Estate, and Hawthorn's fatal car accident on the Guildford bypass forever entangled with that line from Bret Harte's poem on the death of Charles Dickens that they'd studied for O-level English literature at Hele's – 'And on that grave where English oak and holly / And laurel wreaths **entwine**…'

But Rex's father had actually known and had a chance to **befriend** Hawthorn. After Charles King had completed his national service at REME, the Royal Electrical and Mechanical Engineers in Farnborough, and before he and Geraldine had moved down to **Exeter** to be closer to her parents, he'd worked for a couple of years, first as a mechanic and finally as parts manager, in local hero Hawthorn's Tourist Trophy garage in Farnham.

It had meant a lot to them. 'Mike Hawthorn taught your dad to tie a bowtie,' was something that his mother used to say every Christmas; the one day in the year that Charles would wear one.

Rex got into the rhythm of the task, working down the list, checking serial numbers and comparing the clips in the Kayak drive with those listed on the DEF11s – checking the time-signatures that ticked away on the bottom of the screen with those listed. He didn't actually have to watch the assets, thank Christ. Once he'd checked the start time and ticked it off, he'd move the indicator all the way along the progress bar to the last few seconds. It was simple enough work, but you had to concentrate. This wasn't a job he wanted to still be doing in a couple of days' time, so he ploughed on. There were a few errors in Webster's notes, but King himself was getting a bit number-blind himself, so it wasn't surprising if a couple of time-signatures contained transpositions. One serial number had been crossed out and then noted correctly. One hard drive had failed, the whole thing was blank, perhaps from a formatting error or a power outage – it happened – but other than that, everything tallied.

In a funny sort of way, Rex quite enjoyed the monotony of the task, ticking off the time-signatures one by one. But after a few hours of this he realised that he was the only one left in the office. He took the chance to stretch his legs, went to the kitchen and put a jug of coffee on, then remembered the couple of chocolate digestives he'd wrapped in a napkin and pocketed at Gold Support Group. After that, he got so absorbed in the task once again that he didn't notice Lollo coming in, but looking up at around 4 a.m. he noticed that the Detective Chief Inspector's office lights were on, so shouted over, 'Alright, sir. There's fresh coffee in the jug.'

'How was old Heathcliff?' came the shout back.

'Yeah, good. He's quite a character.'

'Aye, him and his fucking curries. I thought you and Cliffy'd get on,' said Lollo. 'He's one of the good guys. We go way back.'

'Yeah, he told me,' said Rex, putting his head down and cracking on.

An hour or so after that was when Webster had turned up.

Rex heard the lift doors open and a stilted 'female' voice saying, 'Sixth floor. Doors opening.' The robotic audio output was followed by a genuine human shout: 'Oi! King, you bastard!'

Given recent events, Rex wasn't particularly surprised.

It had been bound to happen sooner or later, but that didn't mean he just had to sit there and take it.

As Webster barrelled over, fists balled and ready, Rex stood up and stepped sideways to put the desk between them. 'Ed,' he said, remembering some t'ai chi moves and assuming a simple bow stance so that he'd be able to absorb Webster's momentum if he got that close. 'Let's talk about it.'

'I'll give you fucking "talk about it",' said Webster, shoving the swivel chair out of the way and actually taking a swing at Rex before abruptly stopping short and doubling over in pain – 'Fuck!' – as he caught his upper inner thigh on the corner of his own desk.

Rex inwardly winced, and relaxed his posture slightly. Typical Webbo, to shoot himself in the foot like that, the clumsy twat.

That was when Lollo intervened – '*DE*-tective Sergeant!' – and ordered Webster home.

Rex found it a bit of a relief, explaining everything to Lollo: how Jennifer had found out she was Rex's daughter and not Webster's, the genealogy project, her turning up on his doorstep, the whole sorry mess. And the Detective Chief Inspector's response was more generous than Rex had expected.

'Impressive detective work. Takes after her dad, then,' he said. 'The smart one, anyroad.' Then: 'D'you reckon that's it, that's what's been bugging Webbo? Sounds like it could be. If he's going to actually come in and have it out with you like that.'

'Yeah, maybe,' said Rex. 'You've got to feel for the guy. His whole world's just fallen apart.'

'Aye, cuckolded. No getting around that one. Listen, Kingsy, I'm just going for a quick **tom-tit**, then let's bring our catch-up forward, right? Since we're here, like. Half an hour? Then you can fuck off home.'

'Right you are, sir,' said Rex, pulling up his chair and getting back to the job in hand. 'I'm nearly done.'

But something about what had just happened with DS Eddie Webster wasn't quite right.

It wasn't a hunch, or even a thought. It was one of those visceral moments when you suddenly know something and feel it with every bone in your body. Like a shiver that hits you from **head to foot**.

Like when everything in an investigation gets turned **upside down** in a sudden recalibration of the facts.

What if the business with Jen wasn't the reason for Webster's stress?

And was there some **ulterior** motive for his appearing in the office at five o'clock in the morning?

For a start, there was no way that Webster had come in specially to have a pop at Rex, because Rex wouldn't usually be here either.

And if he'd called in asking, any of the EDOs would definitely have let Rex know.

So what had he come in for?

He didn't have his laptop with him, so he wasn't coming back to work after his few days off.

Had he come to pick something up?

Something on his desk?

There was only the usual desk furniture: laptop dock, Anglepoise lamp, and vestigial wire in- and out-trays. There was the Detective Sergeant's notebook, the toaster – a two-bay 'Wavlink' HD docking station – and on a trolley next to his desk the three archive boxes of drives, all bagged and tagged and ready to go back to the evidence store; nothing unusual.

What had Webster been after?

Rex opened the desk drawer. It was filled with sedimentary layers of old stationery, scissors, stapler, empty plastic Sellotape dispenser; non-urgent communiqués from HR, the Police Federation and the pension administrators; one or two overly affectionate old Christmas cards from female colleagues that he obviously hadn't dared take home; charity flyers, promotional teabag samples and other street giveaways; and a used Amazon Jiffy bag, paperback-sized, with – from the weight of it – a book inside. And under all of that the usual mulch of dust and dirt, receipts all grimy and scrumpled, paperclips, leaky biros, little pink or yellow dry-cleaning tabs still on their safety pins, stationery tags, an unused condom in its wrapper, 1 and 2p pieces, and some fluff-stuck Post-its.

Nothing.

Hang on.

As he shuffled back through the various bits of office ephemera, Rex wondered what Webster might have ordered from Amazon. At second glance it felt too rigid to be a book – no give. Perhaps it was a DVD or Blu-ray, a computer game for the girls.

There was a small red plastic ruler at the front of the drawer, the kind you used to get in a school geometry set, and Rex used this and a pencil – force of habit – to poke and prise open the Jiffy so he could peer inside without touching it or removing it from the drawer.

No.

Not a book, or a game or a DVD.

It was a standard-issue, solid-state, 1TB hard drive.

The kind that would slot into a high-performance Timespace DVRX Series CCTV recorder unit.

Not what Rex had been expecting at all, but the slight buzz of vindication soon gave way to a crushing disappointment in his colleague. Whether this hard drive and its contents were intended for what might euphemistically be called 'personal use', or to sell on, who could say. Rex had seen both in the past, and – scarcely believable though it was – he was aware that there was a ready market for this kind of material. He looked back at his notes and realised that he knew or could guess exactly what the serial number on the hard drive would be.

It was still legible there in the desk log too, under Webster's crossing-out.

21: Fougère (Fern)

Rex made his way back to work, still feeling a little the worse for wear after pulling the all-nighter, coupled with the general excitement and the adrenaline, but it had been worth it. When he'd left the station a few hours earlier and walked around the corner to the flat for a few hours' kip, it had still been dark, and a **crescent** moon had been hanging above the rooftops of Theobalds Road to the south. Now he found himself in the lunchtime rush, dodging oncomers. He thought about going to try that **lovat**-green tweed jacket on again, the one that Susan had pointed out in the tailor's window on one of their shopping trips, but maybe that could wait.

He still couldn't quite believe that Eddie had taken a swing at him. Maybe it had been an opportunistic diversion after all, but once Webster had decided to go for it, the intent had been there alright. As Rex reflected on this, two fully Lycra-kitted and helmeted cyclists – more likely these days to be commuting barristers en route to or from Gray's Inn than the cycle couriers of old – one heading north, the other south, avoided collision in the pedestrian throng by each diverting to their own side of a short length of pavement barrier from where they eyed each other with the hostility of jousting knights finding range on their first pass in some medieval **tilt-yard**.

Was that what he and Eddie had been doing all these years? Both just biding their time and staying in range?

Sid's was too busy; well, it was lunchtime, so – Susan's influence again – Rex went into one of the higher-end eateries, with its minimalist **Shaker**-inspired interior design, all whitewash and bare wood, and got the soup of the day: 'Creamy courgette and **chervil** with ciabatta croutons'. Actually, it wasn't bad. But then, Susan was right about most things.

Nearing the police station, he noticed that the line of one- and two-person pop-up tents and repurposed airport luggage trolleys at the foot of the steps had grown and been joined by a slightly larger **bell-tent** that now occupied the curve of pavement at the corner of Richbell Place. In a manner of speaking, Lamb's Conduit Street was now **twinned** with Stroud Green Road by Finsbury Park station – and every other informal tent village in London. He couldn't say he blamed anyone for camping here. Wasn't it all about safety in numbers, and in this case the implication at least of police protection at night? That coupled with proximity to Holborn Library for warmth and bathroom facilities during the day. He could understand the motivation, and he knew that the number of homeless people in London was increasing year on year, even if he couldn't **cite** the relevant stats. He hoped someone in the building was on top of it – he made a mental note to check with Frankie. There but for the grace of God, he thought, as he ducked into the porch of the lower-ground-floor staff entrance on Richbell Place and punched in the code.

Rex took the stairs as usual. Back up to the sixth floor. He had some video to watch.

That was the understatement of the year, as people had once been fond of saying.

Earlier that morning, Rex and Lollo had got the anticipated one-to-one business out of the way as quickly as possible – Rex bringing him up to speed with the domestic situation before outlining the thinking that had led to his discovery a few moments earlier, that Webster might have substituted one of the hard drives from the Operation Kayak surveillance. Damaged or inoperable HDs were a statistical rarity, although, given the sheer quantity used by an organisation the size of the Met, they would turn up every now and then.

'But they're watermarked and wotnot, right?' Lollo had asked.

Rex had nodded. 'I don't know, but let's say that, realising he couldn't **edit** the contents of the HD, maybe he panicked and replaced the whole unit with a damaged drive from another oppo?'

'Aye, it's a theory. Come on, then,' said Lollo, 'glove up and chuck it in the toaster.'

Rex took a photo of the Jiffy bag in situ. Then he took some latex gloves from the dispenser and, holding the Jiffy bag open with the ruler once again, he reached in with thumb and forefinger to remove the hard drive. He held it up so they could both confirm that the serial number matched the one crossed out in Webster's log, then put the hard drive, business end first, into the front **slot** of the toaster.

'What are we looking for?' asked Lollo as Rex moved icons around on the desktop of his laptop and mouse-clicked a few folders and dialogue boxes.

'Fuck knows.'

'How long's the tape?'

'A week,' said Rex. 'If I watch it double-speed and put in enough hours, I could probably watch the whole thing front to back in five, six days?'

'Better get popcorn and make thaself at home, then.'

'First things first. I'll make a copy right now,' said Rex, 'so we can admit the original ASAP. Only take half an hour. Once that's done I'm going home for a kip, if that's okay with you. I'll come back and start fresh at lunchtime.'

While he was talking, Rex walked over to the document station and took a new DEF11 and an evidence bag from their respective pigeonholes, and signed out a new hard drive from the equipment cupboard. Back at the desk, he took it out of the polystyrene packaging and picked at the tab to remove the cellophane wrap, then slotted the new hard drive into the second slot on the toaster. He clicked the 'start' button on a **prompter** that appeared on his desktop.

'Sounds like a plan, Kingsy. Fuck's sake. I always had Webbo down as a bit of a **toper**,' said Lollo, waving an imaginary pint in the air by way of explanation. 'Made allowances because I know he likes to sup on a pint or two. But this? Seems a bit out of character.'

Rex shrugged. He couldn't believe it either. Sure, Webster had always been a bit of a **knuckle**-dragger. He was unreconstructed, yes, but not dishonest. Rex would never have imagined Webster even contemplating something like this.

Until a few days ago, Webbo had to all intents and purposes been going about his business and coming the usual '**merry old soul**' bullshit. It was hard to believe that all the while he could have been actively subverting an investigation.

Cliff Heath's intuition had been right.

But now the good ship Eddie Webster would seem to have run aground on a **reef** of his own making. For a detective of Webster's seniority this was more than gross misconduct; it was a full-on **metaphysical** crisis – a complete betrayal.

When had he made the decision to **exploit** his colleagues' trust like this?

'Out of character?' said Rex. 'Well, I guess we'll find out.'

'Aye,' said Lollo. 'Quick as you can, though, eh.'

Just when King thought the meeting was over, his DCI came out with: 'How's your new lady friend, anyway? Susan, was it?'

'She's fine, thanks.'

'Not seen through your superficial charm and legged it back to Yorkshire, then?'

'No chance.'

'If she gets tired of you and wants a real man…'

'An old one, you mean,' said Rex.

'Aye, well, good luck.'

Rex wasn't sure if Lollo meant good luck with Susan or with Webster's mysterious hard drive. Maybe both, but before he could ask him Lollo brought the meeting to a close.

'Anyroad, I'm clearing the decks for you the next few days, so if anyone gives you any stick tell them to come and **raise** it wi me, Kingsy, okay?'

'Understood,' said Rex. 'Thanks, sir.'

That had been about half five this morning. Now it was later, and there was no more putting it off.

The original hard drive and Jiffy bag were now safely in the evidence vault, and Rex had the only copy, but he wasn't going to watch it out in the open. He'd booked one of the workstations in the 'library' – a password-protected secure space containing partitioned media suites for the viewing of sensitive material. The room felt a bit neglected. An A4 print-out on the wall of the library instructed users to 'Turn off mobile phones'. There was a small and desiccated-looking succulent plant in a pot on the windowsill, and a scrunched-up tissue on the floor beneath one of the office chairs. Along one wall were five empty bookcases, while in another corner stood a dirty orange-coloured reinforced heavy-gauge four-drawer filing cabinet of a type that had once been used for ammunition storage in the sub-basement shooting range, complete with a factory-fitted full-height security bar covering the drawer locks, and two further custom-welded vertical steel rods with padlocked hasps, the keys to which were known to be long lost. It was probably too heavy to move if you didn't absolutely have to; easier to leave it where it was. There was a 'nuclear hazard' sticker on the top drawer, and someone had scratched the words 'CLEAN ME' into the orange paint on a side panel.

It only took Rex a minute or two to set up. He pulled his notebook and the hard drive from his rucksack, plugged the USB from the toaster into the desktop PC, and inserted the hard drive into one of the slots. Adjusted his earphones. A few mouse-clicks to open the Timespace Reviewer application.

Hesitating before he pressed 'play', Rex knew that this two-way split-screen video was going to be his virtual home for the next few days, but it wasn't somewhere he was particularly looking forward to entering. Given even the basics of what he knew about Operation Kayak, it was obvious this wasn't going to be pleasant.

It would not have been an exaggeration to say that anything would have been preferable to this task. He'd rather have scraped away the years of human excrement **caked** onto the cell toilets with a toothpick than watch this. Well, maybe not.

A time code ticked away in the lower right-hand side of both channels: 10.25:01 and counting. On the left channel was an inside shot of the entrance to the Lido Cars minicab office, on the right a wide-angle view of a living room in the flat above the shop, furnished with a couple of tatty three- and four-seater sofas, a large TV and a pot plant: some sort of fern.

Outside on Lamb's Conduit Street, it had started raining. It was pissing down so hard that it was battering the windows. At street level people were scrambling to avoid the near-instant soaking by taking shelter wherever they could: in shops and building doorways, under the canopies of Sid's and Ciao Bella, or, conveniently, in the nearest pub – 'Well, since we're here, what'll you have?' – and in the foyer of Holborn Library.

Upstairs there was no such excitement. In his cubicle in the library on the sixth floor, Rex was eating little wooden spoonfuls of cold soup from the cup, and getting acquainted with the dramatis personae of Operation Kayak. These included, just in the first hour or two on this particular hard drive, at least five of the twelve suspects, all of whom were referred to by the numbers they'd been designated according to the chronology of their appearances in the surveillance, and sometimes by their full names, as well as – informally – by the various nicknames that had been in use prior to a firm ID, e.g. Person 5 or P5, a.k.a. Gary Bell, a.k.a. Big Nose. Victims 1 to 52 were treated with altogether more dignity, and at least spared the nicknames. But while every effort had been and was still being made to do so, a small proportion had not yet been identified.

The footage was crystal clear; black and white but high-resolution.

Playing the video at double speed had a certain distancing effect at first, but it quickly wore off. Rex found that he could take his mind off what was on the screen by simply enumerating who was present at any given time, and by trying to reconcile the major players with their nicknames. But he quickly remembered that this was also fresh material, as yet unseen, and by substituting this hard drive with a blank, Webster had effectively thrown away a whole week's worth of potential evidence.

On a case this size, given the sheer number of people involved and the prolonged nature of the surveillance, it was clear that each of the suspects had committed dozens if not hundreds of serious offences, any one of which, with this quality of evidence, might have resulted in a conviction and a serious custodial sentence. Several of this quality and you had a provable, repeated course of action.

Webster's behaviour was unconscionable.

Rex wasn't familiar enough with the investigation to know the names of all of those on screen, but he felt it was incumbent upon him to note the approximate time code whenever any offences were clearly identifiable: every cigarette burn, every slap and punch, each instance of trafficking, each and every sexual assault that was captured. As day became night and more people showed up, Rex found that if he focused on the TV in the centre of the room it was a way of blocking out at least some of the detail of what was going on around it, beyond mentally keeping tabs where he could on who was doing what and to whom.

Next time he looked up he'd already filled five neatly handwritten pages with the time codes of what looked like clear offences with identifiable perpetrators and victims. He'd email it over to the team once he was finished with the job in hand. But, however harrowing, there was nothing yet to differentiate the footage on this hard drive from any of the others. The officers on the permanent team would know who was who, and be able to request the relevant clips both for evidential and – if they were good enough – ID suite purposes.

For the next few days, Rex would arrive at the station before dawn and still be sitting here when the whole building was bathed in golden evening light from the west.

The one constant 'on the tape' was Dicky Sharp, who'd turn up at eight thirty every evening, and after a quick chat with the controller and whoever was around in the cab office he'd come back out and stand there in the doorway for most of the night.

You could see that most of the men at Lido Cars treated Dicky like a bit of a **retard**, but Rex had to hand it to him, he was sharp as a needle. They'd constantly be jostling him and taking the piss, laughing and waving their hands in front of their noses behind his back or when he wasn't looking, as if there were a bad smell, which of course there was. But for all of that, he'd just be standing there **nonchalantly** doing his job: door security. A bit of a comedown for someone with his ambitions, perhaps, but beggars couldn't be choosers. There he'd be, with arms folded, hands on hips or clasped behind his back, never in his pockets, always in a state of readiness, and never drunk on duty. In recent years it turned out that Sharp had become a **card-carrying** teetotaller – not that he'd taken the **pledge**, just that five nightly pints of the old amber **nectar** wasn't great for his diabetes and increasingly dodgy kidneys.

As he worked through the video, Rex found his respect for Sharp going up, because it was he who every night had been making a mental note of which drivers were in, and who was bringing whom back to the office and when, who was taking whom out 'on deliveries', and who taking whom home and at what time. It was Dicky whom they sent upstairs with a black bin bag when it got quiet around 4 a.m., to tidy up, empty the ashtrays and get rid of the empties, the vodka bottles and the condom wrappers. Dicky who took an interest in the young women, finding out their names and chatting to them on the doorstep when they arrived, asking about school and telling them about his mother.

And it was Dicky who, if he had the place to himself, would carefully put the used condoms into little Ziploc pill bags, and date them, then put them in a Tupperware box hidden in the back of his mum's freezer.

Dicky who wrote it all down in a school exercise book that he kept under the floorboard behind the spare bed in the box room when he got back to the family house in Fullwell Cross in the mornings.

And it had been Dicky Sharp who'd phoned the police and reported the whole thing, thereby filling the gaps in what had otherwise become a dead investigation.

22: Aubépine (Hawthorn)

With a start, Rex found himself looking up at the small patch of **mildew** on the library ceiling rather than at the screen. He'd obviously had a bit of a **cat-nap**, but luckily he'd also paused the video. Five shifts in and he was forgetting what day it was. If anyone had been around to ask how he was getting on, he might have said that it was doing his head in. Maybe it was time to put the kettle on. Stretch his legs and take a leak; splash some cold water on his face. Rex set the laptop to sleep mode, then stood up and stretched.

Well, one thing you could say for Webster going AWOL – and now this recovered hard drive – was that it was a welcome distraction. Talk about a wormhole. There was nothing like watching surveillance footage of utter evil scum committing multiple unspeakable crimes to make you forget your own problems. Although, if anything, it had made him even more anxious about Jennifer's well-being, that these monsters were operating out in the world. How could anyone bear to let their daughters out of their sight for a second?

Not everyone could hack this kind of investigation, of course, and no wonder, but at least these kinds of offences were more widely understood now.

It reminded Rex of something that **Donal** had once said back in Operation Lavengro days about who gets to **wield** power and how. It had been kept out of the public eye for national security reasons, but the structures of bullying and sexual abuse that Lavengro had uncovered were endemic throughout the military of the time. At a departmental level, in the Home Office or the MOD, no one had wanted to believe that not only did grooming gangs exist in the army, but that the power structures inherent in a military chain of command positively facilitated such abuse. It was a toxic combination that went far beyond mere peer pressure. Who would be a whistle-blower or conscientious **objector** within a rigidly hierarchical organisation whose smooth running depended entirely upon blind obedience? Of course, there hadn't really been the vocabulary to describe it back then. As far as most people were concerned, 'grooming' was something that gorillas did in David Attenborough documentaries.

Now, with multiple high-profile convictions, you had to hope that any jury in this **brave new world** might be less likely to stigmatise the victims, to **learn** the lesson, to not instinctively assume it was their character or behaviour at fault and **enact** some misguided knee-jerk disapproval of the victims, some reinforcement of structural sexism, by acquitting the inevitably male offender regardless of rank or status, whether corporate **vice-president** or van driver. Because this was the kind of misogynistic, victim-blaming bullshit they'd been up against. And even now they'd still have to navigate that particular moral **chicane**, and **contrive** to counter such prejudices at every stage of the justice chain, from constable to courthouse.

Things would have to have got pretty bad for Rex to contemplate adding sugar to his tea, but here he was, looking through the cupboard for the box of La Perruche sugar lumps that Jane Milligan in SMT had brought back as a present for the unit from a trip to her holiday home in Brittany a while back. He shook one from the box and dropped it – **plop** – into his tea.

It wasn't all bad, of course. Although, apart from Lollo and Helen, he hadn't been able to talk to anyone about Jen. He hadn't been able to tell Susan about the **Nirvana** 'smiley' T-shirt-wearing teenager who'd turned up on his doorstep with her book about Boudicca and her ironic *Star Wars* rucksack, because he and Susan were still playing phone tag, nor even really had the chance to learn how it felt to say 'my daughter, Jennifer' out loud. That didn't **preclude** telling anyone else, but who else could he tell? Terence was out of town, so one of their occasional catch-ups over last orders in The Coach or The Duke was out of the question. That snatched hour with Jen, sitting in the sun in Coram's Fields and doing the crossword together, already seemed an age ago. She'd asked him what '**Ides**' meant. 'It's a **Roman** date,' Rex had said. 'It's hard to explain. They counted up the days of the month differently back then.' But just because he hadn't really told anyone didn't mean it wasn't real.

But right now, mug in hand, it was back to work. He punched the code into the keypad and then shut the library door behind him. He sat down, logged back in, took a sip of tea and then mouse-clicked 'play'.

Back to Lido Cars.

That was when his phone rang. It was Susan at last, but Rex let the video run while he answered.

'Hey Rex,' she said. 'How are you?'

'Yeah, good. I was hoping you'd **ring**. So great to hear your voice. Lots to tell, actually, but I'll save it for when I see you.'

'Ooh, anything exciting?'

'Very, but it's a long story. Too long for right now – I'm a bit busy.'

'Well, sorry about the radio silence. It's always a bit crazy at work with the year-end coming up. You know.'

'Of course,' said Rex. 'Same here. How are you apart from that? I've missed you.'

'Yeah, me too. Especially today. I love our lazy Sundays.'

Rex smiled. It wouldn't take a truth **serum** for Rex to confess that he was **in love** with Susan. He'd known it for a while, and happily told anyone who was interested.

On the left side of the split screen Dicky Sharp was standing guard, and, just visible through the front door at the top of the screen, the wheels and sills of a car pulled in sharply to the kerb against the traffic. Aye-aye, thought Rex. Who do you think you are? Mike bloody Hawthorn?

'I still think I need a holiday,' Susan was saying. 'I mean, I think *we* do.'

'I like it,' said Rex, his eyes drawn to the screen. 'Where shall we go? Sharm El Sheik? No, you choose.'

'You know where I want to go: the **Riviera**. Jane and Larry got a weekend break to Cannes, and they were saying it's lovely at this time of year.'

On the right side of the monitor, the usual early-evening crew were just getting started. Porn on the telly now, and Person 5 rolling a spliff on an old *Metro*.

'That's a thought…' said Rex. He wouldn't mind sitting in a window seat with Susan next to him, holding hands on the armrest as their plane was pushed back off the **apron** to turn and taxi to the end of the runway en route to Nice or Marseilles.

'I've always wanted to go to St-Tropez!' she said.

On the left, the driver's door of the car opened and someone got out: a stocky pair of legs, shoes and suit trousers. From the way Sharp moved his head, it looked like he was chatting to the guy.

'I'd love that,' said Rex. 'Stay for a bit longer than a weekend.'

'Yes please.'

'Listen,' said Rex, 'I don't mean to **lower** your expectations, but if the weather stays like this, maybe we should take **Terence** up on the offer of his place on the beach. Remember, I mentioned that he's bought a place in Dungeness? Apparently it's been glorious weather out there, and it's all shipshape now. I'm sure I can swing a long weekend off, once I've got on top of this **case**.'

Dicky Sharp on the screen, and opposite him on the pavement still just a pair of black shoes, and the cuffs of some trousers.

'Dungeness?' said Susan. 'Aw, it's so sweet of him to **extend** the invitation.'

'Well, he's a sweet guy,' said Rex. 'As you'll find out.'

On screen, at double speed, Sharp stepped aside and gestured towards the doorway.

'And he's a bit of a perfectionist,' said Rex, 'so his place'll be lovely.'

On screen, at double speed, the guest came fully into shot.

'To be honest, Rex,' said Susan, 'until I see him with my own eyes, I don't think I'll believe that Terence actually exists.'

Rex should have laughed right on cue, but he didn't.

'Are you still there?' said Susan.

No answer.

'Rex?'

He needed to end this conversation right now. He'd explain later.

'Listen, darling,' he said. 'I'm really sorry, but I'm going to have to call you back this evening. Something really serious has just come up at work. Love you.'

'Rex, are you okay?'

No answer.

'Love you too,' said Susan, but Rex had already hung up.

23: Rossignol (Nightingale)

If Rex had sounded shocked it was no wonder. One minute he'd been talking to Susan and idly thinking what an attractive proposition that was: a few days on the beach. A sudden pang to see waves breaking against a stony beach, the smell of salt spray. It was like that Masefield poem, what was it, **Sea Fever**?

They'd done it in English at school.

Susan's voice had briefly lulled him into a romantic reverie, and thoughts of what they might do together. He'd imagined the two of them strolling hand in hand across the shingle to the film-maker turned **gardener** Derek Jarman's cottage, walking among the sea kale beds and the poppies and railway sleepers of a driftwood **extravaganza** that had long outlived its creator, and which Terence had proudly mentioned as one of the local attractions. And come to think of it, Rex had seen the odd spread about it in the Sunday papers over the years. Then, **moving** through a series of disconnected snapshots, he imagined the two of them taking a **gondola** ride in Venice, or on a train, or – perhaps because Susan had once told him that experiencing a Japanese tea ceremony was on her bucket list – wearing matching kimonos and kneeling opposite each other in the tatami-floored room of a tea house with **rice-paper** screen walls—

Fleeting thoughts all gone in an instant.

But the **phantom** on the video player was very much alive, and it was a face that Rex didn't need to **zoom** in on to recognise. But what the hell was Detective Sergeant Edward Webster doing wandering right into the middle not just of a crime scene many times over, but of an investigation and a surveillance operation of the scale and importance of Operation Kayak? An investigation that moreover he was nominally in charge of?

Webster knew his procedures just as well as Rex did. They'd learned most of it together, for goodness' sake. And yet here he was, bold as fucking brass, walking into Lido Cars after a quick chat with Dicky Sharp and – it got worse – going straight upstairs.

It beggared belief.

It wasn't an overstatement to say that this could compromise everything. Two years' work – expensive, specialist work at that – and thousands of person-hours had now been **put on the line**. This was 'suspension, pending further enquiries' territory, or worse. Never mind what it meant for Webster's SIO status, his place at the table for the Gold Support Group meetings. Stepping through the looking glass like this wasn't merely 'below the standard expected', it was deadly serious. Gross misconduct of this nature would almost certainly see Webster immediately and summarily removed from the investigation, and maybe even – temporarily at least – from all other duties. But if this really was what it looked like, then it was hard to see how Webster could carry on being a **copper** at all.

Rex's second thought was for Helen.

Whatever was going on here, you didn't have to be a genius of da **Vinci** proportions to see that it instantly made the situation with Jennifer even more **toxic**.

And didn't this now – the thought struck him like a piece of ice in the heart – also put Jen and Rachel somewhere quite close to actual danger themselves? You wouldn't want any of these freaks dropping round to Helen and Eddie's place on the off-chance.

This was a disaster whichever way you looked at it. And Rex couldn't for the life of him understand what Webster could possibly be thinking, introducing such a high level of risk into both his work and his and Helen's and the girls' personal lives.

But there was no doubt at all about what Rex needed to do.

This was going to have to go upstairs immediately.

And the first port of call in that regard was Detective Chief Inspector **Jethro** Lawrence, even if – after an afternoon catching up on paperwork – he was probably halfway home by now. An East Ender by adoption, Lollo lived in the posh part of Bow. At one time the streets around Tredegar Square had been scheduled for demolition, but Lollo had picked the house up for a song in the early 1990s, after a tip-off from one of his buddies at the **golf club** who worked for a major civil engineering contractor and **road-maker**, that it was looking as if the M11 link road would likely be going via Leytonstone into Homerton instead of feeding into the Mile End Road as had hitherto been projected.

Rex picked up his phone. He knew the number off by heart.

'Aye, you did right,' said Lollo once he was back in the office and Rex had briefed him on what to expect. 'I did have an appointment with some Islay **peat**, but it's already been waiting eighteen years, so another hour or two won't hurt.'

Rex had cued up the clip. He sat Lollo down in front of the laptop and clicked 'play'.

Was Webster drunk? On screen, he lurched into the living room above the Lido Cars office, where at least three suspects were puffing on spliffs and watching porn on the big screen with some of the girls. Talk about out of place. Inappropriate didn't really cover it. There was no sound, so Rex could only guess what was being said, but one of the individuals took a can of something from the fridge and handed it to Webster, while another passed him what was left of the joint. It was grotesque, the sight of DS Eddie Webster standing there, can in one hand, spliff in the other. He was swaying slightly. It looked like he was dancing, if that was the right word, but to what? The music on the porn channel?

'How much more of this is there?' asked Lollo. 'Please, for the love of God, tell me he doesn't—'

'Cop off?' said Rex. 'That's what I thought. Not as far as I can see. Thank fuck. Dances with one of them in a bit, goes off camera briefly, but then he seems to have a bit of a row with this one. Far as I got. Here.'

Rex reached for the mouse and moved the progress indicator forward.

Now Webster was slow-dancing with one of the young women.

On screen, Big Nose leaned in to whisper in Webster's ear, then lifted his chin as if to gesture off camera. Webster appeared to square up to him.

'What do you reckon, sir?' said Rex. 'D'you think they know who he is, or figure he's just some random ponce?'

'Well, if they do recognise him, they're not letting on,' said Lollo. 'But we know that none of them have any form to speak of, so why would they?'

On the right-hand side of the split screen, Webster and Person 5 were engaging in a bit of argy-bargy. No blows yet, just arm-waving.

'True,' said Rex.

'Let's worry about that **anon**,' said Lollo. 'Anyroad, it's **nigh** on impossible to say until we've spoken to the Detective Sergeant, but from the looks of it Sharp knew who he was, even if they didn't.'

'Yeah, but Sharp's a small-time crook who'd worked all the local clubs for years, don't forget. He'll know everybody who's anybody. It's his job.'

Meanwhile, on the left-hand side of the split screen, someone else was arriving downstairs. Dicky Sharp stepped aside as the newcomer strode in the front door without a word. Male IC1, late fifties, bald but with an impressive greying beard, smart black leather blazer, jeans, trainers. It wasn't someone Rex had seen on the video so far. He paused and checked the notes, ran his finger down the list and scanned the two pages of thumbnail portraits, but there was no match. On screen the white male reached out for the banister with his left hand and went straight up the stairs. He looked like he knew where he was going. Like the **stage manager**, come to sort things out. Rex wondered if something about the new arrival looked familiar, but he couldn't be sure.

'Right,' said Lollo, 'I'd better have a formal chat with Detective Sergeant Webster, see what he says under pressure. What d'you reckon. Let's use disciplinary procedure for now. I'll take one of the coat-hangers over to Woodford for a sit-down, man to man. Oh, but Kingsy?'

'What?'

'This'll be a disciplinary matter first and foremost, and I want it by the book, alright? And that means confidential. So don't say owt to Helen? D'you hear?'

'Yeah, yeah, course,' said Rex, distracted by what he was seeing on screen. The new arrival pointed at Webster, then put a hand on his shoulder to shepherd him out.

'Fuck me!' said Rex.

'Eh?' said Lollo.

'This guy,' said Rex, clicking 'pause' and pointing at a detail on the screen. 'Look.'

'Do we know him?'

'Not much. Fuck is he doing there?'

It was unmistakable.

'Remember when I got seconded over to Barnes,' said Rex. 'Operation Lavengro.'

'That bastard?'

He had Lollo's attention now.

'Looks like it,' said Rex.

'Bit of a fucking turn-up, in't it?'

'Not half.'

The first time Rex had met this particular **recreant** piece of shit was in the late 1990s. Show him a line and he'd step over it. Couldn't seem to stop himself. One time he'd been arrested for contempt and criminal damage with a recommendation to **remand on bail**, then he'd started batting for the other side. He'd blended into the woodwork for a bit – a few years in Sri Lanka, then Australia. They'd kept an eye on him, but the last time Rex had seen him had been getting on for a decade ago, when he'd still had enough hair for a grown-out **mohawk**. Rex moved the pointer back and forward on the timeline to find the clearest shot of his face, then keyed in for a couple of screen grabs.

'Best I can do,' he said.

'That's it,' said Lollo. 'Get the bastard logged, and up on the shared drive, eh? And ask around. Someone must have seen him before.'

'On it, sir,' said Rex.

'Okay, change of plan,' said Lollo. 'I'll talk to Webster tomorrow, but I want you to go and have a word with Sharp. Drop in at his mum's place first thing and find out what he knows about Webbo, but nowt else, right? I want that ring-fenced. Do I make myself clear?'

24: Ancolie (Columbine)

Come to think of it, and watching from a safe distance, something about the guy's demeanour – what was it? – reminded Spike of a particular **schoolmaster** at his comprehensive. Not that they looked alike, not at all. This was a science teacher named Ben Whitehouse, who'd obviously fancied himself and was a bit of a smoothie, with his polo necks and corduroy jackets and the racing-green Jag parked outside. Everyone had thought he was a bit of a laugh; irreverent. The kind of bloke who loved Kenny Everett and *Not the Nine O'Clock News*.

Yeah, that was it. Mr Whitehouse – 'Call me Ben' – had been one of those gurning idiots who's always shouting and doing funny voices and impressions.

Hiding in plain sight.

This guy was the same, in that respect at least: a bit of a loudmouth, and catchphrase central. There he was doing it now. Something off the telly – that voice ringing out, loud enough to be heard above the music and the street full of festival-goers heading for the main stage. With a voice like that he could have been selling 'Lovely broccol-eye!' on the veg stall at Berwick Street Market, but here he was: 'mine host', hawker and circus ringmaster all rolled into one.

Last time Spike had seen him was in Greenock Sheriff Court. What was that, seven or eight years back? Or not long after, anyway. The guy had gone so deep he'd come out the other side. But he was still instantly recognisable, even with this new **Vandyke** beard. What's more, it seemed he was still using his cover name. So the ESCU team – the Economic and Specialist Crime Unit – had decided to play along and send his old mucker Spike.

'Plum!' said Spike, catching his eye as he strolled past, looking for all the world like he hadn't just driven all the way down from London in order precisely to engineer this chance meeting. 'Good to see you, man!'

The main thing was that Whitehouse let you use the classroom at lunchtime. He cultivated the idea that it was a kind of sanctuary, a safe space for free thinkers, the elect few. He mimed and made machine gun noises or pulled the pin and lobbed imaginary grenades when he talked about the headmaster or 'the squares'. You could piss about, not like in the school library. Old 'Mary' Whitehouse, as he was known, even kept a few singles and LPs and the old school record player in the storeroom behind the blackboard; mostly just standard party fare – 'Ballroom Blitz', 'Albatross', 'Tiger Feet' – but a bit of pop punk and new wave too. He'd wheel the unit out for end-of-term discos, obviously, but the rest of the time he'd let you listen to records at lunchtimes, on a pair of old language-lab headphones.

'Who have you come as?' said Plum.

'It's me, Spike!'

'Spike, of course. Good to see you, man. Didn't recognise you without your dreads.'

'Shaved 'em off.'

'So I see. Fuck are you doing here?'

'Well, where else would I be?' said Spike, looking around, impressed. 'The old bookstall's grown a bit, then? I like it.'

'Eh?' It took a second, but then Plum twigged and half-turned to acknowledge the enormous marquee behind him. The weather was good and the side panels were rolled up, so Spike could see the bar and the rudimentary stage within, a load of tatty sofas and tables and chairs. People wandered in and out wherever they wanted to, the putative entrance marked only by a painted wooden sign and a duckboard doorstep. 'FREE WHEEL', it said in hand-painted letters. 'This beauty? Yeah, this is me these days. Come and have a drink, mate. It's been too long. I'm doing a revolutionary special cucumber Pimm's today, two pound a glass or fiver a jug: just your classic Pimm's, borage, cucumber and lemonade.'

'Right!' said Spike. 'Revolutionary like—'

'Yeah, exactly,' said Plum. 'The calendar.'

'I remember.'

'And tomorrow's "shallot",' said Plum, 'so it's a free packet of pickled onion Monster Munch with every bar order while stocks last.

Sunday's "absinthe" – bought the spoons and everything. It's gonna be messy. Watch out for the wee caramel brownies, though. One's plenty, two'll have you tripping.'

'Nice one. I'll remember that,' said Spike. 'Go on, then. I'll have a Pimm's for old times' sake.'

Plum turned to catch the eye of one of the bar staff and bellowed the order. Within seconds two glasses of Pimm's with all the trimmings had materialised.

'Blimey, how's that for service,' said Spike.

'In yer eye,' said Plum, raising his glass.

'Cheers,' said Spike. 'So what prompted the move?'

'It was going spare,' said Plum. 'After I last saw you, I went travelling for a bit. And when I got back, I was doing a bit of crewing on the side for Earth Light Sound System – know 'em? Your man Tobias? Learning the ropes. Literally. I figured we could do something a bit different. More like a safe space, somewhere for people to chill out. Well, as you can see.'

'Makes sense. I thought I hadn't bumped into you for a bit.'

'**Lured** me in, didn't they. How about you? Still doing the old… ?'

'Yeah, never-ending,' said Spike. 'You know how it is.'

'For real,' said Plum. 'Protest scene all got a bit too middle class for me; all those posh birds didn't like that I was better at getting headlines than they were. Well, excuse me! I might have read Guy Debord, but I didn't have a country estate where I could let the plebs stay. Sorry, no offence, mate. Which one were you knobbing anyway? Amelia, wasn't it?'

'Yeah.'

'Nice! Got quite serious at one time, didn't it?'

'Ah, well, you know.'

'Wasn't she expecting, last I heard?'

Christ! How did he know that? Well, it didn't matter now. 'Yeah. She lost it, sadly,' said Spike. 'Miscarriage. That did for us. She moved to Australia. Still there, far as I know. Good luck to her.'

'Ah, sorry to hear it,' said Plum, raising his glass. 'Australia? Well, here's to lucky escapes, eh? Nice girl, though. I don't blame you. They meant well, that lot, I s'pose. But at least this is honest graft, 'stead of banging your head against the wall all the fucking time!' Plum turned to survey his domain, seamlessly waving, pointing at, and loudly greeting more than half a dozen folk (what were they, friends? staff? punters?) in the process: 'S'appenin', Jace! Oi-oi, Sy! Megzy-boy!' Then: 'Tell the truth, Spikey old son, it's more like a big family.'

Perhaps there was something in what Plum was saying. Whether you liked him or not, the Belfast man seemed the genuine **article**, maybe a bit too brash, too much of a **hard nut** for the genteel, hippy-dippy landowning tendency within the anti-nuclear and disarmament movements.

'Got talking to Tobias,' said Plum, 'couple of summers back when we were driving up to Temporary Autonomous Zen, and he mentioned that they were getting a bigger tent. I'd got to know this beauty pretty well. Reckon I could put it up in my sleep, so—'

Plum slapped his palm onto one of the stout wooden poles, then reached out proprietorially and nodded to Spike to get out of the way as an **acrobat** and a couple of stilt-walking jugglers hove into view.

'Made him an offer?' said Spike.

'Yeah. "Give us it, or I go to the cops!" Ha!'

'Ha!' said Spike.

'Not really,' said Plum. 'Now I subcontract to the bigger festivals, mainly. It's cushty. Better than traipsing around trying to flog a few boxes of damp books.'

'I bet.'

Rumour had it at one time that Plum had liberated much of his old Free Wheel stock from Compendium Books in Camden when it was closing down. And since it was a convenient rumour, Plum had only half-heartedly disavowed it. Come to think of it, he'd probably started it.

'Come and have a drink later, mate,' he said, lowering his voice. 'Look around. Nice, eh? Take your pick. All the perks **minus** the grief. Candy from a baby, if you know what I mean. D'you know what? I reckon I make more in this couple of months than I used to make all year.'

'You still down Kent way, wasn't it?' said Spike.

'No, we moved. Been wintering in Aldershot the last few years. Bought an old church hall off the Tongham Road if you know it.'

Yeah, I know it, thought Spike, but just said, 'You went back to Aldershot?'

'"Home of the British Army", yeah, I know,' said Plum. 'Does what it says on the tin, though. Fucking squaddies, eh. But we love it, and they love the Irish there now. Not like the bad old days. What about you, mate? Same place? Still up and down to Scotland?'

'Yeah, same. Not been up north for a while, though. Reckon they're doing alright without me. You know what it's like, I just go where I'm sent,' said Spike, truthfully.

'He doesn't even pay them?' said Frank, a colleague from ESCU, in the car later. 'What's in it for them, then: just the tickets and a bit of free face **paint**, some chickpea curry and a dab at the odd **gramme**?'

'In with the in-crowd, maybe?' said Spike. 'Us-against-the-world kind of thing?'

He knew the script, had seen it done. It worked every time. Just surprised to see Plum playing out the old tunes in broad daylight like this. How did it go? You've got a crew of, what, twenty or thirty well-meaning young people. Most of them doing this for the first time. You and your old lady pick one out of the group and open up to them a bit, look after them – lavish a bit of extra TLC – and then one night you lean on them for a bit of sympathy in return. Not too much. Don't overdo it. Just a quick glimpse of poor vulnerable you. They'll lap it up because they feel important. Suddenly they're special, the Lone **Ranger** coming to the rescue, not realising that the next sympathetic shoulder you seek out will be to bitch about them. If you get too bored you can just **expel** them from the movement. The usual rules apply: destabilise, undermine, exclude; bombard them with distracting questions, betray a confidence. **Treat** them badly with no explanation. Shame them. Make it too **traumatic** to stay. It's *so* unfair. But they can't win. They thought they'd been allowed into the inner sanctum, to **bathe** in the oasis, but the caravan's gone ahead without them. Suddenly they're all alone, out in the **open sea**. But then, when you're doing the get-out, everyone mucking in and clearing up, loading the lorry to move on to the next festival, you wave around your wodge of tickets and ask who's in. And you know what? It's predictable as clockwork that they'll be at the front of the queue, trying to get things back to what they were.

'Yeah, well, it's probably easy pickings, right?' said Frank. 'A mate of mine back home used to be a small-time DJ: weddings and birthdays, occasional pub gigs. Had his own decks. Old-style – nothing fancy like today. This was when a light show meant projecting a Super 8 loop of **Steamboat** *Willie* over the oil wheel on a Pluto 500. Once or twice a year he used to do a big house party. And believe me, that guy would get a fuck every time. He didn't even need to try. You'd see him stealing the odd **glance** or two during the night, admiring the scenery, you know, feeling his way, and by one in the morning he reckoned he could chuck Patti Smith's **Easter** on the decks and take his pick of whoever was left. Talk about their favourite C. S. Lewis novels or whatever until sun-up – *Prince* **Caspian** versus *The Voyage of the Dawn Treader* – and that's half the **battle**. Never mind "Dancing Barefoot" – next thing you know they'd be swapping **saliva**. Same sort of thing with this guy Plum, d'you reckon?'

'Oh yeah,' Spike said. 'Classic model.'

'Old Whitehouse is a laugh,' they'd used to say. But it hadn't taken long – half a term? – before his self-defined 'best mates' **remit** had expanded from a few saucy jokes when he came back from the staffroom at the end of lunch to buying concert tickets that they could pay him back for. And not long after that to offering a few of the lads a lift home. Then it was just a couple of the lads. Then it was one. Later, Malcolm – the lucky one, or so it seemed – would talk proudly of stopping off in the woods to look at porn mags side by side in Whitehouse's car. It had all seemed so grown-up. Secret worlds that were revealed in page after page of spread legs and hairy bushes; laughing at the readers' wives. Within a week or two, Malc would confide that he was being told to take one of the mags into the actual bushes for a wank, and he'd obediently comply, coming back to find Whitehouse with a pile of marking on his lap. Then he'd stopped talking about it altogether, and his friends didn't see so much of him any more, but Sir was still dropping in for drinks with Mr and Mrs Drake every other Friday night. His parallel seduction of the parents was note-perfect, executed with the precision of a **surgeon**. He bought a couple of their kittens – they were **Manx cat** breeders – and went to football with Drakey's dad when the Pilgrims were playing at home. He'd tell them what they wanted to hear; suggestions about which topics Malcolm really needed to work on to get the results he needed. He even offered – **oddly** enough – extra tuition once a week, looking at past papers; a special lesson at the end of the day every Tuesday.

'It's not a problem,' he'd tell Malcolm's folks. 'I've got marking to do anyway, and I can easily drop him home afterwards – it's on my way.'

And, of course, they lapped it up.

'It's a shame,' Whitehouse would say to Mr Drake over a pint or two. 'Malc is bright enough to do quite well if only he'd concentrate. He's a good lad, got potential, just needs to apply himself a bit more and stop wasting so much time pissing about with his friends.'

25: Muguet (Lily of the valley)

Dusting himself off in the Costa Coffee toilet, Rex wasn't quite sure how he'd made it out of Dicky Sharp's in one piece. One minute they'd been drinking tea and chatting with his mum, and the next minute the room had started spinning.

He'd got to Barkingside in **double quick time**. Lollo had said 'first thing', but with Dicky Sharp working nights at Lido Cars, Rex knew that he'd be better off letting him get some kip first, so didn't plan to be there much before eleven. He'd finished watching the contents of the substituted hard drive – staying on late after Lollo had finally set off home again for his delayed Sunday evening in front of the telly, then pulling a last **two and a half** hour stint this morning – and there'd been no further unusual incidents on the video, aside that is from the continual, nauseating parade of myriad criminality, violence and abuse that was Operation Kayak's stock-in-trade. But there was little Rex could do about that beyond continuing to note the time codes of each incident, the individuals involved and, broad brush, the offences committed, to at least give the investigative team a bit of a head start once this lost footage was reintroduced into the wider investigation. After that Rex tracked back through the video to Webster's arrival on the scene, the moment his car pulled up outside, noted down the timeline of the incident and took a few screen grabs, all of which he'd send to Lollo so that he could go through it with Webster blow by blow.

Once Rex had tidied up and loaded a couple of things in his rucksack, there was just time for a quick two poached eggs on brown toast and a double espresso at Sid's, before strolling down to Holborn tube station.

Bouncing out to Essex on the Central Line, he took the pen from his inside pocket and opened the newspaper to find the Quick

Crossword. 1 across: 'Why net folks at Delphi? (4,7)'. The question mark told him that the answer would be an anagram of part of the clue, and the ancient Greek location pointed the rest of the way. Before he'd finished writing '**Know thyself**' in the blanks along the top row, he was already scouring the clues for the other two Delphic maxims from the entrance to the ancient Temple of Apollo. Here they were. 7 down: 'Nothing to _____ (6)', first letter 'E', last letter 'S', and 20 across: 'Reburying its urns (anag.) (6,6,4)'. How did it go? Rex crossed out the individual letters in the clue as he spelled out the anagram in the margin: S-U-R-E-T-Y B-R-I-N-G-S... That was it: easy. And it was odds on that the compiler would have continued the theme in further clues. He found 'Plato' first, then 'oracle', and finally 'Apollo', and was finishing the puzzle – '19 down: **Kinsman** (5)', first letter 'U' – as the train pulled in to Mile End station at around 10.30.

If all had gone to plan, at that very moment Lollo would be knocking on Helen and Webster's front door up Woodford way. The interview would be conducted respectfully enough, and Helen would be at work, thank goodness, but it would be clear to Webster that he was under heavy manners from the off, though he might not know quite how much Lollo knew.

It had better not be a damp **squib**. Knowing Lollo's style, Rex was pretty certain that short of giving Webster a **slap** the Detective Chief Inspector would aim to put himself in the **driving seat** – and Webster on the back foot – as quickly as possible. Which was why Lollo had asked Rex to send over the blow-by-blow account and a list of all the key individuals in the Lido Cars ring, and why Rex had wanted to make sure Lollo would have enough material to keep him going for a good couple of hours. Webster must have guessed that they'd found the hard drive, but even then Rex doubted he'd be fully prepared. He wouldn't know what had hit him. Rex tried to feel sympathy for his old colleague, but he failed. He wondered what possible excuse the stupid tosser would come up with for barging into the surveillance operation and possibly worse; what kind of **sanction** Lollo might push for in the disciplinary process that would surely ensue. Aside from obstructing an investigation and theft of police property, it was gross misconduct, surely? Rex was hard-pushed to see how there'd be any alternative to Webster getting the heave-ho. Though he also knew that for a middle-ranking Police Federation member this in itself covered a spectrum of outcomes, from merely bad to much, much worse. But none of which would be good for Helen and the girls.

Stepping out of the ornate red-brick station house at Barkingside tube half an hour later, Rex turned right past a small new-build bicycle parking facility and followed the gently curving Station Approach towards the high street. The combination of mature trees, a brambled embankment, birdsong and a large builders' merchant's yard opposite the station – the smell of sap and warm creosote, of seasoning wood – gave the place an almost rural feeling, which was compounded by a street of well-spaced 1930s semis curving off to the left. It felt a bit like going back in time. Was that why people wanted to live out here? It made Rex want to run in the opposite direction, but maybe that was just him. It was something to **muse** over. With its handy station and a cluster of low-rise red-brick council flats set in communal lawns, some modest terraced houses and shops, what was not to like? And on the crossroads a small and homely church in yellow brick and stone, set amidst trees: Scots pine and oak, and high conifer hedges. Aside from the London brick, it looked a bit like those little churches you'd come across in Norfolk or somewhere. Although as he got closer Rex wondered if it wasn't almost uncannily small. If it weren't for that, and for the traffic, it might have been quite quaint, even picturesque, in a village-green kind of way.

It all made Operation Kayak seem a thousand miles away, but looks were deceiving because this was Kayak's heartland. Well, ten minutes down the road in Romford, but near enough – and that was why he was here, after all.

It was hard to reconcile this scene of apparent suburban tranquillity, probably little-changed since the Second World War, with the continual stream of multiple offences – being not simply perpetrated but performed with relish and transport – that Rex had had no choice but to watch on just that one hard drive. As he walked down Tanners Lane, Rex tried to push the surveillance footage to the back of his mind; to switch it off.

The various housing developments gave way to more spacious semi-parkland and a different kind of architecture. One large glass office building appeared to be the headquarters of the Barnardo's charity. There was the brutalist grey concrete of the Magistrates' Court across the road from a Sainsbury's supermarket, and, on the other side of the high street, Barkingside Police Station.

Barkingside.

It had been notorious at one time.

Rex had first heard of the place during his earliest days on the force.

Every policeman in London knew about the investigations into massive corruption and drug dealing that had been going on at Stoke Newington Police Station in East London in the late eighties and early nineties – even a rookie PC at Holborn as he'd been at the time. Even if such stories had felt a million miles away from Rex's own admittedly, then, limited experiences on the force. It had sounded more like the kind of thing you'd see on TV, in films like *The French Connection*. The very name 'Barkingside' had an even darker glamour within the Stoke Newington scandal because one of the officers being investigated had been transferred here, before being found dead in a Barkingside cell.

It turned out, so the story went, that he'd killed himself with a police firearm.

The police station comprised two buildings or wings, arranged in a rough L-shape and set on the corner of the high street and Mossford Green, a part-residential road running along past the tennis courts and playground on the north-east edge of Barkingside Park and on towards Holy Trinity Church and the cemetery. The presence and function of what from most angles was a rather anonymous-looking building was marked by an antique street light: the archetypal blue lamp, complete with four-sided blue-glazed Victorian lantern and lamplighter's ladder bars. On the high street side was a 1960s concrete-panelled office building, while continuing along Mossford Green was a substantial three-storey extension in orange brick. Between the two buildings was an incongruous bright-blue steel-framed greenhouse-style porch: the new main entrance.

Rex had been in and out of those blue sliding doors a few times himself, over the years. They'd used the identity suites here for some joint out-of-borough investigations. Decent blokes here too, the ones he'd met. But there was no need for Rex to drop in today. Which was lucky because while it might still have looked fairly imposing to the casual viewer, Rex knew that, like many such police stations around the country, Barkingside was operating under constant threat of closure – poor bastards. That depressing drip-drip of demoralising announcements and stays of execution, and with such a reduced staff that the station didn't even have a functioning reception. Instead, a sheet of A4 paper sellotaped to the inside of a glazed panel on one of the former front double doors instructed visitors to turn right and buzz for entry at the vehicle entrance a few yards further along Mossford Green at the far end of the building. You might have to wait a few minutes, but then someone would come and open a little wicket gate to let you in. It hardly enhanced the dignity of the Metropolitan Police, but it was happening all over the country. You couldn't axe 20,000 officers in just a couple of years and not expect that to have an impact. But for a big station like this not even to have a front door? It was demeaning. It struck Rex as low-level heroic that the officers here had adjusted. But he also knew that there was nothing like a bit of siege mentality to bring the staff together. It gave you something to rail against, to kick against the pricks. But still, it'd be enough to drive you mad, having to do that every day. What a waste of time. He tried to imagine how it might work in Holborn if they closed the front door and took away the disability access, so all comers had to use the little side entrance on Richbell Place. It didn't bear thinking about: they'd be queueing round the block all day; officers carrying people up the stairs.

Barkingside High Street itself might as well have been called Déjà Vu Central. It was like a museum of a vanished London that Rex had forgotten he remembered. There was Danny's Pie & Mash, a green-and-orange-liveried Percy Ingle bakery, its window stuffed with cholla, bloomers and iced fingers. There were a few of the larger chains – Boots, Iceland, McDonald's – but plenty of smaller independents too.

A couple of stylishly dressed, professional-looking women of around Rex's age were having a coffee at a table outside Costa. Rex was certain that one of them, slender-limbed and pretty, with fine features and slightly punky, tousled, shoulder-length blonde hair – Christ, she was beautiful! – had given him the glad eye as he walked past. Yes, she'd definitely looked him up and down for a split second. Meanwhile her friend had noticed this too, and half-turned as if to have a quick look herself. Another time he might have stopped for a coffee, a quick flash of the old smile to get the woman's number. But no time for that today. Did he dare, though, to openly look down at the left hand she was using to steady her coffee cup? Yes, he dared – no wedding ring – but kept on walking. He had things to do, and besides, Barkingside might be a bit far to come for a **booty** call.

There was a strange, modernist-looking building at the top of the road, on one side of a large open square just before Rex turned left for Dicky Sharp's mum's place. It looked like something from a science fiction film, as if a 'spinning top'-type flying saucer had landed in the town square beyond the leisure centre, and might have been a 1960s church or mosque, but this copper-vaulted rotunda was in fact Fullwell Cross Library. Take away the Tudorbethan terraces that lined the surrounding streets – and the baggy-trousered skaters taking turns to do ollies and grinds in the square – and you could almost be in Brasilia.

If the high street had been slightly disorientating, Dicky Sharp's mum's house a few hundred yards along Fullwell Avenue was a total time warp. Outside, the brickwork was painted pillar-box red, the mortar picked out in white. The front garden-cum-car-park was crazy-paved with broken pieces of pink and yellow concrete slab, and as Rex walked around the back of Dicky Sharp's slightly battered souped-up silver BMW 3 Series sedan, complete with rear spoiler and some mismatched fender flares – fitted, filled and sanded, but in need of priming and a respray – he saw that a pair of heavily gloss-painted cartwheels, white with red spokes, leaned against the wall on either side of the recessed front porch.

Rex rang the bell. He'd asked their FLO Tommy Bee to leave a message of the 'Nothing to worry about' variety with Mrs Sharp last night, so they'd be expecting him. And he knew better than to flash his badge at the door. He kept a decoy clipboard and a tape measure in his desk drawer at work, which he sometimes popped in his rucksack for just such occasions. If there'd been anyone about, he might have played the old double-glazing-salesman-on-a-follow-up-visit schtick, but as it was, no theatrics were needed.

The front door opened almost before he'd rung the bell. Lily Sharp's hair and eyebrows were as black as her blouse and slacks. And she wore a heavy gold cross and chain over the blouse. Slim and frail, she'd dressed for company. People of a certain age usually did, Rex had found.

'Hello, Mrs Sharp. Rex King.'

'Come in,' she said with a smile that showed off her slightly-too-even **dentures**. 'You found us okay, then?'

'**Seek** and ye shall find, Mrs Sharp. How are you?'

'Been better, thanks for asking,' she said, shifting her weight awkwardly from one foot to the other and back again with a wince. 'He's in there.'

Rex recognised the posture from his own grandmother. 'Bad hip, is it?' he asked as she shut the door behind him and showed him through.

'Well, if it ain't me hip it's me knees, and if it ain't me knees it's me hip,' she said. '**Agony**, it is. Would you like a cup of tea? I just made a pot.'

'Mum, he's the police,' said Dicky Sharp loudly from the other room. 'You don't offer the police tea. No offence, Detective Sergeant!'

'None taken,' said Rex, walking into the living room and shaking Sharp's hand. 'He's right, Mrs Sharp,' he called back out to the hallway. 'We're not meant to, but you know what? I'd love some tea. Milk, no sugar, please.'

'Right you are,' said Lily Sharp over her shoulder.

Dicky Sharp had dressed up too. He'd had a shave, by the smell of it – strong cologne albeit with a slightly astringent uremic base note – and ironed his collarless shirt; put a jacket on. He might be getting on now but he still looked pretty solid. You wouldn't want to have been up against him in a fight in his heyday. Rex could see that he'd have been an intimidating fixture on the door at Hollywood's for all those years. But clearly someone had had a go once upon a time. Looking at Sharp's facial scar up close, Rex could see that he'd been lucky not to lose his sight. Apparently Sharp had been riding shotgun on a debt collection at a domestic address when things had got nasty, and whoever it was had lamped him with the hot iron. The eye itself looked sore. It was bloodshot and weeping. It'd be like having a permanent case of **pink-eye**.

'Nice horse brasses,' said Rex to change the subject while he did a quick risk assessment before sitting down. 'I bet they take a bit of polishing.'

The room was full of knick-knacks and ornaments.

There was a lot to take in.

A dozen or more framed family photos were lined up on the mantelpiece. Among the old black-and-whites of men in suits and hats, and the christening pics and wedding line-ups, were a couple of faded colour pictures of Dicky as a schoolboy, and a larger black-and-white studio portrait of the young Lily Sharp: a **winsome** young woman in her 1950s finery. Next to the clock was a photo of a teenage Dicky Sharp standing with both parents in the porch. He was dressed in the skinhead clobber of the time: tight-fitting Wrangler jacket, Brutus checked shirt, pale-blue denims and cherry DMs.

Hanging in the alcoves on either side of the chimney breast was a rogues' gallery of disembodied heads: detailed and realistically painted plaster sculptures of pirates, gypsies, smugglers, Arabs, a Scotsman, a Sikh.

What kind of **alchemy** was it, Rex wondered, that made one person's trash another's **heirloom**.

'Mum and Dad used to collect 'em,' said Dicky, clearly following Rex's gaze and his line of thought. 'Didn't you, Lil? But it ain't all bad. She likes a bit of Clarice Cliff and all.'

Mrs Sharp didn't answer. She was halfway to the kitchen, but Rex had already clocked the conical cups and saucers in the china cabinet, and the fern pot that took pride of place – complete with lace doily – on the smoked-glass and chromium side table in front of the bow window. If there was anyone left in the UK who hadn't watched *Antiques Roadshow*, they might have mistaken it for a crudely and gaudily painted bucket, but to most people it would be instantly recognisable as a valuable piece of Art Deco china. It was called a fern pot – amazing the trivia you picked up off the telly – not because it was decorated with **frond** and furl of stylised bracken, but because of the plant you were supposed to put in it. In this case, Rex noted, a bright-green maidenhair.

'You've been here a while, I see,' said Rex, nodding at the photo of the teenage Sharp. 'Great photo.'

'Oh, I loved all that,' said Sharp. 'Down the arcade in Wells's record shop every Saturday, I was. All me Desmond Dekker and Prince Buster singles.' He nodded at Rex's Harrington: 'Bit of a natty dresser yourself, eh?'

Rex shrugged, but said nothing. He was the one asking questions.

'Yeah, well. Mum's lived round here all her life. She was a Barnardo's girl.'

Rex remembered the large office building near the police station. 'What, you—'

'Barnardo's – the Girls' Village?' said Sharp. 'Mostly sold off now, over the years, but it was all children's homes down there, sixty acres of it, all set in parks and trees. Beautiful, it was. That's how Barnardo's started. Looking after destitute girls. They had loads of little cottages, each one with a house mother, ten girls to an 'ouse, playgrounds, the lot. All of that down there where the Magistrates' Court is now. There's only a few of them left. It was famous. There was a Children's Church and all. It even had tiny child-sized pews in them days. You must have walked past it if you come on the tube. Course, it's all been turned into luxury flats now, ain't it, what's left of the village, but it used to be massive.'

Mrs Sharp came in with a tray of tea.

'Thank you, Mrs Sharp,' said Rex, picking up a cup and saucer and taking a sip.

'Ta, Mum,' said Sharp. 'I was just telling the Detective Sergeant you was a Barnardo's girl. She was lucky not to have been emigrated to Australia or Canada in them days, wasn't you, Lil. Girls and boys by your time, though, weren' it.'

'Ooh, yes,' said Mrs Sharp. 'Lovely, it was. We had all little uniforms and everything.'

'I can't believe I didn't know about that,' said Rex. 'So was that the little church on Tanners Lane there?'

No wonder it had seemed quaint: it was literally child-sized.

'You wouldn't think,' said Sharp, 'that there'd be six hundred little girls needed looking after, would you, eh?'

Oh yes you bloody would, thought Rex.

That was when it started. Almost imperceptible at first, like the first twinge when you're coming up on acid.

Not now, he thought, taking a deep breath.

'Anyway, Mr Sharp,' he said.

'Ta, Mum – can you leave us alone for a bit,' said Sharp. 'Me and the Detective Sergeant have got things to talk about.'

Rex took the Met-issue laptop out of his rucksack and opened it up.

'You don't mind if I... ?' said Sharp, filling a small china vessel with sterilised water. 'It's for me eye.'

'Not at all,' said Rex. 'Go ahead.' Then he told Dicky Sharp a little of why he was here. He started off by showing Sharp a still of Webster – whom he didn't identify – crossing the threshold at Lido Cars, noting the time and date, and Sharp looking on from the pavement.

'Excuse me a sec,' Sharp said once Rex had finished. He looked up at the Artex ceiling and lifted the eye bath as if it were a loaded shot glass, tipped it up, then held it over the socket for a few seconds. Afterwards he dabbed his cheek with a large paisley handkerchief. 'I had a feeling it might be that,' he said. 'Blimey, where to start.'

It was no surprise that Sharp identified Webster immediately. He'd known exactly who the unannounced visitor was, and why he was there. He even called him 'Webbo'.

Rex felt increasingly detached from the situation. He couldn't quite focus on the meaning of what Sharp was saying, but he tried his best to carry on making notes on autopilot.

For a second Rex wondered if Lily Sharp had slipped him a mickey after all, but he'd had enough counselling over the years to know that he was simply dissociating.

It was 'the policeman's friend': PTSD, the common-or-garden panic attack.

It had started with digestive grumblings, back in Lavengro days.

Ask any policeman that's done child abuse cases or any long-term UCO work. Occupational-stress-related conditions were par for the course: IBS, eczema, hypertension, the lot.

All that pain had to come out somewhere.

When you were investigating pure evil, crimes that really shouldn't happen but you were watching them happen over and over again, an unseen yet pervasive and statistically – sadly – wholly predictable tide of sexual violence lapping away just beneath society's surface, something had to give, and sometimes that something was you.

Sometimes your body started to object, to rebel.

For Rex, what had started as queasiness, or occasional diarrhoea that could all too easily be put down to last night's curry, or poisonous beer from whichever dodgy boozer, had slowly evolved into symptoms not unlike early-onset IBS, before settling into occasional feelings of detachment and disorientation, and panic attacks – like now. Sometimes prompted, sometimes not.

Added to these physical signs, the pressure of managing departure strategies and end-of-tour procedures, whether abrupt or LTP – long-term phased – could often lead to emotional symptoms, like 'missing' your wearies and other activist associates, or the various flexibilities and perks associated with UCO or field operative roles; not to mention living a lie 24/7. What might have seemed like months of mind-numbingly boring discussion of political theory might in retrospect start to seem like fun. A return to normal day-to-day working required immediate adjustments, most of which sounded easy, but in practice could prove hard to manage: the need for circumspection, to avoid recognition by activist associates, of avoiding known areas of association, avoiding likely protests and pickets, or 'bandit country' generally, being able to recognise and deal with paranoia, adjusting to substantial changes of squad personnel in your former workplace, the preponderance of new faces and 'bright young things', of new paperwork and office practices and procedures, all with their corresponding training requirements. Such measures often left former or end-of-tour UCOs with acute anxiety, and feeling additionally disorientated or just plain rusty, but sometimes also questioning the very basics of existence: Why do I have to go to the station in the morning? Why don't I have any dosh? Why do I have to use public transport like all the other lemmings? Wot no expenses? Where's my van?

The combination of such physical and mental symptoms and adjustments could create a volatile cocktail. And with PTSD, knowing what it was, recognising the onset, didn't necessarily stop it happening.

If anything, it made it worse.

By the end of his little chat with Sharp, Rex was almost having an out-of-body experience, but he persevered.

Back out in the fresh air a few minutes later, he'd be splashing bottled water on his face and sitting on a garden wall a bit nearer the high street to get his breath back. Then he'd put the rucksack down between his feet and do some t'ai chi breathing exercises, right there on the pavement of Fullwell Avenue. It seemed to work. Probably turned a few heads, but Rex didn't care. It stabilised things enough for him to get out of there, to shoulder the rucksack and start walking back towards the flying-saucer-shaped library at the end of the road.

As he walked, he would realise with a start that it was the little child-sized church that had done it. The realisation that you can't come of age twice. Once childhood's been taken away, it's gone.

It was the contrast between the idea of that historic Barnardo's Girls' Village – the tens of thousands of young women protected, given a chance to grow up, their lives valued and saved – and the surveillance video from Lido Cars that he'd been watching these past six days, of young women being systematically robbed of that chance, and of their childhoods. Young women who weren't being protected or valued at all, just being used, brutalised, and thrown away.

The two universes simply didn't match up.

It was never-ending.

The list of offences committed on Kayak alone, page after page, the harshness of the language, the multiple crimes committed on numerous occasions by each suspect. And these were just the instances that were known and documented. In addition to the multiple Section 20s – battery, actual bodily harm, unlawful wounding or inflicting grievous bodily harm, causing grievous bodily harm with intent, and wounding with intent to do grievous bodily harm – were countless trafficking offences under Section 2 of the Modern Slavery Act and Article 3 of the Palermo Protocol: the recruitment, transportation, transfer, harbouring or receipt of persons for the purpose of exploitation, the exploitation or the prostitution of others, or other forms of sexual exploitation, namely, causing or inciting a child to engage in sexual activity, sexual touching, intentional penetration of a child, intentional sexual penetration, inciting or encouraging a child to perform sex acts, conspiring to incite children under the age of sixteen to engage in penetrative sexual activity, intentionally causing or inciting a child to engage in sexual activity, conspiring with others to arrange or facilitate the doing of acts that they themselves or others intended to involve sexual activity with a child, conspiring with others to cause or incite children to engage in penetrative sexual activity without reasonably believing that the children were over the age of sixteen, conspiring together with others for the purpose of obtaining sexual gratification by causing or inciting the children to watch themselves or others engage in sexual activity, conspiring with others to cause or incite the said children to engage in penetrative sexual activity, and on and on and on.

For the victims it was a relentless and almost inescapable torrent of violence, pain and degradation, an unspeakable circle of hell right here on earth.

For the perpetrators? Hell was too good for them.

For Rex, just thinking about it again would be enough to—

That was when he'd dived into Costa Coffee to vomit in the (thankfully vacant) customer toilet out the back.

But before all that, Rex couldn't leave the Sharps' until he'd got what he needed. He might not get another chance to come out here again. And as Sharp continued to talk, Rex tried not to hyperventilate. The room started spinning on and off, and gently at first, but Rex concentrated on continuing to take notes and trying to regulate his breathing.

It had happened a few times before, and he'd learned that if he could do that, if he could regulate his breathing, it would pass eventually.

Right now, though, as Sharp nattered away, Rex felt as if he was tripping.

Images flashed in his mind: the blue floral patterns on the melamine mugs at his long-dead grandmother's house... detainee questionnaires: *Yes* ☐ *No* ☐ *Don't remember* ☐ ... sat in the patrol car eating a Twix... a standard-issue, solid-state, 1TB hard drive... half-eaten pizza in its grease-stained cardboard carton... the gingering foliage and bark cankers of *Phytophthora ramorum* infestation in a stand of diseased larch near... a children's church decorated for Easter... derelict halls and landings of the former Cambridge Military Hospital... Nirvana T-shirt and ironic *Star Wars* rucksack... a wooden-handled **bill-hook**... splayed legs emerging from beneath a pile of... detainee questionnaires... *No* ☐ *Bad* ☐ *Neither* ☐ *Don't know/ Can't remember* ☐ *I don't know what this is* ☐ *I don't remember* ☐ *Not requested* ☐.

Rex felt sick; a cold sweat.

Talk about bad timing.

He knew it was showing, but he pressed on and tried to control it, to contain it *Yes* ☐ *No* ☐ *Don't remember* ☐ ... because there was one more thing he needed from Dicky Sharp *Yes* ☑ ... before he could gather up his things and run out of the door. Lollo had said to

ring-fence the conversation *Yes* ✔ … to keep it strictly focused and
not to step on toes. To focus *Yes* ✔ … on the incident with Detective
Sergeant Eddie Webster. But on the journey over Rex had decided
Yes ✔ … fuck Lollo, that he would also *Yes* ✔ … show Dicky Sharp
a still of the other individual.

Find out what Sharp knew about that bastard.

Yes ✔

26: Champignon (Mushroom)

Bent over the hand sink in the tiny airless toilet in the back of the Barkingside Costa Coffee, Rex splashed his face with cold water as best he could in the circumstances, and was thankful that at least he hadn't puked all over Mrs Sharp's sofa, or stumbled in his haste to get out and smashed her smoked-glass tables and her Clarice Cliff collection.

He just hoped that he'd got what he came for; enough to have made the visit worthwhile.

He thought of his hasty exit: scrambling the laptop back into his rucksack, all fingers and thumbs, and practically running out of the door.

He patted his pockets – phone: check, badge: check – and hoped that he hadn't forgotten anything. No, all seemed to be okay, thank Christ. He could do without the embarrassment of having to go back to the Sharps' with his tail between his legs.

Rex pulled a paper towel from the dispenser and wiped his face and hands. He had stopped retching – there was no breakfast left to throw up – and was breathing normally now. He no longer had that jangly feeling of being just about to faint.

He slapped both cheeks to wake himself up.

It was time to face the world, or perhaps just a quiet corner of Costa for a minute or two.

He needed to collect his thoughts and go over the notes – hopefully they'd be legible – before he touched base with Lollo, who'd be well ensconced with Webster right now if all had gone according to plan.

Rex found a table in the rear of the cafe, with the fire exit behind him and a clear view of the street door, and put the rucksack down on the chair next to the wall. He looked around at the large, clean cafe.

It was a recent fit-out, by the looks of things: the grey walls and dark-red fittings decorated here and there with variations on the Costa coffee-bean logo, large black-and-white 'heritage'-style photo panels of rustic Italian village scenes, shiny black tiles behind the serving area, well-spaced black sofas and chairs, and pale wooden tables.

Rex couldn't help wondering what if any relationship the now global coffee platform had with the then rapidly expanding London family business that he and Helen had enjoyed supporting in the early 1990s, with its coffee roastery off a side street next to the railway near Waterloo Station, its couple of dozen cafes and its reliably decent strong mocha blend. It was quite a story: from a family buy-out in 1985 that had still been a source of pride and a regular subject of conversation for the more senior counter staff at the turn of the nineties to a takeover by Whitbread PLC ten years later, which – Rex had read about it in the paper – saw the company expanding to nearly three thousand cafes in thirty countries, and more recently Whitbread's $4.9 billion sale of Costa to Coca-Cola. And what next? He'd heard somewhere that the fragrant old roastery near Waterloo, with its big stainless-steel condenser chimney – a visual and olfactory landmark on those train journeys to Barnes during his secondment to the squad – was now dark, the gates locked. Right now, the cafe he found himself in was more or less empty, but he imagined that, on your average Saturday, and most weekday mornings before work, and most lunchtimes, teatimes, and early evenings, it'd be heaving.

He noticed a movement to his left. It was a barista carrying a large paper takeaway cup that she put down on the table in front of him.

'Excuse me, sir,' she said. 'The ladies over there asked me to bring you a glass of water. They thought you might be unwell.'

'Ah, that's nice. They were right. I'm okay now, though, thanks,' said Rex, glancing around the room for his benefactors. Yes. Thought so. He raised his hand and mimed 'Thank you'.

'Is there anything else I can get you?' said the barista.

'Yes. Can I have a regular English breakfast tea, but leave the teabag in?'

'Would you like any food with that? Egg-and-mushroom breakfast muffin? Smoked-bacon sourdough? All-day breakfast panini? Tuna-melt panini? Roast-chicken fajita? Would you like to see our range of sandwiches and wraps, croissants and muffins, or salads?'

'Sounds great, but no thanks,' said Rex.

'That'll be one seventy-five, please. Drink in or take away?'

'Take away, please. Shall I pay you now?'

'No, it's alright. I'll bring the bill in a minute,' she said. 'Come and pay after.'

'Actually,' said Rex, suddenly feeling hungry, 'have you got any mozzarella-and-tomato panini?'

'Italian mozzarella and tomato stone-baked panini?'

'Yes. I'll have one of those, then, please.'

'That'll be five pounds seventy all together,' she said.

While he waited, Rex sipped the iced water. Wondered how it was going with Webster: how the Detective Chief Inspector would dress it up.

Pen in hand, Rex started leafing through his notebook. Going back over his strange half-hour at the Sharps'.

'Hope you didn't mind our little intervention,' said a female voice a few minutes later. 'Are you feeling better?'

It was one of the women from out front, though maybe not the one he'd hoped. She was evidently stopping by his table on her way back from the loo.

'Not at all. It was very nice of you, thanks,' said Rex with a smile. 'I'm fine. Bad day, that's all.'

'My colleague thought you looked like you'd seen a ghost,' she said. 'Anyway, I don't want to interrupt. We're going back to the office, but she asked me to give you this. Just in case you were wondering who your guardian angel was.'

She handed over a business card, with the green Barnardo's logo on the top.

'Thank you,' said Rex. 'That's very sweet. I'm Rex, by the way.' He read the card, then took out his wallet and opened it ready to pop it in there, and to give her his card in return, but also – mainly – so that she would definitely see his 'badge', his Met warrant card. That would give them something to talk about. Then he looked over at the window to where Thea James – 'Deputy Director of Strategic Partnerships', according to her card – was looking in. He held up her card as if to say 'Got it!' and smiled, held her gaze. She smiled back, then laughed and shrugged, as if to say 'Nothing ventured...'

Rex shrugged too and waved. Then his food arrived, and some metal cutlery wrapped in a paper napkin.

'That's lovely, thank you,' he said to the barista.

'She's one of the good ones,' said Thea James's colleague, nodding towards the street door. 'Anyway, I'm glad you're okay.'

Rex looked back at the window but Thea had gone, and her friend now followed.

Still got it, he thought, tucking in to his toasted panini with renewed appetite. Thea? He could fall into her arms a thousand times. Things had been difficult with Susan – well, up and down anyway, and that wasn't just her journeys to and from York, but pressure of work on both sides, it seemed. Sometimes they wouldn't see each other for weeks at a time. And when they did it wasn't always much better. 'Even when I'm down here I hardly see you,' she'd said on her last visit. 'Even when I'm staying in your flat.' It had turned into an argument.

Maybe she was right and the job was more important. He loved her alright, but perhaps it was time to call it a day; start afresh. But there was no need for any sudden movement. Maybe he could play both for a while. Even though they'd barely met, there was definitely chemistry with Thea. It could be fun.

Yeah, he thought.

In your dreams.

It never worked out like that.

There was no such thing as 'no strings'.

Affairs of the heart were never simple. Relationships were all or nothing; they had to be. But what the hell. It wasn't as if he and Susan were married. If she wasn't here, then what was he supposed to do? One thing about this job, you learned how to compartmentalise.

His phone rang. Talk of the devil, he thought. Susan was a bit psychic sometimes. But no: he recognised Lollo's number.

'Where the fuck are you?'

'Just on the way back now, sir,' said Rex. 'Grabbed a sandwich. How did it—'

... go with Webbo, was what he was going to ask, but he could hear traffic in the background, then Lollo covering the phone and shouting at someone else at his end: 'The fucker's only sat down for a three-course fucking meal!'

'No, I mean where are you precisely?' said Lollo. 'Still in Barkingside?'

'Yeah, Costa Coffee on the high street, sir.'

'Well, get back around the corner, PD-fucking-Q. Sharp has been abducted.'

'What?' said Rex. 'When?'

'Just now! Their number's on special schemes,' said the Detective Chief Inspector, 'so we got a notification.'

'I was only there a second ago,' said Rex, then thought better of it. 'Well, ten minutes.'

'Din't you see owt?'

'Not a thing, sir,' said Rex, but he wasn't about to tell Lollo about his panic attack. 'I'll get back round there right away.'

'You didn't lead 'em there, did you, Kingsy? Or draw attention?'

'No!'

'In his own fucking car and all,' said Lollo. 'Mrs Sharp said she thought it was you as popped back for sommat, so she'd opened the door without a thought.'

'Jesus,' said Rex. 'Okay, I'm on my way.'

'Horse has fucking bolted now,' said Lollo. 'I'll tell you when to bloody go round there. I've not finished yet.'

Rex wasn't about to argue the toss.

'Anyroad, what'd you find out about our friend?'

The meeting was still a blur; Rex hadn't had a chance to go through his notes yet.

'Inconclusive, sir,' he said, improvising to cover his back but immediately regretting it.

'Fuck's sake,' said Lollo. 'I don't need two useless twats on my team. Got one of them inside here already.'

'He knew Webbo, of course... Oh, there was something,' said Rex, desperately flicking through the open pages of his notebook to see what it might be. That was it. 'Sharp said that Webster was looking for a girl.'

Rex carried on flicking, trying to decipher his more-illegible-than-usual scrawl. He tried to think; couldn't read his own bloody writing. 'I'll write it up as soon as I get back.'

'Oh aye,' said Lollo. 'Is that it? Are you tekkin the piss? They're all looking for a girl. That's why they fucking go there in the first place!'

27: Hyacinthe (Hyacinth)

By the time Rex got back round to Fullwell Avenue, the Ilford response team were already in place. He introduced himself, had a quick chat with the Sergeant and gave them his card. He nearly gave him Thea's by mistake, but noticed just in time.

Dicky Sharp had clearly put up a fight, because there was smashed china on the living room carpet.

His mum was still sitting on the sofa. She'd finished giving a statement and must have been in shock.

'I suppose I'd better sweep that up,' she said, but didn't move. 'Richard'll have a fit. I never really liked it, to be honest – all that dusting. But he thinks I do and it makes him happy.'

'Leave 'em to it,' Lollo had said. 'Offer to share your statement if it's useful to them, to set the scene like. But – no offence, Kingsy – there's nowt you can add on the ground. Dicky Sharp's a bit of a face, so they're seeing it as a local affair. They've got an 'ead start because it's on their manor. They've assured me they'll **assess** the situation and keep the Kayak team informed. Reckons he'll just as likely have been roughed up a bit and dumped around fucking corner.'

Rex could imagine that Sharp would have stacked up a few enemies over the years, but with his Operation Kayak hat on he wasn't entirely happy with such a low-key risk assessment. He could hear what Lollo was saying, but he hoped that it wouldn't **backfire**. Regardless of the new strategy, Sharp was still a key witness in a major current investigation, and surely that would also have to be explored here.

'I hope so, sir,' said Rex. 'Because even if we're not putting all our eggs in one basket, we still need him in court.'

'Aye, well,' said Lollo. 'Happen, but he's given us plenty already, to be fair.'

Operation Kayak was weighing heavily on Rex's mind, because

he knew that it didn't even scratch the surface. He didn't want to **do down** any other force, but if this was going on in Romford it could go on anywhere. There'd been high-profile cases in Oxford and Rotherham, but those were just the ones that'd got caught – thanks to some brave parents and even braver victims coming forward, and perhaps a public-spirited witness or two like Dicky Sharp. Rex knew that you could chuck a dart in a map of the UK and wherever it landed – from **St Albans**, **Durham** or **Hereford**, from **Rochester** to **Southwell** to **Carlisle** – you could guarantee **in advance** there'd be an equivalent there too.

And if there wasn't, it just meant that it hadn't been found yet.

It was doing Rex's head in, the evil, the sheer depravity that was going on right under everybody's noses.

He sometimes had to remind himself that life could be fun. Meeting Thea – or almost meeting her – had given him a real buzz, and that kind of excitement was very moreish. But he and Susan had fun too: driving down to **Salisbury** in a hire car for that spontaneous day out at Stonehenge – she'd never been – and listening to 'My Way' by Nina Simone on full volume, or singing along to the *Harder They Come* soundtrack. Or spending the whole day in bed. He had to admit he was looking forward all the more to a few days in Dungeness with Susan – having her all to himself. He'd spoken to Terence first, to take him up on his offer and check some dates, and then he'd rung her back.

'Sorry I couldn't talk yesterday,' he said. 'Something massive came up that I've had to deal with. But I'll try harder, I promise.'

'That's nice of you to say. Well, at least I know what to expect with you,' she said. 'But thanks. It'll be great to spend a decent bit of time together. Tell Terence that I'm looking forward to meeting him. Love you.'

'Love you too.'

It was all arranged. Susan was going to come down from **York** on the Thursday afternoon and they'd get the train over. They could be eating seafood on the beach by teatime. A bit of **crab** maybe, or some prawns, with a crusty French loaf and a bottle of rosé. Rex couldn't wait. For the past few months he'd had an **itch** that only Susan could scratch. How long had it been – a few weeks since he last saw her? If so, it was a few weeks too long. They'd had a bit of a row in the square, and she'd said she didn't know why she bothered, that he never had enough time for her. But surely she knew that it wasn't personal, it was just that police work wasn't a nine-to-five office job. How could it be?

So, a few days in Dungeness it was. Just thinking about it put a bit of a spring in his step.

Rex was well aware that he was a hopeless romantic. Always had been. It must be genetic – but how was that even possible in a complex human organism? Rex tried to remember his biology lessons at secondary school. The human body as a complex multicellular organism. The various hierarchies, from the molecular upwards – cells, organs, whatever – resulting in an entity that's not only able to perform as an independent individual but also feels itself to be a unified self, rather than just a walking, talking bag of crystalline structures, bacteria and multi-kingdom symbiotes. An individual with a sense of self and the power of thought and reflection, the ability to think of futures and pasts, to choose right from wrong and to perform within a society. The idea that a particular gene might simply **encode** a propensity for its owner, if that was the right word – or bearer, host, whatever – to fall in love at the drop of a hat seemed ridiculous. Or to be good at languages, or at drawing. Well, the proof of the pudding was in the eating, as his grandmother had sometimes used to say. But whether due to nature or nurture, if Rex's heart was a temple to **Eros**, in the centre of that temple right now was a **shrine** to Susan. And seeing someone else wouldn't need to change that. He thought of the last time they'd made love. Susan's **smooth** Black skin writhing against him, her nerve-endings **ablaze** as she loudly came with Rex inside her.

He'd double-checked the Dungeness dates with Lollo, and got approval for a few days' annual leave.

'Aye, well go on. You've put in the hours this week, so I reckon you've earned it,' the Detective Chief Inspector had said. 'There's nowt happening with Kayak that can't happen without you for a few days. Just come back Wednesday refreshed, alright.'

'That's the plan, sir.'

'Though I know you'll just be on the nest every waking minute. She's wasted on you, though. You know that, don't yer.'

Helen called Rex at home later. When the phone rang he was just about to go the launderette. He'd spent most of the evening trying to decipher his notes from the interview with Dicky Sharp so he could put them in his real notebook and sign the pages off, send a scan to the Ilford boys as promised. According to Sharp, Webster had been looking for a Hyacinth. Rex realised that Helen might know something about this, but he wasn't about to share the details of the investigation.

Helen was crying. Webster had told his wife about the meeting with Lollo, and about the suspension pending, but now he'd gone to the pub.

Well, that was a start at least, Rex thought to himself. Webster could have lied, pretended to Hel that it hadn't happened. Rex could hear her reaching for a **tissue** at the other end of the line; blowing her nose.

Exactly what or how much Webster had told her was hard to say. Helen seemed more focused on the disciplinary procedure side of things, the temporary suspension on full pay, so maybe he'd only talked effect rather than cause. If that was the case, Rex couldn't imagine what she'd think once she knew the real reason. And she'd find out soon enough. This wasn't going to go away. Of course, Helen was worried sick as it was. And, according to Helen, Jennifer was beside herself, saying it was all her fault. It would have to be something pretty serious for DCI Lawrence and PC Singh to have come all this way for a chat, wouldn't it? The risk to Eddie's career, his pension and everything. What was next? Did Rex have any idea where the procedure went from here?

'Not tempting fate or anything, Hel, but maybe he'll just get put on desk duty for a few months, which wouldn't be so bad at our age.'

'Really?'

'You know the police look after their own. Chances are he'd get a lateral redeployment and keep his seniority. He could go on TeDIU(M) for a bit. That could mean getting some training, maybe even transferring closer to home. And they do say that TeDIU(M)'s the future of policing.'

'Tedium doesn't sound great,' said Helen. 'What's that?'

'You know, the Telephone and Digital Investigation Unit,' said Rex. 'Every force has got one now. They're all the rage. Go in at Ed's level and you'd be running the place in six months!'

'D'you think?'

'I don't even know what this is about,' said Rex, 'so it's hard to say.'

But even as he said it he was aware that Helen knew him well enough to know when he was lying.

'Just a formality, I'm sure,' he went on. 'You know what they're like. There's probably a good chance there'll be a follow-up letter in a day or two and that'll be it and all about it. I wouldn't worry too much, Hel. Cross that bridge when you come to it, eh? Anyway, listen,' he said, clocking the time, 'I've got to run, got to catch the launderette before it shuts, but I'll see what I can find out, okay? And I'll check in with Ed, remind him he's got friends.'

'Okay,' said Helen. 'Thank you. That'll mean a lot to him, I'm sure. Oh, Rex?'

'What?'

'Jennifer might ring you tomorrow. She was talking about coming to see you at the weekend.'

'Ah,' said Rex. 'No go. I've got a few days' leave, so I'll be away Saturday and Sunday.'

'Anywhere nice?'

'Tel's got a new place out in Kent.'

'Oh, nice,' said Helen. 'Give him my love.'

'I will do.'

'Rex?'

'What?'

'Get a washing machine. You're not a bloody student.'

'It's broken,' said Rex. 'I've got to get a new one. But listen, Hel, do tell Jen to call me. That would be great. Can't do this weekend, but I'd love to see her another time.'

28: Râteau (Rake)

Pulling the front door of the flat to behind him and jogging down the stairs, perhaps it was the anticipation of the weekend away with Susan that momentarily rekindled Rex's fleeting and long-dormant teenage interest in matters Viking-related – an interest, incidentally, that he shared with Detective Chief Inspector Jethro Lawrence – but thinking of the coming weekend as he'd pulled on his jacket had conjured a vision of longboats being dragged up onto that broad shingle beach. He could just imagine it. And, according to Terence, it was Vikings that had actually named the place.

While for Lollo the Norse origin of so many place names from his county of birth were simply a source of Yorkshire pride – 'Halifax!' he'd say. 'Huddersfield!' – the young King's superficial interest in Viking history – or imagery, perhaps – had been sparked by a certain cosmopolitan affectation and grandiosity in the music and styling of the UK punk band The Stranglers. He and his schoolfriend Andy had been big fans. Too young to appreciate them during the punk era – though of course they'd heard songs like 'Peaches' on the radio, and seen them on *Top of the Pops* as younger children – both boys had started out by going to Left Bank Records and buying copies of the band's overtly Viking-inspired 1979 album *The Raven*, on the day of its release. From there they had not only followed them **onward** through the quieter and more poppy LPs, but also worked their way through the perplexing back catalogue. For a start, was the first LP called *The Stranglers IV* or *Rattus Norvegicus*? Was the 'IV' a reference to there being four of them? It was confusing. They called it *Rattus* for short. These were still the days when the rarest 7-inch – the limited coloured vinyl, the free giveaway, the picture-sleeve, the Canadian compilation, the US or Europe-only EP, the French or the Swedish translation – and even a *Strangled* fanzine, were still available via the classified ads in the back pages of the *NME*. The first release of *The Raven* had come with a 3D photo on the cover, and contained what seemed to the two twelve-year-old boys to be **clever** songs not just about Vikings but also about things like nuclear testing, genetics and the Shah of **Iran**. Within a few years these songs would come to seem slightly juvenile – not to mention ideologically unsound – to the teenage fans, who by then were looking for a more righteous kind of political intelligence in their music of choice. But the songs had stood the test of time, and in truth it was the schoolboys' enthusiasm and their disappointment that had been childish: what did they expect from a punk band?

They'd missed The Stranglers' more raucous heyday, but still managed to go and see them a couple of times in the early eighties, preferring to get the train up to the livelier gigs in big-city Bristol than the ones in the slightly nearer but less atmospheric Cornwall Coliseum in St Austell, even though the cavernous former indoor tennis courts had the added attraction of being right on the beach.

More recently, this century at least, the Barnes contingent – or a certain demographic thereof – had had a works outing, a morale-building exercise, to see The Stranglers live at the Brixton Academy. Before the gig, the streets of Brixton had thronged with a statistically unlikely number of sixty-year-old bald white men in black leather car coats. The 'Finchley Boys' of legend were now old men. It was like a taxi drivers' convention. Despite having been a teenage fan, Rex had been reluctant to even tag along at first, unsure whether whichever post-Hugh Cornwell line-up it was would even be worthy of the name, and wholly expecting that he'd struggle to greet the set with anything more than the most **backhand** of faint praise. But he'd been immediately and forcibly proved completely wrong: you couldn't argue with that driving sound, those great songs. And as he'd subsequently discover, even the quieter late-period albums could generally be guaranteed to include a couple of absolute stormers, still driven by Jean-Jacques Burnel's 'Barracuda Bass' and Dave Greenfield's psychedelic keyboard licks. And back at Brixton with Donal and the boys – so that dated it – if Rex hadn't recognised some of the more recent material, by the time they did 'Go Buddy Go' he'd been down the front, and before too long he was bouncing around and singing 'Always the Sun' at the top of his voice with the best of them. Then afterwards they'd all piled into a cab and gone back to Rex's and listened to the back catalogue, those childhood records that he'd had to buy all over again, on CD this time.

Before Helen had rung, before he remembered that he'd better get a move on if he was going to collect his service wash before the launderette closed, Rex had more or less finished deciphering the notes he'd managed to scrawl at Dicky Sharp's and now he just needed to touch base with Lollo in the morning and copy them out.

What was the opposite of a smoking gun?

Whatever it was, Rex was wondering if he'd found it.

According to Sharp, Webster hadn't simply been looking for a girl, but for one girl in particular: Hyacinth, one of his daughter's schoolfriends, a looked-after child – 'in care', as Sharp had put it – who'd gone off the rails a bit and disappeared from school. That's what Webster had asked Sharp at the door of Lido Cars: 'Is Hyacinth here?' That's why Sharp had shown him in: because she had been. It suggested that at least he hadn't just blundered into Lido Cars for the **peep show** value or to abuse one of the young women. Although, whichever way Rex looked at it, Webster's actions still raised more questions than answers, chief among which remained, of course: Was he completely fucking **mad**?

What was Webster trying to do, rescue her? To **wrest** her from the grip of the Lido Cars traffickers? If so, there were better ways to do that. And, even if he was, would that be enough to **let** him off the hook?

Rex doubted it.

Besides which, this was all getting a bit too close to home for Rex's liking, because – although Sharpy couldn't have known it – it was no longer Webster's daughter whose schoolfriend Webster had supposedly been looking for, but Rex's. This was Jennifer that Sharp was talking about, and Rex really didn't like the company her name was being spoken in. Rex didn't like it at all. And he was pretty certain that Helen would have a fit if she knew.

Not for the first time, Rex asked himself what Webster could possibly have thought he was playing at. Interfering with an investigation, and perhaps jeopardising it entirely, was hardly a **trivial** matter. How did he think he was going to **get away with it**?

Speaking of which, Rex didn't share the Detective Chief Inspector's blithe confidence in the upcoming SiC report.

'Bound to be sommat in there for them as wants to **abolish** the police,' Lollo had said, 'but I think we'll be alright, son. Don't paint devils on the wall.'

Rex wasn't so sure. He was expecting they'd all get royally screwed by whatever farrago of **newspeak** the SiC report might contain. But then, Rex didn't have Lollo's experience, nor his access to that network of little birds that whispered the weather forecasts – hints and secrets – into the ears of higher-ranking officers.

Bloody hell, Rex had thought he knew Jethro Lawrence, but he didn't know the half of it.

Cliff Heath hadn't held back the other day. Family schisms, the lot.

Rex jogged up Old Gloucester Street and nipped down the alley beside the playground and the pizza place to get to the launderette before it closed two minutes ago. The light was still on, so he was in luck. While he waited he was thinking back to Cliff Heath's stories about his old South Yorkshire mucker. It explained much about Lollo, that was for sure; not least his choice of career. Stories of that winter during the strike of '72 when for a couple of weeks half the street in Cottonley had lived on a sack of **sago** pearls liberated from the primary school kitchen, each watery batch of frogspawn flavoured with half an Oxo cube instead of the customary milk and sugar, or dollop of jam. Lollo's younger siblings had been born that same year too, a couple of weeks before the strike. It was a **multiple birth**, triplets, but one had died. Hard to imagine the combination of grief and **despair** at having two more mouths to feed. The strike couldn't have come at a worse time. Heathy said that the supervisor and a couple of blokes from management had had to cut old man Lawrence's body down from a **gantry** on the washery conveyor, because none of the lads would lift a finger to help a scab, even a dead one. And Cottonley was not even a particularly militant pit. **Cyrus** Lawrence (the name had been popular among several self-educated generations of Lollo's family, and was also Lollo's middle name) had been a staunch supporter of the 'October Revolution' in '69 – a local strike over management's attempts to hamper union meetings – but this time around he'd crossed the line. It explained a lot. Roll on twelve years, and for Lollo the strike of 1984 was always going to be the **second leg** of a grudge match. And if the branch members really had spat on his father's corpse like they said, the young Detective Constable Jethro Lawrence would spit back every night. Every single time he rubbed the **Kiwi** polish into his steel-toecapped uniform Doc Martens, he'd spit on them to bring up the shine and give his boots some extra bite.

Rex couldn't wait to tell Susan at the weekend. It sometimes wound her up just hearing about Lollo, so she'd love all this.

Letting himself back in to Falcon and jogging back up the stairs with his bag of neatly folded washing ready to hang up for airing, Rex thought again of Terence's rhapsodising about the Vikings of Dungeness: 'Denge' meaning to beat or to hammer, he'd said, and 'ness' being the Norse word for a headland.

What did Rex reckon, Terence had continued – might some rebel Viking battle fleet have settled there? To take that strange and inhospitable promontory and transform it into a **rural Valhalla**, a Kentish pirate Utopia? Building a peaceful life of fishery and what little animal **husbandry** was possible, with a bit of wrecking on the side? You could just imagine them, Terence had said, forging tools and agricultural implements from their swords and battleaxes, sheep farming on the marsh, picking banded horsefly **larvae** out of the mud to use for hook bait, setting eel nets, and harvesting the medicinal **leech** from the udders of the old ewes. Did they cannibalise their longboats to make more nimble fishing craft? Did they break up wrecks to make their longhouses? The fantasy took a poetic turn. Did they have fire festivals on the beach, these Dungeness Vikings, with guisers acting out the Norse sagas in Up Helly Aa? Was a **posy** of purple bugloss and white sea kale flowers, he wondered, laid on the stilled breast of some great old Norse warrior before his boat was set on fire and pushed out to sea?

Good old Terence Hobbs. Rex was looking forward to catching up with his mate.

He peeled the plastic film from his supermarket own-label ready-meal **lasagne**, and grated a bit of extra parmesan on top for luck, before putting it in the preheated oven. But now that was all settled, now that he knew when Susan was coming down and that their weekend break was taken care of, Rex had a sudden hankering to see Thea, his new friend in Barkingside. He felt sure that there'd been a

connection. They'd recognised something in each other, and neither
had looked away. He had to check for a second that her business
card was still in his wallet. It was, though of course, if it hadn't been,
now that he knew where she worked, he could always have rung the
switchboard.

Susan wasn't coming down to London until Thursday, and with
Lollo leading on Webster, Binder Singh already making headway
on implementing the new strategy, streamlining the charges for
CPS approval as Clifford Heath had suggested, and the Ilford boys
looking for Sharp, that left Rex in the rare position of having a couple
of weekday evenings potentially free-ish if he played his cards right.
After all, barring some further unforeseen emergency, Operation
Kayak wasn't going anywhere, touch wood. Rex couldn't think of
anyone he'd rather fill the time with than the Deputy Director of
Strategic Partnerships. He'd give her a ring tomorrow morning, and
see if she fancied meeting up for a glass or two of something nice
after work.

He reckoned she'd say yes.

29: Rhubarbe (Rhubarb)

Rex's yen for a bit of an Essex romance did not wholly go to plan. Which is not to say that he didn't get what he thought he wanted – just that it turned out he got a lot more than he'd bargained for.

But then, he wasn't the only one returning to the scene of the crime.

He'd called **Thea** late Tuesday morning, and the **vibes** had been great. Even over the phone they'd immediately settled into a ready rapport that made it feel as if they'd known each other for years. She was busy tonight. It was her turn to host the book group with the girls – 'Sacrosanct, I'm afraid!' she'd said, laughing – but she would be up for meeting at the end of the day tomorrow if he was free?

Rex could have punched the air, but he'd played it cool: 'Well, obviously it's a school night,' he'd said, 'but sure. Maybe we could go for an early drink, or even just a coffee? It'd be nice to chat.'

'Yes, I'd love that,' she'd said. That is, if he didn't mind something in her neck of the woods this time, because by the time she got out of work, blah blah.

'Absolutely,' Rex had said. He didn't mind at all. 'That's great. I'll look forward to it,' he'd said, and meant it. 'I get off at six tomorrow, so I'll just hop on the tube. Why don't I say that I'll be outside the children's church at seven? You've got my mobile number too, now, right?'

She had indeed.

'I'll text you when I get in,' he'd said.

He was almost quite excited.

But there was a lot to get through between now and then.

There were 'i's to dot, and 't's to cross, and Rex knew that these things always took longer than you thought they would. And before any of that he needed to find out how Lollo's chat with Webster had gone, and how the Detective Chief Inspector wanted to play it. And he needed to get that steer before signing off his notebook and getting the scan over to the Ilford team.

Rex needed to think on his feet, but he was good at that.

Lollo had been very clear that he should ring-fence the interview with Sharpy, to keep it strictly focused on Webster, but now Rex figured that he should definitely let the DCI know that Sharp had also confirmed the identity of the other individual on the video.

But getting five minutes with Lollo was easier said than done.

'Can't talk now, Detective Sergeant,' Lollo had said when Rex managed to ambush him in the corridor, mid-afternoon. 'War cabinet meeting with Evelyn and the Comms team.'

And when Rex had raised his eyebrows, Lollo had elaborated. 'Strategy meet to plan SiC response over the weekend.' Not only that, but the meeting agenda had included a Doodle poll for dietary requirements. 'It's gonna be a long'un. Can't it keep, Kingsy?'

In the event, Lollo rang Rex back much later, when he was at home watching *Newsnight*. 'Hang on, sir,' said Rex, reaching for the remote. 'Let me just turn the TV down.'

'Listen to this,' said Lollo. It turned out that the excuse Webster had offered for barging into Lido Cars was that over the past year or so he had developed a dependency on **opiate** painkillers, ever since the high-strength codeine he'd been prescribed for his bad back. He'd been told – or so he said – that one of the lads at Lido was a reliable source, that he usually had codeine or OxyContin. 'Long-short, Kingsy,' Lollo said, 'he'd gone along to try and score. And to be fair, he showed us his stash, and he had a whole bloody chemist's shop worth.'

'But Dicky Sharp told me that Webster was asking for a particular girl at the door,' said Rex. 'Said something about a Hyacinth.'

'Aye, well mebbe that's a code word,' said Lollo.

Not according to Dicky Sharp, it's not, thought Rex. He'd told Rex that Hyacinth was a former schoolfriend of Webbo's daughter Jennifer. A looked-after child who'd gone off the rails a bit, and got mixed up in the scene at Lido Cars. Why would Webster hold that back?

'Are you sure he was being completely honest with you, sir?' said Rex.

'Aye. Everyone on Kayak knows there's a bit of dealing going on at Lido: it's one o' ways they keep girls under cosh.'

'Yeah, I know. But don't you think – isn't there an element of "Well, he would say that"?' said Rex. 'He knows he's bang to rights, so he's offering up the lesser offence? Shouldn't we ask him outright if he had any involvement with any of the young women?'

'**Poppycock**,' said Lollo. 'He weren't playing. He were crying like a baby, between you and me, but he never said owt to us about any Hyacinth. So it looks like we've only got Sharp's word for that, and right now we've not got Sharp. And whatever goes on with the girl, it's beyond range of the camera, right? In other words, he knows we can't prove owt, and he's not offered it.'

'No, but I've got my notes, sir.'

'Are they finished?'

'Just tidying them up now, sir.'

'Because my advice would be to keep it simple,' said Lollo. 'Fewer charges the better, as long as we can mek 'em stick.'

Ever the pragmatist, thought Rex.

'Because,' Lollo continued, 'I hear what you say, Kingsy. But we've already got him on Class A possession, theft, misconduct in public office and obstructing the police. We don't need to add "causing or inciting victims" or "conspiring with others to arrange or facilitate" – he'd be looking at a couple of years at least. We'd have our work cut out to try and prove "intentional penetration", and I doubt he'd cooperate. And you know as well as I do that it's fifty-fifty whether she would. Fuck's sake, Kingsy. He's your mate. D'you think he should be on the register?'

'Well, I'd never have guessed,' said Rex. 'But I suppose he wouldn't be the first.'

'Aye, you're not wrong there, but how far down that path d'you want to go?'

Rex took a deep breath. This was his daughter's home they were talking about now: Helen and the girls. Jennifer was not Webster's daughter, but his. If Rex had his way, they'd throw the book at him. 'All the fucking way, sir, if he's a nonce.'

Lollo's **voice** turned more **solemn**. 'That's **unworthy** of you, Kingsy. Let's not be too **hasty**. I'll admit it don't look great, but he's still innocent until proven guilty, alright?'

But at that moment, Rex realised that Lollo wasn't acting out of concern for Webster. The 'presumption of innocence' guff was just that: nothing personal. There'd not been an ounce of sympathy in the litany of charges. Even though he was now appealing to Rex's loyalty to Webster, it was clear that, for the Detective Chief Inspector himself, any sense of loyalty to a colleague and subordinate – or maybe by now already a former colleague and subordinate – had evaporated.

Detective Sergeant Edward Webster was no longer 'one of us'. He'd transgressed; gone beyond the pale.

It might seem that Lollo was giving Webster the dignity of charging him with a lesser offence, but it was more practical than that. He simply didn't want to throw good money after bad if what he'd got was enough to get rid. There was a part of Lollo that was almost enjoying this now, Rex could tell. The Detective Chief Inspector was flexing some well-practised muscles, like a snake closing its eyes in anticipation as it begins to slowly and mercilessly **constrict** its prey. After this long on the force, it was practically instinctive. Webster was just a tasty snack, an appetiser before the main course.

'So you'll sign off your notes and get a scan over to Ilford by lunch tomorrow, right? And bring me a paper copy for the Kayak file, eleven sharp.'

'Sir,' said Rex obediently. 'One more thing.'

He quickly told Lollo that Dicky Sharp had also identified the other person on the tape. That while he'd had Sharpy there he figured it wouldn't be stepping on any toes.

'Good lad, Kingsy,' said Lollo. 'Thinking on your feet, I like that.'

Rex quickly summarised what Dicky Sharp had said. How the new 'Person 13' fitted in; a kind of *éminence grise*, as Rex understood it, who usually stayed firmly in the background.

'Plot thickens, eh,' said Lollo before he hung up. 'Good work, Detective Sergeant.'

'Thank you,' said Rex. 'Night, sir.'

It was a different and altogether more cheerful Lollo that Rex saw on Wednesday morning, when he dropped off the paperwork. And once business was done, Rex thought he'd make the most of it, and have a bit of sport. See if Cliff Heath was right.

'Aye, go on, then,' said Lollo. He undid his right cufflink and rolled up his sleeve to show an enormous, detailed tattoo of a **dragon** that curled around his bicep. 'Got it off a bloke called Alex in Clerkenwell, late eighties. Took three or four goes, that one.'

Then he rolled up the other sleeve to show – sure enough – a tattoo of a skull in a miner's helmet over a crossed pickaxe and shovel, just like Detective Inspector Cliff Heath's, with a scrolling banner on which was written the word 'The A-Team'. The only difference was that, on Lollo's tat, this was surmounted by a white rose of Yorkshire.

'This one were Aldershot, but all credit to Jeff Jaguar,' said Lollo. 'That guy were old-school. Tattoo royalty, he was, back in the sixties. There were framed black-and-white press photos of his old lady up in the shop. She were in *Guinness Book of Records*. When we got these done, old Tommy Orwell laughed and said it'd be nowt but a blue smear in twenty year. But look: it's a good thick line, clear as the day I got it.'

'Jeff Jaguar,' said Rex. 'What a name!'

'In't it. What else did Cliffy tell you, eh? D'he tell yer what the other blokes had: ASPOM. Arthur Sc—'

'Yeah,' said Rex, interrupting. 'Classic. He told me about your run-ins with the chief mechanic at Camberley and all.'

'Ha!' Lollo laughed out loud. 'Bleedin' hell, Camberley, eh? Fucking bumpkins. Old Heathcliff doesn't know half of it.'

Then Lollo turned the tables and had a pop at Rex's wardrobe, which was a bit unexpected, to say the least. He pointed at Rex's signature Harrington and Fred Perry combo. 'You might be too young to remember, but there used to be a record called "The Oldest Swinger in Town".'

'Eh?' said Rex.

'It'd be a bit of a **wrench** to give up your mod clobber, I know, but being where we are, you've some of best tailors in London **laid on** right here for your fucking convenience. Unless you want to carry on dressing like a fifty-year-old teenager.'

What had brought this on? Rex had no idea, but it was fair to say that Lollo was not given to idle chat. If he said something it was usually for a good reason.

'You've not long left to get DI, and whether you do or don't is not on my say-so, but I'll tell yer this much, Kingsy. Them as gets promoted don't tend to dress like funfair **rowdies** circa 1979. We all know you're working class, lad, so job done. But you wanna grow up a bit and get sommat **bespoke**. Because, let's face it, you're not spending your money on owt else.'

'Can't wear a pinstripe suit in this job, though, sir,' said Rex. 'You can't exactly stop and hang up your jacket before making an arrest. What are you going to do? Give 'em a **bump** on the head with a rolled-up brolly and say, "Excuse me, sir, I'm **predisposed** to place you under arrest if you'll just hold still for a second."'

'Aye, well,' said Lollo. 'That's my advice. Tek it or leave it, son.'

'Fair enough,' said Rex. Then, 'Have you been talking to Susan, sir?' he asked, only half-joking. 'Only she was dropping hints about that green tweed jacket in the tailor's window last time she was down. We went in and tried it on.'

'There you go, then,' said Lollo with the satisfaction of one who's been proved correct. 'You should always listen to a woman. They know. I'd buy it fucking pronto if I were you. That'll put you in her good books, and she'll pay you back in kind. Be worth every fucking penny, that would.'

Later, showered and shaved, with a spray of Floris, in a new, blue Harrington and mustard-coloured Fred Perry, off-white Dockers and blue suede loafers, bouncing along on the Central Line train to Barkingside, Rex wondered how the tasking team at Ilford were getting on. His own panic attack notwithstanding, could he have played it differently at Dicky Sharp's? For a start, if he hadn't been in such a rush to get out, might his very presence have put them off? Or had they in fact been watching, and waited for him to leave before pouncing? Or, worse, had his very presence been the catalyst for the abduction? But he put all of that to the back of his mind when, standing by the lychgate of the children's church, he saw Thea turn the corner. She was wearing a full-skirted yellow-and-gold cotton-print mid-calf-length shirt-dress, and over this a faded blue Levi's denim jacket.

'You look lovely,' he said. Then, with a nod to the church, 'I was reading about the history of this place, Barnardo's and all that, the village. What a vision. It's incredible to think. There must be good job satisfaction, working for something like that.'

'Well, we're all proud of it,' said Thea. 'It's nice to have a job that makes a difference. But then you must feel that way too.'

'Yes, sometimes,' said Rex, resisting the urge to take her hand as they walked back towards the high street. 'Maybe not the other day, though.'

'You were as white as a sheet,' said Thea, laughing. 'I thought you looked like you needed a bit of looking after.'

'Thank you for that,' said Rex. 'I appreciate it.'

'And do you?'

'What, need looking after?'

Rex wasn't entirely green. This was his cue to say something about his relationship status, and he'd been expecting it.

'It's nice of you to ask,' he said. 'I was seeing someone for a while, but she's not in London and it's all gone a bit wrong. I don't think I'm cut out for a long-distance relationship, if you know what I mean. How about you? Well, obviously you gave me your card so I know you're a *bit* interested!'

'Oh damn, is it that obvious?' she said.

'You must have no shortage of suitors, a beautiful woman like you.'

'Thank you. Well, they're not exactly queueing up.'

'I'm glad you gave me your card.'

'Not at all. Thanks for ringing.'

'So: Thea,' said Rex. 'Is that short for something?'

'It can be,' she said. 'You know, Dorothea, Althea, but not in my case. It's Greek for "goddess".'

'Well, there you go,' said Rex with a smile. 'Where's nice around here, then?'

'The Chequers is actually not bad,' she said, pointing to a half-timbered pub on the corner. 'We might see a couple of people from the office, but we shan't be joining them. As long as you don't mind being scrutinised from afar.'

'Not at all,' said Rex. 'Very sensible on a first date.'

'Oh dear,' said Thea. 'You've seen through my cunning plan. Shall we?'

It was a nice **roomy** pub, recently done up, by the looks of it, and filled with the low hubbub of conversation and laughter. There were white tiles behind the zinc-topped bar, and tastefully painted wood panelling. A motley selection of distressed and repainted wooden chairs. Lots of wine on display, spot-lighting, and snacks in large glass jars. It felt like a major brewery chain's focus-grouped idea of what the aspirational young suburban drinker of the twenty-teens might think a revamped traditional boozer aimed at them was meant to look like.

'What can I get you?' asked Rex. 'The food looks good. Do you want to eat something?'

'Not right now, but I wouldn't mind having a look at the menu,' said Thea. 'We can always come back and order if there's anything we fancy.'

Around her neck on a silver chain Thea wore an irregularly shaped silver coin bearing a relief portrait of a woman with classical features, facing left, with a crown of corn woven into her braids.

'That's nice,' said Rex. 'It looks real – not a replica.'

With her full lips and straight nose, the woman on the coin reminded Rex of the disembodied sculpted head depicted in *The Song of Love*, a painting by Giorgio de Chirico. The painting was one of Helen's favourites, and when they were first going out together she'd sent him a postcard of it from a New York trip.

'It's a silver nomos,' said Thea. 'It's from what was the Greek bit of Italy, about 300 BC. It came with a certificate of authentication and a little map and everything. It was a tenth-anniversary present from Trevor, my late husband—'

'I'm sorry for your loss,' said Rex, almost by reflex. 'That's too bad.'

'Thank you,' said Thea, her face briefly stricken with grief. Just a flash, but enough for Rex's trained eye to notice. He wanted to take her in his arms right then, and never let her go.

'When did he die? If you don't mind my asking.'

'Not at all,' said Thea. 'One thing I've learned about bereavement is that you have to talk about it head-on. Ten years ago: cancer. It was brutal, but relatively quick, thank God. We'd been married for nineteen years.'

'I'm so sorry,' said Rex. 'That's really tough. You must have lots of happy memories.' He pointed at the pendant. 'She looks a bit like you, to be honest.'

'That's exactly what Trevor said,' said Thea. 'That's why he bought it. It's **Demeter**, sister of Zeus, the goddess of crops and fertility. The back's nice too.' She lifted the coin and turned it around. 'Look, it's an ear of barley and a griffin.'

'It looks modern,' said Rex. 'Almost a little bit Art Deco, if that wasn't an anachronism.'

'I know. Trev had wanted to **engrave** something on there, but I thought it would be hard to do anything without spoiling it. Besides, I knew what it was for. It didn't need words.'

She smiled. And what a smile it was: Christ! Rex could feel himself falling for this woman. He didn't need a **missal** or a **mullah** to tell him how to **worship** at her gate. On his fucking knees, that's how. Sobbing with gratitude that she had opened herself up to him. Because he knew that was how this was going to go, and if not tonight – a school night, after all, as they'd agreed – then next time.

As it was, after a couple of glasses of wine and a shared fish-finger-and-salad sandwich and chips, they'd gone for a stroll up the high street. Rex wanted to see the library again, or that was his excuse anyway, and to stretch the legs. As they walked, Thea leaned into him affectionately a couple of times, then put her arm through his.

This is the life, thought Rex.

It doesn't get much better than this.

But then it did.

'I don't normally do this on a first date,' said Thea, stepping out in front and turning to face him, 'but do you want to come in for a coffee? I live just up here.'

Without another word they kissed. Rex reached out and put a hand on Thea's waist, and in the split second before he closed his eyes he saw her lips seeking out his, and felt her arms holding him close. A few exhilarating minutes later, she was leading him up a short, checkerboard-tiled garden path to the front door of a terraced house a few streets north of the library, and then into the kitchen for, yes, a small cafetière of freshly ground coffee that was made and poured but mostly forgotten in favour of more kissing and unbuttoning, then of Thea sitting on Rex's lap, and not long after that them going up to bed.

What's more, it turned out that it wasn't a school night after all.

Rex didn't need to get to the station particularly early, and Thea had booked off a half-day in lieu, so they had a bit of a lazy morning, picking up where they'd left off getting to know each other in the early hours. It was one of those glorious moments in a new relationship when your lover is the soul and centre of your world, when your bodies do everything you ask of them, when you almost feel that you could **subsist** on sex and sunshine.

When breakfast toast tastes like ambrosia.

Which is how, mid-morning, Rex found himself walking with a spring in his step back towards Barkingside High Street on his way to the tube station.

As he approached the square between the library and the leisure centre, the sharp clatter of a skateboard and an accompanying yelp of pain and profanity made him turn around. That had to have hurt. It looked as if the same group were back practising their ollies and grinds, and one **skater** was carefully picking himself up off the ground, much to the amusement of all the others.

But it was something else that caught Rex's eye.

Coming around the back of the library, the way Rex had just come, was a slightly battered souped-up silver BMW 3 Series sedan, complete with rear spoiler and some mismatched fender flares – fitted, filled and sanded, but in need of priming and a respray.

He could see from here that the plates had been changed, but that was definitely Dicky Sharp's car.

It wasn't Sharp driving, but it was someone Rex knew.

Person 13. The second individual from the video.

The man whose identity Dicky Sharp had just confirmed in the interview, not that Rex had needed it confirming exactly, but an additional ID didn't hurt.

At this point, the average civilian might have drawn attention to themselves by doing a massive double-take, but Rex's training kicked in and he did the old disappearing act. He tuned in to what was going on around him and became – to the casual glance – just part of the movement and the texture of the crowd in the square. He smiled and said hello to a passer-by while looking over their shoulder at the car, in passing, just to make sure.

There was no doubt.

The guy had certainly aged a bit in ten years, got a bit puffy about the face, but then hadn't we all? He'd put on weight, for a start, and lost all his hair, but now that Rex had got used to the beard, he could see that it was definitely him alright.

Rex got his phone and called it in to Binder Singh on the Kayak team immediately, and then he checked the CRiS number and asked DC Singh to share it with the Ilford boys too.

Talk about a bad penny.

Bold as brass in Sharpy's car, and with all the charm of a twenty-foot **tape-worm** twitching on the table at a toddlers' tea party, head thrashing blindly with hooks akimbo and hungry suckers flaring. Actually, that was doing the unspeakable cunt a favour.

30: Sainfoin (Sainfoin)

'Okay, here's a question for you,' said Terry Hobbs when he returned from the house – scrunching noisily across the shingle – with three ice creams and the half-finished bottle of red they'd left on the kitchen counter. 'When and where were you happiest?' He put the wine down on the pebbles, gently turning the bottle to dig a little hole for it. 'Oh, who wants which?'

'I don't know – **vanilla**? What have you got, Tel?' said Rex.

'Almond,' said Terry, looking at the wrappers, 'white chocolate, classic.'

'Almond, please,' said Susan.

'Whatever's left,' said Rex. 'I don't mind. What was the question again?'

'When and where,' said Terry, 'were you happiest?'

1985, walking hand in hand along the Croisette in Cannes on the French Riviera, thought Rex. The intense light and heat, the sound of the cicadas in the trees and shrubs of the promenade, and the screaming swifts in the air above the town. Seeing a small crowd gathering outside the Carlton to gawp at a pristine sky-blue 1925 **Bugatti** Type 35C that had stopped en route along the coast road from Nice to St-Tropez. The motoring **relic** had looked more like an aeroplane engine on its four huge wheels: all rivets, rods and vents, with a teardrop back and distinctive arch-shaped radiator grille, springleaf suspension, and two tiny semicircular windscreens on the front lip of its stark metal cockpit.

Purpose of this visit from the gods? It wasn't a pit stop, so probably just an opportunity for its windswept driver and passenger (affecting the look of Prince Rainier and Grace Kelly: he in leather flying jacket and helmet, goggles loose around his neck, she in headscarf, with his striped blazer around her shoulders and sunglasses pushed to the top of her head) to show off this great behemoth, and bask in the adoration of the inhabitants of this and every other town along the coast. Someone saying, 'Look, the car in which Étancelin won the French Grand Prix in 1930. The very one!'

It was a happiness that of course had had nothing to do with the car, except perhaps thinking how excited his father would have been to see it, and everything to do with who he had been with, on that long-ago summer morning on the Côte d'Azur.

But Rex kept quiet, and so did Susan, for a moment or two.

Rex was biding his time. He wasn't going to go first.

He didn't know about Susan, but he was thinking: No, Tel, that's not a good question to ask a copper. Anyone else – and maybe most civilians might say their wedding day or when their children were born – but don't ask a policeman a question like that, because chances are they won't tell the truth. Or, if they do, you might not like the answer you get.

And you'd hardly dare ask the same question of a police officer's partner or spouse.

Was Helen happy? Not now, she wasn't.

Had the force brought happiness to her home? Not this time.

Rex hadn't even had a chance to tell Susan about Jennifer yet.

He'd told Thea, though. It felt like *their* news now: part of Rex and Thea's story.

But Webster had brought his troubles upon himself.

Half the journey to Ashford, Rex had needed to leave Susan on her tod, reading the paper and minding the flat whites and pains au chocolat at their table seat, while he'd been on the phone in the carriage vestibule trying to calm Helen down, for the second time in one day. Which turned out to be an impossible task when your hitherto upstanding policeman husband and pillar of the community had been pulled in on what she said they'd called 'a serious disciplinary matter'.

'You promised, Rex,' Helen had said. 'You promised you'd have a word.'

'I will,' Rex had said.

Although, actually, he'd already tried.

But it was too far gone.

Having a word wasn't going to cut it.

And as far as Rex understood it, Sharpy had practically exonerated Webster: he hadn't seen anything, after all. So Rex had kept his notes simple, as per the Detective Chief Inspector's steer.

So whatever else DS Eddie Webster might have blurted out under pressure after that was down to him and him alone. Lollo had been satisfied with the drug score. And with Sharpy now shockingly and permanently out of the picture, there was no one left to contradict that. So it was Webster's word against himself. But something *had* happened with Hyacinth after all, and Webbo had wanted to get it off his chest.

'I'll spare you the details, Kingsy,' Lollo had said, when pressed. 'Charges plural are on file, if you so desire. But it's not pleasant. And, as you can imagine, it were everybody's fault but his own. Stress-related, he said. I told him he didn't know the meaning of the word.'

Lollo was right: Detective Sergeant Eddie Webster was a fucking idiot. But that would now seem to be the least of his character flaws.

For fuck's sake, though. Who'd **defame** themselves?

Plus, however resoundingly wrong-headed Webbo's actions had been in going in, once he *was* in there, sure he wouldn't have wanted to break cover, but that didn't mean he had to get his cock out. No wonder he'd kept it quiet at first. 'When in Rome' was not an adequate defence against a child abuse charge. There was no way around it: at the very least there was clearly 'causing or inciting', and committing intentional penetration.

Rex would bet that Helen didn't know about that bit yet.

Lollo was a cool customer, though.

He'd dropped Webster as easily as flicking a **switch**.

'I'd have to say right now,' said Susan.

Rex nearly spat out his wine, but cleared his throat and recovered quickly. 'That's sweet,' he said. Especially considering that their planned few days away had already been cut short.

'Wow, Good answer!' said Terry. 'Even if you are just sitting on a beach with a couple of old bores like me and Rexy here.'

'Steady on, Terence,' said Susan. 'That's my boyfriend you're talking about.'

'Thank you!' said Rex.

Boyfriend. That sounded good coming from her. Yes, he supposed he was; for now, anyway.

'Besides, you're not such a bore!' said Susan, unwrapping her ice cream. 'Rex was right. You're very good company.'

Terry gave a little stagey bow, with a pantomime flourish as if doffing an invisible hat.

'No, but I suppose I'm a bit of a Buddhist in my own way,' said Susan. 'As far as it goes. I like to try and live in the moment, rather than get sentimental about the past. You know: all of my experiences, everything I've done to date, has brought me to this point, so be conscious in the moment? Well, I try anyway.'

'That's very Zen,' said Rex. 'I can relate to that.'

'Doesn't always work,' she said, laughing. 'I've barely dipped my toe in the water. I don't know too much about it – all the different schools of thought, you know – but there were some meditation classes at work and I kind of enjoyed them. Read a couple of books, that kind of thing. And besides' – she looked around, waving her half-eaten Magnum at the sea – 'here we are. Isn't this place amazing? Don't you just think that life is so beautiful, you just have to embrace it here and now?'

'Hear, hear,' said Rex. 'Did I tell you that I love you?'

'Yeah, once or twice,' said Susan with a smile. 'Love you too.'

'Well, I'll drink to that,' said Terry. 'Top-up?'

'I'm alright for now, thanks,' said Susan. 'But anyway, Terence: your turn. Same question. How about you?'

'I don't know,' said Hobbs. 'I'm pretty happy most of the time because I'm doing a job that I love…'

'Are you joking?' said Susan. 'You're not getting off that easily.'

'I don't know, things like being with friends, finishing something, you know, a job well done: a painting, or a bit of restoration. Going somewhere new? Or maybe discovering somewhere all over again – this place, for instance. Hadn't been here for at least thirty years. There's that moment when you recognise exactly how both you and it have changed.'

'Blimey,' said Rex. 'You two and your mindfulness, honestly!'

'But I don't think I'm answering my own question,' said Terence. 'Because those are more like everyday pleasures, aren't they?'

'Yes,' said Susan, pressing the point. 'So?'

'Okay, I suppose I've had a few moments of pure, unalloyed joy in my life.'

'Can you narrow it down, Tel?' said Rex.

'It's tough.'

'Just choose any one for now,' said Susan. 'It doesn't matter.'

'Okay, well, Rex has heard this one,' said Terry. 'Sorry, Rex.'

'Ah, I know,' said Rex, nudging Susan. 'I've told this one myself a couple of times, Tel. Used it at work.'

'I know. In your "legend", you said. Happy to be of service. At least you asked.'

'I didn't do it justice, though.'

'You had to be there, mate,' said Terry. 'Right. Where to start? Okay, long-short, I went to art school in Leeds, Susan. The Poly, as it was then. This was back in the mid-eighties. We used to go to a lot of gigs, at the poly, at the university union, couple of little clubs in the city centre, wherever. Saw a lot of reggae acts too, out in Chapeltown. Sound system clashes, Saxon versus Maverick Outernational, Jah Shaka – that was the loudest thing I've ever heard in my life – bands like The Gladiators, Sugar Minott, Yellowman, Barrington Levy.'

'Oh, I *love* Sugar Minott,' said Susan.

'There was a club in Chapeltown called Cosmo's. At least it was called that until it burned down. Then they reopened and called it The Phoenix. One time we went to see Eek-A-Mouse – who was big at the time. Oh my God, what a performer. Me and my housemates, Bob and Betty. And we smoked a bit, you know, and walked back afterwards, so it ended up being a bit of a late one. Next day I slept in, and we were all a bit the worse for wear, so mid-afternoon, spur of the moment, Bob suggested going to the pub for a hair of the dog. Not something that we often did, but it seemed like a good idea, to nurse our hangovers and kind of bask in the afterglow of this great gig, so the three of us went down the hill to our local – the Royal Park, if you know it – got our halves of Tetley's or whatever.

'On an evening the place would be packed, and not just with students either. Once a week a retired Al Jolson impersonator and his pensioner mates would hold court in the lounge bar for a big singalong, but this was a weekday afternoon, so the place was dead. We got a table opposite the bar, you know, got my **tobacco** out to make a rollie, and when we sat down, Bet – she's Liverpudlian – looked over and said, 'scuse the accent, "Eh, I'd swear that's Joe Strummer at the bar, with the orange hair." And we looked over and there were these five blokes dressed in black, with, you know, guitar cases, and she was a really big fan, Bet – more of a fan than me – and she said, "Fucking hell, and that's Paul Simonon. It is the fucking Clash."

'And they picked up their pints and their guitar cases and went out the back – there used to be a big garden out the back of the Royal Park – and we picked up our halves and followed them. This was the beginning of May, so the weather was fine. And out the back of the pub there was this veranda and a terrace, and then you went down some steps into a big garden. Just a messy patch of grass, really. And they just lined up on the terrace there and started playing.

'Turned out it was the last-gasp line-up of the band – Mick Jones and Topper Headon had left by this time; Jones was doing Big Audio Dynamite, and Headon was in rehab, I think, from memory, so Strummer and Simonon had replaced them with ex-Cortinas Nick Sheppard, and a guy called Vince White on guitars, and Pete Howard who squatted on the ground and played the drums on a manhole cover. And they lined up on the terrace there and played "Stepping Stone" – the old Monkees song? And we were just open-mouthed, you know.'

'What else did they play?' said Rex. 'I know you told me, years ago.'

'Ha. Nowadays I'd write it down, or someone would just post a live video on Instagram or Facebook while it was happening... But it felt like a **compilation** of all my favourite Clash records – well, some of them. As far as I can remember, they did a couple of tracks from *London Calling* – "Jimmy Jazz" and "Brand New Cadillac" – then they did "I Fought the Law", and "Straight to Hell". Maybe "White Riot". And I don't know if I told you this, Rex, but thinking about it I'm certain they also did a mash-up of "Twist and Shout" and "La Bamba", which isn't on any of the bootlegs or set lists I've seen, but they definitely did. And I know that because I was like "Yeah, I love that song", so the next day I went down to the Virgin Megastore in Leeds city centre and ordered "La Bamba" on record. It wasn't even the Ritchie Valens version. The only version of it you could get new at the time was a 7-inch single on some crappy "golden oldies" label by Trini Lopez.

'I don't know if that was really my happiest moment, but it's definitely up there. We just sat there grinning, perched on the edge of the pub veranda with The Clash playing six feet away. It was completely wild and strange to have this huge band – the kind of band that filled stadiums – playing in the back garden of your local pub. There was no such thing as "unplugged" gigs at the time. They hadn't been invented yet.

'It turned out – we found out later on – that a few days before, they'd set out on a busking tour of the UK: they'd been in Nottingham for a couple of days, now it was Leeds, then in a day or so they'd be on to wherever, York, Gateshead, Newcastle, Edinburgh, Glasgow, Manchester, I think. Not sure they actually played in Manchester, but they were there for at least a night, because a good ex-Leeds University friend of mine who lived in Hulme at the time told me that one of them got off with her flatmate and she had to listen to them fucking all night in the next room. There are bootlegs of some of the other gigs, but not of the Royal Park. They were staying at this mate of Bob's called Scouse's place, a shared house on Delph Lane over in Woodhouse, if you know Leeds. And later that night Bob would sell them a couple of quarters of not-bad Black – something he'd dine out on for years: "Dope dealer by appointment to The Clash!" – sorry, Rex.

'There was some East German punk there, taking photographs. Betty recognised him from around. Maybe this sounds a bit far-fetched, because I thought no one was allowed out of the GDR, right? But I seem to recall a few East German punks hanging around on the scene in university towns at the time, and they were all into photography.'

'For some reason,' said Rex.

'I know! Anyway,' Terence went on, 'somewhere out there – or in some forgotten Stasi file – are photos of us watching The Clash in the garden of the Royal Park. But that's also how I became a "Lopper", as they used to call us. Because later that week I went down to *Leeds Other Paper*, the *LOP*, on Cookridge Street. It was kind of an anti-racist, anti-nuclear, anti-sexist, pro-trade union weekly newspaper, and I asked if they wanted me to review any of these Clash gigs, and I was probably gushing a bit, you know, buzzing with it all. Anyway Mat, it was, let me down gently, said thanks but they'd already got a more critical piece about the gig that focused on CBS – The Clash's record label – being involved in the manufacture of cruise missiles or something. And they were going to go with that, and I can't say I blame 'em. But he said, "Come back tomorrow and help with the proofing, if you want" – so I did. Ended up doing that one or two evenings a week for a couple of years. Drawing cartoons, proofreading, selling ads, doing the listings, pasting up, whatever needed doing. But, you know, I was a painter not a writer, so that's how I didn't become a journalist!'

'Journalism's loss was theatre's gain, I reckon,' said Rex.

'I'll drink to that,' said Terry. 'Anyway, the next day we heard that they were going to play on the steps of the Leeds University Union, where some other band called The Alarm were on. I'm not going to slag them off – they were just another bunch of lads who struck it lucky in the pop charts and good on 'em. Good on anyone who can make a go of it, you know, but the vibe at the time was that they were a bit of a rip-off of The Clash. That's probably a bit unfair, but supposedly that was why The Clash were going to play on the steps outside, to show that they were bigger or something. So, we went along to that and all. And whereas at the Royal Park the day before there couldn't have been more than about twenty people watching on the terrace, the next day must have been knocking on for a thousand.'

Rex was fiddling with his phone. 'Yeah, got it,' he said. 'Look, there's a page on the website, and a couple of photos. It says they played "Cool Under Heat", "Movers and Shakers", "White Riot" and "Clash City Rockers".'

'Give us it here, Rex? Let's have a look,' said Terry, taking the phone and squinting at the screen, scrolling up and down. 'Well, I don't know who they got this set list from,' he said, 'because they opened with a cover version of Toots and the Maytals' "Pressure Drop", and I know that one hundred per cent because as soon as they played the first chords my mate Betty was completely made up, absolutely beaming, because it was her favourite song of all time. Then they played "Garageland", "Johnny Too Bad", "Police on My Back" – yeah, maybe "White Riot" – and after that I'll take their word for it.'

'I love "Johnny Too Bad",' said Rex.

'From *The Harder They Come*?' said Susan. 'Oh God, yes.'

'Wonderful stuff,' said Tel. 'The Slickers. The Clash's version wasn't bad either, to be fair. Especially when you weren't expecting it. I'm pretty sure that gig on the Leeds Union steps didn't last very long, though. I think someone – the rumour was it was one of Chumbawamba – chucked red paint on them from one of the upstairs windows of the Union, to protest about the arms trade or something. So they went around the corner and played at The Fav instead, but we'd had enough by then. Can you imagine? Being blasé about seeing The Clash, for free, for the third time in two days? It's like that Mel Brooks story about Cary Grant.'

'What, "Oh God, not again. Tell him I'm out!"?' said Rex. 'That one?'

'Yeah. So good.'

'Classic,' said Rex.

'Go on then, Rexy,' said Terry. 'Your turn.'

'Well, I can't compete with you two,' said Rex. Although he had some sympathy with Susan's idea of right here and now. And quite frankly he couldn't believe they'd made it here at all.

What a day it had been.

Car chases, the lot.

It really was only this morning, just a few hours ago, that he'd been loved up in bed with Thea one minute, eating her **peach** – a quickie for the road and 'Let's meet up when I'm back' – and the next minute flagging down and requisitioning a car on Barkingside High Street.

Yes, that had actually happened.

Rex had pursued Donal Duffy – a.k.a. Plum, a.k.a. P13 – around the Ilford Gyratory.

It was hardly *The French Connection*, but Rex hadn't lost his touch.

He'd kept pace for a mile or two, before losing the suspect at the Winston Way roundabout, but he figured that if the Ilford boys were quick on their feet they might stand a better chance.

And at that point they'd all still been hoping he'd lead them to Dicky Sharp.

Fucking Donal. How are the mighty fallen.

Rex was glad that the sleazebag had finally come a **cropper**.

Rex and Donal had been a team on the squad back in the Barnes days, until Duffy had gone native during his last four-year stint and let the side down by selling rape victims' witness statements on the side.

Until then, they'd made a decent double act for a while: good punk, bad punk.

That would have been around the time of the new millennium,

the late nineties and early noughties, back when Rex was often working away from home on what Helen – jokingly at first, but then increasingly grudgingly – had used to call 'Operation Spike'.

She'd even tolerated Rex's white-boy dreadlocks – for a while, anyway.

This was back when everyone else they knew had been starting married life and having families. Wasn't that what most people did in their thirties?

Not in Rex's case.

'I'm going to be up in Scotland for a month or so,' he might say. Or Aldershot, or Wiltshire, or Newbury, wherever.

'Spike Ops?' she'd say, at first. 'Well, be good, and maybe phone me once in a while this time.'

'I will, I promise,' he'd say.

Rex had never let on about Amelia, but from the way Helen would sometimes look at him, searching his face for clues whenever he got back from the latest few weeks away, he could tell that she had her suspicions. A slight flare of her nostrils, as if she was trying to detect another woman's scent, or a strange soap.

Rex had taken care not to get caught out like that, though.

And actually, even then Donal had been a dodgy bastard, a right old lech.

He'd once had the nerve to try it on in no uncertain terms with Helen in The Red Lion when Rex had left them alone for about a nanosecond. Whatever he'd said, it must have been pretty bad, because she would never repeat it.

She'd refused to have anything to do with Donal after that.

Said she'd had enough of his relentless lewd tirade.

Rex had realised later that Donal's 'ironic sexual predator' act was like that old saying: If you want to keep something **hidden** you put it on the **mantelpiece**.

But to go from Special Demonstration – okay, so Donal would have probably left with most of whatever pension he'd accrued, even in those circumstances – to small-time festival promoter, to paedo taxi driver and now kidnapper in, what, just a **decade** or so?

Going downhill that fast took real application.

And now he was reduced to running his little harem in Lido Cars and flogging prescription painkillers on the side.

It had taken Webster blundering in there to flush him out.

Well: every cloud.

But if Duffy had found out that Dicky Sharp was a grass, then – leaving aside the hows and whys of that – you could see why he'd want him out of the way.

He wasn't to know that Sharp's notebook and statements had already been admitted, that the damage had already been done.

'Don't blame yourself,' Lollo had said on the phone. 'That course of action would have been well underway long before you turned up on Sharp's doorstep.'

Once he'd lost Duffy, Rex had been just about to drop the Audi TT off at Barkingside Police Station – well, if you're going to requisition a car, you might as well requisition one with a bit of welly – when Helen had called. Had he seen Jennifer yet? Helen asked, because she'd said she was going into town to see him.

'When was this?' said Rex.

'Couple of hours ago.'

Rex stopped short: if he'd just seen Donal, had Donal seen him? Probably not today – there'd been no eye contact made, and Rex had deliberately hung back, not got too close. But the bastard would have seen Rex leaving Dicky Sharp's place on Monday, that's for sure.

And Donal knew where Rex lived.

He'd been round often enough, for fuck's sake, albeit a good few years ago.

But how much could Donal have picked up about Webster and his family during their all-too-brief acquaintance?

Was Webster really so stupid, over however many transactions it had been, that he'd assume this easy intimacy with his new friend and benefactor was protected by some kind of dealer–addict privilege?

Well, frankly, yes, he was.

Could he have blabbed about his personal problems, and mentioned Rex's name, or, worse, Jennifer's?

Rex realised that he wouldn't put it past Webster, with his hail-fellow-well-met schtick, to do exactly that.

And he wouldn't put it past Donal to pay a visit to Rex's flat in Falcon if he'd just made him, as they say. 'Made' as in spotted Rex: recognised him.

'I'm out east on a job,' Rex had said to Helen, trying not to show the twinge of panic he was feeling. 'Barkingside, would you believe. I'd have come and picked Jen up if I'd known. If she calls you, tell her I'll be there in forty-five minutes. Tell her if she gets bored to go to the station, or Sid's. She knows where they are.'

Hanging up, Rex tapped the stereo awake and pressed 'play'; heard a familiar, fast high-hat intro, squelchy distorted bass. Hm, good taste, he thought, checking the mirrors and changing gear. It was The Doors, 'Break On Through (To the Other Side)'.

That'll do, he'd thought, and turned it up.

Then he'd done a three-point turn out of Mossford Green, turned right onto the high street and put his foot down.

He'd figured it would be quicker in the car if he stayed north, came in via Wanstead and Stratford, Vicky Park Road, and then bore right and took the old black cab route through Haggerston and Hoxton, dropping onto City Road that way.

If it came to it, he could leave the Audi in the garage at work.

Forty minutes, The Doors' *Greatest Hits* and a substantial green wave later, he'd parked up in Old Gloucester Street, let himself in and run up the stairs, where he'd found Jen sitting on his doorstep, just like the first time, when he'd happened to drop his clean washing back from the launderette on his way to the office.

Only this time she wasn't reading a book about Boudicca, she was doing the Quick Crossword.

Rex had felt both an overwhelming sense of relief that she was safe – not that, come to think of it, he'd really expected Donal to drop by this very second – but also like his heart was going to burst with pride.

'Oh, hi,' she'd said. 'Unit of electrical current, six letters?'

'**Ampere**,' Rex had said, getting his breath. 'Next?'

'Actually, I'm quite hungry,' Jen had said. 'Are you?'

'How hungry? Sid's hungry?'

'Yup.'

As they walked along Great Ormond Street, Rex said that he was sorry about Saturday.

Jen shrugged, but he could see she was disappointed.

He explained that he was taking a couple of days' much-needed holiday, that he and Susan, his girlfriend, were going to stay at his friend Terence's house in Kent for a long weekend. That Susan lived up in York because she worked at the university there, and hadn't been down to London for a few weeks.

Then he told a little lie, that Susan had said to say she was looking forward to meeting Jen sometime soon. It was a white lie, and it wasn't so bad, because he knew that she would have been if she'd known.

'You'd like her,' he said. 'She's nice.'

'What's up? D'you two have a row?' Jen asked.

Ouch. Was it that obvious?

'Not really. Just that we've both been busy with work, I suppose. I'm looking forward to seeing her, though. Can't wait to introduce you.'

It was all her fault, Jen said, over a plate of smoked salmon and scrambled eggs. She thought that her dad was wanting to impress her. She'd been banned from seeing Hyacinth. Helen and Jen had had a long chat about it. Hyacinth was really clever. She was a looked-after child but she found it hard to do homework at her foster home. So all through the autumn term she'd been coming home with Jen and they'd do homework together after school. Jen said that Helen had begun to notice that Hyacinth was pocketing the odd bit of change, a few pound coins here and there.

'I think Mum figured she must have needed it,' Jen had said. 'She'd leave a fiver out sometimes. And Mum or Dad would usually give her a lift home.'

'Sounds like your mum!' said Rex. 'Very thoughtful of her.'

But then Hyacinth had invited Jen to a party – she was going out with an older boy – and when her father had found out where it was he'd hit the roof and she wasn't to see Hyacinth again, but Jen said it wasn't fair.

'Wasn't at Lido Cars, by any chance?' Rex said, as nonchalantly as he could manage, his blood running cold.

'Yeah, how did you know?'

'Your dad told me,' Rex lied. He didn't want to get Jen's hopes up, and obviously he couldn't say anything about the investigation, but he felt some reassurance was in order. 'I can tell you this much, Jen. It's definitely not your fault. Your dad's right, though. Trust me, you need to stay away from that place. They're not good people. But Hyacinth will be okay. I happen to know that someone called her social worker and asked them to do a proper risk assessment.'

'Who?'

'Bloke called Dicky Sharp,' said Rex. 'An old guy I know who lives out that way. Bit of a geezer, but decent enough, actually. Heart of gold. I spoke to him a couple of days ago, as it happens. He said he'd been worried about all the young women not being treated very well, so he'd got to know them a bit, found out who they all were, and reported it.'

'That was nice of him,' said Jen.

'Yeah, it was,' said Rex. 'Come on,' he said as they walked back to Old Gloucester Street. 'I'll drop you back. Why don't you text your mum and let her know we're on the way?'

'I thought you said you didn't have a car.'

'Just taking it for a test drive,' Rex lied. 'Well, no. Actually, I had to borrow it for work, but they need it back.'

They'd nipped up to the flat to use the loo and so Rex could quickly change and chuck a few things in an overnight bag. He could dump the car in Barkingside and then tube it back to meet Susan at St Pancras International, where they'd hop on the HS1 to Ashford, and from there cab it to Dungeness.

'Here it is,' he said, blipping the locks.

'Cool.'

As Rex opened the passenger door for Jennifer, he looked over at his daughter and remembered something, and he smiled at her with all his heart.

'All **aboard** the *SkylArk*!' he said.

That was it.

The moment Rex had been happiest; bursting with new-found love for the daughter he'd only actually known for a few days.

Terry and Susan were looking at him expectantly.

Quick, think of something neutral to **divert** attention.

'Come on,' said Susan. 'You're not getting out of this.'

Got it.

'Well, obviously I'm going to say when I'm with you, aren't I,' said Rex, doing his best to play for time and sound like he meant it. 'But do you mean present company excepted, Tel?'

'If you like.'

'Okay, it might sound stupid because I don't really follow football, but as a kid it was pretty special when Plymouth Argyle got into the semi-final of the FA Cup in eighty-four.'

'Seriously?' said Terry. 'I never had you down as a particularly **rabid** supporter!'

'No,' said Rex, 'I'm not.'

'I bet your dad supported them, though,' said Susan.

'Yeah. And this was the year after he died. And that was probably part of it: feeling close to my dad, and thinking, God, he'd have loved that, you know? But also, it was a big deal at the time, the FA Cup. Like on Cup Final day the nation stopped what it was doing for a few hours; all the build-up. Even a cynical sixteen-, seventeen-year-old like me. And for them to have got to the semi-final was major, especially for a small team like Plymouth. It was the best they'd done in years. My dad idolised the 1964–65 squad. He had a signed black-and-white photo. I remember it used to hang in the hallway at Spenser Avenue. I grew up hearing their names, and their legendary achievements.

'It was a different world, or maybe that's just the child's-eye view, but it seems to me that it was less complicated being a man in those days. You did your job, and paid your bills. You followed your team and did the pools, watched *Nationwide* and *The Generation Game*, tinkered with the car every weekend to keep it on the road, and saved up for a week away in a caravan somewhere, and that was it, wasn't it? Simpler times. Or maybe not: because that's just the child's-eye view, right?

'I remember when I was a young boy how excited my dad was when the Pilgrims got into the semi-final of the League Cup in 1973–74. I was never really into football in the same way, and by the time I was a teenager it was called the **Milk Cup**, and they were pretty regularly knocked out in the first or second round. But the FA Cup semis in 1984 was different – really special.'

Rex took his phone out of his pocket. 'Anyway, I figured, if you can't beat 'em, join 'em, so I've got the Pilgrims app on my phone now.'

'Eh? I thought you said you didn't follow football,' said Susan.

'I don't, not as such, but it's easier at work to say that you support a club than to explain why you're not interested.'

'Sheesh,' said Susan.

'I know,' said Rex. 'Peer pressure or what. It's not all bad, though.'

'What do you mean?'

'Well, when they got to the League Two play-off **final** in 2016,' said Rex, 'after winning the second leg of the semi-final on aggregate, I actually cheered. Even if Wimbledon beat them in the end. But the way they went on at work, you'd think it was me that had got into the final. It was all slaps on the back and "Bad luck, Kingsy!" Anyway, what I'm trying to say is, if Plymouth ever get anywhere, it reminds me of my dad, even now. Deep down, I am a bit of a Pilgrim at heart. So Plymouth doing well makes me happy.'

'Aw,' said Susan. 'Come here, you big softie.'

'The funny thing is,' said Rex, 'that I'm older now than he was when he died. He was barely forty. Didn't seem it to me then, but he was a young man; in his prime.'

'I'm gonna leave you kids to it,' said Terry, standing and stretching, gathering some of the barbecue things and the empties. 'I'll book that taxi for the morning right now – consider it done.'

'Thank you for everything, Terence,' said Susan. 'I've had a lovely time. It's such a beautiful place. I'm only sorry we can't stay longer now.'

'Thanks, Susan. Yeah, what a shame. But you two are welcome any time. I mean it. Whether I'm here or not. Rexy's got his own key.'

Rex and Susan were each putting their own kind of brave face on it now, but it was true, Lollo's phone call earlier had come as a real blow. After a few minutes absorbing the fact that their precious few days away had been cancelled, Susan had gone for a walk on her own, and Rex went shortly after to catch her up and face the inevitable row. She was furious that Rex had – as she put it – wasted her time. She wasn't going to spoil the evening or embarrass Terence by storming off, but she'd taken annual leave, for *this*? Maybe it was just as well that she'd found out sooner rather than later where Rex's priorities lay.

Rex might have presented a less ruffled front in the face of Lollo's triple-whammy of a phone call, but that was thirty years of training for you, and it wasn't for lack of drama. If World War Three were breaking out, Rex would still be saying the correct, diligent, professional thing, and – right now – role-playing the loving boyfriend. But Sharp was dead, and whatever was coming to Ed Webster was his lookout. It would be rough on Helen and the girls, but they'd be better off without him.

Rex had immediately compartmentalised the bad news about

Dicky Sharp, because that's what you did – although he was gutted, of course.

He'd think about it when he was back at work. Maybe drop a card in to Mrs Sharp next time he went over to Thea's place.

Rex didn't know it yet, but Donal Duffy would be arrested and charged with kidnapping, false imprisonment and a whole pic'n'mix of Section 20s within hours. The bastard wouldn't know what had hit him. Sharp's car, but with false plates off one of Lido Cars' written-off Toyotas, would turn out to have been tracked on the North Circular down to Barking on ANPR and then on the A13 back into central London, a route that would triangulate with the cell tower data on Duffy's mobile to place him in the former but now vacant premises of a large commercial laundry in Grays, Essex.

They'd been after 'Plum' Duffy for a few years now, since the last time he'd fallen off the radar. And there were a couple of historic warrants relating to serious sexual assaults on the festival circuit ready and waiting. The charges were watertight, with DNA, *and* with victims still willing to cooperate. It was enough to scramble the helicopter and cut him off on the way back out of town with a hard stop on Stratford Broadway just off the flyover.

Within twenty-four hours, the Ilford boys would have matched ANPR data with CCTV footage from one of the SOAS cameras on Russell Square showing Dicky Sharp struggling out of the boot of his own car, his mouth taped and hands bound, looking to the left for oncoming traffic and immediately getting hit by a fire engine that was overtaking into the onward lane at speed from the right without its sirens on. Lollo would wince and say that he reckoned it would have been instant, that Sharp had hit the deck like a sack of spuds, but then, thanks to the laws of physics—

'Conservation of momentum,' Rex would say.

'Alright, clever-clogs,' Lollo would say. 'Thanks to conser-fucking-vation of fucking momentum – happy now?'

Long-short, Sharp had shot along the road at ground level, gone head-first into the kerb and flipped over a couple of times before landing head-first again, this time on the cornerstone of the cabmen's shelter. Hard to tell which impact would have caved his skull in; but either way it was *sayonara*, Dicky Sharp. He'd probably already been dead, but if he hadn't been, either of those head traumas would have been enough to finish him off. Poor sod.

Rex had quite liked Sharpy and his mum after all. Enough to know that he was going to volunteer to represent at the funeral.

It was only right.

The team owed Dicky Sharp 'big time', as people were fond of saying.

'One more thing,' Lollo had said, and even at this distance and down the phone line Rex could tell from something in his tone that the DCI was going to enjoy this.

Clearly, whatever it was, he couldn't resist.

'Old golfing mate of mine works in property,' said Lollo. 'Mover and shaker in the growth industry of student accommodation, I kid you not. And I tell you what, we're in the wrong game, Kingsy. Made a fucking mint, he has. Anyroad, he's got a couple of big developments on the go in York, halls of residence like. So I says to him, that's a coincidence, one of my lads has got a new lady friend works in finance at the university there, maybe he should pop in and say hello. Tell her he's a friend of mine.'

'You did what?'

'Her card were on yer desk, wern'it, Kingsy. I didn't think you'd mind—'

Rex had let Lollo say his piece, but now he really had to keep it together, because he wasn't going to let on to Susan. Not now. He wasn't going to give Lollo the fucking satisfaction of ruining their evening twice. And since they were here, for tonight at least, Rex figured that he and Susan might as well enjoy themselves.

In the event, after a bit of a snuggle on the beach, they weren't long behind Terence, clearing up the last bits and pieces and heading for bed.

It was a bit of a turn-on, truth be told.

Rex figured they might as well make hay.

'Wow, someone's pleased to see me,' she said before they turned out the light.

◆ ◆ ◆

As he cut down Judd Street from King's Cross, with Susan now northbound on her train home, Rex got his phone out to check his email, and there it was. An all-staff email from Chief Superintendent

Tabitha Churchill, subject line 'Safety in custody: "Much to commend"'. Well, that was a good start, anyway. He opened the email and had a quick read.

Dear Central North BCU colleagues,

Many of you will remember that last June, Camden BOCU were proud to host and facilitate Safety in Custody (SiC) inspection teams from HMIP and HMICFRS. I would like once again to thank all officers and staff for your diligence and professionalism in expediting an efficient inspection visit. The SiC report was published at 10:00 today – PDF attached. I am personally delighted to be able to tell you that headlines are broadly positive. I quote:

> Inspection revealed an essentially positive picture of police custody in Camden, with generally sound management and competent staff delivering a professional service. There are a number of areas that we identify as requiring further improvement but, overall, there was much to commend.

Thank you, and well done.

Do please read the report in full. I have asked inspectors to make this an agenda item in ALL team meetings next week. Any questions, insights or suggestions, please raise them with your line managers and if they can't answer immediately, we'll get back to you asap.

I am also grateful for the invaluable input of detainees, both on site and in HM Prisons Pentonville, Holloway and Wormwood Scrubs. But I need to draw all Central North BCU officers to paragraph 2.1.3 on page 8 of the attached, which records that:

> more detainees than the comparator said they felt unsafe in detention and had been victimised by another detainee or member of staff.

This is obviously a matter of concern and I have personally been tasked by the Commander, the custody directorate and MOPAC with assessing why such perceptions might exist and whether any remedial action will be necessary. Camden colleagues know that this will be pursued with my usual rigour, and I now look forward to also working closely with Islington colleagues at all levels to achieve these goals.

The report outlines five (5) key areas of improvement, briefly:

Knowledge sharing and IPCC 'Lessons Learned' briefings. Inspectors were assured that IPCC literature is cascaded down through the BCU on a regular basis, so I was dismayed that our custody sergeants claimed to be unaware of these briefings, and did not know how to access the information. (Conversely, Inspectors found good understanding among custody staff on issues and expectations flowing from SDHP – full credit to DCI Lawrence's team for that.)

Cleanliness. While the relative cleanliness in the custody suites at Holborn was commended, it was noted that parts of the Kentish Town estate required deep cleaning, including of mattresses and bedding, toilet facilities. Chronic vermin infestation on both sites was highlighted.

Supervision. Henceforth, Custody will become an agenda item at SMT Performance Framework meetings, and I have this morning requested that SMT make more frequent and regular visits to the custody suites, and encourage more intrusive supervision.

Record keeping. We are committed to better record keeping, particularly about Use of Force Incidents (UFOs). There did not appear to be an overuse of force on either site, but recording was limited.

Oversight and chain of command. I've asked the Detective Superintendent to consult and identify strategies towards steering both the BCU and the wider Police Authority away from its current reliance on 'exception reporting' in our performance evaluation procedures regarding custody, and towards a more proactive business model.

Once again well done, and thank you all for your continued
professionalism and hard work.

Tabitha Churchill
Chief Superintendent, Central North BCU

Fucking hell! Rex had to read it twice.

And then he read that bit again.

Yes, it really did say, 'Inspectors found good understanding among
custody staff on issues and expectations flowing from SDHP.'

SDHP was the Safe Detention and Handling of Persons, SD for
short.

And Rex was station lead on SD.

The irony of all this was not lost on Detective Sergeant Rex King.

He tapped the screen to open the attached PDF, started scrolling
through the document, then thought better of it and typed the word
'death' into the search function. And there it was, in Section 1, under
'Leadership and Accountability', rather than Section 6, 'Causes for
Concern':

There had been one death in custody since our previous
inspection, which had been investigated by the Independent
Office for Police Conduct (IOPC), following which criminal
charges resulted in the acquittal of four officers. Adverse
incidents in the custody suites were recorded and reviewed
properly. Learnings from these were shared with staff, and
organisational learning fed into training as a result.

That was it.

Then under 'Area for Improvement' it simply read: 'The BCU
should ensure that its IT system supports the delivery of custody
functions and minimises system failures.'

Standing on the pavement outside Chilli Cool on Leigh Street, Rex
didn't know whether to laugh or cry.

His phone beeped. This time it was a text from Lollo:

Hope you've seen SIC? SD gets a special mention. That's you
Kingsy, not me. Well done, son. What did I tell you, buy that

f-ing jacket. PS East Area has SIC starting today. Reckon our friend in Barkingsdie will enjoy that. JL

Rex's phone rang again as he was approaching Russell Square. It was evidently going to be that kind of day. He was hoping it might be an apologetic call from Susan, whose train would surely have cleared Ally Pally and the mobile signal dead-zones around the North London tunnels by now, but assumed it was only Lollo again, wanting to crow a bit more. He should crow too – they all should – because if that was the worst the joint inspectorates could do in terms of room for improvement, the BCU had done bloody well. If Jane Milligan from SMT wasn't yet on maternity leave there would definitely be cake and speeches at lunchtime.

In fact, it wasn't Susan or Lollo on the phone, but Helen. And Rex knew what this was about. She was beside herself, crying and barely coherent.

'What's wrong?' said Rex. 'I'm back in London. Literally just got off the train; Lollo's called me back into town. Christ, I've only been away a night.'

'It's Eddie,' said Helen.

Person 14, thought Rex. But he didn't say it. 'What's happened, H?' he said, playing ignorant. 'I know he's been taken off the case – that's why they've cut my holiday short. Have they suspended him without pay now or something?'

'No, it's much **worse** than that,' said Helen. 'He's been arrested and remanded. He's going to be on the sexual offenders register.'

Rex let himself into Falcon and jogged up the stairs, two at a time as usual, door keys in hand. Once inside, he dumped his bag on the bed. There was time for a quick shower – get the smell of trains off his skin – and a coffee, order the new washing machine. Then over to the station for the midday briefing with the arrest teams. After that it'd be up to Russell Square with Bill and Ben to check the Socks were happy, supervise the clean-up and okay the removal of the barriers and incident tape, sweep up the sand. See if Sue Stanza would meet him up at the mortuary on St Pancras Way, then let Tommy Bee know when they'd be able to release Sharp's body.

Then back to the station to tidy up the paperwork and get all the ducks in a row.

With a bit of luck he'd be home mid-evening for a kip, then up at 3 a.m. to coordinate the arrest teams for the Operation Kayak 'Christmas card list'.

Binder Singh had played a blinder rejigging the data, and Cliff Heath had been right: this more strategic approach had paid off with the CPS.

Now, with Duffy's arrest, they needed to move quickly.

In the morning they'd be delivering the warrants: bashing in a few doors, making the arrests. Bringing in the whole Lido Cars crew. Minus two, with Duffy already in custody in Ilford, and Webster – P14 – now in the cells at Barkingside courtesy of the new East Area BCU.

Should all be done and dusted by ten tomorrow morning.

With a to-do list like that, Dungeness already seemed aeons ago.

All that *and* a Safety in Custody inspection in the EA. That was priceless; the cherry on the cake. Rex tried to imagine Webster filling in a detainee questionnaire: he'd be furious. Knowing Webbo, it would definitely add insult to injury.

Served him right, the fucking nonce.

With a fresh cafetière of coffee on the go, and a slice of leftover **treacle** tart from the fridge, a quick shower and shave, clean chinos, new Fred Perry and a spray of Floris, Rex felt a bit more normal and was doing what he'd been meaning to do for the past month: entering his card details for a mid-range Bosch washing machine on the John Lewis website. Jennifer had looked it up on her phone in the car yesterday, and said it was the one they had at home; texted him the link. It had an A+ eco rating and there was a forty-five-minute mixed-load cycle, so that was good enough for him.

While he waited for the bank verification to buffer, there was a knock on the door. 'Hang on,' he said, hoping it wouldn't ask him for his password.

Then, 'I'll be there in a minute.'

This was taking forever.

'Nearly done.'

At last: purchase and delivery date confirmed.

'Okay, sorry about that,' he said, walking over to open the front door. 'Hi.'

'Hey, I wasn't expecting to see you,' said Rex, standing aside so she could come in.

'Sorry I stormed off, Rex,' she said. 'I was frustrated and a bit upset. Not just the holiday being cut short. I just can't believe you didn't tell me about Jennifer. How could you land something like that on me in the taxi? It's almost as if you waited until you knew there wouldn't be time for us to discuss it.'

'Sorry,' said Rex. 'That wasn't the intention.'

'There's so much to talk about.'

'I know,' said Rex.

'Do you want to be part of Jennifer's life?' she said. 'Does Jen even want that? Never mind how Helen's taking it. Has she asked you to contribute financially?'

'No,' said Rex quickly, but then he was suddenly not so sure, and supposed that conversation was inevitable now, whether Helen realised it yet or not.

'Well, don't be surprised. I mean, why wouldn't she? It's so cynical of you to have withheld it, Rex. I feel as if you were playing me. I just don't know what to say.'

'I know. I'm sorry. I wanted to tell you. I tried to call last week.'

'Tried?'

'Sorry. It felt like too much information for a voicemail. Do you want a coffee? I just made one.'

'Yeah, love one,' she said. 'I did actually get on the train and found my seat, but I got off again just before it left. I realised that I couldn't go home without talking to you. There's something I need to tell you.'

'A bit of honesty?' said Rex. 'Yeah, that would be nice. It works both ways.'

She looked puzzled.

'Lollo told me,' said Rex.

'Lollo?'

'Yeah,' said Rex. 'Yesterday, when he phoned. He told me.'

'Told you what?'

'An old golfing chum of his up in York, or something. How could you?'

'...'

'More to the point, why string me along?'

'I don't know about any of Lollo's friends.'

'No, well, precisely. That's the point. He came looking.'

'What point? Rex, I need to tell you something important.'

'Don't bother,' said Rex, 'I know already. What's going on? Who the fuck are you anyway?'

'Oh,' she said, crestfallen, 'that. I'm so sorry, Rex. It wasn't meant to work out like this. Things got out of hand. I fell in love. You know I love you. I show you that, don't I?'

Rex said nothing. She did show him, yes, and not replying broke his heart a little, but he needed to let her finish, whoever she was. He wanted her to have to do the work, to try to fill the void that her deception had just opened up between them.

'It's not that, anyway,' she said.

'But that's enough, though, isn't it?'

'Well, maybe,' she said. 'Yes, probably.' Then she took a deep breath. 'No, there's something else.'

'Well, come on, then, spit it out,' said Rex, irritably. He'd been keeping a lid on this since yesterday. She was taking the piss now.

She didn't mean to, but Susan, or whatever her name was, glanced towards the door for a millisecond – a micro-expression held long enough for an experienced interviewer to notice.

Rex could see that she was having to measure her words carefully.

No, that wasn't it.

This wasn't him looking at her, and perhaps it never had been.

It was her looking at him.

She was closely monitoring his response, and looking for a way out, an escape route, just in case.

And that meant that right now she was wary of what his response might be.

And Rex wasn't having that.

Not at all.

Yet here he was, still standing right in front of her.

He realised that he'd been rooted to the spot.

He was still standing in front of her, and he was still standing a little too close.

Close enough to hold her.

Close enough to kiss her – old habits – although that wasn't what she was worried about, and this clearly wasn't the time.

'It's okay,' he said, as gently as he could manage, arms still by his sides. He slowly stepped back, got another cup out and sat down. 'You can trust me; you know that. You can tell me anything. Look, I just bought a new washing machine.'

'Well, about time. I'm glad to hear it,' she said, reassured by his gesture.

'D'you want some treacle tart?'

'No, you're alright.'

She could read him like the proverbial. They knew each other quite well by now, after all.

Or he'd thought they did, at least. Until last night, when Lollo had told Rex that there was no one by the name of Susan Hollander working in the finance department of the University of York.

He poured two cups of coffee from the new cafetière, then sat and waited; took a sip.

He didn't have to be anywhere until twelve, so she could take her own sweet time.

It was so quiet for those few moments that he could hear the steady duple beat of the kitchen clock ticking on the wall.

He could hear the traffic on nearby Theobalds Road and Southampton Row, and birds singing up in Queen Square.

So quiet that he could hear her take a breath.

'Rex,' said **Annie**, eventually, 'I'm pregnant.'

PART TWO

I

1: Bâton d'or (Wallflower)

The secret of a good relationship was not to have any secrets. Well, not too many, anyway.

Rex and the by now visibly pregnant Annie didn't. They'd declared an amnesty, more or less.

And that was the way they liked it, as they sat – the soon-to-be happy couple – doing the crossword together on the morning of 1 June, the first anniversary of their meeting.

The sun was beaming in through the open window that looked east from Rex's sixth-floor former council flat in Falcon on Old Gloucester Street, and a light breeze ruffled the curtains. Breakfast was toast and coffee for him, and a morning-sickness-friendly lemon tea for her, before Rex – the recently promoted Detective Inspector Rex King of the Homicide and Serious Crime Command at Holborn Police Station in London's Central North Basic Command Unit – went off to work.

But Rex did not **infer** too much from this apparent state of bliss. Not from the engagement ring, a small single diamond in a white-gold mount on a fine gold band, that every now and then Annie would still hold up for either herself or Rex to admire. Nor from the large colour photo on the mantelpiece of the pair of them, arm in arm and smiling on the beach at Dungeness. Rex's old friend Terence had had the photo printed and framed for them. As of this morning it was accompanied by a vintage green Plymouth Argyle **rosette** that Annie had found on eBay and bought for Rex as an anniversary present.

For all the gifts and the romance, the ring, and the obvious pleasure they were taking in each other's company, Rex was well aware that the life he and Annie had decided to share was not some untroubled **elysian** idyll. For a start, their relationship had had its share of **growing pains** – arguments, wobbles and walkouts – with the occasional **obstacle**, or simple **acts** of folly, to be overcome. And despite appearances – a matter of the golden evening light on the Kentish coast, and, in Rex's case at least, Terence's photographic skills – they'd come very close to splitting up on that spring afternoon in Dungeness.

But at least with everything out in the open, if you wanted to know something, you just asked. There was no need for **phone-tapping** or **password**-hacking, for snooping around or for sneaky-beaky subterfuge of any kind.

Conversely, if everything was known, then nothing needed to be hidden. Nothing could be used by the other for blackmail purposes, to **extort** some criminally or perhaps even just romantically favourable outcome by threatening to tell all to, let's say, the innocent and unknowing party.

But it wasn't always easy being honest. Especially when you did happen to have held one or two tiny things back. And, even by police standards, Rex's was a life that, were you able to prise off the lid, would positively **teem** with secrets.

How had they met? At Sid's, the Conduit Coffee House on Lamb's Conduit Street, and on Derby Day, no less: a year ago to the day. They'd got chatting, and taken a punt on each other.

That was the official version, when anybody asked, which they frequently did.

It was not by accident that Annie had been sitting outside Sid's on that fine 1 June morning. Far from shy and retiring, she'd actively sought Rex out, and had her own good reasons for doing so. But falling in love had not been one of them.

But they had. And that was that.

And it hadn't been a surprise for Rex, a few months later, to learn that Annie was pregnant. He'd known that they'd conceived the moment it happened. He hadn't said anything at the time because he hadn't wanted to jinx it, but he'd been certain. It wasn't his first child, after all. Although he was planning to make a better job of fatherhood this time around.

'Seventeen down: "Russian composer",' said Annie, reading aloud from the crossword clues.

'How many letters?' said Rex, expecting twelve for Shostakovich or some such Slavic tongue-twister.

'Six,' said Annie. 'Second letter "L", fourth letter "N".'

'Ah, okay. That's "**Glinka**",' said Rex. 'G-L-I-N-K-A. I don't know his music, I just know the name from crosswords. Terence would probably be able to give you chapter and verse. But it comes up fairly regularly. Oh look, yes, and so sixteen down, "Alexander's land", must be Macedonia.'

'No,' said Annie. 'It's only seven letters, ends in "N".'

'Try "**Macedon**",' said Rex. 'As in "Philip of Macedon".'

So she did.

'Right, I'm off,' said Rex. 'Thank you, darling. So sweet of you,' he said, pointing at the rosette. 'I love it.'

'Thought you'd like it,' she said. 'Have a good one.'

'Unlikely,' said Rex. 'But you never know.'

The thing about impending parenthood, Rex thought as he pulled the front door to behind him and jogged down the stairs to the street, was that it encouraged you to **reflect** on the future rather than the past, to think yourself forwards: into and through the next generation.

But working in the Met right now, it was hard to imagine any future at all.

'Well, it was nice knowing you,' Eric Jinks had said with mock solemnity at the previous afternoon's team meeting, turning to shake Rex's hand after the Central North BCU's Chief Superintendent Tabitha Churchill had broken the news, or confirmed the rumour, which, while not yet entirely bad, was certainly not good.

Rex had slept on the fact that Holborn Police Station was one of thirty-two across London that had been identified for potential closure, but it still didn't sit right. They'd only just emerged from the last restructure and now they were going to have to do it all over again? The numbers were staggering: £600 million already saved, but cuts of a further £400 million now needed, only £200 million of which had been identified. There was only one thing for it: to flog off some prime real estate on the cheap. The only question was which particular piece of central London real estate it would be.

But how long would they have to wait to find out for sure which stations were for the chop?

And why wasn't Kentish Town on the list? The place was a shithole. Or Tolpuddle Street in Islington?

Of course he knew the answer. It would come down to a

straightforward cost-benefit analysis. A thirteen-storey tower on a site of this size, and in a West End location to boot, was worth more to the property market than the other two combined. Simple as that.

The proposed closures were a short-term solution, but were being presented as a thrilling and dynamic digital-age 'offer' to the public. Just think – the spin went – how those savings could be ploughed into modernising a moribund Met. The money that would be freed up to invest in facial recognition, in artificial intelligence, in the expansion of TeDIU(M).

And to judge from the noises that were coming out of MOPAC – the Mayor's Office for Policing and Crime, and the Home Office, not to mention the Closures Working Group, which had recently been euphemistically rebranded as 'Leading for London' – you could be forgiven for thinking that actual boots on the ground were just a distraction from the real business of policing.

According to the draft consultation document that had been accidentally left on a fourth-floor printer and was doing the rounds, the police service could more effectively be delivered by, **inter** alia, hot-desking Ward Officers – 'equipped to work on the go' – by community consultation meetings, by a suite of digital networked tools including responsive social media outreach and reporting, Automatic Number Plate Recognition – ANPR – the various live facial recognition or LFR algorithm pilots, by other AI and algorithm-based prototypes, by TeDIU(M), and by just one front counter in every borough, as opposed to one in every police station. All of which, if the consultation was to be believed, would offer a more efficient, effective and accessible, a more contemporary, convenient and victim-focused service.

It was all very modern and progressive-sounding: digital = good; analogue = bad.

All the more reason, by that reckoning, to close down the 'failed contact points' once they'd been identified. To get shot of the outdated, under-used back-office services, and the inefficient 'analogue' approaches. By which disparagement, a dismayed workforce at the very tall and unmissable Holborn Police Station tower on Lamb's Conduit Street, London WC, had quickly realised the consultation very likely meant *them*.

It was easy enough to blame all this – the wholesale cuts and the closures – on some governmental **say-so**, some **worm** still turning at the Home Office, even after it had already cut 20,000 officers and wrought havoc across the country. But if the Met, MOPAC and the newly formed ACPO successor body the National Police Chiefs' Council – NPCC – generally spoke pretty much with one voice in relation to what everybody else simply called 'the cuts', it also often seemed as if they couldn't **organise** a piss-up in a Grade II-listed former brewery without accidentally-on-purpose demolishing it.

It didn't give a lot of hope.

At times like this, Rex had become used to turning for advice and insight to his superior officer, Detective Chief Inspector Jethro Lawrence: always ready with a **primer** for any situation. That Rex loved to hate Lollo was the understatement of the year. But much as the Chief got on his **nerves**, Rex always valued whatever the Yorkshireman had to say. Not least because he'd usually have the inside gen about whatever was going on. Rex knew that, whatever whisper networks Lollo drew upon, the Chief would have plenty to say about the closure, about the timing of the announcement, and about who'd be benefiting behind the scenes.

So it was a shame that Lollo hadn't been around for a couple of days.

It was uncharacteristic too.

At yesterday's team meeting Rex could tell that Chief Superintendent Tabitha Churchill had not only been covering up for the Detective Chief Inspector but also covering her own arse when, noting his absence, she'd said she understood that he was taking some unpaid leave.

Why she'd felt the need to **prop** Lollo up with what seemed an obvious white lie, Rex didn't know.

But if the old sod had decided to take a few well-earned days off, who were they to argue?

As Rex strolled along a Great Ormond Street that was still busy with the famous children's hospital's night staff clocking out after morning-handover care meetings, his phone beeped.

Oh aye-aye, he thought with a smile, expecting it to be a 'Miss you already!' message from Annie, asking what he fancied for their anniversary supper: steak or **shepherd's pie**?

But the voicemail was from the other woman in his life, Tabitha Churchill.

Jethro's car had been found, she said.

In **Petworth**, West Sussex.

Foul play was suspected. Sightings, search **radii** et cetera all yet to be determined.

Churchill was babbling slightly, and it took a few seconds for Rex to take in what she was saying.

For fuck's sake.

Detective Chief Inspector Jethro Lawrence was officially a 'MisPer'.

When **Little Bo Peep** lost her sheep and didn't know where to find them, all she had to do was leave them alone and they'd come home. But real life wasn't like the nursery rhyme.

They were looking, she said, at a full-scale missing person investigation.

Rex stopped for a moment, and took a deep breath.

The Chief Superintendent was expecting him in her office in ten minutes, and after that he was to liaise directly with the Sussex force.

2: Chamaerops (Dwarf fan palm)

An hour and a half later, Rex King found himself shooing **away** a **pigeon** on the platform at **Clapham** Junction and giving Annie a quick ring while Detective Sergeant Singh went and got them coffees and pastries to eat on the next train to depart from platform 9, the 10.42 Southern service to Portsmouth Harbour and Bognor Regis. They'd take it as far as Pulborough, then get a cab the last couple of miles to Petworth, where Detective Sergeant Melissa Shepherd of Sussex Serious Crime, out of Midhurst Police Station, would be waiting to show them the scene.

With their neat rucksacks and smart casual wear, the two detectives might easily have been mistaken for mature students or middle-class hikers.

At five-ten with a forty-four chest and fit for his age, Rex was wearing a mustard-yellow Fred Perry and a royal-blue Harrington over khaki Dockers and navy boat shoes. Binder Singh was stockier and, now that he was out of uniform, he generally wore sports gear: black Adidas trackie bottoms and bodywarmer worn over a white T-shirt, hair in an undercut with man-bun.

Annie was seriously shocked by the news about Lollo, and more concerned for his well-being than anything else. She was hardly **fond** of the guy. She'd told Rex that she found Jethro Lawrence a little creepy and a lot macho, and she never made any bones about the fact that she hated the way that Lollo always took Rex's loyalty – and his time – for granted. But a happy Lollo generally meant a happy Rex.

'Looking forward to seeing you later,' she said. 'Any idea when you'll be back?'

'I think there's a train just before five. So we could be back around **half seven**, eight?'

'Be careful,' said Annie.

'Always,' said Rex. 'You know me.'

What Annie didn't say, but Rex knew well enough, was that it was always there in the back of your mind when you were living with a policeman: the risk to life and limb.

And what Rex didn't say – as an instinctive point of good professional practice – was that apparently the Sussex team had detected some blood spatter in Lollo's new Jag.

There wasn't yet much else to go on, so the briefing with Churchill hadn't taken long. A patrol car had spotted the dark-blue XE in the early hours, halfway up the tree-lined driveway entrance to West Sussex Nurseries and Wholesale. And when it was still there an hour later on their next go-round, they'd run a check. Once it was clear that the abandoned vehicle belonged to a senior Met officer, they'd immediately escalated.

'Any known enemies?' the Sussex detective had asked the Chief Superintendent, going through the obvious risk assessments. 'A **creditor**? Anyone who'd have a reason to cause him harm?'

'Of course he's got enemies,' Churchill had said. 'Bad'uns too. He wouldn't be much of a policeman otherwise. But no, he's not a gambling man.'

'History of – sorry, ma'am. Any history of family conflict including abuse?'

Rex was glad the Sussex team were playing it by the book, laying the ground for a possible criminal investigation.

Because of Lollo's rank, none of the usual risk assessment categories applied. The very fact of his seniority trumped everything else and made this immediately High Risk, with likely scenarios here including abduction in the conduct of a criminal enterprise, retribution, or murder. So the immediate requirement would be for an urgent allocation of police resources, SMT approval of staffing, the appointment of an SIO, and a media strategy. Was that the way the Sussex team had seen it, Rex had asked. And, more importantly, did they have the resources to deploy?

'That's pretty much their line,' Churchill had said. 'She seems pretty sharp. DS Shepherd's her name. I reckon she'll be SIO. But I want Evelyn on the media. We're talking about that in a minute. I'm not taking any chances with small-town PR.'

'Does she know how long the car had been there?' Rex had asked.

His first thought had been, if Lollo had effectively gone AWOL two days ago, what had he been doing between then and whenever he'd abandoned or been caused to leave his vehicle? His second thought had been: Why Petworth?

'Well, exactly,' the Chief Superintendent had said.

Tabitha had been more candid than Rex had expected. She hadn't entirely been lying at the team meeting. She'd been tempted to say that the Detective Chief Inspector had a **bug**, or that he'd sent his apologies, but neither would have been true. And Jethro *had* asked for special leave a week or so prior, or indicated that he might need some time off. A personal matter, he'd said. Not that he'd actually put in the request, or formally acted on the conversation in any way. But that might be relevant here. What was the personal matter? She should have pressed him on it there and then, said Churchill, instead of simply deferring the conversation to their next one-to-one. And when he hadn't shown up for that, with no word from him or from Becky Fernie, his PA, it had been her first thought that he'd had no choice but to attend to whatever it was, and that, having mentioned it, he'd considered **notice** served. She'd given him the benefit of the doubt. What else could she have done?

Rex supposed she was right.

The journey was a bit of a blur. Binder Singh was acting like a big kid, looking out of the window – 'Wandsworth **Common**!' – and excitedly reading out the station signs at each stop: 'East Croydon!' 'Gatwick Airport!'

'Fuck's sake, I can read!' Rex snapped. 'What's your problem? Have you never been on a train before?'

'You gonna eat that croissant?' asked Singh, pointing at the Pumpkin Café paper bag that sat unopened on Rex's knee.

'Go on, then,' said Rex. 'If it'll shut you up.'

As the minicab pulled up outside West Sussex Nurseries and Wholesale, Rex could see that there was a regular convoy already in attendance. A patrol car, a plain blue Ford Focus and a slightly tatty black Jeep Cherokee were parked up on the verge on the north side of the driveway, and a police forensics van and a personnel carrier on the south side. Blue-and-white incident tape was strung up across the driveway, behind which – chatting with one of the uniforms – was a tall woman, fortyish, with dirty-blonde hair in a ponytail, wearing a black leather biker's jacket, black cargo pants and hi-tops. Detective Sergeant Melissa Shepherd, Rex guessed.

Two Socks – Scenes of Crime – were finishing off preliminaries on the car and making it safe to transport for a full forensic recovery.

'DS Shepherd?' said Rex. 'I'm DI King – call me Rex. And this is DS Binder Singh. Thanks for making time to see us. We don't want to get in your way, but anything we can do. And the gaffer – Chief Superintendent Churchill – asked me to communicate that we can give you any help you need at our end. You're coming up to London tomorrow, I understand. So either Binder or I will show you around.'

'Melissa,' said Shepherd, shaking Rex's hand. 'Thanks.'

Forensics were just finishing off, she said. And the transporter should be here in a few minutes to take the car away. They'd be running diagnostics on the onboard systems, matching up GPS pings with ANPR data and roadside CCTV. But she'd wanted them to see it in situ first.

The Jag was where it had been found – thirty yards up the drive, facing the main road, with its driver's door open. It had been dusted for prints. Shepherd asked the Sock to point out to Rex and Binder where they'd found the blood spatter – mainly on the steering wheel and dash, with traces on the carpet in the footwell behind the pedals. Apart from that, said Shepherd, the car was still showroom fresh.

But something caught Rex's eye.

Something on the back seat.

Something that, if you knew Lollo, you'd know was out of place. It stood out like a Spanish **galleon** in a garden pond.

'What's that?' he said, though the answer was obvious.

It was a copy of *The Job*, the Met's staff magazine. Nothing strange about that, you might think, in a policeman's car. And that's evidently what the Sock had thought too, because he simply shrugged. But Rex knew that Lollo never gave the trade journal the time of day – to him it was a joke. He always called it '***Pravda***'. Originally published by the Met's PR department, the magazine did nothing if not promote the official party line.

'Lollo wouldn't have that rag in the house,' said Rex. 'So I don't know what it's doing here.'

'Oh,' said the Sock, lifting the front cover with a pair of tweezers.

'Okay. I just assumed. It's not recent, though, by the looks of it. It's from 2003.'

'Come on, then,' said Melissa Shepherd.

Using the tweezers and a pen, the Sock opened the magazine at a page marked with a Post-it: a double-page photo-spread of personnel announcements and medal ceremonies, one of which included a fresh-faced Jethro Lawrence shaking hands with similarly youthful Tabitha Churchill.

They were both probably younger in that photo than Rex was now. They hadn't looked young at the time: Rex remembered thinking they were ancient, although they must have been barely middle-aged. They didn't look young now, that was for sure. But policing was like that. If you wanted to make a career out of occupational stress, premature ageing and general ill health, then a job in law enforcement was just the ticket.

'So the vehicle would have driven into the nursery – for what? Expecting to find something or someone? – turned around, but then stopped here for whatever reason?' said Rex.

'Looks like it from the CCTV,' said Shepherd, leading the way. 'But the cameras only cover the yard, not the driveway itself, unfortunately.'

Rex wasn't sure what he was looking at. One nursery was much the same as another: gravel drives and greenhouses; large wooden prefabs. But this one was a wholesaler to local authorities and to the trade, so everything was on a bigger scale. It was a veritable **botanical** garden, all fan palms and cordylines; olive, eucalyptus and cherry trees of all ages and sizes, plus row after row of bedding plants, pansies and pelargoniums lined up for inspection, a **peastick** in every flowerpot. Rex hadn't seen the uniforms at first, but between the rows around twenty officers were silently and systematically searching the place.

They'd been brought in from all over. For Shepherd it had felt like the old days, having this many officers at her disposal.

'There's only one way in or out nowadays,' she said, indicating the fencing that surrounded the site. 'And that's the way we came. We're working on broadening the search area soon as we're done here. Maps are in the shared drive.' She caught the eye of the Sergeant who was directing the search. 'Ted, have you got a sec?'

'Ma'am?'

'Sergeant Thomas, this is DI King and DS Singh down from London. We'll all be seeing a bit more of each other, I expect.'

'Alright, Sergeant,' said Rex. 'Good to meet you. Any joy?'

'You too, sir. No, nothing. But we're not done yet.'

'Carry on, Ted,' said Shepherd. 'We're going back to the station.'

'Right you are,' said the Sergeant.

Shepherd led the way back to the road, and blipped the locks on the Jeep.

'Don't make 'em like this any more,' said Rex.

'I know,' she said. 'It was my dad's. Before they got silly. I want a car, not a tank.'

As they drove through the village, past picturesque stone cottages and spectacular South Downs views, Rex thought back to his meeting with Churchill that morning. His heart had sunk when the gaffer had told him that it wasn't only Lollo's disappearance on the agenda; that another urgent matter had arisen; that Comms Director Evelyn Gummer would be joining them for the last ten minutes. When she added that she'd also taken the liberty of asking Simon Rose, the Police Federation rep, along, Rex had started to worry. He wasn't stupid. Si Rose's very presence would mean that whatever was to be discussed was relatively serious. But even then, Rex hadn't quite been prepared for the life-changing levels of seriousness that it turned out to be.

'I'm not going to beat about the bush, Detective Inspector,' Churchill had said, before doing exactly that. 'And this is an informal meeting, off the record, and our having a chat now is not part of any HR or disciplinary procedure, so Si is here in an informal capacity, same with Evelyn. Let's keep it on first-name terms, okay? My objective here is for us to trust one another and move forward, so we can deal with this out in the open, but on our own terms.'

Uh-oh, thought Rex. Deal with what, exactly?

She took a deep breath.

'Rex, it may or may not come as a surprise to you to learn that we've been notified that you are likely to be called to testify before the Undercover Policing Inquiry into sexual abuse and historical **mismanagement** within undercover policing. It has been alleged by a member of the public in a signed affidavit that while you were working undercover you deceived her into a long-term sexual relationship. It's not gone public, but it will. So I want us to be prepared. I've not seen the statement yet, but you know I'll give it my full attention. Next time we meet will probably need to be with Francis Bland or someone from chambers, of course. But rest assured that we've got your back, Rex. You're a good officer. You were doing important work on a national security issue. You were doing it well, and you were doing it by the book, so I thank you for that.'

'Okay,' said Rex, adjusting to his new life as if it were a stiff new uniform jacket that needed wearing in. 'Well, I appreciate the heads-up.'

Churchill turned to the Comms Director: 'Evelyn, do you want to talk us through current thinking, based on what we've learned from all the others?'

'Sure,' said Evelyn.

While she updated them on road maps, playbooks and lessons learned, Rex almost felt a kind of relief. Mainly this was a sense of security that came from knowing the Met had done this before, and successfully dealt with accusations of this nature, though he knew that the institutional support could just as easily be taken away. But also because it meant that there was one less secret to keep. He'd always had a feeling in the back of his mind that this particular **Highland fling** would come back and bite him on the arse. Deceit? Well, he'd been using his cover name, so he supposed that was **incontestable**. But he had loved her.

Besides, they'd all been at it.

And she'd been gorgeous. But that didn't mean anything. You could come away from even the most beautiful beach with **tar** on your shoe. And Rex was experienced enough to know that not every ghost could be laid to rest by diktat, with a cry of 'Good **riddance**!'

Annie knew about it, of course.

It was ancient history, but it had come up as part of their full-disclosure pact.

She'd be disappointed – it wouldn't be how she'd want to spend the next few years, standing by her man – but at least there were no surprises as far as she was concerned.

His former partner Helen didn't know, although she'd always suspected that Rex was playing away. He'd better tell H pronto. Not least because he didn't want their daughter Jennifer to find out from anyone else – from the press or the socials.

To tell the truth, Rex had always supposed that, with this particular woman now living and working on the other side of the world, there wasn't too much to worry about. Because to all intents and purposes, and as far as she knew, it *had* been a real relationship. And with her having ended it cleanly after that terrible mid-term miscarriage, he'd always – what? – assumed? hoped? thought? that she'd moved on with her life.

Come to think of it, though, how had she found out? Had the UCPI called her, or had she called them? Surely not. Someone else in the movement must have spotted his cover name and broken the news.

Had he been naive just keeping his fingers crossed? Relying on the great trauma of the miscarriage to mask that of the deception, and thinking that she wouldn't want to dig too deep and drag those dreadful memories up again? What could be worse, after all, than having to go through a full labour to give birth to a baby that you knew was dead? She'd lost Thomas – they'd already decided on the name – late in the second trimester, due to **German measles**. Rubella was a rarity in this day and age, but she'd had a peripatetic childhood. Her family had been ANC supporters and anti-apartheid campaigners, exiled from South Africa and travelling to and from Botswana a lot, working at a community centre out in the bush when she was a kid in the early eighties, so she'd missed the boat on some of the usual childhood vaccinations.

'That's the old Petworth Police Station,' said Shepherd now, indicating what looked like a detached mid-Victorian farmhouse with a futuristic conservatory-like wing growing off the side elevation.

'One hundred and fifty-plus years of service,' she said, 'and they'd only just built that new reception when they closed it down. It cost more to build that stupid greenhouse than they ever saved by shutting it. Waste of blooming money. We lost eighteen stations in one fell swoop.'

'I know the feeling,' said Rex. 'They're talking about closing us down. Cuts, eh?'

'Cuts,' echoed Shepherd. 'Tell me about it.'

Two hours later, after meeting the team in Midhurst and making the arrangements for tomorrow, and following a comedy of errors involving miscommunication and a lack of mobile signal, he and

Singh would find themselves back in Petworth, on foot. Having failed to connect with their minicab, they were trying to find the bus stop for the hourly number 1 to Worthing, which Singh was confident would get them back to Pulborough in time for their train.

Some hope. Rex knew all about rural buses.

'She offered us a fucking lift,' he said. 'Why didn't you take it? Or at least wait for me?'

Meeting over, Rex had gone for a quick slash and by the time he'd come back out Shepherd and team had gone. He and Singh had been left high and dry on the police station forecourt.

'Sorry, I thought our travel plans were robust,' said Singh.

'Seriously? A bus? Christ! If you're in the country and someone offers you a lift, you take it, right?'

For Rex, who'd grown up in Devon, this was a blindingly obvious fact of life that had been drilled into him at an early age.

As it was, at six o' clock, with both their phones dead, and walking the few miles to Pulborough, Rex figured that he might as well relax and enjoy it. There was no point getting **het up**. It wasn't every day you got to go for a walk on the South Downs. It was a warm evening too, with skylarks on the wing, noisy jackdaws and, at one point, a sparrowhawk hovering for ages before diving for some unseen prey. The verges and hedgerows were full of cow parsley, and arching sprays of new-growth brambles with their tiny hard fruits already forming. So when they saw the pub, Rex's first thought was for some kind of **libation** to round off the day – an ice-cold Guinness – but also that they could charge their phones so that he could call Annie to let her know they were on their way.

It wasn't the nicest pub – noisy fruit machines and red-faced farm labourers on the lash – but the pint for him and the mineral water with ice and lemon for his colleague did the job. Later they both agreed that neither of them had noticed anyone following them out.

Annie was fine about it. In fact she burst out laughing. 'I thought you were being a bit optimistic,' she said. 'There's bubbles in the fridge, and a fillet steak with your name on it. I'm just watching *Real Housewives*. Nothing's happening without you.'

'Alright. Love you,' said Rex. 'I'll text when we get to Clapham Junction.'

That was when the white van drove past: the familiar racist shout, the homophobic hate speech. There was a swerve and a screech of brakes, and a couple of coked-up far-**right** twats climbed out, fists at the ready, both high as kites on white supremacy and heteronormativity.

Fucking idiots.

Dangerous, yes, but fucking idiots all the same.

'We're police, you dickheads – fuck off,' said Rex, pulling a fast one-two, a punch to the neck and a kick to the groin combo, which instantly disabled the stronger of the pair, but not before bumpkin number two had punched Binder square in the gut and knocked him to the ground.

'Police!' said Rex again, flashing badge and handcuffs in one swift movement before using Singh's assailant's own forward momentum and rising centre of gravity as he pulled a foot back to boot Singh – to trip him and pin him to the ground. With a **knee** in the small of the racist's back, Rex was tempted to break the fucker's arm, but just handcuffed him.

Meanwhile, bumpkin number one had hobbled away and was starting up the van, but Rex had already clocked the registration.

'Leave it, Rex,' said Singh, still winded and having taken a bit of a bang on the head when he'd hit the deck. 'Let's just get out of here. Fuck! You'd think these cunts had never seen someone from **Asia** before.'

'No chance,' said Rex, who was breathing pretty heavily himself, but wasn't about to forget that right now he was Singh's line manager. 'You've got to make a stand with wankers like this,' he said. 'Otherwise who will they go for next? Someone who's not able to defend themselves? What if you'd been on your own? Or someone else they don't like the look of. No, we're calling it in, mate.' He thought for a second, taking out his notebook and checking the time for the incident book. 'Plus I'm not taking any chances: you could have concussion, hitting the deck like that. And then I'm phoning Shepherd. I'm gonna get us a lift home.'

3: Ver à soie (Silkworm)

[REWIND] —

'There's no question about it. If you were going to be tooling around playing cat-and-mouse on the motorways and in the service station car parks of England, chasing from one rave-up to the next, then you might as well enjoy the ride. That's what M.J. used to say. That was his nickname: "M.J.", after Michael Jackson, for obvious reasons. It wouldn't last forever, M.J. said, and since he was driving, he planned to make the most of it while it did last. So I always tried to go with M.J., more often than not. Until I couldn't. The other lads were decent blokes, ▇▇▇▇ and the Inspector, but they didn't have music in their vans. So credit where it's due. He knew I didn't mean it. I was just doing my job. I don't know how he'd got away with it, M.J., but I think he'd slipped one of the mechanics twenty-five nicker to make a few modifications to the fascia and the dash, and chase through the wiring. It didn't get you a fancy finish, in fact quite the opposite, but M.J. didn't care about finish as long as it worked. Twenty-five quid was quite a lot in those days. It'd be more like a hundred now. No, hundred and fifty. Had to work that out: how many pints could you get for a hundred quid these days? Straight up, M.J. told me that they were all refurbed Variety Club of Great Britain minibuses. I didn't believe him, but it was true in this case at least. Obviously it had been resprayed. No, actually, just saying it out loud, I think he must have been winding me up, must have been. But to be honest no one cared what it looked like. It didn't have to look good. I seem to remember that M.J. was annoyed they hadn't forked out on a V8, so as far as he was concerned they were gonna drive those pieces of shit into the ground. It was a pretty decent in-car system at the time, though. Sorry, is this the kind of thing you want? **<Laughter>** You did say you wanted detail. Okay, so what he'd done was ripped out the

built-in mono speaker from the fascia, and made a big enough hole
to accommodate a Pioneer deck and a graphic equaliser. He had an
amp mounted on a metal bracket by his left knee. Not the newest one
he could've got. It wasn't top of the range, but it was good enough;
better than serviceable. Got a bit hot to the touch, but it sounded
great: good and loud. Funnily enough, afterwards I ended up getting
one for my own car, the exact same set-up: FX-K5 deck, EQ1 and a
GM40 amp. Although his had a separate power switch on the dash,
so he could cut the sound quick when he needed to. I mean, you
know. You can imagine how unusual that was. Driving round in that,
with loud music blaring. It was a bit like in that film *Apocalypse Now*,
if you've seen it: the choppers. **<Laughter>** Yeah, surreal. People
would do a double-take, but I suppose they were surreal times. And
I can tell you, M.J. had great taste in music, so we'd never know what
was coming up next: jazz, soul, funk, blues, or some real head music,
Steve Hillage, "Unidentified" – *BOW b-bow-BOM, BOW b-bow-BOM-
BOM* – or Beefheart, The Who, Syl Johnson. **<Several inaudible
words>** All you could guarantee was that it'd be good, whatever it was.
It was an education. Some of it I knew, but it was almost all stuff you'd
never heard of. Definitely not your standard Radio 1 top-forty hits,
or Capital. You'd be like: "Uh?" Then someone would say, "What's
this, M.J.?" And he'd go, "'The Whip'," or "Hamilton Bohannon" – a
couple I remember – or whatever it was. "The Whip" – we loved that
one. The Ethiopians, you know, an old ska band. It could be anything,
but it was never random. M.J. had a DJ's sensibility, and he really put
those tapes together. Loads of weirdly obscure stuff, though. He took
pride in that, I think. I remember these twelve-inch disco bootlegs of
Police records – The Police as in the band – cover versions made by
some guy in New York, that he used to say were ten times better than
the originals. Funkier. I told M.J. he was in the wrong job. Well, not
in so many words. He was just into his music, you know. Maybe we
all were – or young, anyway. There was a lot of hanging around, to be
fair: a lot of time to talk shit. So the cassette would go in. He'd press
"play", and you know: BANG! Every track building the mood, each
track better than the last, every track cranking things up a notch,
raising the tempo, then riding it for a while before going up another
gear. It was relentless, every track a surprise. With the FX's one-
touch reverse, every C90 cassette was a ninety-minute rollercoaster

ride. And when the tape finished, we'd be on at him to play it again immediately. He even used to squeeze in something special to use up any spare few seconds of tape on each side. A bit of Dougal from the *Magic Roundabout* record, or dialogue from *Doctor Who* – "What are *you* doing here?" – or *The Little Prince* in French, or a track off these BBC sound effects seven-inches. "Church bells", you know, "Heavy traffic (trunk road)", "School playground (boys)". He'd apparently got a job-lot when one of the hospital radio stations closed down, along with a big old Garrard turntable. Or the first few bars of a minor-key rocksteady instrumental: an Alton Ellis B-side, or something by Lynn Taitt and the Jets. All timed to perfection – he didn't want to waste a millimetre of tape. Like I said, it was an education. Mind you, I reckon I taught him a thing or two and all. **<Laughter>** "Come on, then," he'd say, once we hit the motorway, slotting a cassette into the deck, pushing the "play" button and turning up the bass. "Let's get this party started." We were just doing a job, and it was hard work, a thankless task, to be quite honest. But those moments stand out in my memory. We felt like kings riding around in that thing. If you wanted peace and quiet you could go with one of the others, with ▮▮▮▮ or ▮▮▮▮▮. You didn't ride with M.J. if you wanted peace and quiet. And in that respect, like I say, there was no one better to have at the wheel than M.J. – no contest. So why piss him off? Can I say that? **<Laughter>** Cut that if you want. Okay, I'll start again: Why would I get on his wrong side? I don't know, but I managed it. Problem was, the guy couldn't take a joke. Serious times, I suppose. Unusual times. It was pretty intense, but that was the nature of the job.'

Sheffield Hallam University, Miners' Strike 1984–85: Oral Histories of a Hidden Strike, 'Part 3: Special Demonstration Squad, March–August 1984' – Officer HN487 [cover name not revealed].

WOODALL

Clifford was always on the lookout for some rare groove. Listened to John Peel when he could, and always made a note of anything interesting. Days off, he'd be flicking through the boxes of second-hand records at the jumble sales and the charity shops, the record fairs and record shops wherever he happened to find himself. Wherever work took him.

He was the kind of record collector who'd make it his business to find out, say, every track ever recorded with The Meditations on backing vocals. And then he'd set about going out and finding them all.

Always happy to ask advice, he kept a notebook with a list of what he was looking out for. Including a few that The Meditations themselves might not have known about. Rumoured pressings that looked like typos if you saw them in the Greensleeves wholesale catalogue, made on the road in fly-by-night deals for a little cash up front: near-miss titles by non-existent artists rubber-stamped onto local label blanks.

He knew the dealers. They'd give him the nod, phone him up or send him a postcard if they got something in they thought he'd like, some rarity or other. And he was earning okay too. And single, still living at home, so usually he'd buy it to keep them sweet. It was how he justified the job sometimes. Okay, so he might not get out as much as he used to, but he wouldn't go without a decent hi-fi. And chances are he'd have already spotted something else he wanted, but he'd play that down: classic haggling tactics.

'Go on, then,' Cliff'd say. 'I'll give you a tenner for it, if you chuck in that Atlantics seven-inch for half-price.'

'Done!'

'You have been,' he'd say with a wink, one Joe Meek rarity richer. 'Cheers, mate.'

But everyone was happy.

They knew what he liked, and they'd probably put that Atlantics single just where they knew he'd find it in the first place, as bait or to sweeten the deal.

Because all the dealers knew what Clifford was into.

His speciality was records with *sounds* on them. As in *non-musical* sounds: a motorbike revving, a car horn, a baby crying, a police car siren, machinery of some kind, a football crowd or football commentary, a dog barking, wolves snarling, protesters shouting slogans, papal visits, Morse code riding on the beat, a game of tennis, or a political speech – and there were plenty of those at the time.

Any artist.

Any style of music.

It didn't matter.

It did something to him.

He couldn't explain it, but it sent a shiver down his spine.

Martyn's theory – Martyn out of Human League and Heaven 17 – expounded to Clifford in a West Bar pub when the band were recording around the corner, was that it were something to do with growing up in Sheffield, being a kid in bed at night and hearing them hammers ringing out down the valley. The sound got into your blood. That and seeing Roxy Music on the telly.

Whoever was riding shotgun up the front would get a running commentary.

'Oh man, listen to this,' he'd say, turning it up. Or, 'The Blockheads were never punks. They're brilliant jazz musicians!' Or, 'It's off that Factory flexi they did, but only the third pressing.' Or, 'Listen! Can you hear that sound? Yeah? Seriously, you must be stoned, then, because I'm not kidding, supposedly you can only hear that particular chewy bass sound if you're stoned.'

Then he'd rewind whichever Isley Brothers track that was, to prove the point, to prolong the enjoyment.

And the lads probably would be a bit stoned too.

But then, this was a loose-cannon outfit, strategic response, inter-agency working. Seconded to the Met: SDS and Special Branch but off the books and outwith the usual chain of command, answering directly to ACPO and the National Reporting Centre.

And, more often than not, a couple of them'd be skinning up in the back, the *Reader's Digest AA Book of the Road* on one of their laps. The ex-squaddies were always the biggest heads. Former 1- and 2-Para from Aldershot, still buzzing from Belfast or the South Atlantic, half of them. They always sourced their gear from higher up the food chain than mere mortals. It was always Afghan Black or Nepalese Temple Balls for them, never just Red Leb. None of them were completely wasted – not yet anyway, not here – but just passing around a little single-skinner every now and then to smooth the edges and keep the lid on. Just enough for a bit of a laugh; to speed the journey, and sharpen the music.

Even Sketch might have the odd toke, sat in the back with his head in a book, but not Clifford; never Clifford.

Clifford was completely straight-edge, though he never made a big thing of it. 'Live and let live' was his motto.

He was so laid-back he was practically horizontal, as they say.
But then, he'd have to be.

'Syl Johnson, that's on Charly Records, from the LP *Is It Because I'm Black*, and that's "Come On Sock It to Me". A new session from, er, Microdisney, and, er, as soon as I find all of the information about the session I'll pa-ha-ha-ss it on to you. At the moment I can't discover it anywhere. This is "Armadillo Man".[3]

TROWELL

To understand Clifford you had to know that the funk and soul scene had been his education. Since he was about thirteen, fourteen, and tall or cocky enough to blag his way in.

Cadging lifts for a few years, or taking the coach, until he passed his test. He knew all the service stations by heart, which coaches would already be full by the time they reached Sheffield, how many Walkman batteries per journey, give or take, and how many sides of a C90 tape would get him by National Express from Pond Street to Leicester Forest East, or from Golders Green to Milton Keynes on the northbound stopping service, or Sheffield to Newcastle non-stop, or Sheffield to Cardiff via Birmingham.

After a few years of that, his licence had been an instant liberation. He'd be borrowing his sister's car – buying his own soon enough – and driving here, there and everywhere for weekenders and all-dayers: Manchester, Burnley, Nottingham, Bolton, wherever.

He loved it.

Walking into a crowded ballroom, nightclub or community centre felt like coming home, whether it was in Blackpool or Wigan, Wakefield or Chapeltown. Hearing music that no one else had got, feeling the floor bouncing underfoot and the bass rearranging your internal organs.

Dancing was what had got him into music in the first place, or dancing as a means of meeting girls, anyway. And he'd been okay at it in those days. He'd had a few moves. Not like Winston, or the lads in Oxford bags and white vests with gold chains around their necks, who polished their shoes and rehearsed their impossibly intricate

---

3   John Peel, *John Peel Show*, BBC Radio 1, 6 August 1986

steps and synchronised routines for months: jazz dancers. Those lads were amazing, robotics, tap, you name it: could have been pros. But at least Clifford didn't tend to trip himself over. He was competent enough that by the end of the night he'd usually find a girl falling into his orbit, and into step; that first glancing kiss.

Couldn't do it now, the dancing, even if he'd wanted to. Not since he'd fucked his cartilage getting tackled that time.

He'd loved the camaraderie of the all-dayer scene. That's where he'd got the idea now, of everyone dressing the part, like the teams on FA Cup day. Because it had still been a big thing on the circuit around that time. Everyone used to go for a similar look; all the lads.

Like one group of lads might all have vintage Levi's, white T-shirts and imported Nike tennis shoes. A few of the white soul boys had wedges, though most of them had a more buttoned-down preppy look with Rick Buckler haircuts, that plastered-down, grown-out suedehead thing. A few had perms. Half the lads wore grey flannel or burgundy pegs, Loake tassel-loafers and argyle socks, short leather blazers. A lot of the Black guys would have a Jheri curl, a looser wet-look perm or short Afros, Light of the World-style. Knitwear and leather jackets, big-textured jumpers tucked into belted trousers. Clifford himself had been a bit more relaxed back in the day: a short Afro and – going out, to Tropical Heatwave down Penny's, or the Blitz – he used to favour a slightly mix-and-match 'mutant disco' vintage look, with shirt and silk cravat, a waistcoat and baggy suit trousers, plimsolls. And a straw hat he'd picked up from the Spastics Society shop. A vintage 1960s suede jacket with tonic lining that he'd found in Ruby Tuesday's on Abbeydale Road.

At that time it had seemed like everyone was into dancing.

There'd be art school skinheads in combats and kung-fu shoes, dancing like it was a martial art. While dipstick dope-smokers in dungarees and Doc Martens, with African-print shirts and Terry Hall haircuts flailed and windmilled around the floor.

Some of the bigger soul boy crews had names, like One-Way, from Farnham or maybe Farnborough.

The Funk Master Generals was another.

They had logos and everything.

The Soulfull Street Rhythm Dancers' logo was like the London Underground's.

Magnum Force all wore matching dark jeans with navy-blue T-shirts that had their name across the top, above a shield that looked a bit like the MG sports car badge.

That's why Clifford had got some T-shirts made now – him and Tully had been joking about the TV show, a gang of do-gooding troublemakers in a van, getting into scrapes, but answerable to no one. That was them, they reckoned.

A few of the lads in the back were probably wearing their T-shirts today.

Clifford had checked the sizes and everything. He'd taken the money up front, cost price. And they'd all coughed up. None had quibbled. Even Sketch played along and chipped in, though he never wore his.

A mate of a mate on the scene had a T-shirt-printing business on Shoreditch High Street in London, making them for bands, and he'd photo-silk-screened the logo from a page of the *TV Times*: 'The A-Team' in red on a black T.

He'd driven up to collect them when they were ready, no sweat.

A bale of T-shirts on the back seat.

This was the life.

Driving was like mother's milk to Clifford. He was never happier than behind the wheel, with decent sounds on a decent system.

Turn the music up and he was in his element.

There was nowhere he'd rather be.

Distance meant nothing to him.

That was the scene he'd grown up in: down to Bournemouth one weekend, and Blackpool the next, or Caister. Birmingham, Derby or Nottingham. Following the Funk Mafia DJs to small-town nightspots across the South-East: Cinderella's in Guildford, Pantiles in Bagshot, Owls in Aldershot. Hanging out and sharing intelligence in the Wimpy at Fleet Services with the Soul Appreciation Society of GB crew. And those guys always had records before anyone else – white labels and test pressings they'd get sent over from the States. Wanting and needing to be ahead of the game; obtaining the unobtainable. Reading the small ads. Getting tips from the older hands behind the decks. It was a two-way street. He used to pay them back by switching them on to home-grown electronic stuff – bedroom indies, small pressings in home-made sleeves, cassette-only releases – that they could take back over in return.

'Obsession' was Clifford's theme tune, off of *The Voice of America*, and a couple of his DJ mates would play a snatch of it if they saw him arrive. Just their way of saying hello.

They'd line it up on the other deck and push that massive descending guitar riff through the mix. Unmistakable.

Confounding the dance floor with the sound of the future.

Dance music no one quite recognised yet.

Sounds they didn't know they loved.

It was like a premonition: a faster tempo and squelches of phased drums.

Some of the lads would look at him like: *You* are into *this*?

You?

Like he was some sort of traitor to the cause.

As if it was just music for white boys.

Well, fuck that. It was black and white, the Sheffield scene. Always had been.

They'd soon catch up, just they didn't know it yet.

'That's Microdisney in a country-ish mood, I would say. Session produced by Dale Griffin, who's written across the top of the session sheet here, "What a good bunch of songs, exclamation mark." More from them, clearly, and also, as I say, our other session tonight from Age of Chance. This is T La Rock **<inaudible>** That's U-Roy on Ujama Records and "I Feel Good". And another one from Microdisney, this is "Half a Day".'

LEICESTER FOREST EAST

Under the bridge and he'd think: Right, an hour and a quarter to home.

On the mantelpiece at his mum's place: colour photos of Clifford and his older sister Karen in school uniform, his parents' wedding day, and his sister's, a couple of his schoolboy medals – under-fifteens, and under-sixteens – mounted on small black Bakelite presentation shields. A miniature gold-coloured trophy of a footballer mid-volley, from the day they beat the West Yorkshire cadets in the northern finals. A framed colour photo of Clifford and the rest of the Sheffield squad running out onto a football pitch somewhere in Friesland, from the championship-winning South Yorkshire first team's friendlies tour of Holland. Happy days!

Propped up either side of a modest carriage-style clock on the centre of the mantel: his mum's Passport to Leisure, and a colour postcard comprising several views of Sydney Opera House, Australia, the card still bent from being wrapped against a cassette in a tightly sellotaped envelope received recently in the post. A message on the back of the card, written in black biro:

Dear Cliff, You probably heard this session already as I know you listen to Peely when you can. But just in case your not yet persuaded of their general A+++ exellence I got my old Canterbury mate Andy to tape it for us. I feel bad about what I did to you in Sheffield last year. In the heat of the moment I thought all is fair in love & war(!) as they say. Well it did feel like a war at times, but now I think that I went to far got carried away & forgot we are on the same team. And that made both are jobs more difficult. No hard feelings mate I hope. See you round the fairs one day Cheers Steve

WATFORD GAP

When he was about sixteen, Clifford had thought about becoming a DJ himself. The career path seemed to be laid out there for the taking, and it went like this: do a few weddings and birthdays with your mobile disco, and somehow you'd end up on Radio 1. Although he had no idea at all what the mechanics of that transition might be. He'd helped his schoolmate John out on a few bookings for beer money. John had bought a dual-turntable unit with integral amp, a couple of cabinet speakers and a panel of flashing lights from his sister's Littlewoods catalogue. The payments had taken half the wages from his Saturday job at Morrisons. Later he'd saved up and bought a second-hand Pluto 250 effects projector, a mirror ball and a pin-spot from Bardwell's electrical supplies on London Road.

One time, they'd been messing around on the decks in the backroom at The Lescar while the regular DJ took a break, and somehow that had got parlayed into a booking to DJ a Christmas party for the South Yorkshire branch of the Communist Party of Great Britain. Which sounded crazy to the pair of them, but really was still a thing. Maybe they'd wanted the regular guy, but the lads didn't care. Excited to have any booking, they'd turned up at The

Rutland Arms as arranged, and carried their boxes of records to the function room upstairs.

Later, he'd made a mental note never to do that again.

For one thing, when they'd got home his mum had been furious. 'You did what? For who?' she'd said, boxing him round the head. 'For *communists*? I hope please God that nobody saw you! You think the police will take you now? You'll be on a list!'

Well, they hadn't looked like Russian spies, but it'd definitely been a more conservative crowd than he'd imagined it would be. Thinking about it, he couldn't remember a single one of them dancing the whole night. The crucial jazz-funk and reggae twelves he was playing had fallen on deaf ears, and even The B-52s' guaranteed floor-fillers didn't liven them up. Luckily John had brought along his emergency supply: a couple of dozen seven-inches usually reserved for senior citizens and the under-fives. Novelty songs, TV themes and golden oldies, singles that were so bad they were bad.

'No, I don't have "I Will Survive",' he'd said for the sixth time, as he faded in Windsor Davies and Don Estelle's 'Whispering Grass'.

John carried on with it, but Cliff stopped helping him out when it became clear that DJing was ever so slightly incompatible with his chosen career. But it didn't stop him raving occasionally, using his annual leave to follow the scene. Earlier that year, on the strength of a rumour, he'd spent some of his overtime on a trip to Ibiza, and got a bit more than he'd bargained for. He'd come back full of unlikely tales of a drug that combined all the best aspects of coke with all the best aspects of acid and none of the bad. A drug that simply made you happy.

No strings attached.

No side-effects.

No paranoia.

No freak-outs.

And honestly that was absolutely the first time he or anyone he knew had ever heard of ecstasy.

It sounded too good to be true.

But the proof was in the pudding.

All of them had sat on the beach at dawn beaming their faces off.

Him and Jane, that little punky dark-haired girl from Leeds he'd met at the airport and ended up hanging out with. They couldn't believe what they were seeing, until they'd joined in and realised, in joyful waves of exhilaration and clarity, that they too were all part of the same divine body; every touch and feeling magnified. They'd fucked just the once. It had seemed as natural as gravity, the ever-flowing rhythm and love of the universe.

Just you wait, he'd said when he got back, to anyone that'd listen. It's coming.

Of course, no one believed him.

But he knew that you couldn't keep a good thing down.

Give it a couple of years tops, and everyone would be doing it.

Other souvenirs had made themselves known more promptly. A couple of days after getting back home he'd woken up in agony, barely able to piss, like his cock was being torn apart. He'd gone to the doctor's sharpish, then tried ringing Jane up to let her know. But she'd already moved on from the Leeds 6 bedsit address she'd given him. Well, he'd tried, and she'd find out soon enough.

Seriously, though, a drug that made you happy.

Once or twice he'd wondered if he'd dreamed it.

It could have been a million miles away.

From that blissed-out, sun-drenched dawn on a Balearic beach to a cold and frosty morning in a lay-by on the outskirts of Newstead, Notts.

A few hundred lads in a field.

Lads who'd soon be needing something to do, though.

It's coming, he'd say.

Just you fucking wait.

Sketch knew; sat quiet in the back. He'd heard the same rumours, he'd said; seen a briefing, but not seen it with his own eyes yet.

Sketch who always had his nose in a book.

Sketch who was a bit of a head himself, and no stranger to non-ordinary reality, who, given the choice, would always drive with Clifford for the music. And, when he wasn't up the front, spent most of every journey sat in the back devouring paperbacks by Carlos Castaneda or T. Lobsang Rampa, or *The Tibetan Book of the Dead*.

What else did they know about Sketch? Sketch with his rat's-tail and his tats and his Captain Beefheart *Doc at the Radar Station* T-shirt, his donkey jacket covered in yellow 'Coal Not Dole' stickers. Not much, but they knew that he was a wind-up merchant, always ready with a wink and a laugh. That he was ex-Merchant Navy, hailed from

Canterbury and cooked a mean lentil daal. That he'd once worked in a pizza restaurant in York and so was of the opinion that garlic should be crushed before you finely chopped it. That he had a kid he never saw, product of a 'too much too young' teenage relationship, who now lived in Canada. That he'd studied economics and history, come up through student politics, and had until recently been living in a squat off Essex Road in Islington, North London. That he was a regular, when he could anyway, at Microdisney's gigs down at Gullivers.

Sketch who didn't have his records with him, what with being on the move, but who was almost as much of a muso as Clifford, who he outranked and didn't let forget it.

Tooling up the M1 motorway, and riding shotgun since Newport Pagnell in order that they could continue their longstanding debate over which was the best Jamaican-artist major-label crossover, today focusing on Jimmy Cliff on Warner Bros (Sketch) vs. Dillinger on A&M (Clifford).

Sketch who would take it way too far today.

And though neither of them knew it yet, that meant that this was the last time he'd be riding with Clifford, music or no music. That was for fucking sure.

'Ah, still in a country-ish vein, that's Microdisney, and that's called "Half a Day". Another very good review for the Ex single, or the package of things, the *1936, The Spanish Revolution* package, with the booklet and the photographs and so on, and of course the two singles. Is it "Record of the Week" in *Sounds*, was it? I think so. This is the track that they care for most. Not my favourite but I thought I'd play it because I haven't played this one before, I don't think: "El Tren Blindado" <inaudible> —'

NEWPORT PAGNELL

'Don't call him M.J., whatever you do,' they'd say, behind his back.

'Don't call him M.J.!'

And they wouldn't for a while. But then someone – usually Sketch – would go and call him M.J., accidentally-on-purpose, and then everyone else would start again too. In spite of themselves or out of spite, or a bit of both.

Day after day, night after night, knowing it wound him up.

M.J. this and M.J. that.

And most of the time he ignored it; water off a duck's back.

Sometimes he'd blow up, but not very often.

There were more important things to think about, for a start.

But a couple of times there'd be someone new along for the ride, and Sketch would take his head out of his book for long enough to drop it into the conversation, call him M.J. again, with a bit of a wink at the others.

It was tactical, designed to provoke.

He was, after all, a bit of a wind-up merchant, was Sketch.

'Oi, M.J.!' he'd say. 'Are we gonna stop at Leicester Forest? There's better machines there. They've still got an original Asteroids. Seriously.'

'Yeah, Sketch,' he'd say, not rising to the bait. 'I know there is, mate.'

And he did.

It was true. There was. 'It's why I always try and stop there, Sketch.'

And, depending on where they were headed, he'd say, 'Yeah, why not', or 'No, we'd better just push on', or whatever.

And they'd go, 'Right you are, M.J.'

And then unsurprisingly if there was a new bloke in the van, not knowing any different, he'd just assume M.J. really was called M.J. and then the whole thing would start all over again.

And it'd be another couple of weeks of everyone calling him M.J.

M.J. this and M.J. that, night after night.

And what did he do?

He did nothing, that's what.

'Ignore it, mate,' the gaffer would say. 'Just ignore them.'

Or someone having a dig, then calling him 'pal'.

That always put Clifford on his guard.

Where Cliff came from, if someone called you 'pal' they weren't being friendly.

And ignoring it was easier said than done, even for the usually unrufflable Clifford.

But that was what he'd try to do.

Go with the flow, like Weeks & Co., was how he put it to Tully.

'They're just showing their own ignorance,' was what his mother had used to say.

And she'd been right, of course, but that wasn't much help when words – 'when' not 'if' – when words turned to fists. The intellectual high ground didn't have a lot to offer there.

'Ignore him,' Mick had said one time, with good intentions. Mick and Charlie were regulars too, bearded ex-Paras with crudely chopped biker mullets. 'He's just trying to get a rise out of you.'

'Mick's right. Don't give him the satisfaction,' said Charlie. 'You know Sketch. He's just joking about.'

But even they'd quickly got bored. 'No fucking sense of humour,' they'd say when he was out of earshot.

And suddenly it's Clifford's good grace or lack of it that's the problem.

Anything for a quiet life, right? But Sketch really knew how to push Clifford's buttons. It was Sketch's way of reminding him who's who. Sketch's way of asserting rank and seniority over the junior Detective Constable.

'Course he does,' the gaffer had memorably said that time. 'It's his job to push people's buttons. And he's on the team, while it lasts, like it or not. So learn from the best, son.'

But even here, on the road, it was all 'M.J., can you—'

'M.J., are we—'

'M.J., what d'you—'

Straight-faced and plausibly deniable, but in full knowledge of what they were doing.

And he'd usually ignore it, because frankly this was still better than working, better than being back at Snig Hill and running the gauntlet every minute of every day, for not being Sheffield-born, for being a 'southern poof', for being Black. Knowing that the gaffer had got their backs and was trusting him and Tully because – as he'd put it on that first trip down south – 'There's prospects for you two here, if you play your cards right.' And understanding that loyalty was a two-way street and all, and having the gaffer's back as a consequence.

Actually, team loyalty cut three ways. And Clifford always knew that Tully – who was built like a brick shithouse – could deck Sketch at the drop of a hat, whatever his rank. All Cliff had to do was ask.

'I always thought he were a sly bastard,' Tully had said the following year, while they were back down in Aldershot for debriefing, waiting in the back of the arcade to get their souvenir tattoos. 'You should have said.'

Clifford ignored the continual provocations, which is what they were, because there was more important stuff to think about, like getting where they needed to go – the rendezvous in the car park at Leicester Forest East or wherever – to compare notes and check the map, to share intelligence and dish out the gear.

Usually he'd ignore it, but occasionally Sketch'd push it too far and then, finally, much as he tried not to, Clifford would blow off some steam. 'Don't fucking call me "M.J." – have some respect! I don't look like Michael Jackson! You know my fucking name!'

'It's meant to be a compliment,' Sketch would say, but that was total bullshit.

Ignoring it didn't make it go away and neither did calling it out.

Being good at your job meant fuck-all too.

There was only one thing that made it go away.

Turning the music up made it go away, for a bit.

But 'One of these days, I tell you...' he'd say. 'One of these days, I won't fucking ignore it.'

And he meant it.

'The ultimate top teen-beat combo, The Fall, of course (still not sure whether that's in the shops, I mean, perhaps we've been playing it too much for a record that isn't available. I mean: is it available? I've not seen any, as I say), and that's "Living Too Late". Micro— That's confusing, that, what I've just said just then, and if it makes any sense to you, well, I'm proud of you. From Microdisney: "Soul Boy".'

TODDINGTON

'What's that you say?' said Clifford, looking in the rear-view mirror. 'Spirogyra? As in the group? *Bells, Boots and—*'

Mick and Charlie were chatting in the seats behind him, and he thought he'd heard talk of the Canterbury prog band. He was a bit too young to have been into them first time around, but he'd picked up a Polydor reissue; knew who Barbara Gaskin was, for example.

'Eh?' said Mick. He had the *AA Book of the Road* open on his lap again, and was trying unsuccessfully, with nicotine-stained sausage fingers, to sweep the crumbs of tobacco out from the deep gutter between verso and recto pages. He'd been stroking his beard and looking at the nature illustrations while he skinned up – 'Wildlife

Sanctuaries by the Roadside' – so it took him a second or two. Then he twigged. 'No, "gyrus", Cliff, mate. It's like a ring for training horses in Roman times.' He had to shout a bit over the sound of the traffic and the music. 'I was just telling Charlie, I wouldn't mind going to see the Roman Fort at Baginton. We've just gone past it: Junction 17. They've got one there. Mudlark mate of ours is involved in the reconstruction.'

'Oh,' said Clifford. 'I thought you were talking about the band Spirogyra.'

'Supposedly it's where the Romans broke in the horses they got off Boadicea,' said Mick. 'I love all that shit: the Romans. Hang on: Spirogyra? Didn't they do "Einstein a Go-Go"?'

'No,' said Clifford. 'That was Landscape. Hang on. Your mate did what?'

But it was too late. He'd lost them. Mick and Charlie were making strange robotic movements and singing along like a couple of schoolboys: 'Einstein a Go-Go'.

'Ah, that's the stuff, eh? Microdisney, and that one's called "Soul Boy". And I always keep a TV monitor on here in the, on the studios, you know, just in case something really interesting happens to some football, or something like that comes on, something that you can really take pleasure in. Of course, it never happens. At the moment, though, there are people trying to reproduce by waving their arms about. Now, my memory isn't awfully good, but I'm sure that's not how you do it. I've got a postcard here which says, er, it's got a Greek stamp on it and it says, "Ha-ha-ha, he-he-he, You're on holiday"— no, "We're on holiday and you're not." Doesn't rhyme awfully well, does it, but it's from Noddy, Johnno, Fozzy, the Slug, the Bish and the Dwarf, who almost certainly are back in the country now and wishing they weren't. I am not, this is true, that I'm not on holiday, and neither am I going on holiday this year, more's the pity, er, but some of my friends have been on holiday, and one of them returned today and brought me a few records, of which the—– I'm about to play you an example. And incidentally if you're listening, Nicky, your phone seems to be out of order. <inaudible> Puzzling, definitely puzzling. That's the Ligament Blub Brothers, though, on Scrundleplatch Records, and they come from Calderwood, East Kilbride. And, er, is this the last from Microdisney tonight? Indeed it is. It's called "And He Descended into Hell".'

SCRATCHWOOD

Today Clifford was playing at home. Usually a rare occurrence, but this was the second time in two weeks. And once again there wasn't going to be time to go and see his mum, or get a change of clothes; not today.

Only two weeks since, there'd been a march in support of a meeting of the NUM National Executive, and that had turned to shit. They'd nearly lost control. But at least they'd anticipated trouble, and had the bodies where they needed them.

'Home? What's that?' someone said, one of the lads in the back, maybe Charlie, and they all laughed. They'd all been away from theirs for so long, up and down the motorways that many times. Sleeping in barracks down south or up at Catterick, depending. Sleeping on the floors of TA halls, waking up to tea urns and toilet queues.

Sketch was laughing too. Although fuck knows where home was for him. You couldn't believe owt he said.

'Sheffield? Love them chimneys,' said Mick.

'Not chimneys,' Clifford said with hometown pride, 'cooling towers. We're coming off well before Tinsley Viaduct.'

Today's 'disco' was at Sheffield City Hall.

A journey that Clifford knew well. He could drive it with his eyes closed.

A journey he'd made a hundred times on a hundred bright, cold mornings just like this one, coming back from a hundred nights out.

Normally he'd be coming off at Chesterfield, glimpse of Hardwick Hall if it was daylight, and the flower stall; through Derbyshire mist, onto the Dronfield bypass and into the south of the city, remembering school trips to Graves Park Animal Farm, through Normanton and Cutthorpe to Lowedges. But not today because he wanted to show them something, any of them that were still awake. He could hear Mick and Charlie, still chatting in low voices in the seats behind, but everyone else had gone to sleep in that dark thirty-, forty-mile stretch with no lights, where the traffic always thinned out. But it wasn't thinning out now and he wasn't coming off at Junction 29, because he wanted to show them something.

Past Junction 30 and he was aware of other coaches, minibuses and double-deckers all jockeying for position and getting into line in the nearside lanes for the Sheffield exits. He knew there'd be buses from Newstead and Bilsthorpe and Ollerton, from Tilmanstone and Betteshanger. And it'd be the same in from the west too, and southbound: buses from Easington and Ellington, from Ashington and Wearmouth, from Fife. Closer to home there'd be double-deckers from Thurnscoe and Cottonley, Dinnington and Armthorpe, and all across the Yorkshire coalfield. And all of them buses would be full.

Clifford who was getting a nose for numbers and logistics, sensing a similar density of coaches to last time. He had a feeling that there was going to be a bigger turnout today than they'd planned for.

No one was expecting a repeat of April's massive showing; not in Sheffield, not again, not so soon. Not with all eyes supposed to be on the big march into scab country next week.

'D'you reckon there's gonna be enough of us?' he'd asked the Inspector when the three vans had stopped at Trowell. And he hadn't been joking. 'How many mobiles have we got?'

The expectation for today, and the planning, had been on the basis that there'd be four or five K, tops. Plus maybe another thousand in home-grown talent: Sheffield Trades Council, local NUM branches, NACODS, Sheffield Women Against Pit Closures, and the other Wives Action Groups, CPGB, RCP and SWP cadres, the university and the City Poly's student unions.

There was a lot of support for the strike in the People's Republic of Sheffield.

Coal was the lifeblood of this place.

Because without coal you didn't have coke.

And without coke you didn't have steel.

And without steel there'd be no Sheffield.

But if there were this many coaches already, the march would have to be more like eight or ten, maybe even twenty thousand strong.

And in a few hours, all however-many-of-them would be mustering on Devonshire Green to march out to the end of West Street and back into the city centre, then halfway down the high street to the cathedral before doubling back up Fargate to Barker's Pool for speeches on the steps of City Hall, over the road from what would soon be the new NUM HQ, which was probably the point.

After which the objective would have to be containment and quiet dispersal via Division Street, back to Devonshire Green and Fitzwilliam Street. To get them all back into buses and on their respective merry ways home, and maybe to crack a few heads in so doing: '*Do svidaniya*, comrades, see you on the picket lines!'

Well, if that was still the plan, Clifford was starting to think, they'd be lucky to get away with it.

He had a nose for it, Clifford, and he reckoned this lot would be a right fucking handful.

There weren't meant to be so many.

Not again.

Not today.

It wasn't meant to be a show of strength; more like a photo opportunity.

Course they'd take the chance to get stuck in, but they'd have to leave the arrests to the regulars.

No visible numbers, naturally.

'Unidentified!'

BOW b-bow-BOM!

Three-man snatch squads, with shields and batons, like Mick's Roman gladiators.

BOW b-bow-BOM-BOM!

Marchers would be on the ground, cuffed and cautioned before they knew what hit them.

BOW b-bow-BOM!

Get them in the mobile cell block ASAP, then get back out to pick the next prisoner.

BOW b-bow-BOM-BOM!

If you believed the brief public statements, both sides wanted to demonstrate that restraint was possible: a statement of intent before the bigger rally in Mansfield on the fourteenth. An opportunity for both sides to be seen to call for calm in the face of escalating violence at picket lines across the country.

They'd be lucky.

Clifford pushed 'eject' and took out the tape.

One hand on the wheel, he reached in and took another cassette out of his pocket, pushed it into the slot, pressed 'play' and turned the music right up.

The sound of this city.

Clifford's theme tune.

Hometown pride was right. He was proud of the music of this town. His town. He was proud to have gone to The Human League's first gig in the canteen at Psalter Lane. They were a bit older, but he remembered the lads from school. Still had the bootleg. Always thought The Cabs were harder, though, and funkier. The sound of the future. And some of the best gigs ever: the Lyceum in '82! He'd said as much to Mal when he'd seen him a month or so back, propping up the bar at The Leadmill with a red bandana tied around his head.

Clifford had been there on a call, and not in his party clothes. He'd happened to be passing in a panda at the end of his shift when Wrenchy had rung in worried about some junkies hanging around the stage door, one of them an ex-stagehand with a grudge, who knew that the venue paid in cash. He'd had a feeling that some artistes who'd been on the bill earlier were going to get rolled for their fee, which came straight out of box office takings.

'I'll take it,' said Cliff. He'd gone along and led them out through the coat check, crawling under the counter, walked them to a different hotel than the usual. A grateful Wrenchy had stood him a couple of double brandies after.

Cliff'd seen Mallinder, surrounded by a group of acolytes, shaven-headed Psalter Lane types, as soon as he'd gone in the bar. The thousand or more students in the place wouldn't have known Clifford was a copper.

Mal knew.

But Mal also knew that Cliff had come to all the early Cabs gigs.

Mal knew that Cliff knew his music.

Mal shared Clifford's esoteric tastes.

The Cabs were into sound and all, and dance music.

Just like Cliff was. He'd idolised them.

They used non-musical sounds in their music: phased field recordings, a redneck cop at a rock 'n' roll concert, Morse code.

That's how they'd got into it in the first place – Mal, Rich and Chris – through their interest in sound. Mal had once told him as much.

That line about no dancing allowed had become a catchphrase for Cliff and his soul boy mates.

That other night in The Leadmill, Cliff had been telling Mal about Ibiza.

Like he didn't know.

The future.

Here it comes.

Someone had once said that to him: You've got to have an obsession. Was that it? Trust your obsession? Something like that.

That lad, couldn't remember his name, was a bit of a tit – Temple ov Psychick Youth type, trying too hard – but it had come to mind several times since, even so.

Maybe there was something in it after all.

Well, if so, Clifford's obsession was sound.

The music of his hometown.

He used to go to all the gigs.

Until he couldn't.

Until he stood out too much.

But he'd still drop in for a cup of tea with John at Red Tape if he was passing. Or for last orders and a cheeky lock-in with Bill and Barbara at The Washington. Or round Mona Lisa's, nights he got off early, to prop up the bar for half an hour. To tap his foot and shoot the shit with whoever was about, whether goth or soul boy. Chatting rare grooves, remixes and in-jokes: who had 'Let's Get Horny' by Hi Voltage on the original New York 12-inch.

Clifford did, naturally, but Rich only had the UK release. That this was also a quiet and skip-prone pressing on a 33rpm EP only added insult to injury.

Raised eyebrows and sighs of relief all round once he'd left, he didn't wonder, but Clifford didn't care.

What's your obsession?

In off Junction 31 so they could come in on the A57; that view of the city as you descend from Intake.

Coming home. He knew the way.

That relentless bass riff.

The lights on the equaliser going with the music.

He knew every note, like he knew every petrol station, and every roadside sapling.

Here we are.

'Look,' he said. 'Oi, Mick, look at this.'

Just for a minute, the whole city was laid out before them in lights.

'You know it's Sheffield,' he said, 'because it's in that bowl.'

Those fast and jittery drums coming in all phased and squelchy.

He recognised every orange street light, every shopfront and factory, every kerbstone, every sooty brick in every building.

Morse code and radio interference riding over the top.

Every street sign and every roundabout, every note was like going home, taking you further in.

That massive descending guitar riff.

Park Square and the flyover, Park Hill Flats – had his mum left the kitchen light on? – and Hyde Park up on the left.

Synths bubbling from one side of the stereo mix to the other.

On the outer ring road past the station, past Dyson House.

The slightly off-kilter vocal.

Between the back of Kennings and The Leadmill, the little mesters and the mills.

They'd got caught short two weeks ago, so this time the former corporation bus garage on Shoreham Street was being used as a 'transport hub', they called it: a mustering point. Easier to keep a place like that secure. The squeal of tyres on the concrete floor. Early starts all round, but with the last of the late frosts behind them at least it was warmer than last week. Diesel fumes from dozens of vans and coaches rising up through the ironwork to the high glazed roof. Hundreds of boots squeaking on the ground. All that noise and smoke in that great echoing space; diesel exhaust and fags; shouting and laughter, letting off a bit of that tension: the pre-match nerves.

PSUs – Police Support Units – from all over. Reinforcements arriving from the West Yorkshire force, from Manchester and Nottingham constabularies.

All the lads piling out of warm vans and coaches, smelling of farts and ciggie smoke. Getting kitted up with riot-style shin pads, and lining up for shield and baton issue. Helmet chinstraps tucked in, for now. They'd only fasten them if they needed to.

Most of the lads in full uniform.

Not the A-Team, though.

And a couple of the local lads did a double-take to see them: 'Uh?' There were audible mutterings about favouritism and tokenism when they saw Tully and Clifford, especially Clifford, out of uniform and chatting with the Inspector. They didn't know that the lads had been singled out for better things; fast-forwarded.

'Lazy fucker,' they called him.

'Arrogant twat,' they said. 'Who does he think he is, eh?'

'Brown-nosing cunt,' they called him, and worse; much worse.

They weren't stopping, though. Only long enough to stretch their legs, to pull on their shin pads and boiler suits, have a cuppa and a fag. Then they'd be up to Rockingham Street to wait it out: the A-Team, but not Sketch.

Him and the other SDS lads who'd driven up with Tully and the gaffer.

All of them covered in yellow 'Coal Not Dole' stickers.

They'd been sharing out a bag of badges – 'Here, you can be "Barnsley Miners Wives Action Group"' – and laughing.

'KENT NUM support the miners fight for jobs.'

'First-Division Geordie Pickets All Out to Win.'

Sketch and the SDS lads giving some lip to the Manchester PSUs who didn't know them from Adam.

Play-acting and getting away with it.

Job's a good'un.

Running up the steps by the old Kennings showroom onto Paternoster Row.

Sketch and that were on their own.

Blending in.

Standard tactics to be deployed.

To make a lot of noise so they'd be heard before seen. 'Maggie Thatcher's GOT ONE, Ian MacGregor IS ONE, da-da-da-DA, da-da-da-DA.' Joining the crowds arriving at the railway station or at Pond Street. The crowds who'd be getting off the buses and the coaches that were parked all the way down Fitzwilliam Street. Fanning out, making like fellow travellers, working the march: hail fellow well met, like. Blending in, and all the time keeping an eye out for that certain element in the crowd: the nutters and the boozers and the brawlers, the racists, the hot-tempered hard nuts, the Tennent's Super and the sweet sherry drinkers. Finding their trigger points: exposed nerves and prejudices. Working out exactly where they wanted to go before they knew it themselves, where they wanted to go but were afraid to. And learning how to wind them up, how to

groom, to coax, and to press precisely the buttons that were needed
to take them there.

Classical moves: take horses to water.

And make them drink.

Like butter wouldn't melt, like he without sin: playing the twats
like a fucking violin.

Geeing them up, getting stuck in.

Casting around for something to throw.

Checking the weight, bringing them with you.

Finding your range, and knowing they'll follow.

Then, 'Come on, lads! Let's get the pigs!'

And lead by example, and chuck the first brick.

CITY CENTRE DISTURBANCE, 27 ARRESTED: PICTURES

Terrified Springfield Primary pupils and parents dodged missiles as
violence associated with the current National Union of Mineworkers
dispute erupted in Sheffield for the second time in a fortnight. 27
arrests were made during rioting on Division Street and Devonshire
Green. Four policemen received minor injuries, and three protesters
were hospitalised; one remains critical. A number of incidents were
reported along the route of Monday's march, and following the
NUM rally at Barker's Pool... At one o'clock, bottles and glasses
were thrown by a large crowd of NUM marchers gathered outside the
Wimpy on Fargate. Miners chanted 'Sieg Heil' and 'Thatcher's boot
boys', while monkey noises were persistently directed at a coloured
police officer.

Sheffield Star, 9 May 1984

'I always enjoy those little asides. That's the last tonight from
Microdisney. "And He Descended into Hell" is the title of it. On
Monday night's programme we've got a new session from Fuzzbox,
and a repeat of our session from Front 242, which went down very
well the first time it went out. If you missed it, try not to miss it
on Monday. This is Keith LeBlanc and various chums from the LP
Major Malfunction, "You Drummers Listen Good" **<inaudible, tape
ends>**'

4: Consoude (Comfrey)

They'd cracked open the **bubbly** when Rex finally got back to the flat around ten thirty.

Rex and Binder had got a cab from Victoria, Rex dropping his colleague off at a thankfully relatively quiet A&E department at St Thomas's Hospital, where Singh could get a once-over and written confirmation of whatever minor injuries he'd picked up in the assault.

Climbing the stairs of Falcon was different now he knew that Annie would be waiting for him. He'd never stopped loving the area. And he'd endured **penury** in the early days, when, on a starting salary, and not too long after he'd been offered and had bought the place on a London Borough of Camden 'Right to Buy' scheme, mortgage interest rates had gone up to fifteen per cent.

Taking off his jacket and hanging it over the back of one of the dining chairs, he'd been about to launch into an after-work debrief, to **recall** the day in all its grim detail and **enumerate** without **gloss** the catalogue of disasters that had made up what had quickly become the day from hell. There was no **swear word** strong enough to express how he felt. What with the potential station closures, with Rex about to be named in the UCPI, and with Lollo going missing, and all of that topped off with Binder Singh being subject to a racist assault out in the sticks, it had been an absolute dog of a day. The cherry on the cake was being challenged in some over-officious **spot check** at the Victoria Station barriers. Some jobsworth twat wouldn't accept their warrant cards as sufficient authority to travel, and demanded they either buy a full-price return ticket there and then or he'd issue them £100 penalty fares each. You couldn't make it up. If you'd asked Rex to think of a worse day in his quarter-century-plus on the job, you'd get a very **short list**.

At least they'd arrested the racists. That had felt good.

Luckily Melissa Shepherd had stepped up. She'd already knocked off for the day, but had come and picked them up and offered them a lift to Gatwick at least. When she'd pulled up in her old black Jeep, 'More Than a Feeling' by Boston was playing on the in-car stereo.

Singh was inspecting a nasty bruise on his arm, where he'd hit the deck. He was developing a swollen jaw and a bit of a bump on the back of the head.

'That looks sore,' said Shepherd. She walked around to the verge and picked a handful of large leaves from a purple-flowered plant that grew thickly along the roadside.

'Comfrey,' she said. 'Put these in a bowl just as they are, and pour half a kettle of boiling water over them. Let it sit for half an hour and then soak a couple of flannels in the tea, and use them as a compress. It's an old remedy; good for backpain and broken bones too.'

'Alright, I will,' said Singh. 'Thanks very much.'

'I say "tea" but don't drink it,' said Shepherd. 'It's poisonous.'

'Is this the automatic?' said Singh, running his hand along the roof of the Jeep.

'Yup,' said Shepherd. 'Noisy but reliable. Should run for a few years yet.'

'Thank you, Detective Sergeant,' said Rex, sticking to formalities once they were underway. '**Else** I think we'd still be walking to Pulborough.'

'No worries,' she said. 'Oh, I forgot to ask you earlier. About DCI Lawrence: any distinguishing features I don't know about?'

'Couple of tattoos,' said Rex. 'That I know of, anyway. He's got a **dragon** on one arm, his right, I think, and a kind of skull and crossbones on the other, up here near the shoulder, with a motto that says "The A-Team", and a white rose of Yorkshire.'

'I pity the fool,' said Singh in a funny voice.

'You what?' said Rex.

'*The A-Team*, innit,' said Singh. 'BA Baracus. "I pity the fool."'

'Excuse my colleague,' said Rex to a perplexed Melissa Shepherd before she drove away. 'He's one of our top lads, usually. I think he might have taken a **dangerous** blow to the head.'

While they were waiting a few minutes for the next train to Victoria, Singh had got a call from the Sergeant at Midhurst to let him know that they'd just now picked up the driver who'd been involved in the assault and the hate crime.

'Good,' said Singh. 'Fucking **dosser**.'

'You understand I have to ask this,' said the Sergeant, 'for Quality Assurance purposes, but would you like to speak to someone at Victim Support?'

That was priceless. Maybe you had to be there, or perhaps it was the adrenaline, but it had the two of them practically doubled over and crying with laughter on the platform there at Gatwick Airport railway station.

'Hey, let's take a rain check on the debrief,' said Annie, with a smile and a **prod** to Rex's shoulder.

Phew, he thought as she moved closer and rested her arms on his shoulders, so she and he were just touching, body to body.

There was still electricity.

'Let's pretend it's a **blind date**,' she said, 'and we're out to impress.'

Rex touched her hips lightly; he knew their power, and knew that there was nowhere in the world he'd rather be. To say he had the **horn** would be an understatement. He didn't just have wood, he had **timber**.

She pressed against him: 'Hello!'

'Bit forward for a blind date,' said Rex.

'Listen, all that nonsense'll still be there tomorrow,' she said. 'But our anniversary won't. Now I've got you to myself for a couple of hours, let's forget about work for tonight and start **afresh** in the morning, eh?'

'Thanks, sweetheart,' said Rex. 'Yeah, you're right. This is much more fun.'

'You've got to **learn** to enjoy the good times,' said Annie. 'And I've got us a couple of fillet steaks if you're hungry.'

'Starving.'

'Otherwise, you know, I could probably rustle up some **gruel** if you really want to kill the atmosphere.'

'I wouldn't care,' said Rex, 'as long as I was with you.'

'Flatterer.'

'Can't help it.'

Annie was wearing a black linen shirt-dress with a twist: full-skirted, the fabric was cut on the bias to accentuate her curves. Disentangling from his embrace, she gave him a twirl. Showed off her small bump.

'I love that outfit. It makes you look all **prim** and proper,' said Rex – and she flashed him a smile – 'but I know different.'

'Thanks,' she said. 'I went to the **salon**. Ashley came along too, remember?'

'Of course! How is she?'

'Check-up is tomorrow. But she's grown so much. And her extensions are a-may-zing, you won't believe. We both got our nails done. Did you notice?'

Rex reached out and pulled her back towards him. To **hallow**, he thought. To sanctify. To worship. Supper could wait. 'Come here, gorgeous,' he said. 'Do you know how much I love you?'

'Look,' Annie said later, after they'd finished their steaks and salad. 'Did you see Jen's card?'

Rex's **first-born**, Jennifer, who was in the middle of her GCSEs and already thinking about universities to apply to, had sent them an ironic anniversary card featuring a kitschy retro photo of a glamorous couple in a **speed-boat**. The man at the wheel wore mirror shades, a navy blazer with gold buttons and a captain's nautical cap, while, reclining beside him in some species of loosely fastened silken dress, his female companion was exposing a large amount of **bust**.

Jen lived with her half-sister and her mum – Rex's ex, Helen – out Woodford way, but had been coming into the **city** centre with friends for a while, and had been to see them a few times. Less so while she'd been concentrating on revision, but she'd been making noises about applying to uni in London, and Rex had pointed out some London colleges – King's, UCL – on their walks around the **area**.

'Is that how she sees us, d'you think?' said Rex.

'Look inside,' said Annie.

Rex did so, and actually laughed out loud. Partly because it was very funny, but also out of parental pride. 'Clever girl. That's just brilliant,' he said. 'I love it. Why didn't I think of that?'

'Happy Annie-versary,' it said. 'Love Jen.'

5: Pimprenelle (Salad burnet)

By eleven thirty the next morning they were letting themselves into Jethro Lawrence's double-fronted 1830s terraced house on Caerphilly Road, part of the Tredegar Square conservation area in Bow, in the East End of London.

'Blimey,' said DS Shepherd, admiring the meticulously restored period detail of inset boot-scraper and coaching door, the recently repointed brickwork and the authentic-looking paintwork. 'Nice place.'

'Don't mind me, Melissa,' said Rex, opening both front-door locks with the same key. 'He'll expect us to be thorough.'

'Thanks,' said Shepherd. 'I appreciate that.'

DS Shepherd, Sergeant Thomas and a couple of other officers had come up on the early train to get to Holborn for ten. Churchill's PA, Frances Charles – Frankie – had set up a meeting room and ordered coffees. Rex had known that it would be a full day after that, and probably quite emotionally testing, so he'd decided to pace himself, which meant not going in before nine thirty for once.

Annie had been right, of course, as always. All the shit was still there in the morning. But as Rex had breakfasted in **silence**, at least he knew he'd slept soundly, and all the better for a bit of what people used to call 'quality time'. They'd even managed another quickie before the snooze went off.

He'd had a vivid **dream**, one that had recurred more or less annually all through his **adult** life, that they were in the South of France, and all of this was playing out against the **blue sky** and the white concrete ziggurats of the Baie des Anges – a luxury **marina** development halfway along the coast between the **race track** at Cagnes-sur-Mer and Antibes – and that somehow, in this dream, all problems could be solved by a magical **coin** that changed denomination depending on the circumstances – now a euro, now a pound coin, now a swimming-pool locker token, or a powerful amulet.

Well, wouldn't that be nice.

But in real life, whichever way you looked at it, this was a monumental crock of shit with **extra** sweetcorn.

At least a decision on the station closures would take a while. Not least because such wholesale restructures and redeployments usually had redundancy programmes, voluntary or otherwise, at their core. So HR were **bound** to be ahead of the game on that. Rex figured it would be coming at them thick and fast, and in short order.

First step would be a series of all-staff meetings with Tabitha Churchill and Si Rose on the **rostrum**, plus someone senior from HR, but with accidentally-on-purpose slightly too few chairs for the number of staff invited. Such were the strategies that HR departments used to give themselves the **upper** hand, by planting a seed in employees' minds that there wasn't enough of everything to go around.

Who was the HR lead on SMT these days anyway? Still Di Malcolm?

Diana and Rex had dated briefly when she'd first moved to London a decade or so back. They'd met in her first week down south, over the buffet lunch at some outdoor mix-n-match Police Federation jolly at Chelsea **Physic** Garden, and something between them had clicked. Her blue eyes were like an **X-ray** machine, Rex remembered. She'd seen right through him, and the two of them had snuck off back to her hotel in St James's Park during the afternoon break-outs to hold their own two-person plenary session. He'd liked her **Scouse** accent, her hard body and her interest in high-end lingerie, and she'd clearly liked his style well enough that they'd dated – or fuck-buddied might be more accurate, and strictly on the QT – for six months or so.

Annie knew all this, of course.

Di had married her personal trainer in the end. And good luck to her. There were no hard feelings, and she and Rex had always given each other the time of day since.

The UCPI would set its own agenda, and there was nothing Rex could do about that, other than wait for confirmation of his hearing date, and to respond truthfully to whatever they might ask him. Or actually to do whatever Evelyn **Gummer** told him to. He'd see the affidavit soon enough and then he'd have to act accordingly, grasp the **nettle**. He knew what was likely to be in it after all, more or less, but it would be interesting to see how she remembered things. It would put him in the public eye, but that was part of the job sometimes, and the pay rise that had come with his promotion would soften the blow. He'd just have to be a **soldier** and do as he was told: keep schtum, and not **spill the beans** too easily.

Most pressing was obviously the case of Detective Chief Inspector Jethro Cyrus Lawrence OBE ('for services to community policing'). Rex had initially found it odd to be referring to Lollo as 'Lawrence' or 'Jethro', but obviously the Sussex team weren't yet on nickname terms with the missing DCI, and in fact an eye for the unfamiliar was important here. Rex knew that he had to follow Detective Sergeant Shepherd's (and to an extent Chief Superintendent Churchill's) lead in treating Lawrence just like any other MisPer, and that meant not taking the familiar for granted, nor leaving anything unspoken.

Melissa Shepherd was already proving her worth. Proactive, willing to **stand up** and be counted, and good at thinking ahead, but clearly working at **optimum** efficiency too. She'd emailed the Holborn and Sussex teams at six with the first draft of her risk assessment, underlining its provisional and dynamic nature, but pretty much covering the bases: welcoming input, confirming the High Risk classification and corresponding resources, identifying interested parties – not too many of those as yet – giving herself and Sergeant Edward Thomas as lead contacts down at Midhurst, and herself as SIO, but with Rex and Binder Singh on the top line too, which was both sensible and thoughtful.

She'd brought three colleagues up to London: Sergeant Ted Thomas from the West Sussex 'PolSer' (Police Search) team, PC Gary Keyes, and a young Detective Constable named Jane Gosling.

Obviously there'd been inter-force formalities to observe, and a cup or three of Building Services' coffee, sweetened by some half-decent pastries that Rex had picked up by way of a welcome, and a thank you to Shepherd for her generosity-over-and-above the previous evening.

Settling in, Shepherd had flagged up that it would be tricky to put Jethro in one of the standard MisPer categories. Was he lost and temporarily disorientated? voluntarily missing? or under the influence of a third party, that is victim of abduction or murder? She wasn't going to rule anything out, but she would be applying the 'missing persons motto': If in doubt, assume the worst.

Local searches were obviously underway in Petworth, and the senior Sergeant Ted Thomas seemed to Rex like a safe pair of hands in that regard. But before they went Sussex-wide, or wherever the sweep of ANPR, CCTV and the Jag's GPS log would lead them, obviously it was first things first. And top of the list was Lawrence's house in East London, because everyone knew that most missing persons are found within the curtilage of their own home. The second priority was to search his office on the sixth floor at Holborn.

After that, things would only get more complicated.

'But complicated is what we want, isn't it,' said Shepherd. 'Plenty of data, right? The more the merrier.'

She was good at 'complicated', and Sussex had the systems and resources to back her up.

Might it be an idea, Churchill had suggested, bringing Lollo's PA, Becky Fernie, into the discussion, for Sergeant Thomas and PC Keyes from Sussex to start on the sweep of his office – 'Becky knows where everything is, right?' – while Rex drove Shepherd, Singh and DC Gosling out to Bow in one of the pool Mini Coopers? Then they could all reconvene back here at the end of the day and look at next steps.

'My thoughts exactly,' said Shepherd.

'I took the liberty, Rex,' said Churchill, sliding over a triplicate vehicle chit that she'd already countersigned. Churchill turned to her PA: 'Frances, do we still look after Jethro's spare key?'

Frankie nodded, and slid a small, sealed manilla envelope out from under her notebook. 'One thing, though, ma'am,' she said. 'Becky and I were just going through the list and we realised that neither of us know the combination for Jethro's safe. I don't suppose...'

Anyone who'd been to Detective Chief Inspector Jethro Lawrence's office would have seen his safe, which while not ostentatiously large was set into the built-in shelving behind him, beneath the window that ran the length of his office and looked out – past a couple of his old rugby trophies, presentation boxes and framed team and other photos – towards East London and the City.

Rex shook his head. He did know it, but he wasn't about to get into all of that now.

Churchill shrugged. 'Just call Banham.'

Lollo's house in Bow was as tastefully decorated on the inside as it was on the outside. Spotless, and sparsely furnished, but with quality pieces: an Eames chair and ottoman, a large flat-screen TV, Bang & Olufsen hi-fi with concealed speakers, and bookshelves full of political and historical works. There was a drinks cabinet containing numerous single-malt whiskies – Springbank, Laphroaig – and some XO brandies, two heavy, antique mahogany cupboards and a striking Arts and Crafts standard lamp in dark oak at one end of an expensive-looking sofa that was upholstered in a golden-hued William Morris fabric.

It was the home of someone who spent money infrequently, but on expensive things. There was art on the walls: paintings and photographs.

'Jethro once told me that when he first moved here it was all artists,' said Rex. 'These streets were half-derelict, they were going to be knocked down for a motorway, so they were being rented out to artists short-term, on the cheap.'

'Hidden depths? What's that,' said Shepherd, pointing above the original and immaculately restored fireplace, 'a **sabre**?'

'No,' said Rex. 'It's the Met's old dress-uniform cutlass. I remember when he bought it, in an auction at Christie's. In Victorian times you'd have had one of those.'

'Actually, in Victorian times, I wouldn't have been allowed in the force,' said Shepherd. 'Nor to vote, or have a bank account. But I get your drift.'

Doors off the hallway included a downstairs loo – empty – and a large walk-in cobble-floored utility area, behind the former coach arch door, containing two sets of golf clubs, hooks for various waxed raincoats and caps, an empty cat-litter tray and a plastic-wrapped wholesale carton of premium cat food, two mountain bikes, a tumble dryer that vented into the back yard, and a chest freezer – also thankfully empty apart from a haunch of venison, vacuum-sealed in plastic to which a raffle ticket was still taped.

The kitchen looked as if it had recently been renovated, but little used: a butler sink and wooden drainer, high-gloss fitted cupboards that contained breakfast cereals, tins and jars of this and that – anchovies, chopped tomatoes, kidney beans – and a few simple ingredients, while drawers of various sizes contained knives and forks, Le Creuset cookware and pristine instruction manuals for the various white goods and kitchen equipment: premium-brand fridge-freezer, dishwasher and washing machine. There was a cat flap fitted to the lower portion of the stable-type door that opened in from the high-walled back yard.

There wasn't much in the fridge: a jar of Dijon mustard, an unopened bottle of Champagne, a litre container of whole milk, butter, a stalk or two of broccoli, and a shortcrust **meat pie** – ready cooked – in a brown paper bag, more the kind you'd buy at a farmers' market or from a quality butcher than from an East End pie-and-mash shop. In the freezer compartment were two unopened bags of supermarket own-brand oven chips, frozen peas, ice cubes and four also unopened loaves of bread.

'Feels pretty impersonal,' said Shepherd. 'Have you two been here before? Is it always like this? I mean, no **disparagement** intended, obviously, but it doesn't feel very lived in. D'you know what I mean? If it was my place there'd be tons of half-eaten jars of pickle in the fridge, and all kinds of crap stuffed into every drawer. Where's all the stuff?'

Rex shrugged. 'Lollo – I mean Jethro – lives for his work, I think,' he said. 'He's at the station all hours, and when he's not he's playing golf. I mean, I do know that he likes to relax with a good war film and a single malt. Likes a bit of Gilbert and Sullivan. But as you know he's got no family, and I don't know if he entertains much these days.'

Upstairs were two large bedrooms, each running the full depth of the house, front to back, with a bathroom on the landing between.

'Nice bath,' said Singh, running his hand around the roll-topped repro vintage **hip bath** that had pride of place on a large recessed square of terracotta tiling inset in the centre of the bathroom floor, and at the centre of which, beneath the bath, was a small stainless-steel drainage grille. The other bathroom fixtures – lavatory, basin, shower – were in heavy reproduction white ceramic, serviced by highly polished copper piping with reproduction taps and fittings in a uniform nickel finish. 'This from that place up on Essex Road?'

'Aston Matthews?' said Rex. 'Yeah, that'll be it.'

One bedroom was obviously the master. There was one half of the large mahogany wardrobe for police uniforms and work clothes, and the other for leisure and pleasure. There were matching lamps on matching bedside tables, and on one of these perhaps some items of recent bedtime reading, to judge by the bookmarks: a hefty hardback – non-fiction – about an old East End **synagogue**, and an interesting-looking book on Norse mythology, that – lifting the front cover to skim the contents – Rex wouldn't have minded reading himself.

The second bedroom contained a made-up double bed and a large antique chest of drawers containing nothing but bedlinen. A writing desk was placed beneath the window overlooking the back yard, with a westward view over gardens and trees, rooftops and outhouses. On the desk was an Anglepoise lamp and a silver MacBook Air. The computer was closed and depowered, switched off at the plug. Shepherd nodded at her PC, who – already gloved up – took a large ziplock evidence bag out of her rucksack.

Next to the desk was a standard four-drawer filing cabinet. Helpfully there was a key in the lock.

'And find out who his cleaner is,' said Shepherd, opening the top drawer of the cabinet and flicking through the suspension files. 'Is there an address book anywhere? Who does he play golf with? Who's his dentist?'

'Surgery on Lamb's Conduit Street,' said Rex, not yet admitting to himself why they might need access to dental records. 'I go there myself. I'll give 'em a ring and get them to email his most recent X-ray and tooth-count.'

Looking around the room, Shepherd said: 'I don't know. It's like the photos on an estate agent's website. It reminds me of a neighbour of my grandparents' when I was very young. He was a good friend of theirs, and a good friend to me. Told me to work hard and not let people – teachers – put me in a "girly" box. Ex-army – served in the Second World War, a widower. He'd worked in town planning after the war: building things instead of blowing them up, I suppose. His house was a bit like this: well ordered, spotlessly neat and tidy, you know, polished shoes and simple pleasures, the occasional pipe and a cup of filter coffee in his case, rather than whisky. And an entire garden given over to the precision cultivation of asparagus, with borders of salad burnet. He was in Italy in the war, I learned later. At the Battle of Monte Cassino. He was lucky to have survived – must have been like hell on earth. Looking back on it now, I think all the order and the routine was his way of keeping a lid on things. Anyway, reminds me of that, a bit.'

Rex shrugged. 'What's our angle here?' He was keen to get going, but wanted to show that he was happy to defer to Shepherd's lead. 'Quick and thorough? Without his phone, the laptop is probably the best resource we've got, but that'll take a while. Binder could take the attic and the outside loo, I didn't see a basement, and I could start checking with the neighbours? How much do you want us to say?'

'Yes, quick and thorough,' said Shepherd. 'I want a standard "open-door" policy. So not a cupboard or a drawer missed. We need as much information, as quick as we can get it. Neighbours-wise, my feeling is: Don't be shy. We say he's missing, and that given his line of work we are extremely fearful for his safety. When did they last see him? Who's his cleaner and what day do they come? Where does he shop, any local farmers' markets or posh food shops? When are the bins collected? Any neighbourhood disputes? Beyond that, improvise. We may not come back for a day or two, so find out as much as you can. Give all of them your card, and stress that they should call you if they think of anything, however small or insignificant-seeming. You know better than me, sir. Central East are giving us four PCSOs to leaflet adjacent postcodes tomorrow and the day after, and if needed we'll do a wider mailshot in a week, but this is a chance for the personal touch, so let's make the most of it.'

A paper-recycling bin in the kitchen was empty apart from the past weekend's Sunday papers: a *Sunday Times*, an *Observer* and the *Mail on Sunday*, and – more personal, perhaps? – estate agents' particulars for cottages in the Yorkshire towns of **Thirsk**, Wetherby, Knaresborough, and the Scarborough and Scalby area.

'Interesting?' said Jane Gosling. She bagged up the brochures, and then spread the newspapers out on the kitchen table, carefully examining them, poring over them page by page, looking for marginalia, doodles or phone messages.

'Rex, when I took down the missing person report from DCS Churchill,' said Shepherd, 'I forgot to ask about sexual orientation. Is DCI Lawrence gay, do you know?'

6: Corbeille d'or (Basket of gold)

Driving back into town, Rex felt a little closer to Lollo the person, but he didn't feel they were any closer to actually finding the (decidedly heterosexual) Detective Chief Inspector. And the disconnect was not good. Any resolution felt far out of reach, and Rex felt bad for being too **nitwitted** to see it.

Shepherd agreed. The information they needed was already out there, it was just that the distribution was **uneven**. It was up to them to read whatever story the evidence was trying to tell them, and find Lawrence as quickly as possible. She knew – they all did – that, whatever the reason for the disappearance, the longer this went on, the statistically less likely a happy outcome became. They'd already lost the so-called 'golden hour', the first twenty-four hours after a MisPer is first reported.

Rex was feeling Lollo's absence already. In the usual run of things, the Detective Chief Inspector would have been Rex's first port of call once he'd had the tip-off about the Undercover Policing Inquiry. Though Rex also knew it would have immediately provoked a **row**.

Lollo had once chucked – and with some force – a canteen **rock bun** at him for less.

'I find that a good policy at work, and one that's served me well throughout my career,' Lollo had said, apropos of nothing, or so it had seemed at the time, 'is to keep thy cock in thy pants.'

For all that Lollo's house had seemed like a blank canvas – **presentable** and tastefully decorated and furnished though it was – if you looked closely, as indeed they had, it gave up many small insights into the Detective Chief Inspector's life and habits: a presentation-framed colour photograph of Lollo with senior detectives from a host of nations meeting US **Congressmen** in Washington as part of an International Policing conference, a DVD box set of The **Forsyte**

Saga, a postcard – blank apart from a capital 'X' (or a hastily scribbled kiss?) on the back – from the Kunsthistorisches Museum in Vienna of Velázquez's **Infanta** *Margarita Teresa in a Blue Dress* that had fallen down the side cushion of the one **easy chair** in his study-cum-spare-bedroom, an Art Deco **brass** bottle opener sculpted in the shapely form of a naked woman, and a gold raffia basket full of cufflinks, dress shirt fasteners and collar stiffeners. In the desk drawer, DC **Gosling** found a folder of paperwork related to the purchase less than a month ago of Lollo's limited-edition Jaguar XE – in retro 1960 **indigo**, so actually quite a rare colour – plus the leather-bound owner's manual and servicing record.

'I wonder how Ted and Harry are getting on,' said Singh as they carried the evidence bags out to the car.

'Who's Harry?' asked Rex.

'You mean Gary?' said Shepherd. 'PC **Keyes**?'

'Oh yeah,' said Singh. 'Sorry, yes: *Gary*. D'you think they've had more luck than we have?'

Somehow, on the journey back to the station, it had emerged that everyone in the car except for DC Jane Gosling was a twin.

'What are the chances of that!' said Shepherd.

It seemed so funny, and really unlikely, but it was true. Binder Singh had a fraternal twin sister, while Melissa Shepherd and Rex were both identical twins, albeit that Rex had never known his brother, who'd died at birth.

'Did you and your sister use to have the same dreams, Melissa?' asked Singh.

'Yes!'

'What's the difference between fraternal and identical, then,' Jane Gosling asked.

'Fraternal twins is when two **ova** are produced and fertilised at the same time,' said Singh. 'Identical is when a single ovum is fertilised and *then* splits.'

For fuck's sake, thought Rex to himself, keeping his eyes on the road. Couldn't they talk about anything other than obstetrics?

He knew that he'd soon know the contents of his own personal UCPI Core Participant's affidavit, but he still couldn't help wondering what kind of sob story it was going to be. The calculated way he'd brushed her knee? Course it was calculating: he'd been trying to seduce her. Or would it be **all** about how **needy** and demanding he was? His **running riot**, romantically speaking, through the protest movement and how he'd taken **advantage** of poor **little unworldly** her. That she'd been **too** inexperienced to know any better. That he'd driven her – wasn't that tantamount to **trafficking**? – to some godforsaken **Nissen** hut on the west coast of Scotland for the express purpose. Not to mention having to bear the overwhelming pain and grief of an unborn child's death alone. How violated she'd felt when she finally discovered the truth. That the humiliation never **fades**. He'd find out soon enough exactly what Amelia Alison Johnson thought about him, and about their relationship. But whatever it was, it would make for uncomfortable reading.

7: Orache (Saltbush)

As he braked for a red light at the junction of Rosebery Avenue and Clerkenwell Road, Rex caught **siren**-sight of a beautiful woman out of the corner of his eye. Turning for a closer look at **holiness**, he found himself staring at his girlfriend Annie.

The car that pulled up next to them at the lights was playing 'Jump (For My Love)' by the **Pointer** Sisters.

'*Love Actually*!' said Singh, doing some moves.

Annie was waiting to cross Rosebery Avenue, arm in arm with a young woman of similar height and build, who wasn't exactly Annie's spitting image, but was unmistakably related. The word '**consanguinity**' popped into Rex's mind from this morning's crossword – 'Blood relationship', 13 letters.

He beeped the horn. But, of course, the carpool Mini Cooper S wasn't familiar to Annie, so why would she even bother to look up?

He quickly wound down the window. 'Hi, you two. You both look lovely. Talk about **ships that pass**—'

'—**in the night**!' said Annie. 'Well, the street!'

'How'd it go, **Ashley**?' said Rex. 'Great to see you. I love the extensions.'

Ashley preened a little, raising her chin and shaking her head with a smile to show off the fruits of yesterday's salon visit. 'Thanks! Yeah, okay, I think.'

'If I don't see you later, give my love to your mum and dad.'

'She was very brave,' said Annie. 'We're just going **along** to Terroni's for ice cream and then do some window shopping in Hatton Garden.'

'Good idea!' said Rex. Then, as the lights changed, 'I wish I could come with you.'

Running out of time and words, he beeped the horn again.

'Bye!' they both waved and shouted.

Later Annie would text:

> R, I know we said **restaurant** but A exhausted, so new **plan** – we
> got TONS of antipasti & parmigiana from Terroni's to dip in whenever
> we want, and baccalà for you. PS Ash is learning guitar! Love you x

Antipasti? Rex was happy with that. It was always quality fare
from Terroni's. To tell the truth, he'd have been happy if Annie had
suggested breakfast **cereal** for supper.

'Is that your daughter?' asked Shepherd.

'No, it's Annie's niece.'

'So sweet!'

Did she mean Annie or Ash, Rex wondered.

'I know – she's the reason we met,' said Rex, sticking to the
official version of events. 'Ashley was in hospital at Great Ormond
Street, and Annie had come down to lend her and her mum a bit of
moral support. Yeah, Annie's amazing too. She's… We're expecting,
obviously.'

Melissa Shepherd actually whooped.

'Annie seems really nice,' said Singh.

Don't say it, thought Rex.

Don't say, 'So what does a lovely girl like that see in an old git like
you?'

But he needn't have worried, because no one did.

If Lollo were around, Rex would have told him that as far as he
was concerned Binder Singh was a breath of fresh air. That the new
Detective Sergeant's non-judgemental, forward-looking and generous
attitude totally justified his recent promotion. And being in a car with
two female officers – one of whom was senior – certainly helped.

Imagine the same fleeting event with four old-school coppers in
the car; the competitive sexist jousting: why tête-à-tête if you could
tourney? It was all so macho and tiring. Certain ex-colleagues Rex
could name would have leched loudly and belligerently after Annie
and Ashley: 'Tits on that!' And probably gone off on one about him
being under Annie's thumb. In such a situation a more pompous Rex
might have needed to decry the **uxorious** label, but there was no one
in the carpool Mini – not Shepherd, not Singh, not Gosling – who'd

be remotely likely to be so confrontational in the first place as to warrant such a riposte. Thank God.

This eastern end of Theobalds Road that was rapidly disappearing into Rex's rear-view mirror had changed a lot. The late-nineteenth-century Gray's Inn Buildings at the top of Rosebery Avenue, with their Francophile mouldings and **chateau** stylings, which had from long before Rex first lived in the area and until the early noughts become notorious **slum** tenements, dens of **vice** and one of the largest squats in London, were practically sparkling since their renovation in the early noughts. Back in the day, Rex had had cause to visit a few and he'd been shocked by the squalor of what had seemed barely habitable cold-water apartments, with smashed-up toilets, foul leakage and condensation, archaic wiring and broken windows patched up with cardboard. It had felt like going back in time. Visiting more recently, it was all underfloor heating and tastefully painted **wainscot**-panelled bathrooms, which looked a lot like progress until you remembered that the demographics who'd needed to live in them when many of the flats were squatted hadn't disappeared; they'd simply been shunted out to benefits factories: warrens of cockroach-infested one-room, one-bed pod-apartments with even fewer facilities in shabbily converted former office buildings on run-down industrial estates off the North Circular, which you could be forgiven for thinking were 'designed' – if you could call it that – less with the well-being of their occupants in mind than to game what was left of the building regs and harvest housing benefit at scale. Such was, Rex often thought, the seemingly almost wilfully misdirected **largess** of the UK government's Department for Work and Pensions, whose velvet glove, if it had ever had one, appeared to have been permanently **riven** from its iron fist.

As he indicated to turn right and right again into Lamb's Conduit Street and Richbell Place, Rex might usually have pointed out to guests that the great two-hundred-year-old plane trees in the Gray's Inn Walks – the expanse of garden behind the high brick wall that ran along much of the south side of Theobalds Road – had been planted to replace an ancient **lime tree** grove that was many centuries older in turn, and which may even have predated the Inns of Court themselves.

Visitors loved all that stuff.

That he didn't do so today was solely due to the fact that his blood had run cold, that he'd started hyperventilating and suddenly felt as dizzy as if he'd taken a hefty **punch** to the head. Never mind the sightseeing tour for the out-of-towners, it was as much as he could do just to keep driving.

For there, fifty or more yards away, just to one side of where his gaze had fallen, and just for a split second, he thought he saw a familiar face in the crowd. It was as if some fleeting, kaleidoscopic confluence of passers-by – movement, light and gesture all in flux – had conjured a face from deep in Rex's past. Although, like the coloured scales in the kaleidoscope mirror, by the time he looked directly at it the apparition had vanished.

Rex had heard of pareidolia, the human or perhaps animal tendency to see familiar images in randomness. And he understood the evolutionary advantages of intuiting the faces of potential predators, but this had seemed – for that split second – to be far more convincing than the pattern of tree-knots in some wooden panelling, or the cracks and stains on a childhood bedroom ceiling.

Maybe it was an acid flashback.

They weren't just a hippy myth.

Is that what this was?

Either that or he was going mad.

For there in the crowd, alive and well and unchanged by the decades, still skinny and suntanned, with a *Taxi Driver* mohawk, Rex could have sworn that he'd seen the young **Milo**.

Who, to give him his due, had unwittingly been the reason Rex became a police officer in the first place.

8: Sarcloir (Hoe)

Rex knew what it meant if a **black cat** crossed your path. That was good luck, wasn't it? Or maybe bad luck? One of the two, anyway, and Rex didn't care which. He liked cats, and he wasn't superstitious.

But that sudden **crisis**, flashback, call it what you wanted – the strange hallucination of a face from the past **amid** the pavement throng on Theobalds Road had slightly freaked him out.

Driving back from Bow, he'd been enjoying the sheer anonymity that the pool Mini Cooper afforded. He hadn't quite realised how ubiquitous they were. Every other car seemed to be a cream-and-black Mini Cooper.

In the back of his mind he'd also been going through random things just seen in Lollo's house: the CD of *36 Chorales for* **Woodwind** by J. S. Bach on the hi-fi, a small tube of expensive-looking Clarins hand **lotion** in the bathroom cabinet, the **oval** mirror in the hall, that hardback edition of the Icelandic **Edda** on the go on the bedside table…

The sudden perception of grave danger, even though conjured in the mind, had thrown him out of this reverie and put him into fight-or-flight mode – that primitive response that buys every creature a few seconds to either **neuter** a **threat** or flee the **fray** – flooding his system with a burst of adrenaline that sent his heart rate flying and blood pressure through the roof. He took care to breathe slowly and deeply, to try and centre himself.

The hormonal call to **arms** would quickly **disperse**, but locking up in the basement garage while everyone noisily got out of the car and the high-security shutter rolled down behind them still felt like an out-of-body experience. The pressure of work was clearly getting to him.

Rex knew that he needed a rest, but he wasn't about to get one any time soon. There was going to be a lot of shit to **wade** through first. And right now he had other more pressing responsibilities, not least to spend the next couple of hours comparing notes with the Sussex team and plotting next steps.

While they were waiting for the lift back up to the sixth floor, DS Melissa Shepherd's phone rang. It was Sergeant Teddy Thomas.

'I'm downstairs, literally getting in the lift,' said Shepherd. 'What is it?'

But she already knew what Ted was going to say. It was the only reason he'd have rung: that the team in Petworth had found something. Nodding, she turned to Rex and gave him a thumbs-up sign.

One of the Midhurst team – a Detective Constable Vic Hoffman – had called the Sarge first thing, while they were waiting for the train up. He'd wanted to check if it was okay to take a few pairs of boots back to the site this morning. He'd woken up convinced they'd been 'thinking in the wrong direction', was how he put it, so had a proposal in need of a **seconder**. What if, in looking for something that had been dropped in the course of the Detective Chief Inspector's possibly flying visit, or in the moments leading up to his disappearance, they had it completely the wrong way around? What if they should in fact have been looking for something that had been there much longer?

'Talk to me, Vic,' Thomas had said, his interest piqued.

'What if,' Hoffman had said, audibly growing in confidence, 'the visit by DCI Lawrence and/or individuals unknown had been to retrieve something that was already there?'

It was just a hunch, he'd said, and he couldn't put it any clearer than that.

'So what you're saying,' Thomas had said, 'is that I was wrong.'

'With respect, sir. What do you think? Instead of someone losing "item X", perhaps they were trying to find it.'

'I always said you were a good officer.'

They'd been searching *the surface* of the nursery site, and drawn a blank. So, to follow Hoffman's line of thought, if this something – 'item X' – that Lawrence or whoever might hypothetically have been trying to retrieve had been left there at some point in the past, given that it was a nursery, you could hide something there and within a relatively short period it would be buried by the artificially accelerated sedimentary processes of a rapidly growing wholesale nursery business.

'That's right,' Hoffman had said. 'Interesting, eh? So whether this process was deliberate or accidental is not the first priority. The first priority is: if that's the case, where would you look?'

'Where would you look indeed,' the Sussex Sergeant had said. 'Go on, then. Quick as you can – leave Ricky on CCTV and take Jamesy with you. And talk to the owner again – what's his name, Edwards? Find out exactly when each of those buildings was erected, and ask to see the plans for each stage of the site's development. Place was a **water-works** for the Petworth estate until the mid-eighties, weren't it, built on the site of an older farm on the back end of the park. I reckon Mr Edwards is exactly the kind of vainglorious tosser that loves talking about himself down the **Marquess** of Granby of a Saturday night, so flatter it out of him if you need to. He'll have them all in a plans chest right there in his office, I'd bet you anything. Get Jamesy to scan 'em on his phone and email them to me soon as.'

They'd spent an hour or two scoping out the site. The Sarge had been correct: part of the nursery had been built in the mid-eighties after the plant had been decommissioned in the late 1970s. Then in the nineties they'd expanded onto the adjacent land, a former hop farm on the edge of Petworth Park proper. It was a family business. He was proud of it. After all, they'd monetised a few dead acres around what had become little more than the goods entrance to the park and the big house.

The current manager was nursery founder Charles Edwards's son. With hard hats on, and using an old hoe for staff and pointer, he'd shown them around. His own innovation, he'd said proudly, was to become the first bark-chip production facility of this size in Sussex, mainly servicing demand from local authorities, and the consumer trade via the wholesale business.

On the northern edge of the nursery site, beyond a **greenhouse** full of **dianthus** in market-ready plastic crates, and the **statuary** section, things took on an altogether different scale with a large concrete-paved apron of vehicle turning space, on which was parked a JCB Midi digger-loader with dozer blade, and three huge **steaming** compost heaps, each the size of a tennis court, contained on three sides by stacked railway sleepers and RSJs. Next to these bays – under a hangar – was a huge piece of plant: a Rotochopper bark-**chip** grinder.

As a way to disappear a body, such machines were a film and TV favourite, but messy to say the least. And running this in the small hours would probably have woken up half of Sussex. But Hoffman had made a mental note to order a forensic inspection in any case, just to rule it out.

This was the old farmyard, Edwards junior had said. He'd had to demolish a derelict hop kiln to expand production.

'What's behind there?' Hoffman had asked, pointing at the perimeter lights and half an acre of wasteland beyond.

'Nothing much. This was where they mulched the old hop bines. They used to creosote the hop poles in there,' Edwards had said, indicating what looked like a large manhole cover. 'Watch out, that's twenty-five feet deep at least.'

Hoffman had been glad of the warning, because the proportions of the dipping bath were deceptive: a low brick perimeter smaller than your average kitchen table surrounding what looked like an inch of still water reflecting bright sky was in fact a deep shaft into which the new hop poles would have been dipped entire before being wired up and set into the fields.

'It's not creosote any more, presumably,' Hoffman had said.

'Enough that it's probably safer left where it is,' Edwards had said, poking it at arm's length with the hoe. 'I've been meaning to fill it in for donkey's years. But no one comes round here. There's no need.'

'Got a pump?'

'Of course,' Edwards had said, taking his phone out of his pocket to arrange it.

'The travellers return,' said Tabitha Churchill, greeting them warmly at the lift. 'How was it?'

'Strange,' said Rex. 'I kept expecting him to walk in.'

'I bet.'

'I know he's a man of simple tastes, but it felt like… How did you put it, Melissa?'

'Like an estate agent's brochure,' said Shepherd. 'But still waters run deep, eh?'

'It was a bit like a classy Airbnb,' said Rex. 'Quality, you know. I'd stay there.'

'We've brought his laptop, among other things.'

'Do you want us to process that?' said Churchill. 'In the interests of time?'

Shepherd nodded.

'Will you deal with the admission, DS Singh?'

'On it, ma'am.'

Ted Thomas and Gary Keyes came out to join them. The Sergeant was ebullient. In the excitement he'd spilled coffee all down his **shirt-front**, but figured one of the Holborn boys would have some spare **togs** in his locker.

'Well done, lads,' said Shepherd. 'Hoffman, eh? Good for him. What did they find, then?'

Thomas held up his phone, but they couldn't all see the screen.

'What is it?' said Churchill. 'For God's sake, man.'

'**Crank-shaft** and engine block from a Ford Transit,' said Thomas.

9: Statice (Sea thrift)

'What do you make of them?' Chief Superintendent Tabitha Churchill asked Rex, when Melissa and the team had gone for their train. 'Is Miss **Puss** out of her depth? Or d'you think they can handle it? I don't need another fuck-up.'

Rex was slightly shocked to hear Churchill speaking this way. He'd sensed some impatience from the gaffer during the meeting to discuss next steps and how the Holborn team might be able to support the investigation, but he'd put that down to her wanting the best for their missing colleague and friend. He hadn't expected her to give them a dressing-down. It had been slightly embarrassing.

Until that moment, Rex had been feeling quite confident of an investigation that had Melissa Shepherd at the **helm**. Nothing had given him pause for doubt. Of course, she had a depleted team down there at Midhurst and Easebourne.

She'd had to repeat that.

'Eastbourne?' Rex had asked.

'No, *Ease*-bourne,' Shepherd had said, 'like "stand at ease"?'

But wasn't that just a fact of modern policing: staff shortages? cuts? reducing waste? everything an opportunity for savings?

Wasn't it the same everywhere?

And since deepest West Sussex was where Lollo had gone missing, Holborn had no choice but to work **hand in glove** with the local squad.

Luckily Rex liked Melissa's style, and her team had seemed conscientious and effective.

'I'm not saying it'll be over by **Ramadan**,' Shepherd had said. 'But I need us to be across this as quickly as we can.'

Rex couldn't help but agree.

'I think they'll be fine,' he said now, to Chief Superintendent Churchill.

'Really? Only fine?'

'Is there a problem?' said Rex. 'Because, if so—'

'I'm sorry,' said Tabitha, 'but like I said in the meeting: It's a great story, but it gets us nowhere. I didn't mean to be **crass**, but you're always going to find something at the bottom of a well or whatever it is. And if you don't know or care what it'll be, then you'll be happy with any old crap. I'm only surprised it wasn't a shopping trolley or a scooter. But isn't it simply confirmation bias: the assumption that this lump of scrap has anything whatsoever to do with DCI Lawrence's disappearance?'

'Yes, exactly,' said Rex. 'That's why I backed you up.'

He'd done the training too. Sat fighting the **lethargy** in a darkened room for two hours, hoping above all that if he did fall asleep he wouldn't snore. Actually it had been less boring than the usual training session. Out of all the Met's instructors, Elsie Beecham was one of the better ones. She did a bit of stand-up on the side, supposedly. Mainly open-mic nights and low-level stuff, but it meant that she knew how to keep you entertained. Long-short, Rex knew that confirmation bias was an issue. You didn't need to be an **oculist** to know that people often only saw what they wanted to see.

At least it happened in all walks of life.

It wasn't just a problem in policing.

Only the other week, Jen had been telling him how, in the nineteenth century, people had been desperate to believe that a series of paths following the line of chalk downs across the south of England was the legendary **Icknield** Way, Boudicca's long-distance marching route from Essex to the **Avon**, but recent research had suggested that this may also have been a romantic myth, albeit one that had been powerful enough to become a self-fulfilling prophecy: any old stretch of path heading vaguely westwards would do. There were hundreds of supposed Icknield Ways.

Rex had proudly told Helen that he hoped Jen was still down for history A-level.

And in policing?

The examples usually given in the media included the demonstrably justifiable criticism that Section 60s – suspicionless stop and search – in areas of high knife crime were confirmation bias in action. That young Black men were disproportionately likely to be stopped simply because of the colour of their **skin**. Or, conversely, that where higher-ranking positions across the force had historically been dominated by older white men, promotions had tended to be given to those who 'looked the part'.

But confirmation bias was a common pitfall in larger investigations too. When you were investigating something, you were trying to tell a story about what had happened. And while the human brain's propensity for joining the dots could sometimes be the detective's best friend, it could also cause problems if the story you wanted to see – your bias – started to dominate, because it might stretch to accommodate available facts or rule out what you didn't want to see, rather than the facts themselves determining the narrative, however unlikely.

So here, today, the fact that Lollo had marked his place in that book of Icelandic sagas with a Zoological Society of London postcard of a **marmoset** did not suggest that DCI Jethro Lawrence had an uncommon interest in the small primates of South America. But what was interesting was the (sadly undated) note on the back, written in a small neat hand:

Dearest J, thanks for a lovely night, sweetheart. Look forward to more monkey business soon. XXXXX

And the question *that* prompted was: Who had **Romeo** been playing **hide**-the-**sausage** with?

Note to self, thought Rex. If Lollo had paid for the tickets to London Zoo, a date might help them narrow down the potential contact.

The example used in the confirmation bias training video was a glamorous high-society wedding on a Caribbean **beach**, where a beautiful, beaming bride and **soigné** groom – a wealthy tycoon, the commentary said – were tying the knot. It was a familiar scene: there was the floral bower, there the guests, there the minister officiating. Rings were exchanged, right there on the sand.

'What are we watching?' Elsie the trainer had asked, pausing the video.

'A wedding,' they'd all said, confidently stating the obvious.

'So what happens next?' she'd said, pressing 'play'.

On screen, the newlyweds were leaving for their honeymoon, when the groom suddenly clutched his chest and dropped down dead.

'Oh dear!' said Elsie Beecham. 'Now, question: What happens to his bride? Will she be okay?'

Cue various stabs in the dark from the assembled cohort about how distraught the grieving widow was likely to be. 'Depends if she's up the duff!' Eddie Webster had said, to general hilarity.

Binder Singh had piped up: 'She'll inherit his money, though! So that'll soften the blow.' And everyone had laughed. He had a point.

'Okay, so here's a few "What ifs",' said Beecham. 'What if that wasn't actually an ordained minister?' She paused to let that sink in. 'What if it wasn't a real wedding at all? What if it was a **morganatic** ceremony designed to lead the woman into thinking she was getting married in the traditional sense, whereas in fact, whatever kind of union this was, she'd legally be entitled to nothing?'

Murmurs of uncertainty in the room.

Then one Islington PC whose name Rex didn't know had piped up: 'Isn't that **Salic** law rather than morganatic, miss?'

'Good question!' she'd said through gritted teeth. 'No, you're referring to the ancient Frankish law of primogeniture, if I remember *my PhD in medieval European history*' – she glared at the constable – 'in which the inheritance goes through the male line, or to the nearest male relative. But let's stick to the subject here. Going back to the video: Whose confirmation bias is being played to?'

'Ours?' Singh had said. 'Had me fooled!'

They'd all laughed again.

'Yes, exactly. And who else's?'

'The guests'?'

'Yes! Anyone else?'

'The bride,' Rex had said. 'Mainly the bride. She's just seen what she wanted to see.'

'Exactly right, Rex. She wanted to get married, and this looked like a marriage ceremony, so that's what she saw.'

'Doesn't mean she's not a bloody idiot!' he'd said.

But wasn't the lesson here that we were all idiots, potentially? Unless we took steps not to be?

Apply this to Hoffman's supposedly great find, and what? He'd been looking, in the most obvious place, for something – anything!

– to support his theory, and, surprise surprise, he'd found something. But the mere fact that he *had* found something didn't make it an important something.

Although it was something quite unusual, it had to be said.

'It wasn't a scooter or a supermarket trolley, though, with respect,' said Rex. But he could see the point Churchill was making.

'Sorry, but some **piffling** piece of scrap metal discarded in a farmyard just doesn't **clarify** anything for me, however much Teddy Thomas wanted to believe it,' she said. 'I didn't mean to be rude to the guy, but unless the CCTV specifically shows Jethro walking over there and trying to fish it out…'

It hadn't been what Sergeant Thomas was expecting to hear, that was fair to say. You could almost hear the **hiss** of the air being let out of his tyres. But the meeting had got onto a more even keel after that. And the Sussex team were nothing if not pragmatic. They didn't mind Churchill throwing her weight around a bit. It was practically to be expected from a Chief Superintendent, and it was balanced out by the rarity value, for a small rural team, of having someone this senior on hand to help open doors and get things done.

'Don't get me wrong, Sergeant,' she'd said. 'That's good solid policework. Well done.'

It was just that, Churchill went on, she was trying to foster a realistic appraisal of the evidence they might actually have. If the importance-or-not of the scrap metal found in the old dipping bath was yet to be determined, and might well turn out to be a red herring, they should focus on the concrete stuff they'd already got coming in: his laptop, bin contents, CCTV, whatever information – from GPS pings to sudden stops – had been recorded on the Jag's hard drive, DNA from the blood spatter, mobile phone data, et cetera.

'I've given you the handwriting sample, Ted,' she said. 'What else?'

'What does it say in the manual?' said Singh.

'Exactly what we're doing,' said Shepherd, cutting in. 'Meeting of coordination and tasking group. Which is us. Notifying Missing People and other relevant agencies. Which we've done – Frankie gave us a good photo. Identifying the need for area searches, and deploying PolSer teams. Check. Then you've got two options. Plan A, you continue to rinse and repeat, and review at one, three, six and twelve months. Or, alternatively, the system works, you achieve closure before that, interview the no-longer-missing person, everyone's a winner, hugs all round, and we all live happily ever after. But in the meantime, let's stick to Plan A.'

'We've got estate agent brochures from Yorkshire,' Gosling said, 'I'm on communication records and bank statements from tomorrow, so I'll roll that into the search. Then transport.'

'Maybe he's planning for retirement,' said Sergeant Thomas. 'He's a Yorkshireman, after all. It's not unusual to want to retire to your **birth-place**.'

'Tabitha's right,' said Rex. 'Let's not make too many assumptions. There'll be lots of data coming in over the next twenty-four to forty-eight, and, we don't want to influence how we read that and start fitting it to any premature scenario-building – right, Melissa?'

Shepherd nodded.

'Besides,' Rex went on, 'the little I know from Lollo, and I'm sure his old mate Cliff Heath at Thames Valley would back this up, is that the DCI is not too sentimental about his hometown. But if there are plans afoot in Yorkshire, Jane'll find them.'

'Of course,' said Churchill. 'Heath's already texted to ask if there's anything he can do. Now earn your spots and get going. And call Cliffy – let's see if he's got any ideas.'

'Consider it done,' said Rex. 'When do we go public?'

'Press conference in Petworth at one p.m. tomorrow,' said Churchill. 'Right, Melissa? My car leaves at eleven and you're coming too, Rex. TeDIU(M) are primed and ready.'

When the Met's Telephone and Digital Investigation Unit was first launched a couple of years back it had been heralded as the future of policing, but it was also something of a retirement home for ex-coppers. Certainly a lot of senior officers ended up crewing the phones. The Police Federation didn't particularly like it; they saw the writing on the wall for future outsourcing. When government was always looking for opportunities to save money, this was a gift: why pay ex-officers top dollar if you could just have a call centre in India or wherever, sorting the wheat from the chaff for a fraction of the cost.

But Rex also knew that you couldn't exactly fight progress – and that this kind of telephone capacity was exactly what you needed when you put out a public call for information. It was the *Crimewatch* effect: every village idiot and their dog would be phoning in.

'We've got a dedicated phone number and we'll be a top-level menu item on 101,' said Churchill. 'TeDIU(M)'ll give us as much capacity as we need through the next forty-eight to seventy-two hours. Evelyn's over at New Broadcasting House editing the packages with the BBC News team right now, and she'll brief us on our lines on the way down. She wants us on the national six and tens. Any earlier and we risk getting lost in Bumpkin Land with the lunchtimes and locals.'

Churchill instinctively glanced at the investigative team from Sussex: 'No offence.'

10: Fritillaire (Fritillary)

[REVIEW AND CUE] —

INT. INTERVIEW ROOM AT ROTHERHAM POLICE STATION —
NIGHT

DETECTIVE CONSTABLE WOODCROFT and prisoner ALAN
REYNOLDS sit facing each other on opposite sides of
a plain wooden table, mid-interview. By the clock on
the wall, it is 10.30 p.m. No one else is present. DC
WOODCROFT is asking questions and noting responses.

> DC WOODCROFT
> How many people were in the car park altogether?

> REYNOLDS
> A lot. It was crowded.

> DC WOODCROFT
> And what was going off?

> REYNOLDS
> A lot of pushing and shoving and that.

> DC WOODCROFT
> What about throwing?

> REYNOLDS
> Yes, it were stupid, a lot of stones being thrown.
> One hit me on the head.

                    DC WOODCROFT
                Thrown at the police?

                        REYNOLDS
                    Yes, and one hit me.

                    DC WOODCROFT
        What about shouting and general abusive language?

                        REYNOLDS
                    Shouting, aye.

                    DC WOODCROFT
                    Did you push?

                        REYNOLDS
                    Not deliberately.

                    DC WOODCROFT
                    Did you throw?

                        REYNOLDS
                        No.

                    DC WOODCROFT
                        Alan?

                        REYNOLDS
                    I shouted, aye.

                    DC WOODCROFT
                And what did you shout?

                        REYNOLDS
        'Arthur Scargill walks on water and Maggie Thatcher
                    is illegitimate.'

DC WOODCROFT
'Thatcher's a bastard'?

REYNOLDS
You said it, mate. Your words, not mine!

Detective Inspector Rex King had to laugh.

And then he had to reread it, and he laughed all over again.

'Your words, not mine!'

Rex King wasn't sat here in the Clean Room next to the third-floor lab at Holborn late on a weekday evening for fun, or for the good of his health, as Lollo had been fond of saying. But as he read through the transcript of a never-broadcast TV docudrama about a public disturbance that had taken place on 7 May 1984 in the city of Sheffield, during the early months of the 1984–85 Miners' Strike, he couldn't help chuckling at the righteous insolence and anger expressed by some of the prisoners.

Detective Constable Woodcroft should have known better than to walk into that one.

It wasn't that important on the scale of things, but Rex was glad that it wasn't only him who'd found it funny.

This wasn't how he had been expecting to spend the few days following what all agreed had been a very successful press conference down in Petworth. By rights he'd now be working closely with Shepherd and the Midhurst team on managing the huge influx of leads the coverage had generated. Shepherd was right: the more data the better, something to really get your teeth into.

Well, he'd got that alright, but from another source entirely.

That's why he was stuck here on the third floor.

It had started with a couple of hefty yellow ring binders open on his desk, and a pencil in his hand, flicking through hundreds of sensitive pages of long-assumed-buried-or-lost police statements that appeared to have been leaked at the very moment they'd all been congratulating themselves, post-press conference, on a job well done.

And that was just the first leak.

They'd quickly realised what exactly they were looking at: lost papers from the abandoned trial of the so-called 'Sheffield 27'.

Twenty-seven striking miners who'd been arrested on trumped-up charges of riot (an archaic offence, dusted off during the strike, that had carried a maximum life sentence) but acquitted on the eve of trial, as the parallel 'riot trials' relating to mass arrests at Mansfield and Orgreave had collapsed. A second Orgreave trial had also been briefed but was never brought to court following the collapses of Mansfield, Sheffield and 'Orgreave One'.

Police and other files relating to these trials had either been destroyed or buried indefinitely, courtesy National Security Provision Article 23 and the Official Secrets Act.

That's what these were. Missing police statements, charge sheets and interview notes from the abandoned Sheffield trial.

The Justice for William Cooper Campaign must have thought it was Christmas.

What was puzzling Churchill was where this particular cache of documents had been hidden all these years.

And here they were, the twenty-seven accused: Seamus Arthur, Lee Atkins, Richard Beese, Kevin Cox, Jack Dean, Robin Downs, Callum Edge, Maurice Etchells, Brett James, Gerry Kent, Roderick Lister, Donald Lowe, Trevor MacWilliam, Neil MacWilliam, Karl Marshall, Anthony McCarthy, Chris Naden, Keith O'Connor, Alan Reynolds, Terence Riddell, George Scott, Edward Servant, Colin Shaw, John Stepney, Daniel Thorpe, Douglas John Wootton and Peter Wright. And for each striking miner charged there was a shadow cohort of police officers – an arresting officer, witnesses, interviewing officers, policemen of all ranks – and a lone duty Chief, Detective Chief Inspector Tony Scrimshaw, holding the fort at Sheffield Central for those few nights a touch over thirty years ago, with the dubious responsibility of rubber-stamping the lot.

As Rex read the files, and entered the officers' names into an open Excel spreadsheet, he found himself imagining what these massed ranks looked like.

A parade of strangers from another time.

Dead now, half of them, most probably. But a few of the younger PCs and ranking officers might still be on the force. They were Lollo's contemporaries, after all.

And Rex had half-expected to find statements from the young Jethro Lawrence and Clifford Heath among the documents, because he had a good idea that 'The A-Team' or whatever they'd called themselves would have been there.

But of those two there was no sign.

Clever sods had obviously kept themselves well away from any action.

Avoided getting their hands dirty.

It had been Tabitha Churchill who'd made the immediate connection with their own current and urgent investigation into Detective Chief Inspector Jethro Lawrence's disappearance. She'd got pinged about the leak as they were driving back from Petworth, via the Met Chief Supers' WhatsApp group.

It was pure gut instinct, she'd tell Gummer later, but knowing what she did about Lollo's past, his early years on the South Yorkshire force, Churchill had suddenly wondered if this might be some kind of – it sounded odd – but some kind of ransom note. The appearance of this material, now, seemed too much of a coincidence not to be related in some way.

It had been Churchill then who'd asked to be put on the circulation list. The way she'd seen it, on the road back from Petworth, the leak would be public soon enough, so she had a night's grace until then. Time to think, and no pressure for her to make any management decisions until tomorrow. There'd been enough to be getting on with, after all, dealing with the PR and logistical aftermath of the press conference.

The trip to Sussex had gone like clockwork, of course. But that's what you expected when there was a pro like Evelyn Gummer in charge of Comms.

There'd also been barely any traffic on the roads. No one had fluffed their lines. And – duly delivered – all relevant soundbites had been snapped up.

Everyone had got what they wanted.

Distractions from loose-cannon local reporters had been nixed. 'No,' Churchill had said to an *Argus* staffer, 'terrorism hasn't been ruled out, but it's important to stress that there is nothing whatsoever – and zero intelligence – to suggest that the Detective Chief Inspector's disappearance is connected to terrorist activity or motives. But we're obviously keeping an open mind at this stage. Next question?'

At one point, just before they started, a little orange butterfly had landed on one of the microphones on the table, and rested for a while.

When people rushed forward to photograph it with their phones, it had fluttered away.

In the car back from Petworth, Gummer had been triumphant.

She'd got cast-iron guarantees from BBC and ITN that they'd be running with the story. And, as the day played out, the conference would get them onto the prime drivetime news-magazine programme, *PM* on BBC Radio 4, and into the second half of both national six and ten o'clocks. On BBC2, *Newsnight* ran with their own VT, while the main package repeated half-hourly through the night across the BBC News channel, and even stayed in the early headlines on Radio 4's *Today* the next morning. These were big wins for the Comms Chief, but it hadn't got them any closer to Jethro Lawrence.

When it had first broken publicly, at lunchtime the day after the press conference, the news that a cache of secret documents relating to the Miners' Strike of 1984–85 had been leaked hadn't seemed of particular relevance to the 'hunt for missing Met cop', as certain tabloids were calling the investigation. But even though the news had been broken by the *Yorkshire Post*, on a tip-off from the Justice for William Cooper Campaign, who had posted all the documents on their website, it was obviously of immediate national significance. And that had placed it firmly in the purview of the Metropolitan Police. Any bearing on the missing person investigation regarding Detective Chief Inspector Jethro Lawrence was not known, but – with her request approved – everything to do with the leak had already landed squarely on Tabitha Churchill's desk, and under the investigation budget code the next morning.

Rex had known nothing of this, of course.

He'd planned to bury himself in Jethro Lawrence's real estate dealings, but first there'd been a breakfast meeting with Simon Rose, the Police Federation rep, about Rex's impending appearance before the Undercover Policing Inquiry. It was to be part planning meeting and part pep talk.

Si had wanted to go over lessons learned in the UCPI thus far, to brief Rex on key personalities involved and to lay out some of the key issues that he thought might emerge. Not to overwhelm him with unnecessary information at this stage, just what might be useful, on a need-to-know basis.

Rose had reassured Rex that, whatever else happened in the inquiry as a result of the identification of a new Core Participant and Rex's cover name being revealed in their affidavit, and him being called to give oral evidence as a state witness, he and Met QC Francis Bland were arguing strongly, and felt confident of winning the point, that Rex's testimony should be held by video link and anonymously. This had come up in conversation already, and was a measure that had been necessarily extended to most other officers, both for their own operational and personal safety, and in order not to jeopardise any investigations – whether ongoing or historic – or indeed any such associated convictions.

All of which had been something of a relief for Rex, but not one that he'd have time to enjoy. For as he and Simon Rose emerged from the tenth-floor meeting room, Churchill's PA, Frankie Charles, had already been waiting for him.

'Did you get my voicemail?' she'd said.

'Hi Frankie. Not yet, no, but I've been in a meeting with Si for the past hour. Long-short?'

'Long-short, the Chief Superintendent wants to speak to you yesterday.'

'Ah, okay. What's it about?'

'It's about time you listened to my voicemails,' Frankie had said, only half-joking.

Despite the forewarning she'd received about the leak, it was not a happy Tabitha Churchill that greeted Rex a few minutes later. Though that didn't stop her having a bit of sport.

'Detective Inspector King,' she said, pointing at the two very large yellow ring binders stacked on her desk, 'I'd like you to meet your new life. I hope you'll be very happy together.'

King had been perplexed. 'I was just—'

'Well, not any more you're not,' she said, filling him in on the basics at least. She didn't want to influence his reading of the material, she said. She wanted to hear what he made of it, off his own bat.

While the events in Sheffield of 7 May 1984 remained less well known than those that would take place in Mansfield and Orgreave in the weeks that followed, there were some who said that the second Sheffield riot should be better known than any of the others, indeed who'd campaigned for decades that it should be better known, who'd campaigned for justice and transparency.

The so-called 'Battle of Orgreave' had produced some of the most memorable imagery of the entire strike, including photographer John Harris's iconic photo of a mounted policeman leaning down in his stirrups with baton raised to beat a female photographer in the head. Orgreave had also become notorious for the creation of false media narratives: the order of events had been reversed in television news footage to wrongly show police violence *following* missile-throwing by pickets, as if the police charges and beatings of pickets had been a response to their missile-throwing, rather than the other way around.

But however bad Orgreave had been, the Sheffield riot of 7 May 1984 boasted one additional macabre statistic that tragically surpassed the violence of Orgreave, and meant that events on that spring day in Sheffield had become catalogued in the darker annals of British policing history. A demonstrator – a striking miner and NUM shop steward from the South Yorkshire coalfield named Billy Cooper, a possible heir-apparent to Arthur Scargill – had died in Sheffield's Hallamshire Hospital from head injuries sustained during the demonstration. No witness had been found to the assault, and no police officer had ever admitted involvement in the striking miner's death.

The intelligence regarding the leak had come from an undercover officer using the cover name Dinah Eden. She was the latest in a long line of UCOs who'd been embedded in the Justice for William Cooper Campaign, as well as in green activist circles in the Yorkshire and Humberside region for the past three years, so an ultra-reliable source.

But even with the heads-up from Eden, the Met were still reading it at the same time as everybody else.

And Chief Superintendent Tabitha Churchill of Central North BCU hated playing catch-up.

So she was delegating that function to Rex.

'I want to know,' she said, 'what, if anything, this has to do with Jethro Lawrence. Or, at the very least, I want to know who's leaked it, and why now.'

'Well,' said Rex, 'let's see if we can't find out, ma'am.'

Detective Inspector Rex King had got used to the fickle switchback of 'following orders' long ago. And when those orders came from a senior officer like Churchill, or Lollo for that matter, senior officers whose competence was beyond reproach, he didn't mind at all.

It was when the orders were imposed from outside the force, which usually meant from above, at the whim of whatever cabinet caucus currently controlled the Home Office or the Treasury, that he'd learned to watch out. Those were the kinds of orders that meant losing 20,000 colleagues at a snap, having your pension fund raided or – as in the latest outrage – having your station pencilled for possible closure.

A few hundred pages of densely typed text in a couple of hefty yellow ring binders he could deal with. But Rex knew that he'd better put on a small show of reluctance, just for form's sake.

As a junior officer going to court for the first few times, he'd been amazed by the powerful memories of the barristers – solicitors too, but barristers even more so. He'd used to wonder how they could digest so much material, then synthesise it into a more or less persuasive argument. He'd supposed it was all part of their legal training. While for him, right here and now, the police training and his wits were all he had to rely upon. Although he had picked up a few tricks of the trade along the way.

What did this have to do with Lollo's disappearance, Rex had asked Churchill when she'd given him the order. And that was about as much push-back as he'd felt able to offer, but he'd had to ask. From the little he knew of Lollo and Cliff Heath's stories about the period, their early years on the South Yorkshire force, he'd already had the idea – and guessed that Churchill did too – that the young officer might make an appearance in here somewhere.

'What's it got to do with—?' Churchill had said, playing along. 'Good old-fashioned police work, that's what! You should try it sometime. And besides, "Lord's My" DS Shepherd…' (which seemed to have become Churchill's new nickname for Melissa) '… has all that well in hand for the minute.'

Churchill was right. And Rex knew before she'd even said it that for the following few days, ninety per cent of the investigation workflow was data entry coming from TeDIU(M). So it made sense that any and all traffic and comms resulting from the press conference, and any actions generated and decisions taken, needed to be focused between the new dream team of Melissa and Evelyn.

Rex knew he wasn't adding any particular value to the larger investigation at the moment. And, besides, as DI he was wasted as a grunt. Detective Sergeant Singh and the new detective constables were more than capable.

And maybe it was because he'd just come out of the meeting with Simon Rose, so was feeling a bit sensitive on the subject, but he was also wondering whether Churchill had been serious when she'd talked about his 'new life'?

Was this it?

Already?

Was he being moved into a non-public-facing career cul-de-sac because of his impending appearance at the UCPI?

Was this kind of desk-based investigation actually his new life, for real?

Was he now just a liability, to be buried on desk duty until the impact of whatever oral evidence he might give could be gauged?

Well, quite possibly.

But he wasn't about to push back on that.

And one thing Rex did know was that the question of whether you were a liability was one you couldn't ever pose. It was a question the mere asking of which would likely produce the positive answer it abhorred. As ever, you just had to keep your head down and do what you were told.

Well, Rex didn't mind a bit of graft. And it could be worse. At least he wasn't being transferred to the purgatory of TeDIU(M) just yet.

'And I'm happy,' Churchill went on, seemingly oblivious to Rex's ponderings, but with the management chops surely to know that she was also planting that very seed, 'to give them whatever room they need to get on with that. So I told them, let's see what comes in over the next few days, and we'll step up as and when needed. In the meantime, Detective Inspector' – she patted the pile of ring binders – 'I think you've got enough on your plate. Don't you?'

Well, that told him. But it didn't mean that Rex had to completely roll over and be happy about it. He was clutching at straws, but he figured he needed have one last stab at getting out of it, and saying – if not in quite so many words – 'Can't someone else do it?'

But if that was the best he could come up with, he was clearly losing his touch. And it was no surprise when Tabitha Churchill stood firm, with a mere, 'Right, then. Let me know how you get on.'

He had to sack off a planned trip to Oxford for a face-to-face with Cliff Heath, which was a shame. He'd hoped to pick Cliff's brains about Lollo, over a pint or two. That little backstreet pub Heath liked in the alley off St Giles that served not-half-bad pizza. Still, it spared them having to shout over all the braying students giving it large. And maybe this way there'd be more to talk about when and if they did catch up.

Rex didn't like that variable much, though. If he did have to rearrange the meeting, it would only be because Lollo had still not been found. And the best thing he could do to counter that possibility, even if he wasn't going to be liaising with Shepherd and the team on an hourly basis, for a while at least, was to get on with the job in hand, however tangentially connected it might prove to be.

There was nothing for it but to start at the beginning, and figure out how the papers were ordered.

There were twenty-seven files in total, alphabetically arranged by the surnames of the accused. Each file comprising a cover sheet, statement by the arresting officer, and further witness statements. Milestones on their post-arrest journey through the legal and custodial system were transcribed in one or more sets of interview notes and evidence statements per individual charged, plus a charge sheet, sketch maps where relevant, and transcripts of interview or interviews, and a back sheet, prepared by the clerk, summarising key information.

It seemed like another epoch, even though, when Rex had joined a very different Met in 1990, the strike – not yet even a decade earlier – had still been fresh in the collective mind. But thinking back, the strangest thing – product of time's relative elasticity, its vertiginous acceleration in relation to the viewer, each year flying by faster than the last – was that to the young PC King walking down what then had still been the fourth-floor corridor, long before this place, and life in general, it seemed, had gone open-plan, it had felt like ancient history.

It was hard to believe, but to the young Rex King, factory-fresh of uniform and with Hendon's North-West London air still in his nostrils, and the police college's ever-present M1 traffic noise replaced by that of Theobalds Road and Southampton Row, Lollo and his peers had seemed like old gits – veterans. But they'd still been relatively young men.

The strike. Then as now, on the rare occasion he'd thought about it at all, Rex felt overshadowed by the enormous scale of the undertaking: on both sides. The sheer teeming complexity and size of the strike spoke to the mindset and the shared culture of a different age, even as its very failure had hastened the passing of that age. Incredible to think that such a huge body of working men (and it *was* men) could unite – well, most of them, anyway – and, speaking as one, dare to challenge both the government of the day and its proxies in the National Coal Board. Rex felt sure – even *Guardian*-reading graduate that he was – that such an undertaking would be impossible either to conceive of or to execute in today's fragmented and divided surveillance society. But there was a symmetry to that equation too. Life and labour had been cheap, and Rex had the distinct and uneasy feeling that even if such a class mobilisation were possible today, there certainly wouldn't be the numbers to police it.

All of this was only reinforced by the two thick yellow ring binders on Rex's desk. What he and the team would soon – but hadn't yet – come to know as 'Leak Number One'. But Rex was well aware that this was just a drop in the ocean, a few scant traces captured from the fleeting events of one afternoon in May, some thirty-odd years ago. Just a couple of hours out of a year-long strike. Multiply that by the millions of man-hours and the sheer effort that the strike had exacted: the lived experience of tens of thousands of striking miners, and their families. Not to mention the collateral damage caused to local communities suddenly starved of circulating cash. And all of that spread across so many sites, networks, groups and organisations, formal and informal, official and grass-roots. And then there was the correspondingly vast body of literature produced, a whole bureaucratic industry dedicated to the strike. The tens of thousands of police statements and charge sheets, the interview transcripts, carbon copies and duplicates, the photocopies, each multiplied and scrutinised by a further multitude of clerks, typists, barristers, judges and juries, not to mention the column inches generated, the newscaster teleprompts, the subtitles, the journalists, the readers: a universe of information and actors.

Well, if Churchill had decided to put him on desk duty, Rex figured that he might as well milk it.

But right now, there was someone he'd rather be with than this lot.

His girlfriend of the past year and a few days.

He thought about that Police Federation weekend he and Annie had been on to Liverpool. Professional development, they'd called it. Too much like hard work to be called a jolly, it had been a networking session for the new inspectors; part and parcel of his promotion, a day and a half of workshops and role-playing, introductory sessions and break-out groups. It had all been a bit too back-slappy for Rex, and most of the supposedly new functions were familiar to him. In the months leading up to the promotion, the soon-to-be Detective Inspector had thought Lollo was taking the piss, getting Rex to do the Detective Chief Inspector's paperwork for him. But Rex realised now that Lollo had been training him up for a while, gently familiarising him with the new levels of responsibility that went with the step-up from Detective Sergeant to Detective Inspector.

Typical Lollo.

Annie had tagged along to Liverpool – partners and spouses had been welcomed, which was a nice touch – and they'd been put up in that old tower-block hotel by the river. Waking up in the morning and seeing the whole of Liverpool laid out at their feet. They'd had the last afternoon free, so had struck out on their own, flipped a coin: heads the Cavern Club, tails Tate Liverpool. Annie had won, or Rex had let her think so. Leafing through the brochure on the train home, they'd made a note to come back and see the Keith Haring.

And now here they were, eking out their first-anniversary celebration for a few more days with some extra treats. Yesterday Annie had picked up a cake from Soho patisserie Maison Bertaux, a local treasure to which Rex had introduced her one cold, dark winter's afternoon. And tonight they were having a takeaway.

It was a perk of the job, or perhaps more a feature, that you never could tell what was coming around the corner. You were never more than a phone call or a tasking meeting away from a sudden immersion in whatever world a new investigation invoked. And you couldn't just tread water, you had to get your bearings quickly, meticulously adhering to and applying the relevant regulations and procedures, and all the while meeting and absorbing the experiences, hopes and grievances of a whole new cast of characters.

In this case, the cast consisted of twenty-seven miners now known to have been wrongfully arrested, and nigh-on a hundred or so police officers of the South Yorkshire constabulary, whose statements and accounts he'd been reading.

Leafing through the hundreds of pages of statements, Rex had found himself wondering what if any aspects of character or personality might be apprehended from the style of writing, from spelling mistakes and vocabulary choices used in reporting the events at the march, which on just a cursory read-through he'd already seen variously described in these accounts as a protest, an incident, a rally, a riot, a raleigh and a melee.

Why bring all of this up now? That was what Tabitha Churchill wanted him to find out. And why these officers in particular? Why the Sheffield files? Why not Mansfield, or especially Orgreave? That's what people really wanted to see, not this motley crew.

He imagined them all mustering for inspection in the main hall up at Sheffield Central, or a city-centre theatre hired specially for the purpose: The Crucible!

In they'd come – left, right, left – the police constables and police sergeants, detective constables and detective sergeants, inspectors, the lot.

Reporting for duty, just like the old days.

Murmurings of indignation.

Wondering aloud why they were here, and what shit had hit which fan.

But they'd probably have a good idea. They weren't stupid. Not your PCs – Rex checked his notes – Nigel Flinton, Clive Kilfoyle and Roger Laye; or your DCs Tommy Wickrow, Brogan Dennet and Edwyn Parley. Not your Sergeants Neil Greenham, Roger Beauchamp and Austin Diamond. Not stupid, your DS Preston Daws, your DS Daniel Whitehouse and your DS Winston Rickman. Nor your Inspectors Tim Membry, Derek Branigan, Bill Needham, Edwyn Custance, Olly Melbourne and Roger Gillingham.

Not stupid, contrary to popular belief.

They'd be half-asleep, though. Rudely awoken and wondering who'd roused them from their slumber.

Dead on their feet and yawning; eyes full of sleepy-dust; air thick with morning breath.

The dawn chorus of belching and farting.

Fag and a can of Coke for breakfast.

Not quite sure what they were doing here.

But of course, sitting there with his pencil in his hand, and with the big yellow ring binders and their hundreds of pages of statements and interview notes opened on the desk in front of him, Rex knew that actually it wasn't them who'd been early-mustered, and put on the spot.

It wasn't them. It was him.

And he needed to get across this as quickly as possible.

After an hour or two of orientation, Rex began skim-reading, then dipping in and reading at random points.

It all looked real enough, if that was in question. Churchill hadn't raised the possibility of the files being forgeries. After all, who would bother? But determining authenticity-or-not had been top of Rex's checklist. And the typing was certainly authentic, as were the typos.

And certainly these were real forms, of a kind he recognised from his own early days on the force: C12s and C12As – 'Statement of Witness' forms and continuation sheets – and C62Bs and Cs, 'Record of Interview' headers and continuation sheets.

As he read, he started to pick out details – who was seen throwing missiles, who punched a police officer – and began trying to memorise some of the names: Seamus Arthur, Lee Atkins, Richard Beese…

By the time he'd finished, Rex would feel as if he was on first-name terms not only with the twenty-seven but with all of the participating police officers too.

If Rex had to make an educated guess as to who these papers had belonged to originally, he'd probably have said that, given the back sheets, it looked like a brief that had been assembled for the defence barristers.

Pencil marks on pages 233 and 234 seemed to support this theory. Someone had underlined several sections of Dronfield Police Constable Anthony Chase's witness statement on the arrest of striking miner Terence Riddell. Passages relating to the fact that Riddell had been holding a piece of wood, which officers suggested in interview he was planning to use as an offensive weapon. The accusation wasn't borne out. Other officers' statements merely recorded that the piece of wood had been on the ground nearby. But PC Chase wouldn't let go of the suggestion, even though, under sustained and leading questioning by Chase and others, Riddell strenuously and repeatedly denied any such use.

Rex knew that a former Home Secretary had admitted to holding back thirty files relating to the Miners' Strike, even as they were rejecting calls for an 'Orgreave Inquiry'. And those stated thirty files had presumably been just the tip of the iceberg, the thirty that they could get away with admitting to the existence of.

Rex wondered what they were afraid of.

Even if law-breaking by the state was exposed, would it threaten national security now? It would hardly lead to tanks trundling into town past the hookah cafes on the Edgware Road. Although it might undermine a general faith in the rule of law, and it would certainly vindicate the strikers, and lead to numerous claims for compensation. Maybe it was cheaper to let everyone die before anyone be allowed to dig too deep.

Even once he'd started to get his bearings in this forest of new information, the scale of the thing was hard to grasp; overview was impossible as yet.

Rex knew that in order for everyone to really be able to articulate their own experiences of those events of thirty years earlier, in Sheffield and in mining communities across the UK, the discourse needed to move beyond the strictures of the typed-up witness statement, the police interrogation transcript; it needed all the living participants to speak and be cross-examined yet still feel some realistic sense of agency and of fairness, to feel that their voice counted after all, and that they could influence either the proceedings or the verdict or both. And to do that would take years. It would take exactly the type of full public inquiry, in fact, that Rex himself was being called to appear before in relation to another historical injustice. And diving into a dog of a task like this was certainly a useful distraction from that; from his own impending appearance at the UCPI.

The contents of these two fat yellow ring binders were also a window into a different world.

Rex wondered what these South Yorkshire police officers might have done differently if they'd had had had the sense, all those years ago, that their statements might be looked at again now.

If they'd had even an inkling that their words might have a life and an audience far beyond the intended Crown Court date.

If they'd had a Scooby Doo that their statements would be preserved, and survive far beyond the intended instrumental purpose of getting-the-convictions-and-be-done-with-it; that their words might outlast even the convictions and the sentences they'd been intended to ensure.

If they'd known all that, how might any such statements they'd given differ from what he was reading now?

He wondered how they were feeling today, any that were still alive. And if any sleepless nights and cold shivers of regret might have been provoked by the story in the *Yorkshire Post*.

DI Rex King could lie with the best of them, but he also had a seasoned interrogator's instinct for evasion, and even reading these witness statements superficially he kept getting a sense of déjà vu. There were things that began to leap out at him: exact word-for-word matches, and unusual phraseology replicated from one statement to the next, spaces for times and dates of charges or events left blank where texts had simply been photocopied from templates. There were obvious failures of process: protesters not cautioned at time of arrest, statements unwitnessed. There were exaggerated descriptions of violence, and too frequent not to mention casual and uncorroborated use of the term 'riotous assembly' to describe a first sight of the crowds. There were obvious discrepancies and contradictions, and what was clearly hyperbole or wishful thinking regarding the volume, timing and source of missiles thrown.

Rex quickly realised that he needed to change tack.

It wasn't enough simply to read these papers front to back and from cover to cover.

Nor just to dip in here and there, or to take one or two files as representative.

It needed a different strategy. And here policing convention would be his friend. Witness statements, especially those written by trained officers, usually obeyed certain structural rules, and it went something like this: Whose statement is this, where are they based, what were they doing there, when and where – noting street names and local landmarks – did any event(s) being reported take place, what happened and to whom, behaviour of suspect, ID of suspect, address of suspect if known, simple broad-brush description of suspect, approximate height, hair colour, clothing. Also noted would be name, rank and number of any other officers present, and actions taken. And if an arrest had been made, then a) the stated offence, and b) whether caution given, etc., followed by the last-known status and location of suspect.

Given such uniformity, rather than simply reading one account after another, Rex's technique was to read them all at once and search for thematic threads, common incidents and vocabulary, the way he'd been taught to do when approaching any complex investigation. Knowing that such impressions could often be fleeting, an ephemeral effect produced in the drift of eye and text, he'd long ago learned to be sure to underline anything that caught his attention, no matter how trivial-seeming, no matter how convinced he was that he'd be able to find it again if he needed to. He'd learned the hard way that you almost never could find 'it' again, because 'it' was often an effect of the text rather than an artefact within it.

He'd read across the top lines, then all the second paragraphs, then the third, and so on.

There was a method to the madness, as the saying went.

'Read-across' was an evidence-gathering strategy that he'd picked up from Lollo, naturally. Along with all the other ways of working that weren't necessarily in the manual. All roads led to Lollo. Except, of course, that right now they didn't.

As investigative techniques went, it was a useful way to quickly deprivilege whatever order had been imposed, any meanings that might be implied by the manner in which papers and cases were collated, and instead to quickly get an impression of the whole, to grasp the overall picture and how it was being represented. It was also an effective way to identify collusion, scapegoating and mutual reinforcement, and to flag potential perjury offences. In such cases the occasional, statistically unlikely knots and tangles of identical vocabulary, syntax and phraseology that sometimes seemed to hop, wholesale, from one account to another, gave an entry point to the interrogator; they suggested planning and conspiracy, and enabled the detective to begin to unpick an alibi or to get at the truth of what might actually have happened, rather than the accused's preferred, sometimes collective, and usually highly rehearsed version of events, that's what.

It was like looking at the same object or event using different levels of resolution to build up a composite image. He'd tried to explain it to Binder Singh once, in the perpetual teatime of the Holborn Police Station canteen.

Take this table. It's just a table: a functional flat plane supported by four legs. You and I are using it right now, he'd said, pointing at his own cup of tea, and Singh's can of Diet Coke, for one of a range of intended purposes, same as this lot. And it's pretty much the same at any time of the day or night.

As they looked around, on one of the other tables a group of young uniformed PCs were excitedly playing cards. A group of women from HR on the second floor were sat in a row by the window, eating from pots of yogurt. While an older officer had propped himself up in the far corner for a quick forty winks.

Rex slapped the table. Go in closer and it's a mass-produced object made from some kind of melamine-faced aggregate board that's been screw-mounted onto – let's see – a spray-painted metal frame and legs, with non-scratch rubber feet. Take a broader view and you see the manufacturing and supply chains, the personnel and the labour contributing to its production, the tendering and requisitions processes. Look again and it's two tones of a warm pinky-grey that harmonises with the refurb architect's colourway for the textured wallpaper and carpet-tile flooring. Now see the shadows it casts when illuminated by the spotlights in the ceiling, or the lifetime of the table, all the nicks and scrapes, or where someone's sat at the same seat every day and picked away at the edging.

Singh was laughing: What was the question again, boss?

But Rex went on: Now imagine we're not looking at a table, but at a disaster or a critical incident. Or any of the big independent public inquiries, where everything from actions on the ground to official workflows and paper trails would be examined again and again, dependencies and chronologies mapped through different lenses and viewpoints from all participant actors and stakeholder groups and at different levels of resolution.

And so it was here, with Binders 1 and 2.

The legals would be looking for anything that might offer an insight into the motivations of the leaker, and for any clear evidence of laws broken. Within the texts themselves they'd be looking at the events being recounted. Looking for familiar and unfamiliar names, for any specific material – it might only be a sentence or two – that someone might use to justify the leak, over and above any possible broad and well-intentioned desire for 'openness' or 'truth and reconciliation'. Above all, though, they'd be looking for anything that might compromise or embarrass the contemporary force.

The NCA cyber team would already be giving it the full forensic treatment, digitally speaking. Putting the documents through optical character recognition software, and rendering it into editable and machine-readable text. The first outputs of which were expected later today. Not only analysing the content but trying to find out where these documents had been hiding for the past thirty-odd years, whose copies they'd been originally, and what route they might have followed in order to be here now. Not to mention the more pressing matter of who exactly had leaked them to the campaigners.

In the meantime, Rex's brief, as he understood it, was more open. To follow his nose and absorb this material as quickly as possible just in case these files might pertain to the current missing person investigation. Unfortunately there were no shortcuts, despite certain niche beliefs to the contrary. What was that newspaper story he'd seen, a year or so back? About the scientific research into the benefits of microdosing psilocybin – 'magic mushrooms' – to enhance cognitive function and learning. The very sensible-sounding theories didn't quite chime with his own diligent youthful research into the matter: the prolonged and hysterical anxiety, fear of intricate pattern, and hallucinations that had included writhing serpents and the certainty that he was being plotted against by paranoid pigeons.

In the absence of sophisticated psychedelics, and since he was going to be sitting here and doing this for a couple more days, Rex figured that he might as well make himself at home, might as well enjoy it. He plugged in his headphones and opened 6 Music on his phone, heard a distinctive fast-paced pop-punk sound.

Good timing.

I'll name that tune in one, Tom, he thought, summoning a once-popular TV game show catchphrase.

Underpinned by Jean-Jacques Burnel's growling barracuda bass, as they'd used to call it, and Dave Greenfield's psychedelic keyboard licks, there was no mistaking who this was. He'd seen them do the song live a few times, and remembered puzzling over Cornwell's lyrics. Who were 'the Rodneys', anyway?

But, more to the point, who were this lot?

He was going to have to get to know them – his new friends – and see what they had to say. They were colleagues of a sort now, however much time had elapsed.

So he might as well welcome them in.

He dragged the blocks of pages back over the stainless-steel arches of the ring binder, and began again, but read-across this time: top lines only.

Right, who have we here, Rex thought to himself. How many policemen does it take to change a peaceful march into a riot? And was whoever killed Billy Cooper among the arresting officers? Were there any witnesses in these pages to the assault that had caused the union official's death?

First up was PC Nigel Flinton. 'I am a Police Constable of the South Yorkshire constabulary presently stationed at Woodseats Police Station.'

Alright, Nige? thought Rex. Was it you?

Next page, Inspector Tim Membry: 'I am a Police Inspector stationed at Woodseats Police Station, South Yorkshire constabulary.'

Then Detective Constable Thomas Wickrow, and so on.

And every few pages, cropping up like the proverbial bad penny, Detective Chief Inspector Tony Scrimshaw's charge sheets. Scrimshaw had evidently drawn the short straw, but he'd certainly been busy those couple of nights. He had a veritable production line going. So many statements to sign that he'd run off identical copies on a photocopier and had someone typing in the blanks, timed and dated only minutes apart, no countersignature, in different stations, different parts of the city. The same typo reproduced on every one: 'I am a Detective Chief Inspectorof the South Yorkshire constabulary stationed at Sheffield.'

Detective Chief 'Inspectorovsky', thought Rex. Christ! You'd get a repetitive strain injury rubber-stamping charge sheets at that rate.

And on through PC Clive Kilfoyle of Woodseats, Detective Constable Brogan Dennet of Barnsley, Detective Constable Edwyn Parley also of Barnsley, PC Roger Laye of Rotherham Police Station. Detective Constable Bryce Dodd and Detective Constable Nathan Atherton, both of Barnsley, South Yorks. PC Edward Peach from Police Support Unit Charlie Echo Zero Six out of Sheffield, Detective Constable Ben Bowman from Barnsley, Detective Constable Phil Bridle also of Barnsley, Inspector Derek Branigan of Rotherham, PC Eric Scrutton of Rotherham, Detective Constable Stewart Brackenridge from Sheffield, PC Leonard Brandon of Woodseats, 'B' Division, and so on.

Rex tapped his foot to the familiar sound of a baby crying in the intro to 'People Funny Boy' by Lee Perry.

Nice playlist.

As he read, Rex started guessing at nicknames. Here was Sergeant Neil Greenham from Woodseats. 'Peace Camp' to his friends. Rex would put money on it.

Here was Sergeant Roger Beauchamp of Sheffield – pronounced 'Beecham' at a rough guess. Then, as he flipped through page after page of Beauchamp's statement, Christ, Lemsip! You didn't have to write a bloody novel. A ten-pager? I think you missed your vocation, mate. I've got my eye on you, though.

Next up, Detective Constable Edmund Toogood from Sheffield Police Station. Too good to be true, Eddie, eh? thought Rex. Then PC David Martens and PC Geoffrey Martens of Sheffield Central; brothers, perhaps? Tweedledum and Tweedledee. Detective Constable Benjamin Knock from Sheffield Police Station, PC Stewart Cameron from Barnsley, Inspector Edwyn Custance of Barnsley Police Station, Sergeant Austin Diamond of Rawmarsh, Rotherham, PC Nigel Walliams also from Rawmarsh and a member of the South Yorks Police Support Unit Charlie Echo Zero Seven, commanded by Inspector Gillingham, Detective Sergeant Preston Daws of City Road, Sheffield, Detective Constable Kieran Precious from Woodseats…

And on and on it went. Rex had stopped listening to the music.

As Rex read-across the statements in the file, he found himself lining the officers up in his mind's eye and trying to guess who was the card player, the Ted, the mummy's boy, the alky, the go-getter, the good officer, the bookie, the pervert, the lech…

The murderer, though? The perjurer? The wrong'un?

They were in here somewhere. Even if they hadn't made an actual arrest that day.

Scrimshaw must have had an idea.

Was it PC Edward Doherty of Dronfield Police Station, DC Antony Sweeting from Sheffield Central, Detective Constable Nelson Le Sueur of Headquarters CID, PC Matthew Halliwell of Woodseats, Detective Sergeant Raymond Daws of City Road or PC Matt Fazakerly from Police Support Unit Charlie Echo Zero Two? Fazakerly was another novelist to boot. His statement ran to eleven pages? Seriously, Zak? thought Rex. You and old Lemsip back there. Hope you got your stories straight, eh?

It was as close as he could get to eyeballing every one of them.

Reaching the end of Binder 2, Rex was starting to feel a bit peckish, but he wasn't about to stop now. Annie had texted earlier to ask if he wanted the usual from Chilli Cool, their regular Szechuan place up on Leigh Street. No rush; they could heat it up whenever he got home.

'Lovely,' he'd texted back. 'The usual would be great. Love you hun.'

That meant soup to start. Hot pepper for Rex, though Annie preferred the wonton. Then he'd have the sliced beef Szechuan style, and gong hao chicken for Annie. And they'd usually share a steamed rice, and a beef-and-pickled-chilli rice noodles, with a side of seasonal veg.

And all of it liberally doused with dried-shrimp chilli oil.

Just the thought was making him hungry, but it would have to wait.

He texted Frankie to see if anyone was already cross-referencing with current HR rolls nationally, to see which, if any, of the officers named here were still on the force. Just in case. And ditto the accused.

He knew what the answer would be: 'Let me know how you get on!'

Well, so be it. He had the bit between his teeth now.

What was that little wooden plaque that Lollo used to have on his desk? A joke old enough to have been on Noah's Ark, but which to the Detective Chief Inspector was as fresh as a daisy: 'You don't have to be mad to work here, but it helps.'

Well, maybe, as he heaved the pages back over the arches of both ring binders and went back to the beginning again, Rex knew the feeling.

He moved down to the second paragraph and read on.

'Since Friday 13 APR 84 I have been engaged in duties in relation to the National Union of Mineworkers Dispute, as Charlie Echo Ten under the command of Inspector Gillingham.'

Next!

'On Monday 7th May 1984 I performed duties in the Sheffield area regarding a Rally concerning the National Union of Mineworkers.'

Next!

'On Monday 7th of May 1984, I was deployed on PSU duties in the Sheffield area, in relation to the NUM dispute.'

Next!

'On Monday, 7th May 1984, there was a demonstration organised by the National Union of Mineworkers. The demonstration consisted of a march through Sheffield City Centre ending at a rally on the car park adjacent to the Devonshire Green, Fitzwilliam Street, Sheffield.'

Next!

'On Monday 7th of May 1984 I performed duties in the Sheffield area in connection with a National Union of Miners rally. I am also a member of a Police Support Unit call-sign Delta Echo Zero Five and for the past nine weeks we have been engaged in the National Union of Mineworkers strike.'

He wasn't going to tell Churchill, but Rex was almost enjoying himself.

He got a WhatsApp from Frankie towards close of play. Yes, he was right: no one was cross-referencing these personnel with HR as yet, but TC says thank you, good idea, please proceed.

Frankie also said that Evelyn Gummer's team had received FOIs to the same effect from journalists on the *Guardian* and *Yorkshire Post*, but they'd delay responding to those for as long as they could. And a PS, just to let him know that the first few raw OCR files were now up on the server.

When Rex took a quick look, he could see that someone at the NCA had gone a bit further still. There were a number of secondary output files, in which they'd sifted the material into various sortable .csv chunks. Here were all the cautions extracted in a single document. They'd also looked for temporal markers — any specific mentions of the time of day — and used those tags and a couple of delimiters to spit out a test sequence of paragraphs in chronological order.

Blimey, they were fast workers.

Now we're talking, thought Rex, almost rubbing his hands with glee as he opened the document and read the first entry.

On Monday 07/05/84 I started duty at **8.20 am** in the morning parading at Sheffield Police Station and my duty for the day was to work with Police Support Unit Delta Echo Zero Four under the command of Inspector Branigan and Sergeant Beauchamp. There were 6 constables and myself in that unit, our instruction were that there was an NUM rally and march in Sheffield and we were to remain on standby away from the demonstration route at Washington Street, off Fitzwilliam Street, Sheffield.

And the next:

At **10 am** Monday 7th May 1984 along with other officers I attended the car park on Fitzwilliam Street.

And as he read the dozens of time-stamped entries, a mosaic image of that fateful day in 1984 began to form in his mind.

Geo-tag this material, Rex realised, and you could watch the whole thing unfold on a – how did they put it? – 'reskinned' Google Map. He'd seen something along those lines a couple of years back. An animation put together for Operation Withern, mapping the spread of the 2011 UK riots, had been shown as part of the presentations at the National Crime Agency launch at Queen Elizabeth Hall.

Rex racked his brain but couldn't remember the name of the agent who'd given the presentation. But it'd be a good place to start. He probably still had the agenda in his email. He wanted to ping them immediately, hit them with a list of requests, but he knew that to do so would fall outwith the terms of the memorandum of understanding between the NCA and the Met. And besides, such a gauche display of enthusiasm wouldn't be respected, and it wouldn't get results. If he played his cards right here, he could have NCA resources on tap, without undue deference or needing to travel over hill and dale to do so. Which meant following the MoU to the letter, and not fucking up the powerplay before you'd started.

He'd need to go through the correct channels – Tabitha Churchill

– and get the nod from the NCA–Met Cyber Working Group. He gave Frankie a quick ring. He owed her a call in any case. The additional problem here – and wouldn't you know it – was that the Central North BCU's lead on the Cyber Working Group had been Lollo. Not because he was in any way a geek or a techno-freak, but because he was a good and fastidious manager who knew his procedure and didn't take any bullshit. Inter-agency working groups were a minefield. They could descend into a mad hatter's tea party if you weren't careful. And Lollo was nothing if not careful.

Rex pressed 'pause' on the radio app and punched in the number.

Frankie picked up immediately.

'Why is it that you only call me when you want something?' she said.

That meant that Chief Superintendent Tabitha Churchill wasn't there.

'Is it that obvious?' said Rex.

They both laughed.

'No, thanks for letting me know about the NCA materials. I'm onto it,' said Rex.

'You're welcome.'

'That's why I called – to check if Tabitha would be happy for me to liaise directly with the NCA team. They're going gangbusters on this, judging by the material they've already shared, so I wanted to strike while the iron was hot, you know.'

'Good question,' said Frankie. 'Understood.'

She was writing it down. Rex liked people who wrote things down.

'See if we can't get a bit of to-and-fro going,' said Rex.

'Sure. I'll ask her when she gets back, and let you know.'

'Thanks. I've got plenty to be getting on with in the meantime, of course.'

'Ha, I don't envy you,' said Frankie.

'All part of the service. I quite enjoy it, truth be told. Something to get your teeth into. Don't tell the gaffer that, though.'

'Too late. I think she already knows.'

Rex sighed, audibly. 'Of course,' he said, 'anything NCA would usually go through—'

Frankie knew what Rex had stopped himself saying.

'Tough, isn't it,' she said. 'That and about fifty per cent of all the workflows in this place. But the Sussex team seem very capable, so Jethro's in good hands.'

'Yeah,' said Rex. 'That DS Shepherd's wasted down there if you ask me. Christ! Tabitha tore them a new one the other day. Listen, Frankie. It's probably too soon to say who's replacing Lollo on the working group…'

'Fancy filling in, Rex?' said Frankie. 'Bread and butter to an old hand like you.'

'Haha,' said Rex.

And a part of him was wondering whether, in the normal run of things, he might be angling to fill that empty chair. Frankie was right: usually it'd be just his style. But not now. Protected and supported though he was in all of this, Rex knew that it only went so far. He had precisely zero chance of getting co-opted onto anything with a UCPI appearance hanging over him. He certainly wouldn't have got the promotion to Detective Inspector now either. Well, it was too late, they were stuck with that one. But with that kind of baggage, not to say the notoriety that might ensue, and the potential it brought for personal and, worse, corporate embarrassment, Rex knew that he was more or less untouchable for the moment. But he wasn't going to say it out loud. And he wasn't going to beg for scraps. Not to Churchill, and certainly not to Frankie. He had some dignity.

'Well,' he said, 'never say "never", eh? In the meantime, if you could mention to the gaffer that, ideally, I'd like to go back to NCA with some requests tomorrow morning? The clock's ticking, obviously. I'll wait until I've got the nod, though.'

'That's helpful, thanks, Rex,' said Frankie. 'Got it. I'll let you know soon as.'

Hanging up, and suddenly sick of the task in hand, Rex pushed back in his chair. He needed to stretch his legs. It had been a long day. What with the stresses of Rex's early meeting with Simon Rose, then the immediate shift sideways into the all-consuming world of Binders 1 and 2, Rex couldn't help feeling slightly dislocated. It felt like one of those days when the points change and before you know it you're trundling down a different track, looking back at where you'd thought you were going.

He jogged down the stairs to street level.

It was good to feel a bit of a breeze on his face.

Lamb's Conduit Street was as busy as ever; bustling with shoppers and a few early commuters trying to beat the rush.

Sid's, a.k.a. the Conduit Coffee House, would be closed for the day by now, but one of the trendier places that Annie preferred – all whitewash and blackboards, upcycled wooden furniture and communal broadsheets – was still serving. He ordered a flat white, a slice of lemon polenta cake and a packet of posh rosemary-flavoured crisps, then sat on one of the high stools in the window. He checked to see if there was a text from Annie, or from Jen. There wasn't, so to clear his head he watched the street go by for ten minutes.

The change of scene gave Rex a second wind. Walking back upstairs to the sixth floor, he figured that while he waited to hear back from Frankie about NCA protocols he might as well put in another couple of hours.

Back to the read-across.

Things were hotting up in Sheffield on that afternoon of 7 May 1984.

It was time for Rex to dive in.

One of us made a radio call for assistance and a short time later police vans started arriving... At this time there were a large number of demonstrators numbering in their hundreds who were being shepherded along Division Street in the direction of Devonshire Green and onto waiting buses and coaches allocated to take the demonstrators home... I became aware of incidents of violence in Sheffield City Centre and as a result of this I went, together with my colleagues to Devonshire Green... The coaches which had carried the demonstrators to a march organised by the National Union of Mineworkers were assembled at Devonshire Green and most had left on their route home leaving twenty to thirty coaches on Devonshire Green and many more on Fitzwilliam Street... Upon our arrival we were met by a scene of complete chaos... Upon our arrival we were confronted with a scene of chaos... Upon our arrival we were met by a scene of complete chaos... Upon our arrival we were met by a scene of complete chaos... I immediately saw a group of youths, perhaps 500 strong, massing on Devonshire Green... In the far corner I saw scuffles break out between police officers and demonstrators... There were large groups of men who were being persuaded to climb onto awaiting buses by police officers... Several coaches were parked on the nearside south of Devonshire Green and police officers were attempting to persuade people to board the vehicles but they were being subjected to both physical and verbal abuse... As the demonstrators were being shepherded along the road sporadic fighting broke out between the demonstrators and the police... On arrival at that location, our Unit was deployed to assist other officers in forming a police cordon on the town centre side of Devonshire Green... Upon my arrival I saw numerous people in the Car Park at the side of Devonshire Green and also outside the Washington pub adjacent to it... Upon arrival at the scene I saw a large number of people gathered on Devonshire Green... At this time a large amount of missiles were being thrown by a large crowd of NUM demonstrators towards the police cordon... On our arrival I saw a large unruly crowd of people some of whom were throwing bottles and other missiles at police officers at that location... There were groups of between ten and thirty males leaving Fargate and making their way towards Division Street... There were groups of between ten and thirty males leaving Fargate and making their way towards Division Street... Some of the men were worse for drink... Some of the men were worse for drink... There was chanting and swearing and general abuse directed against police officers... The terms 'scabs' and 'union breakers' were repeatedly used, together with 'Seig Heil' and the Nazi salute... Some of the men were worse for drink... Sporadic fighting was taking place and missiles were being thrown... There was a large fight in progress on both properties with police officers attempting to stop men from the Rally throwing missiles at them... There was a large crowd of demonstrators on the forecourt... On our arrival I saw a large unruly crowd of people, some of whom were throwing bottles and other missiles at police officers at that location... As officers came to us the throwing of missiles stopped... The crowd began to run onto Division Street and continued acting in an unruly manner and kept throwing missiles... On arrival at that location several minutes later I witnessed what can only be described as a riot in progress... On arrival at the scene the unit was deployed to assist other officers forming a police cordon, in the town centre side of the City Hall and Barker's Pool... On my arrival there I saw an angry mob of about 400 men on Devonshire Green... There was serious disorder... When we arrived at this location there was a large disturbance taking place between demonstrators and police officers... At this time missiles were being thrown by a large crowd of NUM demonstrators towards the police... The majority of the group were shouting and being abusive and were throwing... The majority of the group were shouting and being abusive... There I saw a large crowd of people shouting and being abusive and from in the crowd objects were being thrown towards other police officers in attendance... Whilst on patrol on Fargate I observed groups of demnostrators both walking about the town centre with up to 25–30 youths, men and women and others standing outside public houses drinking from cans and bottles of beer and spirits... Our unit them formed a cordon and other officers went into the crowd removing glasses and bottles from them... As we did so I saw a large group of youths gathering in the Fitzwilliam Street car park adjacent to Devonshire Green, the youths were shouting and being abusive and spilling over onto the pavement... The youths were chanting and shouting and spilling over on to the pavement... I saw a number of officers on the floor struggling with demonstrators... The police vehicle was parked nearby and I alighted from the vehicle and ran to the centre of the skirmish... As we did so, I saw a large group of youths gathering on the Fitzwilliam Street car park... The youths were shouting and chanting and spilling over on to the pavement... The police vehicle was parked nearby and I alighted from the vehicle, together with the other officers, I ran to the centre of the skirmish... At this location a demonstration was taking place made by striking miners... Some of the men were worse for drink... There was chanting and swearing and general abuse directed against police officers... The terms 'Scabs' and 'Union breakers' were repeatedly used, together with 'Seig Heil' and the Nazi salute... I accompanied the groups of men along Division Street to Devonshire Green together with other officers... The mood of the crowd consisting of many 100's was violent, numerous fights were taking place and I saw numerous empty beer bottles or large pieces of wood being thrown about... I would say our unit and one other officer then escorted 100 of these demonstrators back towards Barker's Pool to go up Division Street... The mob was split into two to make numbers easier for escort to buses which we knew were waiting for the demonstrators at Devonshire Green...

This drunken mob numbering well over 100 were all over the road...
We tried to keep the left carriageway clear but this proved impossible...
At one stage an ambulance blue light flashing and its horns going was
unable to move on Division Street... A large group of chanting
youths approached Devonshire Green, swearing and shouting abuse
at the police in the area... As the group approached Devonshire
Green the youths at the head of the group commenced pushing and
jostling two young police officers and other officers went to their
assistance... The men were shouting and chanting threats towards a
cordon of police officers who were attempting to control the crowd...
The whole road for some 200 yards was completely blocked... There
were several groups of men fighting with police officers... Upon our
arrival we were met by a scene of complete chaos... A meeting had
finished and there were large groups of men roaming about many
fighting with police officers and missiles were being thrown at the
officers... The whole road for some 200 yards was completely
blocked... On Devonshire Green was a large group of men some of
whom were throwing various missiles into police ranks... A meeting
had just finished and large groups of men were roaming about, many
fighting with police officers and missiles were being thrown at the
officers... This disorder involved several hundred demonstrators
who were in the main striking NUM Members, numerous bottles
and stones were being thrown at police officers and fighting was
taking place at numerous points at that locus... On our arrival near
to The Washington Public House I saw a large number of
demonstrators on Devonshire Green with a number of police officers
already deployed... I saw that bottles and ~~sto~~ other missiles were
being thrown from the group of demonstrators towards the police
officers, who then moved towards the demonstrators... When I
reached Devonshire Green there was a very large crowed assembled
of about a thousand men who were throwing bottles and bricks and
other missiles at a police cordon... We were immediately redeployed
to Division Street, upon our arrival we were confronted again with
large groups of men... The total number of people on this road
numbered several hundred... The total number of people on this
road amounted to several hundred... The total number of people on
this road numbered several hundred... There were approximately
fifty persons standing on the pavement at the side of the vehicles...

At this time there were a large number of men milling about the total number in the area being in excess of 1,000... On my arrival there I saw an angry mob of about 400 men on Fitzwilliam Street car park... There was serious disorder... The total number of people in this road numbered several hundred... I immediately saw a large group of youths, perhaps 500 strong, massing in the car park... When I reached Devonshire Green there was a very large crowd assembled of about a thousand men who were throwing bottles and bricks and other missiles at a police cordon of about 200 officers... Numerous missiles were thrown as the police moved forward in an attempt to disperse the crowd who were in an ugly mood... At this time a large amount of missiles were being thrown by a large crowd of NUM demonstrators towards the police... While I was on Division Street near the City Hall several bricks were thrown from the crowd in front of me near a stationary bus... I also saw several bottles thrown from this crowd towards a group of police horsemen the bottle burst under the horse causing the horse to shy and rear... This bottle went over my head and smashed near three persons who just laughed and sneered about the incident... The mood of the remaining crowd became agitated... On Devonshire Green at this time several hundred people were causing a very serious public disorder... Bottles and stones were being thrown in the crowd of police officers were I was stood... On the instruction of a senior police officer the cordon advanced along Division Street away from the City Centre and on doing so the crowed began to disperse... At this stage missiles were still being thrown from the demonstrators towards the police... The majority of the crowd began to run along Division Street pursued by myself and other police officers...... On the instruction of a senior police officer the cordon advanced along Division Street away from Devonshire Green and on doing so the crowed began to disperse... At this stage missiles were still being thrown from the demonstrators towards the police... The majority of the crowd began to run along Division Street pushed by myself and other police officers... As we approached Devonshire Green which is adjacent to Division Street I saw that there was a large number of demonstrators gathered there... Walking towards us was a cordon of police officers ~~pushing~~ moving the demonstrators towards our direction... There was a cordon of police officers walking across Devonshire Green towards us... As the demonstrators were being moved in front of the cordon these police officers were having stones, bricks, bottles and other missiles thrown at them by some of the demonstrators... The demonstrators were throwing bricks, stones, glasses and other missiles at these police officers, it was obvious that a serious breach of the peace was in progress... It was obvious that a breach of the peace was in progress... Sporadic fighting was taking place and missiles were being thrown... There were also a number of police officers who were within this crowd who appeared to be having difficulty restraining the crowd... There were also a number of police officers who were within this crowd who appeared to be having difficulty restraining the crowd... I then saw a large number of missiles which were being thrown by the crowd... I then saw a large number of missiles which were being thrown by the crowd who were by this time in a hostile mood... At this time bottles, stones and various other objects were being hurled through the air, directed at police officers present at the scene... All of a sudden I saw a beer glass come from the back of this mob... We all parted and the glass smashed on the ground where we stood... At this there was suddenly a hail of missiles thrown from this mob of demonstrators at us, beer glasses, bottles and beer cans... The crowd was in an ugly mood but it was eventually dispersed... On the instruction of a senior officer the cordon advanced along Devonshire Green away from the City Centre and on doing so the crowd began to disperse... Missiles such as bottles, stones and sticks were thrown at the police by the men on Devonshire Green, beer cans were also flattened and skimmed by these men, at the police... Several police officers were hit by these missiles and I was hit by one of the beer cans, on my chest, but I was not injured... At this time a line of police officers formed across Devonshire Green in order to attempt to control the crowd... In order to control the disturbance, a line of approximately one hundred police officers, with linked arms was formed, diagonally at 45° across the City Centre end of Devonshire Green the intention of doing so being to move the youths/men causing disturbance back towards their waiting buses... In order to control the movement of the men, I along with other officers linked arms and formed a line... Missiles were still being thrown from the demonstrators towards the police... At this time a large amount of missiles were being thrown by a large crowed of NUM demonstrators towards the police cordon... The mood of this crowd was rowdy and violent... On Devonshire Green was a large group of men some of whom were throwing various missiles into the police ranks... The missiles mainly consisted of beer bottles and cans... Various missiles were thrown including bricks stones and bottles and we then moved forwards to disperse the crowd, scuffles took place as the crowd of demonstrators then moved back into the main area of Devonshire Green... While this was happening we were under a constant bombardment from flying bottles and stones thrown from the rear of the crowd... This bottle went over my head and smashed near three persons who just laughed and sneered about the incident... At this most of the men ran backwards about 50 yards and continued throwing the missiles in the direction of the police which often struck officers... The situation I would describe as extremely violent... The group of police officers I was with started to give chase to try and apprehend the offenders of this... At this time I was in the centre of a group pf several dozen police officers who were giving chase to this group of youths... Police reinforcements arrived and together we ran towards the crowd, this caused them to disperse into smaller groups... During the next five minutes a number of violent scuffles and pitched battles took place and a large number of prisoners were taken... We had been instructed to keep our chinstraps up inside our helmets in case it provoked trouble, at this we all removed helmets and put our chinstraps down... Many of the crowd were lashing out with their fists and feet at the police officers... Police reinforcements arrived and police officers ran towards the crowd... This caused them to disperse into smaller groups... Many of the crowd were lashing out indiscriminately with fists and by kicking... Police reinforcements arrived and together we ran towards the crowd... Whilst this was happening we were under constant bombardment from flying bottles and stones, thrown from the rear of the crowd... A greater number of the demonstrators then started chanting and in particular they were shouting repeatedly, 'Maggie Thatcher's got one, Ian MacGregor is one.'... The demonstrators which numbered 130 were shouting, 'Zig Heil', 'Bastards', 'Let's have a go' and other abuse towards us... Some of the chants were 'What's it like to be outnumbered' and 'Maggies Boot Boys' and 'Seig Heil' accompanied by the Nazi salute... I can

remember them shouting 'You'll get what you got at Easington' and
'If you all hate coppers clap your hands.'... All of the abuse was
directed against the police... There were shouts of 'Get the bastards'
directed at us and 'what's it like to be outnumbered' together with
'Pigs'... All the abuse was at the police and I genuinely thought that
there was a common purpose by all these men to direct violence at
us... The crowd were still jeering and chanting and missiles were still
being thrown including large pieces of concrete... If you wanna kick
a copper clap your hands... For approx. half a minute, missiles were
continually thrown at us and I saw several officers hit by the missiles
but I was not hit myself... Some parts of the crowds were chanting,
'If you want to kick a copper clap your hands.'... Our unit was
stretched into a thin 'U' shape around the back of this mob of men,
we were walking alongside and behind the crowd... The whole
incident was an extremely serious confrontation. I have 19 years
service in the police Force and this was by far the most violent and
extreme public disorder that I have ever attended... I have been a
police officer for 17 years during which time I have been involved in
the performance of public order duties of various natures. I can state
that I have never experienced such violence of such magnitude which
occurred without provocation as the events I have described which
occurred on the 7th May 1984. I was genuinely in fear of being
subjected to some physical violence and feared for the safety of
myself, my colleagues and the members of the general public who
were in the area. I believe that it was a deliberate and organised attack
by the demonstrators on the police and I believe had it not been for
the introduction of police reinforcements, there would have been a
greater number of officers injured and to a more serious degree... I
have been a police officer for 3 years and I would say that the events
at Devonshire Green that day were some of the most frightening
moments of my life. I was continually under attack and was at all
times worried about my safety, the safety of my fellow officers and
members of the public who were in the area. As I have said before at
no stage did I ever see any action by the police to provoke the events
of that afternoon...

He was almost disappointed when the phone rang.

Carried along by the rush of voices, and the familiarity of police talk – which hadn't changed much – Rex realised that he'd stopped making notes long ago. And yet he also knew that this composite image was false, or skewed at best. Because from one statement to the next, again and again, there were near-matches and duplications that went far beyond any broad similarities in experience or vocabulary that might be expected when collating diverse views taken at varying times and locations across such a large, chaotic, dispersed, constantly moving and continually unfolding event.

Rex wondered whether the defence barristers had even had time, harassed and under pressure as they surely had been when all of this was heading to trial, to notice this clear evidence of collusion. Was it only now, away from the bustle, the pressure and the exigencies of the courtroom, only now with the latter-day luxury of time and hindsight – not to mention the potential for analysis by sophisticated software – that such properties and attributes were showing up so readily?

It was as if, in the finest of Sheffield traditions, Detective Chief 'Inspectorof' Tony Scrimshaw had been running his own little mester, stamping out not cutlery but convictions.

As far as Rex could tell, the officers involved weren't even trying to hide it. That's how cocksure they'd been, how certain of their power and the support they had.

As he'd been reading, the vision conjured up in Rex's mind's eye had been of South Yorkshire officers sitting in police station canteens and classrooms at Sheffield Central and Rotherham, in Woodseats, Barnsley and Dronfield, writing the statements together during the long hours between arrest, interview and charge. Chewing the ends of their police-issue biros, and working hard to ensure that there were two or more witnesses to every chargeable offence. Yet frequent appearances from one statement to the next of shared syntax and vocabulary seemed to suggest that in some instances – or many instances – the writers were not only comparing notes but might even have been following instructions to use particular words: 'riot', for example. He imagined them sitting facing the front like overgrown schoolboys, taking dictation and copying down certain key phrases from the board.

Here was one: 'You lot kept away during the march when there was more of us than you so you can fuck off now.'

Obviously, Rex hadn't been there. But, it didn't exactly trip off the tongue. It wasn't the kind of thing you'd imagine multiple people saying word for word. But, judging by the number of statements this phrase appeared in, apparently they had.

Yet as he read, Rex knew that the high frequency with which this precise phrase appeared in the collected statements was more than just a statistical anomaly. Let's say one miner *had* said this, in the middle of what was supposed to have been a tumultuous riot situation spread across a large area of Sheffield city centre, exactly how many nearby police officers could realistically claim to have heard it: two or three? And yet there it was, word-perfect, in statement after statement.

And even so, even when they matched word for word, many of the statements – he'd checked – were self-statemented, unwitnessed.

Unwitnessed meant unsound, was how the instructors at Hendon had used to put it in Rex's days as a cadet.

This was a joke.

It was Frankie on the phone.

Yes, she said. The Chief Superintendent had given Rex the go-ahead. He could liaise direct with the NCA team on this, but record-keeping as per the MoU was obviously key.

Frankie had more to impart, though. That Tabitha had asked her to let Rex know that she was certainly mindful of his experience here, and grateful for his hard work as ever, and would be making a decision about who might fill in for DCI Lawrence on the Cyber Working Group nearer the time of the next meeting, and it might be that some sort of temporary co-option would be necessary, but that would be reviewed as and when.

From the form of words Frankie was using, and from a suddenly slightly hesitant and speculative tone of voice that suggested she wasn't talking only to him, Rex could tell that Churchill was also in the room at the other end of the line, listening and nodding.

'Well,' said Rex, 'happy to serve as directed, of course. If needed.'

Though he didn't really care about that now.

It was only half six, so there was time to make one more pass through the files. There'd been no sign of the young Jethro Lawrence yet, but things were getting interesting. Specific offences, and the circumstances of each ensuing arrest, were being recounted.

Here was Woodseats Police Constable Clive Kilfoyle's account of arresting Trevor MacWilliam of Easington:

I went to the Fitzwilliam Street car park where a fight between police officers and men from the Rally was in progress, and I there saw the accused Trevor MACWILLIAM throwing punches at a police officer who was attempting to effect the arrest of a man who was struggling violently. I took hold of MACWILLIAM who then threw punches at me. A struggle ensued and I eventually restrained him by grabbing him by the neck and holding him on the ground. He was then escorted to the police mobile with the aide of other officers. MACWILLIAM continued to struggle until he reached the police mobile where I informed him that he was arrested for being involved in a Breach of the Peace.

Here was the account of another Woodseats Constable, PC Leonard Brandon, of the arrest of Jack Dean of Cottonley:

I then saw a man who I now know to be the accused Jack DEAN. He was shouting 'Stone the bastards' and was kicking and thumping a wooden fencing panel approximately 6'x6' and after smashing it attempted to climb over the remains onto the waste ground by Fitzwilliam Street. Together with PC 622 BRUCE I approached DEAN and said, 'I am arresting your for conduct likely to cause a breach of the peace and for criminal damage. PC BRUCE and myself then took DEAN to the police transit during which time he was struggling. He was then placed in the transit and conveyed to the mobile cell block.

PC Brandon's account was backed up by that of PC 622 Quentin Bruce.

And Rex had to laugh. If PC Bruce wasn't a total hard nut, his life on the force would have been made a misery with a name like Quentin.

He was shouting 'Stone the bastards' and was kicking and thumping a wooden fencing panel approximately 6'x6' and after smashing it, attempted to climb over the remains onto the waste ground by Fitzwilliam Street. Together with PC 724 BRANDON I approached DEAN and PC Brandon said, 'I am arresting you for conduct likely to cause a breach of the peace and for criminal damage.' PC BRANDON cautioned him and he made no reply. PC BRANDON and myself then took DEAN to a nearby police transit vehicle during which time he was struggling violently. As myself and PC BRANDON placed DEAN in the vehicle, he continued to struggle violently and as we placed him in the vehicle my service issue spectacles which I was wearing at the time were banged against the open door of the transit vehicle. The damaged caused to my spectacles because of this action consists of a scratched lens and cracked frame.

And here in Binder 2 was Barnsley Police Constable 818 Trevor McElroy's account of the arrest of Karl Marshall from Burton in Staffordshire:

It was at this time my attention was drawn to two police officers who were escorting a male prisoner across the Fitzwilliam Street car park towards nearby transit vehicles. As these officers approached I saw a man I now know to be the defendant Karl MARSHALL run towards these officers, grab hold of the prisoner's right arm and push the police officer on the prisoner's left with his hand in an apparent effort to free the prisoner. I heard MARSHALL shout 'Take your fucking hands off him you bastard, you're not fucking taking him anywhere', at this MARSHALL was—

Marshall was what?

There was a page missing.

Flipping forward and backward through the pages of Binder 2, Rex satisfied himself that it hadn't been collated out of order. The file jumped from page 174 to page 176, where the story was taken up by McElroy's commanding officer, the Barnsley Police Inspector Bill Needham:

At this time my attention was drawn to 2 police officers escorting a man across the car park towards the police vehicle. I then saw a man I now know to be Karl MARSHALL run toward the officer, grab hold of the prisoner's right arm and push the police officer on the prisoner's left with his hand in an effort to free the prisoner. I heard MARSHALL shout 'Take your fucking hands off him you bastards you're not fucking taking him anywhere.' At this MARSHALL was joined by three other demonstrators and a scuffle developed between the police officers and demonstrators. With PC 818 McELROY I then approached this group and took hold of MARSHALL. PC McELROY cautioned him and Marshall replied, 'Get your fucking arm off my neck.' MARSHALL was then taken to a police vehicle.

Rex could sense himself getting sidetracked and time was ticking on, but a certain morbid fascination had him returning to particular accounts.

Those of Police Constables David and Geoffrey Martens, for instance.

Here was David:

At this time I could see other officers already involved in the melee and several officers were struggling on the ground. Together with PC 306 MARTENS we entered the melee and I saw a Sergeant struggling with a violent prisoner. I then saw a youth who I now know to be the accused Maurice ETCHELLS kick out with his right foot in the direction of the Sergeant. I then indicated to PC 306 MARTENS who was on my right hand side, the accused, ETCHELLS, who shouted 'Leave him alone you bastards, he's done fuck all.' and ETCHELLS lashed out with his right arm and caught me in the chest area. I restrained ETCHELLS who was continuously swearing and trying to break away from us. Together with PC 306 MARTENS I escorted the youth to a nearby police vehicle. ETCHELLS was abusive all the way and struggling and was therefore placed in police handcuffs. I said to the accused, 'You are under arrest for threatening behaviour and will be conveyed to Sheffield Police Station whilst further enquiries are to be made.' Cautioned he replied, 'Fuck off I've done nowt.'

And here was Geoffrey:

At this time I could see other officers already involved in the melee, with several officers struggling on the ground. Together with PC 305 MARTENS we entered the melee and I saw a Sergeant struggling with a violent prisoner. PC 305 MARTENS then indicated to me a man who I now know as Maurice ETCHELLS. ETCHELLS had hold of the Sergeant around his neck. PC 305 MARTENS then went up to ETCHELLS who shouted 'Leave him alone you bastards he's done fuck all.' ETCHELLS lashed out with his right arm, striking PC 305 MARTENS across his chest. I assisted PC 305 MARTENS in restraining ETCHELLS who was continuously swearing and trying to break away from us. Together with PC 305 MARTENS I escorted the youth to a nearby police vehicle. ETCHELLS was abusive all the way and struggling and was therefore placed in police handcuffs. PC 305 MARTENS said to ETCHELLS 'You are under arrest for threatening behaviour and will be conveyed to Sheffield Police Station whilst further enquiries are made.' PC 305 MARTENS cautioned him. He replied, 'Fuck off I've done nowt.'

Even if the Martens brothers were twins, Rex doubted that it was telepathy that had their accounts yielding what he could see, even without the benefit of NCA analysis, was a more than ninety per cent substantial match. Had they written their accounts in the van on the way to the station or around their mum's kitchen table? Less than three hours later Etchells was at Snig Hill, where he was interviewed for twenty-five minutes by Detective Constable Ben Knock. Reminded by DC Knock of the charge of threatening behaviour, Etchells says that they've got the wrong man, and replies:

'I don't know about threatening behaviour all I know I was running for bus and a police officer grabbed me round neck and another grabbed my arm and took me across road put me against wall and put handcuffs on me.'

'Prior to you running for the bus, what was you doing?' Knock asks, before positing the events enumerated in the arresting officer's account, which Etchells refutes at each point. All Knock can do to counter is to ask Etchells whether he agrees that if, as he says, he was alone, then there can be no cause for mistaken identity.

'No they can't have the right person,' Etchells states. 'I didn't lash out at any police officers.'

Nonetheless, and in the absence of course of any corroborating CCTV or other footage, the Martens brothers' brief but mutually buttressing and near-identical accounts were deemed sufficient for Etchells to be detained for a further two days before being charged at 10.25 p.m. on the evening of 9 May with threatening behaviour with intent to provoke a breach of the peace, contrary to Section 5 of the Public Order Act 1936 as amended by Section 7 of the Race Relations Act 1965 and the Criminal Law Act 1977. And that he did together with Donald Lowe on 7 May 1984 at Sheffield in the County of South Yorkshire riotously assemble together Contrary to Common Law.

Charges that, if he'd been found guilty, could have carried a life sentence.

Presumably he was then released, too late at night to be able to catch a train home to Barnsley, and would have spent a chilly night on the platforms of Sheffield railway station, waiting for the milk train; sleeping under mail bags on the parcel platform.

A nice touch.

Just to rub it in.

Rex made another note, then realised that he needed to reframe his questions for the NCA. Now he had the go-ahead he would email them in the morning. Better to be at the top of whoever's inbox first thing than email late and get fobbed off with an Out of Office.

He wasn't so concerned any longer with looking for matches, with paint-by-numbers police witness statements, because they nearly all seemed to have been jointly written. It was the norm, not the exception. Of course, he needed the stats. He couldn't just say he had a feeling that this and that accounts were similar. He needed the data to prove it. But now Rex was following a lead. There was something else he needed to work on with the hotshots at the NCA. He began drafting the email. Keep it simple, he thought: bullet points only. He probably didn't have the technical vocabulary, but he tried to explain as best he could that he wanted to identify the exceptions to this rule.

He wanted anything presented as a direct quotation.

To capture all of the pencil marks or marginal notes that were showing up on the copy.

He wanted to isolate any rogue statements that didn't toe the official line.

Hadn't he just read one account saying the crowd was well behaved?

Contrary accounts, like the officer who suggested, almost by the by, that the throwing of missiles had lasted a mere thirty seconds. Another who made fleeting mention of children going home from school. An officer who reported being told that police were forcing miners onto the wrong coaches: miners from Fife being put on a coach to Merthyr. They needed to look very carefully at the novelists: the two overly long statements. Why were those officers saying so much? What were they hiding?

As well as these contrary accounts, Rex also wanted to isolate and log any oddities: distinctive incidents, vocabulary or imagery that may have only appeared in one statement or interview transcript. He'd found a few already. The ambulance becoming stuck on Division

Street when hemmed in by protesters. Supposed 'miners' (wearing 'Coal Not Dole' stickers) throwing stones and egging others on to follow suit, then showing their badges and making arrests. One group of protesters in a small crowd outside the Wimpy on Fargate heard making monkey noises at around 1 p.m. A Black police officer – 'coloured' in the terminology of the day – who'd been seen by a single prisoner delivering 'a sharp kick' to a floored miner.

Because such moments were only mentioned once, rather than supposedly having been seen by everyone, and because they represented a variance from the limited vocabulary used in the majority of statements, they had a more visceral ring of truth and bore the bright flash and high definition of fresh memories, as opposed to the dull patina of hand-me-down stories.

Rex was also – he realised, after marking several with Post-it notes – collecting jokes.

There were some classics in amongst the interview transcripts.

Rex could see both sides.

In spite of everything he still felt a kind of painful solidarity with this cohort of past police colleagues. Enough to be embarrassed for them, anyway.

But you had to admire the insolence and the wit of one or two of the miners, and how they held up under pressure of interrogation.

File 3 included a transcript of the prisoner Neil MacWilliam being interviewed by Detective Constables Nathan Atherton and Bryce Dodd at Barnsley Police Station. MacWilliam denied interfering in the arrest of another miner, and in doing so he cut to the heart of the matter.

DC Atherton addresses MacWilliam: 'But we only have your word for that, don't we?'

'We only have his word for it!' MacWilliam retorts.

'Who do you mean?' asks DC Atherton.

'The PC who arrested me!'

'But whilst this incident was going off,' says DC Atherton, 'a uniform sergeant also saw the same things.'

'And we've only got his word for that and all,' is MacWilliam's defiant response.

Sometimes the insolence was laugh-out-loud funny.

And one or two performed like true comedians.

One particular highlight, a slow-burning 'gotcha' about Margaret Thatcher, was so good that Rex almost found himself reaching for the phone to share the joke with Lollo, before he remembered.

Annie would appreciate their cool irreverence and righteous insolence.

Maybe he could tell her one or two. But Rex was trying not to take work home with him too much at the moment.

When there was this much going on – the impending station closure, Lollo going missing, and now Rex's being summoned by the UCPI – they'd found that the quick after-work debrief could easily go on all evening, whether there was anything that really needed to be reported or not.

They both knew that at crucial moments and crunch points it could be vital to think out loud, to decompress and to seek your loved one's counsel. But Rex knew that he'd been overdoing it. The new responsibilities and workflows, the workaday routines and modestly elevated peer networks that had come with the promotion had not been unexpected, nor entirely unfamiliar given Lollo's mentoring, even if doing them 'for real' still brought a certain novelty value, for Rex at least.

Annie was proud of him, and so she hadn't wanted to say as much, but there were only so many stories about the vicissitudes – and let's face it the scant rewards – of divisional budget meetings that she could take before her eyes started glazing over.

Nonetheless, proud of Rex's achievements and enjoying his enthusiasm, Annie had indulged him for a while.

But then, late one evening, as Rex was doggedly pursuing some story that even as he told it he was realising might not be quite as funny as it had seemed at the time, he'd caught sight of her reflection in the window at the precise moment that she'd stifled a yawn.

Poor Annie!

That had been a bit of a shock to Rex; a wake-up call.

He'd changed the subject immediately, and been making much more effort ever since.

Annie was the best thing in his life. He wasn't about to drive her away by boring her to death with tedious anecdotes from work.

It was time to knock it on the head, and log off for the night.

He texted: 'On root' (their little joke). 'There in 5. Need anything?'

'Only you, Rexy,' she texted back. 'Hurry home. Got a surprise for you x'

Takeout and a surprise? Now she was talking.

He liked Annie's surprises.

One last thing. He added 'missing page 175?' to his to-do list.

He figured that while he had direct access to the NCA he might as well see how much clout they'd got.

In the event, finding the missing page 175 was the least of what the NCA were able to do.

But Rex's hunch proved to be correct.

Page 175 would in fact include a fleeting reference to PC Trevor McElroy finding an unconscious miner slumped against the wheel of a Doncaster coach in the Fitzwilliam Street car park, bleeding from head injuries. The injured miner was identified as William Cooper, a well-known shop steward from Cottonley, near Barnsley, but the identity of the individual who called an ambulance for the fatally injured Cooper from a phone in the Washington public house remained unknown. As Rex would discover, there were those who'd try (incorrectly, as it turned out) to make the case for it having been PC McElroy himself who made the 999 call. But they couldn't ask McElroy because he'd left the force following the Hillsborough disaster, moving first to Thailand, where he'd worked as a security consultant to UK companies seeking inward investment. He was last heard of retiring to northern Sri Lanka, where more recent attempts to trace him had failed. McElroy was thought to have been killed either in crossfire or in a bombing raid during the final brutal assault by Sri Lankan army divisions on the Tamil Tiger-held Eelam region in May 2009.

But if Rex thought that all of this – what henceforth they'd need to refer to as Leak Number One – was a lot to get his head around, he had another think coming.

But in the meantime, there'd be no prizes for guessing what Rex would dream about that night.

The dreams would be vivid and visceral.

So real that Rex could feel the fist to the jaw, the adrenaline surge.

Booting down a fence to escape from shield and baton blow.

So real he could feel the grit of the road on his face, and taste the blood.

He didn't know Sheffield city centre, so it was a Barker's Pool, a Division Street and a Devonshire Green of the mind that would fill the sleeping Rex's unconscious.

At one point he'd be a protester, running to try and get around a police cordon.

At another he'd be an officer putting a miner in a headlock and flooring him.

Then he'd be everyone at once: the myriad mind of King Mob flooding through the streets and squares of an imaginary city.

Then a shit and a shave, a quick coffee and a banana, and back to work.

'Your delivery's here,' said Jinks, the earlies EDO.

'What delivery?' said Rex.

'I dunno. Amazon?' said Jinks, indicating two – literally – pillow-sized Jiffy bags piled on the chair in the public-facing side of Interview Booth 1.

'Amazon?' said Rex. 'Are you joking, Jinksy? I'm not expecting anything. You know the rules! I wouldn't have it sent here anyway.'

'You're kidding.'

'No, I'm not. For fuck's sake, Eric. How long have you been doing this?'

'Oh shit,' said Jinks, picking up the phone with one hand and hitting the large red button marked 'BANDIT ALARM' with the other. 'Sorry, sir.'

The siren went off throughout the building immediately.

The sustained single thirty-second burst and the warbling tone differentiated the bandit alarm from the continuous ringing of the fire alarm. The building was now on lockdown until the threat was either repulsed or neutralised and the all-clear could be sounded: a ten-second burst of the same warbling tone.

Until then, everybody had to stay put. With the exception of the designated duty wardens, who would be scrambling for the stairs and the relevant departmental attendance lists even as they pulled on their hi-vis tabards. Everyone else had to remain on their floors. There would be no use of lifts, and no one coming in or out.

'Taskforce? This is Holborn desk,' said Jinks. 'We have a suspicious package in reception. Actually, no, we have two suspicious packages.'

Rex rolled his eyes. Statistically, of course, the packages probably didn't contain an explosive device, but who knew if or when some group – perhaps bearing the self-appointed prefix 'Dissident', 'Real' or 'Continuity' – might try and start things up again.

Jinksy must have been half-asleep.

You couldn't just randomly deliver a brace of pillow-sized Jiffy bags to individual police officers. And if you were EDO or, for that matter, in any public-facing role, you couldn't just *accept* random unexpected packages either.

But it was a while since the Letter Bomb Procedure had been in the forefront. And most Met personnel – Jinks included – would have joined the force after the Good Friday Agreement, so never served during the Troubles in any case.

And it was fair to say that more recent terrorist threats had seemed to prefer a more kinetic, hands-on approach than to entrust anything to the vagaries of today's Royal Mail.

There was a tatty laminated flowchart in the ED drawer ('What to look for: *wires, greasy marks on the packaging, an indistinct postmark.* What to listen for: *ticking…*') but Jinks wasn't wholly sure these days who if anyone actually held the key to that blast-proof reinforced concrete pit known as the bomb safe, in the sub-basement under the firing range.

And Rex didn't know either.

His mobile rang. It was Frankie.

'Morning,' said Rex.

'Hi, Rex. Just to follow up, NCA-wise. Lily Atwell will be the lead, and she's expecting to hear from you. Email's lily.atwell – one "T", two "L"s in Atwell – at the usual.'

'Thanks,' said Rex. 'Will do. Hang on.'

He opened his email, found the draft and did as Frankie suggested.

'Okay, done,' he said. 'Where are you? Upstairs?'

'Yes. Typical, eh?'

'I know,' said Rex.

'How about you?'

'I'm stood here looking at two suspicious packages,' said Rex. 'And for some reason they've got my name on them.'

'So it's your fault!' said Frankie, laughing. 'What's in them?'

'Not a clue. Just waiting for Taskforce and the dog team to get here. Hopefully we'll get the all-clear pretty sharpish once they do.'

Four hours later, Rex and Detective Sergeant Binder Singh were gloved up and in paper suits, in a specially requisitioned Clean Room that was retained for just such an eventuality as this, to provide a few hundred square feet of incident-ready real estate next to the old lab on the third floor.

Despite Jinks's protestations, and even though the packages had been addressed to Rex, because the EDO had signed for them, and in absence of any known owner, they were technically Jinksy's property. Rex had made him fill in an MG11 for each of the two Jiffy bags – 'Item 1 (one) of 2x...' and 'Item 2 (two) of 2x Packages contents unknown, delivered to Holborn Police Station front desk by persons unknown' – in order that they might be signed over so that Binder Singh, who'd been brought over on Exhibits, could admit them as evidence.

Working on three spotless table tennis tables acquired expressly for this purpose, Rex and Binder marked out and numbered a masking-tape grid across the surfaces. As each item was painstakingly removed from the Jiffy bag, it would be placed on its own numbered cell, where it would be photographed and a brief verbal description recorded, before being bagged up and individually recorded.

So far so good. But they'd been at it for half a day already, and barely scratched the surface.

And it would take Singh and a team of NCA programmers the best part of two weeks to catalogue the items fully. From the obvious paperwork, the materials appeared to relate to a TV documentary scheduled for Channel 4's generally hard-hitting news, current affairs and politics documentary series *Bulletin*, but never broadcast.

Greenlit in 2011, in the early days of the then still relatively new Conservative government of the day, the episode was to have been titled *The Riot That Never Was: Bulletin*.

It was a docudrama no less, or at least had been planned to contain some dramatic reconstructions.

Drawing on whistle-blower testimony and never-before-seen footage, the *Bulletin* programme-makers had tactically shifted focus away from Orgreave to another key moment of conflict in the strike: disturbances in Sheffield city centre on 7 May 1984 that had left a striking miner dead. A National Union of Mineworkers shop steward from the South Yorkshire coalfield had suffered head injuries that caused his death in hospital two days later. It was the programme-makers' contention that the events in Sheffield illustrated the same modus operandi of politicised policing, violence and evidence-tampering as Mansfield and Orgreave.

There was too much to take in. It was as if he'd been looking at a grainy and distorted photocopy of something and someone had flicked a switch and he was suddenly watching the Technicolor™ movie version with full Dolby Atmos® sound.

The episode had evidently been scripted and cast, with library and other footage sourced and cleared, and had progressed far along the production schedule when, following a raid on the production company's offices by police and security services, it had been pulled and injuncted late in 2014.

This material appeared to include copies and back-ups of everything seized, and perhaps some originals that had been overlooked or hidden. Materials that for whatever reason might have not made the cut, been dropped or trimmed from the film's central narrative.

There were letters, pitching documents and contracts, a heavily annotated working script, pages of notes and a folder containing scans of hundreds of contemporary newspaper cuttings, ranging from national broadsheets and tabloids to local and regional papers, not to mention local independents including the co-operatively produced former pro-trade union weekly the *Leeds Other Paper.*

There were hard drives, CDs and USB memory sticks containing archived emails, and rough cuts of news and library footage.

There was a folder containing approximately thirty 10x8 black-and-white prints that had been taken by a local amateur photographer on the scene. And it was hard to reconcile these rather static images with the descriptions Rex had been reading in police witness statements the previous day. The photos seemed to show an entirely different event. There were no dense and jostling crowds, and no rain of missiles, but police officers and demonstrators standing and talking, officers beckoning and pointing, a bit of pushing and shoving. One photo showed a table placed on what was clearly a paved pedestrianised street, bedecked with collection buckets, posters and placards for the 'Miners Support Fund on behalf of Sheffield Trades Council'. A handwritten note on a sticky paper label on the reverse read: 'Percy Riley on his usual pitch on Fargate'.

There were pages from the photographer's diary, and a letter he'd written at the time describing what he'd called – for his own or someone else's amusement – 'Scenes from a Sheffield Disco'. One photo showed 'PC Plod and our Terry doing the do-si-do', others bore the captions 'Let's twist again' or 'Jive Turkey'. One photo of a miner sitting dazed on the ground with a bloody nose was captioned 'Oops-upside-your-head'.

Later, Rex and Lily Atwell from the NCA would sit and watch CD after CD of news footage. They'd watch the speeches being made on a stage set up in front of the City Hall.

They'd watch footage of dozens of buses and coaches arriving, and of smiling miners piling out of them.

There was footage taken from a moving car. A single shot that showed fifty or more buses and coaches parked in the streets around the west end of the city. Coaches had come from Nottinghamshire and Fife, from Kent and County Durham. Coaches from Newstead, Bilsthorpe and Ollerton, from Easington, Ellington, Ashington and Wearmouth, from Thurnscoe and Cottonley, from Tilmanstone and Betteshanger, and a hundred or more other threatened communities.

With more than ten thousand striking miners in attendance, there'd have been as many as a couple of hundred coaches in all.

They'd watch lo-fi domestic VHS recordings of broadcast news footage that showed miners breaking down a fence somewhere on the west side of Fitzwilliam Street. The newscaster's voiceover telling how miners had broken fences to make weapons, describing striking miners throwing bricks and stones and other missiles to provoke the police, describing the mounted police units charging in response, before officers on foot were able to make arrests.

This was footage that had been edited to support the intended narrative of the day: that the violence had been planned, initiated by the miners, and reluctantly responded to by police in a measured and proportionate fashion.

Everyone who'd been there, every picket and protester, would have known that the order of the news footage had been reversed, but who would listen to them?

Anyone who'd been there would have known that police in snatch squads of three had been violently picking off marchers at will. That mounted police units had charged first in order to split the body of men into smaller groups. That there were rumoured to have been non-police personnel wearing police uniforms, under strict instructions to get stuck in but to leave the arresting to the regulars. That miners had broken fences to try and escape onto the wasteland that ran along the west side of Fitzwilliam Street. That miners had thrown bottles, cans and stones *in retaliation and self-defence*, which of course had only led to more arrests. One or two would have known that the stone-throwing had been initiated by UCOs.

The same techniques would demonstrably be used a week later for the Mansfield demonstration of 14 May, and a month after that by an emboldened South Yorkshire constabulary in the planning and execution of the larger pitched battles at Orgreave. And by other forces at every significant demonstration since, from the Battle of the Beanfield near Stonehenge on 1 June 1985 to the anti-poll tax demonstration – the so-called 'Poll Tax Riot' – in Trafalgar Square on 31 March 1990. And Rex knew this because unlike most of his colleagues he'd been at both of those incidents, and, what's more, he'd attended both as a civilian.

They were two events that it had turned out, chatting one night, he and Lollo had in common. Cliff Heath had already been transferred to Thames Valley but Lawrence had been behind the lines there on the A303 with Tommy Orwell's boys. Dishing out army surplus boiler suits and batons to young farmers, to the beaglers and the beaters, telling them to *Get stuck in!*

Rex's real-life experience had been part of why Lollo had put him forward for the SDS secondment in the first place. 'It's priceless, that is,' he'd said, 'real-world knowledge – London activist experience *and* a ready-made legend. You were there, and no one can argue wi that.'

Meanwhile, Lily Atwell from the NCA cyber team had left Rex a voicemail. He called her back.

'Hi, it's DI King at Holborn. Sorry I missed you,' he said when she picked up. 'Bomb scare.'

'I saw,' said Atwell. 'Everything okay?'

'Yeah. False alarm.'

'So, your email? Keyword analysis and all that?' she said, cutting to the chase. 'Yeah, no problem.'

She began to explain that they'd just need a control sample, which could be a corpus of police statements from a less contentious public order disturbance of around the same period; perhaps a football-related disorder. They'd analyse word frequency in-document first, to isolate any unusual keywords, words only used once or twice, then, by comparing in-document frequency with in-corpus relative occurrence frequency, they'd be able to further isolate a residue of non-common words and unusual or unique vocabulary from the 7 May literature.

'Great!' said Rex. He wondered how to break the news. 'Listen, events have taken over slightly. We've also received a load more material of the same event, it turns out: TV footage, the lot. Came in addressed to me this morning – those were the suspicious packages – and we're still going through it.'

'Oh?'

'We're calling it "Leak Number Two" for the moment,' said Rex. 'It's quite a haul. You might want to come and take a look. I mean, it needs to be seen to be believed. It appears there was a TV documentary in the works a couple of years back. You know, *Bulletin* on Channel 4? It looks like this is everything they'd got, bar the kitchen sink.'

'Wow.'

'I've got DC Singh on Exhibits, and we're taking over the Clean Room here for as long as it takes,' said Rex. 'Get everything catalogued.'

'Hmm,' said Atwell. 'Let me chat to the team and see if we can send someone over to help. Might be worth doing a conservation audit, then look at uploading it direct for rendering.'

'What's that?'

'Basic stuff, really. Put it all in one place, one format, get a crawler going through it to analyse the metadata, pull out any date and time tags in any medium – you know, like we did with the text, but a bit more sophisticated. Reskin Google Maps with as fine a mesh as we need, and run everything through a sequencer. Watch the flow, analyse vectors and turbulence. Bit of AI to fill in the gaps, you know, to help us see the wood for the trees. It looks at buildings, shadows, clouds, direction and temperature of light, wind speed, whatever, to predict where any untagged material fits. Get facial recognition on it and look for any matches. You know: the whole shebang. Then we just press "play" and output it in real time, plus scrobble and zoom functions of course.'

'Scrobble?' said Rex.

'Horizontal scrolling on an interactive progress bar,' said Atwell, 'so you can stop and start and move around in it at will. I take it we're talking about an investigative tool here, a rapid prototype rather than a polished presentation.'

'Yes, precisely,' he said. 'I'll need to get Churchill's sign-off, but I don't think that'll be a problem.'

'She'll know all this, anyway,' said Atwell. 'Woman's a legend.'

'Yeah, I know. But listen, this reminds me of that Operation Withern presentation from the NCA launch – d'you remember? All bells and whistles, amazing! It blew everyone away. Was that one of yours?'

'Before my time,' said Atwell. 'But I'm aware of the work. I only came over from Rathbone Square about six months post the NCA launch. And to be fair, if they were playing it at the launch, most of that work would have been done by the old Policing Improvement Team coders. Kind of a parting gift. But a few of my old Facebook colleagues would've crunched the metadata on those Withern convictions for you at their end.'

'Great,' said Rex.

He could remember when what was now Rathbone Square had been the Royal Mail's Western District Office on Rathbone Place. Rex couldn't quite decide if the transformation of Rathbone Place from the post to social media, from pen, paper and postage stamps to such a radically different scale and degree of information economy and surveillance, seemed apt or sacrilegious or both.

'But it's basically the same tech, you're right,' said Atwell. 'Same three-screen format. We'll bring a couple of workstations over, obviously. Same principle, probably, just a bit slicker now because we're getting better at it, and there's more to play with. Plus the machines are faster. Obviously, what you're looking at, we'd be drawing on a limited pool of data, and from the analogue age. So we're missing all the evidential gold from mobile phones: second-by-second movement, comms, photos, who's calling who…'

This wasn't news to Rex, he'd seen mobile tracking plotted in real time across city-wide demonstrations, but his blood still ran slightly cold at the thought. 'I'd like to add the witness statements to the mix too,' he said. 'Watch the flow of prisoners around the city? See how fast they're being processed. See if any particular station is skewing the stats.'

'Absolutely,' said Atwell. 'No problem. Bring it on.' She thought for a second. 'This Clean Room – I presume it's networked? Relatively up-to-date?'

'Pretty sure,' said Rex, looking at the trunking, a kind of digital dado rail that circled the walls at waist height.

'Well, we'll come and test it. May need to bring the engineers in and upgrade you. How many workstations could we get in there? Four?'

'Easily,' said Rex. 'Floor space might be an issue, though. Once you've seen it, let us know what you need and we can have whatever furniture and docking stations brought in, I don't know, probably tomorrow morning at a pinch.'

'Great,' said Atwell. 'But no bother. We'll bring in our own kit.'

'Even better.'

'We're used to parachuting in,' said Atwell. 'We'll be there in forty minutes to scope it out.'

'Okay, see you then.'

'Oh, one thing, just to check, is the material stable?'

'Yeah,' said Rex. 'Binder Singh's on it. He's scrupulous – best Exhibits Officer we've got. We've just admitted the lot, and he's going to start bagging and tagging.'

'Great,' said Atwell. 'But cease immediately, no disrespect. Don't touch *any* of the media now until I get there. We'll need to do a full conservation audit first, to see what if any archiving and restoration needs there are before we copy everything. We'll bring the portable tape kiln. No use playing an old VHS tape if it gets chewed up first time, eh?'

'That's music to my ears,' said Rex. 'By the book is how we like it. I reckon we're secure until then.'

'Roger that. See you in a bit.'

'Yep, see ya.'

He debriefed Singh on the call, and did a quick visual check that they hadn't already fucked up. No, thank Christ. Then sent the DS off for some coffees from the canteen. They'd better get used to this room. It looked as if they were going to be here for a while.

Amongst the plethora of items in Leak Two, he'd recognised one thing immediately: a stack of A4 papers, folders one to twenty-seven. Not dissimilar at first glance to the witness statements that had comprised Leak One, and which he'd been poring over the day before. He wondered what process he was looking at here. In a trial of that magnitude, with multiple defendants, how many copies would have been made? There'd be file copies and back sheets for each of the clerks in whichever chambers it was, plus one set for each of the barristers on the defence and prosecution teams. Would each of the individual accused also have a copy of their own particular file? He'd better check the legal procedure with Francis Bland or his clerk.

Detective Inspector Rex King was still gloved up.

On a hunch he carefully lifted the pages and rifled gently through them without disturbing the stack.

Page 175 was missing here too.

Then he leafed forward through the papers until he reached File 20.

Yes!

On pages 233 and 234 were the same pencil annotations to the witness statement of Dronfield PC Anthony Chase in the form of underlinings of certain passages that described the accused Terence Riddell holding a piece of wood. In the following pages were more annotations, hand-drawn asterisks and underlinings of Chase and other officers' accusations that Riddell had been planning to use the piece of wood as an offensive weapon. An accusation that Rex knew, because he'd read the interview, would be strenuously and repeatedly denied by Riddell under sustained pressure and leading questioning by Chase and others.

Rex could see that these annotations would have been made by the defence barrister or their team, because they were certainly to Riddell's advantage. Together they demonstrated that none of the officers had actually witnessed *any* attempt to use the stick as an offensive weapon, and in fact only Chase had even claimed to have seen Riddell holding it.

Had the trial not collapsed en masse, Rex had a feeling that the defence had been feeling lucky with Riddell. Perhaps they'd felt that there was enough here to have him acquitted. And perhaps that could have precipitated other acquittals, because all the charges were demonstrably nonsense.

No wonder the whole house of cards had come tumbling down.

And there was one thing of which DI Rex King was now certain.

This wasn't just another run-out of the same documents, collated for another actor in the trial, but an actual copy of the exact same set that comprised what they were now referring to as Leak Number One: Binders 1 and 2, which now seemed paltry, piffling by comparison with this new tsunami of data.

Standing there in the Clean Room, hearing Singh's footsteps coming down the corridor outside, Rex felt that familiar sudden rush of elation that came with any solid breakthrough, but he wasn't about to show it.

He turned away from the table and looked out at the buildings on the opposite side of Lamb's Conduit Street. Then without thinking he evened up his feet, settled into a standing meditation stance, centred his breathing – *breathe in, and breathe out* – and took a moment to gather himself.

In the fluorescent-lit offices over the road, shirtsleeved men and women were working at their desks, talking, typing, looking at screens.

Rex already knew the origins of Leak Number One, though he hadn't let on, hadn't said anything to Churchill or any of the others, and wasn't about to.

Now, more than that – and this was beyond doubt – he also knew with absolute stone-cold certainty the identity of the South Yorkshire constabulary whistle-blower at the heart of the *Bulletin* documentary.

And he knew that one other person would know it too. Wherever he was.

The door squeaked as DS Binder Singh elbowed his way in with the coffees.

'Alright, Kingsy? No sugar, isn't it.'

'Yes, Binder. Milk, no sugar. Thanks,' said Rex, turning back from the window.

He took a sip of the coffee and thought for a second.

He looked at his watch, then added, 'Okay, she'll be here in twenty minutes. Buckle in, mate. I think this is going to be fun.'

II

II

11: Bourrache (Borage)

[REWIND] —

It would be a fable to confound **Aesop**, or maybe more like a tragedy: when **nymph** turns Nemesis.

Rex leaned back in his seat as the plane accelerated and took off. The cabin rumble and the sound of the undercarriage hydraulics added to the sense of anticipation. But always at take-off there it was in the back of your mind: the tiny statistical possibility of system failure.

And the knowledge that if anything went wrong, you'd be **toast**.

To take his mind off it he looked out of the window and counted swimming pools. Rex had always found it both soothing and surprising, flying out of Gatwick and seeing so many people, rich as **Croesus**, with their own pools. He loved this time of year. May, when all the leaves were on the trees once more. Then he found his eye drawn to the out-of-town hotels, supermarkets and business parks serviced by the motorway. The M25 away to the north and just visible in the haze until concealed again by cloud.

And now they were flying blind.

He'd planned to travel light, his single **hold-all** safely stowed in the overhead baggage locker, but he wasn't travelling alone. Who exactly he was travelling with was another matter entirely. And she'd brought a ton of baggage.

He hadn't even known her for a year, but Rex's **horse sense** had well and truly deserted him. Who'd have thought **Calamity Jane** here – in the seat next to him, and holding his hand no less, who'd enjoyed last night's pre-holiday treat of *Ravioli di borragine e ricotta* just as much as he had – was herself an **agitator**, with a mission as yet unclear. Though step one had clearly been to **pursue**, to seduce, to **envelop** him in a loving embrace. And then what?

Rex was not unaware of the irony. So this was what it felt like to discover that the person you've come to love is not who they say they are. You could **adhere** to your own codes of behaviour and assumptions all you liked. Minding your own business in your own little world. Only then to discover that you are utterly beholden to the machinations of agencies and imperatives unknown.

But isn't that always the case? Like the deep-sea **diver**, unaware of the **gale** blowing on the surface? Or the **inmates** of some asylum, so involved in the comforts and assurances of their own private rituals that the power struggles of the wider world go unnoticed, until a giant hand reaches in and takes the roof off.

It was such a shame they'd have to end it, although Rex couldn't see what choice he had.

But you can't dump someone who's not really there. You can't ghost a ghost.

That was what this trip was about. There'd need to be a bit of – like the song said – *getting to know you*. But for real this time. A long weekend to work things through, well out of reach of work. Which for Rex meant being well out of the reach of Lollo.

And what exactly was in it for her?

That was what Rex hoped to find out. Because right now, with the plane banking to turn towards the English Channel, he was all too aware that he could neither **impugn** nor **construe** motivations that remained as yet so resolutely hidden.

Like in that old parlour game. If you'd asked him a month ago what **sort** of animal his lover was and why, he might have said a **Persian cat** – beautiful, languorous and sensual – but now, and as far as Rex was concerned, she was a bitch who could be bought with a **dog biscuit**.

It **sticks** in the craw – he thought to himself – being so thoroughly deceived.

Rex had always thought of himself as the outsider. A **black sheep** in the force, one of the good guys, going against the institutional grain. But this unexpected turn of events had made it clear that he was not an outsider at all. Or if he was, it made no difference. He was simply fair game. And for all his tradecraft, he was transparent enough to have been played. He'd been well and truly outmanoeuvred.

He was the one who was meant to dish it out, not be on the receiving end.

He knew all this, but still it wouldn't be easy.

He'd grown to love even her scent, and the bottle left on the shelf in his bathroom. Once or twice he'd even given a quick squirt into the air when she wasn't there, just to feel her presence in the flat.

But now he felt manipulated, groomed. It was textbook ingratiation: step by step, the imitation of intimacy.

And it worked too; every time.

First you leave a toothbrush, then a bottle of perfume, and maybe your favoured brand of coffee. And before you know it you've become part of the warp and weft of the target's life. And it's not even that they simply can't imagine how they ever got along without you. More than that: they start projecting you into their own future. He knew how these routines went, but that hadn't stopped him falling for them, and for her.

She was wearing the same scent now. She'd bought the *parfum* in duty free. But it was a wonder that those **aromatic** floral notes on that cinnamon-and-sandalwood base didn't turn sour, when all along the lies had been seeping from her every **pore**.

12: Valériane (Valerian)

[FAST-FORWARD] —

The investigation was a **dead duck**, every road a dead end. And it didn't matter how many times the Chief Superintendent might lose her temper or pull rank, they still hadn't found Jethro Lawrence.

To say that Detective Sergeant Melissa Shepherd was **disappointed** with the lack of progress investigating the 'ambiguous disappearance' of the senior Met officer hardly covered it. Right now she wanted nothing more than to drive down to Bosham with a box of basics, pull shut the hatch on the **companion-way** and take that two weeks' annual leave she'd had to postpone. Maybe treat herself to a nice steak and a glass or two of wine to wind down on the first night, but then just live out of tins, drink soothing herbal teas and not set foot on land for as long as she could manage. To sit out on deck on a **calm** summer night with a good book, getting bitten to buggery, and then to pull down the hatch and listen to some **Elgar**, or – current favourite – the RCA recording of Verdi's operatic *Othello* with Plácido Domingo. It made a change from the rock 'n' roll she played in the car, that got her through the working day.

She didn't consider herself the yachting type, but with much of her childhood spent at her maternal grandparents' house in Chichester, boats had simply been a fact of life. They'd even had sailing lessons at school, and somehow, when the wind had changed, she'd found that the love of sailing had stuck. And while it didn't wholly **vanquish** the old vicissitudes, she'd found over the years that a few nights afloat could temporarily **offset** them.

What was it about this investigation? You could hardly call it a **mess**. That was the problem. It was too neat. He might as well have been abducted by aliens.

Looking for Lawrence had been like looking for a non-existent needle in a haystack. A month after the disappearance they'd had to **halve** the number of officers on the case, so now it was just Shepherd, Keyes and Gosling down in Sussex, with whatever PCSOs they could blag, and King and Singh on hand as and when needed in London, with Chief Superintendent Tabitha Churchill apparently swanning in and out whenever she felt like it.

Stupid cow, thought Melissa – with her instinctive mistrust of the motivations of any top brass – thinking she's still a detective.

When Churchill, DI King and Evelyn Gummer had swept into town for the press conference it had been almost comical, like royalty visiting.

Shepherd and King had exchanged knowing glances.

King was alright. He seemed like a stand-up guy. Though there was now supposedly a bit of a cloud over his head with the UCPI, for those in the know. And lately he'd been almost impossible to get hold of.

While he'd still been part of the investigation, Sergeant Teddy Thomas, still rankling from the bollocking he'd received on his first visit to Holborn, but more confident of the **mores** on his home turf, had taken to calling Churchill 'Her Majesty'. And Melissa had not attempted to correct him.

'Aye-aye,' he'd said under his breath as the chauffeured Met Range Rover purred to a stop outside the Old Dairy housing development. '**Queen's Flight**'s arrived.'

But it had been an eye-opener to have the sophisticated PR machine of the Met at their disposal. Melissa Shepherd liked Gummer. And the Comms Chief's media strategy had certainly worked. It was the only thing that *had* worked, in as much as it had put the investigation on the news. And what that meant these days was that a single BBC News package edited for both BBC Sounds and TV use was recycled dozens, no hundreds, *thousands* of times through the following twenty-four hours on all platforms, not just the six and tens, but all BBC News channels, commercial local radio and the World Service, the BBC News and ITN websites and social media. If you were alive in the UK and not in a coma that week, you'd have seen numerous variations on this theme. A clip of the press conference, with a montage of footage showing Jethro Lawrence speaking from the podium at an ACPO conference a few years back, or leaving the High

Court after giving evidence in the trial of the three officers acquitted of the unlawful killing of Trevor Tennyson. A prerecorded interview with Churchill outside New Scotland Yard, telephoto footage of Lawrence's abandoned car in the tree-lined nursery driveway, and an appeal to the public from Shepherd, who was quickly and quite frankly sick of the sight of herself.

ITN had a slightly different slant, while Channel 4 News played up Lawrence's early days in the South Yorkshire force – unearthing footage of a young and **studious**-looking Lawrence in shirtsleeves as part of a South Yorkshire contingent in the background of the press conference following the arrest of Peter Sutcliffe.

The campaign had had the anticipated effect: the phones hadn't stopped ringing. It seemed as if every freak in the country had phoned the hotline to unravel their particular pet conspiracy theory, then posted it on Facebook or Twitter. The disappearance bore all the hallmarks of Mossad, they said. It was the Serbs. It was the Iranian Revolutionary Guard. It was the Iraqis. It was the Russians. It was the Syrians. It was the Saudis. It was Al-Qaeda or Daesh or IS, or some factional power struggle therein. It was related to Brink's-Mat. It was the lizard people. It was MI5 or MI6. It was a hoax. Many suggested that it was related to the death of David Kelly. Others invoked the unsolved murder of Jill Dando. It was trafficking gangs, organised crime, or the IRA. Or all three working in cahoots. Numerologists, telepaths and mediums weighed in. Flat Earthers. Details of Melissa Shepherd's clothing and her appearance were interrogated; were rated; were inappropriate; were a sophisticated code. Bot farm accounts implicated Lawrence in conspiracy theories involving members of the Royal Family, the EU, the UN, the WHO, the IMF, the World Bank, NATO, Jeremy Corbyn, and George Soros. All of it mendacious time-wasting nonsense, but it all had to be processed, sifted, logged; each source cross-checked and verified, their respective motivations quickly assessed.

So Gummer's strategy had worked in one way, but in every other sense it had drawn a great big zero. They were still no closer to actually finding the missing DCI. Within forty-eight hours of the press conference any official reference to the investigation or the police appeals to the public would be accompanied only by the image of the abandoned car, its open door taunting them. They needed a new approach.

The Detective Chief Inspector hadn't been Shepherd's first missing person, but he was the only MisPer she hadn't found – or found the remains of – within the magic one month.

While Teddy Thomas's team continued to search in woodlands to the east of the nursery and in nearby Petworth Park, Sussex had also drafted in a more senior PolSer Coordinator from Brighton, and working together they'd redone dogs and aerial, the full 3D routine – up and down, side to side – but all teams had failed to identify any further target areas. Lawrence's not being a West Sussex local made it challenging to create a sense of public ownership of the search.

But then Gummer had earned her salary. She and one of the BBC News editors had concocted a classic shoulder-to-shoulder lateral search against the backdrop of Petworth House, more for the cameras than with any hope of actually finding anything. Any police officer with a modicum of experience knew that such searches were usually counterproductive: destroying more evidence than they found, with research showing that participants generally lost focus and concentration within 500 metres. But the PR value of this footage – a police operation in the grounds of a beautiful stately home – was undeniable, and the 'Downton effect' thus created did **allow** them to leverage a further thirty seconds of airtime not only on the nationals but around the world. The video clip and a single defining photo (a line of police in traditional 'village bobby' tit-head helmets and hi-vis stretched across the lawn, with the baroque majesty of 'the English Versailles' in the background) had gone viral – Gummer showed them the stats. There'd been hundreds of thousands of posts and shares every minute. But the story itself had slipped off to a regional-only graveyard, before drying up entirely. A reconstruction was discounted. Why **hire** in an actor when there's nothing to see but a dark car on a dark road on a dark night. Perhaps if Lawrence had been driving a classic old Mk2 it might have been memorable. With their distinctive domed cabin, chrome flash and rasping engine, those beauties could still stop traffic – park one anywhere and it'd draw a crowd – but it would take the **secular** zeal of a fanatical motoring enthusiast, or the dispassionate gaze of an ANPR camera, to remember seeing a modern Jag XE.

Airport protocols had been actioned, but when Lawrence's passport had turned up in the first office sweep, they hadn't been pursued.

Whether Lollo had been the **author** of his own disappearance or it had been **accomplished** by some as yet unidentified individual, or band of **merry men**, was uncertain. And Shepherd still hadn't ruled out either possibility. Although no explicit preparations for departure seemed to have been made, and the fact that all known phone, email and bank accounts had immediately flatlined suggested a worst-case scenario.

So what did they have? That a phone call had been received on Lawrence's personal iPhone from an untraceable mobile number – most likely a burner – on the evening before he'd vanished. That according to the Jag's data cache he'd made an emergency stop in a CCTV blind spot on Chrisp Street in Poplar while driving back from the Canary Wharf Waitrose at 9 p.m. two days before that – but scraps of fox fur and vulpine DNA in the wheel arch seemed to account for that. There'd been a flurry of excitement when the carpet in the vehicle's boot was found to be damp, but a quick search of Jaguar forums showed that water **ingress** into the boot floor of an XE was a not uncommon issue, even on special editions.

In spite of the investigative inertia, Shepherd felt as if she'd got to know Jethro Lawrence quite well: the tasteful décor of his early-Victorian terrace, and his taste in classical music. But she knew that this was an illusion: she didn't know him at all. And she still didn't know what had happened. But the simple fact of the matter was that on the night in question he'd driven direct from Bow to Petworth, via the M25 and M23, as far as the Pease Pottage interchange, where he'd picked up the A264 and A272 – pretty much the route Shepherd had driven in reverse when she'd given Rex King and Binder Singh a lift back to Gatwick on day one. Keyes had pulled in representative footage of the vehicle at almost every stage of the journey, plus ID and photos from half a dozen speed cameras.

So he'd driven fast, garnered enough speeding offences to lose a civilian their licence, but that didn't mean much.

He had a fast car; a new toy, moreover. So what?

It seemed that the last thing Lawrence had done at home that evening had been signing an online petition to **oppose** the building of a **casino** near the Ragged School Museum on Copperfield Road, opposite the Mile End sports ground. Hardly the actions of a desperate man.

It was starting to look as if all they had left was PC Hoffman's engine block and crank-shaft, which both turned out to be from a circa 1980 OHC-type Ford Transit.

'OHC?' Shepherd had asked. 'Enlighten me, please.'

'Overhead cam shaft, ma'am,' said Hoffman. 'As opposed to overhead valve – your two basic varieties of Transit at the time. OHC being simpler, and more powerful.'

And on further inspection, the question that these automotive parts posed was not yet whether they were relevant to the investigation, or why someone might **dump** Transit van parts in a hop-pole dipping bath in West Sussex, nor even whether they'd come from the same vehicle. The question was why someone had gone to the bother of removing the serial number from the engine block.

Take that, Tabitha Churchill.

13: Carpe (Carp)

[REWIND] —

As soon as they'd checked in and shut the door of the hotel room behind them, Rex and Annie would drop everything and do what any couple with their relationship on the ascendancy would do. But first they had to land.

The plane began its descent then turned when it hit the coast. Rex craned his neck to look out of the window, searching for familiar shapes of coastline and mountain. Did everyone do that? Strain to reconcile what they were seeing – mountains, parched Mediterranean landscape, terracotta rooftops, a coast road – with something half-remembered? How long was it since he'd last been here? Both too long and long enough.

From the moment they'd flown past the red **radar** scanner at the end of the runway and touched down, the air had taken on a different quality. There was something about the smell and the heat and the light; the brightness of the sea, and a quality of the air that he'd forgotten.

It was beautiful. It felt like coming home: to **bask** in this heat and sun for a few days.

And suddenly Rex had a new earworm, sung to a long-forgotten soca beat: 'Feeling Hot, Hot, Hot' by **Arrow**.

'Well, that was easy,' said Annie as they waited in the line for a taxi. 'Getting away.'

If the heat had made Rex instantly relax, the sun-warmed skin and the **dewy** sheen of sweat was also making both of them feel horny. Although, right now, everything was making them feel horny. Even being pregnant was making Annie feel horny, at least when she wasn't feeling sick. And the fact that Annie was pregnant was making Rex feel horny. It wasn't only vanity, the confirmation of his continuing virility, but also that they didn't have to worry about Annie getting pregnant any longer, so could have as much unprotected sex as they wanted. They threw each other **sidelong** glances in the back seat of the cab from the airport, her hand on his knee, shoulders brushing.

Rex had gone for his monthly haircut the day before.

'**Thatch** on you,' the barber had said. 'That's a good thick head of hair.'

'Glad I don't take after my dad,' Rex had said. 'He went bald in his early twenties.'

'You sure he's your dad?' the barber had joked.

'Don't!' said Rex. 'That actually happened to a friend of mine.'

As the taxi sped up into the hills, both of their ears popped.

It was starting to feel like a holiday.

It wasn't a holiday.

There was more to it than that: much more at stake than simple relaxation.

Annie, if that's what her name was – and he'd seen her passport now, the one she was fanning herself with – had promised to tell him everything. And in return she'd asked the same of him.

Well, what was Rex going to say to that? He knew this was something that had to be done, that it was a task to which no man could be appointed in his **stead**. So he'd said *Yes.*

But Rex was a policeman. He could lie with the best of them.

The other condition Annie had imposed was to go abroad, that the negotiations should take place out of reach of Rex's work, so no one could **boss** him about. They would take that break they'd been promising themselves, and she didn't want Lollo spoiling it.

'Okay,' Rex had said, 'it's a deal. Where?'

'South of France?' Annie had suggested. 'Flights to Nice are really cheap right now.'

'I have an idea,' he'd said. 'Trust me?'

A place from his past, he'd said. Somewhere that meant a lot to him.

'I'd better trust you,' Annie had said, looking down at her bump. 'Considering.'

Rex's usual style was not to allow anyone to **delve** too deeply – not even Helen had been allowed too close. But now, if he and Annie were to move forward together, the opposite was needed. So that was what they were going to get, overlooking an azure sea: a **torrent** of truth. No, torrents **plural**: a two-way street, in which no honest thought or word would go **unheard**.

But that could wait, because between them and the hotel there was a bric-a-brac market on a few tables around the village-square car park, and they thought they may as well amuse themselves by browsing one or two of the stalls, since it was on the way.

But a bit of teamwork was required here too.

Rex was in his element, and attacked with the training of a child who'd been brought up knowing how to work a good jumble sale. He was also slim enough, lifting his hold-all above the fray, to squeeze **edgeways** between the stalls, while Annie-and-her-bump was content to saunter at more of a distance, pulling her wheelie-case behind her and pointing things out for Rex to investigate.

Rex began flicking through boxes of antique postcards, which included a full set of glamourous 1960s modernist advertising photographs for the Citroën DS, and older black-and-white pictures of farmers, peasant children, women in national costume, and churches.

All of life was here. There was a set of **Indian** brass cups, dope dealers' scales, the long-separated constituent parts of various archaic coffee makers, stuffed freshwater fish mounted in dusty tanks of glass and mahogany, a cardboard box of **Zeus**-brand derailleurs, handlebars, bottom brackets, seat pins and sundry other vintage bicycle components. There were snuff boxes, cigarette lighters, a 1941 J. M. Dent & Sons Ltd edition of James Boswell's *The Journal of a Tour to the Hebrides* – with **Doctor Johnson**, of course – that still bore the imprimatur, classifications and loan record from Ruislip Library, and was due to have been returned on 11 August 1962. There were two boxes of detective novels, translations of Agatha Christie. On one table was laid out a history of the French Revolution in thirteen volumes, a single character on the spine of each spelling out 'LA*REVOLUTION'. There were umbrella stands, coat racks and coal scuttles, countless wine glasses and other glassware – jugs, bowls and vases – categorised by size and colour, aquaria and goldfish bowls, a tall pale-blue enamel jug or pitcher, miniature copper saucepans of arcane shape and function, and a box containing dozens of brightly coloured school-issue fountain pens. There was a framed colour print of an **osprey** coming in to land on its treetop nest, and, bizarrely, a recently published colour prospectus for the proposed **Swansea Tidal** Lagoon.

Annie bought a small and decoratively moulded velvet-lined **shellac** jewellery box, that felt impossibly light to the touch.

'What are you going to put in there?' asked Rex.

'Not sure yet,' said Annie. 'Maybe it's not for me.'

Rex showed her a large unframed black-and-white photo mounted on board, of a cowboy at a rodeo.

'**Lasso** you,' he said. Was that a song lyric? He couldn't remember.

'Look,' said Annie with a nudge, pointing out the stuffed, mounted and rather moth-eaten head of an **eland** that plainly needed a bit of TLC. 'He's got the horn. Poor thing.'

'I know how he feels,' said Rex.

'Shall we check in?' said Annie.

'Is that an **educated** guess?'

They'd made love the minute they got to the hotel room. First with Annie **bestride**, and then from behind. **Cramp** in his leg forced a change to sideways for a bit, then Rex on top, and bloody hell she was practically **double-jointed**.

Hot, hot, hot, indeed.

This was going to be quite a week.

It was just a shame that he was going to have to spoil it.

14: Fusain (Spindle tree)

[FAST-FORWARD] —

When Rex's phone rang, he was on his way to meet Tabitha Churchill, **Francis** Bland QC and Evelyn Gummer. It was D-Day, affidavit day. He hadn't read it yet, but they would have done. At least it got him out of the Clean Room for an hour or two.

'King,' he said, habitually, but he knew who was on the other end. 'Hi, Melissa. How's it going?'

With Lollo still missing, and Rex moved sideways, he had been content to let DS Shepherd take the investigative lead, but to **ably** assist if and when needed. As their respective roles and responsibilities had **crystallised**, where others might have bridled, Rex hadn't resisted, and it hadn't taken long for him to **settle** into the more collegiate position – when he could – of long-distance sounding board.

Shepherd was impressive. Her grasp of police process at every level was **masterly**, and Rex had told her, during at least one of their chats, that he could do with excellent officers like her in his own division. That she was wasted in Sussex. That even if not Holborn, there might be more prospects for promotion in the Met.

'Thank you, sir,' she'd said. 'I'll take that as a compliment. But there's important work to do down here too, you know.'

'There is,' Rex had conceded. 'It's just spread more thinly.'

But this wasn't one of their scheduled catch-ups. They weren't due to talk until tomorrow.

'Listen, I can't talk for long, Melissa,' said Rex. 'I'm just going into a meeting' – he paused for a second to find the most neutral phrase – 'on an unrelated matter.'

'Understood,' said Shepherd. 'It can wait. Just wanted to give you the heads-up. For God's sake don't tell Churchill, and I don't know how this is likely to **unfold**, but I'm coming round to the "cockamamie speculation".'

Rex laughed. He knew exactly what she meant.

It was their shorthand for Hoffman's idea. A phrase that had been coined by an incandescent Tabitha Churchill during her unwarranted putdown of Teddy Thomas in Meeting Room 6B – regarding the crank-shaft and engine block's relevance to the investigation, and Hoffman's seemingly groundless, a priori assumption that the missing Detective Chief Inspector Jethro Lawrence's presence at the nursery was thus somehow related.

'In cloud-bloody-cuckoo-land, maybe,' she'd added.

Well, she would say that, and it may have been a 'cockamamie speculation', but what else did they have?

Today's meeting was in Churchill's office, the inner sanctum on the tenth floor, and it had started without Rex. Pre-meets were not generally a good sign, but not unexpected in the circumstances.

'Go in,' said Frankie.

Rex's pet theory, or one of them, that the higher up the Met you went in terms of rank, the more **mannered** and idiosyncratic – décor-wise – the office, was borne out by Churchill's, which had been furnished with flair and **elan**. Rex supposed that the laissez-faire organisational attitude towards grand, antique desks in cherry wood and leather – as here – and to green-gold-and-white-striped wallpapers, the antique rugs and the personal selections of prints and paintings from the force's own not insubstantial art collection, was intended to somehow soften the pain of higher rank. The **nearer** you got to God, it would seem – or his representative on earth, the Commissioner of the Metropolitan Police – the more such symbols or consolations of power were required.

Rex had been up here before many times, of course, but not in quite the current strained circumstances.

It was a chance to look again at Churchill's pick of the Met's collection. On the wall behind her desk was a large nineteenth-century map – hand-drawn and coloured – of the old Bow Street Sub-Division, the Met's and UK policing's historical heartland, with its famous Runners. The Sub-Division stretched from Charing Cross Road to the Royal Courts of Justice, and from the River Thames up to Theobalds Road. Basically the rooftops that you'd see out of Churchill's office window if you craned your neck to the left a bit. There were also framed First World War-era black-and-white photographs of the Met's first female police cadets – dressed to the **nines** in their 'fruit bowl' helmets and Sam Brown belts – and of the telephone exchange at Scotland Yard; and 'Sefton Returns', a colour photograph of the army horse that had survived terrible injuries in the Hyde Park bombing of 1982, being led, **riderless**, to inspect the large pile of public donations sent during his recovery.

Rex remembered seeing the bombing on the news, and in the papers. It had seemed remote, the pictures carefully edited to spare the full horror.

Now, of course, like any police or emergency services officer who'd found themselves on duty during the terrorist attacks on London's public transport network that became known as '7/7' – 7 July 2005 – he knew exactly what it might have been like for those on the ground.

Rex took a seat, and Churchill nodded in greeting. There was no need for introductions; they all knew why they were here.

The Chief Superintendent had evidently elected to be **postmistress**, delivering the bad news. She pushed the brown envelope across her desk toward Rex.

He undid the string fastening and took out the document, in full knowledge that in doing so his life had just changed, and taken on a yet graver, and soon more public, aspect.

If he felt nervous, it was more the **fear** of making a wrong step.

It was like that old childhood game of **Mousetrap**, where one false move sets off a chain of events – activating all manner of marbles, springs and levers – until the plastic basket drops…

No, that wasn't it. Because the false step had already been taken, and long ago.

That Rex was sitting here right now was the culmination of decisions made in the stress of the field nearly a decade and a half earlier. And the challenge here wasn't to avoid setting off the trap, whose machinery trundled inexorably towards him at this very moment.

That ship had sailed.

No, the challenge here was to dodge or deflect whatever **dessert**, just or otherwise, the machine had in mind for him.

And if you had to choose a team to help you do that, you couldn't do much better than the three people sitting in front of him: Chief Superintendent Tabitha Churchill, Met Comms Chief Evelyn Gummer and Francis Bland Esq. QC, as Rex would come to know him from his email address autofill on Outlook. If Lollo weren't missing, he'd probably have been here too, in his capacity as Rex's line manager.

'Shall I read it now?' Rex asked.

'We'll give you time to read it in full later,' said Churchill. 'Francis, do you want to outline the process – what you're looking for at least in the first instance?'

Now it was Bland's turn to dispense gifts, as he slid a pack of fluorescent highlighter pens and a wodge of Post-its across the desk.

'Yes, certainly,' he said. 'We're not asking you to spin a tale, DI King, or to ameliorate the contents. You're a senior police officer, not a **perjurer**. We're all grown-ups. These things happen. Put two red-blooded and similarly sexually orientated adults together in a confined space for long enough and they will often tend to find reasons to fall in love. I'd suggest that once we're finished here you take the rest of the day to read this through carefully. You could make a useful start by highlighting anything you fundamentally agree or disagree with. Use a different colour for each. I don't know, green for yes, pink for no. But also look for events and descriptions where your own recollections of the time are at variance with the claimant, mark them out and note down your version on a Post-it.'

'Okay,' said Rex. 'Understood.'

'But by all means,' said Gummer, 'have a quick skim-read now. We can give you five minutes. And tell us any first impressions – how it makes you feel.'

Gummer's gift was a box of tissues that he hadn't noticed until now.

Did they expect him to cry?

It was probably par for the course, but he wasn't going to give them the satisfaction.

'I don't suppose you still have your notebooks from the period in question?' said Bland. 'Obviously completely understandable if not.'

Oh yes, thought Rex, I've still got the notebooks alright; but he said nothing.

He quickly scanned the ten-page document.

IN THE UNDERCOVER POLICING INQUIRY

WRITTEN OPENING STATEMENT of

Helen

For a moment the room began to spin: Helen?

Helen had fucked him over?

He'd been expecting to see the name Amelia; not Helen, but Amelia Alison Johnson.

But then he read on.

'For the purposes of this inquiry,' it began,

I have been given the name 'Helen'. I have been granted anonymity, and invited to become a Core Participant in the Undercover Policing Inquiry because I was deceived into a long-term sexual relationship by an undercover officer in the SDS/NPOIU whom I met within the Peace Movement and know only by his cover name of Martin Thorn.

Phew!

Thank Christ for that!

It *was* Amelia.

But that was weird. Why would she take the name Helen? It could only be to have a pop at his ex. And that rang warning bells. Rex's mind started racing. How had Johnson found out the name of his former partner? How long was she going to be in the country? Were Helen and the girls safe? How quickly could they get special schemes put on their phone numbers? They'd have to be told—

Tabitha Churchill, perhaps knowing a little of Rex's personal life, said quietly but firmly, 'A technical point, DI King: Core Participants are allocated their inquiry aliases alphabetically and at random. The only way they could have any say in it would be in the unlikely event that they coincidentally drew a match. And I don't believe that's happened. Not to date, anyway.'

Rex nodded, 'Sure', keeping the overwhelming sense of relief to himself.

The affidavit was rather impersonal, but 'Helen'/Amelia was recounting events and meetings that he remembered well.

Rex found that he missed her, and the life they could have had together, a life that briefly had seemed to be opening out before them.

Was that the kind of feeling that Gummer was looking for? Genuine and lasting affection? It would be an unexpected gambit, perhaps.

Turning the pages, Rex was looking out for names at first, and significant public events and people. They were all here: **Plum**, the Hackney anti-nuclear protests, his and the Core Participant's not-so-accidental meeting at the anti-Iraq War march of 2002, **Tobias** the UCO masquerading as a rave impresario.

There was a lot about Scotland, of course.

And as well as the obvious stuff, she'd highlighted the trip to **Arran** that had really cemented their relationship, the visit to the Pitlochry Dam and **salmon ladder**. How he'd seemed strangely **recalcitrant** at first, but then his moving in with her, and how she'd introduced him to her friends. That *their song* had been 'Sex Bomb' by **Tom Jones**. She wrote about his reaction when she'd said she was pregnant. His proposal of marriage. His frequent disappearances, and her suspicions that he was having an affair.

Now the shock of the contact, and discovering that he hadn't even been a real person, but a police officer doing a job.

That two of the most cherished years of her life had been a lie. And all the years since, when she'd punished herself, thinking it was her fault things hadn't worked out.

That she'd worshipped and adored him, and he'd shamelessly allowed her to demonstrate her love.

That she was now glad in retrospect that she'd miscarried.

That the revelation had made her loathe and despise the baby they'd lost, whom she'd so loved.

That she'd contemplated suicide on more than one occasion.

That she now mistrusted authority, mistrusted the police and other state institutions, and found it hard to make new friends. That she questioned the reality of even her existing friendships, knowing that there was a high likelihood that others among her friendship groups and in political circles would be undercover police officers.

That she felt completely and utterly violated and abused.

That this was nothing short of a sustained and institutionally sanctioned rape.

Rex was taken aback. He hadn't expected that.

He had really loved Amelia.

He'd loved their unborn baby too.

When he'd proposed, he'd meant every word of it. He'd even thought their relationship was strong enough to withstand his cover being blown.

He shuffled the papers and put them down on the table in front of him, then sat there in silence for a moment or two.

To fill the time he reached out and lined the document up neatly with the Post-its and highlighters.

Getting his thoughts in order too, was the message.

He recognised the names, certainly, he said.

And that his first impressions included feelings of genuine warmth and lasting affection, which had taken him slightly by surprise. As far as he was concerned, Johnson – 'Helen' – and he really had been in love.

That he would do as Bland suggested.

That there were several points of variance and interpretation he could see, even just on this cursory read-through.

That he did still have his notebooks in a safe place.

He said all of this, and showed no outward sign – that was his training kicking in – but inside he was reeling. Churchill was mouthing something about next steps, but Rex wasn't taking it in at all.

'Anyway, we'll put that all in an email,' she said, rounding up.

The meeting was over.

Rex noted the change in tone.

'Thank you, ma'am,' he said. 'Francis, Evelyn.'

He put the affidavit, Post-its and highlighters into the envelope.

'Thank you, Detective Inspector,' said Bland. 'It's difficult, I know, but an officer of your calibre…' He left the sentence hanging.

'It'll work out,' said Churchill, forcing a smile. 'I'm glad we've made a start. It's always simpler when you can see what you're dealing with.'

'Let's keep this confidential for as long as we can,' said Gummer.

'Understood,' said Rex, standing and taking the package from the desk. 'Thank you all.'

As he was about to turn and exit the room, to leave the team to their inevitable debrief, he looked again at the pictures on the wall, and remembered something Lollo had said, some insight into Chief Superintendent Tabitha Churchill.

'Were you there, ma'am?' said Rex, nodding at the photo of Sefton, but meaning the hideous and bloody aftermath of the Hyde Park bombing itself.

She clearly wasn't expecting that. With a sharp intake of breath and an involuntary flash of moisture in her eye, Churchill steeled herself and nodded, before turning back to the papers on her desk, and to Gummer.

'Very good, ma'am,' said Rex, with an outward solemnity that belied his inner delight.

He'd found a weakness in Churchill's armour.

But he wasn't going to push it.

Not unless he needed to.

15: Civette (Chive)

[REWIND] —

Annie squeezed his hand and looked around them as the taxi did a quick three-point turn in the lay-by before kicking up a small cloud of dust and disappearing back the way it had come.

Rex pointed at a narrow lane that turned sharply off the main road then turned again out of sight.

'Down there?' she asked.

'I think so,' said Rex.

He was lying, of course, which wasn't exactly in keeping with their plans for the day, but Rex knew exactly where they were. It wasn't a garden path he was about to lead Annie up, but a long, shaded track lined with oak and olive trees and prickly-pear cacti, at the end of which was – what? – either a dead end or the future.

And a precipice.

How did that work?

How to get from here to there?

And would both of them make it back?

It was a test of nerve.

Full disclosure, that's how.

It was 9 a.m. by the new nineties-retro-styled plastic **Swatch** that Annie had bought him at the airport. Warm, but not too hot, with the cooling touch up here of a sea breeze. It would be cooler still, Rex remembered, in the thick shade of the trees that overhung the track. The air was filled with the constant chirping of myriad unseen cicadas. For Rex it always seemed like a geological or atmospheric effect, the very sound of heat. A sonic soup, bright and pointillistic, which at certain times of the day would line the entire Mediterranean basin, from shoreline shrub to high karst, from herb layer to hilltop.

Someone had once told him they were edible, and rich in oil. That in **Tudor** times they'd been considered a luscious sweetmeat.

There was no one around. They could be almost anywhere in Southern Europe, although of course the illusion of tranquillity and solitude might be shattered at any moment by a coachload of tourists, by a stinking dustcart, or a wedding convoy like the one they'd seen in town when they were walking to the hotel the day before. A procession of thirty or more beribboned cars, all blaring their horns as they drove from church to the wedding reception. Other drivers honking their congratulations. Mere pedestrians, Rex and Annie had stood hand in hand on the roadside, smiling and waving as the celebration passed.

They'd seen a few early-risers leaving the hotel in 'rambler' chic': khaki shorts and T-shirts, stout walking boots, Aussie-style hats, high-tech walking sticks. But that wasn't Rex or Annie's style. They weren't the type to wear matching fleeces, or to buy their clothes from camping shops; to carry a multi-tool or a spare **tent-peg** in the lightweight cargo-pant pocket.

Annie was wearing a loose dress in green-and-gold slubbed linen, with a broad and floppy white sunhat. Rex was in his usual **barrow boy** uniform of Fred Perry and off-white chinos – minus Harrington – although, when they'd gone shopping together on Jermyn Street, Annie had coached him towards a more contemporary cut with a narrower leg. 'Body like yours,' she'd said. 'You might as well flaunt it.'

Who was going to argue with that?

Yesterday they'd taken the day off. Once they'd arrived at the hotel, fucked and showered, they'd both needed to decompress. Annie was no **slouch**; she'd immediately gone to the communal bookshelf in the hotel lounge and, after weighing up *The Admirable Crichton* by J. M. **Barrie** and *The Moon's a Balloon* by David Niven, she'd chosen a foil-jacketed **potboiler**. She'd then spent much of the day reading in bed, while Rex had gone out for snack supplies – bread, olives, cheese and tomatoes, sparkling water – and to make them a reservation for later.

Mission accomplished, the afternoon had passed quickly.

Later, the air-conditioning inside the restaurant had been positively **polar**, so they'd moved out onto the terrace. The simple bistro-style supper had comprised an **entrée** of rabbit terrine for Rex and grilled sardines for Annie, followed by the special, roast **capon** served with a **Patna** rice pilaf and what certain friends of his had used to call *une salade grecque.*

After dessert, coffee and brandy, Rex had caught the waiter's eye and made the universal gesture of scribbling on some invisible tablet held aloft. While they waited for the bill and the card machine, he'd suggested that they might go for a walk in the morning. Not so much a yomp, more a leisurely stroll.

'Love to,' Annie had said.

That was good, because they had work to do, and Rex had a feeling that some air, and walking side by side, the forward motion, might be more conducive to the task in hand than sitting down face to face.

It wasn't meant to be an interrogation, after all.

Well, it sort of was. And Rex was going to find out what he needed to know if it killed him, or her, but they might as well be leisurely about it. He figured that if you were going to play a serious game of truth or dare, a game of real brinkmanship, you might as well up the stakes and do it on the edge of an actual precipice.

Then, if it all got too much: whoops!

The first bounce off the side would probably break your neck.

He found the possibility strangely calming.

This morning, his love for Annie renewed, Rex had awoken humming the chorus of the old Temptations song 'You're My Everything'. The falsetto vocals were well out of his range, but he couldn't get it out of his head while he showered and shaved. He sang it sotto voce while he dressed, and whistled it on the way down to breakfast.

'Anyone would think you were in a good mood,' Annie had said, cracking the top of her boiled egg.

Actually, the previous night's calm had evaporated and Rex had felt as nervous as the apocryphal **cadet** at their first **autopsy**, but he wasn't going to say that. 'They'd be right,' he'd said, draining the glass of cold **orange** juice she'd poured for him, then tearing off a hunk of fresh bread and using it to shovel up the golden, chive-sprinkled scrambled eggs. 'How about you? You look rested.'

'I slept like a log,' Annie had said. 'Once I got used to that **bolster**.' 'How's your egg?'

'Delicious. State of these, though.' She pointed at the colonial-era **sepia** photographs of Kalahari **Bushmen** that lined the walls.

'Christ, sorry about that,' Rex had said. 'We'll get breakfast out tomorrow?'

If we get through today, he thought.

It was not a foregone conclusion.

But now here they were. The track hadn't used to be metalled, but Rex figured that once they cleared the corner this tarmac would give way to the rutted dusty path he remembered. He'd had a hankering for that long-remembered walk, past dry-stone-walled olive groves with gnarled thousand-year-old trunks and tethered goats. They'd follow in the ancient footsteps of the countless generations who'd scuffed or ridden donkey-back along these paths, who'd kicked up the same sun-dappled limestone dust, or booted a pebble off into the undergrowth, batted away the occasional horsefly and smelled these same strong scents of thyme, fenugreek and oregano.

'Shall we?' said Rex.

'Lead the way.'

'Even better,' he said, falling in step beside Annie and taking her hand. They were in this together. He was thinking about what they were walking into – the **overlap** between past and present, and why: their baby, their future.

'Okay,' said Rex. 'I'll start.'

This wasn't the time to **haggle**.

A bit of **bulldog** spirit was needed.

'Remember back in **April**?' he said. 'That was totally my fault. I didn't know she'd actually come round, but I carried on seeing her for a month or so after I told you I'd broken it off. I suppose I was still digesting our news. And you'd gone back to York, so I was feeling lonely.'

'What? Crazy Woman?' said Annie, remembering the late-night phone calls and the screaming match on the balcony. 'Oh, that figures.'

'She wasn't crazy, just disappointed,' said Rex. 'A lovely woman, and justifiably angry. I led her on. It wasn't fair. That weekend when I said I was at the Police Federation conference, we took a weekend break to Birmingham and the **Walsall** Art Gallery. I'm sorry.'

'Are we going to apologise for everything?' said Annie. 'Is that how this is going to work? Because it's going to get really tedious.'

'No, you're right. Maybe we can just—'

'Take it as read?' said Annie. *'Please.'*

Rex still felt bad about Thea; using her like that. She *was* a goddess. He remembered them both standing in the gallery and holding hands in front of a miraculous painting of a blank sheet of paper that had been folded and unfolded. ***Octavo,*** it was called, by – Thea had leaned forward to read the label – the Scottish painter Alison Watt.

They'd marvelled at it for a few minutes: the illusion.

Rex had wanted to fall into it, to feel the smooth glazed surface of the paper against his cheek.

Tabula rasa, he'd thought. She'd been standing beside him, the back of her hand against his. If only I could start again with you.

Thea's skin cool as paper to his first kiss.

'She was very sweet, actually,' said Rex, squeezing Annie's hand as they neared the first bend, where a house he didn't remember blocked their view of the track beyond. 'I could have loved her, if I didn't already love you.'

'Not so much, though,' said Annie.

'No, you're right,' said Rex. He wasn't stupid enough to argue the toss. 'Not so much.'

'That wasn't so bad,' said Annie. 'Okay, my turn.'

Rex braced himself for a shock that never came.

He must have made a mistake.

It wasn't Annie's confessions that threatened to **up-end** his world right now. Well, of course they might well do, but right now it was the view down the track once they'd cleared the corner.

This wasn't it at all.

He wondered if he'd made a mistake. Where were the olive groves? The **stubby** cacti? And the giant, spiky succulents the size of a small car?

He must have misremembered.

Where even was the dusty track?

16: Buglosse (Bugloss)

[FAST-FORWARD] —

And now Melissa Shepherd couldn't get hold of Rex. He hadn't 'vee-essed' their regular weekly catch-up (as Shepherd's mother had used to put it: 'VS' for 'very sorry'). It just simply hadn't happened. Shepherd had found herself sitting by the phone like a lemon.

It was unlike DI King. He was usually on the dot.

After fifteen minutes she'd texted Singh – 'Hey B, Is Rex about, do u know? Let me know. Melissa'.

Then she'd called Churchill's PA, who said that, ah yes, the Detective Inspector was currently dealing with – how did she put it? what was the particular form of words she'd used? oh yes, that was it – 'an unrelated matter'.

It was a fob-off that she'd recognised; **light** but firm.

As far as Frankie knew, she'd said, he'd be back at his desk tomorrow.

So in the absence of catch-up and consensus, what did Melissa Shepherd do, on her tod in Midhurst Police Station? She did what she'd learned to do when she was writing her dissertation back at Brighton **Polytechnic**: she made a mug of tea and a **bite** of toast, turned on the radio (right now a **ragtime** special on BBC Radio 3, and, coming up, the first of four concerts featuring various highlights from the 'Big Guitar Weekend'...), undid the top button of her **jeans** and went back over everything, that's what.

Of course, back in 1991, she'd been a **chainsmoker** too, with a steady stream of gone-out rollies needing to be relit. But she'd given up when she was doing her PGCE. It was partly the waste of money that her impoverished-student-self had resented, but she'd also realised that constantly stopping to make another roll-up didn't actually help sustain her concentration after all.

But apart from that, the MO was the same. To reread, to find the thread, to rebuild the **pyramid**, block by block, to see something she might have missed, to **annotate** her own annotations.

Every time Shepherd went through the files, a new detail would snag her **interest**. So what did she **espy** this time? The contents of Lawrence's bathroom cabinet: Gillette razors, a **styptic** pencil, a pot of Aveda Men hair **clay** and some moisturiser. Among the papers on a bill-spike in his kitchen had been recent-ish receipts for a bunch of **pussy willow** branches from the florist's up the road at Lauriston, and a Deliveroo order of **flatfish** in **parmesan** crust for two from Wright Brothers; a Waitrose recipe card for sausage-and-chilli pasta **bake**.

There were questions raised that she still hadn't been able to answer: With whom had he shared that meal of Dover sole? For whom the catkinned twigs? – those things lasted weeks, but there was no sign of them in the house – and just whose Clarins hand cream was that?

These and other suggestions of the presence of a perhaps significant other were intriguing, but no one had been able to shed any light on Lawrence's romantic life.

Did he make his moves to that copy of Art Blakey's *Witch Doctor* LP? A record that it just so happened had also been in the Jag's CD player the night he'd disappeared. It was good driving music too – with that hypnotic walking bass and high-hat cymbal ride it certainly got you there. She'd downloaded it, and could well imagine The Jazz Messengers played loud on a decent in-car hi-fi while Jethro sped through the deserted tree-lined streets of Sutton and Leatherhead towards the M25 and whatever it was that had awaited him or been set in train in Petworth.

And then the things that didn't seem to fit: Andrew Morton's biography of **Diana**, an old *Vogue* **Fashion** Supplement, a **scarf** – more a pashmina – that still bore musky perfume scent, a YouTube video still open on his browser of Zinedine Zidane's left-footed volley for Real Madrid against Bayer Leverkusen in the UEFA Champions League Final of 2002. Yes, astonishing. *And?* The well-kept planters of echium and lavender outside his kitchen window.

Was DCI Jethro Lawrence gay? Well, of course Shepherd had had to ask.

Not as far as Churchill knew, came back the answer. But he did keep his personal life to himself, she'd said.

When Shepherd had asked Rex the same question, and told him Churchill's answer, he'd shrugged, surprised. Lollo was straight as they come, he'd said. Always had a twinkle for the ladies, confident and charismatic, never backward in coming forward. Maybe Churchill hadn't seen him in action. He could charm the birds out of the trees, and frequently had. But no, Lollo hadn't spoken of a current love interest. Rex would give the gaffer that.

Fat lot of use they were, then.

The truth was, the more Melissa Shepherd felt she was getting to know the missing Detective Chief Inspector, the closer she got, the more he was seeming to slip through her fingers.

17: Séneve (Charlock)

[REWIND] —
'Well, I never *cheated* on you,' said Annie.

Rex was about to protest.

'Yeah, yeah, I know,' said Annie, stepping back off the road, holding on to a chain-link fence to keep her balance on the sloping bank. 'Never say never, but not in that way, anyway.'

Rex followed, sharpish. They'd heard the lorry before it loomed around the corner: a clattering engine, several noisy changes of gear and a horn sounding on the road behind them. Rex raised a hand in acknowledgement as he and Annie stood to one side. Lizards skittered away into the scrubby undergrowth of bramble and verbena that surrounded the naked rock.

At least some things don't change, thought Rex.

These flat slabs peppering the landscape were, Rex remembered, some sort of ancient clastic rock, lava or pumice. This one, gently sloping, created a natural terrace. It was the kind of place you might have sat early in the morning smoking a cigarette and watching the sun coming up. At least, if this three-storey holiday apartment complex wasn't now blocking the view.

What must she think of me, Rex wondered. Promising her a scenic stroll, then bringing her to *this*. But of course Annie – having no expectation – was completely unperturbed.

Rex, however, was dumbfounded.

He recognised every twist and undulation of this track, the slight drop as it turned to the right, the gentle swing to the left before it dropped again. But the track was now metalled, and instead of ancient olive groves and shaded scrub it led past fenced-off yard and white concrete shed, and on through a hotch-potch of small-lot piecemeal suburban ribbon development, just like everywhere else in this part of the world.

Maybe it wasn't the first place you'd think of for a day out, but Annie wasn't a mind-reader. She must have assumed Rex had his reasons. It could lead anywhere: to lunch in some off-the-beaten-track restaurant, to a jeweller's workshop, to some rare vantage point. Who knew?

Well, Rex knew, and he wasn't saying. Not yet, anyway.

They had too much else to talk about.

Full disclosure.

Maybe it was more truth and reconciliation than truth or dare.

Beginning a new life together by being totally honest, with each other at least, about each of their pasts.

Rex had started with something small, a recent brief infidelity, but Annie went straight in. She had more fundamental truths in mind. The lies she'd told were of an entirely different magnitude. Now that they needed to think about their future, and the future of their child, there was something that she really needed to get off her chest.

Something about how she and Rex had met.

On Derby Day, not even a year earlier.

Yes, of course her niece Ashley had been in Great Ormond Street; that much was true, but little else.

It wasn't a long walk, but they took it slowly because there was a lot to take in.

Rex had a bottle of water in his rucksack, some peach-flavoured iced tea and some of the local brioche. Annie's morning sickness was receding, but still the sweet and buttery-tasting bread had been the only food in the bakery window that hadn't made her want to projectile-vomit.

If Rex had thought he could remain in charge of their own particular truth and reconciliation process, he'd been wrong.

Some houses were flush to the road, occupying tiny, narrow-fronted plots like in the sloping streets of any Mediterranean hill town, while others sheltered behind shaded terraces and carports, or were screened by high walls and hedges, some with small front gardens, others with electronic gates and security cameras.

Rex had completely lost his bearings, but a promise is a promise: total honesty and no judgement.

Telegraph poles and electrical cables followed the line of the road, and interlaced overhead.

Where once had been a gate into a scrubby enclosed field, a neglected vineyard, was now a lane down which clustered yet more nondescript shallow-roofed one- and two-storey houses: satellite dishes, cars parked in front of each of them.

It was no different to any other development, any other swathe of cleared woodland. That was how it worked: the trucks and cranes and hard hats moved in, and value, hard cash, was created out of potential. And was it Rex's imagination or were some of these houses unfinished? There was a lot of rough-cast concrete, naked brick and metal roller-shutters. Or were these just varying combinations of the vernacular architecture of the area: stuccoed walls – some white, some pink- or orange-painted – with shuttered windows, and terracotta-tiled roofs, aluminium awnings, grapevine verandas, blue-and-white house numbers.

And through it all, Rex and Annie walking hand in hand and taking turns to confess.

They walked and talked, stopping every now and then to sit on a wall and have it out: to explain, but without trying to justify, to admit but not to apologise, to acknowledge without needing to excuse.

Not therapy, but pragmatism.

The only way forward.

Where once had been a great patch of prickly-pear cacti was now crazy paving, potted geraniums and a two-car garage.

The mature fig tree, and the old wall that you could stand on to pick them, was now in someone's garden.

Where once the scent of thyme, fenugreek and oregano, of wild mustard and of dust scuffed underfoot, now the ripe and rotten stink of purple-lidded communal rubbish bins, of foul-smelling nappy sacks baking in the heat. Broken glass on tarmac around a bottle bank.

Where once had been silence but for swift cry, frog croak or cicada song – depending on the time of day or night – the haunting cry of a black woodpecker echoing around the hills or the distant mew of a buzzard soaring high above, now was just the buzz of engines and power tools, music on the radio, television, some poor bastard coughing uncontrollably, and the distant sound of children's laughter and splashing water.

And then an as yet undeveloped lot the width of two houses, containing two great old olive trees and a breeze-block shed, an oil tank on concrete supports, some prickly-pear, and beyond that two small patches – you couldn't call them fields – of tilled land behind rickety improvised fencing. Plastic bags hanging from the branches of a dead tree.

Irrigation ditches dug to catch the run-off from the paved road.

Sawn-off olive stumps, and fan palms.

Some smaller holiday lets, clustered around a communal yard.

Behind a chain-link fence, an Astroturf five-a-side football pitch.

As they walked, the plots started getting larger, and the road widened in front of a broad-fronted, three-storey orange house with green-painted shutters standing in a large cypress-planted garden.

Ever the policeman; always, too, the risk assessment to be performed. As they walked, Rex couldn't help noticing the cameras. Hidden in small black glass domes, on top of pole mounts or on wall brackets on the corners of buildings, at gate and door, complete with movement trackers and halogen lamps: domestic security systems. This wasn't any longer the primordial, pre-digital and unsurveilled landscape he remembered.

'Smile,' he remembered, 'you're on *Candid Camera*!'

There would be no getting in and out of here unseen, he realised, so quickly recalibrated the threat level and his expectations accordingly: Severe not Critical; responses Heightened not Exceptional. Black Special or Amber in old money.

A substantial house on a corner, with a huge dining table and pizza oven on the terrace. Its garden filled with an eccentric assortment of ornaments: large terracotta jars, garden gnomes, faux-classical statuary, plastic flamingos the size of a man, brightly painted wagon wheels.

Next door, a sign on an orange wall – 'Biergarten' – tables and chairs visible through hedging; simple mosaic decorations on the stucco, and a stack of air-conditioning units. A steep driveway and a silver four-wheel-drive vehicle parked high off the road. Corrugated plastic roofing across a terrace that was larger than the market square of the average small village.

They'd paved paradise alright. But what Annie was telling him was even more disorientating.

For Rex it was a double mindfuck.

To find out quite how much he had been played; the kidder kidded.

But he wasn't outdone yet.

Rex still had bigger fish to fry, and he knew now that if that was the worst she could do he'd be able to bring Annie onside.

But still, her revelations coupled with this near-complete transformation – or erasure – of a place he'd thought he knew, and from which he'd intended to draw strength, had done the opposite. This walk into a part of his past. Something he'd been saving for last.

But why stop at double-whammies when you could have a triple, and the last was by far the worst. Rex was not prepared at all for what awaited them at the end of the road.

He'd expected a precipice: a thrill! the urge to jump! pretending to push or be pushed!

He'd thought he was ready for anything, for mutually assured destruction in treacherous terrain that he knew at the highest resolution and she didn't, but he'd been wrong.

No, *this* was wrong.

It was indecent.

Off the scale.

Bandit country.

He stepped back, as if to turn away, but he couldn't take his eyes off it.

At the end of the track was a newly constructed turning circle, freshly laid tarmac with bright new road markings, clean white concrete kerbs and box-fresh black-painted drain gullies.

And beyond that?

18: Houlette (Shepherd's staff)

[FAST-FORWARD] —
Notwithstanding the 'cockamamie speculation', as **Churchill** had so charmingly put it, that Detective Chief Inspector Jethro Lawrence's disappearance at that Petworth nursery was somehow connected to the vintage automotive parts dredged up nearby, what Melissa Shepherd wanted to know, given the 'missing persons motto' – if in doubt, assume the worst – was who exactly, beyond the hundreds if not thousands of hardened career criminals he'd put away in the course of a long and distinguished career, might have had sufficient **grudge** against DCI Lawrence to not only wish but actually do him harm.

If she ever was granted a **minute** or two to **chat** to DI King (and he'd had **no time** the next day either, the 'unrelated matter' still his **plea**), this was what she planned to ask him.

One night she'd dreamed of her late father, as she did occasionally. Jim Shepherd had been a **Stockton** lad, a solicitor, staunch Labour supporter and dogged political point-scorer all his life. A portrait of Clem **Attlee** had hung above the fireplace throughout Melissa's childhood.

Where her schoolfriends had gone to Cornwall or to France for their summer holidays, or even to Wittering or Bognor Regis, the Shepherds had gone to the North-East of England, where they would traipse from one distant relative's living room to the next. She and her sister – 'the twins' – would have to amuse themselves by reading through back-issues of *Titbits* magazine and watching *World of Sport* (or *Reader's Digest* and *Grandstand*, depending on which side of the family it was). There'd be day trips out to the windswept beach at Bamburgh Castle – picnicking on cheese-and-tomato sandwiches, crisps and flasks of tea – or to Stephenson's Cottage by the Tyne, or the industrial museum at Beamish. She remembered looking at the various steam engines and looms, the **shuttles** in their display case, and practically dying of boredom. It wasn't fair, they'd said. Their schoolfriends were wearing bikinis on the beach, and here they were looking at nineteenth-century **rent** books and truck tokens in a museum, or touring the industrial **districts** of Tyne and Wear.

'Great railway journeys of the world,' she'd once joked, 'Thornaby to Redcar.'

But now she was glad of it. She knew what working people had had to put up with; how far they'd come and how hard they'd had to fight. It had stood her in good stead.

In her dream she and her father were listening to the wireless – as he'd used to call it – as news of Harold **Wilson's** victory in the 1974 general election was coming in, and in that dream the report cut to Wilson's victory speech.

'Mr **Pitt**! Mr **Disraeli**! Mr **Gladstone**! Harold **Macmillan**!' thundered the Member of Parliament for Huyton, Lancashire, waving his trademark pipe in the air. 'Edward Heath, can you hear me? Edward Heath, can you hear me? Your boys took a hell of a beating!'

Both her father and her mother had loved the radio comedies. Life would grind to a halt for half an hour in their house when the first notes of the 'Minute Waltz' were heard, or the theme for *I'm Sorry I Haven't a Clue*. And **nobody** had been a bigger fan of *Round the Horne* than Jim Shepherd. Broadcast long before her time, it had seemed the stuff of legend to Melissa when she was a child.

That was why, when her dad had gone for his last extended stay in hospital, she'd splashed out and bought a CD Walkman for him, and a ton of batteries, together with the four-CD box set of all the episodes. By then he'd lost the finer coordination and basic dexterity required to operate something quite so fiddly, but that was alright as long as she was there to rest the headphones on his ears and press 'play'. And now, some of her fondest memories were of her ailing father in his hospital bed, crying with silent laughter at the camp escapades of Julian and Sandy – respectively Hugh Paddick and Kenneth Williams – in which they would joyfully **mangle** the mores of that week's **chosen** profession or pastime, one week lawyers, the next bookshop owners, into a tissue of innuendo and double-entendre. She hadn't really got it until one visit when he'd thrust the Walkman into her hand, and insisted that she listen to the 'Bona Law' episode.

'What?' she'd said, puzzled. 'As in—'

This had been her father's cue to explain Polari, the gay slang which Horne's programme – and Julian and Sandy's 'criminal practice' – had popularised and taken into the austere living rooms of post-war Britain.

'Oh, that,' said Melissa. 'I thought you meant the 1922 Prime Minister.'

He'd looked at her askance, but, as she told him, you didn't get to be in the Midhurst Tigers, the top-scoring pub quiz team at The Greyhound two years in a row, without knowing that **Bonar Law** was the answer to a couple of fairly regular questions about British Prime Ministers.

Now she had inherited the CD box set of *Round the Horne*, and still listened to it every once in a while on the boat when she wanted to remember her dad. Just thinking about listening to it brought tears to her eyes.

When Melissa called DI King the morning after that, she'd still gone straight to voicemail.

Fuck's sake, she thought. You can't get the staff.

19: Luzerne (Lucerne)

[REWIND] —

A sign picked out in black Art Deco ironwork letters against a broad expanse of white concrete and glass said '**Mandalay**'.

Rex was **agog**.

Not to be overdramatic, but he'd finally made it back to a sort of personal holy **grail**. Not the only **high-water mark** of his early adulthood to be sure, but one of several. The chance if not exactly to drink again from this **chalice** then at least to honour it, and to share the memory with Annie, even if it was the last thing they did.

He remembered an early-evening **tipple** long ago, as twilight fell. Listening to Grace Jones and UB40 – *always* Grace Jones and UB40 – on the bar **stereo**. Or looking for the local weekly **jazz** programme at whatever **kilohertz** it was on the radio. That one time, singing along to the Sex Pistols – 'Frigging in the **Rigging**' and 'Belsen Was a **Gas**' – but being one-upped and out-punked by the German bourgeois whose tape it was, who'd also claimed to have a pair of genuine **plaid** bondage trousers from SEX. An English girl singing 'Summertime' in a breathy, bluesy voice. Waiting for the stable hands to finish grooming the horses so Helen could go riding up in the hills. Trying to **waylay** one of the many stray cats **with** a **saucer** of cream.

He wasn't sure what he'd been expecting. It would have been unreasonable to suppose that nothing would have changed since he'd last been here, but this was monstrous. It was as if some **eldritch** spell had wiped a chunk of Rex's past from the face of the earth; and, worse, made it the **butt** of an indifferent joke.

But it wasn't only Rex's past that had been trampled on.

What kind of ghoul? what oligarch? what **bowlegged daddy-long-legs** in what **two-step** with death would **prowl** these tree-lined hills and cliffs in search of just A. N. Other **riparian** plot, yet choose to lay its ghastly **hat** here of all places, to **adopt** this of all sites to **expedite** what banal vision in brutalist white, to squat **ghostly** on this cliff edge like a grotesque and outsized concrete cuckoo crushing a tiny nest?

As if to answer his unspoken question, the large metal gate rolled smoothly to one side, offering the bright-blue flash and reflected shimmer of swimming pool beyond, as a white Swiss-registered Humvee with blacked-out windows and Lucerne licence plates growled past them and the automatic gate slid shut once more behind it.

'You okay?' said Annie.

'Not really,' said Rex. 'It's a long story.'

'It always is. You and me both. But look at me.' She caressed her bump. 'We've got plenty of time. I'm not going anywhere.'

Rex couldn't say anything for a while.

And then he could.

Then he told Annie everything.

20: Hémérocalle (Daylily)

[FAST-FORWARD] —
Doodling **angular** abstract shapes on the pad, Melissa Shepherd waited for Alice Day from the South Yorkshire constabulary's HR department to answer the phone.

She'd put in a request for Lawrence's old personnel file from before he moved to London. She wasn't looking for anything in particular, just hoping something might **crop up**. She was planning to keep an eye open for anything unusual: **errant** behaviour, ancient grievances and long memories. Did he ever **depart** from the manual? Were there any extended or unusual absences? Evidence of gambling? Admittedly, all of these were unlikely, given his current rank.

As a rule, police HR records were thorough, recording everything from training modules completed to sickness absences. From **tetanus** jabs to taking too long a tea break, from postings to promotions to PIPS qualifications: all of it was grist to the hungry HR **mill**. And even for those early years in Lawrence's career, Melissa was expecting the usual hefty folder. So she was surprised to get a voicemail from Alice in the HR department up in Sheffield, saying there was a problem, and could she give them a call back.

The South Yorkshire constabulary's 'music on hold' was Scott Joplin's '**Maple Leaf** Rag'. It reminded her of watching *Ask the Family*, a television quiz show from her childhood that even in those days had seemed resolutely old-fashioned in its promotion of the white nuclear family, and which had latterly used the ragtime hit as its theme tune. She and her sister and father had used to enjoy watching deadpan host Robert Robinson on evenings when their mother was working. Dad in his **armchair** and the girls on their Christmas-present beanbags on the floor, with a bowl of Angel Delight for **afters** in front of the telly. They would keep score themselves most weeks. To see who could get the most answers right.

'Which Elizabethan playwright was **knifed** to death in a Deptford tavern?' Robert Robinson might ask.

'Christopher Marlowe!'

'Good girl,' her father might say, ruffling Melissa's hair.

Same with *University Challenge*. No wonder she was now **captain** of the quiz team.

But at least the Joplin had nudged her 'Oh Carolina' earworm to one side.

She'd had Shaggy's dance floor cover version going round her head since Rex, in reinforcing Jethro Lawrence's heterosexuality, had described 'Lollo' grinding along to it with someone called Jane Milligan at a station Christmas party, back in the day.

'Talk about "dirty dancing",' he'd said. 'And Jane in her batty riders – blimey.'

Oh, jump and **prance** yourself, she'd thought. I bet you loved it.

'Hello, HR.'

'Oh, hello,' she said. 'Is that Alice Day? This is DS Melissa Shepherd down in Midhurst and Easebourne.'

'Eastbourne?' said Alice.

'No *Ease*-bourne. Midhurst and *Ease*-bourne,' said Shepherd for the zillionth time. 'Like "stand at ease"? Sorry I missed your call. I was hoping to check something in Detective Chief Inspector Lawrence's personnel file, and I just got your voicemail saying there was a problem?'

Day told Shepherd that Detective Chief Inspector Jethro Lawrence's personnel record for his time on the South Yorkshire force simply didn't exist. It seemed that those had been the days of paper files, which could more easily be lost or destroyed than digital.

'There was a fire,' said Day. 'It could be that they were destroyed in that.'

'My God,' said Shepherd. 'When was this? I hope no one was hurt?'

'No, luckily it was contained pretty quickly,' said Day. 'We only lost a couple of archive boxes. Electrical fault.'

Oh aye, thought Shepherd. She was hardly a **neophyte**, and it wasn't that she'd **thought** the goods would be served up for her on a plate, sliced and **diced**, but she wasn't expecting to have hit this particular brick wall quite so quickly.

She thought back to her degree, and the second-year philosophy elective. Syllogisms had not exactly been her **strong point**. How did they go? First came the major **premiss**, then the minor, then the conclusion.

All men are mortal.

Harry Secombe is a man.

Therefore Harry Secombe is mortal.

Well, *was* mortal. He'd died yonks ago, rather proving the point. But back in Melissa's student days, the **dotty** ex-Goon and presenter of Sunday-evening television fixture *Songs of Praise* had been a household name, so presumably the lecturer had been trying to be topical, or to keep the class awake. They'd had a **vote**, a show of hands to see who'd agreed or disagreed with the statement.

Then, to illustrate the danger of false logic, the lecturer had pointed out of the seminar room window at Marlborough House, an eighteenth-century mansion with neoclassical stylings, on the opposite side of the Old Steine.

'**Doric** columns are from ancient Greece. Those are Doric columns. Therefore this is ancient Greece. Right?'

Wrong!

But what was the logic of Lawrence's missing personnel file?

Maybe something like:

If someone doesn't want something to be found, they hide it.

Something appears to have been hidden in this instance.

It would **figure** therefore that there might be something to hide.

Might? It seemed like a **certainty**.

Of course the **inverse** *might* be true and there was an innocent explanation – 'Would that it were… Would that it were,' as quizmaster Robert Robinson used to say – but it would **beggar** belief.

Jethro Lawrence's personnel file hadn't been transferred with him to the Met. She'd checked. So why would the South Yorkshire constabulary HR department have lost or destroyed his records, 'in a fire' or otherwise?

Bugger the car parts! Was this what she'd been looking for? This wasn't merely a gap, or a wilful omission in the record. It felt like more than that. Not exactly a lead, not yet. But all Shepherd's instincts told her that it could be the beginning of something: a fruitful place to look.

21: Trèfle (Clover)

[REWIND] —
Luckily Annie was a good listener.

And whether it was good for the soul or not, Rex had confessed.

Sitting there on the clifftop with Annie, looking out to sea, he'd told her everything.

Shameful things from deep in his past that he'd never thought he'd be able to tell anyone.

'We'll have to send Helen and the girls a card,' said Rex later. 'Not sure if I dare show her this, though. She'd freak. I can't believe they were allowed to build here.'

The beach at the foot of these cliffs beneath them had been the site of a massacre, a once-celebrated last stand by the last few dozen Italian 'Acqui'. Remnants of the *33ª Divisione di fanteria*, who in small boats under cover of darkness had sailed up the coast from Cephalonia to Corfu, escaping certain death in the massacre of September 1943 in which more than five thousand Italian prisoners were shot and three thousand drowned by the notorious *1. Gebirgs-Division* of the Wehrmacht. They'd somehow miraculously survived those nights afloat only to die right here two weeks later at the hands of Corfu's occupying forces, the equally infamous *104. Jäger-Division*.

When he and Helen had visited all those years ago, there had been a simple embossed tin plaque commemorating the fact in English, Greek and Italian, affixed to a whitewashed boulder set next to a simple and also whitewashed one-room fisherman's hut, daubed in blue paint with the word 'ενοίκιο'.

Rex wondered whose **tom fool** idea in whatever planning department of the regional division it had been to erase that modest memorial and allow such an ostentatious architectural display of disproportionate wealth in its place. Money talked, of course. But had

they even known or cared, when their **spades** broke the soil of this
sacred **hectare**, that people had died here?

The last time Rex was here, he and Helen had found the place by
accident, the summer after graduation, the year before he'd joined
the police. Hard to believe, but back then it had been seriously off the
beaten track. A woman they'd got chatting to on the boat over from
Igoumenitsa had told them which bus stop to get off at. She'd said
that the track from the main road didn't look like much, but that it led
to the most amazing beach.

She'd been right, but she hadn't mentioned the hut.

Because Rex and Helen were very much in love, they'd thought
'ενοίκιο' must mean something romantic, but it simply meant the
shack was 'for rent'.

So they'd asked up at the taverna and it had turned out that until
recently a young couple from London had been staying there – they'd
overwintered illegally, staying longer in Greece than the permitted
three months – and while there weren't many home comforts it
was sparsely furnished and relatively clean. Nadia from the taverna
arranged it so that staying there would only cost them the equivalent
of about two pounds per day. So they'd paid for two months on the
nail, then gone back to pack their rucksacks and check out of the
hotel, dropped by the taverna to borrow a blanket from Nadia, then
walked the last couple of miles on that rough track through an ancient
and unspoiled Mediterranean landscape, past fields and olive groves
that had been several millennia in the making.

Inside the hut there'd been barely room for the old iron bed, one
chair and a bookshelf upon which were ranged the essentials: a little
battery-powered transistor radio, an old wine bottle, its neck encrusted
with candle wax, a copy of *Under the Volcano* by Malcolm Lowry, a
pocket torch, a pack of playing cards and an ashtray; a camping stove
and a mocha pot. An oil lamp hung from the single rafter. There
were hooks on the wall, and no windows except for a small and milky
glazed panel in the door that they mostly left propped open, with a
lump of driftwood for a doorstop. Outside were a weathered wooden
bench and a small rusty folding table. Nadia had lent them a couple
of heavy glass beakers from the taverna.

Of course, they had to go up to Corfu Town to the stuffy, upstairs
office of the bus company to change the return date on their tickets.

They'd also had to get used to checking the bed for scorpions whenever they came in, but it was clean and dry and it smelled of sun-warmed stone and old wood. In the winter it must have been a different story.

It had been an idyllic couple of months. A long walk up to the village every morning for bread, tomatoes, yogurt and honey, for coffee, and to use the English-style flushing toilet at the taverna; a rarity in village Corfu at that time. Then they'd walk back in the afternoons – cutting bunches of grapes from the vines as they passed – to read in the shade, or go down to the beach to swim or to sunbathe. And on the evenings when they didn't walk back up to the taverna for a simple supper and a bottle of retsina, they'd stay on the beach. Standing in the shallows, they'd run their hands through the water to marvel at the phosphorescent plankton. Or they'd sit on the sand and watch the lightning flash of storms far out at sea, talk for hours and count shooting stars. Later they'd sit on the bench beside the hut to play backgammon and smoke Karelia cigarettes, to drink brandy and snuggle up by the light of that oil lamp.

Hard to imagine now, with all the bars, deckchairs and tavernas lined up along the shore, that back then even this beautiful beach had been completely undeveloped. There really had been nothing here. And from Monday to Saturday the place had been deserted.

Sundays were different.

Mid-morning, before it got too hot, there'd be a procession of motorcycle trailers and donkey carts bringing the elderly women, the grandmothers and widows of the village. Holes would be dug on the higher part of the beach, into which deckchairs would be placed so that the women might sit down and be buried up to their shoulders in the hot sand. A small black parasol would be pushed into the sand next to each of them. One or two family members would stay to feed them sweetmeats and give them cups of water from a glass pitcher. When Hel had asked Nadia about it later, she'd told her that this went on every weekend throughout the summer. The heat was a traditional remedy for rheumatism.

At teatime, the families reappeared to dig the women out, dust them off and drive them back up the track.

When Helen had had an upset stomach one night, Nadia's mother gave Rex a bowl of spent coffee grounds soaked in lemon juice. Nadia explained that Helen should eat it all.

Back at the hut, Rex had spoon-fed her the bitter mixture.

In the morning they'd been woken early by a small earthquake. Hel had still felt a bit shaky, but the coffee grounds had worked.

To return the favour, and earn a little money, Rex had then spent the last two weeks of the holiday helping Nadia's father Spiros down in the olive grove. The family were building a house, and now that the reinforced concrete shell of ground and first floors was complete, there were piles of bricks, door and window frames, lumber, bundles of steel rebars, buckets and tools to be moved up onto the first- and second-storey slabs.

Rex had reluctantly accepted the small daily payment of a couple of thousand Drachma – not even four or five pounds – in cash from the till each evening, but on top of that when he'd arrived on the site at 8 a.m. on those few mornings, Nadia's mother had sent Spiros along with breakfast and lunch for them both. Two bags of freshly fried sardines – that morning's catch – a small loaf of bread and a bottle of domestic wine each. Water came from a well that had been dug in the modest grounds. A donkey was tethered in the shade at the back of the site. At 4 p.m. Helen would come to meet him, Spiros having promised them a lift back up to the taverna where supper was on the house: moussaka and chips, feta salad and more wine.

A glass of the family's home-made *tsipouro* for a nightcap.

A few yards beyond the hut had been the cliff edge, where a precipitous old partisans' path zigzagged down to the beach. Back in the day, Rex and Helen had tried their hardest to make that vertiginous descent, but they'd only tried the once, and it had been so terrifying that they'd had to inch their way back and go the usual long way around.

So quite what he'd expected today, Rex didn't know. Surely he hadn't really been thinking of that precipice as his way out. More likely that choosing to come here had simply been a kind of displacement, an unconscious strategy by which the physical danger might mask the greater personal and material risk of full disclosure. And wasn't coming back here, rather than one or two other places he could think of, itself a kind of displacement or transference?

Well, if so, the strategies had worked.

Rex felt like a weight had been lifted.

Just to have been able to *say* that thing he thought he'd never be able to tell anybody.

It was a hurdle he'd known they'd needed to overcome if he and Annie were to spend their lives together.

He felt slightly foolish, though. How naive to have expected that the hut would still be here.

They were aghast to discover, at the foot of the cliff an hour or two later, that the villa even had its own private elevator down to the beach.

As to the formerly precipitous old partisan path: that was gone too. No trace remained.

Back in the day, the safer route had been to walk perhaps half a mile north along the clifftop, to where a broad river valley rich with vineyards, olive groves and maize fields cut through the sandstone below the village of Marathias, the river trickling onto the beach through beds of reed and bamboo.

Back up on the main road, where the cab had dropped them off those few hours ago, Annie didn't need to **cajole** Rex into having a drink. They stopped to get their breath back at the same little taverna Rex remembered.

He wondered if Nadia was still here. And, if so, whether she'd recognise him. Whether she was still alive.

They sat at a table outside, where Rex had a cold beer, a local lager although it came in a **Stella** Artois-branded glass, and Annie a sweet coffee.

'Acropolis Adieu' by Mireille Mathieu was playing on the stereo. It seemed as if it had been playing forever. How long was it since he and Helen had been here – a couple of decades at least?

It was hard for Rex to reconcile that all of this development – the complete suburbanisation of an ancient and seemingly timeless track down through the old olive groves, a track as old as human habitation – could have happened in such a relatively short period of time.

'Don't come the innocent with me,' said Annie, laughing. 'You helped build the first house. It's practically your fault!'

They'd tried to find that first house as they'd walked back, but it might have been any one of them.

Last time Rex had been here, this road past the taverna had been a dogleg in the main road, but main road it certainly had been. Now the traffic and the buses north and south sped past a little way up the hill. And there were new shops and new tavernas up there too. Leaving what had been the village centre stranded like the oxbow lakes Rex remembered from geography at school; created when a meandering river has rerouted to a new path of least resistance.

It made Rex feel hopelessly **dated**. He'd thought about asking the young waiter when it had all changed, but he thought better of it.

Besides, he knew the answer. There'd been no one moment. It was simply a matter of life going on, a process both **cyclic** and haphazard. A continuous unfolding in time that needed no **totem** – no 'millennium bridge' or commemorative bypass – to mark it.

Come to think of it, the waiter was probably Nadia's grown-up son.

Sitting there in silence with their drinks, and a little *mezze* – taramasalata, pitta, thinly sliced *pastourma*, olives and a saucer of oil – Rex and Annie were both taking stock of the day's revelations.

The pact they'd made, their amnesty, their truth and reconciliation process, his and her **blunt** admissions, were forcing him to recalibrate their relationship, and fast. Though her **status** as his lover, his life partner, the woman who was expecting his child – his third, if you counted little Thomas – was unaffected.

Rex had always known there was something special about Annie. Even before Lollo had stuck his oar in. It hadn't seemed so at the time, but he'd done Rex a favour; cut to the chase. They'd got on immediately – well, of course they had, she'd seen to that – but something had really clicked on that road trip down to Stonehenge and the South-West.

The more Rex found out about Annie – and today he'd got a whole heap more than he'd bargained for – the more he liked her.

Liked?

Loved.

And with what he knew now, Rex couldn't be sure if that was in spite of how she'd played him, or because of it.

She was his type alright.

Beating him at his own game.

Nearly.

But then, **flightiness** or coquetry had never appealed to Rex. Even what people called '**model** good looks', though Annie certainly had those. Rex preferred loyalty and long-term commitment; knowing someone was there for you. He'd always rather an interesting conversation, or a moment of shared experience, than a fluttering of the eyelashes.

Lately he'd been wondering if any of Annie's conversations up to this point had been for real. But now that he *knew* it had all been for show, he found he didn't care.

Not quite everything, perhaps, but mostly. Not habitual, but strategic: she'd only lied when a lie was necessary. He knew well enough how it worked. So that was okay, then. And he'd done far worse.

This woman, though.

Truly, if he loved Annie any more than he did right now, he'd be down on one knee. Then their first day back in London they'd be up to Camden Town Hall for a **licence** and choosing rings in Hatton Garden before tea. Actually not a bad idea, thought Rex. Don't rule it out.

The stories she'd told him today: her activism, the campaign, asking for his help, playing him like a violin.

How she'd got into it.

Her university days in Sheffield: postgraduate research and radical student politics in the Arts Tower.

Creating a book club and embroidery circle for cover was particularly impressive, if true. And no reason now why it wouldn't be.

Decanting trustworthy individuals one by one from a compromised campaign group. Randomising responsibilities: chairing, choosing the titles each month, being **postman**. Confounding any fakers that slipped through the net by choosing only the best, most staunchly feminist or Black writers: Marge Piercy and Octavia Butler, W. E. B. Du Bois and Frantz Fanon. Selecting books that the casual reader might find heavy going, but which were mother's milk to them, hardcore as they were: Henry **James**, say, or the full text of *An Enemy of the People* by **Ibsen**, and kicking out anyone who hadn't read the books in full, each month, no crib notes allowed. Then everyone tasked with choosing one book, and making an embroidery patch of the front jacket. No UCO was going to put in that much psychic labour. They'd watched them make their excuses and fall away.

In one year you've made half a patchwork quilt.

Two years at most and you've completely laundered your cell.

It was utter genius.

Rex was thinking about his and Annie's adventures these past few months, not yet a year: driving over the **Tamar** Bridge at dawn on their way to the Eden Project last summer.

Or the night before that, running around a decidedly damp Bristol city centre, the British Isles buffeted by remnants of Hurricane **Bertha**, when she'd realised she'd forgotten her make-up bag. They'd spent a fruitless hour looking for Black hair and cosmetics products in the **Cabot** Circus shopping centre, before finally getting directions to a great little shop on the Horsefair.

That had been real.

And Rex could honestly say that in that fleeting moment, holding hands and jumping over a puddle in the wind and the rain, he had almost never been happier.

Now, by the time Rex and Annie got back to the hotel, they were too late to choose from the menu, but glad to take whatever came.

As it was, the last mouthfuls of Annie's delicate mussel *kritharoto* – the local **risotto** – were ruined by the late addition of a generous **seagull**-shit garnish: seafowl **spoils** seafood shock! The perils, they supposed, of eating al fresco. And it wouldn't have been more **comical** if she'd been wearing a **gum boot** on her head. But it completely grossed them out, splashing too in Annie's antiemetic **Sprite**.

'Oh, yum!' she said, scooching her chair back. 'Shall we?'

The waiter gave them dessert on the house: a plate of baklava, two sweet coffees and two glasses of brandy.

Once they'd settled up, and looking deep into each other's eyes, Rex proposed a toast: to them, to love, to seal their pact.

He realised now that she'd been trying to tell him last year; given him a clear signal.

Hadn't she?

She'd seen right through him. Wasn't that what it was about?

What at the time had seemed a strange conversation, as they'd toured some ancient manor house and gardens in Devon on the way back from the Eden Project.

Hidden in the Elizabethan panelling: a **priest's hole**.

At first it had reminded him of one of Donal's unspeakable jokes from back in the day. He'd had to stifle a giggle, but wasn't about to repeat it for obvious reasons.

'Shall we be naughty and get in,' she'd whispered, leaning on his shoulder. 'Pull it shut and let the tour go on without us?'

'Nothing I'd like more,' Rex had said, 'but I don't think we'd fit.'

'Maybe you're right.' She had touched a hand to his cheek and gently turned his face towards hers. Then, with no warning, that piercing look straight into his soul. 'Better to hide in plain sight, eh?'

22: Angélique (Angelica)

[FAST-FORWARD] —
At last Melissa and Rex had scheduled a phone meet for eleven or so, whenever he got out of whatever it was.

DS Melissa Shepherd had decided that she would take the call out of the office, as long as there weren't too many people about. The PCSO at the station had been a right **pain** all morning, so she'd needed to come outside just to clear her head. She'd treated herself to a takeaway coffee – latte, no sugar – and was sitting on her favourite bench (yes, she had a favourite bench) watching a **flotilla** of ducklings bobbing up and down in the **shallow** water of the newly restored South Pond, by the Chichester Road.

About once a week she'd actually take her lunch break. And she'd usually get a takeaway coffee from Gartons, and come and sit here for ten minutes, then walk along the waterside of the medieval pond and over the little footbridge to the Grange and back to the station via the library, sometimes dropping in to change or renew a book or two. When she worked on Sundays she might have a wander around the antique market. But today, what with the investigation and the PCSO driving her **round the bend**, she hadn't been concentrating, and found herself at the Costa up on North Street, and had to backtrack.

She'd been remembering her friend Margaret's fortieth birthday celebrations at the **Rose and Crown** over in Cuckfield back around Easter time, and wondering where she should have hers come September. She was godmother to Mags's two children, James and Suzy, eleven and twelve. It was a role that she'd resisted at first, despite her childhood church-school-fostered faith, but then had come around to.

'Who else am I going to ask?' Mags had said. 'You're my oldest friend.'

This was true. They'd been younger than James and Suzy were now when they'd met at Midhurst Church of England Primary.

Melissa found that she enjoyed being a godparent immensely: the choosing of special cards and gifts, the regular visits to Mags and Alistair's place, where for the past nearly ten years she and Mags had ritually marked each of the children's heights on a door **jamb** in biro, just as Mags's mum had done with them when they were little girls. When James and Suzy were still toddlers, she'd **proposed** annual day trips to London. Introducing them to one or other of the great London museums, then decamping to the nearest park for a picnic and a run-around.

Returning to the matter in hand, Melissa wondered whether the phone call would actually happen today, or whether she'd be fobbed off again. The Detective Inspector had been easy to work with at first. Experienced, proactive, strategic, politically savvy – office politics, anyway; he'd been a useful foil to Tabitha Churchill's pomposity, and almost fastidiously punctual.

So why the sudden change?

Melissa made up her mind to ask him. She didn't want to get too personal about it, but thought she might just drop in a casual 'Everything okay?' near the start of the conversation.

See what his response might be, and take it from there.

She wondered whether the mysterious 'unrelated matter' that kept getting trundled out as an excuse had anything to do with his upcoming appearance at the Undercover Policing Inquiry.

Although Melissa had notionally been working with Detective Inspector Rex King for a month or more, she wouldn't have said she'd got to know him particularly well. He'd been personable enough, though, and quite entertaining company, within certain parameters at least. And she could definitely say that he'd never overstepped any mark with her, nor been anything but diligent and conscientious in his dealings with others in the team. But he played his cards close to his chest, that was for sure.

Of course, this hadn't stopped Melissa from forming a few opinions.

First of which was that the DI was seriously punching above his weight with that beautiful girlfriend of his. What was she – fifteen, twenty years his junior? And pregnant too. He'd find that a bit of a struggle at his age. It wouldn't be too bad now, but fast-forward ten years and he'd be mistaken for the grandfather. A few more and she'd soon find herself wiping *his* arse, unless she had the sense to get out while the going was good.

But you didn't get to any kind of rank in any force – let alone the Met – without being an operator, and King had clearly been through several **mills** and come out unscathed. But from where Shepherd was sitting, King's connections seemed to have mainly come from the very person that they were now looking for. Lawrence's team had seemed invincible. But without the Detective Chief Inspector, what was left? How would DI King fare now, without the protection of his precious 'Lollo'? Rex certainly seemed unflappable, but what did they say about chickens? **Behead** one and it only **keeps** running for so long before collapsing.

For Rex's part, the nagging anxiety of the inquiry was taking second place to the investigation, but his forthcoming appearance meant that he was starting to get used to waking up at 3 a.m., his mind racing.

The prospect of his appearance, and reading the affidavit of the Core Participant (the person he was now having to get used to referring to as 'Helen' rather than 'Amelia' so that he didn't unwittingly breach her anonymity in the hearing room and find himself in contempt), seemed to have opened up a whole new part of his brain that now permanently cycled through every jot and tittle of her statement and his own version of the same events: rehearsing answers in his mind. But Rex had been here before with Tennyson. He was experienced enough to know that this was a standard-range response.

Simon Rose had promised Rex some training. It was the least the Police Federation could do. Rex was hoping he'd be coached to within an inch of his life.

The real **Helen** had written with news of **Edward**, Rex's one-time Holborn sidekick, the former Detective Sergeant Ed or Eddie Webster, better known as Webbo. The postcard had got caught up with the junkmail, and Annie had only found it when she'd tossed the past two days' worth of fast-food flyers and cards from local minicab companies into the recycling.

Rex read it while he made the coffee.

Helen had used to like sending postcards, and they were usually pictures of art, from one museum or another. He still had a few of her cards from years ago, in the letter rack on his mantelpiece: Rubens' sketch of Christ preaching to the fishermen at **Galilee**, Rixens' *Death of Cleopatra*, showing both the Egyptian queen and her first handmaiden **Iras** dead, while Charmian – herself about to die – adjusts her mistress's diadem in a last futile attempt at dignity. Plus a few cards with paintings by Helen's favourite: Giorgio de Chirico.

'That's quite a collection,' Annie had said when Rex showed her.

'I like them,' said Rex. 'Didn't seem any point chucking them.'

'It's very charming. She has good taste.'

'In art, maybe.'

This latest one was a picture Rex knew. It was a painting at the National Gallery that they'd often looked at on their regular visits many years earlier: *La Gamme d'Amour* by the French painter Jean-Antoine **Watteau**: *The Scale of Love*.

A bust of Pythagore – Pythagoras, who else? – overlooks a woodland scene in which a man in theatrical costume plays the lute to a young woman who is seated on the ground next to him holding a musical score. The inexorable consequences of love play out over time – mathematically, is the implication – in several tableaux receding into the far-distant landscape.

There was no code intended by Helen here, Rex knew; no **metaphor** or secret message. But she'd certainly expect him to remember the picture from their shared past in early adulthood, her 'growing-up', as she had once rather graciously put it.

She was writing to let him know that Edward had been transferred to HMP Belmarsh, and was most likely to serve out the rest of his sentence there. But that she and the girls were well in spite of everything – they'd had a girls' day out in London, hence the card. Not that they'd forgiven Ed, and none of them could face seeing him after he'd **admitted** what he'd done, but they'd written back at least. Her usual sign-off: 'Take care. Fondest, H.'

There was a PS that Jennifer was looking forward to seeing 'you two' – him and Annie – again soon.

Well, the feeling was mutual.

At her party, Mags had tried to set Melissa up with a friend of Al's: Vic, a **cabinet-maker** from Bosham. Nice guy too – the quiet and sensible type – which made a change from the usual cocky **alpha**-male man-boys that she'd once seemed to attract. Bit of a hunk, actually. He looked a little like that Irish actor in **Thor**: Volstagg was the character, but what was the actor's name? They'd had a slow dance to that Bob Dylan song. He'd been talking about how, after nearly twenty years doing something he loved, he'd wanted a change – to stay in the same line of work but also to give something back. Ray Stevenson, that was it, the actor. Anyway, he'd needed a steadier income for a few years to keep up the maintenance payments while the kids – a boy and a girl – went through uni, so after a bit of soul-searching he'd gone to uni himself, done a PGCE. Now he taught on the furniture-making course at Chichester College. He still took the occasional commission, but wasn't chasing his tail quite so much.

It seemed almost too good to be true. And there was no DV history. She'd checked.

It was a mystery that he was single, but maybe it was just that he was a bit bruised from the break-up. She should have grabbed him with both hands, of course, but instead she'd got a bit **tiddly**, dropped one of her earrings into the **borsch**, and gone into full make-'em-laugh, self-deprecating mode. All of which still, if Mags was to be believed, hadn't quite succeeded in making her totally repellent.

'Go on, give him a ring. He thought you were really nice.'

But Melissa hadn't wanted to be the first one to text; hadn't wanted to seem desperate. Then work and life had taken over for a bit, and now it was July.

Sod it. She'd text him quickly, just before her scheduled phone meeting with Rex. That way she wouldn't overthink it.

Hi Vic, hope you're thriving. Sorry been so crap – work blah. Shall we meet up for that drink while the evenings are light? I can't remember which nights you're free. Be lovely to see you. Melissa ☺

She regretted sending it immediately – should have signed off with an 'X'.

Bugger it. He could only say no.

Or ignore her. Well, he'd been doing a pretty good job of that already.

Pull yourself together, woman.

She took a deep breath, and then phoned DI King, half expecting it to go to voicemail.

'King,' he said.

'It's Melissa,' said Melissa. 'You're a hard man to get hold of.'

'Hi Melissa. Yes, apologies for that. I've been working on—'

'Don't tell me,' she said. 'An "unrelated matter"?'

'Yeah.'

Melissa wondered what the big secret was. And then it clicked: desk duty! You're in the shit and you've been grounded, you stupid cock. But she just said, 'Frankie told me. Anyway, glad I've got you now.'

She told him about the brick wall she'd hit with South Yorkshire. That she'd **applied** to them for Jethro's HR records and found they'd been accidentally destroyed. What did he think? Did Rex know anything about – she forced herself to use Lawrence's nickname for the first time – Lollo's life before London? Anything controversial? Hillsborough?

Where to start? thought Rex. 'Well, everything was controversial back then,' he said. 'But no, he was out a few months before Hillsborough. Secondment to the Met in eighty-seven, full transfer eighty-eight.'

'Did he get any grief for being a **carpet-bagger**?'

Rex knew what she meant: coming in to lord it in an area where he had no connection. 'No, because he only came in as DC. And he was still playing rugby at that time – second fifteen. Fly-half. So he was a popular bloke.'

He wanted to say, 'Didn't you see the photo in his office?' but measured his tone: 'There's a photo in his office, I'll scan it if you want. Up and down to the sports grounds in Esher all the time, I gather. No-nonsense, kept his nose clean and worked his way up the ranks. The person you probably want to speak to,' he went on, 'is Cliff Heath over in Thames Valley. The two of them were mates. He's a bit younger than Lollo, but transferred out of Sheffield at the same time.'

'I'm ahead of you,' said Shepherd. 'You mentioned him before.'

'Oh yeah,' said King. 'So I did. Well, there you are, then.'

'No, sadly not,' said Shepherd. 'And it turns out Heath's file is missing too. It was in the same box as Jethro's: "Transfers 1986–89".'

'Seriously?' said Rex.

'I know,' said Shepherd.

'Why not give Heath a call? I mean, he did say if we needed anything to give him a shout.'

'I'll do it now.'

'I'll ping over his mobile number. Hang on… Oh, one more thing, though, while I've got you. That "unrelated matter"…'

'What about it?' said Shepherd.

'Turns out it might not be unrelated after all,' said Rex. 'Can you come up?'

23: Canard (Duck)

[PAUSE] —

Shepherd may have left the voicemail, but it was Rex that Cliff Heath called back first. He was sitting at his desk and idly flicking through the papers in the wire in-tray. If anyone had asked, Rex would have told them he was procrastinating.

'Alright, Cliff,' said Rex, picking up as soon as he saw Heath's name on his screen. But he could hardly hear the Detective Chief Inspector for wind buffeting the mic. 'I can't hear you very well, mate.'

'…' said Heath.

'Can't. Hear. You,' said Rex.

'…' said Heath, then: 'Hang on… Okay, I've come inside. Better?'

'Much,' said Rex. 'Where are you, Cliff?'

'Glastonbury **Tor**. We needed to take a break: press "pause" and recharge the spiritual batteries.'

Rex wasn't expecting that.

'Serious? Respect, mate. Didn't think you were into all that.'

'Well, you know,' said Heath, 'there are more things in heaven and earth than your whatever.'

'Amazing place, though,' said Rex, remembering a couple of times he'd made the **trek**, back in the day.

'Holy, they reckon…' said Heath.

Rex couldn't be certain, but it sounded like Heath's voice was breaking up a bit, before it was lost to gusting wind noise once again.

Glastonbury sometimes had that effect on people, and Lollo's disappearance had clearly hit Cliff hard. Maybe he was rediscovering religion. He wouldn't be the first to seek consolation from a higher power. Rex could imagine what he might be saying. He'd told the stories himself, about Joseph of Arimathea making a pilgrimage after the crucifixion, or even of Christ as a young man, blessing these shores.

Or was there more to it than that?

Cliff Heath and Jethro Lawrence went back a long way. Compadres on the South Yorkshire force. They weren't the same intake. Rex had assumed they were at first, but Cliff had put him right. No, Jethro had been four or five years senior to the young Heath, who'd looked up to him like an older brother. And then – with some aptitude or potential spotted – they'd both been plucked from obscurity, picked out for better things. Guided by the legendary Inspector Tommy Orwell. Heath's mum must have been proud. And the young Black constable from Park Hill Flats must have thought all his dreams had come true: one-to-one mentoring, fast-tracked for promotion, training and qualifications over and above, opportunities for advancement. And then suddenly they were playing with the big boys, with as much responsibility as they could handle.

Friendships, careers, professional associations and networks forged in the heat of the strike. And then that nifty bit of footwork from Orwell or the powers that be, which saw them airlifted out: Cliff gone Detective Constable and moved to the Thames Valley force, Lollo likewise to the Met.

You always were light on your feet, Cliff, thought Rex. You've said as much yourself.

He pictured the two of them, the young Heath and Lollo, playing a quick game of kickabout or keepy-uppy on the Polo Fields at Aldershot while they were down there with Orwell and Christ knows who else, which other agencies, recruiting muscle.

'Come back inside,' said Rex. 'Cliff!'

'… Sorry, yeah,' said Heath. 'That better?'

'I can't hear you if you poke your head out, mate.'

'So Bethany thought we should get away for a couple of days. Tune in to the spiritual side of things a bit, you know. Consult the **oracle**. And where better to do that?'

'Take stock,' said Rex. 'Good for you. Listen, I meant to say congratulations. Lollo was singing Bethany's praises, before—' Don't go there, thought Rex. 'Tell her I'm looking forward to meeting her one of these days.'

'Thanks, Rex, I will. She's right here… Says the same. But Lollo…'

His voice tailed off for a second. Then, 'I hear congratulations are in order with you and your lady friend. Said you're settling down at last. What's her name? Susan?'

Oof, Rex felt that. So that wasn't all Lollo had told Heath.

Heath knew.

Well, of course he did.

Thanks, Lollo, he thought. But he couldn't say he blamed him. It was a good story. There was a poetic justice to it.

'Annie,' said Rex. 'Her name's Annie. Thanks, Cliff. Nice of you to say. Yeah, that's right. I thought it was about time; can't play the field forever! Looks like November. We'll send you both an invite.'

'Nice one, thanks. Aw, I'm pleased for you. Hang on.'

Was he losing him again?

'Cliff?' said Rex. He was getting bored now. And resumed leafing through the papers on his desk: memos, back-issues of *The Job*, invitations, conference papers. When was he ever supposed to have the time to file this stuff? It was tempting to simply chuck the lot in the bin. In the unlikely event that there was anything really important in here, and some vital task that had gone unactioned as a result, someone would soon make a fuss. You could guarantee it.

'I'm here,' said Heath. 'Bethany sends her best too. She wants to know how you proposed.'

'On the beach,' said Rex. 'In Corfu. Agni, if you know it. God, it's so nice there – first time I'd been in years.'

He heard Heath relay the news to Bethany. 'Aaaaw, that's nice,' he heard her say. 'How romantic.'

'She says "How romantic"!' said Heath. 'Love Greece. I'm really pleased for you both.'

'Anyway,' said Rex, 'what can I do for you, Cliff?'

'Yeah,' said Heath. 'That DS Shepherd down in Eastbourne gave me a bell, but – well, for one thing I'm on annual leave. But any chance of a word in your **ear** before I call her back? I'll still be on leave, so keep it on the down-low, but we're coming up to town tomorrow first thing. I could do a quick lunch, maybe.'

Rex let the 'Eastbourne' thing slide. It wasn't his fight: he couldn't be bothered. You'd think it would be worth Melissa Shepherd's while to transfer just so she didn't have to say 'No, *Ease*-bourne, as in "stand at ease"?' a million times a day. 'Usual?' he said. He fancied a curry. It had been too long.

'Sounds good,' said Heath. 'Twelve thirty? I won't **detain** you for too long.'

'My treat,' said Rex.

'Thanks, mate.'

Rex hung up. Then grabbed the top half of the papers from his in-tray and dumped them in the grey steel wastepaper basket under his desk. That just left – he riffled through what remained – more of the same! A selection of spoiled statement forms, staff appraisal papers, couple of certificates of attendance from last year's Compliance Training Cocktail Session (GDPR, Equal Opps, 'Prevent'), detainee questionnaires and random bumf left over from the SiC inspection, a bunch of raffle tickets.

There were also Gold Support Group papers.

And among these was a folded sheet of paper, bearing Lollo's handwriting: a note.

It wasn't addressed to anyone, certainly not to Rex.

Was this what they'd been looking for?

Well, he'd touched it now, so it was too late to keep it completely clean, but Rex carefully removed the other documents, then stood up and went to get an evidence bag from the cupboard, and some latex gloves. He took a photo of the item in situ, and then carefully placed it in the evidence bag and logged it.

'Maybe it's nothing,' he would say in his email to Shepherd – copied to Singh and Churchill – 'but it looks like a suicide note to me.'

All three of them emailed back immediately.

Rex's mobile started ringing.

Then his desk phone.

The next day, standing on the pavement outside the Ravi Shankar Bhel Poori House on Drummond Street at the allotted time, Rex hadn't recognised the slim Black man walking towards him in sports jacket and slacks until he reached out to shake hands and said, 'Rex, good to see you.'

Egad!

Talk about **visually** arresting.

Rex didn't know if it was the Tarot reading, or Bethany, but Cliff Heath had had a serious makeover.

Gone was the wrong-vintage shoulder-padded jacket in burgundy leather.

He'd lost what had to be two or three stone, and what's more he'd ditched the syrup.

He looked like a **hard-boiled egg** with a face.

'So how's the investigation going?' Heath asked as they waited to be seated. 'Any progress?'

Rex was going to have to steer the conversation carefully, but he'd made up his mind that he wasn't going to share too much, certainly not yesterday's potential discovery.

He shrugged. 'I wish I could say we've found him. But it's slow progress. I think DS Shepherd wanted to pick your brains, though. Not sure what that's about. South Yorkshire days, maybe?'

'I'm hearing good things about Shepherd.'

'Yeah, she's good. Wouldn't mind having her on the team up here, to be honest,' said Rex. Then he decided to change tack. 'Married life obviously suits you, Cliff. You look ten years younger. Seriously.'

The waiter greeted them, then turned and headed for the staircase up to the mezzanine.

'"Lead on, O master of the Caravan",' said Heath, quoting what Rex recognised as an old **Flecker** poem that he too half-remembered from school.

'Love the hair,' said Rex. 'Or lack of. Much better. It suits you.'

Heath rubbed his bald head proudly.

'Yeah, it's funny,' he said. 'I used to take a lot of trouble over my hair, even when I started losing it. No, *especially* when I started losing it.'

'You used to have it in the old Jheri curl back in the day,' said Rex. 'Lollo told me.'

'Yeah, I was a proud Soul Man. Still am. I loved to look the business.'

He looked pointedly at Rex's jacket: '*You* know what I mean. Taking care of appearances.'

'Yeah,' said Rex. 'You've got to be posh to dress down at my age. I'd just look poor. Can't understand these blokes who look like they've been dressed by their mum. Skinny posh boys in crumpled shirts and bed hair, clutching their cuffs, with their trousers at half-mast. People'd think I was a tramp if I dressed like that.'

'Tell me about it,' said Heath. 'There's definitely a type. I live in Oxford, remember: they're everywhere. But then, here I was thirty, forty years later – no disrespect – and I was thinking "Keep the faith", until I realised that *the faith*, whatever it was, had long ago stopped giving a shit about me.'

'Ha,' said Rex. 'I know exactly what you mean.'

'But I tell you what,' said Cliff. 'It took me a long way in this game, that wig.'

'Eh?'

'It distracted people. They'd drop their guard without me having to lift a finger. I say wig, I mean wigs plural. I had a **batch** made. And they're not cheap. But I suppose I got sick of being a cheap laugh, the source of other people's **entertainment**. And Beth, God bless her. Beth encouraged me. Put a tiger back in my tank.' He patted his now flat belly. 'Three months on the keto! Gym three times a week! I didn't think I could do it. Well, I'm allowed the occasional treat. It's amazing what you can achieve with the support of a good woman. As you'll find out.'

'I already know,' said Rex. 'A partner in crime? You bet. What are you going to have, Cliff? The usual?'

'Always. You?'

'Yeah, that buffet is giving me the glad-eye. But I'll have a salted lassi if the waiter comes before I get back.'

'What else did Lollo tell you?' asked Rex once they'd eaten something. He'd been wondering how best to break the news, but then thought Fuck it and came right out with it: 'Did he tell you about the TV programme?'

Cliff shook his head. 'What programme? Tell me what?'

So he hadn't. That was a significant omission. But Rex wasn't about to do Lollo's explaining for him.

'Look at this,' he said, taking his phone out of his pocket. Opening up the photos, he tapped and then unpinched to zoom in on a grainy image pulled off a digitised frame of Super 8 film: two young men in boiler suits and helmets, visors up, faces just visible, but – once you knew who you were looking at – completely recognisable.

Rex hadn't expected the image to have such an impact.

A range of emotions played across Cliff Heath's face for the full ten seconds that it took him to absorb the photo. And then his whole posture altered, and he fell forwards slightly as if winded, as if he'd been punched. Then, with a deep breath, the DCI composed himself, straightened up, pushed the phone back towards Rex.

'Operation **Fieldfare**,' said Heath.

'That what it was called?' said Rex. 'That I didn't know.'

'No one does. That was taken care of. Yeah, me and Tully. I told you about all that, didn't I.'

'Aldershot, right?'

'Yeah, well, war stories tend to get a bit exaggerated. Where'd you get that from, anyway?'

'He didn't tell you, did he,' said Rex. He was puzzled.

Previously Heath had almost boasted about their exploits down in Aldershot: the PSUs, the A-Team, them and Tommy Orwell, inter-agency working. Recruiting extra muscle among reservist ex-Paras who were only too happy to answer the mythic call of Sir Francis Drake's drum, that spooky **sentinel** of national threat. Up at the crack of dawn and convening out the back of Leicester Forest East northbound. All the lads pouring out the back of an army **lorry** that first time. Most in unnumbered boiler suits, helmets and visors, army boots, riot-style shin pads. Everyone piling into the vans. A little something to keep them awake. A few SDS lads in donkey jackets and jumble sale clobber from the Oxfam shop, festooned in yellow-and-black 'COAL NOT DOLE' stickers, making themselves scarce and off to hitchhike on the slip road, to blend in. Fellow travellers, to the untrained eye at least. Agitators and agent-provocateurs, who could work the targets like beaters at a pheasant shoot: funnelling them towards the jaws of defeat. If only they knew. Gulling them into behaviours and choreographies that were guaranteed to make them stand out in the crowd. And they'd want it too. Keen as primary school kids with their hands up – 'Miss! Miss!' – squirming with the desire to be the one picked to answer a question. Then, before they even know it, they're high and dry, ripe for the plucking, ready to be picked off, clattered. Three-man snatch squads coming down on them like a ton of bricks. Cuffed and cautioned. Next!

'You've got to understand,' said Heath. 'It wasn't like some stately **sea battle**, conducted at a distance. It was a ruck, a proper **light-infantry** skirmish. Hand to hand. There was proper racism then too. Proper. Your generation wouldn't understand.'

Well, that was **unfair**: Rex knew only too well that a picket line or a protest wasn't exactly the Garden of **Eden**. He'd seen his share of neo-Nazi pricks too. He wasn't Black, though. He knew that; knew the difference.

'It was a different time,' said Heath. 'It was rough out there. See a brick flying towards you, what are you going to do?'

Rex nodded.

'You duck,' said Heath, 'and then you retaliate! Well, you've been there, mate, I take it.'

Rex shrugged. 'Part of the job, Cliff, unfortunately.'

'Yeah,' said Heath. 'You develop a sixth sense, as a body of men. You can contain it, nip it in the bud. But then something happens. You've learned your lesson and you don't wait for it to come to you. You put the boot in first. You get stuck in, but you leave no trace. You leave any actual arresting to the regulars. And we were bloody good.'

Rex nodded. He knew that Heath had been seen making an arrest on the day, so his hunch had been correct: the apparent arrest was for show, to get a UCO out of schtuck.

'The A-Team,' said Heath. 'That's what we called ourselves.'

'I know. You said,' said Rex. He understood.

How to **behave oneself** is not always the priority.

Sometimes it's just about implementing a strategy. Well, that and your training. Always your training.

Other times it's pure survival instinct that takes over, despite everything.

You get carried away.

Rex knew where this was going.

He recognised the sleepless nights, the rehearsed lines.

Anxiety was a great weight-loss programme too; the best.

But this wasn't some mere **foible** that Heath was talking about.

And it was **anathema** to Rex, even now, but he took care not to show it.

'Yes, it wasn't pretty,' said Heath. 'Yes, it wasn't pleasant. Yes, there were casualties. On both sides.'

Fuck, thought Rex.

No wonder.

No wonder you both got moved sideways.

No wonder someone had decided to **edit** the HR record.

It was about time he brought Melissa Shepherd up to speed.

Because, let's face it, she could talk to Heath until she was blue in the face, but he wasn't going to be able to tell her anything useful. Not voluntarily.

And Heath clearly didn't realise that Lollo had stitched him up like a kipper.

'Oh my God!' said Rex, scooping up some rich, red *idli* with his paratha. 'Good call, Cliff. You've got to come to London more often. I've missed this place. *So* good.'

'I know,' said Heath with some satisfaction. If he'd noticed Rex's switcheroo, he didn't let on. He was probably glad of the change of subject. 'Forty-odd years I've been coming here. We used to come down to Laurence Corner for uniform requisitions, me and Tully, and this was the perk.'

'Nice work if you can get it.'

'You can imagine. We felt, I don't know: special? Two lads on the town, *and* we were getting paid for it.'

'I bet,' said Rex, smiling, empathising, like the practised interrogator that he was. But in that moment Rex knew that, even now, Heath didn't see that they'd both been played, back in the day.

'Beth's not so keen, to be honest,' Heath went on. 'Says it doesn't agree with her, but this place *is* London to me.'

So, Operation Fieldfare, eh? Rex could imagine the young lads down from Yorkshire. Big-eyed boys having a laugh in The Smoke. Reversing their van into the gate out the back of Laurence Corner. The initials 'FF' chalked on a pallet of 'army surplus' Dutch police boiler suits. Loading up. Skimming a pony in discount-for-cash, enough to cover a curry and a few pints before they headed back to the M1.

Leaving the restaurant, Rex had the unshakeable impression that, for all the usual bonhomie, the positives – the makeover and the connubial bliss, the acceptance of baldness, and the spirituality – the Thames Valley Detective Chief Inspector had seemed slightly more absent than usual, **fretful** even. Which prompted Rex to wonder whether Heath's new-found spiritualism was just a front, or a genuinely held response to the rapidly changing circumstances.

Remorse does funny things to a person.

Heath would have seen the leaked papers a month back, so would have known – even if they were a bit close for comfort – that he and Lollo didn't figure in them. But if Lollo hadn't warned him, how would Heath know what the leak hadn't revealed, the truth that was now bound to come out sooner or later?

Maybe Lollo hadn't needed to warn him.

Maybe he already knew.

Was that it?

Fuck!

Was it him, then, back in the day?

Was it good old Cliffy Heath who'd got stuck in and danced a jig in **hobnails** on Billy Cooper's head?

24: Mélisse (Lemon balm)

'HOW… *COULD*… YOU?'

Sobbing and screaming – 'HOW… *COULD*… YOU?' – right there on Lamb's Conduit Street, just at the foot of the police station steps, Jen could barely get the words out. 'You're,' she sobbed, 'just… as… bad… as… my—'

Ouch, thought Rex, wincing at the comparison-to-come: that hurt.

But then she really let him have it.

'—*DAAAAAAGGGGHHHH!*' screamed Jen, uncoiling a full-handed slap around his face as she did so, and putting her whole weight behind it. It was perfectly placed for maximum whiplash of fingers on cheekbone, while the heel of her thumb caught him right on the nose.

All that money Helen and Webster had spent on childhood tennis and karate lessons for the girls had clearly paid off. And Christ, did the humble-bragging Webbo use to bang on about it at the time.

Momentarily disorientated by pain and shock, Rex couldn't see straight until Jen was already a hundred yards away and powering off up the road towards Coram's Fields. He'd really have to run if he wanted to catch up with her, but it was probably best not to push his luck. She knew her way around, and – on that evidence – wasn't about to take any shit from anyone.

It wasn't what you wanted, to be slapped in the face like that. But a part of Rex was proud of his daughter, impressed even. He supposed that such a display of anger was to be expected, just he hadn't expected it quite so soon, right here and now. Nor for the physical expression of that anger to have landed quite so precisely and with such force.

He could understand it, though.

Why wouldn't she be angry?

Helen and the girls had already been let down badly enough. 'And then some,' as the saying went. They had every right to have expected better from Rex.

They shouldn't have found out like that, in any case.

But he'd been expecting better too.

Other Core Participants and former UCOs appearing before the UCPI were being protected, so why wasn't he?

Amelia – the non-state Core Participant – had been afforded anonymity in the story, which had broken on the *Guardian* website the previous night, being referred to only by her UCPI alias of 'Helen'. But Rex's dual UCPI designation of HZ9122/EN9122 (the 'H' prefix referred to a posting to the Special Demonstration Squad, the 'E' to the National Public Order Intelligence Unit) had been listed as a future contributor to the inquiry. Not only that, but they'd broken Rex's cover name of 'Martin Thorn', and published a photograph of him marching, complete with face paint and short dreads, in the massive Stop the War protest in London in 2003. Helen would have shown Jen some old photos, so clearly Jen would have recognised the photo in the paper. And he could only imagine how upset Helen must have been to see her name being invoked, or echoed, in his accuser's randomly allocated alias. The photo used by the *Guardian* had been taken by a Scottish friend of Amelia's just south of the Cenotaph on Whitehall, but was already credited to a picture agency. He'd been marching arm in arm with Amelia at the time, though she'd been cropped from the picture used by the paper. She'd already been identified as a target by UCOs in the anti-nuclear movement.

Rex's cover name of Martin Thorn had been stolen from the birth certificate of a SIDS baby in deepest Essex who'd died at ten days old. Obviously they wouldn't have called it SIDS at the time. Someone in the campaign had evidently been digging around and found the little one's death certificate.

It was always a risk, even with this tried-and-tested method.

Amelia hadn't exactly been the first target that Rex had got close to. So who was going to come forward next?

Simon Rose had texted Rex late last night to let him know that his cover was blown.

'I'm so sorry,' Annie had said when he got off the phone, giving him the hug of all hugs. 'It's just not fair.'

They'd all been hoping Rex would be able to give evidence anonymously, like most of the other ex-UCO state witnesses. But clearly someone had other ideas.

'D'you think you'd best call Helen right now?' Annie had said. 'Better she finds out from you.'

Rex knew she was right, but it was with heavy heart that he'd called Helen's number.

He'd meant to phone and give her the heads-up before the shit hit the fan.

Of course he had.

He really had.

But instead he'd just kept putting off the inevitable.

Truth be told, he'd felt sure that, even if they lost the battle on anonymity, he'd have a short period of grace: a little more time before his name would seep out into the public domain.

She'd answered on first ring with a cheerful 'Hi Rex', before realising that there could be no good reason for him to be calling at 11.30 p.m.

Dear, sweet H. Her first thought had been for the baby: 'Oh my God, is everything okay? How's Annie?'

But then the temperature of the call had dropped quicker than a polar vortex. Helen had been on her laptop chatting with a friend when he called, so had gone straight to the *Guardian* site, where – for the moment at least – 'Spycop Martin Thorn' was the top-trending story.

'You bastard,' was all she'd said, before slamming the phone down.

And really, if anyone had reason to slap him in the face it would have been Helen. Here at the very least was confirmation at last that Rex had been having an affair, just as she'd suspected. Time would not have softened that blow at all.

And yes, he did still think of it as a love affair. Even when it had gone tits-up; even now.

Rex gingerly touched his cheek, hoping there wouldn't be a bruise.

He hadn't known Jen was coming; hadn't expected to be ambushed.

He'd only stepped outside to meet DS Shepherd, who'd called to say her train had got in to Victoria. He was expecting her any minute.

He hadn't planned to see Jen until the weekend, when she and her little sister Rachel, her half-sister Rachel, had promised to drop by for tea and cakes with Rex and Annie on their way home from shopping in the West End.

They were both excited about the baby – that had been the purpose of the trip. Helen had told Rex that the girls had been discussing what 'baby things' to buy: whether something useful from Boots or a higher-quality offering from Liberty.

Rex had been touched. He'd introduced Jen to the high-end Arts and Crafts department store on a previous visit.

Well, that wouldn't be happening now.

He wondered if he'd ever see his daughter again.

But there was no time for Rex to mope. He'd suggested to Melissa that they have a quick coffee over the road when she arrived. He wanted to brief her on Leaks One and Two, and bring her up to speed before introducing her to Lily Atwell and the NCA coders with whom he'd spent the best part of the last month. It had taken a long time, but they'd finally made a breakthrough, and he wanted to share it as soon as possible.

And here she was, just crossing over from the Theobalds Road end.

'Ouch!' said Shepherd. 'I saw that. Are you okay?'

'Yeah, I'm fine,' said Rex. 'That's Jen, my daughter. She's not a happy bunny today. No, sorry, that's not fair. She's angry with me.' He thought for a second. 'And justifiably so.'

'What I think it is?' said Shepherd. 'I saw the news, obviously.'

'Yeah,' said Rex. 'And totally my fault for not giving her and her mum a heads-up in time. MPF rep only tipped me off last night. He was apoplectic. We'd gone for anonymity. I wasn't expecting my cover name to come out quite so soon.' Rex thought for a second. 'If at all, to be honest. But I thought we'd have a little period of grace. Didn't think I'd be named. I'd been advised to give family and friends fair warning. Let them know they might hear things about me. That some of it might be true and some might not be. Just so they were prepared.'

'And how did that go?'

'Not well,' said Rex, 'evidently.'

'Funny thing is, I'd wondered if it was something like this hanging over your head,' said Shepherd, 'or a disciplinary of some sort, when you kept saying you were working on "an unrelated matter". It smacked of disciplinary. I thought, aye-aye, someone's under heavy manners here.'

'The day they transfer me to TeDIU(M) to die is the day I'll worry about that.'

'Bless 'em, though, eh?' said the Sussex Detective Sergeant. 'Fate worse than death, sat on your arse all day.'

'Haha, yeah – bless 'em,' said Rex. 'Never say never, but it wouldn't suit me.'

'Listen,' said Melissa. 'Just to clear the air. I assume the best of colleagues unless proved otherwise. And call me old-fashioned, but I believe in something called "innocent until proven guilty".'

'Thanks,' said Rex.

'Don't thank me yet. Heaven forbid, but I'm just extending the same benefit of the doubt that I'd expect from you, right?'

Rex understood, but was grateful nonetheless for even this measured consideration.

'We're on the same team, after all,' said Shepherd. 'For now. And we were doing okay, right? You've been pretty straightforward with me, as far as it goes.'

'Thanks,' said Rex. 'Yeah, I try.'

'It's not a good look, though. But you don't need me to tell you that. Everyone's gonna know your face now – everyone. And that's never good. Hard to see how you could continue in a public-facing role.'

'Yeah,' said Rex. 'I know.'

'TeDIU(M) might not seem so bad after a year or two of this. And that's if you can last that long with this hanging over your head.'

'Christ! Kill me now.'

'How are you bearing up?'

'One day at a time,' said Rex. 'But, you know, Annie and I are still getting married. Still having a baby. All of that. Life goes on.'

'Have you set a date yet?' she said.

'Yeah, November. Just having the rings made in Hatton Garden now. Nothing flash: matching plain bands.'

'Where? Any idea?'

'Gray's Inn,' said Rex, instinctively pointing an arrow's trajectory in a vaguely south-eastern direction from where they stood. 'Just over there. Lovely little chapel. You know, it's one of the old medieval Inns of Court: Gray's Inn, Lincoln's Inn, Inner Temple. It's a perk of the job that technically I'm entitled to get married there.'

'Are you serious?' said Shepherd.

'Yeah, straight up,' said Rex. 'Because the station is built on land that was leased to Rugby School by Gray's Inn – I mean, we're talking sixteenth century – technically one of the senior Holborn lads is nominated *Custos Grayorum* for a three-year term. Apparently it means "Guardian of Gray's"! Originally it was a sort of peppercorn agreement for the school to supply a nightwatchman. Now it's entirely ceremonial, you know, *cementing the bond between offices of the law* and all that.'

He laughed and shrugged. Shepherd was good. She'd taken his mind off…

'I mean, I've only just started,' he went on, 'but from what I can gather you don't actually have to *do* anything, just go to the odd remembrance service, "Ancient Amity Dinners", that kind of thing. Plus you're entitled to attend chapel services every Sunday, to have lunch with the porters and to get married there. I don't think anyone's ever taken them up on it, because normally the chapel's booked up a couple of years in advance, but they've had a cancellation on the Saturday of remembrance weekend, as long as we don't mind their flowers already being in for that. What are the chances! Annie said since I'd gone DI it was a good excuse to buy a new dress uniform. She wants me to wear it for the wedding.'

'I bet she does,' said Shepherd, laughing. 'Custard— what was it?'

'*Custos Grayorum*,' said Rex. 'Lollo did it back in the day; said it was a right laugh and all. I don't know how he swung it, but he put me up for it when I went D—'

Rex's voice cracked and a cold shiver went through him.

That was when the penny dropped.

His lip trembled.

He tried again: 'When I went—'

But, choked up, he found he couldn't get the words out.

Already red-eyed and sniffing from Jen's slap, a by now flushed and flustered Rex was suddenly rendered speechless by a gesture that he hadn't even noticed at the time.

Of course Lollo had known that Rex and Annie were expecting.

Rex had told him.

The first thing he'd asked was when Rex was going to pop the question.

That was surely the only reason he'd have swung the *Custos* appointment Rex's way: precisely so they *could* be married there.

Call it Lollo's wedding present.

With a visceral shiver of emotion, Rex fought back the tears.

He didn't know where to look.

Here he was, Detective Inspector Rex King of the Homicide and Serious Crime Command, Central North Basic Command Unit of the Metropolitan Police, standing in the street with a junior officer – only just a junior, but a junior all the same – and about to fucking cry.

'You alright, sir?' said Shepherd. 'Get you anything?'

Feeling foolish at his sudden show of emotion, Rex drew on a well of righteous anger to pull himself together. It took a minute, though.

'Yeah,' he said. 'Thanks. I'm okay. Must be a bit slow. I got put up for the Gray's Inn gig when I went Inspector. I've only just realised that he'd probably have put me forward for it so we could get married there.'

That wasn't all that Rex had just realised, but it was enough for Shepherd – for now, anyway.

And she was impressed too. 'Oh, how sweet,' she said. 'What a nice thought. He's just gone up in my estimation.'

'Kind of a wedding present,' said Rex. He knew that he could trust Shepherd. 'Just touched me for a second, that's all. That's between you and me.'

'Understood, sir.'

But Rex knew that it had been more than just a wedding present from his old boss and mentor.

It had been a parting gift.

Whatever else had been going on, Detective Chief Inspector Jethro Cyrus Lawrence OBE had wanted to see one of his lads right.

He must have known, even then.

That if he wasn't going to be *at* the wedding, he still wanted a hand in it.

That was the moment that Rex knew for certain.

And even though it had always been a possibility (it was the 'missing persons motto', after all: If in doubt, assume the worst), the sudden certainty came as a bit of a shock.

'No worries,' said Shepherd. 'It's that kind of day.'

'Tell me about it.'

'Just to wrap that up,' said Shepherd, 'before we get into it. Our dealings have been fairly limited, but if your legals think you need a character witness in any shape or form, don't hesitate to give them my name.'

'Thank you for saying that, Melissa,' said Rex, mentally adding it to the list of things he needed to discuss with Francis Bland at their meeting later on. 'I really appreciate it. I'll mention it to them.'

'Least I could do,' said Shepherd. 'I'll go first. We've had a development; yesterday afternoon.'

'Oh?' said Rex.

'You'll remember that DC Gosling was tasked with going through the ferry manifests of all South Coast ports, tracing West Sussex drops in the paperwork, cross-checking ANPR and chasing the hauliers back to source. Taken bloody ages, of course. Well, finally one landed. We've got a Romanian truck made a drop at Petworth Bulk the evening of the disappearance: German earth-moving machinery, heavy plant. He was dropping off two new leases – no one actually *buys* anything outright these days, it seems – and picking up a couple of the old fleet, which refurbed sell on outside the EU, Bosnia or wherever. Obviously the drop takes a while all told, but job done by ten p.m., so he parks up in the lay-by on Haslingbourne Lane for a few hours' kip. He's up about three a.m. to set off in good time for the five a.m. sailing, Newhaven–Dieppe. And listen, we didn't want to trouble you with it so went to Frankie, who was very helpful and put Jane onto some Romanian PhD students at UCL SSEES, you know, the—'

'School of Slavonic and East European—'

'—Studies, yeah,' said Shepherd, 'and had them interpret.'

'Good work,' said Rex. 'And?'

'He picked up a hitchhiker. A farmer, he thought. Or, at any rate, a bloke who'd come over the fields, apparently – there's a public footpath – and asked for a lift to Newhaven.'

'Lollo?'

'Don't know yet. Right kind of age, maybe. Jane's had the postgrads translate the MisPer kit too, and is pinging it all over to police in Bucharest via Foreign Office liaison today, so they can do it properly.

And she needed to run the covering email past the Romanian speakers first. First-class work, actually. And quite right too: we don't want to introduce any ambiguity. She's shown real initiative.'

'Yes, of course,' said Rex, momentarily lost for words. Then: 'No, quite. Well done, Jane.'

'Exactly. Thank you. I'll pass that on,' said Shepherd. 'She'll appreciate that, coming from the Met.'

'Thank you. Yes, outstanding police work. Please pass on all of our thanks. Fingers crossed, then.'

'Exactly,' said Shepherd. 'Right, then, your turn. What was it you didn't want to tell me on the phone?'

'Let's get that coffee,' said Rex, pointing to Sid's and leading the way. 'And I'll fill you in a bit before we go up. It's a bit of a rabbit hole, to be honest. We weren't sure if it was connected. It was just one of the gaffer's hunches.'

'Oh, right,' said Shepherd, obviously still rankled by the unnecessary dressing-down her sergeant had received from Tabitha Churchill a full month before. 'So Her Majesty's allowed to have hunches? Just us lesser mortals that can't?'

'Something like that,' said Rex, rolling his eyes. 'It was a good'un, though. Progress too, I think.'

'I'm all ears.'

'Remember those papers that got leaked a month back,' said Rex, crossing over. 'The Justice for William Cooper Campaign: "Who Killed Billy Cooper?" and all that.'

'Yeah,' said Shepherd. 'The ███████████ of the Miners' Strike.'

'That's it,' said Rex, opening the cafe door for Shepherd. 'It opened the floodgates, I can tell you. Had to bring the NCA in on it. Anyway, I wanted to give you the headlines first, so you know what to expect.'

◆ ◆ ◆

A dozen or so of them had been gathered in the tenth-floor conference room on that Sunday morning the previous November. As was customary, there'd been a representative of every department in the old Camden BOCU: Lollo, Si Rose, the still at that point Detective Chief Superintendent Tabitha Churchill, Comms Chief Evelyn Gummer, Jane Milligan from SMT, Sue Stanza for the Forensic

Medical Examiners, Jinksy taking a turn to represent the BOCU's St John Ambulance Corp of which he was the non-active Secretary, Rex for Serious Crime, Di Malcolm from HR. There was the elusive Angela Soul from Building Services, and the Met's Deputy Chaplain, Barry Lincoln – his first time officiating at Holborn – and standing next to him with arms clasped behind his back and holding not the standard short brass infantry bugle but a longer cavalry trumpet was ex-Life Guards bandsman, now Family Liaison Officer, Tommy Bee.

Each of them with their departmental wreath, to be displayed here for a week or two, then put back in the cupboard until next year.

Frankie was giving out the orders of service – which had been printed with embossed lettering on white card – and quietly telling everyone individually that they were welcome to join the Detective Chief Superintendent for sherry in her office afterwards.

While they waited, Rex looked at the war memorial that was fixed to the white-painted wall. It was a simple rectangular dark oak plaque, as might adorn the walls of many a late-twentieth-century public institution. It was charged top centre with a Queen Elizabeth II 'star and crown' Metropolitan Police badge, on either side of which were the dates '1939' and '1945'.

Below this the inscription was painted in gold lettering, protected by a pane of clear Perspex:

IN HONOURED MEMORY
OF
THOSE FROM THIS STATION
WHO GAVE THEIR LIVES IN
THE WORLD WAR

Then came twelve names:

C.M. BROWN	P.C. 384
E.W. BROWNE	W.R.P.C. 610
P. BULL	S.C. 167
K.G.F. FRIMAN	W.R.P.C. 658
A.E.W. GARDNER	P.C. 162
T.J. GARDNER	P.C. 259

F.G.R. JEFFRIES	P.C. 438
W.B. McLAREN	P.C. 315
G.A. RAYMENT	P.C. 438
H.S. STAGG	W.R.P.C. 410
A.T. SPROSEN	P.C. C.I.D.
F.G.E. TAYLOR	W.R.P.C. 368

Rex wondered, and not for the first time, whether the two Police Constables Gardner were father and son, or brothers (although as soon as the service was over he'd immediately forget this, as happened every year). On a much earlier Remembrance Sunday the young Rex King had asked the then Detective Sergeant Jethro Lawrence what 'WRPC' meant. He'd wondered if the 'W' stood for 'Women', but wasn't sure if they'd had women in the Met in those days. Well, now he knew the answer to that one, as did anyone who'd been in Tabitha Churchill's office.

'"War Reserve",' Lollo had told him. 'And "SC" is "Special Constable", I presume.'

'Oh, right,' the younger Rex had said.

'But there were women in the Met since the First World War,' Lollo had pointed out. 'Best you know that.'

Beneath the names, and in the same painted gold lettering, was a quotation from the Act of Remembrance:

"AT THE GOING DOWN OF THE SUN
AND IN THE MORNING
WE WILL REMEMBER THEM"

The service had been timed to coincide with the national minute's silence, so at the appointed moment Barry Lincoln cleared his throat and then began the introduction: 'We give praise to Almighty God,' he said, 'whose purposes are good; whose power sustains the world he has made; who loves us, though we have failed in his service; who gave Jesus Christ for the life of the world; who by his Holy Spirit leads us in his way.

'As we give thanks for his great works, we remember those who have lived and died in his service and in the service of others; we pray for all who suffer through war and are in need; we ask for his help and blessing that we may do his will, and that the whole world may acknowledge him as Lord and King.'

As Lincoln's introduction drew to a close, there was a short pause before a sombre Detective Chief Inspector Jethro Lawrence stepped forward:

'... and what doth the Lord require of thee,' he said, reading Micah (6:8) – the King James Version – from the card, 'but to do justly, and to love mercy, and to walk humbly with thy God?'

♦ ♦ ♦

'So you can pause it here with the touchscreen like *this*,' said a by now paper-suited Rex. He and Lily Atwell were giving a similarly dressed Melissa Shepherd a tour of – how had he put it? – the 'rapid prototype' they'd spent the past month building. He had a few crumpled A4 pages of notes in his left hand, and with his right hand tapped the 'scrobble bar' – he called it – that ran along the bottom of all three large flat-screen monitors mounted on the Clean Room wall. 'And burrow in wherever you want,' said Rex, checking his notes. 'Let's say [*TAP*] this ambulance at four fifteen p.m.'

He dragged and threw the thumbnail over to the left-hand screen, then unpinched a few times to enlarge a photograph of a standard South Yorkshire Metropolitan Ambulance Service vehicle of the time, a high-top square-backed long-chassis Ford Transit, in the standard 'jam sandwich' livery of the time. It appeared to be turning onto Division Street from Rockingham Lane.

'This photo is from the *Sheffield Star*,' said Rex. 'It wasn't used in their photo feature, but they sent all their negs in after Cooper's death. They're logged in Sheffield's evidence store, but missing, presumed lost, until' – Rex pointed at the Aladdin's Cave of evidence laid out on the table tennis tables behind them – 'they showed up here. We've been through them with a fine-toothed comb, facial recognition, the lot, and we get the victim William Cooper walking down Division Street towards Devonshire Green at three fifteen, and then the last sighting is in the cordoned crowd at three twenty. The vehicle was Code-Fourteened from Middlewood Ambulance Station at four oh one. Fifteen-minute journey, give or take.'

He gestured at the whole array: 'Beauty of this is that you could email that item, or the whole cluster, to yourself – I mean, "in-group" only – but you could also check on all the dependencies. So the 999 call came from the Washington pub here at three fifty-six. And, by the way, the call was made by persons unknown on the landlady's home phone in the hallway out the back, not the payphone in the bar; that was busy. So we think the call must have been made by a regular customer, a local who'd have known the layout of the accommodation. But the landlady was upstairs watching *Sons and Daughters*.

'You can see the personnel involved, befores and afters, call up all the different views of that time and place, all the witness statements it appears in, blah blah.' As he spoke, Rex was tapping and swiping a bewildering number of pop-ups and drop-downs to illustrate each of the potential pathways he was describing, and corresponding documents and thumbnails popped up at different points along the timeline. 'Lily's the expert, but just to give you an idea.'

'Oh shit,' said Melissa Shepherd. 'Is that *the* ambulance?'

Lily nodded.

'For Cooper?' said Shepherd.

'Yeah,' said Rex. 'For Cooper. Thought we'd better cut to the chase, or we could be here all day.'

Actually he'd wanted to cut right to the chase and show Shepherd the Super 8 freeze-frame of the baby-faced Jethro Lawrence and Cliff Heath leaning on the bonnet of a Ford Transit carrier that wasn't mentioned on the muster rolls. But he'd thought they needed to show the workings-out first. Didn't want to make it look too easy.

'Ten others were called through the afternoon,' said Atwell, 'but only for walking wounded, so they never needed to come further inside the incident perimeter than Barker's Pool to the north-east, or the bottom end of Fitzwilliam Street at the south.'

Rex tapped again, reading off the screen and directing what seemed at first like a – like a what? – a blizzard? a tangle? a forest? a wave? – a moving cluster of pop-ups and thumbnails that rose and fell – yes, a wave that rose and fell – in response to his touch as he dragged a slider along the scrobble bar, any one of which, if tapped, unpinched, swiped and flung (a short-fling to open 'item X' in a mid-sized pop-up on the screen above, long-fling for a larger window), would open up its own thicket of branching pop-up 'stubs' in turn, and any of these could be similarly flung out of the central screen onto the left or right screens and watched or read full-size. Rex seemed to know this material inside out. He and Lily Atwell had obviously been living and breathing it for weeks, but Melissa Shepherd could see that it was going to take a while to get her eye in.

'Three fifty p.m. Here's where,' said Rex, consulting his notes and turning the page, then tapping, swiping, unpinching and flinging as he went, 'we started to see *the incident within the incident* rippling out. Seamus Arthur [*TAP*] arrested at three fifty by PC Nigel Flinton from Woodseats for trying to prevent a coach from leaving. Keep that time in mind. Ground Zero – as we're calling it – is next to the rear nearside wheel arch of a Doncaster-bound coach parked and stationary at the north end of the Devonshire Green car park somewhere between three thirty-five p.m. and Arthur's arrest at three fifty. According to PC Flinton's witness statement here [*TAP*; *UNPINCH*; *SHORT-FLING*] Arthur climbed onto the front grille and held on to the windscreen wipers as the coach was overtaking a double-decker bus. When the coach stopped, he climbed up onto the front offside tyre and leaned into the cab shouting at the miners within to get back off their bus to fight. But [*TAP*; *SWIPE*; *SHORT-FLING*] move forward to Seamus Arthur's interrogation at Rotherham Police Station by Detective Constable Thomas Wickrow at twelve eighteen p.m. the next day [*TAP*; *SCROLL*] from File 1, Binder 1: "There was a chap hurt," says Arthur,' said Rex, reading off the interview transcript. '"His nose was bleeding. I went to help him and there was somebody already with him. I was asking driver to help us."

'"Don't you think by stopping the traffic in the way you were, you were only causing more trouble?" Wickrow asks.

'"I can't say as I was, no," says Seamus Arthur in response.

'Then,' said Rex, with a quick glance at his notes, 'we move to Folder 3 of Binder 1 [*SWIPE*; *TAP*; *SHORT-FLING*] and we've got a witness statement given on the day – sadly it's unwitnessed; you'd be surprised how many of these statements are unwitnessed – by Inspector Melbourne of Barnsley, Oliver Melbourne, Olly to his mates, who says [*SCROLL*], "At three forty-five p.m.... the Unit was deployed to Devonshire Green where numerous buses were parked and members of the National Union of Mineworkers were walking to their buses after demonstrating in Sheffield City Centre.

I arrived at the car park on Devonshire Green with my unit. Stones and glass bottles were being thrown at the police. Near one of the buses I saw one demonstrator on the ground with a headwound."

'Remember,' said Rex, 'William Cooper didn't die from his injuries until the ninth of May.'

'Of course!' said Melissa. 'So if that's Cooper the assumption is it's just one more miner with cuts and bruises.'

'Yes, maybe so,' said Rex, 'but if that's Cooper, then on Olly Melbourne's authority, an Inspector no less, that's Cooper already down at three forty-five, five minutes before Arthur's sighting.

'Then we move to PC Edward Peach's witness statement on the arrest of Richard Beese – Binder 1, File 4 [*SWIPE*; *TAP*; *SHORT-FLING*; *SCROLL*]. Beese was not cautioned by Peach at time of arrest, three forty-two, because Peach claims he was being jostled, but arrival at the mobile cell block is logged at three forty-seven p.m. And, questioned at Barnsley Police Station the next day by Detective Constable Ben Bowman, Beese says [*SWIPE*; *TAP*; *SHORT-FLING*; *SCROLL*], "I crossed Devonshire Green and starts walking to find some of my mates for cars. I see one of them on ground by Donny bus, with two or three coppers around him." So that's at least three minutes *before* Olly Melbourne. A sighting also corroborated by Gerry Kent – File 11, Binder 1 – interviewed at seven fifty p.m. the next day by Detective Sergeant Daniel Whitehouse and Detective Constable Cameron Knock at Sheffield Police Station here [*SWIPE*; *TAP*]. And note that Beese and Kent are immediately arrested by PSUs from different stations. They're on completely different custody pathways from the off. So – this is vitally important – Beese and Kent have not been able to speak or to compare stories at this time. Then Beese gets into an altercation with a policeman making another arrest – for which he himself is arrested – and there's no further mention of the miner on the ground. But triangulate that with this black-and-white time-stamped Portacam footage, we see Beese – in this distinctive hooped jumper – crossing the road at three forty p.m. So we think Cooper Ground Zero is between three forty-one and three forty-two p.m. And we thought we had it because the accused Roderick Lister interviewed by DC Philip Ramshaw at Rotherham Police Station eleven fifty-eight a.m. in File 12 talks about a "kid" on the ground by an unidentified bus "getting a bit of a kicking" but Lister's already away in the mobile cell block by three twenty p.m., so it's a different incident. Same with the *quote* "coloured officer" *unquote* – pardon my French – who's seen "delivering a sharp kick" to a man on the ground. That was outside the Wimpy on Fargate, way over here' – Rex pointed towards the north-east of the incident zone – 'at two forty p.m., and appears to be related to sections of the crowd making monkey noises at the Black officer.'

'Charming,' said Shepherd. 'You wouldn't think—' she began saying, but then let it go.

'I know,' said Rex. 'But just because they're striking miners doesn't mean they were all fervent anti-racists, unfortunately.'

'No, I suppose not.'

'There weren't that many Black miners in the NUM. If you get my drift.'

'Shit,' said Shepherd. 'I hadn't thought.'

'So here's a funny thing,' said Rex, moving on to the next page of his notes. 'The protester in that incident at the Wimpy appears to have been seen being arrested by the same Black officer, because [*SWIPE*; *TAP*] the accused Keith O'Connor is arrested by Sergeant Keith Allnut of Woodseats for trying to interfere in said arrest. Interviewed by DC Philip Ramshaw – that name again! – in Rotherham Police Station at eight thirty a.m. on the eighth of May, O'Connor says, "Me and me mate were outside Wimpy. One of Kent lads was getting kicked by the coloured officer, and I went to pull him out of scuffling because that's what it was." "So one of your mates was scuffling with police?" Ramshaw asks. "No, a Kent lad. Not so much scuffling as he was on ground. And I tried to pull him out of it, I had hold of him twice you know," says O'Connor. "It was all happening so fast I can't really tell you in detail." "Tell me what happened then," says DC Ramshaw. "Well," says O'Connor, "I don't know because the next thing I knew someone had their hands around my throat."

'But there's no paper trail of that supposed arrest. My theory? The so-called "Kent miner" on the ground is a UCO, and they didn't want to lose him into the system, as it were – too much hassle. So the "arrest" might just have been for show and they'd have *accidentally-on-purpose* let him struggle free on the way to the mobile.'

'Did you say something about student footage?' said Shepherd.

'Yup,' said Atwell. 'Students. Who'd have thought it: students to the rescue.'

'And a radio ham,' said Rex. 'Listening in to police radio from an attic up the top end of Penrhyn Road, who just happened to tape the lot.'

'Rex told you about the *Bulletin* documentary, I take it?' said Atwell.

'That got pulled? Yeah, he did.' Melissa Shepherd sat down. 'Bloody hell!' she said. 'Is this what you do all the time, then, Lily? This level of kit is unreal. It's like science fiction. We've got one flat-screen down at Midhurst… But I could count the times we've switched it on with one hand; and two of them were for football. Seeing all this makes me feel like we're working in a different century. How many people have you had on this?'

'We've had six coders from my team,' said Atwell, 'working in teams of two on eight-hour shifts round the clock, plus the team back at Tinworth Street. Andante's only ever as good as the metadata, really. And with this much analogue material, a lot of that has had to be input by hand. I mean, this is the first time we've used Andante to review historic and archive material in this way, so it's a bit of a road test – which is good, we need to push it, and it means I can offset part of this with my training and development budgets – but it's holding up fine so far.'

'Sci-fi! That's what I said, Melissa,' said Rex. 'What's that film called?' He waved his arms at an imaginary screen. 'But now I've got used to this as an investigative tool I want to use it on everything. Chance'd be a fine thing. Hang on, though, I haven't finished yet. We've got the *Bulletin* VT editor's hard drive, so we've been able to let Andante unscramble their edit, tag each shot for time, location, direction – who's behind the camera in some cases, facial recognition – and redistribute the lot through our timeline.' Rex tapped a button on the left-hand screen and a whole new set of thumbnails – both colour and black and white – populated the bar like a deck of cards, each slotting into place, one after the other, across the screen from left to right.

'It's great, but I don't get it,' said Shepherd. 'All of this doesn't seem to have anything to do with Lollo's disappearance any more. Or am I missing something? What exactly are you two investigating here?'

'Oh, didn't I say,' said Rex.

The Sussex Detective Sergeant shook her head.

'Murder,' said Rex.

◆ ◆ ◆

Listening to Met Deputy Chaplain Barry Lincoln, and to Lollo's reading, Detective Sergeant Rex King found himself looking past his colleagues and out of the tenth-floor windows at the dazzle and drear of the November sky. Fast-moving clouds were coming in towards them from roughly the south-west, reflected in the shadows that flickered across the rooftops and elevations of Covent Garden, Holborn, Bloomsbury, Soho and Fitzrovia.

Lollo always took the annual remembrance service very seriously, and encouraged others to do the same. As miners, his father and grandfather had been in an essential profession, but his pacifist grandmother had been a military nurse on the front line… which as far as he was concerned represented a higher order of gallantry altogether: to have gone into that maelstrom unarmed. Aside from his ceremonial stint as *Custos Grayorum* a few years back, when he'd have been needed in the chapel at Gray's Inn, Lollo had attended the Holborn service religiously year in and year out since his transfer to the Met, whether it was his name on the rota or not. He never bunked off as others might, nor tried to foist attendance on an underling.

Rex couldn't help wondering how many other small workplace remembrance services were going on in public buildings and works across London and beyond at that same moment, in barracks, bases and regimental chapels, yes, but also in places of public service, in hospitals and railway stations, schools, colleges and universities, postal sorting offices and theatres, waterworks and telephone exchanges; in lifeboat, ambulance, fire and police stations.

Of course, too, at that moment, Rex knew there were the larger civic functions taking place outside in all weathers at war memorials great and small, on village greens and in town centres and town halls across the capital, and the country. Memorials that had been raised by public subscription after the First World War or the Second, in churchyards or on village greens in once-bucolic outer London boroughs. Some of those monuments now barely visible, stripped of viable scrap metal, dwindled and encroached upon by road-widening schemes, by signage and illuminated hoardings. Seen through steamy top-deck windows by front-seat pilots on North and South Circular bus routes: the crosses and cairns, plaques and plinths, angels and allegorical figures, obelisks and cenotaphs, briefly red-wreath-wracked by November's sentimental storm-tide, then untended again for another year. Bronze Tommies whose static gazes now fell onto controlled traffic flows, with modern 'wait times' subject to real-time adaptive sensor control adjustment, where once they'd gazed upon milepost and cattle trough; upon triangles of grass, kempt except where the wall barley's flea dart harvest ripened bushy beyond the mower's reach around white-stone post-and-chain boundaries, all long-vanished.

But alongside those larger civic functions and hidden from public view, how many small, local workplace gatherings like this one? How many staff giving up their Sunday mornings once a year – whether from a sense of duty or job description; drawing the short straw – to come together cross-generationally and remember fallen colleagues with archaic, local-variant surnames. How many workplace chaplains stepping forward again, as the Met's Barry Lincoln was now, to recite the 'Act of Remembrance'—

Melissa Shepherd looked around the large third-floor Clean Room. It had taken a second or two to work out what this set-up reminded her of. It certainly didn't look like any prior investigation she'd seen. Nor in fact like any kind of policing she'd been privy to up until now, but whatever was going on here certainly took the job to a whole new level, and a whole new budget scale to boot, she didn't wonder.

The Science Museum, that was it.

It reminded her of that exhibition they'd seen at the Science Museum a couple of years ago. She and Mags had taken Melissa's godchildren James and Suzy to the Science Museum, and down in the basement there'd been a large and brightly lit white room and all these big tables, each piled up with rubbish for the sorting. Yes. For a month, every single item of rubbish or recycling disposed of by museum staff and visitors was being photographed, analysed and reckoned-with in some way. She couldn't quite remember. It had been a touchy-feely, artsy-educational, visitor-participation kind of thing, and the kids had *loved* it. They all had.

This – the scene in the Clean Room – looked a bit like that.

On the three table tennis tables at one end of the room, the evidence was bagged and tagged and ready to go to the store. All of it, hundreds or maybe thousands of items, had been photographed and catalogued, and any media content – digital or analogue – had now been conserved, duplicated, scanned or in many cases migrated onto some more stable archival format, and saved on the shared drive. Workflow targets had been mapped onto the large wall-mounted whiteboards, scribbled out, and exceeded.

Good luck to them, thought Melissa. It must have been a management nightmare. No wonder Atwell had brought her own team over.

What would it cost, Shepherd wondered, an investigation like this? Probably more than the entire annual budget for her station. You probably could have kept the little police stations at Selsey and Steyning open too, for less money than this was costing. And for what, really? She'd grown to like and admire the missing Detective Chief Inspector Jethro Lawrence in his absence. But she'd all but given up hope of actually finding him.

DS Melissa Shepherd had been assuming the worst for a while. And now it seemed that King and Atwell's attention had shifted too.

Showing Melissa some of the analogue assets – Super 8 and 16mm film, obsolete video cassettes and reel-to-reel tapes, cassettes, piles of paper – Lily Atwell had proudly informed Shepherd that the digitisation process had been a – how had she put it? – *museum-standard conservation operation*. Yes, that was it: 'museum-standard'. Those were exactly the words she'd used.

Melissa had been surprised. And in that moment, the flash of recognition, she'd very nearly blurted out that *Yes!* it reminded her of the Science Museum. This funny exhibition— But she'd stopped herself; kept schtum, and just nodded: 'Wow.'

The video cassettes and film reels weren't even the half of it. Thousands of items were now logged and indexed. Each with its own invisible cloud of metadata. All completely beyond the capacity of any one individual to work through and read, let alone to apprehend in full, unless you had a spare year or two. But looked at through the lens of the NCA's Andante software, you could conduct it like an orchestra, instantaneously. And here was Rex, like the Sorcerer's Apprentice, conducting – across a wall-mounted triptych of large flat-screen monitors – a forensic reconstruction of a civil disturbance that had taken place in Sheffield city centre on 7 May 1984, drawing on sources as diverse as leaked witness statements relating to twenty-seven wrongful arrests, and a TV documentary that had been halted mid-production but which itself had drawn on the usual archive news footage and outtakes, but also whistle-blower testimony, scripts for dramatic reconstructions of key episodes, and now – it seemed – a load of never-before-seen footage that had been shot on location on the day by Sheffield City Polytechnic students who'd just happened to be doing a documentary film-making workshop in the city centre while all this was going on.

Rex had made her laugh over at Sid's. Before they'd had to get suited up to go into the Clean Room.

Melissa had said something about it all sounding like 'three-dimensional chess'. And then she'd laughed and told Rex how she could remember watching *Star Trek* as a young kid, with her dad. And how, in those innocent days, 'three-dimensional chess' had seemed the absolute height of human complexity.

'Complex?' Rex had said. 'I'll give you complex. Try ten-dimensional. Come on, let's get back. I want to introduce you to Lily. You'll like her.'

Shepherd had finished her tea, then followed him back outside.

'Hang on,' she'd said. 'Look at me a sec.'

Rex, recognising some maternal tone in Shepherd's voice, had done as he was told. He'd stopped on the pavement outside Sid's, and chin up, eyes on Shepherd, turned his head slowly from side to side.

'Bit red,' she'd said, 'but I think you've got away with it. A black eye would have started showing by now.'

'It looks like your textbook South Yorkshire fuck-up,' Rex had said as they'd walked back over to the station from the cafe. 'By which I mean a total failure of policing. Even after April's near-riot, they believed their own hype and policed it like a standard 404, which meant they failed to recognise it as a Critical Incident even when it was happening right in front of their faces.'

'Really?' Melissa had said without a hint of sarcasm.

'Yeah. I don't know what they were thinking. It ticked near enough all the boxes for a CI even *before* Cooper was fatally injured. Offender status notwithstanding, obviously, because we can't say for sure who struck the blow.'

All the boxes? Shepherd had thought, mentally conjuring the Critical Incident checklist from CIP training; the games of 'Critical Incident Bingo'.

Media Interest? – *check*.

Failure to follow standard operating procedures/policy? – *check*.

Wider community issues? – *check*.

Serious injury? – *check*.

Significant damage? – *check*.

Local interest? – *check*.

Regional interest? – *check*.

National interest? – *check*.

Vulnerable victim? – *maybe not*.

Prominent victim? – *check*.

Repeat victim? – well, an NUM shop steward at that time? – *check*.

Repeat location? – *check*.

Repeat offender? – unknown – okay, she'd give Rex that.

Prominent offender? – unknown – *ditto*.

Large number of victims, though? – *check*.

Policing error? – *check*.

Minority community issues? – *check*.

Prominent location? – *check*.

Police misconduct? – probably? – *check*.

Failure within the criminal system? – *check*.

Victim from within the police service? – well, hate speech wasn't a crime back then, but okay – *check*.

Offender from within the police service? – probably? – *check*.

Political interest? – *check*.

How about the LSIs?

Likely significant impact on the victim? – *check*.

LSI on the family? – *check*.

LSI on the community? – *check*.

'Okay, I'll give you offender status,' Shepherd had said. 'And vulnerable victim? – well, not really. Other than that, though, what box didn't it tick?'

'Criterion *numero uno*,' King had said as he punched the entry code into the keypad on the staff entrance on Richbell Place, surprised that Shepherd had missed the self-evident truth: 'Death!'

Melissa had face-palmed. 'D'oh!'

'Because… ?' he'd asked. (Lollo had trained Rex well.)

'Because… that didn't come until two days later,' Shepherd had said, though she'd had to think about it for a second.

'Precisely. Cooper's death is registered when his ventilator is switched off at six p.m. on the ninth of May in the ICU at the Royal Hallamshire Hospital. But other than "Death" you're seventy-odd per cent of the way to a CI full house, *and* all three LSIs. Yet, even then, there's clearly no lessons learned beyond arse-covering, no training updated, no institutional memory whatso-fucking-ever. Because roll on five years and the next time you're facing a 404 that's rapidly turning to shit, it happens again, only more so, ninety-six times over. But it starts with Cooper. No, actually, it starts back in eighty-one with thirty-eight fans in the Leppings Lane end injured in a crushing incident at the Spurs–Wolves semi. In a stand that hadn't had a safety certificate since seventy-nine. What's wrong with just doing your fucking job, eh? Those poor lads never stood a fucking chance. And by eighty-nine you really do have a full house. Because *you're* now the repeat and prominent offender.'

Shepherd had looked at him blankly. '"You" in this case being… ?'

'Us. Well, South Yorks.'

There'd been a pause.

Say it out loud, Rex had thought; you've got to keep saying it: the date that goes down in the Universal History of Infamy and the rollcalls of hell. 'The fifteenth of April 1989.'

Shepherd had known the date. 'Hillsborough,' she'd said.

Rex had nodded.

Shepherd had felt a chill.

A boundless chasm had opened up beneath them: the weeks and months of anticipation building through that whole unbeaten cup run that had come to a head on 18 March, when Liverpool had beaten Brentford at home 4–0, taking them into the semi-finals, a season's worth of early starts and coach journeys round the country coming good, the scarves and the singing, the service stations, the buzz of pleasure and excitement and a kind of heaven on earth turning to puzzlement and surprise and disbelief, indignation and pleading, and the agony of suffocation and pissing yourself in pain and fear, of loss and grief and darkness and blood and shit and lies upon lies upon lies upon lies upon lies and enough stone-cold culpability and shame – *you would think* – both individual and corporate to last several eternities.

Rex had knocked at the door of the third-floor Clean Room, before reaching down to open it and offering DS Melissa Shepherd into the brightly lit space beyond: 'After you.'

◆ ◆ ◆

'Let us remember before God,' said the Met's Deputy Chaplain Barry Lincoln, 'and commend to his sure keeping: those who have died for their country in war; those whom we knew, and whose memory we treasure; and all who have lived and died in the service of mankind.'

Rex, thinking, as instructed, as ever, of those whose memory he treasured – and glancing around the room at Lollo, Tommy Bee and Jane Milligan, at Simon Rose, Eric Jinks and Tabitha Churchill, at Evelyn Gummer, Di Malcolm, Sue Stanza and Angela Soul – noticed that, although the Deputy Chaplain was holding the Order of Service as if reading from it, his eyes were firmly closed. He was reciting the act from memory.

'They shall grow not old as we that are left grow old,' said Lincoln. And Rex wondered if it was about time to lay to rest some ghosts from his own distant past. If it was time to embrace the living; this beautiful woman who had stepped into his life.

Meeting Susan had been a miracle. Sitting outside Sid's that morning, Derby Day no less, worrying about her niece in Great Ormond Street Hospital. First they'd fallen into that easy and instant rapport, and by the end of that very same day they'd fallen into bed. She'd felt almost too good to be true, but here she was, still in his life. Sure, the relationship had its challenges – not least that she still lived up in York. Combined with the pressures of his work, it made it hard to plan anything, and anything you did plan tended to fall apart at the last minute. But he understood that she didn't want to come to London and be financially dependent upon him – she was actively looking for work, but he was confident she'd find something, and in the same line of work because London was not short of universities –

'HEIs', as Susan called them. He hadn't understood at first: 'eight-chi-eyes', what's that? – and, let's face it, from what Susan said, if there was a cohort of university staff that was needed more than ever these days it certainly wasn't your actual academic and teaching staff. Her horror stories of zero-hours contracts, casualisation, disempowerment and institutional abuse. The growth areas were in finance and requisitions, estate management, Pro-VCs, lavish salaries funded by pension contribution holidays. She'd put in for a support role at one of the London colleges.

They'd said, 'Don't you think you're overqualified?' and Susan had said that she'd been thinking things were so bad she'd have to get a job in a chocolate shop, so this would be a sight more up her street than that.

'Age shall not weary them,' said Lincoln, 'nor the years condemn. At the going down of the sun and in the morning. We will remember them.'

'We will remember them,' said Rex, said Lollo, said Tommy Bee, said Jane Milligan, said Simon Rose, said Eric Jinks, said Tabitha Churchill, said Evelyn Gummer, said Di Malcolm, said Sue Stanza, said Angela Soul: all joining in with the customary sotto voce chorus of observance.

Tommy Bee stepped forward and – looking a few degrees above the horizontal, as if this was to be sounded for the benefit of the farthest men on the battlefield – he brought the long cavalry trumpet close to his lips. Then, as part of the same movement, he slowly raised his right elbow until his arm was horizontal and wrist bent, so that he was reaching down to hold the trumpet from above. This was a habit from his own military service, whether on Horse Guards Parade or in 'Afghan'. Days when 'sounding the call' in full dress uniform had required him to hold the regiment's pendant banner clear of horse or body. There was a pause as he took a breath, then: contact. For a fraction of a second all you heard was Bee's breath and the spittle that sprayed through the mouthpiece into the elongated curl of brass tubing and the final, open trumpet flare beyond.

Then he found the note.

And what a note it was.

Talk about a fanfare for the common man, thought Rex.

Being ex-Household Cavalry, Bee didn't customarily play the more usual, well-known tune of the B-flat 'Last Post' (although of course he could, he had the standard bugle back at home, and had done so on countless occasions when instructed), but by special request of the Chief Superintendent and with the permission of the Metropolitan Police Chaplaincy, the less well-known E-flat call used by British cavalry regiments.

If you weren't expecting it, it could take you by surprise, this simple call, with its echoes – in the opening and closing bars – of the huntsman's horn.

Of the assembled company, only Barry Lincoln was here today for the first time, and he knew what was coming. But even then, Rex thought he saw the Deputy Chaplain flinch slightly as that first, less familiar G-below-middle-C rang out clearly in the air. The hundred-and-twenty-odd notes ending, in the stuffy air and muffled acoustics of the tenth-floor vestibule, with that final sustained G.

A faint echo ringing down the stairwell.

Who could say what thought-acts had filled the minute's silence that followed.

It was a silence you could get lost in.

And with his head bowed, and without looking at the others, Rex had wondered what if anything they each had to hide.

◆ ◆ ◆

While Lily Atwell nipped out for a comfort break and Rex checked emails, Melissa Shepherd walked slowly and in silence around the evidence tables. She was trying to take it all in. There were more than two and a half thousand items, all told.

Ziplocked evidence bags containing everything from hard drives to 10x8 black-and-white contact sheets, to gigantic ancient video tapes in obsolete formats, and tiny plastic reels of Super 8 and 16mm movie film. Amazing to think that all this ancient media was now *in the system*; not only that, it was what they'd just been looking at, whizzing through it in – what had Atwell said? – *ten* dimensions in the NCA's interactive AI. Why 'Andante', though? Shepherd had wondered. She thought she remembered from childhood piano lessons that it meant 'slowly'. But there was nothing *slow* about this.

Was it just that it sounded good? Yeah, probably.

As she slowly paced around, hands clasped behind her back, she was trying to mentally process everything they'd thrown at her so far. And it felt familiar. This thoughtful kind of looking-but-not-touching, *was* like a museum or an art gallery.

'I know they're called "exhibits",' she said, 'so I'm really stating the bleeding obvious here, but it actually *is* like an exhibition. Not paintings, I don't mean. You know, modern art.' She looked around. 'Big white space. Stuff on tables. Hi-tech screens.'

'Yeah. Plenty of that round here – galleries – if that's what you're into,' said Rex, looking up from his phone. 'Used to be, anyway.' He remembered going on a call with Webbo years back: 'Cool Britannia' time. There'd been a break-in at a little gallery next to the old Reuters building. 'The proper stuff, I mean,' he continued. '"Contemporary art", they call it now. What's your interest in that, then?'

'Kids,' said Melissa. 'Well, godparent duty.'

'Nice,' said Rex.

'Yeah. It is. We do at least a couple of London museum trips every summer, and the kids like Tate Modern. There's always something new to see, and you can get a ferry.'

'Yeah, we've done that,' said Rex. 'Me and Annie.'

Back in the day, when he and Webbo had arrived at the premises on the call-out, they'd been greeted by the proprietor – who'd introduced himself as 'the gallerist' – a well-spoken, tall and friendly, jovial kind of guy. Well, you probably had to be in that game, to part people from their money. But sort of jovial and serious all at once: lots of big words, and sharp as a tack.

Rex thought about telling the story to Melissa, but he wasn't sure it was worth anyone's time. It was good, though. The gallery had been down an alley, or a service road, in a brick-built, mid-sized single-storey, former light-industrial premises. In that part of Clerkenwell it could once have been anything, from a printer's, to rag trade, to a machine shop or a clock factory. It'd probably stood empty for a decade or so before being turned into a high-end contemporary art gallery.

They'd walked in and been taken aback to find that the whole space inside had been crammed with helium balloons, floor to ceiling. You literally couldn't have got more balloons into the building. A burglary? Rex couldn't quite imagine how the individual concerned had been able to find *anything* amidst all this, much less nick it.

But Webbo hadn't been able to contain himself. It had pressed all his buttons. 'Bloody hell,' he'd spluttered. 'What dickhead done this?'

Quick as a flash, the gallerist had shot back: 'It's the dickhead that stole my fax machine and my laptop that *I'm* bothered about, if you don't mind.'

And he'd been right.

There was an important lesson there: stick to your job, don't come the armchair art critic.

Over by the evidence tables, Shepherd stopped to read a document through the plastic. Not a press clipping, but an A4 print-out of a web page, dashed and dotted with yellow highlighter.

CONSPIRACY OF SILENCE OVER COOPER DEATH

South Yorkshire force to be criticised for culture of 'omerta' over the death of NUM shop steward William Cooper in Sheffield 28 years ago.

A forthcoming documentary in the Channel 4 *Bulletin* series is expected to criticise the South Yorkshire constabulary for a continuing 'conspiracy of silence' over the death of Barnsley area NUM official William Cooper from head injuries sustained during a controversial rally in support of the Miners' Strike of 1984–85 that took place in Sheffield city centre on 7 May 1984. On that day, 27 protesters were arrested and charged with 'riot', although the trial collapsed alongside parallel 'riot trials' for Mansfield and the so-called 'Battle of Orgreave', amid allegations of wrongful arrest, assault, and flawed police procedures.

The documentary, *The Riot That Never Was*, will show new evidence suggesting South Yorkshire officers, together with members of so-called 'spycops' unit the Special Demonstration Squad and military reservists, working secretly on the scene from carriers referred to as 'Rogers 1, 2 and 3', were responsible for the death.

The documentary will be aired later this year, amid counter-claims that the South Yorkshire constabulary has changed. This despite the fact that no convictions have resulted from the Hillsborough Inquiry and Operation Resolve investigations.

The *Bulletin* programme will, for the first time, air testimony from a South Yorkshire constabulary whistle-blower.

Programme-makers say there is an 'indication' that one officer in particular was responsible for Cooper's death, but whose name has been redacted from the documentary. And that there was a 'deliberate and sustained attempt to conceal the presence of the carriers at the scene, both on the day and subsequently'.

Speaking in London, a Metropolitan Police spokesperson said that UK Police as a collective body rejected the findings of the documentary that South Yorkshire and/or Special Demonstration Squad officers were responsible for Cooper's death, but added: 'I am particularly sorry that we can't bring it to that definitive point where we can absolutely say what happened, why it happened, and what was the legitimacy or otherwise of that.'

The spokesperson added that there is not sufficient evidence to prosecute anyone for the brutal attack on Cooper, who had attended a march and rally in support of the National Union of Mineworkers dispute, nor to prosecute anyone who might have conspired to conceal the identity of any such individuals.

Cooper's son, David Cooper, said: 'This documentary shows what we have always believed, that my father was killed by one of the officers whose names have been withheld from the public domain over all these years.'

The documentary-makers said that the identities of the officers who they believe travelled to the Devonshire Green, Sheffield, car park where Cooper was attacked, in unregistered patrol vans known only as 'Rogers 1, 2 and 3', remain undisclosed in the documentary, despite the fact they are thought to have attended an open inquest two years after Cooper died.

It is thought that the redactions have been made either because the programme-makers have not found conclusive evidence that the officers were the most likely to have inflicted the fatal blow, or because they do not wish to prejudice any resulting or future criminal prosecution.

It is known that South Yorkshire Inspector Thomas Orwell was in charge of three carriers, SDS Units known as 'Rogers 1, 2 and 3', on the day of Cooper's death and throughout the first months of the NUM strike. Orwell died in 2005, having resigned from the force in 1994 to join his brother's financial publishing business, after criticism of his relationship with the tabloid press in the aftermath of the Hillsborough disaster in which 96 Liverpool supporters died.

According to a long-serving Labour MP interviewed for the programme, the South Yorkshire constabulary have a culture of 'covering up', while a serving officer said that the force had a 'code of silence' akin to organised criminal gangs.[4]

Detective Sergeant Melissa Shepherd felt a mixture of shame and recognition, but quickly pulled herself together.

'So all of this' – she gestured at the tables – 'was given to us by the documentary-maker? Is that right?'

And they evidently didn't have too much trouble finding it, she thought to herself. So why didn't we?

'Rob Langdon,' said Rex. 'Producer and director. Yeah, exactly. His initial contact went into my spam folder, so it took us a few days. All except "Binders 1 and 2". You know, the, um, police statements, the court papers: Leak Number One, as we called it. The programme-maker came forward independently when they saw the news about Lollo.'

'What's the connection?' said Shepherd. 'Why break the silence now? And what's all this got to do with DCI Lawrence?'

'I thought you'd have guessed that already,' said Rex.

When the minute's silence was up, Tommy Bee brought the cavalry trumpet back to his lips, as he had done so many times before, elbow uppermost in that same overarm stance, to sound once more the 'Reveille'; again, by special request, the less familiar E-flat cavalry trumpet variant.

Was the assembled congregation – standing in a silent semicircle by the lifts in the tenth-floor vestibule of Holborn Police Station – oblivious to the events that would overtake it the following summer? Each of them holding their respective wreath, recycled from the last

---

4 'Conspiracy of Silence Over Cooper Death', *Yorkshire Herald*, 22/12/2013, 22.56 (online editions only – withdrawn 23/12/2013, 06.00).

time or ordered in anew, and each waiting for the moment when – once the final notes of the 'Reveille' had died away – they would, with the exception of Metropolitan Police Deputy Chaplain Barry Lincoln and Tommy Bee, and starting with Chief Superintendent Tabitha Churchill, take their turns one by one to step those few paces forward on the grey carpet tiles to lay said wreath behind the short brass rail on its narrow ledge beneath the old war memorial.

But surely those events would already have been 'in train' (as Tabitha Churchill might herself have said, of projects, initiatives or investigations already well commenced). Although the question of who knew what and when might be a more difficult one to answer.

But what was it that fell almost unnoticed from the pocket of Lollo's rarely worn dress uniform trousers, as with the wreath held in his left hand he pulled a large paisley handkerchief out of his right trouser pocket to blow his nose before squaring up his chin and stepping forward?

Standing next to Lollo, with his head slightly bowed, and readying himself to stoop and pick up his own wreath, Rex saw the fluttering movement out of the corner of his eye, and as the Detective Chief Inspector repocketed the hanky and stepped forward with wreath now held in both hands, Rex kneeled as if out of respect, as if he'd noticed a lace had come undone. It had landed next to his shoe, smaller than a postage stamp: a tightly folded piece of paper.

In one smooth movement, Rex calmly picked up the pocket-burnished scrap and held it between his third and little fingers and palm as he tidied his laces. As Lollo stopped and laid his wreath, and by the time he'd bowed his head for the customary couple of beats, Rex had already straightened up, picked up his wreath, and placed the scrap of paper unread in his own left trouser pocket. And before Lollo had quite resumed his place in the line-up, Rex was already beginning to step forward, wreath in hand, to sombrely take his own turn.

◆ ◆ ◆

Rex didn't say anything to Atwell, but he'd been spending so much time on Andante – poring over Rob Langdon's documentary footage, even after she and the coders had left for the night – that he'd started thinking like a TV producer, dreaming increasingly unlikely trailers and programme blurbs. Last night's dream had been particularly vivid:

Who's Spying on the Spycops: Bulletin (Channel 4) goes undercover in the UK's two most notorious spycop squads and finds evidence of institutional sexism, racism, corruption and abuse. Reporter Gina McQueen went undercover in the police as PCSO then agency staff for a decade before being made permanent. McQueen then went incommunicado for a year in order to gain access to safe houses and dark sites across the capital. Her extraordinary secret camera footage shows spycops sharing pornographic footage of surveillance subjects, using racist and sexist language, and leaving the privacy and dignity of both fellow officers and the victims of crime often ignored. McQueen exposes the spycops' official and unofficial 'trade craft' manuals, and how so-called 'restriction orders' and super-injunctions are used to prevent scrutiny, and in so doing finds layers of deception still operating in the modern Met. The NPOIU and SDS earn millions from police and Home Office budgets, and have already been told to make improvements. McQueen is now believed to be in hiding. An emergency safeguarding plan is now in place after the programme-makers raised their concerns with Her Majesty's Inspectorate of Constabulary and Fire & Rescue Services (HMICFRS), the Home Office, and other agencies.

In the dream he'd been reading this press release at his desk on the sixth floor, before walking into the old library, where he'd been horrified to see that the old orange ammunition-store filing cabinet with the 'nuclear hazard' sticker wasn't there in its usual corner. The carpet tiles still bore its imprint: a deep impression in the fibres, as might be made by an extremely heavy weight only recently moved. He'd run to the window in desperation, from where, looking down to street level, he saw two men using a hydraulic pallet truck to lift the heavy cabinet into the back of an unmarked Luton van. He'd turned and run full tilt for the stairwell; raced down two or three steps at once, burst out of the staff entrance onto Richbell Place and a deserted Lamb's Conduit Street just in time to see the van turn left at the junction with Theobalds Road. As it did so, a familiar face turned to look back at him from the nearside passenger window of the cab—

Rex had woken up sweating, his heart pounding.

He got up and went to the bathroom, splashed his face and drank a small glass of water. He leaned on the sink for a moment, then assumed a standing meditation stance – sinking slightly onto bent knees, hands gently spread in front of his body, palms inwards, with middle fingers pointing at each other – and centred his breathing for a few minutes.

'You okay?' Annie had said when he got back into bed.

'Yeah, bad dream,' Rex had said. 'Go back to sleep.'

Atwell's 'comfort break' was taking longer than expected.

But Melissa Shepherd was in no hurry. There was plenty still to take in. According to Rex's summary, the abandoned *Bulletin* documentary from which most of this evidence had been sourced was – or would have been – built around interviews with a whistle-blower from the South Yorkshire force. She'd not seen it yet, but Langdon had filmed tens of hours of interviews in a darkened room and protected their – his – identity further by using a voice actor. The whistle-blower had given them copies of the original muster rolls, and 'starting line-ups' for the day, plans that were drawn out on Ordnance Survey maps of the city centre that listed and placed all the PSUs present on the day, showing the positions of the various units and divisions before, during and after the march, around the rally itself, and to manage the safe transit of the crowds afterwards. The PSUs from Barnsley and from Rotherham, from all the Sheffield subs, large and small, from City Road, Woodseats, Dronfield and Attercliffe; the mounted units in from Cudworth.

But among all this there was no note – and no trace – of Rogers 1, 2 and 3.

And if there'd been two thousand officers in attendance, the hundred or so who'd actually given witness statements and been directly involved in arrests and chain of custody, the hundred or so in Binders 1 and 2 of Leak Number One, were only five per cent of the total. But still, scanning the muster rolls, the lists of personnel, alphabetically or by station and unit, there was no record of Jethro Lawrence here.

Looking from table to table, a photo caught Shepherd's eye: a 10x8 black-and-white photographic print from the archives of the *Sheffield Star*, according to a paper chit and the rubber stamp on the reverse. It was a photo of local 'radio ham' Frank Cross from Hunter's Bar. Cross had had a thirty-foot antenna in his back yard at the time. The picture had been taken to accompany a news story celebrating Cross's having received and logged the final telemetry signal from the failing US space station Skylab before its disintegration in the atmosphere above the Indian Ocean and Western Australia on 11 July 1979; clippings from the *Sheffield Star*, *Yorkshire Post* and *Daily Mirror* also supplied. In the photo he was sitting at the desk in his Penrhyn Road attic facing a big old – possibly home-made – radio and transmitter set (a 'rig' and 'TX', in the amateur radio lingo of the day). On the exposed brick wall behind him hung the various necessary certificates and licences ('wallpaper', in radio ham speak), and that year's Bardwell's calendar. And amidst these was a framed embroidery sampler of 'the Radio Ham's Commitment', upon which the text of that short address or secular prayer was framed by an arrangement of cross-stitched antennae, Morse switches and electrical symbols. Sewn, Shepherd wouldn't wonder, by Mrs Cross on the long lonely evenings while Frank was upstairs:

> Let us pledge ourselves anew to radio,
> To communicating with our fellow men and women.
> That we may listen to, acknowledge, and reply to others,
> and support those working toward mutual understanding
> and clarity of signal on any frequency,
> and for the peace and welfare of all nations.
> *Key up! and copy.*

Stapled to this was another evidence bag that contained eight grey plastic TDK C-90 cassette tapes in their crystal cases, and another containing a pile of Cross's Sheffield City Council-issued QSL cards. 'G8 ALW' was the call-sign, which with Cross's address was printed in red on the back, over a black-and-white photo taken from within the city's once-famous Hole in the Road. Inside the cards, verso, facing the correspondence form, someone in the Town Hall had evidently had the wit to place a decent plug for the city itself. Good thinking when you considered that such QSL cards would be exchanged by post or by hand with other radio hams around the world following any on-air contact ('QSO'). So why not give the place a bit of a puff? 'Sheffield,' it said in bold black type over a mustard-yellow ground, '… the emerging city of the North.'

Yorkshire's largest city and the finest shopping centre in the north of England.
Europe's cleanest industrial city, where the grime of yesterday has been ruthlessly eliminated.
The city of quality, with an unrivalled reputation for skill and craftsmanship.
The friendly, trouble-free city, unfamiliar with industrial strife and student unrest.
The city dominated by trees and flowers, and surrounded by countryside of exquisite beauty.

Shepherd snorted in amusement.

'Haha, I know,' said Rex, beating her to it. '"Unfamiliar with industrial strife"! Good one! They'd have had to rewrite that after this, I reckon. The programme-makers tracked him down. Good old Frank, he was scanning the police radios all day: twelve hours' worth. He'd had them buried in a biscuit tin in the garden ever since. It's a miracle they survived. Programme-makers didn't know what to do with it, there's so much of it, but when we dropped his audio into Andante, everything fell into place. It just plays out right before your eyes. You hear the commands and then *boom*: a couple of minutes later the cordon is formed, the carrier moves, the horse units charge, the snatch squads go in, the arrests start.'

They heard footsteps outside, and someone punching in the Clean Room keycode.

'Right,' said Lily Atwell as she pushed open the door. 'Sorry about that. I was needed on a conference call. Oh, you found Frank Cross, I see. What a star! Him and lovely Gerry Bannerman. They don't make 'em like that any more. Where were we?'

'Film students?' said Melissa, putting down the evidence bag. 'Wasn't it something about a film workshop?'

'Exactly,' said Atwell. 'Bannerman's film workshop group.'

And while Rex lined it up, she told Shepherd that the producers of *The Riot That Never Was* had built the programme around three new approaches: whistle-blower testimony, dramatic reconstructions of police interrogations, and some never-before-seen footage of the demo that had been shot on 16mm and Super 8 film, as well as black-and-white video, by a group of film students from the art school of the former Sheffield City Polytechnic on Psalter Lane in the Banner Cross area of the city. They'd been doing a film workshop in town that day with one of the Psalter Lane lecturers, a long-haired and affable educationalist, author, folk musician and independent documentary film-maker named Gerald or Gerry Bannerman. They'd shot the rally, the actual speeches, on two Bolex film cameras, using a Nagra tape deck and boom mic for sound. Another of the students had been shooting establishing footage on a Sony Betacam portable video camera and battery pack, while yet another had shot a dozen or so cartridges of Super 8 on a borrowed Braun Nizo.

'Rex, do you wanna do the honours,' said Atwell. 'Maybe start with—'

'Super 8 panning shot at fifteen thirty-five?' said Rex.

'Precisely,' said Atwell.

With all wreaths now duly laid, and having collectively pledged to serve God and all mankind in the cause of peace, for the relief of want and suffering, and for the praise of his name; and having asked for guidance by his spirit – none of this from memory, but with all of them reading the words aloud from the Order of Service – and for wisdom, courage and hope and for him to keep them faithful now and always AMEN. With the various blessings having been enumerated, half a dozen further Amens chorused, and a full-hearted, primary-school-cadenced sing-song rendition of the Lord's Prayer – 'the power AND the glory' – in its now slightly old-fashioned wording (Lincoln and Churchill both favouring the 1968 Service), Rex nipped to the loo en route to the post-Remembrance Ceremony drinks. He carefully unfolded the scrap of paper and scanned it on his phone, then emailed the jpeg to his non-work account.

It wasn't anything special; just a phone number:

......
TABBY CAT =
07885970760

Well, a phone number – about a cat?

How disappointing.

At the very least, Rex had been hoping for some skullduggery.

Rex knew that Lollo's beloved old off-Siamese tomcat had died three or four years back. Miles (short for 'Miles Davis', or short for 'Mile End' – he'd heard Lollo swear by both) had been a gift from a former soap-star neighbour of Lollo's (in what had by then become the swanky Bow Heritage Area) whose pedigree 'Modern Wedge' kitten, as they were called (and Lollo had bored them all absolutely shitless with Siamese cat lore at the time), had briefly strayed one evening. By the time they'd found out she was a queen, she'd been too far gone to spay, and had given birth to an unplanned litter. Apart from the green-eyed Miles, the resulting kittens were apparently passable 'Appleheads' – a stockier Siamese variety, more resembling the physique of your average cat – and made great pets, although were obviously no good for breeding.

In any case, Miles had been the apple of Lollo's eye for a decade or more. So if he'd been thinking of getting a new one it would hardly be surprising.

Could that be right?

Rex would have to try calling the number later from the pay-as-you-go burner that he kept in his desk drawer: a not-so-smart phone that he'd bought a year or two back for the sole purpose of using as a decoy when asked to supply a mandatory phone number in online forms, and which was now of course plagued by dozens of daily spam calls and texts.

Once he'd oh-so-carefully refolded the scrap of paper, Rex placed it gently back into his otherwise empty right trouser pocket.

Now he just had to find a way to get it back into Lollo's pocket.

Short of simply reaching in there for an affectionate fumble, he wasn't entirely sure how such a delicate operation might be successfully executed.

He'd just have to take his chances.

He flushed – for appearance's sake – washed his hands and activated the all-too-audible hand dryer, then exited back out into the vestibule and followed the sound of chit-chat over to Churchill's office.

Frankie's desk in the anteroom had been cleared and now bore just a tray of sherries, a carton of orange juice and bottles of still and fizzy mineral water. Building Services had provided teas and coffees in pump-action beverage dispensers. On another tray were laid out a number of smoked-salmon-and-cream-cheese beigels cut into quarters, fresh from the Brick Lane Beigel Bake that morning. Churchill had recently moved to one of the big Georgian piles by the river in Limehouse, so she'd no doubt have got her driver to stop and pick them up on their way in this morning.

In the office proper, Deputy Chaplain Barry Lincoln was looking at the historic photo of the first female Metropolitan Police officers that hung on Churchill's wall, pointing out some detail of the uniform to Frankie.

Lollo was holding court with Di Malcolm, Evelyn Gummer and Jane Milligan, regaling them with some tale of derring-do, by the looks of it. While Tommy Bee – red-faced and chatting slightly over-animatedly with Jinksy – seemed to be on a bit of an after-show high. 'Post-Dramatic Stress Disorder', as Rex's non-copper mate Terence had once called it ('Why do you think actors drink so much?' he'd said). And in his line of work he would know.

Judging by the empties on the table beside him, Bee had started knocking back the sherries. It looked as if the Act of Remembrance had dredged up other souvenirs of his time over in 'Afghan'.

'Lovely playing, as ever,' said Rex. 'Everything okay, mate?'

'Oh, thanks, man,' said Bee. 'Yeah, fine, thanks.'

Judging by his boozy breath he'd already drunk a fair bit. Without knowing who in the station Bee's AA sponsor might be, Rex didn't feel able to offer much help, so he said something blandly positive while making a mental note to send for psychic reinforcements and to check with Winston Edwards who the sponsor was for next time, if there was a next time.

'It was beautiful, Tom,' said Rex, 'really dignified. I always forget. Thank you.'

He looked around for Barry Lincoln, to have a private word before the Deputy Chaplain fucked off, and get him to have a private word in turn with Tommy Bee. What were chaplains for, after all?

As he walked over to join in with whatever it was that Lollo, Di and Jane were finding so amusing, Rex saw that Lawrence was reaching for the hanky in his pocket.

A move that might give Rex a tiny window of plausibility.

'Nice office, isn't it,' said Rex, with his hand in his pocket, grasping the scrap of paper between middle, third and little finger and palm, ready for when he chucked some bait in the water. 'Hi, all. What's with the horse? Anyone know?'

Hanky in mid-air, Lollo looked not at the photo of Sefton like everyone else, but over at Churchill, who was now leaning on the corner of her desk talking to Barry Lincoln.

'Sefton,' said Lollo. 'Survived the Hyde Park bombing of 1982. The gaffer was there, bless her, well—'

Lollo blew his nose.

'I think you dropped a receipt or something, sir,' said Rex, bending as if to pick it up, a little sleight of hand, then standing to hand it to Lollo as he turned back. Don't overplay it, he thought. 'Seriously? I didn't know that. Must have been like hell on earth.'

'—aftermath, anyroad,' continued Lollo. 'Aye. Absolute bloody carnage doesn't do it justice.'

If he was surprised to see the scrap of paper that Rex was offering him, he didn't show it, not even a flicker, just took it, hanky still in hand – 'Oh, ta' – and put it into the breast pocket of his shirt. Then Lollo blew his nose one more time and replaced the hanky in his trouser pocket, all the while continuing with his story.

'The gaffer was in one of the first carriers on the scene,' said Lollo. 'A vanload of graduate entry programme cadets who just happened to be coming in from Hendon on Edgware Road for training at St James's Park. They were coming up to Marble Arch when they heard the blast, and were on the scene in seconds. Talk about a baptism of fire. The gaffer once told me there were that much blood it warmed the air. The heat, she said, coming off all them dead and dying horses.'

'Oh, excuse me,' said Rex, putting his hands up. He'd just spotted Lincoln making his getaway. 'I need to catch the Deputy Chaplain; get him to have a word with Tommy Bee – try and encourage him to go to a meeting. Anyone know who Tommy's sponsor is?'

'Eh?' said Lollo, looking round to see the increasingly red-faced and agitated Family Liaison Officer. 'Oh, aye. Well spotted.'

'Barry?' said Rex. 'Hang on.'

Behind him he could hear Lollo saying, 'Aye, he's a good'un—'

'Here they are,' said Rex, unpinching to enlarge the pop-up window: a freeze-frame of Super 8 film. 'As Lily said, according to all the muster rolls, registers, maps and action plans for the day, they shouldn't be here.'

Shouldn't be, but were. He almost hadn't recognised them at first. It was one short, moving shot, unused by Langdon, its value unrecognised, the crux of which lasted less than a second, and was further compromised by being seen through the distinctive coarse grain of Super 8 film. But the sun had been out that afternoon, so there was reasonable definition.

And there they were.

Unmistakable.

Standing in front of the bonnet of a carrier parked beside an end-of-terrace shop – and was that another carrier just visible behind, its bonnet poking out from around the corner? – blue Ford Transit minibuses, with windscreen grilles, the visible number plate on the first of which had until six weeks earlier – they'd looked it up – been registered to the Variety Club of Great Britain. Approaching the end of their useful life, they'd been sold on at British Car Auctions down in Blackbushe, Surrey.

'You're joking!' said Shepherd.

'He's not,' said Atwell. 'DVLA records have the log book transferred to a company called Able-wellco Ltd.'

Standing in front of the first carrier, leaning on its bonnet, squinting in the light, were the two Sheffield PCs.

'Obviously that's Lawrence on the left,' said Rex, 'and Clifford Heath. Both stationed at Snig Hill, Sheffield Central, but at this point in time they and Tommy Orwell – Inspector Thomas Orwell – are on secondment to Special Branch for Operation Fieldfare.'

In the image they looked fresh-faced; laughing and chatting. Lawrence with arms folded, leaning back, with the open driver's door behind him. A number of other figures just visible in the shade behind.

Shepherd wasn't quite getting it. 'So... what?' she said. 'Disabled kiddies' minibuses bought at auction by... *not* the South Yorkshire constabulary?'

'No,' said Atwell, 'bought by an "off-the-peg" shell outfit called Able-wellco Ltd, which is set up, according to Companies House, in January 1984, then acts as subcontractor in a number of ACPO and inter-agency requisitions, capital expenditures and other disbursements relating to the policing of the strike, before being dissolved December 1985. Although the final year's accounts were never submitted.'

'Who's actually employing them here, then?' said Shepherd, the penny now dropping.

Christ! she thought. No wonder she'd got nowhere with South Yorkshire's personnel records – mysterious fire, my arse.

'Given that there's a gap in their records,' she said, 'is it Sheffield still, or ACPO? Is it, what did you call them: Able-wellco? Are they technically police officers at all at this point?'

'Still South Yorkshire paying their wages, we *think*,' said Rex. 'But you know the rest on that score. We didn't bring Heath in yet; wanted to wait for you. Do it together. And yes, still technically police officers, although their particular chain of command comes direct from ACPO and on upwards, in the first instance at least, not the Sheffield management structure or standard command. According to the whistle-blower, the others in the unit are a mixture of Special Demonstration UCOs and Army reservists, ex-1- and 2-Para out of Aldershot.'

'Does Heath know that we know?' said Shepherd.

'Yeah, but not how much we know,' said Rex.

'And this is from one of the student films?'

'Yup.'

'Where are we in relation to Ground Zero?'

'A matter of feet,' said Rex, 'and no more than five minutes. Andante [*TAP*; *SHORT-FLING*; *UNPINCH*] places the vans in Westhill Lane, *here*' – Rex pointed at the map that had opened in a new pop-up – 'which runs from Eldon Street *here* down to Devonshire Green, servicing the backs of the shops and the flats above. The backs of the buildings you can see beyond the carriers front-on to West Street. The sun's out, and those shadows give a time of fifteen thirty-five to fifteen forty p.m.

'According to Bannerman's notes,' Rex went on, consulting his own notes and pointing out locations on the map, 'the students had more or less finished filming for the day. They'd just popped into Rare and Racy, a book and record shop *here*, Langdon's bought a book and he tucks the receipt inside – where it still is; plus his SYT bus ticket home, that's all been admitted as evidence along with his witness statement – then they come out and one of the other students wants to use up the last minute or so of film. So she shoots *this*: a slow three-sixty-degree pan, clockwise from this spot *here* on the pavement opposite. Deceased, sadly. The Donny coach is right behind her *here*. You'll see it in a sec when I play the film. A 1969' – Rex looked at his notes – 'Leyland RTC, registration 433MDT, with route 11A and destination West Bessacarr still on the blind. The Cottonley bus – Cooper's bus, in other words, a double-decker – is in the next rank behind it, *here*. Then the student group depart the scene in a westerly direction onto Cavendish Street *here*, and disperse, before Bannerman returns twenty minutes later with a couple of the cameras – one Braun Nizo Super 8 and one Bolex – and a bag of used Betamax cassettes left over from a previous workshop and a few reels of fogged film stock and leader. Around four thirty he's questioned by another PSU while filming Super 8 and 16mm down on the Fitzwilliam Street side of the green. Bannerman gave them some blarney about updating his Sheffield City Polytechnic promotional film to show the political life of the city, and how that tied in with his film work for the English Folk Dance and Song Society, but it didn't wash. Forced under pain of arrest to give up the film, he reluctantly agreed. But—'

'It's not the actual film?' said Shepherd.

'Exactly,' said Rex. 'Press photographers are all in a makeshift pen on the other side of the police cordon on Division Street way over *here*. Meantime, when it emerged a couple of days later that a protester had died, they'd hidden the footage. First – so Langdon told us – in the boot of a derelict Frogeye Sprite in a Hunter's Bar garage belonging to one of the sculpture technicians. From there it went into the safe in the Psalter Lane finance office, presumably for what Bannerman quite reasonably decided was the students' and his own safety. Bannerman, as you'd imagine, swore the students to silence, and never breathed a word. And they were right to be scared, because three weeks later there was a burglary in the comm arts block at Psalter Lane, in the course of which all the locked cupboards and filing cabinets in Bannerman's office were broken into, and a crate containing a dozen or so U-matic cassettes, and Super 8 and 16mm film reels, was stolen, presumed destroyed.'

'Whatever the burglars might have thought they were getting,' said Atwell, chiming in, 'the material stolen from Bannerman's cupboard was in fact student work submitted for second-year assessments. Caused a stink at the time. Still comes up on the alumni Facebook page.'

'Haha,' *Bulletin* director Rob Langdon had said when interviewed by DI King the previous week. 'Lucky them, having to sit through all of that: hours of structuralist arty wank. And that was just mine.'

Langdon knew all of this, it turned out, because he'd been one of the students on the workshop. He'd told them that he put his whole career and work ethic down to his time at Psalter Lane, kept in touch with Bannerman and the other tutors.

Had it ever been screened, *The Riot That Never Was* would have included the first public airing of the student footage – though not the Ground Zero panning shot – which though patchy in quality by professional standards did nonetheless fill in vital information about the day that had been missing or withheld from other accounts. Langdon could have had no way of knowing the true value of that one shot.

'So Bannerman,' Rex continued, 'processes the film himself, and somehow manages to keep all this safe and under wraps until he sadly dies in 2007 – greatly missed by students and colleagues past and present, et cetera – when his widow contacts ex-student Langdon and asks if he wants this mysterious box of old film she's found in the loft, a few tapes in which had his, Langdon's, name on. He does. Happy to help. Then, when he does get a chance to look at the material, he realises what it is, and in 2010 decides to put a cryptic ad in the personals in *Private Eye*, to see what if anything might come out of the woodwork.'

'Hence the whistle-blower?' said Shepherd.

'Hence the whistle-blower,' said King. 'But even they were surprised the footage had survived, apparently. We'll skip the rally itself,' he said, 'and go straight to fifteen thirty-five. Look, if I play the three-sixty pan in slow-mo [*TAP*] you'll see she starts with the

PHANTOM AT THE FEAST

camera pointing down towards the western end of Devonshire Street, then comes around slowly past the turning to Westhill Lane and the individuals in question, past Devonshire Street shopfronts, Rare and Racy there, then you can clearly see the back of the police cordon further east along Devonshire Street towards Division Street pushing the crowd onto the green and away from Eldon Street; she comes around and coming up now you'll see the Donny coach just a few metres away parked in – look! there! – *this* group, with coaches from Newstead, Bilsthorpe, Ollerton, Tilmanstone and Betteshanger. No one either side of the Donny coach as far as we can see. So Cooper's not yet arrived on the scene, though he's only a minute or two away. And in the row behind are buses from Easington, Ellington, Ashington, Wearmouth and Fife. Double-deckers from Thurnscoe, Cottonley – Cooper's pit, as I said, and Lollo's hometown – Dinnington and Armthorpe, then "Pay and Display" sign, pavement, and back to the starting point facing west.'

Rex stopped the segment and it returned to the thumbnail image: a freeze-frame of Heath and Lawrence.

'It's only from the whistle-blower's interviews with Langdon, and this image,' said Atwell, 'that we even know Orwell's unit is in Sheffield. But once we know that, it's corroborated by Frank Cross's tapes.'

'If you look hard enough, anyway,' said Rex.

'Too right,' said Atwell. 'On the day, all the official PSUs have your standard two-letter, and one- or two-number call-signs like Charlie Delta Zero Five or whatever. This lot seem to be designated "Roger" precisely to be able to operate under the radar.'

Shepherd didn't know whether to nod or shake her head, so she did both. That made sense. Call yourself 'Roger' and any comms would be easily mistakable for standard RVP or radio voice procedure, where 'Roger' usually meant 'Received'.

'Hmm,' Shepherd snorted. 'I bet they thought they were really clever, eh?'

'Yeah, so any to-and-fro,' said Atwell, 'just sounds like general chat, or the answer to a question we're not hearing. After today, Rogers 1 and 2 are never seen again, and they're down to Roger 3, and the SDS lads started hitching a ride with different PSUs, and/or under their own steam. But we understand that Heath and Lawrence continued working with Orwell around the fringes of the NUM dispute, answering to an unknown chain of command, and with a roving brief that went on to include the organised surveillance and harassment of arrested miners' defence teams, breaking and entering, the lot.'

'So that's where Binders 1 and 2 come in?' said Shepherd, getting the hang of it.

'Exactly,' said Atwell. 'The papers were in an item of post stolen from the home – in Adel, on the outskirts of Leeds – of one of the defence barristers on the "riot trial", as they were known. Annotated by a pupil. Langdon's got the identical set from his whistle-blower. He used the interview transcripts for his dramatisations.'

Shepherd looked over at Rex, who just nodded and shrugged his assent.

'Then, to further the unit's plausible deniability, within a few months both officers had been moved sideways from the South Yorkshire force to long and successful careers in different regions: Heath to Thames Valley and Lawrence to the Met; lucky them. But we've got three further clear sightings of Roger 3 on the seventh of May, three bites of the cherry in Cross's scanner recordings. One around two forty-five directing them to north side Devonshire Green car park. Which makes sense because according to the whistle-blower that's Orwell; Roger 3 is in command of the special unit—'

'"The A-Team",' said Rex. 'They called themselves "The A-Team", after the TV show. An itinerant unit that roved around—'

'Looking for trouble,' said Atwell, 'you might say. But yes, "The A-Team". Charming, eh? So Orwell's in radio contact with whoever, and commanding the unit; Lollo's driving Roger 1, Cliff Heath's Roger 2. And in addition to Roger 3 in the audio we've now got the visual.'

'So, what?' said Shepherd. 'You've got this bloody A-Team hanging around here, Cooper blunders into their purview and—' At this she punched the palm of her hand.

'Not quite,' said Atwell.

'They're ordered to support the cordon,' said Rex. 'At two thirty-three. Three vanloads, remember – six each that travelled with Orwell and Lawrence, two with Heath, plus the officers themselves. SDS lads are long gone by this time, infiltrating the crowd, and left to their own devices to hitch a lift or get home best they can. But most of them run over the road mob-handed between the parked coaches to get to Devonshire Green proper, where they go into snatch squad 'triplets', they called them, to pull demonstrators out of the crowd, or just to get stuck in. No arrests, remember? No paper trail. But Heath and Lawrence are hanging back, whether ordered to or not we don't know. Meanwhile, we think that Cooper maybe gets separated *down here* – he's jumped the fence over to the waste ground on the west side of Fitzwilliam Street, runs up towards Cavendish Street, then crosses back over towards Devonshire Green car park, only to find himself on his tod behind police lines. It's just pure bad luck. So he makes towards where he knows the Cottonley bus is parked, turns a corner and gets into an altercation with "Individual One" at Ground Zero: an assault that the whistle-blower – Lawrence, we now know – witnesses, but seems powerless to intervene or stop.'

'Who's "Individual One"?' said Shepherd.

'That's what we want to ask Heath,' said Atwell.

'Why did Langdon come forward with all this now?' said Shepherd. 'And why direct to you, Rex? What pulled his chain?'

Rex and Atwell looked at each other with puzzled expressions, as if incredulous that Shepherd hadn't figured it out yet, so self-evident did it seem to them, who'd been immersed in this world day and night for the past four weeks.

'Sorry, I know it's a lot to get your head around,' said Atwell.

'The whistle-blower had told Langdon to do it; to get this material to me, in the event...' said Rex, expectantly. He was still in training mode, his sentence trailing off so Shepherd could fill in the blanks. Why else did she think she was here, after all?

But that wasn't good enough for the NCA agent. '*The whistle-blower had told Langdon specifically to contact DI King in the event of anything happening to him,*' said Atwell pointedly, finishing Rex's sentence, for the avoidance of any doubt.

'Oh,' said Shepherd. 'Bloody hell. Seriously? Oh, I see.'

III

25: Fromental (Oat grass)

Picture the **homely** scene: Rex was in the kitchen with Annie. One of them, in yellow Marigolds, was doing the washing-up *and* the rinsing in the new Ikea double-sink and drainer. The other was taking their turn to dry, with a bright new linen tea towel bought – along with the little bags of lavender in the clothes drawers – on a recent Mediterranean holiday.

Rex would have liked to move with the times, but Falcon being a 1959 block of flats, not even the whole of **human** ingenuity could create sufficient space in that kitchen for a dishwasher. No, not even the slimmest of slimlines. There was barely room to swing Rex's brand-new Bosch washing machine as it was.

And don't even think about a tumble dryer.

Chopin's Piano Concerto No. 2, Larghetto, was on the radio, played by a prodigiously gifted fifteen-year-old soloist with the Ukrainian National Symphony Orchestra, from a recording made in **Kiev** in 2005.

Annie was slowly getting into classical music and even opera, despite herself, what with Terence tipping them off to concerts in Wigmore Hall or St John's Smith Square, or sharing his occasional Royal Opera House comps. And to a fair few of which, after initial reluctance, she'd even gone alone, when Rex – 'So sorry, my sweet!' – just couldn't get away from work, which was almost – every – time.

She'd got used to him calling to say he'd left the tickets with **Eric** Jinks on the Enquiry Desk for her to pick up en route.

'Stood you up again, has he?' Jinksy would say.

'Haha,' she'd say. 'Have to call my fancy man instead.'

But Annie didn't mind.

It was okay.

Rex wasn't getting off the boat.

Not now she'd climbed so fully and wholeheartedly aboard, and with another passenger on the way, to boot.

And on the dining table next door, the recycled bistro-chic: a candle burning steadily in the empty bottle of first-anniversary **Champagne**.

And Annie knew – more or less – what she was getting into, by this time.

Even if Rex didn't quite.

As Annie lifted the last dinner plate from the **plate rack** to dry, and Rex picked the last piece of diced **carrot** from the trap, he found himself wondering when exactly they'd last had carrot in anything. Perhaps that *puttanesca* Annie had rustled up two nights before.

This being a block of forty-two households, each discharging daily so many statistically predictable litres of wastewater, sewage and waterborne detritus: swollen grains of rice or oat; coffee grounds and old tea; each unavoidable smear of cooking grease that had melted and emulsified in each sinkful of hot water and detergent only to catch on inconvenient calcifications and solidify within just a few feet of its rapidly cooling journey down to ground level and beyond. With all of this 'content' (as the drainage experts called it) rushing down with each **flush** and each yank of sink- or bath-plug into mostly nineteenth-century sewers, it was obvious that this iron tree of industrial-age domestic life, the multiple branching drains of an ageing modern building like Falcon, would be prone to blockage, to the snagging and inexorable build-up of plastic baby wipes at soil pipe junctions, to the swelling of absorbent 'sanitary items', to the fatberg in the **drain pipe**.

But not today.

Today it was all flowing away just fine. The alarming rising and falling of water levels in collective toilet bowls, the slow back-ups and the sudden sucks, now long forgotten until the next time, the next call to the Camden Council emergency number on speed dial: 'Hi, it's me again. From Falcon,' Rex had said last time. 'Have a guess.'

But **cripes**! What events had been set in train all those years ago, to roll along unseen or be shunted into what sidings, until rerouted by what blind and mystic **signalman** to emerge from what **tunnel** at this very point in time: now, today?

They say that trains will only run on suitable tracks, but if that's **true** – and it's a big 'if' – the question might be rather: Who had laid such tracks and why?

What strange concatenation of events was it that led to this moment, when Rex and the now very obviously pregnant Annie were having a kiss and a cuddle while she hung up the tea towel? What ancient double-cross was it that had both led to and belied this happy scene, ripening just as surely as **fruit** on the **cane**, to come out and kick you in the nuts when you least expected it: the dawn **raid**, the slap, the summons. The Core Participant who's emerged to **implicate** and to **aver** that Martin **Thorn** – of course, she still only knew his old cover name – did deceive into a sexual relationship, **molest** and abuse said 'Helen', who, after miscarrying, did then flee the UK with **heaviness** of heart and lightness of womb to lead the life down under of a wounded **introvert**, eking out the almond milk and a meagre **salary** in the overheated attic of a Kings Cross (Sydney) pub conversion.

So, really? Must the **track suit** the train? Or is it in fact the train itself which as it travels must create its own? That first seeks out the path of least resistance; that surveys its likely gradients then levels its own ground and painstakingly makes its own bed; that next most carefully but with unthinking ease lays down the necessary subgrades, formations and ballasts upon which to place what sleepers or ties it needs to take its own load.

Identifying and grooming the target. With each betrayal and each lie, every nuanced omission, and each hand placed on each, by definition, less powerful knee.

Rex remembered how he and Amelia had celebrated when she'd found out she was pregnant. He as in 'Martin Thorn', anyway. But the feelings had been real enough. They'd been dancing around her kitchen to that great mix tape of Terence's (although of course 'Marty' had claimed it as his own), singing along at the tops of their jubilant voices.

'You take a little piece of steel
and you put it in the ground.
John Henry sang, he said, Lordy what a sound!'

Well, if John Henry was a steel-driving man, then Rex was too. The truth was that it was he who'd made the running all those years ago. He who'd surveyed the terrain, mapped its contours, marked out the road, then driven in the spikes, laid the track and set the train in motion.

There was no blind signalman of fate. And however much Rex might have liked kidding himself that he was a victim of circumstance, these had all been conditions of his own choosing and making, a course of action that he had most willingly and wilfully pursued, all the live-long day.

And with Rex now both called out by 'Helen' *and* beaten at his own game by Annie, no less, would it be too **arch** here to **note**, in bold **italic** type, that *what goes around comes around*?

26: Martagon (Martagon lily)

'**Mumbles**, though,' said Rex.

'Sorry?' said Atwell.

'Heath – he mumbles on the phone,' said Rex, searching for the Thames Valley DCI's mobile number among his recent calls, and remembering the last time he'd called Heath and found him down on Glastonbury Tor getting spiritual. 'Easily distracted. He's better face to face.'

They were bringing Heath in; with kid gloves, of course, out of deference to his rank and status. They'd briefed **Tabitha** Churchill, who was going to actually make the call before sending through the paperwork.

They'd quickly decided that Rex was too close to Heath, while having an NCA agent making contact out of the blue might cause alarm. Not that Heath was considered a flight risk per se, but Rex had mentioned how uncharacteristically emotional he'd seemed recently, and so they figured that the mild flattery of a personal call from the Chief Superintendent might soften the blow, be less alarming and thus more conducive to ensuring his cooperation.

Rex and Lily had played Churchill the whole thing on **Andante**.

She was almost as impressed with the tech itself as with the forensic reconstruction. She'd seen a corporate demo of the beta version at last year's Facial Recognition Conference, but that had been deployed at a live event – a small demo on the steps of Bow Magistrates' Court – not a historical one. (And when the highlights of that beta demo had been cascaded down to team meetings, Rex had enjoyed pointing out that the clips were set to 'Something Good' by **Utah** Saints.)

How had Churchill responded to the news about Heath?

She'd been mildly surprised, but agreed with the strategy.

Was it only surprise she'd shown, though? To the seasoned eye, she'd appeared to **deflate** slightly, to wobble for a fraction of a second, a micro-expression that only an experienced interrogator might notice; an experienced interrogator like Rex.

'Impressive work,' she'd said, which was about as effusive as the Chief Superintendent ever got.

It wouldn't do to storm up the M40 mob-handed. It would give the wrong signal. They felt more comfortable just asking him to come in for a chat. That way they could get a feel for the nature of any alibi. If pushed, they felt, he might just open up. Rex and Lily Atwell had been talking strategies already, with both favouring an indirect approach, to make him stretch a bit, rather than a **full pitch** to the leg stump, to use one of proud Yorkshireman Lollo's cricket analogies.

A full toss would be too easily put away by an experienced hand like Cliff Heath.

Put it to him too straight and he'd likely **regress** into some **righteous** and uncooperative state.

Of course, Rex would have preferred to have a long and leisurely chat with Heath over a **mango** lassi and some **potato** poori at the Ravi Shankar, but the more formal alternative would also need to be an offer that Heath couldn't well refuse.

And Heath would be the one bringing reinforcements, no doubt, in the shape of his Police Federation rep and legal representation.

'Oh, that reminds me,' Churchill had said. 'Rex, did you hear from Francis Bland? He thinks you'll be called to the UCPI during the parliamentary **recess**, so that's a good thing. We'll discuss it later. Sorry, Lily. Please continue.'

Whether Heath's legal representation would be Thames Valley's brief or one privately engaged was moot. Because even if they weren't quite at the stage of being able to say, 'Clifford **Moses** Heath, I am arresting you for *blah blah blah*', they at least had a theory.

And now, too, they had evidence that put Heath squarely in the frame in Sheffield.

He was already responsible for one assault on the day, outside the Wimpy on Fargate, albeit of a Special Demonstration Squad officer, who'd himself now been statemented.

During the rally, Heath and other Roger 2 personnel had been parked up first on Surrey Street, down by the former Sheffield

Independent Bookshop (much to the consternation of the staunchly left-wing and NUM-supporting shop assistants), before they were ordered to regroup with Roger 1 on Westhill Lane. By this time, Orwell and Roger 3 were back at the mustering point in the former tram shed. Even without the UCO's statement, other sources corroborated that Heath had been the only Black officer on Fargate. He was one of only four Black and one Asian officers active during the entire incident, and they'd all been accounted for: PCs Delroy Osmund out of Rawmarsh with other personnel from PSU Charlie Echo Zero Seven, and Devon Bendix from Deepcar crewing the mobile cell block in Barker's Pool, DS Winston Rickman from Sheffield Central arresting Karl Marshall on the other side of the cordon, while DC Jaideep Bahmani had already taken the first group of prisoners back to Rotherham, where he was processing and interviewing for the rest of the day, and into the following morning.

They also had Heath on film at 15.35, within feet and seconds of Ground Zero, and they needed him to fill in that gap of a minute or two. Had Cooper been racially abusive too? Making monkey noises like the group on Fargate, or worse? Was it really as simple as that? Would that have been enough to provoke an already riled Clifford Heath to **stove** in Cooper's skull and scarper, leaving the Cottonley shop steward bruised and bleeding, unconscious on the tarmac there by the Donny coach for ten minutes, a steady **dribble** of blood from his **ear-hole**, before person unknown called the ambulance from The Washington? Vamoosing out of town, then him and Lollo keeping mum all these years? Having each other's backs? Well, they might not have lived in each other's pockets, but they'd known each other since Heath was sixteen.

It was easily done in the heat of the moment.

The heat of the moment could make you do all sorts, as Rex – victim of his own **libido** – knew only too well.

And Heath wouldn't have the fatherly protection of Tommy Orwell now, as he'd had back then.

Rex and Lily knew they had enough for a chat, at least.

How they would play it was 'run the film' – as they'd started saying when talking about the Andante output. To call it a 'film' seemed catchier than the Andante developers' preferred but metaphor-stretching 'Ten-Dimensional Interactive Moving Probabilistic Analytical Networked Investigation and Surveillance Tool'.

Hopefully, if they ran the film first, that would blow Heath's mind for starters, catch him off guard.

Then they would talk around the edges of that gap in their knowledge, starting with the incident on Fargate, then gently coaxing the DCI through the events of the next two or three hours. Testing him to discover what he might be prepared to give up.

They'd soon find out if they had 'aught or nowt', as Lollo – still more 'thee, thy, thou, thine' than 'eeh bah gum' – had used to say.

Do it right and Heath would sing like **Sinatra**.

Do it wrong and he'd clam up like Clark **Gable** in *The Secret Six*.

What they didn't know was how Heath would respond to the news that he'd been stitched up by the old South Yorkshire mucker he'd known since his **teens**.

And now here was Frankie, interrupting.

Rex knew what she was going to say almost before she opened her mouth.

And Churchill knew it too, judging by the way she seemed almost to buckle at the knee.

'Sorry to interrupt, ma'am,' said Frankie. 'But I thought you'd want to know soon as.'

It was bad, if not inconclusive, but not wholly unexpected.

The Seaford Ice & Fisheries Co-operative Society, to whose premises Melissa Shepherd was presently making haste, was exactly the type of small, local, **profit-sharing trader** that was increasingly being squeezed out of business by **fat-cat** fishery quangos – 'arm's-length' near-to-government bodies, founded by **letters patent** or Royal Charter, and usually to blame for most things; at least if you asked the co-op members (whose opinions would be readily volunteered even if you didn't). Shepherd knew fishermen, and she also knew from experience that even in the current tragic circumstances she wouldn't get out of there without a lecture.

A partial human skull – not completely skeletonised, with some flesh and hair, and fatty deposits remaining – had been found tangled in the crab pots of an old Newhaven **sea-dog**, who'd taken it straight to the Seaford Co-op fridges for safe-keeping, and was now apparently waiting for Shepherd in the King's Head on Pelham Street.

Whether this would in fact prove to be the final human remains of Detective Chief Inspector Jethro Lawrence of course remained to be seen. But once she'd taken possession and a witness statement – with a borrowed Styrofoam cool-box strapped in safely on the back seat, with the music turned up, and with all the windows opened as far as they'd go – Melissa would be driving to the lab in Brighton just as fast as she respectfully dared.

27: Serpolet (Wild thyme)

Maybe it was not so **cut and dried**.

It was a **shaken** Detective Chief Inspector Clifford Heath who greeted DS Melissa Shepherd and DI Rex King in reception at Holborn the next day.

But that didn't mean anything, because they were all a bit shaken.

If it did turn out to be Lollo that the fisherman had found, what a loss it would be.

It's what they'd all been aiming for, to find the Detective Chief Inspector, but now that the **winning post** was in sight there was absolutely nothing to celebrate.

Rex had nearly slapped Jinksy last night, the disrespectful fucker.

'How to get ahead in policing,' the EDO had said. Then, when Rex hadn't laughed, he'd kept on going: 'Look on the bright side: if it is Lollo they won't need a very big **urn**.'

'You'd better stop fucking digging, Eric, I swear, or—'

But thankfully Jinksy had taken the hint. And Rex knew at heart that Jinks's insolence was well meant. Few officers had more respect for Lollo than the EDO. Jinks owed Lollo his life, or the will to keep living it, at least.

Frankie – thoughtful as ever – wanting to soften the blow if it came, had got some nice flowers for the gaffer and for Becky Fernie: a small **egg basket** each, full of golden **alyssum**, white freesia, pink and yellow peonies and a yellow-and-pink-blush rose that Rex when he saw it later would describe as 'rhubarb and custard', but which Frankie would assure him was the hybrid tea variety known as Peace.

She'd chosen it specially; figured they'd both be upset.

In Lollo's absence, Becky had already been acting up a level. She'd moved to the eighth floor, where she was doing SMT exec admin during Jane Milligan's maternity leave. And making a good job of it too, Rex had heard.

The Sussex Coroner was on the case this morning. Melissa Shepherd had pinged her Lawrence's dental records for comparison. Shepherd was on the tube from Victoria right now, and she'd tipped off the Coroner that she'd be travelling and in meetings for most of the morning, so only to text if it was a positive ID. Although the Chief Superintendent had made the order of the day clear to Shepherd and to everyone else. Heath's interview had to be the priority.

Frankie hadn't bought flowers for Rex, but later that day – once they knew for sure – he'd return to his desk on the sixth floor to find a little plastic pot of locally produced **honeycomb** waiting for him. It was from the Duke of Bedford's beehives in the Montague Street Gardens. They sold it in the adjoining hotel. Next to it was a sweet card from Tabitha Churchill – a postcard of the Georgian giraffe house in London Zoo. The message on the reverse had clearly been dictated to Frankie – Rex recognised her handwriting – but the thought was the main thing:

Dear Rex, I'm so sorry for your loss. JL always thought and spoke very highly of you, as I think you know. Take a day or two compassionate leave if you want. Here anytime if you want to chat. We're going to miss him.
TC

But that was later.

'You're looking well, Cliff,' said Churchill, whose policy of flattery had now carried over into her being part of London CN BCU Serious Crime's welcoming party.

If Met Comms Chief Evelyn Gummer hadn't been seconded onto the MOPAC Closures Working Group and sub-committee to spearhead its 'Leading for London!' rebrand for the next week or so, she'd have been here too. Because she and Churchill both wanted to keep a lid on this for as long as possible. If this could be kept under wraps until Silly Season too, then all the better.

But, as it was, Gummer was currently sequestered in the board-room down at Tower Bridge trying to figure out how to spin the impending forced closure of thirty-two London police stations as a positive. The story being crafted was that the closures were purely about cutting **overheads** and improving public access to police services.

The Closures Working Group was lucky to have her.

It wasn't all that great for Rex, though. If his UCPI appearance hit the fan, he'd want to know that Evelyn Gummer would be controlling the message, whether Parliament was in recess or not. He didn't quite trust anyone else to care half as much. And no one else was half as good as Gummer.

'Have you lost a bit of weight?' said Churchill, to lighten the mood while they waited.

'Three stone,' said Cliff with evident **delight**, turning sideways-on and patting what had used to be his belly, 'in three months. Bethany calls me her **Chippendale**.'

That was an image Rex didn't need: Cliff Heath in stripper **get-up**: all cuffs and collars. Quick, change the subject.

'Off the curries, eh?' said Rex. 'A bit less of the old **ghi**?'

'No,' said Heath, 'that's the thing! I can have as much curry as I want, just without the rice and naans. No carbs at all is the **stipulation**. Well, you know. You're allowed the odd chip.'

'Oh yeah. Cauliflower rice and whatever. Annie's into all that too.'

'Yeah, for real,' said Heath. 'I'm not gonna **lie**. I didn't think I'd be able to **sustain** it for more than a day. I thought I'd be faint with hunger by lunchtime, you know. Tell the truth I did feel a bit **drowsy** on day three or four, once I started burning up the old body fat, but you get used to it. Now I'm five days on, two days off. And even on the days off I don't tend to have a blow-out. Bethany got this book, see. And we took the plunge. She said it was now or never. She didn't want to lose me. You should see *her*, though! I said she was beautiful as she was, but she wanted to do it together, bless her.'

'Well, it worked,' said Rex. 'I was telling Annie that I didn't recognise you the other day!'

No one seemed to be in any rush to head up to the third floor.

'How about you, ma'am,' said Heath. 'Got any holiday plans?'

'Two weeks in **Paris** come September,' said Churchill. 'I always wanted to go. The Louvre and whatnot. You?'

'Andorra,' said Heath. 'Spain somewhere: the Pyrenees. Isn't it one of those little principalities like Liechtenstein or something? I don't know, to be honest. Bethany booked it. Place called **Encamp**. She'll take a pile of books. She's into that Inspector **Rebus**. Got the lot, she has. That's her idea of fun – police work!'

They all laughed.

'Camping, d'you say?' asked Rex.

'No, that's the name of the town, *Encamp*. I think so. We'd better not be camping, I can tell you.'

'Right, who are we waiting for, then?' said Rex.

'My rep?' said Heath.

'No, they're here,' said Churchill. 'Both of them. I didn't know Thames Valley use the same chambers as us – good of them to support you like that. I gave them the meeting pod off the sixth-floor landing. Do go up if you want. Frankie'll show you. We're just waiting for Melissa Shepherd and Lily **Atwell**, and we'll be up directly.'

'Who?' said Heath.

'She's NCA,' said Rex. 'Lily Atwell. Amazing work. You'll see.'

If Heath's heart sank at the thought of the National Crime Agency raking over his past, with everything that entailed, he didn't show it.

When the door opened and Lily entered, they could hear the booming bass and skittering **high-hat** of an old jungle track blasting from a passing car. A reggae DJ sample was repeating in the mix: 'Yo! You have a licence fi play this?'

Heath turned in surprise. 'Bloody hell, that takes me back.'

'Nineties sound?' said Rex, thinking of his own raving days. He'd had to be into it. It had been part of his legend.

'No, the eighties,' said Cliff. 'That sample.'

But inside, Heath now knew that he'd run out of time.

And here was Melissa Shepherd too.

Right now, in the minute or so they had, how could Heath even begin to tell Lollo's protégé – this young Detective Inspector – about growing up in Steel City, the electronic music capital of the world. Okay, Rex was a decent bloke, but what did he care about the funk and soul all-dayer scene that Cliff had grown up in? About driving back into the city over Intake at dawn, and seeing the lights spread out beneath you. About looking up at Park Hill Flats, to see if his mum had left the kitchen light on for him; her way of saying hello even if she was out at work.

And how could he possibly tell King about having the exact same sound system bootleg that DJ Krome and Mr Time must have sampled for the very track that they'd just heard on a car stereo outside?

It was the kind of story you needed to be sitting down for with a fellow traveller in the pub, to **recollect** over a drink or two, and even then probably not.

He remembered the shock and surprise he'd felt on first hearing that DJ Krome and Mr Time sample. Having his own past, and his own personal mythology, handed back to him on a dub plate, on the radio, a decade later. Because believe it or not, Clifford had actually been at that very soundclash when those famous words had been uttered.

For real.

But who cared, other than him? No one, that's who.

He'd got the train over to Leeds for Saxon versus Maverick Outernational in the Chapeltown Community Centre, Leeds, May 1985. Man like Papa Levi, Tippa Irie, Daddy Colonel, Trevor Sax, and Musclehead. Saxon in the area. Speed rapping. Cocoa Tea on the turntable, Jah know. Echo Minott and Mikey General for each and every Leeds-ite.

A legendary clash.

It was not that long after him and Tully had come off Operation Fieldfare. While they were biding their time and waiting for their payback, for their transfers out of South Yorkshire and onto the fast track.

Leeds had had a better sound system scene than Sheffield. He'd used to swap rest days and take the train over. He'd seen Jah Shaka the month before; and plenty a **group** like The Gladiators, and the Mighty Diamonds. Eek-A-Mouse!

How to explain walking back through the fields and factories of the Meanwood Valley at dawn, lying in the grass, your ears absolutely ringing, smoking the last scrap of sensi before you walk back down to the station. Terrys All-Time was gone by then, burned down they said, so it'd have to be a quick bacon butty in the Merrion Coffee House, which opened early on weekdays.

He'd found a leather jacket after Saxon that night. A decent black leather blazer that someone had dropped on Scott Hall Road there! Checked it over to make sure no one had shat in it and there was nothing in the pockets, no blood and no weapons. No needles. No H

or Ki. No, it was clean, or as good as. Then he'd put it on, and it had
fit him like a glove. Could have been tailor-made. He'd worn it home,
then worn it for years.

His mate over at Fox Records kept the bootleg sound system
cassettes under the counter, and young Cliff would go and buy
whichever one a month or two down the line. This would be a dead
cert. He'd been hassling the guy: 'Saxon versus Maverick in yet?'

And when it did arrive, he'd listened to it so often the magnetic
tape had broken and he'd had to rethread what was left back onto the
spool.

'Yo! Yo! Yo! Operator! Yo! You have a licence fi play this?'

He knew the words off by heart. But he'd run out of time

So, standing next to Rex there, with DS Shepherd bounding
across reception with her bag over her shoulder and her right arm
outstretched to shake Lily Atwell's hand, Heath just laughed, and it
sounded like this: 'Hyik-yik-yik-yik.'

'Oh man,' he said. 'Rex. Those were the days, eh? Innocent times!'

Innocent? thought Rex.

Exactly what kind of denial are you in, mate?

But go on, then, have it your way.

At least it was the last time, thought Rex, that Heath would be
laughing for a while now. So there was that.

Or it should have been.

And, hands up, Shepherd knew she'd fucked up the second her
phone buzzed in her bag.

She realised immediately that she'd given Heath an out, if he was
quick enough to take it.

If?

What was she thinking?

A survivor like DCI Clifford Heath?

Of course he was quick enough.

He'd had to be.

And it was a shame, because up to that point it had all been going
so well.

Once they'd got upstairs, and were sitting around one of the now
empty table tennis tables in the Clean Room – no need for paper suits
now, with everything cleared off to the evidence store – Churchill
had kicked things off, thanking everybody for their time and making

it clear that this was just a conversation, that Heath wasn't under caution.

But – and here she tilted her head to one side, sympathetically – since it was now explicitly clear from the evidence that he and the then PC Jethro Lawrence had been the sole persons in the immediate vicinity of 'Cooper Ground Zero' – William Cooper's arrival next to the Doncaster coach in the Devonshire Green car park shortly after 15.35 – they just needed a little help filling in the gaps.

They'd found the reservists, the former 1- and 2-Paras from Aldershot. They were a loyal bunch, the Paras. Close-knit and always ready to answer the call. Charlie was dead – heroin overdose in 1998 – but Mick was still around, still into the Romans, volunteering as a centurion at Vindolanda. Still enthusing about practising 'Testudo' shield formations on the playing fields at Hendon.

Of course, she'd continued, they'd have asked Orwell if they could. And while DCI Jethro Lawrence was still MIA, at least pending final confirmation, he did appear at least to have told Rob Langdon all he knew: chiefly that he saw the fatal blows being delivered, that he'd failed to intervene to stop it, but that he was unable to recall or to identify the officer in question, because said officer had had his back to Lawrence.

And yet, Churchill went on, there were only two officers actually present at Ground Zero by that time: 'Jethro and you. Isn't that right?'

She was partly bluffing, of course. Although, to be fair, this discussion hadn't really been designed to elicit a great deal from Heath, but to demonstrate to him and his team – to the Thames Valley's barrister and Heath's Police Federation rep alike – the wealth of 'circumstantial-plus' evidence that was currently pointing his way. It was a threat, in other words. To either play along and manage this with them, or to put his reputation and the planned life ahead with the lovely Bethany at even greater risk, if or when they decided that this could all go public. After all, that happy retirement was wholly dependent upon Heath's generous pre-1995-rates final salary pension, with its old Civil-Service-rates portion. He wouldn't want to be gambling with that.

Although it was fair to say too, but Churchill wasn't going to say it here, not now, that for all his experience as a documentary director,

Langdon hadn't had the benefit of NCA agent Lily Atwell and her Andante ten-dimensional AI coders. As a result, Langdon had clearly been over-reliant on the whistle-blower, who'd very much been able to set their own agenda. To say what they wanted Langdon to hear. To make Langdon tell the story that the whistle-blower wanted him to.

But in Lollo's absence, Churchill went on, maintaining her intimate tone, the responsibility had now, sadly, fallen to Heath.

They'd let him read the UCO known as HN487's witness statement. His account of being assaulted by Heath on Fargate, the fake arrest to get them both out of schtuck. But this had been met with an indignant response from the Thames Valley Detective Chief Inspector: 'Steve Kenchington? Are you kidding? The guy's a racist. He made monkey noises! He incited an already agitated crowd to racially abuse me! A hundred pissed-up and angry miners making monkey noises. D'you know what that sounds like? Or the risk of it? The danger it puts you in?'

They didn't, of course.

'Listen,' Heath went on. 'Besides, Sketch wrote to me and apologised a year or so later. Sent me a damn mix tape – from Australia! I've still got his letter.' He looked at the barrister, who raised his eyebrows then made a note. '*He* apologised to *me*!'

They'd also shown Heath and co a quick flash – top page only – of a much longer interview with Kenchington, about Operation Fieldfare; his (or HN487's) UCPI hearing transcripts; and his anonymous contribution to someone's PhD-by-practice oral history project on the role in the strike of the Special Demonstration Squad.

Then, just in case Heath thought they were basing everything on the testimony of one perhaps discredited former SDS officer, Atwell and Rex had shown them the Able-wellco Ltd investigation. And then they'd only shown them, but pointedly not allowed them to read, the full two-hundred-page transcript – festooned with Post-its and highlighter as it was – of Lawrence's on-camera interviews with Langdon.

'D'you know what each and every one of those Post-its is?' said Churchill, placing her hand on the top page. 'Or can you guess?'

No one said anything.

'A nail in your coffin, Cliff, I'm sorry to say. That's what. Each one of these Post-its clearly points to you. And all from the mouth of the man you thought was your oldest friend. How does that make you feel?'

'Makes me feel like you're trying to paint a picture, to be honest,' said Heath. 'I think you're trying to frame me.'

Then and only then they'd 'run the film' on Andante, and given DCI Clifford Heath the full works. You'd think they were trying to sell him the system, by showing him everything it knew about his movements on the day: his own personal critical path to the fatal encounter with Cooper; his position in relation to the A-Team; the other Fieldfare personnel; their carriers in relation to all the other PSUs, and in relation to the crowd which, with Andante playing at twice-real-time, seemed to swarm raggedly from Barker's Pool down Division Street to Devonshire Green and Fitzwilliam Street, spilling into every side road as it moved west on the map. They toggled the filter to show crowd density based on police witness statements, and the much-reduced crowd density based on analysis of photographs and the film students' documentary footage; continuous missile-throwing versus a thirty-second burst. They'd shown him exactly what they knew, culminating in the Super 8 film still of him and Jethro Lawrence standing in front of the carrier at the corner of Westhill Lane at 15.35, the 999 call from the Washington public house, and the period when the emergency vehicle turning onto Division Street from Rockingham Way was delayed by the protesters and the police cordon, before Rogers 1, 2 and 3 left Sheffield city centre at speed, hitting the M1 after final contact at 16.35 precisely.

That was when Shepherd's phone vibrated.

She'd forgotten to turn off notifications.

She reached for it in alarm, but it was too late.

The damage was done and Shepherd knew it.

She flushed and blushed blotchily from cheek to cheek and down past her collarbone to her chest.

No one said anything, but they all knew what that meant.

That this wasn't just any old text message incoming.

It was the Coroner's Office, texting to say she'd made a positive ID.

Churchill glared at Shepherd in frustration.

And no wonder.

The gaffer had been right after all.

They'd never know the truth or otherwise of whatever they were going to get now.

And with that, with no one left to protect, and without further **ado**, Detective Chief Inspector Clifford Moses Heath caved.

Clifford Heath blabbed.

Or did he?

28: Faux (Scythe)

People used to be fond of saying that a dying person's life flashed before their eyes. That when your appointment with the Grim Reaper came, some mystic slideshow allowed you to relive or at least to review your every mortal moment as if fast-forwarding through a video of your life. Others maintained – based on the popularly published testimonies of those who claimed to have survived a 'near-death experience' – that some great and beneficent presence in the form of an all-enveloping light would draw you into its **glow**, and that perhaps this very same bright and godly light might turn you away if it were deemed not yet to be your time.

The ancient Buddhist texts attributed to eighth-century mystic Padmasambhava that comprise *The Tibetan Book of the Dead* codify the rituals and experiences of those last shining, thrilling, blissful moments when the Bardo of the Clear Light of Reality which is the Infallible Mind of the Dharma-Kāya is experienced by all sentient beings.

More recently published research in the field of neuroscience posits that a burst of coordinated activity, particularly of the 'gamma oscillations' popularly known as brainwaves, might flood the dying brain with imagery and experience, a memory-retrieval process perhaps more akin to dreaming or a psychedelic trip.

And yet despite humanity's long history and its beliefs, faiths and cultural expectations, all of this remains unknowable. It is a truth that we're destined each alone to discover for ourselves, and to take such very hard-won knowledge with us to the grave.

And so it was with the suicide of Detective Chief Inspector Jethro Cyrus Lawrence OBE, who, as the Sussex Coroner would later confirm, voluntarily entered the waters of the English Channel somewhere on the Sussex coast, in full possession of all mental and physical competencies and agencies, himself therein to drown.

As to the manner of this entry: whether he ran out onto the beach like a kid on the South Bay sands in full anticipation of the water's cold embrace and swam out fully clothed, we must assume, past the point of no return, or walked into the water sombrely with pockets full of heavy pebbles, or hurled himself from one of that most beautiful county's many great cliffs into the roiling tide far below, none could say. Although it would later be recorded that the absence of any ante-mortem cranial fracture mitigated against the latter possibility. And with prevailing winds and coastal currents on that Sussex coast being what they are (notwithstanding the impacts on the Coroner's longshore-drift or 'LSD' modelling of known and licensed offshore dredging operations that were in train that spring) his entry would most likely have been points substantially east of Selsey Bill.

Other than that – with only a skull remaining – the statutory inquest didn't have a great deal to go on. But through the respective offices, persons and submissions of Senior Officer (Grade 3) Lily Atwell of the National Crime Agency, of Detective Sergeant Melissa Shepherd of Sussex Police (Midhurst and Easebourne) and of Detective Inspector Rex King of the Central North London BCU – and each of their teams, both separately and collectively – it might have been possible for the police and the Coroner to come to some sympathetic and sufficiently coherent or compelling understanding of events. With such an effort contributing, perhaps, to an easing of the path of the late Jethro Lawrence toward his mastering the Great Body of Union that he might appear in whatever shape will benefit all beings whomsoever, and that his own consciousness now in reality void and his intellect shining, and blissful these two in the inseparable union of the Dharma-Kāya state of Perfect Enlightenment, that he may serve all sentient beings which are infinite in number as are the limits of the sky. This much at least – even if she lacked the precise vocabulary – was Annie's unformed hope, and likely too the especial hope of her fellow enthusiastic dabbler in entry-level Buddhism and New Age philosophies Clifford Heath. Although neither of them knew it of the other, nor had they yet – at this stage – even met.

But for DCI Heath, London-bound again at a steady seventy on the M40 from Oxford, the teachings of the great mystic Padmasambhava and how they might enable him to make some holy intercession on his dear late friend's behalf were foremost on his mind.

As to his intentions, he'd left a garbled message with DI King that had not yet been returned, so hoped he'd see him there. But it was at that moment, with red kites wheeling overhead in search of roadside carrion, as Cliff Heath turned up the music and sang along at the top of his voice to 'Mr Soul of Jamaica' Alton Ellis and his 1973 hit 'Lord Deliver Us', and with the spire of St Giles Church in the roadside village of Tetsworth fast disappearing in his rear-view mirror, that the Lord did indeed deliver Cliff Heath, from a Vauxhall Zafira that in overtaking a Transit-trailer combo in the central lane of the northbound carriageway misjudged and clipped the rear of said trailer, which immediately jack-knifed and in so doing launched the Zafira, now slowly spinning on its horizontal axis, clear over the central reservation, rising past the horrified Cliff Heath's offside and through the turbulence of his very wake – where, had he been driving a second slower etc., etc. – and directly into the path of the southbound carriageway's oncoming afternoon traffic, where it collided in mid-air with the mid-section of the front of the cab of a brand-new Dutch-registered Scania S-series 16-litre V8 unit hauling a container-load of medical equipment from the Black Country to the Netherlands, and immediately burst into flames. A double fatality (both drivers, instantly; RIP) and resulting pile-up that would close the southbound carriageway behind Heath for the rest of the afternoon.

His own near-miss and the haunting moment of eye contact that he'd shared with the puzzled Zafira driver had only reinforced a stunned and shaken Clifford Heath in the importance of his spiritual mission.

While for Jethro Lawrence six weeks earlier, give or take, speeding down to Petworth in the early hours in his special-edition indigo XE with *The Witch Doctor* by Art Blakey playing loudly on the in-car hi-fi, Blakey's skittering high-hat marking out a rhythmic and rebellious counterpoint to the inexorable march of time and white supremacy like a stone skipping lightly across the face of the ocean and into the oncoming tide, the procession of lights and deities and obeisances delineated in the *Bardo Thödol* was all yet to come.

He had enough on his plate as it was.

Not least of which was the break-up with the person he now realised might well have been the love of his life, and the promise of chaste **abstinence** and supreme loss of face to come. Now he'd had the very best of the best – and, oh, how he had had her – what could the bereft and grieving Jethro Lawrence possibly want with the rest?

Lollo had lost his precious Tabby Cat; his irreplaceable one.

Never more to slink across the floor and purr upon his knee, nor spoon in his bed.

Never more to walk hand in hand around the zoo together, nor to listen teary-eyed to the original cast recording of ***Chicago***.

To kiss and be kissed; he was going to miss that.

Driving round to her place late at night.

To cuddle and be cuddled.

Or her texting as she set off, and thirteen minutes later – long enough for him to finish whatever work he was doing and freshen up – that familiar light rattle on his front door.

To lick and be licked.

Then dining butter-fingered in bed on asparagus and Brie!

To nuzzle up and be nuzzled up to.

Fucking till his dick was raw.

To gently nip and be oh-so-gently nipped back in return.

Working their way through an as-new copy of *The Joy of Sex*.

To bite and be bitten.

Then up on the kitchen table, with her feet on his shoulders.

To tease and be teased was not the half of it, oh no.

Not with his precious Tabby Cat.

But then, at work, nothing. The ability to act like nothing had happened.

It was their secret. And therein lay the problem, though it had taken him a while to see it.

Of course Rob Langdon was always going to ask Jethro Lawrence about Orgreave. It wasn't, he'd assured him, the focus of the film. They wouldn't be touching on it in any detail – though it would be impossible, of course, not to mention it briefly to put events in Sheffield in context, as part of a continuity – but *had* he been there on 18 June 1984?

This was a month or two before Langdon started filming, when, for a couple of weeks running, the film director had driven out to Bow on Lollo's rest days and they'd sat in his kitchen and chatted. They'd been long days too: fuelled by pots of strong tea and plates of gingernuts. Dark when they'd started, and dark again by the time they'd finished. Langdon sketching out loose notes and diagrams in longhand in a large A4 notebook.

Maybe he'd just presumed that since Lollo had been at the Sheffield and Mansfield riots, so-called, then he might have had the full set.

'I'll be making a few notes while we chat,' he'd said when they'd sat down. 'It's purely personal. I'm not going to quote you. It's just an aide-mémoire, okay?'

Lollo had nodded his assent. He'd already signed a contract so felt all bases were covered. He'd asked his former soap-star neighbour and fellow Siamese fancier to recommend an entertainment lawyer. They hadn't met up, in the event, but they'd spoken on the phone a couple of times, and the lawyer had made a couple of suggestions for Jethro's protection, taken out some of Langdon's wiggle room.

'Are you sure you want to do this?' the lawyer had asked finally. 'Then this is probably about as good as you'll get.'

Orgreave? Jethro had seen the great coking plant often enough. Looming in the distance if you knew where to look: the enormous line of coking ovens and sintering plants dwarfing the village; the pipelines and steam vents, sulphur-dioxide removal works, the coolers and the top gas heat-exchangers, the gasometers and distillation plants, the conveyors and the hoppers and the loading bays and the lorry parks.

And, on the day, it had been the backdrop to a theatre so large and fast-moving that no one, not even the heli crews, had had a complete overview.

Jethro had memories, just like everybody else. Although, if he was honest, he wasn't sure where his own memories and the collective memory – of newspaper photos and TV news packages – had started and stopped.

Lines of police banging their long shields with their batons, and the cry that came up in response: 'ZULU! ZULU! ZUUUUUUUU-LUUUUUUUU!'

Six hundred coppers of all ranks chasing pickets up Highfield Lane, in two waves, each three hundred-strong, with mounted units, short-shield groups in riot gear and vehicles coming up behind.

Some poor bastard who'd been kicked in the face by the muscle in a three-man snatch squad. Arm broke by baton blow, blood pouring out of his nose and a cut above his eye as he's dragged through a break in the lines and led away; fiftieth arrest of the day.

'I'm arresting you for riot, son.' Get them in the mobile cell block ASAP, then get back out to pick off another likely lad. Anyone'll do. Cunts wouldn't know what'd hit 'em. A forget-me-not for good measure. That's what they called it: a forget-me-not. A sharp kick from the toe of a boot in the small of a back. As precise as you can make it. As precise as a hammer hitting a nail. It'd only leave a little blue bruise, but they'd be feeling that for years. They'd remember you. They'd think twice.

No visible numbers, naturally. That was all part and **parcel**.

'Get stuck in!' That were the battle cry of Inspector Tommy Orwell: 'Get stuck in, lads!'

Them mounted units from Cudworth going in full tilt.

Stick that in your fucking pipe and smoke it, Scargill.

Getting stuck right in. Fighting for their lives, it had felt like. A fight to the death. But a fight engaged in full confidence that they'd set and baited a trap.

Come into my parlour, said the spider to the flying pickets.

But they hadn't officially been there, no.

If pressed, Lollo figured he could tell Langdon the partial truth that the NRC had quickly determined that their particular brand of disruption and **incitement** was better deployed elsewhere. That it were more effective at smaller picket lines; grass-roots gatherings. He could say that he'd done the same training as the Orgreave lads, but that were it. New kit meant new safety routines, you see, and new tactics with which to become familiarised. They'd all done short-shield sessions with ex-army trainers over Preston, or down at Hendon.

If pressed he'd say that, anyroad.

'Orgreave? No,' said Lollo.

You're not bloody blaming me for that, he'd thought, shaking his head.

Not that they'd officially been at Sheffield for that matter, nor at Mansfield.

It wasn't strictly true, of course, but Jethro had figured that this truth was a bit too complicated, so he'd stuck to his guns: 'No,' he'd said again for good measure. 'Though I know a few thousand lads as was, and they did a damned good job under extreme duress. Next question!'

When Langdon had nipped upstairs to the loo, he'd left his notebook open on the kitchen table. It was intentional. He was signalling to the

Detective Chief Inspector that he'd got nothing to hide; no reason to be secretive. 'Trust me like I trust you' was the message.

Jethro had slid the notebook around and carefully taken a look. Several loose leaves and stapled A4 print-outs had been inserted between its pages. One was a typed list several double-sided pages long headed 'VO montage 1 – agency photos b/w to select'. Lollo only managed to read the top page, upon which the first item was ringed and highlighted, while some entries had been crossed out. Lifting the cover sheet, he could see that throughout the document other options were ticked, roughly circled and/or underlined, with the words 'to Susie' or 'Susie to action'.

J8405TP1s — Mounted Policeman attacking Lesley Boulton, Orgreave 1984. Police mounted on horseback attacking Lesley Boulton from miners womens support group WAPC. 18 June 1984
Medium: b/w photo
Date: 1984 AD (C20th AD)
Description: Miners' strike 84-85, Lesley Boulton, Orgreave, Battle of Orgreave, Orgreave coke works mass picket, Miners' strike 1984, Sheffield South Yorkshire,
Photo credit/clearance: John Harris/Report Digital

SAA5656267 — Ambulance employees assist Arthur Scargill, the wounded president of the NUM (National Union of Mineworkers), to an ambulance, during heavy fighting between police and miners in Orgreave, England, June 18, 1984 Medium: b/w photo
Date: 1984 AD (C20th AD)
Description: Miners' strike 84-85, Arthur Scargill (b.1938) British trade union leader, Orgreave, Police
Photo credit/clearance: Nationaal Archief/Collectie Spaarnestad/ANP/Pynis/ Bridgeman Images

unknown — Orgreave June 18 1984, striking miner George 'Geordie' Brealey with large sideburns and wearing a toy Police helmet 'inspects' the line of police officers close up. Officers wear full uniform with helmet chinstraps fastened and no ID numbers. Nose to nose, Brealey gazes impassively at a uniformed officer standing inches away.
Medium: b/w photo

Date: 1984 AD (C20th AD)
Description: Miners' strike 84-85, George Brealey (d.1997) striking miner, Orgreave, Police
Photo credit/clearance: Don McPhee/Guardian CHECK RATES FOR MULTI-REGION FILM/TV/STREAMING

84052440 — British police use riot shields and helmets for the first time in an industrial dispute at the Orgreave Coke works during the 1984-85 Miner's strike. Police in riot helmets with long shields run up a grassy bank, pickets in foreground look on. 29/05/1984.
Medium: b/w photo
Date: 1984 AD (C20th AD)
Description: Miners' strike 84-85, Police, Orgreave, first uses of riot gear
Photo credit/clearance: Martin Jenkinson Image Library

1406514a — Mounted Police move in on striking miners picketing at Orgreave Coking Plant near Sheffield. Six horses galloping across field, miners in background.
Medium: b/w photo
Date: 1984 AD (C20th AD)
Description: Miners' strike 84-85, Police, Orgreave, Cudworth
Photo credit/clearance: Pete Lomas/ANL/Shutterstock

1406922a — Miner's Strike 1984: An injured picket with blood streaming from his face after violence erupted at Orgreave Coking Plant, talking to ambulance worker, holding shoulder of police officer in riot gear.
Medium: b/w photo
Date: 1984 AD (C20th AD)
Description: Miners' strike 84-85, Police, Orgreave, injured
Photo credit/clearance: John Sherbourne/ANL/Shutterstock

And so on.
Did it give him pause, Detective Chief Inspector Jethro Lawrence, seeing what was on top of that list? That sole surviving photo from a strip of negatives that once upon a time he personally had cut into tiny pieces and flushed down a Snig Hill shitter?
Did it fuck.

He already knew he was sailing close to the fucking wind.

Opening at another page, headed 'Background', Lollo saw that Langdon had bullet-pointed a few key facts and figures, and what looked like questions for follow-up.

National Smokeless Fuels Ltd = wholly owned subsidiary of the NCB?

Orgrv = 83% of male employment in area, 61% of total – any data for a) decommissioning period, b) do we know labour demographic now?

Agreement to continue minimal coke supply to BS Scunthorpe to maintain blast furnaces/BS jobs, Q1) When was quota first exceeded and 2) av. weekly excess thereafter? 3) 30-wagons p/d? less? more?

Daily intelligence re picket numbers: Police/security service infiltrators in NUM, how many? Handlers? Route to NRC?

Infiltrators/sleepers in other unions: ASLEF? GMB? Electricians? How long? How high up? All the way? Nat Exec level? Post-war CPGB as sleeper farm?

Any known audio of Thatcher 'attempt to substitute the rule of the mob for the rule of law' quote? Or briefing by Ingham?

Someone had crossed out 'Ingham' put a ring around 'audio' and written 'Banbury speech, 30/05/84 —ITN' in red biro. 'Susie!'

Q. How many times – and frequency – the word 'riot' used in TV news coverage from beginning of strike to 18/06? Needs complete audit of BBC and ITN archive ASAP. Who? Georgia? 2-person job?

Et cetera.

Hearing Langdon flushing the loo and running the tap upstairs, Jethro had slid the notebook back into place. He liked Langdon and supposed that the director wouldn't have minded him snooping like that, but he wasn't going to push his luck and be too brazen about it.

By the time the director had settled back down at the table, taken a sip of tea and picked up his pen – 'Okay, where were we?' – Lollo had decided to give him something.

'The lads,' he said, 'used to call it a "forget-me-not".'

'A what?' said Langdon.

♦ ♦ ♦

'Call yourself a crossword nut?' said Annie.

She and Rex were sitting outside the taverna on the beach in Agni. Behind them was a hillside of cypress trees and in front of them the clear blue water of the Ionian Sea lapped gently onto the pebbles.

'Okay, show me again,' she'd said.

So Rex had shown Annie the photo on his phone again: the scrap of paper that had fallen out of the trouser pocket of Lollo's dress uniform, at last year's Remembrance Sunday ceremony.

He told her that he'd tried calling the number but it had turned out to be merely one of a bank of consecutive phone numbers servicing the UK wing of a leading global industrial lighting supplier. Maybe it was a quick note made at some high-ranking function he'd attended; a preferred supplier for some major Met lighting requisitions? Or, if not that, then perhaps he'd written it down wrong, or it was just random doodling.

Annie was looking at him askance.

'You sure about that?' she said.

Rex looked at his phone again.

......

TABBY CAT =
07885970760

'Would you ignore that equals sign if it was in a cryptic crossword clue?' she asked.

Christ.

Annie was right. The number of times he'd shown her how to recognise the different types of crossword clues, and here he'd not even thought to look at it that way.

Knowing how to read the clues was half the battle.

He'd shown her how to identify the pointers for anagrams, or for 'hidden clue', 'reverse hidden word', 'repetition' or 'alternate letter' solutions; to spot the 'deletion' or the 'container' clue; the 'initial letters' ploy; the spoonerism, the 'moving letter' and the 'substitution' clues; ditto the homophone, the 'charade', the joke, the thematic sequence, the girl's or boy's name, the standard- or double-definitional…

'Eh?' said Rex, not quite ready to concede the point.

'Would you, though? I bet you wouldn't. It's not just random. It's got to be a "pointer" here, don't you think?'

'Maybe, yeah…'

But she was right; one hundred per cent.

Bessacarr? Why did he have to go and say Bessacarr when he could have said owt?

Should have said nowt.

Lollo was in Orgreave alright, but he'd had Bessacarr on the brain all day.

He'd never even been to the shithole.

Kid only asked where he were from and of course it were first thing as popped into his head. He couldn't well say Cottonley.

The dickhead were only making conversation; idle chat to fill a momentary lull.

Fucking twat.

Himself not t'other.

First time he's put on the spot and he goes and forgets his own legend, never mind his training.

He'd have made a fucking useless UCO.

It'd have been easier to have come in uniform.

It'd have been easier not to have come at all.

Bessacarr!

He'd thought that would satisfy the lad, but it only encouraged him.

'Oh aye,' he'd said, this lad, standing up and peering over the garden wall to see if the coast were clear. 'There's a load of Donny lads over yonder, d'you know 'em?'

'Aye, probably,' he'd said, willing him not to push it.

'There *was* a load of Donny lads, anyroad. Hang on, I'll get 'em.'

In the end he'd had no choice but to deck the twunt. Wasn't

expecting him to fight back, though. Must be losing his touch. Turned into a proper scrap wi young'un.

Note to self, he thought later, legging it up Highfield Lane: Stick to your fucking legend. And if you can't stick to your legend, change the fucking subject, turn it back on them.

Note to self.

'Note to Benny.'

He could laugh now. But that's what he'd thought Stanford had said, back in the classroom at Castle Green.

'Note to Benny.'

You had to laugh. And the teacher had been looking right at him when he'd said it and all.

Benny? What? Simple lad off *Crossroads*?

Shiny-faced farm boy with a woolly hat and ruddy cheeks, and not two brain cells to rub together?

Who you calling fucking Benny?

Even worse, he hadn't only thought it, he'd actually said it too – 'What d'you mean, Benny? Do you think I'm stupid?' – begun to get up. The sound of chair legs scraping lino as he'd half-stood: 'You calling me Benny?'

'Sit down, son. SIT DOWN. No, it's Latin in't it,' said the instructor, mentally recalibrating – Christ! – exactly how much work he had to do to knock these lads into shape. They were worse every year. And he were only talking basic literacy, nothing fancy, just basic literacy, and personal hygiene, some of them, the correct use of soap. And *this* **lout**, what to do with this one? How to get him to control his temper, to channel it? He were supposedly a grammar school boy and all; a rugger bugger. Presumably his low attainment in the classroom had been tolerated for his achievements on the pitch. And he might well be expecting the same treatment here. But if he was, he had another think coming. And John Stanford had thought all of this and a countermove in the time it took to spell it out on the blackboard, and to point at each word while he said it.

'**Nota bene**. It literally means "note well", or "take note" – so when I said it just then I meant: "This next bit is important." And remember that, because when you see the initials "NB" in a manual, or on a form you've to fill in, that's what it stands for: *nota bene*, take note, look out for this and be sure to note it well. And I were talking to the whole class, not just you, Jethro Lawrence. And you should know me well enough by now to know that I'm not in the business of singling people out or calling 'em names. Understood?'

'Yes, sir,' he'd obediently replied, schoolboy habits not forgotten.

Jethro shuddered to think of it, even now. He'd been that embarrassed he'd still come close to clobbering Stanford just to save face. Better to lash out than to cry.

After class, Mr **Stanford** had taken him to one side and told him he was giving him extra homework. And it took him by surprise because he'd expected a ticking-off, but how Mr Stanford had said this, it were like it were a good thing.

It were because he had potential.

It were praise not punishment.

Mr Stanford had told him to go and join the Central Library on Surrey Street, that he'd to borrow a book a week – 'story book or encyclopaedia's up to you' – and write a short report about what he'd read; bring it in every Monday. 'This is not optional, Jethro Lawrence,' he'd said. 'Fail to do this, miss even one week, and I'll fail yer, son, and you're out. Understood? I'll bring you a letter tomorrow and you go down there lunchtime, right? Choose your first book. No excuses.'

Well, he'd done as he were told.

Next lunchtime he'd taken Stanford's letter and stepped for the first time into the **polite** halls of civic engagement, education and self-improvement. And it were fair to say that, once he'd got into the habit of it, he'd not looked back. Although after that he'd quickly learned to stay in the reference library and do most of his reading there, if he didn't want the piss ripped out from the lads. He chose kids' books at first – books about dinosaurs and Vikings, simple tellings of Greek or Egyptian mythology, Aesop's Fables.

One lunchtime he'd been dismayed to find that either he or they had lost his library ticket, and they'd started him off reading newspapers while they issued another. 'Just sit there and read the papers,' they'd said. 'It won't take a minute.' And so he had done.

Thinking back now, he wondered if Mr Stanford hadn't given them a ring and put a word in; asked them to keep a lookout. He must have. Probably did the same thing for all the hopeless cases every year. He'd have known about young Jethro's troubled past, about his father. It'd have been on file.

Then one day he'd clocked there were records there and all, and a record player in a booth. He'd seen some folk listening on them big grey headphones. Long-hairs and student-types waiting patiently in turn to listen to a whole LP. You could borrow them – them as had a record player at home; them as had a home at all. Him having neither, not really. And he didn't know where to start, what to listen to and what to read, and he'd been too proud to ask. So he'd used to look at the books and records on the returns trolley, and let others do the recommending for him. He'd used to lift front covers and check how many stamps they had. And if there were a lot of stamps it meant it were borrowed a lot. And if it were borrowed a lot that meant it must be good.

And that's how the young cadet would pass a couple of hours on his rest day every week. Hunched over whichever book it was he'd chosen. And once he'd plucked up the courage to choose a record and join the queue, there was the added bonus of listening while he read. Well, for both sides of an LP at least, or longer if there was no bugger waiting. Going with whatever the returns trolley turned up: jazz and folk records, musicals and opera, from Gilbert and Sullivan to Thelonious Monk, or strange Himalayan folk music. Some he'd never hear again, while others – post-war jazz, and Gilbert and Sullivan – would stay with him for life. He'd write up his brief reports for Mr Stanford in a school exercise book he'd bought in the newsagent's on Surrey Street.

He'd never thanked Mr Stanford at the time, but you never do, because at the time you don't realise the stakes, or exactly what it is you're being given.

He pitied those who hadn't had a Mr Stanford in their lives.

But he also knew that he'd let Mr Stanford down.

He'd let Mr Stanford down big-time.

He'd not lifted a finger.

He could weep.

Bessacarr?

Well, he weren't gonna say Cottonley, were he? They've long memories in Cottonley. It wasn't the Class War of '84 that was at stake here, but '72.

And then Cliff Heath and a couple of others were pulling him off the kid. They picked the lad up and all.

He dusted himself off and spat on the ground at Jethro's feet. 'Fuck are you, grandad?'

'Oh aye. Want some more, do yer?' said Jethro.

'Fuck off, you old git,' the lad said. 'What's tha fucking problem?'

'Come on, then! Want some more, eh?' said Jethro, wiping his face on the back of his hand, checking for blood.

'Stupid old bastard!'

But the lad was already being bustled away by his mates.

Truth be told, Jethro Lawrence always was a hard nut. But he'd passed his eleven-plus, just about. Scraped through, at any rate. The results had been waiting when they'd got back from Aunty Pat's, that bright summer in Scarborough, 1962. They'd stuff their faces every breakfast – Weetabix, bacon and egg, toast and jam, then out the door, leaving grease to **congeal** on 'Hedgerow'-**pattern** crockery – and not go back to the rooming house near the castle until after dark. Tea was haddock and chips from Fishpan at five o'clock every day. Whitby scampi for his mum. And ice creams from Alonzi's if they were lucky. Dad disappearing into The Nelson for an hour while they played on the beach.

Those summers it seemed like they were always running up and down steps. It were steps to the beach, steps to the castle, steps every-bloody-where. Steps into the past, to dingy cobbled streets, steps into the future, the bright neon of beach and funfair.

On the way home he'd used to race his dad up Custom House Steps, and to be fair by the end of the week his dad'd beat him.

Aunty Pat were Jethro's dad's cousin. Born and wed in Cottonley, she and Ron had moved out to Scarborough after he'd had an ankle crushed in the tipper mechanism of a freight truck in the washery. He'd not lost his foot, but he'd not been up to the physical demands of the job after that. He'd had to wear a calliper and a reinforced boot for the rest of his life, and he hadn't wanted to be behind a desk at the pithead, so they'd bought a place in Scarborough with what little compensation, on a street called Paradise. They'd turned it into a guest house for six months of the year – she the landlady, he the handyman – and earned more in them few month than he'd made down the pit in a year.

'It's called "Paradise",' his father had said, 'because this used to be the harshest bit of town, and the meanest land. The worst fields with the thinnest soil, Pat said. Good for nowt. That's why they built these houses here: cause no bugger wanted it. And it's why they've such big gardens. To give the poor folk as lived here chance to grow owt.'

But there'd been a lesson in all this too.

Young Jethro were tough enough to be a miner – no question. His father told him so. Sat on the beach right there, his breath sour from the pub, while Mum paddled and splashed in sparkling shallow water. But Cyrus Lawrence wanted more for his lad, he said. A job wi prospects. Where a bright lad could climb up through the ranks instead of wearing his sen out in the dark, underground.

'Leave it, Tully,' said Clifford Heath. And Jethro looked at him and was about to say sommat but he had to laugh. There were grass stains on the knees of Heathy's tight grey flared slacks. His Mickey Mouse T-shirt was riding up over his hairy gut, his jacket covered in yellow 'COAL NOT DOLE' stickers, and his wig had gone wonky in the fray.

'State of you,' said Jethro, himself red-faced and panting in his ice-washed jeans and black plimsolls. His own gut was hanging out of a Fred Perry he'd borrowed off Rex, which was now half pulled off, torn under one arm and stretched out of shape from the fight.

'You can fucking talk,' said Heath.

Both of them breathless, laughing, like the old days.

When him and Heathcliff had been just regular young constables on the beat.

Before all this.

Before Tommy Orwell had taken them under his wing.

That one time him and Cliffy Heath had spotted Martin Fry out of ABC – lanky lad in a black leather jacket with a big blond quiff – filling up his red Ford Mustang convertible in the Shell garage at the bottom of Ecclesall Road.

They'd strolled over to admire it, with its soft **cream** leather interior, and he'd just nodded and went, 'Alright, Clifford, how's your mum?'

Cliff'd known him from the clubs, see, or over Disco John's, when Martin had first moved from Stockport and used to hang about at gigs in his trademark long brown leather coat selling his fanzine. Cliff still had a few copies. They'd all be sat round his mum's kitchen table for tea and toast, Delroy Wilson's swinging vocal syncopation on the music centre: To live in a – how did it go? – a beautiful house?

Sommat like that. Sommat about you better got money? 'Who's this, Mrs Heath?' Martin had asked.

Turned out it was a flying **visit**. Decent bloke, though. Other local lads made good might have laughed or run a mile, or blanked you completely. But, to his credit, Mart had made no bones about seeing Cliff in uniform now instead of on the dance floor.

Man's gotta live, in't it.

'Yeah, she's okay, thanks,' said Cliff.

'What's that, a V8?' said Jethro, running a hand down the nearside wing.

'This is Tully,' said Heath, introducing his mate.

'Alright, Tully,' said Martin. 'I'm Martin. Aye, 1964 V8 Mustang 289. Eh, coming to Comsats Friday, Cliff? I've got a couple of plus-ones.'

'No,' Cliff said, 'I'll be on lates, Mart. Bound to be a good'un, though.'

'Oh, right. Yeah.'

'You stopping long?' said Cliff.

'No, just till the weekend.'

'What system you got in there, Mart?'

'Don't ask,' said Martin. He burst out laughing. 'Bloody RadioShack, look!'

They all laughed.

'Bloke I bought it off wasn't into music. Gonna replace it with sommat a bit more powerful. What d'you reckon, Cliff?'

'Pioneer all the way,' said Heath. 'If I were buying now, I'd go FX tape deck, equaliser, and GM-series amp if there's room, subwoofer in the fuckin' boot.' Then like a twat he'd said, 'Not cheap, though, Mart.'

Martin had gone to say something, skipped a beat, frowned for a sec, then shrugged.

'Reckon I can afford it, Cliff.'

'Oh, aye,' said Cliff. 'Happen you can.'

Tully had ripped the piss out of him for weeks after that. '"*Not cheap, though*"! Tha fucking knob. Bloke's a fuckin' pop star. Course he can fuckin' afford it! Not scrimpin' and savin' like regular folk, is he, eh?'

One of the producers, with her hi-vis and her clipboard, her mobile phone, ran over in a panic.

'Is everyone okay?' she said. 'We were worried this might happen. You know: stirring up old memories. It's like Howard said at the briefing: it's meant to be a re-enactment, not a rematch?'

'Briefing?' said Heath. 'Oh, up Oakwell? No, missed it. We only got in for the rehearsal yesterday morning. I live in Oxford now and he's London. He's mates with Michael and James.' He pointed at Lollo. 'Works round the corner.'

'Oh, wow,' said the producer. She took a slip of paper from the clipboard and handed it to them: an address and a map. 'Come and join us for drinks afterwards. If you need more, see one of the assistants.'

Over at the foot of the field, they were getting a few retakes in the can.

A 'miner' pretending to be Geordie Brearley in his toy police helmet was walking along the lines with his hands clasped behind his back, taking the piss and inspecting the line, looking down his nose like a Sergeant Major.

The line of riot police, four deep, were all banging their shields with their batons. The director walking along the line with a sort of circular Steadicam-type contraption – as broad as the steering wheel on a 1969 Leyland RTC bus – with a video camera mounted in the centre, shooting close-ups.

And the shouted response from pickets: 'ZULU! ZULU! ZUUUUUUUU-LUUUUUUUU!'

A **nominal** 'copper' who'd appeared next to the producer, a former miner but now dressed as a tit-head, turned to her and laughed and said, 'They thought it scared us, that banging sound, but really it just used to get us revved up.'

People were milling about by the production company's Portakabins and trailers in the corner of the field. Or by the catering vans in the other corner. *Gladiator* and *Starship Troopers* on repeat in the green room-cum-beer tent. Some blokes were watching telly over a pint or two in plastic glasses. Loudly sharing war stories. And in the vast blue marquee, wardrobe assistants were sorting through the racks of clothes and uniforms, piles of shields, batons, helmets, the works.

And outside, as if by **magic**, there's no coking plant looming over the rooftops and overshadowing the town: no great line of coking ovens and sintering plants, no sulphur-dioxide removal plant, no coolers or top gas heat-exchangers, no gasometers, no conveyors and no hoppers, no loading bays or lorry parks; only hills and sky.

Lollo didn't recognise the place.

Asda was gone; or moved, anyroad. The old manageress had been fierce, but even she couldn't stop two hundred pickets on a booze raid.

No mobile cell blocks. No convoys of carriers parked along the side of the road for two mile or more; so many it were a job to guard 'em.

Not the actual battlefield, neither.

That were long since subsumed by yonder open-cast pit; in part a clean-up operation: scraping off several square miles of slag to extract any waste coal residue and remove a geology toxified by more than a century of leachates and coking wastewater run-off; the ammonia nitrogens, tars and phenols that were by-products of the coke-making process.

So they moved over the railway bridge to the big field behind the houses, with scaff towers for camera positions.

What there was were folk camping in the field, and St John Ambulance stations.

There were Maltby Miners Welfare Band, and a host of re-enactors. Jethro had read the list on the call sheet in wonder: The American Civil War Society, Anmod Dracan down from Redcar, Archaic Events, Arrierre-Ban Historical Enterprises, Armies of the Potomac and Northern Virginia, The Balhag Warriors, Bills and Bows, The Blazon Knights, Buckingham's Retinue, The Chatham Home Guard, The Colchester Historic Enactment Society, The Diehard Company, Victorian Military Society, The End of the Roman Age Society, The English Civil War Society, The Escafield Medieval Society, The Essex Militia, The Fauconberg Household, The Fort Cumberland Guard, Gascoignes Fellowship, Hands of Time, The Historical Enactment Group, The Historical Maritime Society, The Hoplite Association, Independent World War Two re-enactors, The Invicta Military Preservation Society, Lace Wars, Legio II Augusta, Livery and Maintenance, The Napoleonic Association, The Mid-Gard Marauders, Pershing's Doughboys, Regia Anglorum, The Ringwoods of History, The Roman Military Research Society, The Sealed Knot,

The Second Guards Division (Red Army), The Southern Skirmish Association, The Troop, T.I.M.E., The Tudor Group, The Victory in Europe Re-enactment Association, The Vikings (NFPS), The War of the Roses Federation, The World War Two Living History Association, 21eme Regiment d'Infanterie de Ligne, and The 47th Foot.

And there was plenty of folk had come to see the filming: locals and art-lovers over from Sheffield, shipped in on special coaches from Manchester and Leeds, or up from London, and stood along the edge of the field behind a double layer of fencing for their own safety: artists and gallery-goers, painters and sculptors from Yorkshire Artspace and Blast Lane Studios, from St Paul's Street in Leeds, performance artists and administrators, Artangel folk, gallerists, Visual Arts Panel, local art world luminaries, museum keepers and collectors, representatives of the various funding bodies and sponsors with their plus-ones, critics from the broadsheets and art mags, Jarvis Cocker in a crocheted woollen cap. A flicker of recognition.

Jethro and Cliff Heath were here to make up the numbers in a massive **arts** project.

A re-enactment that could have been designed to reinforce the idea that the real event hadn't been theatre. A last hurrah before the name of Orgreave is wiped off the map by a man-made lake, four thousand new homes, a manufacturing park, two primary schools and a windswept waterfront that will be described in the developer's literature as 'stunning'. The whole place renamed 'Waverley'.

Stunning like electro-convulsive therapy: the collective memory erased.

And this time Tully and Heathcliff were on t'other side, playing striking miners. With Rex and a few other UCOs **incommunicado** in the crowd. He'd come as a punter. Him and half a dozen other Public Order lads, that Irish nutter, keeping a weather eye, man-marking a couple of militants, RCP and Socialist Worker, rump-CPGB members that might want to stir up trouble, or hijack proceedings to make a point.

Visitors' parking was all along the lanes into the village, where carriers and coaches had once parked. Today there were just a token two or three old-style blue-painted police transits, hired in from a prop house and parked up at the entrance to the field.

Not Rogers 1, 2 or 3, but close enough to have made the old A-Teamers look twice.

Now there were marshals with hi-vis tabards and clipboards, there to offer interpretation or to point the way. Handouts upon which the project's more provocative sponsor – Murdoch's *Sunday Times* – was absent.

There was a crowd of a few hundred all spread out along the edge of the field and gawping from behind a double cordon of orange crowd-barrier tape strung through steel fencing pins, Tannoy horns on poles, bunting, Frankie's 'Two Tribes' playing over the PA, ice cream vans. The whole thing felt more like a summer fête, with bad weather to match. And the artist and instigator Jeremy Deller – on first-name terms with everybody, but not yet a household name – walking down the other side of the cordon in a white bucket hat and green anorak, with 'Access All Areas' lanyards around his neck and a video camera in his hand, smiling and chatting to people in the audience. Telling them that this wasn't the actual field, that the coking works used to be *over there*, where the open-cast mine now is, and this was as close as they could get, but *that's* still the railway, and *that's* the actual bridge there, the bridge that the pickets were chased over on the day.

And that's still a line of several hundred tit-heads coming towards you over the brow of hill, re-enactment or not.

Earlier the Assistant Re-enactment Director-cum-MC had been explaining the 'Testudo' – the tortoise – the Roman shield formations, the snatch squads, and how the lines would break to allow the mounted units through. And how sometimes they'd pretend to break the line, just to watch the miners run in terror, in anticipation of a charge.

He'd describe a tactic, and then you'd see it recreated.

The line would open to let the snatch squad through: pick a target – anyone'll do. Some poor bastard clattered, cuffed and cautioned before they knew it.

And when the horses come, you'd better get out of the bloody way and fast. Good-natured or not. You've no time to calculate **momentum** when two thousand deadly pounds of police and public-order-trained Percheron is galloping towards you at thirty-odd miles per hour.

Lads playing pickets weren't taking any chances.

As soon as the lines broke, they ran back up the hill as fast as they could.

The MC was telling how TV news had reversed the order of events – bricks first, police retaliation later – when on the day it had been t'other way around. But today's bricks were made of spray-painted foam around a woodblock core that added just enough weight that you could throw them; film props.

Down the side of the field near the gate there were men sat in deckchairs at trestle-table stalls, former miners, pensioners now, one selling home-made fairy cakes, another selling courgette seedlings in little pots for £1 each, another marmalade and jam, local honey, another with second-hand books and DVDs.

Folk looking out for their mates in the crowd of pickets playing football with tops off like on the day, though now it was overcast and drizzling.

'There's Uncle Pete!'

'There's Tim!'

One of the production company's runners saw Deller on Highfield Lane and told him that a fight had broken out between a former miner and a former police officer in one of the gardens. Nothing too serious, he'd said, just tempers fraying. No one pressing charges. You could see how it had happened: stirring up old memories. It was one of several on the day. And there was a bloke with maybe a broken ankle or a bad sprain sitting on a coal bunker up by Highfield Lane too. The lad had fallen awkwardly off the kerb and someone else had stepped on his foot as they were running. The ambulance was called and – true to life – it was unable at first to get through, for all the crowds on Highfield Lane.

And then it was done and they just needed to get a few more shots in the can. The audience shepherded from field to village street.

The money shot took a couple of takes: a mounted police officer riding in with baton raised and leaning low out of his stirrups to strike at a female performer standing in a front garden near the bus stop who began to raise her arm to protect herself before someone behind grabbed her shirt and pulled her out of the way. The man standing next to her raises his battered Canon AE-1 – complete with 28mm wide-angle lens – as if he's taking John Harris's iconic photo. But there's no film in the camera, and that was where the re-enactment ended. There'd be no film processed, no police boot cropped from the right-hand side of the image, no prints sent off to the agency, no reproduction in the *Observer* of 24 June, no silkscreened poster made by *Leeds Other Paper* and Alternative Publications on Cookridge Street, no official complaint about police brutality filed, with that negative offered as incontrovertible evidence, no harassment of Boulton or Harris, no solicitor acting for Boulton, no one disputing in Parliament or the press the veracity of this photo, not this time.

There'd be no break-in at the solicitor's office to steal the negative; not this time around.

And when it was all a wrap, to a ripple of applause, the re-enactors now swelling the audience that lined the streets, the surviving members of the local branch of the National Union of Mineworkers proudly marched their banner through the town.

There was not a dry eye in the place; even the coppers.

It was nice to be a VIP, thought Lollo, as he, Cliff and Rex joined Deller, Figgis and the Artangel crew, friends and family, funders and participants who'd been invited to a post-gig do at the Miners' Social Club, a short drive away.

Just time to drop by the wardrobe marquee and get out of their costumes.

Lollo nodded to James and Michael on the way in.

'Jethro,' they said, warmly shaking his hand. 'So glad you could make it. Help yourself to food and drink.'

As they went towards the bar, he heard someone saying, 'It just shows the level of engagement this project has got. I mean, he's a senior officer now. That someone like that is willing to step into a miner's shoes today! Oh, no, he's Met. Come up from London specially. We've known him for years. Used to drink in The Duke when we first moved to Eyre Street Hill. Not your typical copper. He's a bit of an art collector, lovely place out in Bow. But during the strike he was in PSUs on the South Yorkshire force. Oh, um "Police Support Units", I think: PSUs. Anyway, nice bloke. Likes opera!'

There was a tab behind the bar, and trays of ham sandwiches and slices of cold black pudding were laid out in the side room, like at a wake.

Like a wake?

It was a wake.

They'd felt like VIPs back in the day too. And why wouldn't they. Tommy Orwell had spotted their potential, picked them out from the ranks, and fast-forwarded their careers.

Wasn't that how the story went?

They were untouchable.

But it wasn't up Snig Hill that Operation Fieldfare had been hatched, nor in New Scotland Yard, or the offices and meeting rooms of the Palace of Westminster, but around a modest pine kitchen table in 'The Downs', a rose-covered red-brick grace-and-favour cottage near the Ranger's House in the back end of Petworth Park. The high-security temporary home of Major General **Timon** Cholmondeley-Potter, then in charge of special forces in Northern Ireland. The Major General – a top-five target of the Provisional IRA – lived an anonymous and closely guarded life in a cluster of buildings set in half a mile of open country, and protected by cattle-grids and closed-circuit TV, by motion sensors and trip-lights on all approaches. Round-the-clock protection from three ten-man light infantry platoons on a continuous rolling rota of eight-hour watches in outbuildings front and back, and able to mobilise in seconds to identify and neutralise any threat, any attempt, any incursion or attack.

They'd walked right in.

And Inspector Tommy Orwell might not have got a salute, but he got a curt 'Sir' from the platoon's commanding officer.

Heathcliff and Tully hadn't actually been sat around the kitchen table in Petworth; they'd shuffled about in the doorway until it was made clear that they should go outside for a cig with the Major General's protection detail. While plans were being hatched inside, they were out in the garden comparing the relative merits of rugby league v. rugby union, the nightspots of Aldershot v. the nightspots of Sheffield, but they'd picked up some of it; you couldn't help it. The scale of the operation.

Once, standing outside the back door, Tully had heard Cholmondeley-Potter laughingly referring to 'the apes' – needing to keep the apes how did he put it? 'to keep the apes at arm's length', something like that – but he'd said nowt to Cliffy Heath because his first thought was that the insult was directed at his Black colleague. But only later, back in Aldershot, once plans had started taking shape and training was underway, did he realise that the two-star officer had been referring to the muscle, the reservists, the ex-1- and 2-Para personnel who'd be joining their unit.

Well, that made sense, in an 'ours is not to reason why' kind of way.

They were ex-squaddies, after all.

They were there to follow orders, not to be party to whatever machinations produced 'em.

Now he knew differently, of course.

It had only dawned on him years later that the apes old Chimney-Pot had been referring to were him and Heath. He'd just been too arrogant to see it.

The Major General couldn't understand why Orwell would have brought them along, and he certainly didn't approve.

But it wasn't their fault.

What did they know?

Heathcliff and Tully were just a couple of young coppers who'd been flattered into thinking they were something special. When wasn't it truer to say they'd just been a pair of outsiders, singled out by Orwell and groomed into loyalty?

Battering that mechanic to within an inch of his life in Camberley hadn't been a misdemeanour for which Jethro had needed to be shown lenience; it had been desirable, a necessary qualification.

Still here, though, weren't they?

Apes or not.

Tommy Orwell had been drummed out of the force. While the heavy-smoking Major General Cholmondeley-Potter was long gone: dead of emphysema within six months of his investiture in the Queen's Golden Jubilee Birthday Honours. Well, at least these two, Heath and Lawrence, had been survivors.

Better than that: these apes had both made Detective Chief Inspector.

He'd bumped in to a much-reduced 'Sir Tim' (for short) years later, in the early noughts.

Time flies.

It was in St James's Park, on the day that Jethro and eleven others across the Met had been made up to Inspector. There was a bit more pomp and circumstance in the Met in those days. There'd been a reception for the whole cohort at New Scotland Yard. Full dress uniform had been required, not least for a colour photo of the dozen new Inspectors that had appeared in the next issue of *The Job*. A print of which had been obtained, framed, and hung in Jethro's sixth-floor office.

It was a bright, clear spring day, with leaves just showing on the trees, and after the jollies and the small talk had concluded, and fortified by the selection of sandwiches and savouries on offer, he'd decided to milk it a bit and walk back to Holborn. He'd cut through the little alleyway that led to Birdcage Walk, then over into St James's Park.

As the footpath curved around the flower beds opposite Horse Guards, and the people thinned out, he'd found himself falling into step with a gentleman in morning dress – cut-away black tailcoat, grey striped trousers – who'd been walking ahead more slowly, with a stick and a slight stoop. As he'd passed, he'd turned and seen the slab of colours worn on his left breast, then recognised their wearer.

When Jethro had wished him a 'Good afternoon, Sir Tim', Cholmondeley-Potter had stopped before replying, as if unable to walk and talk at the same time.

Jethro had stopped too.

'Good afternoon,' he'd said, after a second or two's pause, then: 'Were you just at the palace too?'

The voice, though cheery, was hoarse and weakened, the face hollowed but unmistakable. Sir Tim was frailer than Jethro might have expected, but still gave the impression of being sharp as a tack, his eyes still bright.

'No, sir,' Jethro said. 'Presentation for us new Inspectors at the Yard.'

'Oh, I see,' the Major General said, eyeing the two silver stars on the policeman's epaulettes. 'Congratulations. How many of you?'

'Twelve of us,' said Jethro. 'Ten men and two women.'

'Jolly good, then. Onwards and upwards.'

'Indeed,' said Jethro.

'You're a Yorkshireman,' he said. 'Where from?'

'Cottonley,' said Jethro, 'near Barnsley, South Yorkshire, sir.'

'Mining country.'

'Yes, sir. Once upon a time.'

'I had the pleasure, in my UNPROFOR days,' said Cholmondeley-Potter, 'of working with the Prince of Wales's Own Yorkshires in Bosnia. Now that was a fine body of men.'

You had the pleasure of working wi me and all, thought Jethro, but he said nothing.

'"Shootbat", we called them,' the old man continued. 'Because they tended to be, well, I'm not saying "trigger-happy", but they were reckoned to be somewhat robust in their approach, as I'm sure you know. So what brought you to London?'

'Fast-tracked for promotion back in the eighties,' said Jethro. 'In those days, the brightest and best tended to get shared around.'

Major General Sir Timmy drifted off for a second, then, with a smile of paternal affection forming on his face: 'My daughter,' he said – and probably not for the first time – 'tells me I have to walk every day.'

The statement had the confident tone of a well-used conversational gambit. Maybe he was not so sharp, after all.

'She's quite right too,' said Jethro. 'Should do more of this myself.'

'Good idea,' said the Major General. '"Use it or lose it" is what Laura says.' Gathering his thoughts and his breath, and half-turning his head to acknowledge the scale of the undertaking, how far he'd come, he smiled and said, 'She's a good girl, but either this park is bigger than I remember or I've got slower. These damned legs.'

'Need any help, sir?'

'No, thank you,' he said. 'That's my car just pulling up now.'

Jethro glanced at the black Daimler.

'Then I won't keep you, sir,' he said, with a nod of 'Good day' as he stepped away and made to continue on his way.

'And to you, Inspector,' said Cholmondeley-Potter with a smile of affirmation. 'Keep up the good work.'

Jethro knew that it would take Major General Sir Tim a good five minutes to walk the thirty yards or so to his car, but he could see that, yes, that must be his daughter Laura waiting in the back, ready to jump out and assist. He nodded and smiled warmly as he approached.

She smiled gratefully and mouthed 'Hello' through the glass, then, as Jethro paused, wound down the window, letting out a faint waft of a perfume that carried a fine, clear note of night-scented stock.

'Hello,' he said, taking off his cap, leaning down so they were on more of a level. She was dressed up too. 'How are you? The Major General's on good form, I see.'

'Thank you,' she said. 'Yes, he is. He was a Brigadier when he retired, you know.'

'Oh,' said Jethro. 'I hadn't realised. Name's Jethro. Knew him of old.'

'Well, some days are better than others. And this was a good day, and a treat for me to come along, but once we get him home it'll take him a few days to recover.'

She was a handsome woman too, with her fair hair worn up and a dimple on her chin; bare shoulders and pearls, and black mascara surrounding bright blue eyes. Whatever the occasion at the palace – an Armed Forces luncheon? – he could see that she'd been there too. Mid-forties, he guessed, with a twinkle in her eye and an open smile. They were both looking, he realised, at each other's faces, at each other's mouths. In other circumstances they might have found an easy rapport, and sought each other's glances out across the room.

They'd have plenty to talk about.

And she'd have been around university age back in the day. Coming back to 'The Downs' for the holidays. Where might she have gone: Oxbridge? Or, failing that, Bristol? Durham? Exeter?

He wondered if she'd known quite what her father did for a living, beyond the ceremonial functions.

Job? he wondered. Something in publishing, or a steady rise up through the charitable sector? Children? Husband?

No ring now, anyway, so she was some fool's loss.

She was the sort of girl he'd have asked to dance more than once if he'd seen her at a wedding. He could almost feel the layers of silk and damask shifting against her hip beneath his touch.

She was the sort of girl a man could hold and fall in love with on a spring afternoon like this, in their glad rags.

Then later in some hotel room, with her skirt hoiked up and his trousers on the floor.

So close and yet so far.

A good and honest, loving, giving English rose. What more could any man want?

'Well, I'd better leave you to it,' said Jethro. 'He's very proud of you.'

'Thanks for taking a minute to chat,' she said. 'He'll have enjoyed that. And it'll give him something to talk about later. You know, it's really surprised me. How some people just stare. They look at the elderly as if they're monsters. But it's a special time if you're able to slow down and take a bit of care. I've learned to find the things we can enjoy doing together: little moments of pleasure. Do you have elderly parents?'

'No, sadly not.'

'Oh, I'm sorry,' said Laura. 'I didn't think.'

'You've no need to apologise. He's lucky to have you,' said Jethro. 'Anyway, very nice to meet you, Laura. And to see Sir Tim again.' He thought about introducing himself more fully, but instead he held her gaze a beat or two longer than was decent, and she held it back. Then he smiled and nodded, and said, 'Ma'am', before putting his cap back on and continuing on his way.

As he strode up towards The Mall, he could hear the car door opening behind him, and the warm words of greeting and praise as Laura stepped out to help her father into the back seat beside her.

Jethro knew that once they were comfortable in the car – with seatbelts on, and walking stick stowed at his side – and as they turned left at the lights and drove away back up The Mall, Sir Tim holding on to a leather grab-handle above the window, she would ask her father, 'Who was that policeman? Do you know him? Jethro something? He seemed to know you – called you Major General.'

And of course her father wouldn't know, but at least he'd be able to say, and with some authority, 'Yes, he's one of the Met's new Inspectors; a Yorkshireman. There are twelve of them this year: ten men and two women. "Shootbat", we used to call them...'

But that would be enough to go on.

Enough for her to find him if she wanted to.

Maybe she'd look for a news story later, and recognise him in a photo; or look up his shoulder number and find some excuse to call.

He hoped so.

'Two women? Well, that's *some* progress, then,' she'd say as they reached the end of The Mall and the driver swung left towards Belgravia. 'I suppose fifty-fifty's too much to ask for.'

◆ ◆ ◆

Annie was right, of course.

'What if it's not a phone number,' she said, 'but a straightforward substitution cipher?'

'"A equals one, B equals two" type of thing?' said Rex.

'Yeah, but starting with zero instead of one?' said Annie. 'The key is the adjacency of the "T" and the zero, isn't it?'

She was good. Rex wanted to say that he'd taught her well, but he felt a bit of a fool.

As if Annie had needed to be taught anything.

It was him that had been too eager to see the obvious.

A phone number – as if!

What had he been thinking?

'If "T" *equals* zero,' said Annie, way ahead of him by now, 'what does that make "A"? Hang on: U, V, W—' She counted off the letters on her left hand.

Rex started counting it out on his fingers too.

'"U" would be one,' said Annie. 'So "V" is two, then— W, X, Y, Z… Yes, so if "A" is seven, eight would be "B"! 07885 *is* "Tabby". You can see him counting them off – these little dots. I'll bet you anything the last bit is a partial date: seventh… 1960? But I'm not sure that's important. Could be anything. This is standard password methodology, no? But if so, the password for what?'

Rex shook his head in a show of sad pride: 'Not a password,' he said. 'Not one I know, at any rate.'

'Oh, right,' said Annie. 'Of course. So what, then?'

Rex smiled, remembering an old phrase of his father's, one that had used to infuriate him beyond measure as a child, hoping now that it would wind her up too.

'That's for me to know,' he said, 'and for you to find out.'

Yes! he thought, mentally punching the air, and imagining some signature victory dance around the corner flag of his mind.

He knew what this was for.

It had to be.

He'd sat and looked at it often enough.

But he wasn't going to let Annie win as easily as all that.

◆ ◆ ◆

She'd been one in a million, that was for sure: his Tabby Cat.

The problem was that Jethro hadn't known if he'd exactly wanted it to be a secret any more – not for good, anyroad. He were nothing to be ashamed of. He considered himself quite a catch, did Detective Chief Inspector Jethro Lawrence.

She took his breath away.

He'd wanted everyone to know.

She were that brazen.

He'd even asked his Tabby Cat to marry him.

They'd been down to Dorset for a dirty weekend, and he'd taken a ring with him.

It was always a dirty weekend with that one.

His mother's engagement ring. A little velvet box hidden in his washbag.

He'd wanted some commitment, wanted to make things right, at this stage in their lives, not to add complications, but to avoid them.

But he hadn't fully understood that maybe this was it.

That time she'd walked naked to the bathroom and come back with his **shaving tackle**. She'd lathered him up and shaved his balls. It had taken ages. It was almost unbearable, but he'd trusted her completely. Then she'd handed it to him so he could do her.

On the beach by Durdle Door, he'd got down on one knee and proposed.

'Oh, Jethro,' she'd said. 'I don't know what to say. Can I think about it for a day or two?'

'Course you can,' he'd said, careful not to let his disappointment show. 'Take all the time you need.'

Yes, they'd been flirting for a while before it had finally happened – albeit plausibly deniably, imperceptible to others' eyes – and they'd both known it. But still, it had fair taken his breath away the first time she'd reached over to slowly and oh-so-deliberately drag her fingernail along his hot and heavy **hornbeam**, from hairy root to shiny tip, through the stiff serge of his dress uniform trousers, and then left her hand there to hold and squeeze. And all this as they'd waited in the back of a staff car outside a Met reception over Millbank. Her holding him, and him ever-hardening in her hand until he thought he'd burst. And her, bold as brass, looking him right in the eye all the while until – with no dangerously jerky or sudden movements, just a cessation of touch, and a simultaneous adjustment in her seat – she'd let go. And she'd done so a split second before Met Comms Chief Evelyn Gummer noisily opened the nearside door and sat in the front passenger seat, and regaled them for fifteen minutes with whatever gossip she'd picked up: who'd said what, who was on the way up or down, in or out, what whichever Assistant Private Secretary to the Minister for Policing really thought about the MOPAC chair's PA (hint: those boys had been an item once upon a time, yes, really), and which way whichever wind was or might be blowing.

Gummer – always with an ear to the ground – wasn't only good at controlling the information flowing out of the Met, the conversations that the organisation was driving, but also at divining, tapping into and converting (into 'sales', into power, into ammunition, into reach) the information flowing within it. Well, maybe she was losing her touch because nothing was as good as the juicy gossip that was going on right under her nose right now, and she'd only up and missed it.

Gummer had seen nowt, thank fuck, but Lollo had had a hard-on for the rest of the fucking day.

He'd even tried to buy Paradise. A place for them to retire to. A cottage had come up just along the road from Aunty Pat's old place. Course it were all chi-chi now; more like the bloody Dordogne than North Yorkshire. Heaven on earth! And you could still get haddock and chips from Fishpan. London fish suppers didn't compare.

But she'd said no, and not before lining up the ultimate humiliation for her soon-to-be ex: 'Jethro, you wouldn't just give this critical path a once-over for me, would you?'

And worse, after the break-up, after snatching all that away from him, to have been able in all seriousness to delegate to him – *to him*! – BCU lead on the MOPAC Public Access Consultation now known as 'Leading for London!' It beggared belief. The consultation was a poisoned chalice if ever there was one, a game of such bad faith and sophistry that, while he wasn't exactly destined to lose, it would be impossible to win – odds so stacked against the interests of the police and public both.

She'd not been able to dress it up.

She'd not really tried.

And that time he'd not been able to conceal the dismay on his face.

'Of course I can,' he'd said. But like a fool he'd not been thinking.

He'd just been trying to please her in that potent moment when he'd thought – hoped – that she might still say 'yes'.

'Thank you, Detective Chief Inspector,' she'd said. 'If you could have any comments and amends on my desk Monday morning before SMT, that'd be great.'

Whoops.

If he'd been looking for the writing on wall, there it was.

'It's not you, Jethro, it's me,' she'd said later, over a functional one-course supper in a quiet corner of Pont de la Tour.

She'd really said that.

'I thought we'd both agreed that it was just a bit of fun. It was fun, wasn't it?'

Spare me the fucking clichés, he'd thought. Nothing is 'just a bit of fun' at my age.

'I think we both want different things out of our retirements,' she'd said, sliding the little velvet box back across the crisp cotton tablecloth. 'But thank you, Jethro. I'm sorry.'

She'd paused for a second or two, then delivered the coup de grâce: 'I think it's best if we slow down a bit. Give each other a bit of space.'

Her car had been waiting outside and she'd offered to drop him home, but he'd said no. He had some fucking dignity.

There'd been tears in Jethro's eyes as he'd walked blindly home, lost in thought. Quite what route he'd taken he couldn't tell you.

That she could switch it off, just like that!

It wasn't only the humiliation of the rejection – that was bad enough. But now – to top it all off – he'd found himself gulled into somehow being responsible for the delivery of that steaming turd of a MOPAC consultation. It was a line-management nightmare.

Lined up to take the rap, more like.

And who was his line manager?

Christ! Now he'd be at her desk on Monday begging for scraps and hoping he'd done his homework. Because she was a hard taskmaster, was Tabitha Churchill. He'd seen how she'd turned on people before. Many was the night he'd been called on for emotional and professional support; given her a shoulder to cry on; nodded while she'd bitched about whoever it was that had let her down this time. But he hadn't imagined that he'd be next. If he hadn't dotted his 'i's and crossed his 't's she'd send him away with a rocket up his arse, alright. Not his naughty Tabby Cat any longer. Never now to be whatever power couple he'd imagined: driving down to Glyndebourne with a hamper in the summer, or poring over the programme for the Proms. Now she'd be quietly slagging *him* off to the next sympathetic ear. And she'd enjoy it, and, worse, so would they.

◆ ◆ ◆

'She said "yes",' said Rex, smiling broadly.

He'd wanted to tell Lollo as soon as they'd got back from holiday. And he'd known Jethro would be pleased, but still the Chief's enthusiastic response had surprised him.

'Of course she did,' said Lollo, reaching out to shake him warmly by the hand. 'Good lad. Of course she did.'

Twenty years ago news like this might have warranted a drink in the office, or a toast at least. Not in these more serious times, though. But when he'd got home later on, half a case of Champagne had just been delivered.

'Look!' Annie said, reading the card that came with it.

He'd told Lollo all about the proposal.

How they'd had lunch on the beach at Agni, then gone for a paddle. There were jet skis out on the water, and further out – against a backdrop of the Albanian mountains – a couple of big cruise ships on their way from Venice down to the Peloponnese. In the clear water around their ankles were quicksilver shoals of tiny fish darting hither and thither. But then Rex had spotted something else. He'd looked again.

'What is it?' said Annie.

He bent down, reached into the water and carefully moved some pebbles. He half-expected it to be broken glass or a sharp bottletop that had caught his eye, glinting in the shallows.

But it wasn't.

It was much more exciting than that.

And the timing was perfect.

Surely it was a sign; an omen.

Something to really seal the deal.

'I don't believe it,' he said as he showed Annie the heavy gold wedding band in his hand.

Some fat-fingered fellow must have lost it, because it was a big'un. There was enough gold here to make two respectably sized wedding rings. And right now it would have to do. He'd take it to one of the jewellers on Hatton Garden when they got back, and see what they suggested.

It was a plan.

Rex had got down on his knees there and then on Agni beach; kneeled down in the limpid and gently lapping water. So what? His trousers would dry out soon enough in this heat, and he could rinse out the salt back at the hotel.

He'd held the wedding band up with two hands, didn't want to risk dropping it back in the sea. 'Annie, will you marry me?'

Well, what else was she going to say?

It was too big for her, of course, but she'd slipped her ring finger into it nonetheless.

'Good lad,' said Lollo again. 'I had a feeling this one would make an honest man out of you.'

'Thank you, sir,' said Rex. And he wondered whether even his own father – God rest his soul – would have been happier to hear about his and Annie's engagement. Was that a tear in the Detective Chief Inspector's eye?

Rex often thought of his own parents, frozen in time in the early 1980s. They were so young when they died, he realised now.

Annie's theory – which she spelled out again as she opened the box and took out a bottle of vintage Champagne to show Rex the label – was that not only was Jethro a bit of a father figure to Rex, but that Jethro in turn treated Rex a bit like the son he never had.

And she was probably right.

Christ.

But Rex and Annie were madly in love. MAD as in 'mutually assured destruction', Cold War babies that they were. Each knew too much about the other.

As they'd waited in line – cabin baggage only – to board the EasyJet back from Corfu Airport, the ring safely stowed in his washbag, Rex knew that 'going forward' – as Tabitha Churchill liked to put it in her all-staff emails – this was now the basis of their pact. The rock and the foundation upon which their relationship was now built.

Because Annie knew everything – but *everything* – about Rex.

And Rex – thanks in part to Lollo having his back – knew a fair bit about Annie too.

Or at least he thought he did.

So much so that in all seriousness he'd wondered, that couple of days ago, when the taxi had dropped them off for their long walk, he'd wondered whether both of them would make it back. It would have been so easy for one or other of them to lose their footing on that old partisan track and tumble-bump down the sheer sandstone cliff to a certain death.

Well, that would have simplified things for all concerned.

But if he'd really allowed himself to think that through, he mightn't have been sure which of them it would be. Who'd push who?

Instead he'd opted for a different kind of pressure: a post-traumatic show-and-tell. More of a tit-for-tat, I'll-show-you-mine-if-you-show-me-yours approach; not an attack but a deliberate letting-down, brick by brick, of his defences.

And it had worked.

Or it had seemed to.

◆ ◆ ◆

Frankie had kindly texted to tip him off that a strictly embargoed draft copy of the Coroner's Record of Inquest and Conclusions into the death of Jethro Lawrence had been received in-house to allow for some pre-planning of press.

Churchill had seen it without letting on, and now Rex wanted to see it too.

He'd drop his old friend and the BCU's Assistant Director of HR Di Malcolm an email.

Di wouldn't let him down.

In such cases, when the deceased was a high-profile public figure, the Coroner's Office was generally happy to work together on a carefully worded announcement. But even then, Rex knew that he was not likely to be on the circulation list.

Besides which, with all hands needed on deck comms-wise to spin the 'Leading for London!' launch on the coming station closures into a positive news story about increasing public access to the police, publication of the Record of Inquest into Lollo's death was lower priority. It was being pushed forward a week or so, precise date and time to be confirmed. The clock was ticking, but it wasn't as if Jethro Lawrence was going anywhere. And Rex was certain that Churchill and Gummer would be looking for a minimum of a couple of days of clear water between the 'Leading for London!' campaign and the Coroner's report. Not to mention, further down the line, the potential release of any possible negative outcomes from the leaks, and any ensuing investigation into Operation Fieldfare, or link to the death of William Cooper.

Melissa Shepherd's investigation into the Detective Chief Inspector's disappearance had been ring-fenced, de-escalated and defunded, personnel and resources reallocated pending its closedown. Her exit strategy would involve collation and submission of the inevitable report (costings, impacts, etc.), a facilitated sit-down debrief with the London team (flipchart to capture ideas, headlines, lessons learned, etc.), and working with Evelyn Gummer at London CN to draft a statement that would ultimately be supportive of Churchill's official word, yet neutral and passive enough to work across news and social platforms. She'd had a few goes already, basing her attempts on the standard condolences template: 'On behalf of the West Sussex Force I would like to extend/offer/send our deepest/fondest/heartfelt/sincere sympathies/condolences/good wishes to our Metropolitan Police colleagues and to the friends and family of Detective Chief Inspector Lawrence. It has been our sad yet proud privilege to—'

Rex emailed Di Malcolm.

Sure enough, Di emailed him back within seconds.

Here you go. Dx

Rex took a deep breath and opened the attachment: the Coroner's Record of Inquest.

It was tough to see the conclusions that she'd written there in black and white.

It brought it all home somehow.

Name of Deceased (if known):
Detective Chief Inspector Jethro Cyrus Lawrence OBE

It is not proposed in this conclusion to set out the law relating
to suicide. But two key points need to be made in the context of
conclusions. First, Parliament has decided that suicide should
remain as a short-form conclusion. The word 'suicide' is expressly
used in the Rules. It is therefore my judicial duty, when suicide
is proved on the evidence, to record the conclusion of suicide
according to the criminal rather than the civil standard in law.
It would be wrong, for example, to record either a) an 'open'
conclusion or – in the case of a serving police officer – b) a 'service
death' (that is when the deceased was killed in the line of duty),
when the evidence of suicide is clear. Secondly, suicide must never
be presumed. It is my duty to make express reference in each case
of possible suicide to the two elements which need to be proved:
(i) that the deceased took his/her own life; and (ii) the deceased
intended to do so (or, put together, 'he/she intentionally took his/
her own life'). Having given all the material that's been sent to me
the most careful consideration, I've concluded that the evidence
that DCI Lawrence took his own life is overwhelmingly strong.
Further, there is nothing I've seen that supports any allegation that
DCI Lawrence was subject to foul play, or that his death was the
subject of any kind of conspiracy or cover-up. Reviewing witness
statements and evidence, I am satisfied that both elements have
been proved here to the criminal standard of proof—

Rex scanned the meat of the thing… 'suicidal ideation and
behaviours'… blah blah… 'confirmed whistle-blower'… blah blah…
'leaks traced to subject's mobile phone'… 'presence of nasal mucus
in blood spatter found on the scene would be consistent with nose
bleed'… blah blah… 'no family or significant attachments'… blah
blah… 'parting gifts, they felt'… blah blah… 'signed suicide note –
quote "Can't take it any more" unquote – found hidden among papers
on a colleague's desk'… blah blah… 'positive ID from witness'…
blah blah… 'last sighting on Railway Approach outside the ferry
terminal'… blah blah… 'dredging activity'… Then Rex cut to the
final paragraph:

Those findings of fact here lead me therefore to the following
inevitable conclusion. I am satisfied to the relevant standard of proof

that Jethro Cyrus Lawrence took his own life and that he intended to do so. For the purposes of the law I must therefore record the formal conclusion as suicide.

◆ ◆ ◆

Rex pulled the front door to behind him and jogged downstairs to where he knew Police Federation rep Simon Rose would be waiting for him on the pavement outside.

It was 11 a.m., but it was dark.

Building contractors had encased the whole block of flats in scaffolding, over which blue nylon netting had now been stretched, robbing residents of their views and putting flats and balconies alike into a permanent twilight that was going to take some getting used to, as long as it lasted.

The scaffolders – did they have to shout so much? – had been hard at work for about three weeks, but that was just the overture to several months of works to be done, for which – as one of the roughly sixty-five per cent of leaseholders in the building, as he now explained to Si – Rex was being royally rinsed to the tune of £15,000.

'Ouch!' said Si, then changed the subject. 'So when did you first meet DCI Lawrence?'

They walked up to Queen Square, then turned left along Cosmo Place towards Southampton Row.

'Soon as I joined,' said Rex. 'He was DS Lawrence back then, and struck the fear of God into us. And he's been a constant in my working life ever since, barring the odd secondment...'

Rex paused, and they looked at each other. It was precisely because of just such a 'secondment', in this case to the National Public Order Intelligence Unit, that today's rehearsal was even necessary.

'As I say. Barring the odd secondment, he's been my line manager for most of that time.'

'Blimey,' said Si. 'I didn't realise. I'm sorry for your loss.'

'Thanks, mate,' said Rex. 'Yeah, it's hard to get used to.' He thought for a second, then said, 'Lollo *was* the Met for me.'

Rose was leading the way to one of the big hotels on Russell Square, where the Police Federation had hired a function room for a week of optional but strongly advised coaching sessions for any still-serving officers from the Met and elsewhere who'd been scheduled to give evidence, written, oral or otherwise.

'Basically,' Si had said, outlining the offer to Rex a couple of days previously, 'it's available to any officer or manager who's been called to give evidence as part of Phase Four of Tranche Two of the inquiry. We don't want you going in there unprepared.'

Phase this, tranche that: the vocabulary had sounded bizarre at first, but Rex was getting used to it. Phase Four of Tranche Two was to be devoted to Core Participants, UCOs – undercover officers – and managers from SDS and/or NPOIU 1997–2008.

They'd laid out the tables and chairs more or less as they would be in the Thistle Marble Arch Hotel on Bryanston Street, where the actual inquiry was taking place.

Francis Bland QC and a couple of his pupils would conduct the questioning based on transcripts from Phase Three, and they had a video camera and monitor set up for feedback and training purposes. Si Rose had already given Rex a folder of bumf, plus a notebook and a Police Federation pen. The folder bore Rex's designated number on it rather than his name.

He'd sent himself to sleep reading through the pack in bed the night before.

One document comprised a slightly daunting compilation of sample questions that other UCOs had faced to date, more or less. They ranged from those designed to elicit basic one-word answers – yes, no; dates and times – to some that were more fine-grained than he'd been expecting. He'd run through them, just the first few anyway, thinking about what he'd say.

When did you join the Metropolitan Police as a Cadet?

That was easy. Accepted autumn '89, joined and commenced training Easter 1990. Rex still had the letter which had been addressed to him c/o Coptic Street in the filing cabinet at home.

When did you become a full Constable?

Graduate entry accelerated training programme, so – he had to think about this – first Monday in January '91? Christ! Probation completed January '92. He could double-check.

Were you aware of the presence of undercover units either by name or by any slang terms prior to your posting?

He'd read a tatty paperback of Serpico *as a teenager (had he bought it at a jumble sale, or a charity shop? one or the other) so Rex would have assumed similar existed in the UK, but certainly not the extent nor the targets.*

Can you recall the exact date of your posting to SDS/NPOIU?

Roughly, but again he could check and make a note, have it to hand if that was allowed. Was it allowed? He'd already been given an aide-mémoire of cyphers and pseudonyms they'd pulled together for witnesses who were due to give evidence about individuals thus identified to date. So if he could have an aide-mémoire for that information, presumably he could have a note of key dates to hand. He'd ask Si tomorrow.

What was the duration of this or any other undercover posting?

Again, he'd have to double-check exact dates, but he'd kept all HR correspondence religiously.

Did you make colleagues in your prior role or post aware of any such posting?

No.

Following your posting to SDS/NPOIU and on return to any prior role or post, did you get the impression that colleagues had been made aware of the reason for your absence from said prior role or post?

No one had said anything, but he'd sensed that colleagues knew.

Was your absence ever referred to?

Not overtly, no.

Were you or any other UCOs to the best of your knowledge ever referred to as a 'hairy'? And if so, how did you respond?

He'd heard the term, but never directed at himself. A hairy? He'd have decked them, probably.

Can you recall the name of the officer who referred you?

That was easy: Lollo. Detective Chief Inspector Jethro Lawrence.

What if any experience of public order policing did you have prior to your posting to SDS/NPOIU?

Prior to becoming a cadet, more like! thought Rex. And Lollo had known it. 'What's a legend?' Rex had asked. Seriously! He'd been at the sharp end on 1 June '85, ran for his life, it had felt like, then escaped riding pillion a few miles on the back of some biker girl's Honda 125; an angel by any other name, she'd happened to ride past just in the nick of time and had a spare helmet in the box. Then he'd been in Trafalgar Square on 31 March '91. He'd been waiting for his police training to start mid-April, just after Easter. He'd not gone to the whole demo, but strolled down Charing Cross Road from Coptic Street and caught the tail end of the speeches. He'd broadly disagreed with the poll tax at the time – who hadn't? – and figured he'd be safe if he stuck to the edges, more spectator than participant. Knew better than to get himself arrested. He needed that job; needed the protection it would bring.

He was in a few of the library photos if you zoomed in far enough.

He'd checked.

And he'd certainly be in the police photos.

There, among a handful of figures standing on the raised dais beneath the portico of the National Gallery. He's the one in the white Fred Perry and faded 501s, in Adidas hi-tops with an olive MA1 slung over his shoulder. Watching carriers reversing at speed to split the crowd – it was a wonder no one had been killed – then mounted units charging and the crowd scattering; moving as one like a murmuration of starlings; returning a useless fusillade of half a dozen two-by-one sticks that had become separated from their placards, then turning as one and running, scattering. The general unspoken principle being that a baton is a baton, you need to put some distance between you and it, as far and as fast as possible. He'd got out of there sharpish before things had got really nasty. The trouble hadn't reached as far as Centre Point; not gone much north of Leicester Square tube.

He wouldn't tell them this, but the very next day, 1 April 1990, he'd been back doing a door-to-door market research gig on St George's Estate on Cable Street, trying to earn a few quid before Easter to tide himself over. Jogging up and down the stairs of those St George's tower blocks and low-rises. Pie and mash for lunch every day from that place by Shadwell tube: that was the life! He'd been told to knock on every door. Not allowed to take no for an answer. Showing his ID: 'Market Research, can I come in and ask you a few questions, please?' They'd been encouraged to be persistent. More than that, they'd been instructed not to take no answer to mean that no one's home, but to knock until someone opened the door. The view from some of those flats: a bird's-eye view of News International. He remembered a young professional woman in stockinged feet pointing out where all the picket lines had been in '86. That was when Murdoch's printworks had been moved from Fleet Street to the new secret site in Wapping, where seven hundred men could now do the work of seven thousand. The print unions had been lured into a costly dispute, the closed shop and so-called 'Spanish practices' swept away in one fell swoop.

He'd jacked it in after that. But on that April Fool's morning, the first person who'd answered the door to him had been an actual card-carrying communist. A ninety-five-year-old East End Jew and bona fide Battle of Cable Street veteran, living in low-rise sheltered housing on the St George's. He was listening to his box set LP of Brecht and Weill's Threepenny Opera *when he showed Rex in. It was there on the coffee table, and one of the discs was spinning on the turntable, the 'Ballade von der sexuellen Hörigkeit' coming out of oversized but puny Soviet speakers.*

'Ah,' Rex had said, 'this takes me back', and sung along! 'Das ist die sexuelle—'

And, with the ice broken, it was the old man who'd brought up what was already being called the Poll Tax Riot. And when Rex had said he'd been there, the old man had said, 'Son, it's nothing new. I've been protesting since I was younger than you are now, and let me tell you they always, always, always end like that. The police always go in with violence.'

'All fairly straightforward, I think,' Simon Rose said cheerfully.

'That's easy for you to say,' said Rex.

The way this was going to go, Si had explained while they waited in the hotel lobby for the lift up to the conference suite, was the standard workshop method: they'd record his answers, a few at a time, then play them back to see what improvements needed to be made. Practise a few, then tape them again. Rinse and repeat.

He skim-read a few more questions while Si set up the video camera on a tripod, plugged in the monitor.

How much time did you spend at Barnes Common, Camberwell New Road, or Vincent Square prior to your deployment?

Can you describe what assistance, formal training, or handover period you received or experienced prior to your deployment?

Can you recall any assessment of your suitability for the role being undertaken either formally or 'on the job' prior to your actual posting?

Can you describe the nature of any 'reading in' time allocated to you prior to your posting, and if so, was there any monitoring of your progress in this regard?

Were you issued with or given access to anything that could be described as a 'Trade Craft Manual' or e.g. any volume or volumes outlining your role, responsibilities, and 'ways of working' as an Undercover Officer? If so, please describe said volume or volumes and their location.

What assistance was given and by whom in the creation of your 'legend'?

Were you involved in the procurement and/or administration of any cover documents in support of your cover name or legend or that of other UCOs?

Were you involved in the procurement and/or administration of safe houses?

Were you involved in the procurement and/or administration of cover accommodation?

Were you involved in the procurement and/or provision of additional manpower resources in support of the clandestine bona fides of other SDS field operatives?

During your posting, to whom did you report and by what means? Please answer fully.

Can you describe the nature and frequency of any 'welfare calls' you were required to make?

How did you explain or justify such regular observances to any surveillance subjects?

Did you liaise with the Transport Department over the procurement and disposal of suitable vehicles for yourself or other Undercover Officers?

Did you have a role in registering vehicles in your cover name or the cover names of other UCOs?

Did you attend regular gatherings with other UCOs at Barnes Common or Vincent Square?

Did you attend regular gatherings of either a work or social nature with other UCOs at any safe house?

Did you share knowledge or information about ways of working with other UCOs at any safe house or gathering?

During the period of your posting, who were your supervisors?

Did you yourself undertake any supervisory or tasking role during your posting?

Did you have any role in producing or processing written reports of public order incidents?

Did you liaise with other UCOs in the production or processing of written reports of public order incidents?

Did you include your own cover name in any such reports, and if so can you recall any examples and/or any justification for so doing?

Can you recall any modification – stylistic, grammar, substance, etc. – that were made to any written reports you produced?

Was it your responsibility to source or to add Special Branch or Security Service file references relating to any individuals named in any written reports you produced, and if so how would such work be undertaken?

Did you have any other direct contact with Security Services during the period of your posting?

Did you have any direct contact with the Office of Surveillance Commissioners (OSC) or RIPA Secretariat?

Were you aware of the presence of any Security Service personnel in any of your postings?

Were you made aware of any Quality Assurance procedures, operational standards, or monitoring by Authorising Officers, Controllers, Handlers or Managers?

Were you made aware of any 'departure strategy' or End of Tour procedures, operational standards, or monitoring conducted by Authorising Officers, Controllers, Handlers or Managers?

To the best of your knowledge did you or any of your contemporaries ever provoke or encourage a third party to commit a criminal offence?

Were you arrested, tried or convicted in your cover identity?

Were you involved in or did you actively participate in any incidents of public disorder or violence in your cover identity?

Did you report on any legally privileged information and/or the activities of any elected politicians?

Did you develop close relationships with any informant(s) or POIs during your posting?

To the best of your knowledge did you or any of your contemporaries engage in any sexual activity whilst in your cover identities?

To the best of your knowledge did you engage in or enter into any long-term sexual relationship(s) with any CIs or POIs during your posting?

If yes, please detail all such long-term relationships entered into including with any CIs or POIs during your posting.

Did you report on intimate or sexually explicit details of any such relationships?

'Christ, Si,' said Rex. 'This is going to take days.'

He was worried about how Annie was going to take his appearance at the inquiry.

She'd promised to come along and give him moral support. And he knew that fundamentally there'd be no surprises in it for his fiancée because he'd already told her everything.

He hadn't held back.

They'd made a pact, after all.

He'd told her how he and Amelia had met, the growing relationship and moving in together, her becoming pregnant. He'd told her about the awful miscarriage, and the heartbroken Amelia's move to Australia.

Annie had listened patiently and without judgement.

They'd followed some of the inquiry proceedings online, to familiarise themselves with how it all worked.

But there was a difference to hearing something bad in the abstract – as part of an intimate and respectful two-way conversation between life partners, told in words of your own choosing – and the loaded and provocative context of an official inquiry. Having every hurtful detail spelled out for you; being in effect the bad guy, and if not in the dock, then certainly in the hot seat.

It wasn't a trial. He had to keep reminding himself of this. Not yet it wasn't, anyway. But it would be an ordeal for all concerned.

'Don't worry,' said Si Rose. 'I know it's all a bit daunting. But you're in the same boat as everyone else. We'll take it one step at a time, okay? And hopefully, even if we can't work on all your answers, this process will give you a few tools and skills that'll make the whole thing more manageable for you.'

'Okay,' said Rex. 'Understood. Thanks, Si. Yes, that sounds really helpful.'

You're good at this, thought Rex.

Rose had a very reassuring manner: warm, open and empathetic. He could put you at your ease. If he wasn't a police officer, Si would probably make a good counsellor, or the feel-good facilitator at corporate planning away-days.

'We'll do a couple of the easy ones for warm-up,' said Si, 'to work on things like tone. But then we're going right into those last few. It sounds tough, and it won't be easy, but if we can spend a couple of days on those I'll be happy. Because that's the heart of the matter, right? And I mean, I know it's personal, but not to put too fine a point on it, Rex, in your case, that's what everyone wants to hear about.'

That's about the size of it, thought Rex. It was going to be a long couple of days. He was partly dreading it – embarrassed in advance for what he was going to have to tell Si – but then again, who hadn't had a break-up?

Romantic victim of circumstance that he was, Rex was also very grateful, and he was a pro. He was determined to work hard, to give it all he'd got and get this right.

'Right,' said Si, looking up and pressing the 'record' button on the camera: 'Here we go. Couple of warm-ups: When did you join the Metropolitan Police as a cadet?'

That was easy. 'April 1990,' said Rex. 'The Tuesday after Easter.'

'Was it Clifford Heath?' Langdon asked.

They'd been recording all day, the room hot with lights and machinery.

Jethro hadn't been expecting that.

'Did Clifford Heath kill William Cooper, accidentally or otherwise?'

Jethro had already given the producer everything he knew.

It hadn't really been a riot, not full-blown. The deployments had been a pre-emptive tactic to create the appearance of one, though. To create fear amid conditions in which you could plausibly arrest anybody and charge them with riot. And even though it had happened later, Mansfield had gone to trial first. And those charges of 'riot' had started to look fairly shaky when it turned out that several dozen parents had been taking their children home from school right through the middle of it, and they hadn't seen a riot. Miners and police, yes. A bit of argy-bargy, maybe. Shouting, yes. But a full-blown riot? No.

Langdon had shown Jethro the Super 8 footage of him and Heathcliff at the foot of Westhill Lane. The two of them leaning on the bonnet of the carrier known as Roger 1, looking across at the union-hired buses lined up in the Fitzwilliam Street car park, having a crafty ciggie behind the lines and watching the cordon do its work over on the green, while the second cordon was coming up Fitzwilliam Street to pen the demonstrators in the square.

The other lads had all run over, as instructed, to get stuck in, but him and Heathcliff had hung back to watch it all play out for a bit, from a safe distance, like.

It had been Tommy Orwell who'd questioned Bannerman, and made a note – 'Gerald James Charles Bannerman – No Further Action' – but a couple of days later he'd suggested that Heath and Lawrence go up Psalter Lane in the early hours and take a look; nip in through the art school canteen fire escape, which he'd arranged would be left on the latch, then up to the offices on the second floor of the comm arts block and remove anything that looked like it had been shot on the day. To have a poke around Bannerman's place near Endcliffe Park and all, while they were at it.

Guaranteed anonymity, Langdon had said.

It were in his contract wi production company.

One minute him and Cliffy Heath had been standing at the foot of Westhill Lane.

And the next he was watching a man stomping William Cooper to a lingering death, consciousness never to be regained.

Watching but doing nowt to stop it.

William Cooper, who had not grown old as they'd grown old.

Cooper, whom age had not wearied as it had wearied Jethro Lawrence and Clifford Heath.

What a fucking waste.

Had he been in denial all this time? Kept it to himself all these years out of some sense of misguided loyalty?

'Was it DC21502 Clifford Heath?' Langdon asked again, the cameras rolling this time.

In the third-floor Clean Room, Rex punched the air like Plymouth Argyle had just won the triple.

'What's that?' said Lily Atwell, looking up from her laptop.

'Got him,' said Rex. 'We've bloody got him.'

'Well, it weren't me,' said Detective Chief Inspector Jethro Lawrence.

He was confident in the contractual understanding that he'd be unrecognisable, but the confidence had been misplaced. His features were pixelated and his voice was to be substituted by an actor in the final footage, but that didn't make any difference to King and Atwell. They had all the contracts and the shooting logs.

'It weren't me, I can tell you that,' said Lawrence. 'But I watched it happen. I saw him do it, and I froze and did nothing to stop it. I didn't lift a finger. And I can truly say I've never for one moment forgotten it nor forgiven myself for that.'

When Detective Chief Inspector Jethro Lawrence stood up from his desk with that week's *Private Eye* under his arm and turned and nodded to Rex to indicate that he was off to collect his *Daily Mirror* from the front desk, Rex was ready. Usually that would give him half an hour, regular as. The cleaners started at 5 a.m. and usually took their time, but today one of them was already buffing the floors in the stairwell, and he could hear two more starting work on the fifth floor. That meant he had maybe fifteen minutes max before they got to the sixth. He took some latex gloves from his desk drawer. Then, as soon as he heard the lift doors opening way down the shaft, he opened the photo on his phone, then strolled over to Lollo's office.

How did it go?

......
TABBY CAT =
07885970760

He unpinched the photo to enlarge the number, put the phone down on the desk. Perhaps it was because he was rushing, but the gloves wouldn't go on smoothly, and had to be pulled on one finger at a time. It seemed to take forever. Then, holding the phone in one hand, he carefully tapped in the numbers on the keypad.

The sequence that they'd thought at first was a phone number. Well, anyone could be forgiven for that.

The red LED switched to green, like the key-card mechanism on a hotel room doorknob. Rex grabbed the handle firmly and pulled it down – yes! – to open the safe door.

He was in.

At that moment Rex's mobile rang.

It was Lollo's number.

In the building's early-morning quiet he could hear the distant sound of the lift doors opening and closing down in reception, and the sound of the lift beginning its ascent.

Shit! Was Lollo coming back upstairs? Had he forgotten something?

Rex shut the safe door and stepped out of the DCI's office.

'Alright, sir,' he said.

The lift stopped at the fifth floor – he could hear the automated voice. After maybe thirty seconds the doors closed and it continued up.

'Sixth floor,' said the automated voice. 'Doors opening.'

Shit! Rex realised that he was still wearing the latex gloves.

The doors opened.

'What can I do for you?' he said, holding the phone between ear and shoulder so he could rip the gloves off and kick them under his desk.

'What are you doing?' said Lollo.

Shit!

'Right now?' said Rex, playing for time. 'Two things.'

'Two things?'

'Yeah,' said Rex. 'This and that.'

The old ones were the best.

'Very funny,' said Lollo. 'No, just if you get a chance can you give that bloody "Leading for London!" policy doc a once-over for us? It's on my desk in an orange envelope.'

'Yes, sir. Of course I can. Anything I should be looking out for?'

'Just get a feel for it. Bloody time-wasting crap. And see if you can think of some other poor bastard as might be better suited to leading on it than me. Any suggestions gratefully received. Oh, it's confidential, but if you could accidentally-on-purpose leave it in the photocopier outside Si Rose's office, and run off a few?'

'Alright – will do.'

'Doors closing,' said the automated voice.

Nobody had got out.

'I'm off,' said the Detective Chief Inspector, 'to see a man about a dog.'

'Right you are, sir,' said Rex.

'I should be back in for tasking by eleven,' said Lollo. 'But if I'm not there by ten to I want you to deputise, right? I've emailed Becky to let her know, but she's got a dentist appointment first thing so won't be in until ten thirty.'

'No problem, Chief.'

'So you've got the place to yourself for a bit,' said Lollo. 'Hold the fort for us, son.'

'Will do, sir. Is that everything?'

'Aye,' said Lollo. 'Anyroad, you've got my number if owt else comes up.'

'Yes, sir,' said Rex. 'Bye, sir.'

'Oh,' said Lollo. 'Remind me, next time I see you, I've got something for you. An early wedding present. Just a little something.'

'You didn't have to, Sir.'

'I know I bloody didn't,' said Lollo, ending the call.

Christ! He didn't half go on sometimes. Now Rex only had ten minutes before the cleaners got here.

He pulled another pair of latex gloves from his desk drawer and went back to the picture on his phone. Tapped in the number and opened the safe door.

Before he touched anything, Rex took a photograph of the contents. He'd be able to put everything back just so.

There wasn't much in there.

He'd been expecting… Well, *what* exactly?

There were only a few things, all on a central shelf: a letter, a small – ring-sized – velvet jewellery box, a few sheets of loose A4 and a large pile of what looked like printed A4 papers wrapped in a tattered manilla envelope.

The letter had been sent to Lollo's home address on Caerphilly Road in Bow, London E3. Recently too, by the looks of it. The postmark was indistinct, but both paper and envelope were bright and fresh, unlike the brown paper of the manilla envelope that had gone kid-glove soft with crease and wear. The pile of papers – unbound and without staples, as far as Rex could see – was perhaps six inches high. The whole held together by two elastic bands.

Okay, thought Rex. Priorities: letter first.

It was unusual to see a hand-addressed envelope. It looked like a personal letter. Who sent those any more? Helen had been a real one for letters back in the day, he remembered; and postcards. It was a nice habit. When had everyone stopped doing it?

He carefully opened the flap and slipped what turned out to be two pages of matching cream laid notepaper out of the envelope and scanned the contents onto his phone.

He recognised the handwriting, which was small and neat, written in black fineliner.

There was no time to read it now, but he could see from the word 'SORRY' in capital letters that it was a 'Dear John' letter, and – turning it over to the last page – he could see who it was from.

The maroon velvet jeweller's presentation box contained a simple engagement ring: a small single diamond in a white-gold mount on a fine gold band. It looked old and hardly weighed a thing. He took a photo of that too.

Then he thought again and put it back in its velvet box, and put the box in his pocket.

If Lollo ever opened this safe, Rex wanted him to know that he'd been here; that he'd understood.

Or he thought he understood, anyway.

Wasn't that what he'd meant about a present?

Later Rex would reflect back on this moment with the knowledge that he'd been practically following orders. This was surely what Lollo had wanted him to do. He'd given Rex both the invitation and the means. He'd been asking a favour and Rex had been only too happy to oblige.

There wasn't time to scan so many documents here and now, so Rex put the pile of papers from Lollo's safe face-down on the desk and swapped the contents of the envelope for a similarly sized pile of random papers from the recycling. He put the decoy pile into the envelope and back in the safe. Just on the off-chance that anyone else decided to take a look inside the safe in the next couple of hours.

He checked their relative positions against the photo he'd taken, then closed the safe door, making sure he heard it click shut.

Five minutes later he was in the old library scanning the papers onto a clone of Lollo's phone, one page at a time in file batches that he emailed via the DCI's old Hotmail account to Annie's duff email address. It took him about two hours, all told, and it killed his back, bending over like that, but he got into the rhythm of it, did most of it on autopilot. Without needing to read the contents, he could see that the papers mostly comprised C12s and 62s – interview and witness statement forms – from a small number of Sheffield police stations dated variously through May, June and July 1984. He didn't have time to read the materials now, but he'd noticed that each file had a cover sheet and a back sheet, and each page looked to be numbered in the top right-hand corner.

When he'd finished, Rex powered off the phone and walked over to a dirty, orange-coloured, reinforced, heavy-gauge, four-drawer filing cabinet that stood in the corner. Of forgotten provenance, it had been there since forever, and might once have been used for ammunition storage in the cage of the now defunct sub-basement shooting range. There was a 'nuclear hazard' sticker on the face of the top drawer, and the words 'CLEAN ME' had been scratched into the orange paint on a side panel. After pulling on a pair of latex gloves, he took the keys out of his trouser pocket and first unlocked and put to one side a factory-fitted full-height security bar covering the individual drawer locks, then two further padlocks that fixed additional custom-welded steel rods. This done, he unlocked the third drawer down and placed the phone on top of the files that were stacked inside. Then he closed and locked first the drawer, then the two padlocks, before replacing and locking the central security bar.

By the time Binder Singh jogged in at his usual 8.30 a.m. and had showered and changed and was at his desk logging on, the papers were back in Lollo's safe, the decoy pages back in the recycling, the latex gloves were in the bin, and Rex was making coffee in the office kitchenette and perusing the 'Leading for London!' info, twelve stapled copies of which he'd also left in the fourth-floor printer, for maximum reach.

There would be a disturbance in the force this morning, alright. Once Si Rose got wind of the official confirmation that Holborn was a candidate for closure.

DI Rex King didn't know it then, but Detective Chief Inspector Jethro Lawrence would not turn up for the tasking meeting at 11 a.m.

He would never see the Detective Chief Inspector again.

Slightly breathless from the run – quicker over open fields, but he hadn't dared – and opening the manilla envelope to remove the papers inside, he'd seen that on the top of the pile was a cover sheet: 'FILE 1 – <u>SEAMUS ARTHUR</u>'.

'Bingo!'

'That them?' said Heathcliff.

'Aye, I reckon,' said Tully. 'Thank fucking Christ.'

Their plant in chambers had tipped them off that the witness statements would be going out to the defence barristers on the Sheffield and Mansfield trials this week. Heathcliff and Tully had been out in the fields near Adel – off the Otley Road – every morning, staking out one of the Sheffield brief's houses and waiting every day for the post van to appear. Targeting the most out-of-the-way and the least overlooked had seemed a good bet at the time, but they were starting to feel conspicuous. It wasn't like a busy city street where the station's old pale-blue carpool Rover 2000 could blend in, so they'd been parking a few fields away in a passing lay-by that had tree cover, and they'd taken turns to yomp over there. It was only a couple of hundred yards as the crow flies, but considerably longer if you were sticking to the hedgerows. That was when you'd actually got there. It was a good hour or more's drive from Snig Hill, so they'd been on the road by a quarter to six every day – but Heathcliff didn't mind. At least the Rover had a cassette player.

Doing this journey, Sheffield to Leeds, reminded Clifford of driving up with a carload of pals to Futurama at the Queen's Hall. They'd been to both days; taken sleeping bags and kipped on someone's bedsit floor up Hyde Park in the Brudenells. It had been a matter of local pride to catch Clock DVA on the Saturday and stay over for Vice Versa's last gig as a three-piece on the Sunday. A half-hour set low down on the bill in the early afternoon, or supporting the Young Marble Giants, had seemed like the fucking big time: little did they know. What a line-up, though. They'd stayed on for the headliners Siouxsie and the Banshees on the Saturday but bailed after The Psychedelic Furs on the Sunday – it wasn't going to get any better than that. And with 'Flowers' still ringing in their ears, they'd piled into the cars and driven up to Terrys All-Time, and joined the queue for a debrief over chip butties and tea with Martin, Steve and Mark before the drive back to Sheffield: everyone singing 'Jazz Drugs' at the tops of their voices. It were light by the time they'd got back.

Only a few years ago, but already it felt like the distant past.

The barrister, Fiona Harrington, and her family lived in a farmhouse down a private road in the fields out beyond Adel golf course. The 'letterbox' – such as it was – was an old wooden potato crate placed in a niche in the inside wall of a barn-cum-garage set at a blind angle beside the house, which made things a bit easier. They hadn't had to break in, at least.

Not this time, anyway. Though they'd done it before. Been through her knicker drawer and all: suspenders, the lot.

Not this week.

They'd just had to be quick, was all, because the post came at any time after a quarter to eight, and on weekday mornings she'd check the box at quarter past. That was when – regular as clockwork, at least on days she wasn't in court – they'd hear the front door slam and the car on the gravel, then she'd pull up to open the five-bar gate and pop into the barn to pick up the post, which she'd throw onto the front passenger seat before driving out to drop the girls off on her way into Leeds, at one of the posher prep schools on the Otley Road.

And all of this just to cause a bit of distraction and delay; to try and throw the defence barristers off their stride.

It was an undeclared policy of special measures that went to the top and was applied to everyone involved, from defendants and their families on up. Measures that ranged from conspicuous phone-tapping to low-level harassment of legal professionals in the form of parking tickets, ill-timed paging announcements in court, targeted traffic stops, and expenses claims disputed or delayed. All of it plausibly deniable, but effective distractions: net result an hour lost here, a day or two there. Or a week, in this case, by the time Harrington called the clerk to ask where the files were and was assured they were in the post. Phoning again the next day, and the next. It all added up to additional stress and delay at a time when they should have been prepping what was a complex case in face of overwhelming paper evidence. A case in which every charge was backed up with up to half a dozen cast-iron witness statements.

Cast-iron as in all the witnesses were serving police officers, and thus witnesses of the utmost probity.

And they all painted the same picture.

As long as you didn't look too closely.

But Tully and Heathcliff were looking very closely indeed, because they needed to make sure they didn't make an appearance themselves.

◆ ◆ ◆

Rex went up to the sixth floor to see what the fuss was about.

He could hear a voice intoning something rhythmically but couldn't quite make it out. Poking his head around the door of Lollo's office, he found Detective Chief Inspector Clifford Heath in some disarray, sitting in Lollo's office chair and reading aloud from a sizeable A4 print-out.

"'O nobly-born',' he read on, beckoning Rex to come and join him. 'Come on, son! I don't know where he's got to, so I figure I'm gonna read the whole lot two or three times. They say that if the body's not here to speak to, you can sit in their chair and have contact with their spirit that way.'

'What is it?' said Rex.

'*Tibetan Book of the Dead*,' said Heath.

He pointed at his place on the page, then picked up where he'd just left off: "'*O nobly-born*, until yesterday each of the Five Orders of Deities had shone upon thee, one by one…'"

Rex didn't know about Cliff's own near-death experience on the M40 earlier that day. He looked at the newly svelte Thames Valley DCI, half expecting him to stop and say, 'Only joking!' And, after a bit of a giggle and some mutual shoulder-slapping, to get on with some proper work.

But he didn't.

For Clifford Heath, this clearly *was* the business of the day. Right now nothing mattered more to him than making whatever prayers and observances might ease Lollo's path through the various – what was it? Bardo? in his presumably eternal journey towards—

Well, Rex wasn't wholly sure what the destination was, but he reckoned he'd find out soon enough.

"'… *and thou hadst*",' said Cliff insistently, pointing at the relevant spot.

Rex joined in too, with a shrug. Oh well, he thought, remembering one of his grandmother's old sayings: In for a penny…

He was a little uncertain at first. The language felt new and unusual to him, after all. But then, figuring that this was a holy text, to be treated humbly and with respect, and that his dear Annie – with her sincerely-held Buddhist leanings – would definitely approve, and with Clifford's frequent nods and clenched fists of encouragement, he got into it.

"'… and thou *hadst* been set face to face, but, owing to the influence

of thine evil propensities, thou wert awed and terrified by them and
hast remained here till now. If thou hadst recognised the radiances
of the Five Orders of Wisdom to be the emanations from thine own
thought-forms, ere this thou wouldst have obtained Buddhahood in
the Sambhoga-Kāya, through having been absorbed into the halo of
rainbow light in one or another of the Five Orders of Buddhas. But
now look on undistractedly. Now the lights of all Five Orders, called
the Lights of the Union of Four Wisdoms, will come to receive thee.
Act so as to know them. O nobly-born, on this the Sixth Day, the
four colours of the primal states of the four elements, water, earth,
fire, air, will shine upon thee simultaneously..."'

Thirty years ago, on Devonshire Street beside the Doncaster bus,
Jethro Lawrence had watched while a man was kicked to death.

And what's more, he'd done nowt about it.

It had felt like he were underwater.

Or as if he were watching a film in slow motion.

Not only did he not try and stop the lad, he didn't even want to try.

A feeling of serenity.

A feeling like he was floating somewhere nearby.

An intense and mystical light.

Jethro Lawrence's OBE.

He'd had a phone call from the palace, sounding him out.

Of course he'd accepted.

Then the invite had come in the post. The size of a decent hardback
or a seven-inch single, on stiff card.

Tabitha Churchill and Rex had joined him for a celebratory supper
at Ciao Bella when he got back from the palace.

He'd almost had an out-of-body experience then too.

Meeting the Queen.

His imposter syndrome kicking in.

His fear of being caught out.

Him being just a working-class northern lad.

'I'll ask you again,' said Tabitha Churchill.

That was when Cliff Heath broke.

It wasn't him, he said. It was Tully.

Tully just wouldn't stop kicking the lad.

It was Cliff who'd made the phone call. What else was he going to
do?

He'd run down to The Washington. He'd been a regular back in the day. They all were – all the musos. He'd even picked up a couple of teapots for Barbara the landlady on his travels, seaside antique shops passed on the way to or from whichever weekender; Bridlington or Skeggy. But she was watching telly upstairs, so he'd asked Suzy the afternoon barmaid if he could use the phone. Police business, he said, didn't want folk to hear, don't tell anyone. 'Course you can, Cliffy love,' she'd said. 'Come through.'

And she'd kept her word too.

And across the decades the ethereal umbilicus that's been tethering Jethro Lawrence's consciousness to his body pulls him back in.

'Eh! Look!' said Cooper, turning corner of Donny bus and catching Tully's eye. Instant recognition and a note of mockery in his voice.

He'd been taken through line, but had wriggled free and got onto wasteland off Fitzwilliam Street and figured he'd get back to buses from there.

He'd thought he were lucky one.

He'd thought he'd escaped.

But he'd recognise another Cottonley lad anywhere, especially this'un.

'Look!' said Cooper again. 'It's that blackleg bastard's lad! What you doing here, eh? You're on wrong fucking side, tha fucking son of a blackleg cunt, tha fucking scab.'

Well, that were it.

He'd gone **down** wi first fucking punch.

29: Fraise (Strawberry)

'All set?' said Francis Bland QC.

The weeks had flown by.

Lollo's funeral had come and gone the previous week.

Now it was Thursday and Rex's appearance at the UCPI was scheduled for the coming Monday: 11 a.m. at the Thistle Marble Arch.

He was expected there at 9.45. The additional time was to allow for security clearances, and other process.

He'd finally phoned Helen to have 'the chat' last night. Sitting next to Annie on the sofa and holding her hand for moral support while he did so. He felt terrible having to rub it in like this, especially after everything Hel had been through this year. But the alternative – that she'd find out from someone else, or in the papers – was unthinkable.

It had been bad enough when his cover name and photo had been leaked, and by association the confirmation of her suspicion that he'd cheated. She'd been furious. It was a fair guess that her reaction to this would be worse.

He'd told Hel of the risk that his real name could be confirmed in court, and thus in all recorded proceedings and transcripts, and likely then wherever the subject came up, for ever and a day. He'd told her that the UCPI chair hadn't acceded to their request for full anonymity. He said he supposed that the cat was out of the bag now anyway, but this would obviously mean that the earlier leak would be corroborated. And with Rex's – or Thorn's – identity confirmed, he'd also start to appear alongside all the other former UCOs on the various campaign websites. The inquiry generally was being ignored by TV and radio news, thank Christ, and Comms Chief Evelyn Gummer, who remained hopeful that it being Silly Season might save them from too much print scrutiny, but you could never tell.

'Right,' said Helen eventually. 'Does Annie know about all this?'

'She's right here with me now,' said Rex.

'Hi Helen,' said Annie, just loud enough for Rex's ex to hear.

'Well, that's a good sign. Tell her "Hi". There's no point arguing about it. I'm sick to death of the lot of you. I'm just glad you're going to have to be honest for once in your bloody life. But I can't promise that Jen will take it so well. She won't hear your name mentioned. But I'm going to have to tell her this too now, so thanks a lot. I suppose you realise that she'll take it out on me.'

'Yes, of course. I'm sorry,' said Rex.

'Are you? Christ! Like she hasn't already got enough on her plate.'

'How is she?'

'What do *you* think? I suppose she's okay, considering,' said Helen. But she clearly wasn't about to let Rex off the hook by leaving that hanging. 'Considering she's lost two fathers in the space of a few months and is just about to start Year 12. Thank God she did well in her GCSEs. And you haven't even written to her. It's pathetic! Just drop her a bloody line or a card, you selfish prick.'

Then she'd hung up.

Annie had given him one of her meaningful looks.

'Okay, okay,' Rex had said. 'I'll write to Jen at the weekend.'

But even as he said it, Rex knew that wasn't going to cut it.

'Herbal tea?' said Annie, getting up from the sofa and walking over to the kitchen to fill the kettle.

'Please,' said Rex. There were some postcards in the drawer: Stonehenge, Corfe Castle, Concorde flying over Clifton Suspension Bridge. 'I'll do it now. Got any stamps?'

Now he'd come to Bland's office in **chambers** for a final scheduled pep talk.

Annie would be waiting back at Falcon with the car – official business so Rex had booked one of the carpool Minis – ready to hoof it up the M1. Because between now and Monday there was also the small matter of Lollo's ashes being scattered tomorrow.

They were driving up tonight and staying over, while Churchill, Gummer, Frankie and Becky Fernie would be flying in on Friday morning.

Frankie had shared Gummer's call sheet with Rex so that he and Annie could synch up with them in Scarborough tomorrow. The bigwigs were going from Battersea **Heliport** to London Heathrow, then from Heathrow to Leeds Bradford Airport. The Chief Commissioner of the South Yorkshire force would be picking them up landside for the hour or two's drive over the Yorkshire Moors.

They were renting a Georgian mansion in the old town for the night. Rex and Annie had found a cosier place around the corner for two nights, and would be driving back down south first thing Saturday. The weather was forecast to be good. Had it not been for the UCPI on Monday, Rex would have suggested to Annie that they stay on **awhile** afterwards, but they both felt – and Francis Bland agreed – that it would be better to have the whole of Sunday to prepare, to be calm and have a bit of family time at home. To spoil themselves a bit.

A few others from the station were going up by train. It might have been tempting to join them, but Rex and Annie had fancied a bit of alone-time before the shit hit the fan.

Not everyone who'd wanted to was able to get to Scarborough or take a Friday off. So there was to be a small reception back in London on the Tuesday evening. They'd booked the downstairs room at Ciao Bella – where else? Melissa Shepherd was coming up for that, having sent apologies for Scarborough. More than that, said Frankie, eager to share some gossip: Shepherd had asked if it would be okay to bring someone.

One of Lollo's old flames had called too, Frankie said. The daughter of that Major General, 'Sir **Chimney-Pot**', as the tabloids had called him; the chain-smoking old soldier who'd been in the news a lot during the Bosnian War: UNPROFOR Top Brass. She and Lollo had dated for a while in the mid-noughts. That was before Frankie's time, but Rex nodded. Yes, he remembered meeting her once or twice; a lovely woman. What was her name? Laura, that was it.

Unreconstructed as ever, Lollo had referred to her as his 'bird'.

'Tail on that, I tell thee,' he'd say to Rex when she was out of earshot.

Laura had seen the announcement in *The Times* and phoned to see what was happening. She wanted to pay her respects, informally at least.

That was nice of her.

Lollo hadn't treated her very well in the end, if Rex recalled correctly.

It was still taking Rex a while to get used to, and get into the habit of, thinking about Lollo in the past tense.

Bland's office looked out over the leafy Gray's Inn Walks. Rex had had the tour now, as part of the induction to his honorary posting as *Custos Grayorum*.

On one of the polished wooden window seats in Bland's wood-panelled office, and positioned to catch the light that flooded in through the large Georgian sash, was an enormous **amethyst** geode resting in a **chromium** stand. It was huge: twice the size of a rugby ball. Bought, Bland had told Rex when he'd asked, from a dealer in São Paulo a couple of years back.

'Yup. Ready as I'll ever be, I suppose,' said Rex. He'd brought the info pack and the notebook that Si Rose had given him. The notebook had a simple strawberry design on the cover.

'Glad to hear it,' said Bland. 'Just be humble, answer fully but seriously, thoughtfully. Measure the question first; don't rush in. You don't need me to tell you! You're a senior officer, so let all that experience and professional care shine through.'

'That's more or less what Si Rose said.'

'I know,' said Bland. 'He's good, isn't he.'

Rex nodded. The **practice** runs with Si Rose and team had really helped. He'd had four day-long sessions in total. He didn't know if that was good or bad, but it had been useful. Plus they'd fitted in a couple of breakfast debriefs at Sid's.

After all that prep he found he was at least able to think about his impending appearance as part of Phase Four of Tranche Two without feeling entirely **nauseous**.

The inquiry had become a personal **Hellespont**: a challenging and turbulent distance to be covered in a single continuous and dangerous effort. It would take all of Rex's strength, discipline, stamina and cool technique to get to the other side without it becoming a **rout**.

But he had survived other such grillings, after all.

And now, thanks to Si Rose's careful facilitation, his iterative, workshopping approach – 'Let's try that again!' – Rex was relatively confident that if he could only stick to the plan he'd be okay.

He felt that at least he'd got the correct, respectful and passive tone down pat: a verbal and behavioural **carapace**, born of experience and procedural confidence, that without appearing to **omit** anything relevant might still look more like diligence than evasion. It would enable him to evoke and embody the modest, measured but surefooted and broadly based professional capabilities and capacities of the senior policeman.

More than this, though, the workshops had been grounding for Rex, in what was otherwise a time of personal and professional turmoil.

The process had been invaluable.

It had reminded him of the importance not just of police work generally but undercover work in particular. He'd been selected for his abilities, after all. Lollo—

'No! Too **chummy**! Keep the tone formal.'

Si had thought for a second, then added: 'But do feel free to choke up a bit when you mention DCI Lawrence. The man was like a father to you, after all! You're an orphan. Let's use that, Rex. We're not looking for **pity** here, but it'll humanise you. No offence. We all feel that it's useful here for you to flesh out your story. The tendency otherwise, with a repetitive process like this, is to **homogenise** the experiences of UCOs and Core Participants alike. We need to show that you're all different. You're all individuals; you especially.'

My mentor, the late…

Well, it wasn't difficult to get a bit emotional about the poor bastard.

… Detective Chief Inspector Lawrence—

'That's better!'

The late Detective Chief Inspector Jethro Lawrence, God rest his soul, had put Rex forward and personally endorsed his secondment. He was a bit of a father figure, to be honest. Hard to impress, though. And didn't suffer fools gladly. So if he complimented you for something, some job well done, or singled you out for an opportunity, that was high praise indeed. If he didn't like something, he'd soon send you away with a **flea** in your ear. He'd spotted that Rex had the policing talent and the qualities necessary to engage in duties that were unpalatable, yes, not pleasant, certainly, but which concerned the safety of children and young people. And duties that had also proven vital not just to the national interest, but that went to the very heart of our national security.

'Aaaand: cue national **anthem**!'

Rex had stopped and looked over to the Police Federation rep.

'Not really,' Si had said. 'But don't lay it on too thick. "A matter of national security" is fine.'

National security blah blah. In the case in question, Rex had been actively monitoring individuals who would literally – no, who *did* literally – dismantle the UK's defence capability through a misguided and quasi-religious zeal…

'Love it, carry on!'

… a threat that had been compounded, moreover, by a rhetorical sophistication that had enabled them to bamboozle a small-town Scottish magistrate into granting an acquittal.

And that meant that they were still out there: the enemies within.

'No! Too strong. Leave it at "zeal"; don't *criticise* the judgement, Rex. You're here to uphold the law, not to critique it. That's not your area of expertise, or responsibility. Wouldn't it be better to demonstrate some sort of continuing professional interest? Maybe simply mention, if you can, that as far as you understand it, it's… How can we put it? How about that it's… among a raft of acquittals currently being appealed. Just plant a seed of doubt.'

That meant that they were still out there. Individuals who'd been perhaps unwittingly radicalised by elements on the fringes of the Peace Movement into knowingly following criminal courses of action.

'Yes, better.'

Of course, the fact that the 'elements' that had been doing the radicalising had themselves in many cases been UCOs was to be studiously avoided.

'Frame it as if you're thinking about the future rather than the past?' Si had said.

Okay, so, thankfully… there was a new generation of UCOs out there now. A new generation facing new national challenges.

'Good! Go on.'

And wasn't this inquiry as much for their – for the country's benefit? – for their benefit. Yes. All this was for their benefit. So that the UCOs of today – and this was why on balance he was glad to be able to speak out in the open, without the shield of anonymity – the new generations of police officers ought to be able to learn the lessons on offer here rather than repeating the mistakes of the past.

'Good, yes. Allow the pastoral role of the senior policeman to shine through. Channel your inner Lollo! Love it!'

Speaking personally, when working undercover he'd found it important to empathise and to understand the motivations of these individuals, in order to be able to report fully. But unfortunately he'd got too close. Put simply, he'd had the all-too-natural misfortune to fall head over heels in love with his POI.

And she with him.

He'd been a victim of circumstance as much as she.

If that was bit of a stretch, Si had let it go.

Two star-crossed lovers indeed. But what did anyone expect? If you put two healthy young people into an enforced and prolonged period of intimacy, they were almost bound to fall in love. Wasn't that the entire premise of *Heartsick Holiday*? Had Si seen the latest series?

'Christ! Don't say that, Rex!' Si Rose had almost choked on his coffee. 'Concentrate on what you know, and a bit less of the pop psychology, eh? The press would have your guts for garters – and the Met's – if you tried to compare undercover policing to bloody *Heartsick Holiday*.'

Whoops.

'Jesus!' Si had continued. 'That's the whole point of the programme, but it's not the ethos of undercover policing. Fuck's sake, Rex!'

'Sorry, I got carried away.'

'Well, don't! Stick broadly to what we agree, okay? No ad-libbing, or improvising. You've got to concentrate every second, Rex. Do you understand? Don't try and be clever or amusing, and *never* say something off the cuff, however tempting, because it will *always* backfire. Remember that right now at least you're speaking from within the heart of the Met. You're a senior officer of the first **tier**. The kind of officer that people want to see in the Met: mature, diligent, capable, unflappable. Someone who can help steer the **ship** through a storm. That's your audience here: council tax payers, and the victims of crime. I want you to give them confidence. Remember that. I don't want you to suddenly find that you've talked yourself way out onto a limb here.'

'Sorry. Yes, of course.'

'Because we'll never get you back in. You'll be on your own.'

'Understood.'

'Okay, let's try that one more time: To the best of your knowledge did you engage in or enter into any long-term sexual relationship(s) with any informant(s) or POIs during your posting?'

Some time later, Rex realised that he'd been gazing out of Bland's window at the great plane trees in the Walks outside.

'Well, Francis, I must say,' he said, 'that going into this I'm glad to know you've all got my back.'

Francis Bland looked at Rex and frowned briefly.

'Well, I think we've given you the tools you'll need,' said the QC. 'And I have confidence that you'll use them effectively. Think of it that way, rather than some sort of blank cheque.'

Oh.

'I'll be there, of course,' Bland continued, 'but my client here is the Met, you understand.'

'Of course, yes,' said Rex. 'Message understood.'

Rex knew how it looked to have support withdrawn.

Between postings in 2001, Rex had been one of several plain-clothes detective constables tasked to join the Westminster PSUs guarding the various party headquarters during the general election campaign. He'd often find himself outside Conservative Party HQ on Smith Square, and during those few weeks he'd grown to be on nodding terms with the then Tory leader, William Hague.

They had a decent cafe in the church there too, in the crypt. And often there'd be classical musicians doing their get-ins or tuning up and rehearsing for concerts.

Lollo had once told him – manly advice – that the concerts in St John Smith Square were a reliable, safe and effective venue for a first date. 'Believe me, son. A couple of concerts and they'll be eating out of your hand.'

As was the case with all the major political party headquarters during the run-up to the election, there were a couple of PSUs stationed on the square, together with a BBC Outside Broadcast unit. All the major news channels had their cameras set up 24/7 in the pen outside, with tech support in the van, and their reporters on call in nearby hotels, ready to take the rain covers off and respond to any breaking news story.

That much was standard for every general election, Rex had learned.

But then, one morning, with more than a week to go until election day, Rex had turned up to find that the OB unit was gone and the pen was empty: the cameras and the reporters had all been redeployed to the respective headquarters of the Labour and Lib Dem parties.

Rex and the PSUs were redeployed too, of course. Police presence was pulled back to two PCs on the doorstep. So Rex never saw what if any impact it had on Hague and the team in Conservative Central Office and on party morale generally to know that the world's and the country's attention, and with it any prospect of victory, had evaporated overnight, never to return. You didn't need a PhD in **psephology** to predict that Hague would lose the election, and lose it big.

Rex and Annie had hit the traffic somewhere north of Junction 10.

Up ahead, the northbound carriageway was reduced to two lanes between Junctions 12 and 15a, with all entry and exit slips closed, except between Junctions 13 and 14 where traffic was down to a single lane.

Neither of them had thought to check.

Traffic was moving, but slowly.

The radio announcement said that this was due to roadworks connected to the building of the Northampton Gateway Construction Project, whatever that was, with other closures and diversions likely to continue into September.

'Quick,' said Rex, 'call the Cones Hotline!'

'The **Cone** what?' said Annie, looking askance at him.

'Sorry. Showing my age. John Major? You know!'

She didn't.

'The Cones Hotline. It sounds **pathetic**, but it really was a thing in the early nineties: a traffic cone hotline. As if it was roadworks that were causing the recession. A hotline, in the days before anybody had mobiles. Well, I mean, apart from the odd *executive*. I mean, what's the use of a hotline if you can't report things in real time?'

'Before my time,' said Annie. 'I mean I remember John Major, but—'

'I suppose it was a "dead cat",' Rex said. 'Isn't that what they'd call it now? Bugger the interest rates, let's talk about traffic cones instead! Bloody John Major. I can't believe he was screwing whatshername at the time.'

'Did I tell you,' said Annie, 'that **Alaric** called?'

Annie's brother-in-law.

'How are they?'

'They're fine,' said Annie, 'I suppose. But they're worried about me.'

'Really?'

'Yeah. Jane's coming on Monday, to give me a bit of moral support.'

'That's nice,' said Rex as they inched forward in the queue. 'So she should. The more the merrier.'

'He thinks,' said Annie, 'or they both think, I should leave you.'

'Well, I suppose I can understand that,' said Rex. 'And what did you say?'

'I told him that you'd offered me an out, but I'd said no. I told him what I'd told Jane: we're getting married and nothing's going to change that.'

'Thanks,' said Rex, reaching left to squeeze her hand. 'Look, it's going to be a tough week, so if Jane and Larry being around will help you – us – get through it in one piece, then that's great as far as I'm concerned. Not that it's down to me, of course.'

'That's sweet of you,' said Annie.

Later, as they emerged from the single-lane section and the traffic started to flow a little more easily, Rex said, 'I was saving this for later, but I had a strange call too today. Well, not *strange*: unexpected.'

'Oh yeah?'

'Becky called me,' said Rex.

'Remind me?'

'Becky Fernie. She was Lollo's PA, now acting up for the SMT? I don't know if I told you, but Lollo had asked her – I mean years ago – if she'd be the executor of his will. Getting his affairs in order, I suppose. Like you do. He used to listen to that *Money Box* programme on the radio in his office.'

'Oh, right. And?'

'All characteristically well organised, of course. Anyway, a bit of a surprise, but it turns out I'm mentioned in the will.'

'Actually, I'm not surprised,' said Annie.

'Yeah, I suppose not,' he said. 'But guess who's getting most of it, though. Well, the **cash** part of the estate, anyway.'

30: Bétoine (Bethany)

It was only when Annie appeared at the Undercover Policing Inquiry that Rex realised the **dreadful** truth: he'd been gulled.

But he didn't show it. That was his training kicking in. A horse-necked demon straight out of Cliff Heath's *Tibetan Book of the Dead* could have manifested in the hearing room with a thunderclap and a cloud of purple smoke and Rex wouldn't have flinched.

But just because he didn't show it, didn't mean it hadn't happened. And even now, walking down the steps into the basement of Ciao Bella, he felt that something irrevocable had happened, the full meaning and implication of which remained as yet unclear. But something had been broken, a Rubicon crossed, and it was almost a surprise and something of a relief when Rex got a little cheer from the friends and colleagues gathered in the restaurant's lower level. It broke him out of his mood.

Rex raised both hands and smiled, acknowledging the goodwill, but with a shrug and a self-deprecating shake of the head. It was a nice thought – very sweet of them, actually, and of course he was grateful – but he wasn't sure it was appropriate. They weren't here to celebrate the successful – could you call it that? – completion of his appearance before the Undercover Policing Inquiry, after all, even if in other circumstances such a celebration would certainly have been called for.

Well, it might have looked like a success from where his colleagues sat, but they didn't know the half of it. And besides, this wasn't about him. It was a wake for their dear departed Detective Chief Inspector Jethro Cyrus Lawrence.

He scanned the sea of friendly faces. It was quite a turnout, from the station and beyond. Everyone was here.

Lollo would have loved it.

He'd have been holding court, but instead he was the **phantom** at the feast.

That familiar presence seemed now to be just out of sight. His voice forever just beyond earshot.

The funeral itself had been private.

'A private family funeral' was how they'd agreed to put it. Not that any actual family had come, but there was no need to rub it in. Frankie had made contact, but of Jethro's immediate relations and contemporaries there was only one surviving sister-in-law and a handful of grown-up nieces and nephews. Flowers had been sent, a small arrangement: 'RIP uncle Jethro from Jean and the kids'.

In the end it had been just Rex, Clifford Heath, Tabitha Churchill, Frankie Charles, Eric Jinks and Becky Fernie who'd gathered in the front row of the smallest chapel at Golders Green Crematorium in North London. Frankie had ordered some flowers too. They'd thought of a mixed arrangement, but in the end had gone for single-**bloom**: a spray of white roses, of course, which had been laid on the full-size cardboard coffin.

The celebrant had welcomed them. Her speech was short, but not perfunctory. She'd clearly done some research. And Becky and Tabitha had been on hand the night before to read the draft and fill in a few gaps. Then Rex had read Henry Fothergill Chorley's lyrics to 'The Long Day Closes' – by one half of Lollo's beloved Gilbert and Sullivan – and Becky had done 'Psalm 23'. They'd all sung 'Hills of the North, Rejoice' to a backing track played over the chapel hi-fi. The service went far better – everyone said so – than any of them could have expected.

'If anyone asks,' Tabitha Churchill had said in the car on the way back, 'and they will, we'll tell them it was a small family funeral, and leave it at that.'

They all agreed. There was no need to shame Lollo any further.

Not now.

Best to give him this moment, at least.

The long shadow of shame would reach him soon enough.

There was a decent turnout tonight; plenty of familiar faces.

Si Rose was chatting to the Forensic Medical Examiner, Sue Stanza.

Frankie had tipped off Rex that Sue was desperately upset by Lollo's death. She'd seen her share of suicides; perhaps more than any of them. Each one less a single act than a catalogue of injuries, sometimes all too visible, that recorded a painful and quite often protracted **tussle** between life and death. She knew that it was almost never the quick and easy way out that some people assumed, and that death didn't always win, not right away. She'd also seen the false hope, the tearful relief, and apologies sobbed in apparent survival that could sometimes even then be cruelly snatched away in agonising organ failure days later. Like all of the late Detective Chief Inspector's friends – if they thought about it – Sue Stanza hoped that death had come quickly for Lollo, that once set on that path he hadn't suffered too much.

Tabitha Churchill was already here too, at the centre of a small group that included Comms Chief Evelyn Gummer and good old Jane Milligan, who in theory was still on maternity leave but wouldn't have missed this for the world.

And there was Melissa Shepherd and her chap. When Rex had spoken to her on the phone a couple of days before, Shepherd had told him that they were going to make a weekend of it. Vic had got them tickets to Bloodstock up in Derbyshire. Twisted Sister were headlining, on their farewell UK **tour**. She and Vic were glamping and everything. Vic had booked them a tepee.

Rex was glad Shepherd had been able to come. She'd done right by Lollo, and been such a staunch colleague over the past two or three months that he felt as if he'd known her for years. They could have done a lot worse. He liked her what-you-see-is-what-you-get attitude, her practical, methodical approach to police work, and her respectful management style.

He'd sung Shepherd's praises to Churchill; made a case for the impressive Sussex DS moving to the Met. At his suggestion, the gaffer had begun sounding her out for a transfer. But – 'with all due respect, ma'am' – although she was flattered, Shepherd hadn't wanted to pursue it. She was 'too much of a country mouse', apparently, and – as she explained to Rex later – frankly, a station with a staff of six was enough for her. To say she'd been disillusioned by the decision to shelve and not go public with the results of the Cooper investigation didn't really cover it. She clearly wasn't cut out for the political aspects of high-level policing.

Besides, Melissa was thinking of putting down more roots in her little corner of West Sussex, not pulling them up. She was taking the budding romance slowly, but it had potential. And she was well aware that these kinds of second chances at life-partnership didn't come along too often.

Rex could certainly relate to that.

But even if she had been tempted by Churchill's offer, there'd be little point entertaining such a proposition now, given the latest 'Leading for London!' announcement, and the fact that there was nowhere any longer substantively to transfer to. Not to mention the inevitable programme of early retirements and redundancies. She could hardly swan into a new job in Central North while others were losing theirs.

Rex scanned the crowd. There was Frankie, and Becky, whose secondment to SMT had in the past few days been made permanent. So she'd be okay, at least. Whatever else happened, in the topsy-turvy, self-justificatory world of Metropolitan Policing there'd always be a Senior Management Team, even if they had no one left to actually manage.

He raised a hand in greeting to Binder Singh, who raised a glass back. DS Singh was growing in confidence every day. Lollo had been right about that: splitting up Bill and Ben. He'd promoted Singh and left Jimmy Rattle in the ranks, but not before seeking Rex's advice on the matter. Rex had been surprised when Lollo had told him he'd realised too late that he'd royally fucked up with Eddie Webster. He'd promoted the partnership rather than the individual, and he wasn't about to do that again.

Clifford Heath had brought the lovely Bethany, and what a catch she turned out to be. The new slimline Heath who was talking to Rob Langdon looked ten years younger, a different man.

Rex had passed Langdon's contacts to Frankie and asked her to be sensitive. Langdon had seemingly got quite close to Lollo while making the programme, and came across as a decent enough bloke. As long as he didn't start poking around. Rex presumed that Langdon would have had enough of the police for a while.

There was Jinksy – an almost permanent fixture at the front desk this past decade. Stiff-legged, but off his crutches for the moment. And there was Di Malcolm from HR, with Barry Lincoln, the Met's Deputy Chaplain. The family liaison officers were sticking together in the corner, FLO Coordinator Winston Edwards and a sober if red-faced Tommy Bee among them.

Everyone was here.

Well, not quite everyone.

He scanned the room again.

There was no sign of Annie.

Rex hadn't seen her since the hearing yesterday, in fact; and didn't know if he'd ever see her again. He half hoped he wouldn't, though it would be better to keep her where he could see her. But this lot didn't need to know that. Rex wasn't about to hijack Jethro's night by burdening anyone else with his problems: the psychic chasm of cold dread, of gut-churning fear and doubt, uncharted and immeasurable as yet, that had suddenly blinked into existence, and then just kept on growing. Adrenaline kicking in as Rex had instantly cycled up through the threat levels, from Substantial through Severe to Critical; responses already Heightened now Exceptional.

If anyone asked, he'd already decided he'd just smile and say that Annie would be along later.

Ciao Bella indeed!

Best foot forward, Rex raised his chin and gave a little salute in greeting to their host, Ciao Bella's patron. **Profuse** as ever in his hospitality, he'd just supervised the bringing down of the antipasti for the buffet – two great platters filled with freshly cut prosciutto and salami, with olives and mozzarella balls and cherry tomatoes, with bruschette and crostini – and was now looking with extravagant and vocal delight at the baby photos on Jane Milligan's phone.

The walls of Ciao Bella were busy with murals and knick-knacks, and framed photographs of Italian celebrities and movie stars, with musical instruments and movie posters; the Italian *tricolore* a recurring **motif**. Rex had almost stopped noticing them, but tonight he was seeing it all afresh, like a first-timer. What a place. He couldn't count the number of times they'd eaten and drunk here. Nor, sadly, how many of those times it had been at Lollo's behest or with the Chief picking up the bill.

Rex knew the menu inside out; knew the staff. There wasn't your usual turnover of waiters. Most of them had been here for years. It was a family affair. The patron chatting to customers, and other family members in charge of the till, or the bar. A pianist tinkling the ivories for a few hours in the early evening. And every year a fundraiser for the children's hospital.

Rex's 'usual' was *Spaghetti al Cartoccio* 'with the White Wine sauce'. Seafood and spaghetti in white wine – never the tomato sauce! – cooked in, and served in, a paper bag. You needed a large napkin for that one, not just a standard serviette. *And* the finger bowl.

Lollo used to have the *Scaloppa Milanesi* with a side of *Spaghetti Bolognese*. That one wasn't actually on the menu, but very traditional. They'd always smile if you asked for it like that. Lollo had told Rex that *Scaloppa* was often served that way in Italy.

All rounded off with a grappa *digestivo*.

A constant flow of conviviality: the leaving dos and Christmas dinners, the big birthday parties and the little birthday suppers, the book launches, the wedding anniversaries and the office crushes, the eighteenths and the fiftieths, the twenty-firsts and the university acceptances, the exam results and the graduations, the engagements and the job offers, the celebrations and the spillovers, promotions and retirements, the departmental debriefs on the occasion of this or that successful conviction or oppo concluded.

Where would they go now?

Who could say where they'd all end up.

Jethro's disappearance and death, protracted as it had been, had already seemed like the end of an era, but now this?

Rex was glad he'd still been up in Scarborough when the news broke on Friday. After scattering the ashes they'd all gone for fish and chips at Papa's. And he'd had the foresight to book in a day's leave to lick his wounds following Monday's UCPI appearance. Not quite the long weekend that you'd choose, but at least it meant that he'd missed the all-staff email and some of the emotional impact.

No good news ever landed at 4.45 on a Friday afternoon.

The **rescript** – to coin a Catholic phrase – had been handed down from on high. The unholy trinity of the Home Office, Scotland Yard and MOPAC had spoken with one voice. Holborn had been selected. The station was set for a fast-track closure, with no power of **veto**.

First of all the front doors would be closed 'with immediate effect'.

Holborn would cease to be a public-facing building.

Then the various functions and departments would be tied up, or merged with and out-housed to Kentish Town or Tolpuddle Street, with an accompanying programme of staffing reductions through redundancies and early retirements. Within six months all that was envisaged to be left on Lamb's Conduit Street would be a TeDIU(M) call centre, a number of bookable meeting rooms, and the custody suites, which would remain as the Central North BCU's only 24/7 custodial facilities, with contingency capacity to be provided by Kentish Town, by Tolpuddle Street and by the British Transport Police premises on Tottenham Court Road.

That was the plan. But cells and a call centre could be anywhere. Meeting rooms could be subcontracted from a Southampton Row hotel for less.

Surely this'd all get sold off for luxury flats. How long until the hoardings went up? The architectural CGI illustrations? Would the policing history be obscured or would it get turned into 'heritage' and be bundled into the sales pitch? Or maybe a bit of both.

What would it be called? Not The Station. That's too close. Metropolitan? How about The Metropole? Hadn't the estate agents had a bash at rebranding Holborn already? Midtown, they'd called it: a Manhattan-lite fantasy. Maybe they'd revive that into the bargain: Metropole Midtown. That had a ring to it. Rex could just imagine it: concierge at the front desk, underground parking, cycle garage and e-scooters on the podium, a gym in the shooting range, swimming pool where the cells were. And once you went upstairs, most of the inner partitions had been ripped out in the last refurb, so the developers could carve it up any which way.

'You lucky thing, Rexy boy,' said Jane Milligan, squeezing past Di Malcolm and Barry Lincoln, and reaching out to clink glasses. 'Becky told me. Did you know?'

Word was getting round, then.

Good news travelled fast.

'Hey, Jane, congratulations!' said Rex. 'What a sweetie! Frankie showed me the photos. Oh, that. No, honestly, I had no idea. He kept it to himself. I can't really believe it.'

'When are you moving in?'

'If we can get in before the baby, I'll be happy,' said Rex, sticking to the simple version of the story. 'We've got the keys already. We were over there on Sunday.'

'Must be a bit weird,' said Jane. And she was right.

Rex hadn't been there since the search.

'House and contents' was what it had said in the will. And they'd decided that a lot of it would be sold, or given to some upcycling charity.

It would have been weird to keep everything; a little macabre living in a dead man's shoes.

Some of the art was worth a bit, though. Lollo had bought it before the artists were well known. They were going to keep a couple, but put most of it into one of those 'British Contemporary'-type auctions at Christie's or Sotheby's. But it was a lovely place, and that was a genuine Eames, and a decent pine kitchen table from Peter Jones. You'd struggle to find a better one today. And the narrow refectory table and benches in dark oak were English Civil War period, Lollo had once told him.

And there were, after all, some fine wines in the storeroom.

And of course there was some good Sheffield cutlery: Viners' 'Chelsea' pattern, two canteens' worth.

They'd decided they'd give one of the canteens to Cliff and Beth as a belated wedding present.

'Viners,' he'd say. 'The best. I remember the factory. Up back of Moore Street substation.'

'Yeah, Jane. It is a bit weird,' said Rex. 'There's a couple of things need doing. Nothing major: new boiler, lick of paint. Got to do the baby's room. We figured we'd do it all now while it's empty and before—'

'When's it due?'

'A month or so.'

'Better get your skates on then!'

'Tell me about it,' said Rex. 'I mean, Christ! So generous and unexpected. But I'd rather have him around any day. We'd have asked him to be a godparent.'

'Aw, he'd have loved that,' said Jane, not quite slurring, but with the slightly exaggerated mannerisms of a woman who's just had her first glass of wine in six months. 'He loved you in a way. You probably don't know this, but he used to call you "Sexy Rexy". Not to your face, of course. I mean, not in a sexual way. It was his joke – used to make him chuckle. It was an old shop in Sheffield or something: Sexy Rexy. Anyway, things are hard enough. You can't be looking a gift horse like this in the mouth, not with a baby on the way.'

'That's what Annie said,' said Rex. 'She's in proper nest-building mode.'

'Oh, is Annie here?' said Jane, looking around excitedly. 'She must be huge.'

'Haha, yes. The bump is bigger than her. No, not yet. She'll be along later. We'll come and find you.'

'Bit of a wrench, though,' said Jane.

Rex shrugged. More than just suiting him, Falcon had been a central part of his identity, a well from which he'd drawn a lot over all these years. He'd given a lot to this little patch of 'Holborn–Bloomsbury borders' – and it had given back too. With its proximity to work, this motley few blocks on the north side of Theobalds Road had been for Rex a source of – what? – not just stability and a certain local pride, to know and be known in your neighbourhood, but also power, and safety. With that connection gone, what would be left? If the station no longer owed him anything, then he owed it nothing back.

'I don't know, Jane. Feels like a good time to move on, I suppose. And besides, we're keeping the flat. Well, sort of.'

'Good for you,' said Jane. 'You deserve it. I'm happy for you. How was the funeral? Was it awful?'

'No, it was nice,' said Rex. 'Just family.'

'That's nice,' said Jane. And if she had been contemplating probing further, she'd evidently decided against it.

'Yeah,' said Rex.

'Bloody Jethro,' she said. 'Stupid sod. Why didn't he say something? Why did he do it?'

'I know.'

Although Rex did have some inkling of why. A perfect storm of shame and consequences, some of them criminal – on the back of what now read like some fairly deliberate and irrevocable bridge-burning – all of which had been about to wreak havoc on Lollo's life and work. But Rex wasn't about to say so here. And, as far as he knew, with Jethro's suicide now confirmed by the Coroner, the investigation into Cooper's death was effectively mothballed for the moment at least. The Andante hard drive had been filed away at the National Crime Agency, locked in a digital drawer pending some future political expediency in its revival. Rex knew that the Met would have no compunction about chucking the late Detective

Chief Inspector under a bus if ever such a move seemed useful. But he hoped they'd leave a decent interval between now and then.

Rex had his own 'insurance policy' filed away too, just in case he ever needed it. 'Ammunition', you could call it; locked away in plain sight pending a move to Tolpuddle Street or wherever he found himself at the end of all this. Among it his own collection of edited highlights, and one of the NCA Andante coder's back-up hard drives, plus his own audio, secretly recorded on a Zoom he'd hidden behind one of the flat-screens, of Cliff Heath's off-the-record conversation. There were other things in there too: his duff passport and driver's licence, a small metal cashbox he'd not opened since leaving Exeter that contained still somebody else's vital documents.

'Result!' said Jinks, who'd joined them, clearly oblivious to the topic of conversation.

'Have you guys met Melissa?' said Rex, drawing Shepherd into the conversation. 'Who led the search. Melissa! Come and meet Jane. I think you must have met Eric on the Enquiry Desk, but this is Jane from SMT. Jane, this is Melissa Shepherd from Midhurst and Easebourne.'

Shepherd shook the hands that were offered.

'Eastbourne?' said Jane. 'I love Eastbourne.'

'Yeah,' said Shepherd. 'Me too.'

Jinksy was clearly a bit pissed, but who could blame him. The Met had just told him that his public-facing 'analogue' role as Enquiry Desk Officer wasn't needed or valued in the brave new world of 'digital' policing.

Analogue? That had rankled for a start. Made him sound like some clapped-out old cassette player.

The idea that the job he'd put his heart and soul into on the front-desk front line for ten years could be replaced by an app, by a Dedicated Ward Officer on the street, by a 'digital strategy', a web form, a call centre, a series of Ward Panels, Safer Neighbourhood Boards, by LFR, ANPR, TeDIU(M) and social media outreach, by artificial intelligence, and an annual consultation meeting with community representatives… Charming! The suggestion that a move away from bricks and mortar and a visible 24/7 police presence on every high street would somehow make people in their moments of need feel safer and more 'engaged' was frankly offensive.

Clicks and algorithms were no substitute for boots on the ground.

'You gonna sell the flat, then?' Jinksy went on, "Cause if not, I heard that Chrissie Charlock and her lady are looking for a one-bed rental in Zone One.'

'Not quite sure yet,' said Rex.

On the drive up to Scarborough, he and Annie had discussed what to do with the flat. It might take some careful diplomacy, but he thought Helen would see sense eventually. It was a couple of years away yet, but it could mean Jen would be set up, for uni and beyond. And, in the meantime, some rental income would help plug the gaping hole in the household finances of what was now and perhaps forever would be a single-parent family.

The important thing was that Rex would be able to take responsibility and do right by his daughter. She'd recognise that later.

Or maybe she wouldn't, and would hate him for it forever.

But either way, when Annie had suggested it, he'd known immediately that it was the right thing to do.

Talking of things wreaking havoc, where *was* Annie, anyway?

Rex had practically fallen off his chair when she'd turned up at the UCPI. Not that he hadn't been expecting her. He'd known she was coming; she'd promised. But Christ almighty, that was quite an entrance. And that had just been for starters, the precursor to a moment of cataclysmic clarity; of recognition. That was it. Not just the shocking realisation that he'd been duped, but the understanding – instinctive and absolute – of how.

'Excuse me, guys,' said Rex.

He'd spotted Heath getting in line for the buffet, and decided to go and join him.

'Hi Cliff,' said Rex, picking up a napkin-wrapped knife and fork. 'Lollo would have loved this.'

'I know,' said Cliff, proffering two plates at the server, for a helping of lasagne and a tong-full of green salad on each. 'He's here in spirit, though, eh?'

'Well, his spirit'll be in a better place thanks to you, Cliff, I reckon,' said Rex, following suit.

'It was the least we could do.'

'Annie was impressed. I told you, she's well into her Buddhism.'

'Is Annie here? I can't wait to meet her,' said Cliff, motioning with his two plates a direction of travel, to where Bethany had commandeered some chairs in the corner. 'Come and join us.'

'Not yet,' said Rex. 'She'll be along later.'

'When are you moving?'

'Soon as we can.'

'I bet that was a bit of a surprise.'

'You're telling me.'

'He recognised something in you, Rex, I think. No sob-stories, but he thought you'd done well to overcome losing your parents so young or whatever; to reinvent yourself.'

'He said that?'

'Well, in so many words,' said Cliff, handing a plate of food to Bethany, and a knife and fork. 'Here you go,' he said. 'Look who I found.'

'Rex!' said Bethany. 'At last! Ooh, is Annie here?'

'Bethany,' said Rex. 'So good to finally meet you! No, not yet, she'll be along later. How are you doing? Remind me, we've got a little belated wedding present for you two next time we see you.'

Half an hour later, before dessert and at Tabitha Churchill's cue, Rex picked up a knife and lightly tapped the stem of his wine glass. The Chief Superintendent was standing at the foot of the stairs and putting on her reading glasses, a piece of paper in her hand.

'Hello everyone,' she said as the room quietened. 'I'm so pleased that we can all be here this evening to remember our dear friend and colleague Detective Chief Inspector Jethro Lawrence OBE, to give him his full title. Or Lollo, or just plain Jethro to many of you. And I'm delighted that Detective Sergeant Shepherd' – Churchill gestured towards Melissa, who was leaning back against Vic with her arms folded and half a glass of white wine in hand – 'if any of you haven't met, who led the investigation down in Sussex, has been able to join us too. On behalf of us all at Holborn, I'd like to thank you and your team, Detective Sergeant. Good job. Thank you.'

'Hear, hear!' said Rex, leading a ripple of applause.

'A couple of other thank yous: to dear Felice and Patrizia, always here to feed and water us in times of happiness and sadness. Bless you both. Thanks also to Becky and Frankie for organising everything – and I don't just mean this evening.

'I've been really touched,' Churchill went on, 'to hear from some of you in recent days and weeks, and to learn just how central and instrumental to your lives and careers Jethro was. Whether that was his "putting a word in", his hands-on management style, or his mentoring and guidance. I hope Rex won't mind me repeating what' – she turned, and Rex nodded and shrugged at the same time, as if to say *Go ahead* – 'he told me a couple of weeks ago, that for you, Rex, as for many of us, I suspect, Jethro *was* the Metropolitan Police. And I don't think there can be a finer tribute than that.'

She paused for a second.

'But I'm going to have a go.'

Everyone laughed.

'Detective Chief Inspector Jethro Lawrence was an outstanding police officer and a fine friend; steadfast of purpose and broad of shoulder. Qualities that should be **commonplace**, but certainly – in my experience, anyway – are not. Jethro could be frank! He didn't suffer fools gladly, as you will all know, but that was always, always driven by his faith in every one of you; his desire to get the very best out of his officers. And he was right. He knew what you were capable of, and didn't rest until you knew it too, and until you delivered. And you *did* deliver, you do deliver, time and again. And one thing I know for certain, because Jethro told me personally, is that he took a great deal of heart from all of your achievements over the years.

'In his personal life Jethro was a proud Yorkshireman, and a keen rugby fan and golfer. He was also partial to settling down with a bit of Gilbert and Sullivan and a good book. Sorry, I should say Gilbert and Sullivan, a good book and a few fingers of Glenmorangie, or Laphroaig, or Springbank…

'While at work he rose to the challenge of any task that the job and the Central North BCU could throw at him.'

'Hear, hear!' said Winston Edwards.

'Or so we thought, perhaps. And I hope we didn't take him for granted. But may I say, please, folks, this is a tough job we all do. And it's a job that can and does take its toll on our mental and physical health. But if you're ever feeling as if you can't cope, do please please please reach out and talk to somebody. My door is always open. And I don't need to remind you that the Samaritans poster in reception isn't only there for the benefit of the public. I've asked SMT to work with me and develop a well-being and mental health awareness programme that we'll be rolling out in due course. But more of that later.

'I know,' Churchill continued, 'that, like me, many of you will remember Jethro Lawrence most fondly and with the utmost gratitude and respect for the earnest compassion and courage of his leadership and quick thinking in the field on what we now know as "7/7", and the diligence under extreme duress that helped lay the ground for Operation Theseus. For which services, indeed, he was awarded the Commissioner's Commendation for bravery above and beyond. As indeed were a number of our officers at the time, including Sergeant Jinks. Who I'm pleased to say is still with us. And who, as I think most of you will remember, had been coming into work on that Piccadilly Line train on the seventh of July 2005, and who helped others to safety before succumbing to his— to *your* own life-changing injuries, Eric. And Eric, you've also told me that Jethro's support and encouragement, his regular visits down to Headley Court during your rehabilitation (visits, I may say, that he kept very much to himself, and undertook in his own time), and his going the extra mile in identifying a role more suited to your new circumstances, were central to your finding the confidence and fortitude to return to work. I know that you – as Jethro did – have always worn your Commendation pin with pride. And justly so: thank you.'

Red-eyed, Jinksy waved away the attention, drawing a round of respectful and affectionate applause. Someone, it sounded like Jimmy Rattle, shouted, 'You're in there, Jinksy!' and got a bit of a laugh.

'And I hope,' said Churchill, 'that Jethro's brand of compassion, how seriously he took that pastoral aspect of his role and his rank, will be an example to all of you in your careers and in your dealings with your fellow officers going forward.

'Speaking of which—'

No, don't, thought Rex. Don't go there. Not now, for Christ's sake. But she did.

Just as he knew she would.

'—Friday brought us mixed news. I know that Detective Chief Inspector Lawrence worked very hard on the "Leading for London!" consultation, that he couldn't have done more, in fact. And I also know that he was personally devastated that he'd been unable on all of our behalves to secure the future of Holborn within the BCU.

Though I reassured him, because I know, as you will too, that he'll have done his level best in face of an intransigent MOPAC and Justice Minister.'

How convenient! thought Rex.

He was stunned at Churchill, but knowing what little he now knew of their relationship he could quite believe it. You absolute bitch, he thought. That decision was done and dusted long before you palmed it off on him, and you know it.

Lollo was a safe pair of hands, not a miracle worker.

'But when,' Churchill went on, 'the Met is told by government to look for real estate savings, I'm afraid it really does come down to Location, Location, Location.'

If she was trying to get a laugh, she didn't succeed.

'I'm sure,' she continued, 'that, following his example, wherever each of us end up, we'll meet the coming challenges – and, for many of us, the new colleagues or the new opportunities – with the kind of courage, tenacity, sense of duty and respect that Jethro taught us.'

Evelyn Gummer started to clap, but no one took her lead.

Come on, wrap it up, thought Rex. Don't fucking milk it.

You've made your point.

You've passed the buck, and not even made a particularly good job of it.

Right now, he couldn't have loathed Tabitha Churchill more.

'Teflon Tabitha', the press called her, referring to the Chief Superintendent's inexorable rise, and her seemingly untouchable status. But Rex had faith that one of these days she'd get what was coming. That someone somewhere would move against her, would have the right ears and the clout to set whatever wheels in motion to **oust** Tabitha Churchill from some as yet unwalked **corridor** of power.

Until then, the only way was up, baby.

But if and when it did come – one day, her inevitable fall from grace – he hoped it would hurt like hell.

Because when she finally got her comeuppance, Rex planned to enjoy every minute of it.

'On Friday,' she said, 'as you'll all know, we had the privilege of scattering Jethro's ashes in the waters off Scarborough. It was a lovely day. The sun was out. And I know that many of you would have been there too if you could have been. But, as Rex will confirm, it was a very small boat.'

Rex looked around at everyone and nodded, smiled. 'All aboard the *SkyLark*!' he said, to a ripple of recognition and laughter.

'It *was* called the *Skylark*,' said Churchill. 'And you were all there with us in spirit. As many of you know, Scarborough was a special place for Jethro. He told me that when he was a boy he thought it was heaven on earth. Even as an adult: "Paradise", I think he called it.'

'Scarbados!' said Jimmy Rattle, and everybody laughed.

'Indeed,' said Churchill, with a smile. 'And I happen to know that Jethro had been planning to spend more time there during his retirement. He'd had his eye on a lovely little place. Well' – now her voice wavered, and she choked a little – 'he got his wish in any case. And by the way, he did use to go on about it, I know, but I'm sorry to say, he *was absolutely right about the fish and chips*. Best in the world!'

That did get a laugh. Lollo was a typical Yorkshire-fish-and-chips bore.

'You keep going on about dripping,' Rex had once said, recycling an old joke remembered from the school playground. 'You should just go to the doctor's and be done with it.'

'So, everyone,' said Churchill, 'please raise your glasses, and join me in a toast to the memory of our very esteemed and greatly missed friend and colleague Jethro Lawrence: *To Lollo!*'

'To Lollo!' came the chorus of replies.

'Right,' said Churchill. 'I'm going to shut up now, and I think Cliff is going to do us the honours with some music for a bit. Thank you, Cliff.'

There was a ripple of applause, before Clifford Heath, now stationed behind some decks and speaker stands in the corner, faded up the intro to ska classic 'The Whip'.

Detective Chief Inspector Clifford Heath of the Thames Valley Police didn't DJ very often these days, for obvious reasons; almost never, in fact. And to say he wouldn't have minded turning the volume and the bass up a bit was something of an understatement. But he was happy to play a few tunes for his old mate Tully, and never let it be said that he didn't know how to start a set! The Ethiopians' effortless vocal over that harsh, metal-bashing groove – what are they playing? rail spikes? – by guitar pioneer Lynn Taitt and the Jets was a little bit of him right now. And it set the tone for a couple of hours of ska, rocksteady and lovers rock. Next he was lining up 'I'm Still Waiting' by Delroy Wilson. The former child star's mum was *his* mum's second cousin back home. Her dad's cousin. For real! Then maybe something **saucy** by Prince Buster. Sure, for this lot he'd have to throw in the occasional crowd-pleaser: 'Common People' or 'I Will Survive'! That was a lesson learned many moons ago, DJing for… Good grief! The local branch of the Communist Party, was it?

Well, the less said about that the better.

Communists?

Oh my days!

His mum, may she rest in peace, had nearly had a fit.

Thankfully that one had never got out.

Although she'd been right: it almost certainly meant that his name'd be on a list in a file somewhere.

Thank Christ it had been before the days of computers and cross-referencing, or he'd have been hoofed out of the police before he'd even started.

Luckily, no one had thought to care about the young Black soul boy putting on a show behind the decks. He'd thought he was so cool, barely out of school and swaggering around Sheffield in his Flip! zoot suit and kung-fu shoes, with a tatty straw hat on the back of his head.

In the years since, it had occurred to Clifford more than once, however, that among the thirty or forty supposedly card-carrying communists who'd been present upstairs at the Rutland Arms that night, in what was still then affectionately known as the People's Republic of Sheffield, at least four or five of them, or maybe more, would have had to have been active UCOs.

Rex was talking to Vic about work. Honestly, he could see the appeal of a job where you were working with your hands, teaching a craft.

'Woodwork teacher?' said Melissa. 'He's being modest. Vic's a cabinet-maker, and a good one.'

'Oh, we'll know where to go, then,' said Rex. 'If we need anything for the new place.'

Rex envied the guy. That was a good honest job if ever there was one.

Vic asked Rex how he'd got into joining the police.

'By accident,' he said. Then told Vic how he'd been looking for work and there'd been an ad in the *Camden New Journal*, some graduate recruitment scheme, so he'd written off for the form. Thought he'd do it for a year or so, but quickly discovered that he liked police work.

It was what he'd always said.

It wasn't the whole story.

But then, who had time for the whole story? Other than Annie, anyway.

His fiancée – if she *was* still his fiancée – really was a good listener. She'd had to be.

Never mind looking for work in HE; he'd suggested that she should retrain and become a counsellor or a therapist.

'Or join the police,' he'd said. 'There's always vacancies in TeDIU(M). I'll put in a word.'

'Nah, you're alright,' she'd said.

Vic was growing on Melissa. She was enjoying the simple pleasures of doing things together. Whether that was driving up the M23 in the **Jeep** with the music on loud, singing along to 'Ramblin' Gamblin' Man' by Black Oak **Arkansas**, or headbanging to that bootleg CD of Iron Maiden live at the Bristol **Hippodrome** in '84.

She was enjoying no longer arriving everywhere as the singleton.

Having someone ask how she was, and meaning it.

Sometimes, when she was with Vic, she could forget the loss of her father for a bit; little moments here and there. Maybe her grief was turning a corner.

Rex had pulled her aside the first chance he got.

'Just in case I don't get to say it later: thanks for everything,' he'd said. 'Doing right by Lollo. I know that Tabitha didn't make it easy for your lads.'

'I don't know why she kept sticking her oar in,' said Melissa.

'Well, that's just her style, I suppose,' said Rex. And if Melissa hadn't figured that one out for herself, he wasn't about to tell her. 'Anyway, thank you.'

'That's nice of you to say, Rex. I feel like I just kept control of the paperwork, really. It was that fisherman who did the finding.'

'Yeah, well,' said Rex. Then he changed the subject. 'Listen, this lot don't know yet, and maybe never will, so keep it to yourself, but I thought you needed to know that Lollo left the rest of his estate – the cash part, a decent amount too – to the **Cooper** family.'

'Oh,' said Melissa. 'I see.' She looked crestfallen; took a deep breath and blew it out slowly. 'Blimey, so that's as good as a—'

'Yeah,' said Rex. 'But through some blind trust he's set up. So it'll be an "anonymous benefactor" and the family can take that however they want. And if they do find out… Well, I just didn't want you to be surprised if it ever did go public and they tried to make a meal of it. Frankly, I wouldn't blame them. But as far as I know, Evelyn reckons the Met'll not be making an announcement. If challenged, they'll say it's a private matter. And I mean, you can't prosecute a dead man. The family could always spunk the lot on a civil case to press the point, but I hope they don't. Technically speaking, I'm not sure Lollo was exactly working for the police at the time anyway, certainly not as part of any publicly accountable chain of command.'

'Different era,' said Shepherd. 'Blimey. Well, I mean – money's no replacement.'

'No, but as apologies go, it's—'

'—better than a poke in the—'

'Right,' said Rex.

Clifford Heath had slowed it right down, and in the centre of what was now a dance floor, documentary director Rob Langdon was slow-dancing with Laura Cholmondeley-Potter to Tyrone Taylor's 'Cottage in Negril'.

Rex felt a quick **buss** on his right cheek, and turned – blood running instantly cold – to see Annie. He wondered what she was playing at; what her game was.

But he knew exactly what her game was, because he'd been there himself.

And she must now, surely, know that he knew.

Because she was good. He'd give her that.

What he didn't know was just how far she was prepared to push it, and if or when she'd use what she knew about Rex against him.

He wasn't going to let on, though. 'Hi hon,' he said with a smile, reaching out to take her hand. 'I was wondering if you'd make it.'

'Wouldn't have missed it,' said Annie. 'Tell you later.'

Would she? Really? He hoped so, but he'd heard that one before.

'Annie, Melissa; Melissa, Annie,' said Rex, making the introductions. 'And this is Melissa's partner, Vic.'

'Hi,' said Vic, shaking Annie's hand. He looked as if he didn't mind at all Rex taking the slight liberty.

'Well,' said Shepherd, nudging her chap, 'it's early days yet, but he's growing on me.'

'Oh, hi Melissa,' said Annie. 'Rex speaks very highly of you! I think we sort of met before. You were in the car?'

'Yes!' said Melissa. 'Blimey, that seems an age ago. I didn't think we'd end up here.' She paused. 'Well, it's always the worry, but—'

'I know,' said Annie. 'Poor old Lollo.' Then, to Rex, 'How's everyone taking it?'

'As well as can be expected. Putting a brave face on it, as you can see. I think you missed Churchill's speech? Had its moments, but wasn't too offensive. To be honest, the rest of them have had a while to get used to the idea of Lollo not being around. I think everyone's more upset about the station. It's all got lumped in together. Everyone's worrying about whether to apply for their own job or to take voluntary redundancy or whatever. Sorry, I don't want to bore everyone with our troubles.'

'Oh yeah, sorry to hear about that,' said Vic. 'Melissa just told me. That's terrible. When's it closing?'

'Front desk closed already,' said Rex. 'So it's no longer a "public-facing" building.'

'Christ!' said Annie. 'They don't hang about. What on earth is Eric going to do?'

'TeDIU(M), probably.'

'Ugh. Could be worse, I suppose,' said Annie. 'But he'll miss the variety, I bet.'

'Stuck in a stuffy call centre,' said Melissa. 'Rather him than me.'

'Cliff's devastated about Lollo, of course,' said Rex. 'Said he'd always seen him like an older brother. That's why Bethany, his wife...' Rex looked around the room and pointed. 'Over there, with the red hair? That's why Bethany suggested he do the music. Give him something to do, she thought.'

'He's great,' said Annie. 'I love all this stuff. Maybe he could do our wedding?'

Our wedding? thought Rex. Seriously? Still? But he only said, 'Ha, yeah. That'd be a turn-up! Let's ask him. He's dying to meet you. When I told him you were getting into Buddhism, the beginner's mind and all that, he said something like, "Oh great! Another 'stream-enterer': the more the merrier" – or something like that. "Stream-enterer"? Does that sound right?'

'I think so,' said Annie. 'The four stages is what they call it. Him and Beth are coming, though, right? They've got the date?' Rex shrugged yes.

'And you two, Melissa,' said Annie. 'We'd love it if you could both come. Invites in the post soon, but it's the fourteenth. The Saturday before Remembrance Sunday.'

'Love to,' said Melissa. 'Rex was telling me about Gray's Inn. Sounds proper.'

'Yeah,' said Annie. 'It's proper, alright.'

Rex put his arm around her shoulder, felt hers around his waist.

It felt good and bad at the same time: love and fear combined.

It felt like coming home and walking into the jaws of hell all at once.

He didn't let it show, but he'd presumed she was a goner. That, mission accomplished, she might have done one, and bolted. He'd hoped so, in some ways. Because he feared the implications of her staying.

What was this new feeling, exactly? Was this what life was going to be like from now on?

He was possibly as scared as he had ever been, but he was as thrilled as he was scared.

Before Annie had pulled a fast one, the thing that Rex had been most nervous about at the Undercover Policing Inquiry was the prospect of seeing Amelia in the public gallery. As a non-state Core Participant with cover name 'Helen', she'd given her statement to the inquiry in an affidavit sent from Australia, but Si had told Rex that they now knew for certain from current UCOs in the Women Against Secret Police Surveillance campaign – WASPS – that she was planning to attend. This was where Francis Bland's tactical blunder over Rex's wasted application for special measures began to show itself. Because he hadn't been granted full anonymity, she'd have had access to the time and date of his appearance for about as long as he had.

Her affidavit had made sobering but perplexing reading.

Put simply: her version of events wasn't how he remembered it. The chronology stacked up more or less okay. But in her statement his every action was depicted as being of de facto evil intent. He came across as insincere, manipulative, a sexual confidence-trickster who strategically and calculatedly set about dismantling her defences brick by brick. His every action had been planned, staged and self-conscious, as he relentlessly and falsely – and ultimately successfully – insinuated himself into her life, her affections, her bed, and her body.

Rex's unspoken personal justification, that he'd been young, dumb and full of cum, was starting to seem disingenuous even to him. It didn't even sound naive; more like a downright lie. He'd tried it on Francis Bland and Si Rose, and it hadn't flown with them, that was for sure. Thankfully, they'd advised against. There'd been sharp intakes of breath and much shaking of heads.

But he maintained that he had fallen in love with Amelia, and that their real mutual attraction had placed him in an impossible situation. He couldn't admit that he was an undercover officer without jeopardising an ongoing investigation, one that had national security implications. It had been a double bind. But Amelia was just his type and he – the real Rex: Rex the person, rather than Rex the police officer – shared her beliefs.

It would be sailing close to the wind, but he could always freely admit that he'd felt more like an imposter in the police than in the Peace Movement. It wouldn't be a lie.

And it wasn't like he'd had this whole **harem** going on, like some of the other UCOs.

Yes, he admitted that he'd acted **improperly** at the start; taken advantage.

He shouldn't have allowed any intimacy to develop, shouldn't have deliberately created the conditions in which his presence and attention could be misinterpreted.

He could see that it was an abuse of his power.

In common with all of the female Core Participants deceived into sexual relationships, 'Helen' didn't know – couldn't have known – what exactly she was consenting to.

And that meant she hadn't consented.

In her affidavit, 'Helen' claimed that she'd been shocked to discover from WASPS activists that her relationship with Martin Thorn had followed the same pattern as all the others.

The similarities were alarmingly obvious.

She asked whether these were behaviours laid out in some lost chapter, volume or binder of the Special Demonstration Squad's so-called 'Trade Craft Manual' – only one volume of which had been leaked, she'd seen it – or whether they were part of an unwritten culture. Were such ways of working shared informally between officers? As well as providing cover, was the abuse of women a product of institutional sexism? Was it a tolerated form of team-building behaviour? Or perhaps all of the above?

She told how he'd started love-bombing her, with shy smiles and eye contact.

The way he'd **bombard** her with flowers, gifts and text messages. She'd been flattered at first. Who wouldn't be?

He was good-looking.

They were both adults.

Adults fall in love.

More than that, adults *look* for love.

She'd been looking for love. What was wrong with that?

And in Martin Thorn she'd thought she might have found it.

She discussed him with friends.

They all thought he was really nice – a dish.

Here they were: Spike and Amelia! They made a lovely couple; everybody said so.

They'd been fellow travellers, after all. Both active on the anti-nuclear scene for so long that it was a wonder they hadn't found each other before!

And Martin Thorn's attentions? Why would she think that these were anything other than what they seemed? Such male attentions were a part of life that, as a woman, even as a feminist, she'd been brought up to recognise and understand, and to accept at face value as signifiers of romantic interest. She didn't need to reciprocate if she didn't want to, but in this instance she'd had no reason to doubt his intentions, and the feeling had been mutual, or so she'd thought. And even if she'd known the extent of undercover police activity within the movement, she could hardly have suspected that *she* would be a target, going about her life and harming no one as she was.

The course of action for which she'd been charged and acquitted had been a spur-of-the-moment thing, partly egged on, or in fact actively facilitated, by Thorn. Even if – in a misguided attempt to protect him – she'd minimised any such role at every stage: in her questioning, her statement, and her defence.

His relentless performance of interest had been sustained and convincing, but all of it was false. All of it, the months of closeness, his apparent bashfulness, his loving attentions and ministrations, what had seemed like spontaneous care, thoughtfulness, sensitivity, his depression and periodic disillusionment with the Peace Movement, was ultimately a knowing strategy, an act undertaken to maintain and strengthen his cover, and in order to groom her into a caring role and into a romantic and sexual relationship…

Rex wondered if that was really what had happened?

He could see that, yes, maybe he did have a tendency to shower his beloved with tokens and demonstrations of affection. Certainly when he was in the early stages of a relationship. But didn't everyone do that?

But relationship it was, and real in almost every way; ninety-nine-point-nine per cent.

It had gone on for a while, first as a bit of a fling and then as something more serious, until Amelia's miscarriage had rent their world **asunder**.

And besides: she'd left him.

It wasn't him fucking off 'to Australia' when his posting was coming to an end, but her – for real, and for her own reasons.

And if someone hadn't posted a list of UCO cover names that included 'Martin Thorn' on the WASPS Facebook group, she'd have been none the wiser now.

Rex was convinced that their relationship had been more than real.

He felt sure, too, that it would have been strong enough to withstand the breaking of his cover.

He could have pulled the ultimate switcheroo, and it would still have been *him* sitting in front of her, after all.

He knew that now, because he'd done it with Annie.

He'd taken off the mask, and – miracle of miracles – she'd still loved him.

Or so he'd thought the previous morning, as he set off on the forty-five-minute stroll along to the Thistle Marble Arch Hotel.

Before Annie had pulled the rug out from under his feet.

And yet, here she was, brazen as you like, acting as if nothing had happened.

As with other state witnesses, the Police Federation – in the shape of Simon Rose – had offered to book Rex a taxi for his appearance before the UCPI. Rex had said thanks but no thanks, that he'd prefer, as ever, to walk.

It was one of the pleasures of living where he did.

Given the choice, he'd always sooner walk to all but the most serious of grade-A calls, and even those he could usually reach more quickly on foot than in a car.

But this was different.

It was a pleasant morning, not too hot for the time of year, and after a cooked breakfast and a coffee (no time for the crossword today), a hug and a kiss and a 'You'll be fine!' from dear Annie, the stroll through Fitzrovia along Goodge and Wigmore Streets to Marble Arch would do him good. Annie had gone over his outfit the night before. It was a shirt-and-tie day, a chance to wear his new jacket. The walk would give him time to run through his notes, and to practise his answers. Better that than having to make polite conversation with a cabbie. If he got there early, he could always grab another coffee and go and sit in nearby Portman Square for a while to clear his head.

Rex pulled the flat door to behind him and, in the half-light of the scaffolding, jogged downstairs to the street.

The info pack he'd been given made it clear that the UCPI was a public inquiry, held in the public interest, where state and former state witnesses would be afforded an opportunity to account publicly for their actions.

The well-being of all participants, whether Core Participants or state and former state witnesses, was declared – in a message from the inquiry chair – to be paramount. To this end, state witnesses like King and other past and present UCOs were afforded a discreet entrance in the hotel's underground car park, and once inside the hotel they had exclusive access to certain non-public areas. While non-state Core

Participants – those who might consider themselves, for example, to be 'victims' – had access to all public areas and were greeted by inquiry staff at a table in reception, and given passes, welcome packs, bottles of water, packs of tissues: made to feel special.

The info pack also made it clear that video recordings of the inquiry's proceedings would not be published, nor would proceedings be live-streamed. And, on a related note, that while smartphones, mobile phones and other handheld personal communication devices *could* be brought into the hearing room and any overflow room or waiting area, their *use* was proscribed in certain ways.

Such considerations – for privacy, and dignity – had also formed part of the various preliminary protocols that Rex had undergone in recent weeks. As Francis Bland had explained to him, if it could be demonstrated that giving evidence publicly might undermine the safety and security of witnesses and their families, threaten current or past investigations or convictions, or matters of national security, it was possible for witnesses and/or their counsel to apply for certain measures to ensure anonymity: closed hearings, giving evidence by video link, real *and* cover name anonymity (in which cases, venue and date would not be publicly announced), etc.

In conference prior to the twenty-eight-day deadline for such applications, Francis Bland and Si Rose had advised that in their opinion it was better to apply for the minimum of such measures: just the dual (real and cover name) anonymity. Rex had gone along with their recommendation, so had been slightly dismayed to learn a week or two later that the request had not been acceded to. The inquiry's only concession being that, since King was a serving police officer, his real name could be withheld – he would be identified only as HZ9122/EN9122 – but his cover name(s) would be stated on the record, and the date(s) and time(s) of his appearance(s) would be published in advance.

It was a tactical blunder, though it hadn't seemed likely to backfire at the time, but one that he now realised he might live to regret. Perhaps they were hanging him out to dry after all. He shouldn't have listened to them; should have insisted. If it had been down to him, they'd have gone in with all guns blazing and asked for everything. At least that way they might have come away with something. As it was, when Annie asked over breakfast how he was feeling, he'd said –

using the moderate language of the senior police officer – that he felt slightly more exposed than was ideal.

From the car park, a number of signs pointed the way to the segregated waiting area, and a series of rooms that for the duration of the inquiry were made available for witness counselling and meetings with legal advisers. All such rooms were furnished with the ubiquitous pump-action beverage dispensers for teas and coffees, trays of cups and saucers, jugs of milk and iced water, and baskets of individually cellophane-wrapped high-sugar-content long-life choc-chip cookies.

From these non-public areas, behind a free-standing hessian-lined office partition or screen, a single door opened directly into the hearing room. An A4 print-out was pinned to the non-public side of the screen:

UCPI

HEARING ROOM BEYOND THIS POINT
YOU ARE NOW ENTERING A PUBLIC AREA

'Annie? So good to finally meet you,' said Tabitha Churchill, shaking hands with Annie. 'And very many congratulations on your engagement.'

'Aw, thanks,' said Annie.

'Show her the ring,' said Rex.

Annie raised her left hand – fingers up, palm in – and waggled her fingers.

Rex smiled proudly.

He'd been wondering how Churchill would react when she recognised that simple and distinctive engagement ring, a small single diamond in a white-gold mount on a fine gold band. But if she did recognise it, she didn't show it.

Well, you can't kid a kidder.

And perhaps in concealing her surprise she'd overcompensated, because she didn't show even a modicum, the bare minimum, of polite pleasure either.

Well, that was his answer.

Worse, it was a dead-eyed Tabitha Churchill that looked Rex in the eye, betraying neither emotion nor interest, but patiently and passive-aggressively waiting for him to break the silence.

It was a winning strategy from the Chief Superintendent. He'd have to remember it and give it back buttered if he ever found himself talking to a weakened Churchill in some future moment of crisis.

'It was Jethro's mother's,' said Rex. 'He gave it to me the last time I saw him. Of course, I didn't know then that it would be the last time.'

'I know it would have meant a lot to him,' said Churchill.

'Yes, so I gather. We're very grateful. He told me that once upon a time he thought he'd found a woman worthy to wear it, but he'd been proved wrong.'

'Oh dear,' said Churchill. 'Poor Jethro.'

'Or not,' said Rex, as lightly as he could manage. 'You know Lollo. He kept his love life to himself, and I didn't want to pry, but he seemed fairly cheerful about it.'

'Good for him,' said Churchill. 'Old men, you know, are prone to making fools of themselves in matters of love. I'm glad he saw the light.'

As Churchill turned away, Rex and Annie allowed themselves a quick glance of conspiratorial delight.

Just like old times.

As if the last couple of days hadn't happened.

Was he just putting on a show or had Rex forgiven Annie?

That depended.

It depended whether her lies had bottomed out yet.

Her barefaced audacity had astounded him.

And whether he'd forgiven her or not was moot, because right now he realised that he loved her all the more for it.

It had certainly been an odd experience, giving evidence.

Even at the moment 'Helen' a.k.a. Amelia had walked into the hearing room at the Thistle Marble Arch Hotel and they'd unavoidably made eye contact, Rex had almost imagined that just a look from him would still be enough to make her melt into his arms and back into love with him. And for a split second he was surprised and slightly puzzled to find his trusty old mojo wasn't working, and that the machinery of mutual desire which had once animated the space between them was now inert. What did he expect? To pick up where they had left off?

How exactly would that have played with Annie?

Once upon a time, Rex had convinced himself that he'd loved Amelia. No, but he really had. And they'd been going to have a child! He had been genuinely thrilled about that when she'd told him. Even though, for some reason, he hadn't been the first to know. She'd told a friend before she'd told him, which had felt a bit weird at the time; disrespectful, maybe. Was that it? He'd put that to one side, immediately reconciled himself to the fact of impending fatherhood, flung his arms around Amelia and said 'Wonderful' or some such.

Or had that just been Martin talking?

It had been hard to tell sometimes where Rex King ended and Martin Thorn began.

And thinking about it practically, even with such life-changing events already set in motion, he'd seen no reason to end things with Helen there and then.

There was plenty of time for that: a good six months' grace. Rex's two parallel lives could trundle along side by side for a while yet.

Both were fictions, after all.

And now, all these years later, it appeared that he wasn't the only one living several lies at once.

'Backstage' at the UCPI, Rex waited for Francis Bland to give him the nod. He was first up after lunch.

When the moment came, he took his place in the hearing room, seated between Bland and Simon Rose. Then the ushers opened the door to allow the public back in. There were maybe thirty seats and Francis told him that most of them would be taken up by WASPS campaigners – Women Against Secret Police Surveillance. They were there every day, to support each other, to bear witness, to become the very public to whom the UCOs would be held to account. Rex averted his gaze and stared into the middle distance. He didn't want to meet anybody's eye. But he'd been drawn to Amelia immediately; something about her gait or posture had been instantly recognisable, and still attracted him. He couldn't help but turn. She looked good. She was slightly tanned, older and somehow leaner about the jaw, dressed in a grey business suit with a dark top and sensible court shoes rather than her formerly preferred uniform of Breton shirt and dungarees. She had greying shoulder-length hair now instead of a punky crop or her later up-do. As she walked into the hearing room their eyes met, for the first time in how long?

There was no magic.

No romance.

No electricity between them.

But Amelia immediately faltered, lost her footing, went weak at the knees. Rex wondered if she was about to faint, right there in the hearing room.

He guessed that she wouldn't be the first.

That's why the St John Ambulance were there. A pair of them sitting by the door.

They weren't needed in this instance, because before Amelia could fall a woman rushed to her side from somewhere behind.

He didn't show it, but he was shocked by Amelia's indifference to him, by the absent expression that had met his exploratory gaze, the way she'd averted her eyes.

The friend steadied Amelia, then put a comforting arm around her, ushered her to a front-row seat and sat down beside her.

Amelia was gently sobbing, and the friend held her hand.

He couldn't take his eyes off Amelia.

It was the T-shirt that he saw first.

Amelia's friend was wearing a black-and-yellow WASPS T-shirt: Women Against Secret Police Surveillance.

A slim Black woman in a WASPS T-shirt and with Afro hair, holding Amelia's hand and comforting her.

A slim but actually now quite heavily pregnant Black woman in a WASPS T-shirt.

He'd recognise that bump anywhere.

She'd caught Rex's eye, sought it out: met his gaze and stared him down.

Annie.

Annie in a WASPS T-shirt, sitting next to Amelia and staring *him* down.

She held his gaze, unblinking, for what seemed like hours, but could only have been a matter of seconds.

Rex stared back impassively.

He didn't show his shock: that was his training kicking in.

His face betrayed no emotion, but inside he was frantic, his mind racing through the options, struggling to interpret the evidence of his senses.

Annie had lied.

Her big confession!

Their pact!

Had all of it been a lie?

With a start, Rex knew who had circulated the list of cover names on the WASPS Facebook group. He realised that, when he'd called her bluff, Annie had simply used the revelation of her involvement in the Cooper Campaign as a feint, used it for bait.

And he'd fallen for it.

She hadn't been after Lollo, after Justice for Billy Cooper.

That had just been a bonus.

She was after Martin Thorn.

And she'd found him.

Played him at his own game.

Is that what she thought?

But Rex drew confidence from the knowledge that he still had something up his sleeve. It wouldn't be a surprise to Annie; he'd told her everything, even if she hadn't quite returned the favour. But one of the things that had kept him going in the past couple of days was the knowledge that, if the hearing in any way threatened to go tits-up for him, he could always break cover completely, and come clean right here – end the performance of a lifetime.

Just knowing that he had a nuclear option had given him the confidence that he could do whatever he needed to do to get through this.

Knowing that he could play his trump card, his get-out-of-jail-free card.

Knowing that he could tip over the chess board.

It would be bridge-burning, scorched-earth behaviour.

Suicidal even.

Only to be used in extremis.

Maybe he had more in common with the late departed Lollo than he'd thought.

But then Annie did something else.

Something that made him question these assumptions and strategies even as they were forming in his mind.

Without moving a muscle, slowly and deliberately, and without breaking the steady gaze that was locked eye to eye with Rex, and unseen by Amelia or anyone else in the hearing room, Annie winked.

And not quickly either.

She unmistakably and unambiguously winked at Rex, and then the barest flicker of a smile, before she turned and looked back at Amelia, whispered something and gave her distressed friend's arm a brisk and comforting rub.

And then the moment was whisked away.

An inquiry official tapped the microphone on the desk in front of her and opened the session:

'Welcome back to Day Three of Phase Four Tranche Two of evidential hearings at the Undercover Policing Inquiry. My name is Alba Triana. There is no fire alarm testing this afternoon. If a fire alarm does go off, please follow the fire exits and make your way to the muster point located at the Hard Rock Hotel, Great Cumberland Place. On arrival, please make yourself known to a fire marshal, who will be wearing a high-visibility jacket and will be keeping a register of all attendees. The fire marshals will also be responsible for informing everyone of when it is safe to return to the hotel in liaison with the representatives from Thistle Hotel. I now hand over to Deputy Chair Christopher Moggford to recommence today's proceedings. Deputy Chair.'

'Thank you,' said Moggford. 'Now, for the benefit of any new arrivals, may I reiterate what I said this morning, and what I usually say to those in the public gallery. You may use any handheld electronic device for the purpose of communicating silently what you have seen and heard in the hearing room, but only after ten minutes have elapsed since the events that you are describing; you may not use your device for recording or photographing our proceedings. There is a formal note on the desk in front of you which sets out fully the terms of what I have just summarised.'

The Deputy Chair turned to the inquiry solicitor.

'Ms Caine. Now we're going to hear the oral evidence of HZ9122/EN9122, and if there's time the summaries of the evidence of HP9350 and HP9085?'

'Thank you, sir,' said Caine. 'Yes, first we'll hear oral evidence from HZ9122/EN9122, cover name "Martin Thorn". And then – if there's time – I will read the summaries of HP9350 (no cover name released) and HP9085 (no cover name released), both of whom will not be giving oral evidence. For the record I need to point out that HP9085 is currently serving a ten-year custodial sentence relating to a conviction obtained since he left his former state employ in the SDS. He gave evidence under oath at Her Majesty's Prison Lewes as witnessed by counsel for the inquiry's office. The conviction is on an unrelated matter.'

Caine turned to Rex and said, 'HZ9122/EN9122, can you confirm your cover name for the inquiry.'

So Caine was to be his interlocutor, for the next however long.

He studied her face, looked for a way in, and relaxed, remembered his by now well-practised tone: 'Yes, it's Martin Thorn,' said Rex.

'Cheers,' said Vic, shaking Rex by the hand. He and Melissa were wanting to get off, so they'd been around the room seeking out Tabitha Churchill, Binder Singh and Frankie in turn, and now Rex, saying their goodbyes. 'Good to meet you. Sorry about the circumstances. Jethro seems to have been quite a guy.'

'Yeah,' said Rex. 'Certainly was.'

'I can see he'll be missed,' said Vic. 'Not something you can say about everybody. Anyway, we're off. Staying up in North London with a couple of Melissa's old uni friends.'

'Nice one,' said Rex. 'Enjoy the gig. Melissa says you're camping.'

'Well, glamping,' said Vic. 'No point roughing it at our age.'

Now it was Melissa Shepherd's turn.

In theory Shepherd hated Rex.

She hated him for what he stood for.

She hated him for what he'd done.

'Cheers, mate,' she said. 'See you around.'

He'd deceived a woman into a relationship, and used her for cover.

Melissa had read the UCPI transcript this morning.

Of course she had.

And she knew, too, that Rex would be well aware that she'd read it.

He wouldn't have expected anything less.

Of course she'd have printed off the PDF of the previous afternoon's proceedings and read the lot.

The evidence given by a former UCO who'd been granted only

partial anonymity and was referred to by his cover name of Martin Thorn and/or the inquiry designation of HZ9122/EN9122.

It had made for grim reading.

It had made her feel vulnerable and angry, and more than a little unclean by association.

Thorn's version of events had been self-serving, to say the least. And his declaration of undying love, right there in the courtroom, for the Core Participant who'd been his victim, had been both bold and utterly repellent. It disgusted her.

It was like an act of violence in itself.

Another one.

Adding a foul insult to the victim's very real injury.

Melissa imagined it would have landed home too. He wouldn't have said it if he didn't think it would have an effect.

The brass neck on the guy.

But he'd clearly done what he needed to do.

He'd done just enough to plant a seed that *he* was some sort of victim of circumstance, and to throw doubt onto elements of the Core Participant's account.

Of all the UCOs who had given evidence to the inquiry so far, this one bucked the trend.

She had left him, after all.

As if that made any difference.

But he'd exploited that fact; amplified it.

He'd been heartbroken, he said, to have lost a baby and a life partner in one fell swoop.

As if that really made any difference.

As if that cancelled out the offence.

But still, only partially protected as he was, he was stuck with it now.

That photo of Martin Thorn the crusty protester in a camo boiler suit and army surplus boots would crop up now whenever Spycops or the WASPS campaign were googled, whenever they were mentioned in the press.

Melissa Shepherd hated Rex in theory. She was only relieved that she didn't have to work with him now, so there was no need to move forward in this grim new knowledge. Prior to his giving evidence at the inquiry it had been different. It had been fine. She'd been able to give him the benefit of the doubt. She hadn't known, hadn't seen, hadn't imagined exactly what kind of creep he was.

It was a total mindfuck.

Because Annie was lovely, the feeling was that he couldn't be all bad.

Maybe he'd changed.

And yet this appalling behaviour had been played out, and in public, only yesterday.

This was him.

It was him then, and it was him now.

Later she'd bend Vic's ear about it, and maybe they'd simply VS the wedding invite nearer the day, but that was a decision for another time. For now she decided to hold her metaphorical nose, and pretend it was still last week when she hadn't yet known any of this.

She gave Rex a friendly hug, for old times' sake.

'Congratulations, you two!' she said. 'And good luck with all that... You know: the cuts. I'm sure you'll land on your feet somewhere.'

Rex was grateful for Shepherd's confidence, but couldn't ignore the slightly barbed tone. Would he land on his feet? Right now, to tell the truth, he wasn't so sure.

'We'll figure it out,' he said. 'See you in November, I hope.'

'Yes, I hope so,' said Melissa, taking the path of least resistance.

Would that be the next visit to Ciao Bella, Rex wondered?

Probably, although it would be touch and go as to which would come first. His and Annie's wedding reception or all of their leaving party?

Would Holborn go out with a bang? Or with a trickle of increasingly depressing and ever more sparsely attended shindigs until everybody was sick to death of leaving dos, then poor old Billy No-Mates at the end gets none. Life at work would become a near-daily round of chipping in for collections, and signing leaving cards, of tearful farewell speeches with drinks and cake at the end of every shift. Navigating the restructure would become a full-time job.

Of course they'd be back here all the time.

With Jen here; assuming that all went to plan.

Just try to keep them away!

His daughter Jen, in a couple of years, safe and warm in her flat in Falcon.

They'd have to take her to the Coptic Street Pizza Express to celebrate, to Fryer's Delight, to Ciao Bella. To Bradley's and The French.

Our place, thought Rex. No, our places: bars, cafes, meeting places.

All our restaurants, plural: the function not the brand. Now he got it.

An old joke.

It was part of what it was to be human.

The never-ending flow of food and conviviality, a bubbling spring of comings-together, a movement, a distribution, an irruption, a temporary change in population density, a twilight chorus of chat and celebration, hellos and goodbyes; that human need for company and the flow of conversation, for drink-splash, light and warmth. The billions of comings-together, like an eternal and statistically predictable daily tide, rising and falling as dusk's shadow tracked across the earth's surface.

For good or for ill.

Had he knowingly exchanged information about ways of working – or sexual relationships with targets – with other UCOs and field operatives in safe houses or at other gatherings?

Of course he had. Boys will be boys!

And if Annie was here, that meant she didn't mind, or that she was happy to let bygones be bygones.

But of course Rex knew that there was more to it than that. Annie's tolerance meant something else too.

A logical truth that he'd been avoiding for a while, chosen not to look directly at, but which was now inescapable.

She was here because it had been her job to be here.

He was well aware of that now.

It takes one to know one.

Their pact had perhaps not been quite as equal as he'd hoped, and he'd given her a lot more than she'd bargained for, and now he had no way of knowing if she'd use all of that against him at some point in the future.

But he could live with it if she could.

They'd cross that bridge if they needed to.

And, after all, if a further coup de grâce was coming, for the time being it would be in her interest to keep him safe, or plump and ready for the chop anyway.

And that gave him breathing space.

It gave him time.

And he was not without certain insurances. Ammunition, if you like. 'SDS TRADE CRAFT BINDER 1' among them, which he'd liberated from Barnes Common a couple of days before the station's decommissioning and planned demolition was announced, and a 16TB Andante hard drive.

And, bless him, Lollo's promised final gift would turn out not to have been the ring or the house, but a stout brown envelope – post-dated and addressed to Rex in Lollo's hand – that would be hand-delivered to his front door on the morning of the wedding by a pupil in Francis Bland's chambers. Upon closer inspection he'd find that it contained copies of all Annie's personnel records, her personal file and copies of all her duff papers – duff passport and driver's licence, rent agreements and car insurance, a disciplinary file, written reports from within the Cooper campaign, reports in which, of course, she herself (or her duff) figured, and minutes of Office of Surveillance Commissioners (OSC) and RIPA Secretariat meetings. To be locked away you-know-where, with his other insurance policies, and his back-up; his nuclear options.

They'd certainly done Lollo proud tonight, but it was time to scoot.

Not by far the last to leave the party at Ciao Bella, Rex and Annie pulled the door open and, realising that another couple had been just about to enter, they stood back and let them come in, exchanged inaudible pleasantries, before stepping out onto Lamb's Conduit Street.

'You okay, hon?' said Annie, sliding her arm into his as they walked north, towards Great Ormond Street. 'Seem a bit quiet.'

'Yeah,' said Rex, leaning into his fiancée, hardly able to believe that she still was his fiancée. 'A lot to take in, that's all.'

Well, that was the understatement of the year, if not the century.

'How do they think it went?' she said.

So, no apology, then; no explanation – not yet.

He realised that he couldn't be sure if it was Annie asking the question or her duff, or her duff's duff? – how far did it go? – but that right now he didn't care which it was.

If he thought about it, masks off, he might not be totally sure who she was asking, either.

Or who it was, right now, as they walked arm in arm up Lamb's Conduit Street, that was measuring his own reply. From now on, that would depend upon who they – singly or collectively – were talking to.

Well, he could take it if she could.

'Okay, I think,' he said, adjusting to the shifting sands of their new shared reality, but speaking from the heart, whoever's heart it was. 'Think I took them by surprise, anyway. They weren't expecting me to be quite so proactive. I just figured, you know, fuck it! Attack is the best form of defence. Anyway, I thought Tabitha was civil enough tonight, give or take. And I didn't milk it, so I don't think she knows that I know. I've already had emails from Si *and* Gummer. Both saying, you know, Well done! Onwards! kind of thing. And according to Frankie I'm being co-opted onto the Met–NCA Cyber Working Group. Recommended subject to NCA ratification, anyway. Hopefully Lily will put a word in. I mean, one day at a time, eh? But not dead yet.'

He smiled: 'How did it go down with the girls?'

'Tell you later,' she said. 'But you certainly put the cat among the pigeons. You can imagine. The WASPS are going to have your guts for garters.'

He laughed.

She laughed too, and pulled him closer to her side as they walked.

Somewhere in the distance a dog barked; a siren. There was a burst of music and chatter as a pub door opened and closed.

Lamb's Conduit Street, London WC1, was still surprisingly busy for the time of night.

There were couples out walking hand in hand, or arm in arm; some just off home, going for the tube or to catch a bus; waiting for a taxi; popping into The Lamb or The Perseverance for last orders.

It was crowded, but then this wasn't just any old London thoroughfare. It was a village street. The village street of Gray's Inn, of Great Ormond Street Hospital, of Chancellors Court, of Phoenix, of the whole post-war Tybalds Close Estate: Blemundsbury, Springwater, Richbell, Windmill and Falcon.

And for a short while at least, only a few decades in the scheme of things, it had been the village street and home of Holborn Police Station.

For even less time than that it had been his village street too.

He was going to miss it.

As they walked, he thought about telling her that at one time this had been the very northernmost edge of London in these parts, with clear views across the fields to the hills and farms of Hampstead and Highgate. That the street was named after William Lambe, who'd dammed the River Fleet and built a conduit, in reality an open pipe or gully, to supply water to the City of London. That Lambe had gifted one hundred buckets to the women of the area so they might draw free water from his fountain. That the old Rugby School Leases map showed that this public fountain had been located precisely between the first two shop- or housefronts north of the Long Alley, precisely where Ciao Bella was now. That what was now Ciao Bella had always been a watering hole and meeting spot.

But he didn't.

Because right now, after all that, after all these years, to be silent was all that was left.

Silence, or something very like it – an adjective, a verb, a state of being or imperative mood – really was the only solution that remained.

[FAST-FORWARD] —

The lights in Holborn Police Station reception and several of the upper floors are still on, but all of the plate-glass vestibule doors have been locked, and further secured by short lengths of medium-gauge galvanised-steel chains, wrapped and padlocked around each pair of inner door handles.

Lengths of opaque white lining paper have been roughly cut from a roll and taped in overlapping vertical strips to the inside of the glass.

Between this improvised screen and the glass itself, a small number of notices printed on A4 paper are taped to the glass, face-out:

NOTICE

THIS POLICE STATION IS NOW CLOSED
THE NEAREST 24/7 POLICE STATIONS ARE

ISLINGTON   CHARING CROSS
2 Tolpuddle Street   2 Agar Street
London N1 0YY   London WC2N 4JP
Underground: Angel   Underground: Charing Cross

IF YOU HAVE AN APPOINTMENT WITH A MEMBER
OF STAFF OR A CONTRACTOR IN THIS BUILDING,
PLEASE CONTACT THEM DIRECT TO ARRANGE
ACCESS

And:

Directorate of
Legal Services HAS MOVED
Please call ████████████████
(Mon–Fri, 9 a.m.–5 p.m.)

And:

Leading for London!
Careers Workshops
Please wait at RICHBELL PLACE entrance

Inside, unseen, the reception area is full of broken desk and filing
cabinet components, shelving units, broken office chairs of all periods
post-1962, unclaimed archive boxes, crates full of old hanging files,
sundry items of office equipment – laptop docking stations, desk
furniture, stationery, a broken flipchart easel – five crates filled
with orphaned leads, power supplies and multi-gang extension
leads, printers to be scrapped, twenty large blue plastic crates full
of redundant Cisco 7000-series office telephones to be collected for
refurbishment, photocopier components and toner cartridges, paper
sacks of confidential shredding for incineration, orange sacks of

paper and plastic recycling, a medium-sized Banham safe with door unlocked and ajar, stacks of fireproof acoustic tiles removed from suspended ceilings on each floor during a now-completed survey of air-con ducts, waste pipes, sprinklers and other services.

Stacked two-high on the old Enquiry Desk are a dozen or so cardboard removal boxes, overlooked or yet to be collected. All taped up, marked 'FRAGILE' and labelled either 'K' for 'KENTISH' or 'T' for 'TOLPUDDLE'.

Behind the desk stands a dirty, orange-coloured, reinforced, heavy-gauge, four-drawer filing cabinet of a type that might have once been used for the storage of ammunition in the sub-basement shooting range, complete with a factory-fitted full-height security bar covering the drawer locks, and, running vertically on either side of this, two further custom-welded steel rods with hasps and padlocks. Someone has scratched the words 'CLEAN ME' into the orange paint on a side panel. A black-and-yellow 'nuclear hazard' sticker on the top drawer is partially obscured by a 'Documents Enclosed' A5 clear-plastic 'sticky', containing a shipping or removals invoice, and the item's intended destination.

On the wall above this, hanging **mute** and unseen, is a sheet of white A4 photocopier paper upon which has been written by hand, in capital letters, with a dried-out, blue-black whiteboard marker:

WILL THE LAST PERSON TO LEAVE
THE METROPOLITAN POLICE
PLEASE TURN OUT THE LIGHTS

Afterword

The Holborn Police Station depicted in these pages shares only some external features and a location on Lamb's Conduit Street, London WC1, with the real Holborn Police Station. All internal layouts, command structures, personnel, procedures, operations, investigations, inspections, software, etc. are entirely fictional. Ditto other forces and stations mentioned. The cuts to police in recent years – as to other public services – are, however, all too real.

The Safety in Custody inspection, process and findings depicted here are wholly fictional, but use terminologies derived from the many joint police custody inspection reports 2008–2020 published by the HMICFRS and the Justice Inspectorates.

Readers seeking information or support regarding deaths in police custody are directed to the work of the UK charity INQUEST – www. inquest.org.uk – which monitors deaths in custody and provides 'a specialist, comprehensive advice service to bereaved people, lawyers, other advice and support agencies, the media, MPs and the wider public on contentious deaths and their investigation'.

References to the Hillsborough disaster of 15 April 1989 on pages 452 and 459 predate the Coroner's ruling of 2021. Remembering the 97 – YNWA.

The protests and acts of sabotage taking place in and around Her Majesty's Naval Base Clyde on Gare Loch (a.k.a. 'Faslane') in Part One are fictional, as are all protesters and perpetrators shown here, but the protests are partly inspired by, and set against a backdrop and a tradition of real blockades, occupations and peace camps, in particular here the work of the Ploughshares anti-Trident movement, Menwith Peace Camp and broader anti-nuclear movements and protests in the UK. Readers wishing to find out more are directed to the excellent 'Peace and Non-violence Reading Lists' maintained by Housmans, London, radical booksellers since 1945.

The accounts in Part One of The Clash arriving in Leeds in the early days of their UK 'busking tour' of May 1985 are based on events at which I was present. Set lists discussed are based on my own contemporaneous retellings, and are supported by recordings that have emerged very recently.

The Sheffield NUM rally of 7 May 1984 described in Part Two never happened. It is imaginary, a work of fiction, as are all persons and incidents depicted therein.

Similarly, the Undercover Policing Inquiry (UCPI) that takes place within these pages – including all rehearsals, preparation, briefings, questions, personnel and participants – is entirely fictional, but has been approximated to my best endeavours based on published structures, vocabularies and syntax, locations, and the likely behaviour of my characters in that situation.

The cameo appearances in Sheffield locations in Part Two, of Stephen Mallinder from the band Cabaret Voltaire in Chapter 3, and Martin Fry of ABC in Chapter 28, are fictionalised versions of factual events at which I was present. John Peel (1939–2004) quotations are from a home-taping of the sixth 'Peel Session' featuring the band Microdisney, first broadcast on the *John Peel Show*, BBC Radio 1, 6 August 1986. These transcripts are reproduced here with the express permission of John Peel himself, for which I was and remain very grateful. Peel's permission was granted in an answerphone message ('Hello, message for Tony White, it's the music-loving John Peel here…') left by him in response to a request I'd made by letter in 1995 to use these precise links in a work of fiction. It has taken this long to find a 'worthy vessel' (to paraphrase William S. Burroughs).

Both *Phantom at the Feast* and the preceding novel *The Fountain in the Forest* are mapped out against the ninety days between the end of the Miners' Strike in March 1985 and events near Stonehenge on 1 June that same year. Ninety days = ninety chapters across the two novels. On 1 June 1985, and with considerable violence, 1,300 police prevented a large convoy of travellers from reaching the Stonehenge site, thereby preventing the Stonehenge Free Festival of 1985 from taking place. Initially reported as 'the Battle of Stonehenge', that ambush became better known as the Battle of the Beanfield.

Phantom at the Feast (like *The Fountain in the Forest* before it) is in part inspired by the work of Oulipo, the *Ouvroir de Littérature Potentielle* (or *Workshop for Potential Literature*), founded in Paris in 1960, whose members – including Italo Calvino, Harry Mathews, Georges Perec and others – proposed and demonstrated the use of 'constraints' in the production of literary works. As well as using the Revolutionary Calendar, the novels are written using an Oulipo-inspired lexical constraint: namely, a 'mandated vocabulary' comprising the solutions to successive *Guardian* newspaper crosswords of March to June 1985. Character names, locations, events, the stories told throughout this novel and the preceding volume have emerged from, and literally been produced out of, that predetermined list of words.

Why?

In the mid-1980s I would do the *Guardian* Quick Crossword every day. Researching these novels and the period in general took me to the national newspaper collection at the British Library (and the collection of the local independent *Leeds Other Paper* held in Leeds City Library). Reading old copies of the *Guardian* on microfiche, I found myself drawn to the paper's back pages and those crosswords once again. As an experiment, I redid just one crossword, nearly thirty years after I'd first completed it. I'd thought it might be fun, but I hadn't been prepared for the rush of memories and associations that were unleashed in the process.

As well as finding myself re-immersed in the habits and the lexicon of the period, I discovered that this small daily act of puzzling and decoding and writing out of solutions had been firmly woven into the warp and weft of my own lived experience of those days. So perhaps those same crossword solutions would also offer a way back in now: a richly authentic historical seam to be mined. I tested the method with a novella, *Dicky Star and the Garden Rule* (2012), which was commissioned to mark the then twenty-fifth anniversary of the Chernobyl disaster of 1986.

Each crossword yields, in effect, a twenty-odd-word linguistic 'time capsule', a cultural 'core sample' exposing what Sukhdev Sandhu in his *Guardian* review of *The Fountain in the Forest* called the 'collective lexical unconscious of the period', complete with a pantheon of historical figures that here includes Doctor Johnson, Tom Jones and a selection of past UK Prime Ministers. I have sought to retain variations in common usage, hyphenations, etc. of the time. As with *The Fountain in the Forest*, words drawn from this mandated vocabulary are emboldened in the text.

Thus, as noted above, each chapter of *Phantom at the Feast* is written using all of the solutions to *Guardian* Quick Crosswords, respectively, from 3 April to 1 June 1985 (*Guardian* days only, so excluding Sundays), and in order of their appearance in the text, as follows:

Part One
Chapter 1
Relax, free, each, foreseen, horseshoe, breakthrough, Red Sea, Rosyth, globe trotter, rook, titans, town planning, resemble, obsolescence, utterly, reheat, clip, three-foot, hack-saw, taxi rank, bacon, arboreal. (Solutions to *Guardian* Quick Crossword No. 4,675, 3 April 1985)

Chapter 2
Yes sir, amends, decamp, griddle, Ashanti, guillemot, egret, Tobago, opera, modulated, dry cell, grain, Andre Previn, Malcolm Sargent, Thomas Beecham, Simon Rattle, elitist, elegy, gratis, laser, doormat, Iceni. (Solutions to *Guardian* Quick Crossword No. 4,676, 4 April 1985)

Chapter 4
Anent, national, drapery, produce, cave, coloured, landfall, scenery, smite, self-help, cold comfort, gross, transaction, chicken feed, crib, pity, play, heave, skylark, delivery van. (Solutions to *Guardian* Quick Crossword No. 4,677, 6 April 1985)

Chapter 6
Criteria, regard, quit, fractious, not so hot, scones, comb, hunchback, Notre Dame, Victor Hugo, Quasimodo, denude, debase, Icarus, genocide, dreamy, scramble, arum, aboard. (Solutions to *Guardian* Quick Crossword No. 4,678, 8 April 1985)

Chapter 7
Awful, self-deception, Lansbury, mainstay, wink, note, gallows, sin, monster, mar, vista, lean-to, nine lives, hollyhock, neat, larboard, trainees, Norman, Oakham, Nairobi, ransack, moment of truth,

tragic, flop, unfit, nasal. (Solutions to *Guardian* Quick Crossword No. 4,679, 9 April 1985)

Chapter 8
Incurred, Rubik, kayak, dik-dik, oak-leaf, Jura, musketry, Pawnee, Kinross, Crufts, bravado, alack, Evelyn, chock-a-block, kink, Trevor, kinetic, king-maker, ordain, Kabaka, subeditor, Hackney, Kerouac, Arkle, Danube. (Solutions to *Guardian* Quick Crossword No. 4,680, 10 April 1985)

Chapter 9
Dicky, limit, Goldwyn, Mayer, vegan, odd-ball, fag-end, Ilford, shaver, eyelid, unfortunate, hot iron, flawed, cameo, law-suit, Nehru, trammel, Antigua, milch, really, darken, fumble, wayside, renal, partitioned, outlive. (Solutions to *Guardian* Quick Crossword No. 4,681, 11 April 1985)

Chapter10
Vaunt, lull, inane, snigger, pellet, flamenco, without tears, journal, gold leaf, November, balsam, daub, Repton, expound, riddle, glue, get off my back, stand pat, peasant, well-dressing, wandering Jew, logic, limb, appal. (Solutions to *Guardian* Quick Crossword No. 4,682, 12 April 1985)

Chapter 11
Overstatement, aid, teetering, underdog, even, trade gap, sceptic, suspense, floating voter, cue, vary, plan, invite, Lavengro, Aldershot, parade, catchee monkey, focus, giddy, mesh, seaman, nudist, to hell and back, retinue. (Solutions to *Guardian* Quick Crossword No. 4,683, 13 April 1985)

Chapter 13
Crew, Andromeda, blue blood, heal, implement, peril, tale, free wheel, cram, polite, Leonid, strip, Dedham, sleek, stud, isosceles, profiteer, foster, germ, milk teeth, ration, pigeon, stockpile, Kabul, rustle, pucker, Eden, tier. (Solutions to *Guardian* Quick Crossword No. 4,684, 15 April 1985)

612 TONY WHITE

Chapter 14
Run-around, Hobbs, enable, hydrant, numb, scorn, soluble, aspirin, nasal, hurrah, apostrophised, looks, Eamonn, Basil Rathbone, sheet, Botha, on shore, chamber, rosette, indeed, avow, ormolu, Atlanta, sweat shop, opossum, social. (Solutions to *Guardian* Quick Crossword No. 4,685, 16 April 1985)

Chapter 15
Sol, amble, crock of gold, tariff, too, iceberg, hailer, flag of truce, pragmatic, regulator, college, listening, rug, unfair, hippo, boiled egg, outfit, age of reason, anger, ire, anaemia, breath of air, freshen, gorse. (Solutions to *Guardian* Quick Crossword No. 4,686, 17 April 1985)

Chapter 16
Titanic, cream bun, iced, chocolate cake, sweetbread, ouzo, instant coffee, Kent, aloof, defiant, lovable, tithe, Campden, urban, grin, fridge, tinned, fruit salad, cadge, vitamins, hackwork, bedazzle. (Solutions to *Guardian* Quick Crossword No. 4,687, 18 April 1985)

Chapter 17
Leaf, Shanklin, bowl, wither, turnip, whip-cord, snowball, pine, bucket shop, raid, oftentimes, prospect, knot, disaster, bird bath, Nile, avid, champion, vanguard, degree, new society, ends, petit fours, honest. (Solutions to *Guardian* Quick Crossword No. 4,688, 19 April 1985)

Chapter18
Copra, inner man, once, gallon, tanglewood, opus, peacock, Beeching, hoots, staid, step, drag, saga, literacy, Heathcliff, briefly, sheath, goal-post, smoke-screen, esparto, allegro, hood, fudge. (Solutions to *Guardian* Quick Crossword No. 4,689, 20 April 1985)

Chapter 20
Yonder, tempt, violent, topsy-turvy, pumpkin, unfit, turn turtle, iota, hear hear, pike, trout, gainful, lido, outbreak, noise, burr, Fangio, entwine, befriend, Exeter, tom-tit, head to foot, upside down, ulterior. (Solutions to *Guardian* Quick Crossword No. 4,690, 22 April 1985)

Chapter 21
Crescent, lovat, tilt-yard, shaker, chervil, bell-tent, twinned, cite, edit, slot, prompter, toper, knuckle, merry old soul, reef, metaphysical, exploit, raise, caked, retard, nonchalantly, card-carrying, pledge, nectar. (Solutions to *Guardian* Quick Crossword No. 4,691, 23 April 1985)

Chapter 22
Mildew, cat-nap, Donal, wield, objector, brave new world, learn, enact, vice-president, chicane, contrive, plop, nirvana, Star Wars, preclude, ides, roman, ring, serum, in love, riviera, apron, lower, Terence, case, extend. (Solutions to *Guardian* Quick Crossword No. 4,692, 24 April 1985)

Chapter 23
Sea fever, gardener, extravaganza, moving, gondola, rice-paper, phantom, zoom, put on the line, copper, Vinci, toxic, Jethro, golf club, road-maker, peat, anon, nigh, stage manager, recreant, remand on bail, mohawk. (Solutions to *Guardian* Quick Crossword No. 4,693, 25 April 1985)

Chapter 24
Schoolmaster, Vandyke, lured, article, hard nut, acrobat, minus, paint, gramme, ranger, expel, treat, traumatic, bathe, open sea, steamboat, glance, easter, Caspian, battle, saliva, remit, surgeon, Manx cat, oddly. (Solutions to *Guardian* Quick Crossword No. 4,694, 26 April 1985)

Chapter 25
Double quick time, two and a half, know thyself, kinsman, squib, slap, driving seat, sanction, muse, booty, dentures, seek, agony, pink-eye, winsome, alchemy, heirloom, frond, bill-hook. (Solutions to *Guardian* Quick Crossword No. 4,695, 27 April 1985)

Chapter 27
Assess, backfire, do down, St Albans, Durham, Hereford, Rochester, Southwell, Carlisle, in advance, Salisbury, York, crab, itch, encode, Eros, shrine, smooth, ablaze, tissue. (Solutions to *Guardian* Quick Crossword No. 4,696, 29 April 1985)

Chapter 28
Onward, clever, Iran, backhand, peep show, mad, wrest, let, trivial, get away with it, abolish, newspeak, sago, multiple birth, despair, gantry, Cyrus, second leg, kiwi, rural, Valhalla, husbandry, larvae, leech, posy, lasagne. (Solutions to *Guardian* Quick Crossword No. 4,697, 30 April 1985)

Chapter 29
Thea, vibes, opiate, poppycock, voice, solemn, unworthy, hasty, constrict, dragon, wrench, laid on, rowdies, bespoke, bump, predisposed, roomy, Demeter, engrave, missal, mullah, worship, subsist, skater, tape-worm. (Solutions to *Guardian* Quick Crossword No. 4,698, 1 May 1985)

Chapter 30
Vanilla, Bugatti, relic, defame, switch, tobacco, compilation, peach, cropper, hidden, mantelpiece, decade, ampere, aboard, divert, rabid, Milk Cup, final, worse, treacle, Annie. (Solutions to *Guardian* Quick Crossword No. 4,699, 2 May 1985)

Part Two
Chapter 1
Infer, rosette, elysian, growing pains, obstacle, acts, phone-tapping, password, extort, teem, Glinka, Macedon, reflect, inter, say-so, worm, organise, primer, nerves, prop, shepherd's pie, Petworth, radii, Little Bo-Peep. (Solutions to *Guardian* Quick Crossword No. 4,700, Friday 3 May 1985)

Chapter 2
Away, pigeon, Clapham, fond, half-seven, creditor, bug, notice, common, galleon, Pravda, botanical, peastick, mismanagement, Highland fling, incontestable, tar, riddance, German measles, het up, libation, right, knee, Asia. (Solutions to *Guardian* Quick Crossword No. 4,701, Saturday 4 May 1985)

Chapter 4
Bubbly, penury, recall, enumerate, gloss, swear word, spot check, short list, else, dragon, dangerous, dosser, prod, phew, blind date,

horn, timber, afresh, learn, gruel, prim, salon, hallow, first-born, speed-boat, bust, city, area. (Solutions to *Guardian* Quick Crossword No. 4,702, Monday 6 May 1985)

Chapter 5
Silence, dream, adult, blue sky, marina, race track, coin, extra, bound, rostrum, upper, physic, X-ray, Scouse, Gummer, nettle, soldier, spill the beans, stand up, optimum, sabre, meat pie, disparagement, hip-bath, synagogue, Thirsk. (Solutions to *Guardian* Quick Crossword No. 4,703, Tuesday 7 May 1985)

Chapter 6
Nitwitted, uneven, row, rock bun, presentable, Congressmen, Forsyte, infanta, easy chair, brass, gosling, indigo, Keyes, ova, all, needy, running riot, advantage, little, unworldly, too, trafficking, Nissen, fades. (Solutions to *Guardian* Quick Crossword No. 4,704, Wednesday 8 May 1985)

Chapter 7
Siren, holiness, pointer, consanguinity, ships that pass, in the night, Ashley, along, restaurant, plan, cereal, vice, tourney, uxorious, chateau, slum, wainscot, largess, riven, lime tree, punch, Milo. (Solutions to *Guardian* Quick Crossword No. 4,705, Thursday 9 May 1985)

Chapter 8
Black cat, crisis, amid, woodwind, lotion, oval, Edda, neuter, threat, fray, arms, disperse, wade, seconder, water-works, marquess, greenhouse, dianthus, statuary, steaming, chip, shirt-front, togs, crank-shaft. (Solutions to *Guardian* Quick Crossword No. 4,706, Friday 10 May 1985)

Chapter 9
Puss, helm, hand in glove, Ramadan, crass, lethargy, oculist, Icknield, Avon, skin, marmoset, Romeo, hide, sausage, beach, soigné, morganatic, Salic, piffling, clarify, hiss, birth-place. (Solutions to *Guardian* Quick Crossword No. 4,707, Saturday 11 May 1985)

Chapter 11

Aesop, nymph, toast, Croesus, hold-all, horse sense, calamity, Jane, agitator, pursue, envelop, adhere, diver, gale, inmates, impugn, construe, sort, Persian cat, dog biscuit, sticks, black sheep, aromatic, pore. (Solutions to *Guardian* Quick Crossword No. 4,708, Monday 13 May 1985)

Chapter 12

Dead duck, disappointed, companion-way, calm, Elgar, Othello, vanquish, offset, mess, halve, mores, Queen's Flight, studious, allow, hire, secular, airport, author, accomplished, merry men, ingress, oppose, casino, dump. (Solutions to *Guardian* Quick Crossword No. 4,709, Tuesday 14 May 1985)

Chapter 13

Radar, bask, arrow, dewy, sidelong, thatch, stead, boss, delve, torrent, plural, unheard, edgeways, Indian, Zeus, Doctor Johnson, osprey, Swansea, tidal, shellac, lasso, eland, educated, bestride, cramp, double-jointed. (Solutions to *Guardian* Quick Crossword No. 4,710, Wednesday 15 May 1985)

Chapter 14

Francis, ably, crystallised, settle, masterly, unfold, mannered, elan, nearer, nines, riderless, postmistress, fear, mousetrap, dessert, perjurer, plum, Tobias, Arran, salmon ladder, recalcitrant, Tom Jones. (Solutions to *Guardian* Quick Crossword No. 4,711, Thursday 16 May 1985)

Chapter 15

Swatch, Tudor, rambler, barrow boy, tent-peg, slouch, Barrie, potboiler, polar, entrée, capon, Patna, cadet, autopsy, orange, bolster, sepia, bushmen, overlap, haggle, bulldog, April, Walsall, octavo, up-end, stubby. (Solutions to *Guardian* Quick Crossword No. 4,712, Friday 17 May 1985)

Chapter 16

Light, polytechnic, bite, ragtime, jeans, chainsmoker, pyramid, annotate, interest, espy, styptic, clay, pussy willow, flatfish, parmesan, bake, witch doctor, Diana, fashion, scarf. (Solutions to *Guardian* Quick Crossword No. 4,713, Saturday 18 May 1985)

Chapter 18
Churchill, grudge, minute, chat, no time, plea, Stockton, Attlee, shuttles, rent, districts, Wilson, Pitt, Disraeli, Gladstone, Macmillan, nobody, mangle, chosen, Bonar Law. (Solutions to *Guardian* Quick Crossword No. 4,714, Monday 20 May 1985)

Chapter 19
Mandalay, agog, grail, high water mark, chalice, tipple, stereo, jazz, kilohertz, rigging, gas, plaid, waylay, with, saucer, eldritch, butt, bowlegged, daddy-long-legs, two-step, prowl, riparian, hat, adopt, expedite, ghostly. (Solutions to *Guardian* Quick Crossword No. 4,715, Tuesday 21 May 1985)

Chapter 20
Angular, crop up, errant, depart, tetanus, mill, maple leaf, armchair, afters, knifed, captain, prance, neophyte, thought, diced, strong point, premiss, Harry, dotty, vote, Doric, figure, certainty, inverse, beggar. (Solutions to *Guardian* Quick Crossword No. 4,716, Wednesday 22 May 1985)

Chapter 21
Tom fool, spades, hectare, cajole, Stella, dated, totem, cyclic, blunt, status, flightiness, model, licence, postman, James, Ibsen, Tamar, Bertha, Cabot, risotto, seagull, spoils, comical, gum boot, sprite, priest's hole. (Solutions to *Guardian* Quick Crossword No. 4,717, Thursday 23 May 1985)

Chapter 22
Pain, flotilla, shallow, round the bend, rose and crown, jamb, proposed, mills, behead, keeps, Helen, Edward, Galilee, Iras, Watteau, metaphor, admitted, cabinet-maker, alpha, Thor, tiddly, borsch, applied, carpet-bagger. (Solutions to *Guardian* Quick Crossword No. 4,718, Friday 24 May 1985)

Chapter 23

Tor, trek, oracle, ear, detain, egad, visually, hard-boiled-egg, Flecker, batch, entertainment, fieldfare, sentinel, lorry, sea battle, light infantry, unfair, Eden, behave oneself, foible, anathema, edit, fretful, hobnails. (Solutions to *Guardian* Quick Crossword No. 4,719, Saturday 25 May 1985)

Chapter 25

Homely, human, Chopin, Kiev, Eric, Champagne, plate rack, carrot, flush, drain pipe, cripes, signalman, tunnel, true, fruit, cane, raid, implicate, aver, thorn, molest, heaviness, introvert salary, track suit, arch, note, italic. (Solutions to *Guardian* Quick Crossword No. 4,720, Monday 27 May 1985)

Chapter 26

Mumbles, Tabitha, andante, Utah, deflate, full pitch, regress, righteous, mango, potato, recess, Moses, stove, dribble, ear-hole, libido, aught, thou, Sinatra, gable, teens, profit-sharing, trader, fat cat, letters patent, sea-dog. (Solutions to *Guardian* Quick Crossword No. 4,721, Tuesday 28 May 1985)

Chapter 27

Cut and dried, shaken, winning post, urn, egg basket, alyssum, honeycomb, overheads, delight, Chippendale, get-up, ghi, stipulation, lie, sustain, drowsy, Paris, Encamp, rebus, Atwell, high-hat, recollect, group, ado. (Solutions to *Guardian* Quick Crossword No. 4,722, Wednesday 29 May 1985)

Chapter 28

Glow, abstinence, Chicago, parcel, incitement, lout, nota bene, Stanford, polite, congeal, pattern, cream, visit, nominal, magic, arts, incommunicado, momentum, Timon, shaving tackle, hornbeam, down. (Solutions to *Guardian* Quick Crossword No. 4,723, Thursday 30 May 1985)

Chapter 29

Chambers, heliport, awhile, chimney-pot, amethyst, chromium, practice, nauseous, Hellespont, rout, carapace, omit, chummy, pity, homogenise, flea, anthem, tier, ship, psephology, cone, pathetic, Alaric, cash. (Solutions to *Guardian* Quick Crossword No. 4,724, Friday 31 May 1985)

Chapter 30
Dreadful, phantom, bloom, tussle, tour, profuse, motif, rescript, veto, commonplace, oust, corridor, saucy, jeep, Arkansas, hippodrome, cooper, buss, harem, improperly, bombard, asunder, mute. (Solutions to *Guardian* Quick Crossword No. 4,725, Saturday 1 June 1985)

Acknowledgements

Above all, thank you to my wife Sarah.

The writing of *Phantom at the Feast* was supported by an Authors' Foundation grant from the Society of Authors, 2018; and by the KURS Association in Split, Croatia, through its Marko Marulić residency programme for writers and translators. I would also like to acknowledge the support of Arts Council England through the Arts Council Emergency Response Fund: for individuals, 2020.

For foundational support for the research that led to the commencement and planning of this novel I need to again thank the Department of French at King's College London, where I was creative entrepreneur in residence, funded by Creativeworks London, and a visiting research fellow from 2013–15. I am grateful to Dr Sanja Perovic of King's College London, author of *The Calendar in Revolutionary France: Perceptions of Time in Literature, Culture, Politics* (Cambridge University Press, 2012). I would also like to thank the artists Stuart Brisley and Maya Balcioglu, for approaching me in 2012 to initiate a discussion about Brisley's own use of the French Republican Calendar in a number of his performance art works dating back to the early 1970s; and for their hospitality in Dungeness in August 2014. During those illuminating conversations between 2013 and 2015, Brisley once observed that for him the ten-day week of the Republican Calendar provided a frame within which a revolutionary performance might happen. A simple insight but catalytic both for this novel and (from 2018) *The Fountain in the Forest*.

I salute Sheffield's pioneering artists and musicians.

I'm very grateful to my friend Tim Etchells for generously allowing me to make use of notes and personal correspondence from 2001.

With warmest thanks to the Sarah Such Literary Agency, to Maxim Jakubowski, Jamie Hodder-Williams, Polly Halsey, Victoria Chapman,

Claudia Bullmore, and the team at No Exit Press and Bedford Square Publishers, to Fiona McMorrough and Annabel Robinson at FMcM, the Such family in particular Elizabeth and Freddie Such, Mathew Clayton, Mark Ecob, Silvia Crompton, Chris Dorley-Brown, Maja Vrančić of the KURS Association in Split, Borivoj Radaković, Edi Matić, Marko Gregur and Vinko Radovani for their hospitality in Croatia, staff and students of the Fine Art department of the former Sheffield City Polytechnic 1986–89, Giles Lane, Cathy Naden, Alida Bremer, Hannah Redler, Barbara Campbell, Deborah Chadbourn, Forced Entertainment, Jonathan Main, Bronac Ferran, Jeremy Deller, Artangel, James White, Xanthe Rann, Sarah Miller, Elizabeth Magill, Andrew Wheatley, Jamie Taylor, Lee Brackstone, Popbitch, Philip Bebb, Deborah Bellis, Dave Read, the late David May, and Andy Hall (RIP); and last but not least, to the readers who have posted photos, and messaged me about *The Fountain in the Forest*, and asked when this one was coming. Your enjoyment and your words of support (and your patience) mean a great deal to me, thank you.

Tony White, London, 19 Thermidor CCXXXII

If you enjoyed *Phantom at the Feast*, stayed tuned for
The Fountain in the Forest, coming December 2026.

When a brutally murdered man is found hanging in a London theatre,
Detective Sergeant Rex King becomes obsessed with the case. Who is this
anonymous corpse, and why has he been ritually mutilated? As Rex digs
deeper into the crime scene, the investigation begins to unravel, refusing the
logic of a conventional murder inquiry.

Clues fracture into symbols, witnesses contradict themselves, and the case
starts to mirror Rex's own buried past. The search for the victim's identity
becomes inseparable from a more troubling question: who, beneath the
certainty of his badge and rank, is Rex King himself?

Shifting between Holborn Police Station, an abandoned village in rural
1980s France, and the violent clash between state power and counterculture
at Stonehenge's Battle of the Beanfield, *The Fountain in the Forest* reimagines
the crime novel as something stranger and more daring. At once a
gripping police procedural, an avant-garde experiment in language, and a
philosophical meditation on liberty and identity, it is an iconoclastic novel
of rare ambition.

'White joins a handful of contemporary writers who are proving that
the novel has never been more alive. He is a serious, engaging voice
of the modern city' *Guardian*

'*The Fountain in the Forest* sets the author and his readers a bracingly
high bar' David Collard, *TLS*

'An engaging plot allows plenty of room for radical yet accessible
interventions... That all these stylistic fireworks can illuminate several
rich plot lines, each with multiple twists, which an attentive reader
will enjoy disentangling, is the best vindication of experimental prose'
Financial Times